I0762117

THE FRENZY SERIES

5TH ANNIVERSARY EDITION

CASEY L. BOND

THE PLAGUE OF DARKNESS

Then the LORD said to Moses, "Stretch out your hand toward the sky so that darkness spreads over Egypt—darkness that can be felt." Exodus 10:21

FRENZY

PROLOGUE

MERCEDES BRUSHED MY HAIR BACK FROM THE SIDES OF MY FACE AND KISSED my forehead. The scent of pine soap clung to her skin. We'd washed in the river this afternoon, splashing in the sunshine and forgetting the ominous task that night would bring with it.

"I don't want you to go," I told her.

She smiled. Mercedes' smile could disarm the most hateful of people. I was sure it could even calm the rough seas mentioned in the books she taught me to read. "I'll be fine. There are other people with me."

"And a night-walker."

"They aren't how you imagine. The night-walkers are....intense, but they've never threatened, only helped us. People like to perpetuate fear and cause drama where there isn't any." She let go of my hair.

"Will you wake me in the morning? When you come home?"

Mercedes chuckled. "Porschia. You and I both know that you'll already be awake. Will you please try to get some sleep?"

"I'll try. It's just hard with you being gone."

"Mother, Father, and Ford will be here."

I shook my head. "They aren't you."

"I love you, too," she replied. "I promise to come straight home to you, after the morning rotation and after I grab our rations. You know we need them. This winter's been terrible."

My stomach growled.

"How are you not afraid?" Tears welled in my eyes. I wished so much that I had an ounce of her courage.

"I've done it before."

"One night, Cedes."

"Now, I know what I need to do. It isn't a bad thing. It isn't dangerous. And I plan to volunteer again and again. As long as we need it and they accept me, I'll be fine. It's seriously no big deal, Porschia. Maybe one day you'll go with me."

"Father won't allow it."

She winked at me. "Father won't always be there to stop you. Now, I have to get going. Evening rotation starts soon."

"Love you," I told her, hugging her one last time.

"Love you back. Listen, stay in your room." She knew Mother's mood had been sour all day.

ONE

Mother wore her manipulative face this morning, my least favorite. She blew out a long breath, filling the air with the rancid scents of disappointment and aggravation. That was her modus operandi: out with the bad, in with the good. But Miranda Grant never found enough good. She could never inhale enough hope or contentment to keep her from suffocating. So she struggled through every second of the day, a perpetual frown thinning her lips, a rigid frame and cold, dismissive eyes.

She yelled more often than not, reminding me I was more the cause of her disdain than the utter despair we found ourselves in. The world had gone to shit and she didn't ask for this life. But then again, none of us did. Mother handled it more poorly than everyone else—her moods and actions swinging violently back and forth across an invisible pendulum. One moment she would dismiss me without so much as a glance or flippant gesture, and the next she would strike out. But I learned to use the reflexes I was given, snatching her wrist before her hand could make contact with my cheek.

This morning, she chose the well-trodden path of disdain when she should have been mourning. If I knew my mother, she would soon go into fix-it mode because she knew better than everyone else in Blackwater about what was wrong with the world. All anyone had to do was ask her. And if they didn't ask, she would gladly offer the solution in detail, at which point I would gratefully fade into the background and sneak away. Her voice was like nails on a chalkboard. Hearing it often enough, I was sure, would make my ears bleed.

I tugged down the sleeve of my hand-me-down dress until it grazed my wrist, almost reaching to where it should ideally lay. Mother leaned against the Formica countertop, assessing me. Her steely blue eyes took in every detail, every stray thread; the way the dress didn't and would never fit me the way it had my sister. I would never measure up to Mercedes; never fill her shoes, literally and figuratively. My sister was beautiful, petite, and full of life. She was happy; the embodiment of everything Mother thought should be mixed together to create the recipe of the perfect woman, the perfect daughter. I was her exact opposite.

Where Mercedes had been short and curvy, I was tall, and my bones protruded indelicately. Where her hair looked like golden honey in summer, mine was a dull, light brown and dry like the withered stalks of corn in winter. She was light and I was too much like my mother. I was dark. But unlike Mother, I wasn't miserable. I just had a different outlook on life, different goals than those she had chosen for me. And unlike my sister, I wasn't afraid to voice those aspirations, to carve my own path. Unlike my sister, I was alive. That fact alone made Mother hate me.

Mother cleared her throat and offered a slight smile, tucking an errant strand of silvering hair back into her tight bun. "You look terrible in her dress." I stood taller, despite the words that should have made me cower. She noticed. Wrinkles formed around her tightly pursed lips and she narrowed her eyes. I tugged on the sleeves again. I was too tall for Mercedes' dresses, too tall by several inches, but they were all we had so they would have to work. To Mother's chagrin, I would wear them proudly. They were all I had left of Mercedes. All that was left of her light were her ebony dresses, the signature of all Colony women.

My feet carried me through the kitchen and out the back door before more venom could spew from her mouth. Ford wasn't ready yet, but thankfully he was awake. While Mother was greeting me so warmly this morning, I'd heard the weary floorboards creaking overhead. He'd just rolled out of bed. Ford was fourteen going on twenty. Over the summer, his voice changed, turning deeper. He had changed, too. Just this spring, he was tall and lanky, limbs too overwhelming for his frame, but he grew up over the summer. He developed muscles, larger than any pubescent boy should have, and he grew in other ways, too. Ways that couldn't be seen from the outside. Ford was more mature than most of the gangly boys he called friends.

Through the meager harvest and canning season in late summer, he helped in the garden without complaint, often for hours on end. He began to beg Father to let him join the rotation early, wanting to practice his archery skills in real life. His goal was to take down several bucks or a large bear to garner enough meat to give every family a healthy portion.

Ford also helped our neighbors with their gardens and chores, especially the elderly and infirm. While his few friends giggled about girls and ran around town, Ford kept his head down, and his tenaciousness didn't go unnoticed. Just last week, the Elders announced his apprenticeship working with the Colony's livestock. It was an important position in our community. What livestock we were able to breed were all we had to sustain us, should things get epically worse. And things, it seemed, were heading in that direction at a rapid clip.

I was glad I didn't see him this morning. Hearing the growling of his empty stomach was driving me crazy. It didn't bother me when my own howled and cramped, but Ford was still young. He was my baby brother, and younger siblings should never go hungry. Mercedes whispered through the wall vent more than once that she could hear my stomach rumbling from the other side of the wall that separated our beds. Her powerful voice would later fade, heavy with the despair we all felt but could do nothing about.

I eased the door closed behind me and stepped outside. Fog hung thickly in the air, a damp, silken blanket that covered the black earth underfoot. My leather boots sank into the mud with each step. It had been too dry during the spring and early summer, but late summer and fall was unseasonably wet, causing the river to swell and flood out of its banks. Our house was one of the closest to the water, so it was one of the first to flood. We were one of the first families to lose the majority of the crops we'd spent so much time tending. Everything planted in the front yard was lost, which meant we would only have the back yard gardens' bounty to last us through the season and to provide food throughout the winter.

Trudging toward the rapids on leaden legs, I mentally prepared myself for the ceremony. It had been exactly one week since Mercedes left on the hunt with four other people. There were two men, one woman, one teenage girl, and Mercedes. The others returned without her, telling a horrific tale—a nightmare we all lived. She had been bitten by an Infected. The others in her party couldn't risk helping her, even when she screamed and clawed into the black mud beneath her. They ran and didn't look back, thankful to make it back to the crossing themselves, heaving for breath and thankful they'd made it. Why they weren't accompanied by a night-walker was beyond me. It was part of the treaty, and until that night, the treaty had never been broken.

The sound of rushing water over smoothed rocks pulled me from imagining my sister's fall. To most people it was a soothing sound, but to me, it was an awful reminder that Mercedes would never cross those rapids again. The smell of rich earth and fresh water mixed with the crisp leaves that blanketed the ground everywhere, leaving the branches above bare and cold. Like macabre fingers clawing toward the sun, they stretched toward the North Star that peered down from the lightening morning sky.

Surprisingly, Father was already waiting at the calm pool beneath the nearby waterfall. It wasn't the largest fall along this river, but it was wide. The pool beneath the spilling water was pristine and calmed the ripples that the fall pushed outward. It was one of nature's juxtapositions. Rage met temperance. Ferocity met timidity. Life met death.

All of those lost from and mourned by the Colony were honored here in this pool, so it seemed that Mercedes' farewell was even more fittingly held here. It was the spot that we swam in as children, and where we bathed to rid ourselves of the dark, miry earth before Mother had a fit. It was her favorite place, where she would come to think, and where Noah had stolen her first kiss. Noah – the boy she'd loved since childhood, the boy who had grown into a man-- the man she planned to marry this winter.

Standing alone near the water's edge, I watched the swirling torrent just beneath the falls and let the rush of the water fill my ears. A waterfall of my own flowed steadily down my cheeks, spilling onto my dress drop by drop. Fresh. It smelled so fresh here. None of the Infected were across the bank, because their rot wasn't present. Her rot wasn't present.

The Colony considered her dead, but the truth was far worse. She wasn't dead. She wasn't really alive, either. Mercedes was Infected now, and would begin to decay. Her pearly white teeth would yellow and chip off as she gnawed on blood and bone, sometimes animal, sometimes human, but always anything she could grab hold of. Her golden hair would thin, falling out in great clumps. I'd heard rumors from expeditions that chunks of hair littered the briary woods. Her skin would mottle and her muscles would weaken. She would remain a walking skeleton, her only concern her next meal, only barely surviving until something bigger came along that she couldn't escape. Then, *she* would become the meal.

And if she ever were to catch a human, ever bite a human, she would infect them and spread her curse to another. The most humane thing, the Elders said, was to find the Infected and eliminate them. But the Colony was in survival mode now. Winter had just begun. The gardens were mostly barren, and though we stored what food we could spare our stomachs during the spring, summer and fall, there wouldn't be enough to keep everyone from going hungry over the coming cold months. The priority would be hunting for meat that everyone would share, but that wouldn't be quite enough for anyone. However, the meat would keep us alive until the last snow fell and we could begin planting again.

Feet shuffled in the tall grass behind me. Every resident, unless ill or physically handicapped, was expected to attend the farewell ceremonies. Most wanted to attend, to pay their respects, or so they claimed. In reality they wanted to gossip, to ferret out their fears of the Infected that lay just beyond the river. Fortunately, farewells didn't happen that often. We'd only had three this year until now, and those three colonists died of natural causes.

Mercedes was the fourth. Oh, how Mother wailed when she learned of Mercedes' fall. She cursed and screamed and questioned why it couldn't have happened to me or to Ford. Then she raised her hands toward the heavens, called us liars, and demanded that we leave her house and not return. Ford didn't outwardly flinch at her words, and I wouldn't allow myself to. Not anymore. Instead, we came here, to the river.

Ever the peace-keeper, Father scolded her and called for the physician to give her a tincture to calm her nerves. He made excuses for her behavior and apologized on her behalf, though Ford and I both knew she wasn't the tiniest bit sorry for her actions or the poisonous words that poured so easily from her mouth. I wished there was a remedy for bitchy. Mother desperately needed that.

To Father, Ford, and me, Mercedes wasn't dead. She was living, and though it was a half-life we wouldn't wish on our worst enemies (not even upon Mother), she was still alive. I took solace in that. Somehow, the knowledge that she was fighting to survive despite the infection was more comforting than covering her corpse with six feet of heavy, ebony soil. She was on this side of the grave, even if just barely. Even if only temporary.

Someone had to find a cure at some point. If she could just hold on. . .

As the trio of Elders, clad in white robes that draped from their bent bodies, stepped toward the water, I backed away. Too close now to discreetly bury myself in the midst of the gathered crowd, a sea of black and white cotton, I stopped and listened. I watched the flowing water, refusing to give credence to the words of old men who had no idea what it felt like to lose a family member to the Infected, who sought no cure and saw no hope in the future.

Survival was a necessity, not a way of life. They'd given up, and so had everyone else.

I couldn't allow myself to listen to their propaganda. I listened for Mercedes and I heard her laughter in my mind, in the memories that she still lived on in. She would stay vibrant and healthy there until I died. I wished I could transfer them to someone else so I could to keep her alive forever.

Once the old men were finished taking turns speaking about Mercedes, whom they knew very little about because they never cared to get to know her while she lived amongst them, the residents, friends, and acquaintances formed a line to the river. Each stepped forward to utter a prayer for her. Some threw dried flowers into the dark water. Stiffened petals and stems gathered on the surface, some overlapping the others until they became heavy and sank together to the river bed. All two-hundred thirty-seven residents prayed that my sister would die swiftly. That was what they prayed for: mercy. But my thoughts were unmerciful and it was eating away at me slowly. I was the only one who asked her to hang on, who willed her to keep trying, to live, for me.

It was selfish. I was selfish.

But I didn't care. I couldn't bring myself to wish for death, however merciful, to find someone I loved.

I knew that I should stand with Ford, but he was lost somewhere in the crowd. Mother and Father were, too. They didn't need me and I didn't need them either. It had been a long time since I fit in with my family, if I ever did. Now, none of it mattered anyway.

Small crowds of people lingered, chit-chatting merrily about how much food they were able to preserve, of all the fall crops they pulled from the earth in the past month, their predictions for the winter snows, and how they were thankful that the night-dwellers weren't able to attend farewell ceremonies. When the treaty was made, there was talk of a wall being erected to separate them from us. No physical wall was built, but a wall stood nonetheless; invisible, dividing the two creatures. No human crossed the barrier into their section of the Colony, and no night-dweller crossed unless it was to take part in the rotation.

My father caught hold of my elbow as I walked toward home. Carson Grant sighed and raked a hand through his graying hair. "Your mother wishes to speak to you before you go."

I sighed heavily. Of course she did.

"Okay." My teeth were clamped together so tightly, I thought they might splinter.

"I—" he stopped his words abruptly. My eyes urged him to complete the thought, but he clamped his mouth closed and nodded in the direction of our home. When he released my elbow, I walked away, my boots sinking deeper into the miry clay. I would rather walk for a thousand days through this mess than be forced to look into my mother's face today.

TWO

Our house was two stories of once-white, aluminum siding, with old furniture stuffed into every corner of every room, and a rusting metal roof that sounded like the tinkling of wind chimes when rain hit it. When Mother and Father were first married, they chose this house together. Not all houses had been claimed back then, and it took several generations to build the population to the paltry number the Elders so often boasted about. At one time, a family had filled the walls with love. Mother removed that warmth, that love, which hung upon the walls in the form of memories, of family portraits and finger-paintings. She gutted the house, throwing out anything that wasn't useful, ordering Father to set it on fire. And he did.

I wish I could have seen what 'happy' looked like before the flames devoured it. The old Victorian house had a long porch on the front with paint that was chipping and peeling, revealing withered posts and boards. It was like seeing the skeleton of an unhappy thing.

Mother was waiting on the porch for me, arms crossed over her chest, mouth and brows pulled into tight knots. "You took your time and wasted mine."

"You had such big plans this morning, Mother?" Mother never did much of anything anymore. She refused to leave our home, or even the sanctity of her bedroom, more often than not.

She waved one arm, impatiently motioning for me to join her. Each step creaked underfoot. "Do you hear that?" she asked.

"The sound of dilapidation?"

She snorted in dismissal. "The sound of your footsteps burdening even the strongest of wooden planks. I think you could stand to eat a little less, Porschia."

My stomach was gnawing on itself, and now it wanted me to chew her face off. I was thinner than the porch rail that my fingernails dug in to. I wished it was her skin.

"In fact," she continued, "one of two things needs to happen today. You need to arrive at dinner with a viable prospect for a husband, or you need to be accepted into the rotation."

Loudly grinding my teeth, which I knew she hated, I stared at her. She knew I had no prospects, and there was no way I would be accepted into the rotation; not so soon after Mercedes' fall. She snarled her lip in response. "Your brother needs your rations."

I snapped. "He has Mercedes' rations!" Not to mention that I always wrapped some of my food in a napkin and slipped it to him beneath the table. While his eyes told me he didn't want to take it, his hands accepted, too hungry to refuse.

"He's still growing and you're old enough to marry, old enough to have your own house and garden and pull your own weight."

My mouth gaped open. "I don't pull my own weight? When was the last time *you* got your fingers dirty, Mother? Or your shoes? When was the last time you canned food for your family? Carried laundry to the river? Left your bedroom during the daylight hours? Hmm?"

She waved me off. "You'll get your own rations with a husband, and you'll add to our family's rations if you are accepted into the rotation. Earn your food or go without. It's that simple. I won't have you ducking out of the rotation and embarrassing this family again!"

"I did *not* duck out of the last one! I was anemic, which the physician said was the result of malnourishment! It wasn't anything I could help, Mother."

"No, and Mercedes took your place instead. And see where that got her?"

Guilt. That was how Mother won wars.

"I didn't ask her to, and neither did the Elders. She volunteered to go. She loved to hunt, but loved to be away from you most of all." I left her audible gasp behind me and stalked off toward the center of Blackwater Colony. Anger burned the skin of my face. I didn't need a husband, but perhaps I could find one. And I would enter the rotation, because if I didn't learn the art of seduction fast enough or get knocked up so that a guy had to marry me, I would starve without rations. Mother would see to that. She was going to punish me, every moment of every day, for Mercedes' fall to the Infected.

THE SUN'S RAYS WERE BURNING OFF THE FOG, FILTERING THROUGH THE almost-bare trees. Most of the leaves had fallen, leaving only a few still clinging to their branches. It was the tannins in those dark leaves that made the water run brownish-black, but clear. It was the silt from the river that gave the land its darkness. Everything in this place was cursed.

I headed toward town. Staying at home wasn't an option. No one would be at Town Hall for another hour, at which time they would accept applicants for the new rotation. It started in two days. Choices were made quickly, and those choices were final. The Elders either chose you or excluded you. There was no negotiation, regardless of how desperate your plight. Everyone was desperate here.

My feet found the crumbling concrete road, whose twin yellow lines snaking down the center of the pavement were almost faded and chipped. They were useless anyway, just like the cars that once crowded these streets, the rusted skeletons sitting abandoned in yards, only good for the animals who sought shelter in their cubbies and compartments. Mother wasn't excited about having children at all, so she told Father to name us. Father? Well, he wasn't imaginative. There was no meaning behind our names. Mercedes, Porschia (though spelled more femininely), and Ford. We were named for the three rusting vehicles that were parked in our back yard. I think all but the navy blue Ford pickup were rusted well before the infection spread, long before people left this place in search of something safer--a safety they would never find. Their frames were almost eaten in two. No traces of paint were left.

Blackwater was not really a town. The real town lay beyond the tall concrete flood wall that now served as our border and protector. No, Blackwater was the forgotten section of a larger city. It was the area reserved for the citizens who couldn't afford to live within its boundaries, so they bought cheap pieces of land; land that flooded. Land that no one else would dare inhabit. But within this small outskirt, sandwiched between the wall and the river, the founders of Blackwater saw the very real potential for safety. And they were right. Within our Colony, we were safe. It was only when we stepped foot outside that danger could reach us.

There were only a few houses between my best friend Meg's house and mine. Her house was made of brick, but with only one story, her family lost their belongings with each swell of the river. They'd gotten better at stuffing things into the small attic space, piling things on countertops, and at saving what they could. My knuckles found her door. After three quick knocks in succession, Meg's smiling face was staring at mine. Freckles dusted her porcelain skin and made the red glow of her hair that much more lovely. She was kind and happy, and that sort of happiness radiated through her so naturally it was like sunlight. Before you knew it, you were a kitten, purring contentedly in the sill, warmed by her light.

"Oh, no. What did she do now?" Meg understood about Mother, not because I'd told her, but because Mother never hid her true self from Meg while she visited me. I think that in Mother's eyes, Meg was damned by association and not worthy of her carefully constructed façade.

She ushered me inside, her skirts stopping Priscilla, their cat, from escaping the house. There were few pets left in Blackwater, and Priscilla was one of them. Most found their way outside. Those that wandered would cross the trees that crossed the river or drown trying. Those that crossed into the forest were prey for bigger animals or the Infected.

I eased the door closed behind me, earning a meow from Priscilla, who'd already forgiven me for not letting her outside. She brushed back and forth across my legs. "Priscilla!" Meg admonished. "You're getting her skirts all hairy!" Meg scooped up the white ball of fluff and carried her to the back of the house, closing her inside a bedroom.

"She was fine," I told Meg.

"She'll have your bottom half completely white before long."

Meg was an only child. Her parents were loving and supportive; everything that my own were not. They always offered to let me stay the night or join them for dinner, which I might need to take them up on soon if I didn't bring a boy home for dinner or get chosen for the rotation. They weren't home, which meant they were likely still chatting with neighbors at the riverside.

Meg led me to the kitchen table and sat me in a wooden chair while she busied herself by filling a kettle of water and shoving it into the coals below. It would bubble in no time. "We need tea," she said simply, as if the answer to life's problems could be steeped from the leaves she cultivated from her window boxes.

"Do you know if Jonah is still interested in a... marriage?"

Meg turned around, her dark skirts swishing and her eyes wide. "Why do you ask about him?"

I swallowed. Though she knew how bitter and hateful my Mother was, she still wouldn't understand the demands or threats made this morning.

Her brows relaxed and she turned, removing the screaming kettle from the coals and filling two mugs with steamy water. I could smell the herbs: chamomile and lavender. Honey. She sighed as she handed me my mug and sank into the seat across from me. "Jonah isn't looking for a wife any longer. But if he was, he wouldn't be a good match for you. He's too quiet."

"I might not have the luxury of waiting to choose someone good for me. Besides, he's a nice guy and I thought he was ready to settle down. It's almost winter." All marriages happened in the winter when the Elders and colonists were the least busy.

Meg's cheeks turned red. "What I mean to say, is that Jonas asked *me* to marry him."

My eyebrows shot up and I smiled, shoving away from my seat and wrapping her in a hug. "Congratulations!" I squeaked.

Meg's eyes were guarded when I pulled away from her. "Do you like him?" she asked tentatively.

"No, I don't like him like that." I sighed, dropping back into my seat. "It's Mother."

She nodded and sipped her tea.

"Will she choose for you if you don't?" *No, she doesn't care that much,* I wanted to say. She would just see me starve. She would push me to cross the border to find food because she wanted me to be Infected—to be rid of me. Mother wanted revenge.

"I doubt it. Don't worry about me."

I glanced at the clock and realized that my visit, though it seemed short, had taken much longer than I thought. "Um, I have to go. Thanks for the tea, Meg." Abruptly, I stood up and hugged her, making a hasty retreat before she could ask where I was going. Meg was terrified of the rotation and had never entered it, but she had the luxury of food and love to surround her and no need to put herself into it. But she was kind and didn't want me to enter it, either. She would throw a fit or cry if I told her my true intention, so I did what I did best. I ran away.

THREE

Town Hall was another short jog up the concrete road. Meg followed me as far as the porch. She called out, asking where I was going so early in the morning and telling me I could stay with her. I knew that, and I didn't mean to be rude by leaving so abruptly, but I literally could not lie to Meg. She would have an absolute conniption if she knew where I was going next and what I was about to do. I couldn't handle her pleas or tears.

As much as she was my friend, she'd grown to be Mercedes' as well, and Mercedes' infection devastated Meg. She wouldn't approve of me stepping foot across the boundary. I thought about the night-walkers, about how lucky they were. They could come and go as they pleased. They were strong and fast and immune to the infection that took away family, friends, and neighbors. *What would Mother think if I brought a night-walker home for dinner?*

Walking down the street, watching the shadows in the windows of the houses, candles being extinguished, people welcoming the day, I took a deep breath and tried to calm myself. I needed to be chosen. If my blood was strong, I would just have to convince them to let me enter the rotation. I knew it was highly improbable, because my parents just lost a daughter and the Elders wouldn't want them to lose a second child, especially so soon. Maybe I could sneak a drop of someone else's blood somehow. Stab them with my hair pin?

Before I knew it, I was stepping between the twin oaks that lined the walkway to Town Hall. According to the sign that hung askew next to the front double-doors, the building used to be a church: Blackwater Church of God. I tried the handle and found the doors unlocked. The moisture outside had already seeped into the fabric of my dress. I shivered, wishing that the sanctuary had a fire place. The ancient boards creaked beneath my feet with each step forward. *I think you could stand to eat a little less, Porschia.*

The room was empty, save for the colorful shafts of light being cast all over from the sun on the intricate stained glass windows. The flapping of wings overhead startled me, and I jumped forward and into the nearest pew. Doves made a nest in the bell house and a wide crack in the ceiling exposed the beams overhead. The small, steel bell swayed back and forth overhead. I hadn't heard it ring since I was a child. It only sounded when someone or something dangerous breached our boundary—and only if someone could make it here in time to sound the alarm.

The door opened and closed behind me and the boards groaned again. It was Saul Daniels. I sighed. He was one of only a handful of people my age. My mind spun. I knew he wasn't dating anyone, unless it was a very recent thing. If I wasn't accepted into the rotation, maybe he would want me instead. I made sure that my hair was braided nicely this morning for Mercedes, but now it would work to my favor.

He stood in the row behind me and I smiled brightly at him. "Saul, I didn't expect to see you here."

He nodded, narrowing his eyes and brushing a too-long piece of light brown hair out of his eyes. "I think I'm even more surprised, especially given the events of this morning." No doubt he had been at the farewell. Everyone was.

"Thank you for coming," I muttered, turning around in the pew and facing the altar.

A warm, strong hand found my shoulder. "May I sit with you?"

I scooted over to make room for him and he settled beside me with a sigh. "I'm really sorry about Mercedes."

"No one's sorrier than I am. I had applied for the rotation because Mercedes did it two weeks before, but my blood floated so she made application. She was a great hunter." I sniffed, trying to stop the tears from welling up in my eyes.

He placed a comforting arm around my shoulders and pulled me closer. "She was. I wasn't with her that night, but I went out with her once before." Saul paused, both of us watching the dust motes flurry through the colorful rays in front of us. "Why are you here?" he asked in a gentle voice.

For some reason, I was having trouble with my masks of late. I couldn't lie to Meg, and now found that I couldn't lie to Saul either. I'd known him all of my life. We were the same age and ran in the same circles, but had never been close. Maybe it was the gravity of the day, the farewell, or the thoughts that spun in my mind of how to get Mercedes back, or maybe I was losing it, but I told him. All cards were placed on the table. "We need the food. I need the extra rations."

Swallowing my pride with a huge gulp, I stared forward.

I could almost hear his brow furrowing. "You're going hungry, Porsch?"

"Yes, and at the same time, not exactly." I tried to smile through tears that wouldn't be held back. How did you tell someone that yes, you were starving, but that your parent still intended to deny you what little portion of food you were relying on?

I began to laugh. From somewhere dark, it bubbled up. "I either need a husband or I need to get into this rotation."

"Or what?" his voice rumbled.

"Or I'm going to cross the border and find food myself."

He blew out a tense breath. "Not a good idea."

"Not many options available to me, Saul," I said shortly. He nodded and startled at the sound of someone slamming the door open behind us, and then of people filing in. The three Elders were scattered among the intruders, shaking hands, nodding excitedly, with smiles stretching over their faces as though nothing in the world was wrong with this arrangement. Nothing at all.

Saul leaned over and whispered in my ear, "You know there will be a night-walker here, right?"

My eyes widened. "What?" Saul nodded. "I didn't see them when I applied the last time," I whispered back.

"You didn't make it far enough into the process." His blue-gray eyes bored into mine. I'd never been close to a night-walker. I'd seen them from a distance, across the invisible border that the townspeople erected all those years ago, and I knew that one accompanied every rotation party that crossed the boundary. They were supposed to protect the humans from the Infected, although if I ever found the vampire who failed to save my sister, I would run a stake straight through his heart. There are only a few in Blackwater. It has to be one of them. "Just thought I'd warn you in case you didn't know." In case Mercedes didn't tell me, he meant. And she didn't.

The doors slammed closed behind us and everyone found a seat, with the exception of the Elders, who stood regally at the front of the room. There were ten others besides Saul and me. Only five were needed.

Three entrants were surprisingly old, three of the oldest men in the Colony and also among the most respected, other than the Elders, of course. Maybe their blood would float. *Maybe mine would.* How would they hunt? Their legs bowed and their hands shook with palsy.

One woman and man were my parents' age and lived on the other side of the Colony. Mary and Timothy Brown. They held hands and smiled as if this was a normal part of their day. They had only bore one child, and he was married and already in his own home. They didn't need the extra rations.

"You know how this works?" Saul asked, brows knitted with concern.

"Mostly." I straightened my back.

"Five people will be chosen. Each person will be assigned to a vamp, maybe two. Their numbers fluctuate for some reason."

My heart skipped a beat. "Two?" Saul nodded. "Mercedes never mentioned two. Actually, she didn't tell me much at all about the feedings, just about the hunt itself."

He leaned in. "She was trying to protect you."

Now no one could protect me.

Elder Yankee stepped forward and explained the process. Each of us would need to cut our fingers, letting the blood pool. A healthy drop would be placed into a clear vase of water. If it floated, you were automatically eliminated from the culling.

"Culling?" I whispered.

"They're harvesting us."

That was sick, but eww. It was true.

Elder Yankee, a tall, slender man with peppered hair, continued. "If your blood is healthy, you will be assessed for physical agility. Based upon those findings, we will choose the five needed for the supply. Those who are chosen will get double the rations during the two-week rotation and will have to leave the Colony each night to hunt. We need meat. We need meat so desperately. You all know this, so I cannot stress to you how important your job will be if you are chosen." Thick truth filled the air, pushing out every sound but roaring silence.

"We, of course, will go into greater detail if you make it past the first obstacle. Please form a line."

With that, everyone shuffled from the pews into the aisle, waiting their turn in line. As I suspected, the three most elderly persons were disqualified quickly. They were anemic, like I *had* been, like I prayed I wasn't now. Their blood floated. Having had no meat in weeks, it was no wonder that our bodies lacked iron. And why did the blood-suckers need iron-filled meals anyway? Couldn't they go hunt meat for us and then we would have enough food and be tasty, too?

I folded my arms over my chest, ignoring the tugging of the sleeve on my forearm as it rode up too high, unable to fit any farther up my arm.

The dismissed left the hall immediately, shuffling out with conceding smiles. I wondered if they just came to hang out or if they really relished the thought of being vamp food. A shiver crawled up my spine. Saul and I were next. He motioned for me to go ahead of him, so I stepped forward. Elder Beckett smiled, his wiry, white eyebrows curled like caterpillars, making him seem less scary. "My dear, I don't think it's a good idea for you to be here, what with Mercedes falling so recently."

"I want to be."

He stared at me and pondered my words for a moment. "Would you like me to do it?"

I nodded, biting my lip. This was going to suck. I closed my eyes and held out my right forefinger. A zip of lightning and it was all over. When I opened my eyes, a tiny cut was present and blood was pooling inside the fissure. I squeezed the end of my finger and hoped with everything in me that my blood would be good enough this time. *Please sink.*

Holding my finger over the vase of bloody water, I squeezed a fat crimson drop into the pool and watched. My heart stopped. It hung in the water, neither floating nor sinking. I looked at Saul, who was too focused on the drop to acknowledge me. I looked back and finally, finally, it began to sink ever so slowly to the bottom of the vase, leaving a pink-tinged tendril streaming behind it.

FOUR

FOUR OF THE TEN OF US WERE ANEMIC. THAT LEFT SIX TO FIGHT FOR FIVE spots. The odds weren't nearly as bad as I imagined, but of the six who were left, all were physically fit for the most part and seemed to be at the top of their game. I wasn't out of the woods yet.

In addition to Saul, there was a middle-aged couple who lived a few streets away from me, a familiar-looking man who looked to be around thirty, and a boy who had to be his son. Surely they wouldn't send them together. What if the unspeakable happened? Maybe I did have a chance.

Elder Beckett ushered the four who were dismissed to the door, thanking them for volunteering and urging them to please come back next week to apply. As quickly as he pushed them out the door, a large wooden door behind the pulpit swung open and through it entered a night-walker. He was tall and muscular but lithe, even in his movements. His hair was dark, but not completely black. It was the color of the soil, of the silt that stained the black water. His skin was pale and he was young, or at least he looked it. They were all rumored to be hundreds of years old.

When he strode into the room, it was as if he owned it. Every eye was on him. He kept his features passive and stepped toward the Elders with an extended hand, which they accepted with smiles. "Thank you for coming, Roman," Elder Yankee and then Elder Brown said in turn.

The night-walker smiled at the men who ran our Colony. His teeth were perfect pearls, and I gasped when I saw his fangs. They were longer than I'd imagined and looked sharp on the ends, needlelike and dangerous. My gasp drew his attention and his eyes locked onto mine. They weren't red or black or weird at all; they were brown-black, like his hair; beautiful, framed by sooty lashes and brows.

The vampire turned his attention back to the Elders, who asked us to come forward. As silly as it seemed, they asked us to balance on one foot and then the other. We jogged single-file around the perimeter of the room. No one faltered. If this was the test for agility, no wonder people were being caught by the Infected. It would take more than a jog around a room and basic balance to avoid the newer ones, especially.

We were asked to line up at the front of the room. I didn't miss how the three sets of rheumy eyes looked at me. Yellow-white mixed with pity and dismissal. They were going to send me home. I clenched my fists, pressing my lips tightly.

Saul nudged me. "How soon do you need a husband?" he whispered.

"As soon as possible," I admitted without looking at him. I was still staring holes into the old men in front of us.

Clearing his throat, Saul said, "Let's do it. Marry me."

My mouth gaped open and I tore my eyes away from the Elders. As my gaze slid toward Saul, who was standing to my left, my eyes made contact with the vamp's. The night-walker shook his head once, almost imperceptibly. Then he said something to the Elders to which only they were privy, followed by the shuffling of feet and clearing of throats. "This is quite unorthodox," one muttered, but I was too busy watching the vamp to pay attention to which Elder had spoken.

"Well?" Saul questioned with a nudge.

Elder Beckett began talking. "It seems we need six for this particular rotation. You've all been accepted. Report to the pavilion tomorrow morning before sunrise for the first feeding. If you're new, please take one of the papers on the table at the back of the room. It will explain the process and expectations. Tomorrow night, you will all leave the Colony together and go on a hunt to find food. Get some rest. You'll need it." After Mercedes fell, the hunts were cancelled. We needed to find meat. We *would* find meat! I would help!

I turned to Saul, who was smiling. "You're in!" He picked me up and spun me around, my dress whirling around my legs. My laughter mixed with his as I hugged his neck. Maybe being married to Saul wouldn't be so bad after all. He was handsome and obviously kind, but why would he agree to such a crazy proposal?

When he sat me back down, I could see the night-walker over Saul's broad shoulder, watching me with a strange look on his face – half dare, half amusement. I turned and headed toward the table in the back to pick up one of the informational papers. I needed to know what I was in for.

Saul caught my arm. "Get your paper, but I want to talk to you about it all. Some things aren't quite right," he whispered conspiratorially.

"How would you – OH! You've been before. I'm stupid. Ignore me."

Saul stopped in his tracks and stood straight. "You are not stupid, Porschia. Don't put yourself down. I have a feeling you get enough of that from other people."

He was right. I swallowed and squeezed past a couple of the others who were milling around. The table had one last paper on it. Someone would need to hand-write some more. Before we stepped outside, Tim Brown poked his head around the corner. "Can you two wait outside for a sec? We just want to meet with everyone before tomorrow if you have a few moments."

Saul and I both agreed and stepped outside. The fresh air, now warm from the sun that burned away the cool mist, was exactly what I needed. We weren't inside for more than a half hour, but when you were so vested in something, time slowed to a crawl. It was during that time that stress and worry and fear crept into your mind and body, wearing you down, eating and clawing at you from the inside out.

HOLDING THE PAPER TIGHTLY, I LET THE SUN'S RAYS WARM MY SKIN, FOR once thankful of the dark fabric of my dress. In the summer I loathed it because it drew in the sun. Saul stood a few feet away. "I wasn't kidding," he said softly.

Now that I'd made it into the rotation, the urgency of finding a husband wasn't as severe. I had seven days before I had to begin worrying again. "I know," I answered. "And I'm grateful, but I have a new proposal."

He offered a lop-sided grin and stepped closer. "What's that?"

"Let's get to know each other better over the next week and see if you're still interested."

Saul nodded thoughtfully. "I accept."

The paper in my hands rattled, drawing my attention from him. I was about to read about what was expected of me when the door of the hall swung open wide. Mary Brown filed out, then Tim, followed by the father/son pair. Everyone shook hands politely.

Tim and Mary were kind people, well-suited for each other with similar senses of humor, and obviously in love. She teased him about keeping up with her in the woods, and he suggestively indicated that he couldn't wait to see her in "those pants" again. I made a mental note to borrow clothes from Ford. Dresses weren't going to cut it.

Tim's blond hair was receding and his stomach was slightly paunched. He was shorter than Saul by several inches, but his rosy cheeks and ever-present smile set me at ease immediately. I envied Mary's shorter stature and rounded hips. Her hair was dark brown like mine, but streaked with glittering silver in a few places.

Victor Freeman and his son James had beautiful dark chocolate skin and hair. They stood tall and lean by each other's side and wore the same serious expressions. To them, this was no game. It was no game at all.

Victor spoke up. "I think we should make a plan for tonight. We have one week and need to provide as much meat as possible to the Colony. I've been teaching James about snares and traps. We can set those tonight in hopes of catching game throughout the week."

"That sounds like a great plan," Tim offered. "We should split into groups of two to cover more ground. Saul and Porschia can head east, Mary and I will head west, and you and James can set traps to the north, carving a path between us. That may flush any animals out and send them running toward one group or the other. It'll increase our chance for success."

The paper in my hands began to rattle. "Is it common to split up?"

Victor shook his head. "No, but it's been so long since a team brought enough meat to feed the entire village that it's a necessary evil. We need to make this work." The lines in the skin of his forehead deepened. He was right to be concerned.

Saul patted me on the back. "We've got the east. Right, Porsch?"

I looked at the confidence radiating from him. He stood tall and I felt sure he'd protect me even if the night-walker who escorted us wouldn't. "Yeah," I agreed.

The Browns and Freemans said their goodbyes and strode away toward their respective homes. Saul nudged me. "Let's go over your list. There are some things you should know."

FIVE

In scrawling, hand-written print, the word 'Rotation' stared back at me.

Rotation

The rotation began when the treaty between the night-walkers and Blackwater Colony was signed. You have been chosen for the rotation. Your duties are as follows:

1. Present yourself at the pavilion before dawn and just after dusk each day of the seven day rotation. You will be partnered with a night-walker. You will provide him or her a small amount of your blood. Despite rumors you may have heard, Night-walkers do not need much to survive on. They will only take what is required, as per our treaty.

2. After you've provided blood in the morning, you may report to Town Hall to collect your extra food rations for the day. Please stay well nourished. This will make you and your blood healthy and desirable.

3. You will be expected to leave the Colony at night to hunt. The other members of the current rotation will go with you. A night-walker will escort and guard you, as night-walkers cannot be harmed by the Infected. As per the treaty, for another layer of protection from the Infected, you will be gifted a special ring from the night-walker with which you partner. He or she will explain the significance of the ring.

That was all the paper said. There was no information about hunting, skills that might come in handy, about the Infected, or what to do if you encountered one—nothing.

My mouth was hanging open, so Saul nudged it closed. "What questions do you have? I can see your brain working."

"What do you do if you see an Infected?"

Saul swallowed. "Run. It's all you can do."

"What if they attack you?"

"You fight back and use the ring as a last resort." Saul looked away uncomfortably.

I grabbed his arm. "You've encountered them?"

He nodded. "I've seen them, but we ran. We got away." My sister didn't.

"Are they terrifying like everyone says? Rotting?" I choked on the word, praying my sister wasn't suffering.

Saul shook his head. "Mercedes wouldn't be yet. The newly-Infected are even more frightening, though. They still look human. They're slower than we are, but they're much faster than an older Infected. And they still think. They smile. It's scary as hell."

"So, some magical ring is supposed to keep me safe? This is insane." I wiped away the sweat that beaded on my temple.

Saul pushed a strand of hair away from my face and tucked it behind my ear like he had done it a hundred times. "It's not the ring, it's what the ring holds. And it isn't magic, it's a curse."

"What does it hold?" I asked in a trembling voice that matched my fingers and knees.

Saul shifted on his feet and crossed his arms. "Vamp blood."

My eyes widened. "You're kidding."

He shook his head slowly. "No, I'm not kidding, and if you drink it you'll become one of them, so make sure there's no other way. Not that I think you'll need it. I'll be with you. I promise to keep you safe, Porschia."

I swallowed and nodded. It was the only way to answer. My voice would have cracked and so would I. Crying in front of Saul would have weakened me in his eyes, and I needed him to know I was strong, that he could count on me. I was glad I could count on him.

He nudged me. "Hey, want to have dinner with me tonight?"

"No," I rushed to answer. I wouldn't take pity food from anyone. "I'm fine."

Saul shifted uncomfortably, shoving his fists into his pockets. "It's not that. I just thought it would be a nice way to get to know each other."

"Would tomorrow be okay?" I asked, knowing that I wouldn't be able to make anything for us without the extra rations. "My family will be excited to know that I got into the rotation." With a fake beaming smile, I pleaded with him silently to understand.

"Sure. We can eat before we have to feed the night-walkers and then we'll be ready for the hunt."

The thought of needle-sharp fangs biting into my flesh made my skin pebble, but I pasted on a smile and accepted the awkward hug that Saul offered in goodbye. "I have to get to work. I start my apprenticeship today." He smiled proudly.

"Doing what?"

"Carpentry."

"That's wonderful, Saul!" This time, my smile was genuine. "I'm still trying to find a job that I can't screw up, so today, I have to work for the seamstress." I cringed, knowing that yesterday I poked my finger more than I imagined was possible in one day. Maybe I could collect the blood today and my vamp partner could drink it that way instead of...

"Have a good day. I'll see you in the morning at the pavilion."

"You too." He walked away, looking back twice over his shoulder at me, a smile on his face.

WALKING QUICKLY TOWARD MRS. DILLINGER'S SHOP, I TRIED TO KEEP MY mind from spinning. One week. One week to be fed upon, to hunt game for the Colony, to have rations, for Saul to spend time with me and decide if he really did want to marry me. *He would probably change his mind.*

The few houses that weren't needed for shelter were used for shops or storage, not that any currency was exchanged. Everyone had a job. Everyone had needs, so people used whatever skills they possessed to help their neighbors. It all came down to working for the good of the Colony. We had to help one another. Father said that since seeking refuge in Blackwater, no one had ever received word from an outside community.

The walkway to the shop was made of river stones. My boots followed them to the door where I knocked gently before entering. "Come in,

Porschia." Mrs. Margaret Dillinger worked alone. She used to take in clothes and projects from the women who could no longer sew, the arthritis having gnarled their fingers. Yesterday, I saw that hers were twisted, too. Her steps, even down the hallway, were careful and deliberate. She led me through the house and showed me everything, explaining in detail where the supplies were located. I spent much of the day either fetching those same supplies or poking holes into my fingers.

Inside the door, I untied and stepped out of my muddy boots and climbed the wooden staircase. Mrs. Dillinger was a widow, stern but kind. Her hair was gray and she wore glasses with frames that were too big for her face. She explained about her arthritis, how it crippled most that it afflicted, but she swore that staying busy kept her hands from drawing up altogether. Her legs were another story.

The woman wore her wrinkles proudly, telling me that she had earned each and every one throughout her nearly eighty years on this earth. She'd lost all but one of her three children; one in an accident, and one to the Infected. Her youngest son lived in town with his wife. Their two children were married and lived in town, too. The amazing thing was that she didn't let the losses weigh her down. Having one son left, she doled out all of her love and attention on him, his family, and their extended families. She had a legacy to be proud of.

Right to business, Mrs. Dillinger straightened in her chair and pushed herself up, hobbling toward a bed where a bolt of fabric was unrolled. "You did well hemming the men's pants yesterday. I think you have potential. I'm going to show you how to measure someone for a dress and how to cut the pattern based on the woman's measurements."

"Okay." I cringed, thinking of how badly I blundered yesterday. How this woman thought I had any potential at all was beyond me.

A white envelope with the picture of a dress like mine on the front was on the bed on top of the fabric. "You're my guinea pig today, Porschia. Hold your arms out. I'll measure you to show you how to measure someone else."

With my arms stretched wide, she measured my bust, waist, and hips with a tape, scratching each number onto paper. She showed me how to use the guide on the back of the envelope and how to cut the fabric according to the delicate pattern. "This isn't going to last much longer, is it?" I asked.

Mrs. Dillinger smiled. "Nothing lasts forever. And, to answer your question, no. The pattern is almost useless. But if I could teach someone else how to measure and cut, that person could learn from me and carry on without it." With a meaningful glance aimed my way, she smiled. I was probably her last resort. She had no other apprentice.

Avoiding her eyes, I admitted, "I've failed at everything I've tried so far."

Mrs. Dillinger's fingers stilled. She held her needle tightly between her thumb and forefinger and looked up at me. "What else have you tried?"

I sighed, looking up at her. "Baking, basket-weaving, working with the smith. The animals hated me. I think they knew I was scared of them. The only thing I can really do is clean."

Mrs. Dillinger narrowed her eyes. "Nothing wrong in cleaning. I'm sure there are a lot of folks who could use help in that area. But I think you can do this. You'll just have to set your mind on it. If you don't give up on learning from me, I promise not to give up on teaching you. The most important thing is to be patient and not give up on yourself."

She was right. I tended to give up too easily when things didn't come easily. The hunt would be no different. I'd never stepped foot out of Blackwater. I had no idea what to do, but Father might be able to help me. I would just have to avoid Mother long enough to ask him this evening. But no matter how hard I tried to quiet my stomach, it roiled. Mother made it clear that I wasn't welcome at my own home, even though by some miracle I had managed to meet her demand. No matter what, she would still find a way to push me out. Standing on my own two feet was my only option at this point.

"Thank you for teaching me. I'd like to learn."

Mrs. Dillinger nodded and told me how to pin the pattern to the fabric, how to gently cut each panel, and then how to arrange them in order. She never stepped in or chastised, just offered guidance that was firm, but not demanding. In a place I felt sure that failure would find me again, I found hope.

SIX

When the sun crept below the hills beyond the Colony and Mrs. Dillinger and I were both squinting to see our work without candlelight, she stood up and pressed her hands to her lower back. "Time to go home, Porschia. I know you won't be able to work as long tomorrow, but if you want to come and do a little bit, that would be fine."

Tears stung my eyes. I knew I wouldn't be able to go home after the morning rotation. I nodded and choked out, "Thank you."

"Are you afraid?"

I was, but I was more afraid of walking out of the shop's door and facing my own. "A little. I know it's silly."

"Nonsense. Fear is what keeps us alive when we're in danger. It's nature's alarm system. Don't ignore it just to save face."

"Have a good night," I told her, tugging down my dress sleeve.

"See you tomorrow."

I rushed down the steps and eased the heavy wooden door closed beside me, making my way across the wooden porch planks and over the river rock to the cracked concrete beyond. Several people passed me and I nodded in greeting, but kept plodding toward the house. When I drew near, I could see the soft glow of candlelight flickering in the windows.

Fast footsteps came from behind before I could turn around. "Hey, Porsch!" Ford's squeaking voice called out as he threw his arm around my shoulder. He was taller than me and chattered excitedly about his afternoon tending the animals and how Father had arranged a few jobs for him in town.

"How was Mr. Jent?" I teased. Mr. Jent was a crotchety old man who loved to bark orders and tell dirty jokes, even to my fourteen year old brother.

Ford just laughed. "Same old. I chopped wood for him all morning. You can imagine the jokes that stemmed from that alone." I smiled but slowed as we approached the corner of the yard. "Mother's happy," he offered gently.

"Why?"

"Seems that you getting chosen for the rotation benefitted our dinner table tonight."

"What? I don't get extra rations until tomorrow."

He shook his head. "It was one of my deliveries this evening. Fresh chicken sounds good right about now."

My breath left in a whoosh. "A whole chicken?"

Ford sniffed the air so I did too, and my mouth began to water at the scent of fried chicken wafting from the house. "Hey, uh, listen," Ford started tentatively. "About tomorrow, please be careful out there. Don't leave the night-walker. They can keep you safe. I don't know what happened with Cedes, but just stay with the vamp."

I nodded, watching his Adam's apple bob up and down. He'd barely mentioned her since she fell ill. "Think Father will help me learn a few things?"

"Like what?"

"Crossbow or knife. Something. Anything."

Ford's brows nearly touched. "I think he will. At least, I hope he will." Father had been distant since Mercedes' accident. He was pulling away, constantly making excuses to avoid being home. Mother harped about it constantly when she wasn't raging at me. Luckily for Ford, he was her baby – her youngest – and being a male in the Colony, the least likely to disappoint her. He was a good kid, strong and hard-working. Opportunities were open for him everywhere.

Ford tugged me toward the door. Tiny remnants of splintered wood clung to his gray pants, the shoulders of his white shirt, and a few strands of his sandy hair. "You should wash up," I told him before he opened the door with a grin.

"Where's the fun in that?" He loved to ruffle Mother's feathers.

Somehow the odor of the animals he tended this afternoon had seeped into his shirt and I covered my mouth and nose with my hand. Mother would be livid, but not at me. I smiled at my baby brother. Diverting her attention was his goal. I loved him for that, for his heart.

Ford groaned when he entered the house. He followed his stomach to the kitchen and I couldn't help but follow mine. Mother was hovering near the pan over the fire as the meat sizzled and popped happily.

"Smells great, Mother," Ford said, plopping into a chair at the table. Mother turned to look at him, her smile fading when she saw me standing in the room. She wiped her hands on the pale apron at her waist and turned away again.

"You made the cut. I'm surprised that they would want you, Porschia." Her words were like tiny sticks shoved beneath my finger nails. They hurt like hell but wouldn't kill me.

Ford straightened. "You should thank her, Mother. If it wasn't for Porschia sticking her neck out, we wouldn't be eating tonight and we all know it."

Mother whirled around, finger pointing at Ford, ready for a fight, but Father's booming voice silenced her as he stepped into the room. "He's right. Leave her be, Miranda."

Dinner was tense, spent chewing meat that was much too hot because we couldn't wait to get something into our empty stomachs. It burned the roof of my mouth, but I couldn't eat fast enough. I tore at the tender meat, ripping skin from bone, swallowing gristle and all. The bones on our plates were just that, completely cleaned. Chicken was all we ate because we had plenty. After next week, we would be starving again.

"You get your extra rations tomorrow?" Mother asked.

"After morning rotation."

"Bring them home right away before you go to Mrs. Dillinger's shop. You *are* still welcome there, right?"

I gritted my teeth. "Yes."

"Good. Just leave them on the porch for us."

Father didn't have time to show me his crossbow or how to use a knife that night. He made an excuse that a neighbor a few streets away needed his help and hurried out the door, leaving us gaping at his retreat, but he did wake me when the sky was still black as pitch. The stars twinkled in the clear sky and on the ground, a fine layer of frost was laid. It wasn't the first frost of late fall, but I still wasn't quite ready for winter.

"You can take my lamp if you'd like," Father offered as he led me down the steps of our house. I shoved my boots on and laced them up.

"Thank you, but I can find the way." We only had one lamp, and Ford or Mother might need it.

I stood back up and looked at the lines on his face. They seemed deeper this morning than they did last night somehow, or maybe it was just a trick of the candlelight. Father held a handkerchief out to me. "For strength."

"Thank you." I took it, feeling something soft beneath the fabric.

"I want to see you before you hunt tonight. I'll show you what I can this evening."

All I could do was try to smile and ease the door open quietly. Greeted by the frigid air, I shivered as I left him behind.

"They won't hurt you," he called out to me.

"I know." I *didn't* know, but hopefully my false bravado calmed his nerves. In me he saw Mercedes, his daughter who entered the rotation, left on a hunt that she'd been on half a dozen times, and never returned. He saw loss, anguish, and regret. He saw hopelessness.

SEVEN

THE FROZEN EARTH CRUNCHED LOUDLY BENEATH THE TREAD OF MY BOOTS as I made my way toward the pavilion. I didn't own a coat and Mother had locked Mercedes' room after she fell. I couldn't take Ford's because he would need it when he woke up. Stuffing my hands in the pockets sewn into the skirt of my dress, I balled my fists, hoping to cling to the warmth inside.

A bitter breeze blew against my back, parting my hair against my nape and whipping it into my face.

"Where's your coat?"

I jumped and screeched, clawing out toward the voice. Saul stepped out of the shadows, holding his lamp up, illuminating his ornery grin.

"What are you doing out here? You don't even live near here!"

He chuckled. "No, but you do. I thought we could walk together. I thought you might have some questions about this morning."

The harsh breath that left my body made a warm plume of steam. "It's going to hurt, isn't it?"

Saul fell into step beside me. "Actually not really—not like you think." He smiled and raked his fingers through his hair. "If they lick the area before they bite, it numbs the skin. You don't feel much more than a pinch."

"And they always numb it?"

"That's been my experience," he answered honestly.

"How many times have you been in the rotation?"

He sniffs. "Eleven." My eyes widened. That was a lot of blood and time outside the Colony. "Not every hunt is for food."

"What do you mean?"

"The bolts of fabric that you sewed yesterday? That came from town, from inside the flood wall. In the summer, they send you in to forage for supplies. Most stuff is depleted now, though. When it's gone, it's gone. A long time ago, people used to go beyond the forest where the farms were to look for lost or forgotten livestock. That's how we have the ones at the barn."

The barn was close to the river, near the night-walker section of town, beyond Mercedes' favorite section of the river but before the cemetery. Though mostly defiant and numb yesterday, I remembered the nickering of the horses, the bleating of the lambs. There were cows, goats, chickens, ducks, and pigs. Animals were only slaughtered when it was absolutely necessary, which was why the chicken in our kitchen was such a surprise yesterday.

"Did you enjoy your chicken last night?" I asked, glancing over at Saul, who was removing his jacket. "What are you doing? It's freezing."

He smiled and tucked the warm wool around my shoulders. "I know, but I've been warm for a while. It's your turn." He paused. "Do you think you can borrow a coat for the hunt? It's going to be really cold tonight."

"I can get Mercedes' old coat. It's just... I didn't want to wake everyone this morning."

He looked ahead at Town Hall in the distance. It looked worse at night. The wooden siding that used to be white was peeling and some boards were missing altogether. It was slowly falling apart. And yet it fit in this place, the breaking down of something once holy and revered.

"What chicken?" he asked.

I stopped in my tracks. "Um, Ford delivered a chicken from the barn. He said each of us were gifted one."

Saul stopped with me and ticked his head back. "Maybe they overlooked us or something." He searched my eyes. If Ford did what I think he did, I was going to kill him before the Elders learned of his theft and punished him. "I won't say anything," he gently reassured me, motioning me forward. The sun was slowly lightening the sky to the east, now somewhere between dark blue and light. Stars were still winking down upon us, but dawn was going to make her majesty known in a short time.

"So the night-walkers can't be in sunlight, right?"

Saul nodded. "I think that's why the 'before dawn and after dusk' feeding times. That, and you never see them walking the streets during the day."

The pavilion was little more than a concrete square with a three tiered water fountain in the center that was taller than I would be if I stood on Saul's shoulders. It hadn't run in years, and the water that was left was stagnant and filled with rotting leaves and larvae. There were concrete benches around the perimeter of the square, and that was where we met Victor and James and where Tim and Mary found the four of us waiting impatiently. Even the normally-jovial couple was quiet this morning.

I shrugged Saul's jacket off when I saw the night-walkers approaching from the other side of the pavilion. There were six of them. I thought only five lived in Blackwater. No wonder they needed another person for the rotation.

Like a gaggle of geese, Roman was at the head, at the center of the vee, while the others trailed behind him at either side. It was intimidating. James eased closer to Victor and Mary to Tim. I didn't know if they even realized they were doing it. Fight or flight was an innate response, and everything within was screaming at me to run in the opposite direction. Eat or be eaten, and we were offering ourselves up for breakfast.

Roman's dark hair was disheveled, but it didn't detract from his looks at all. His eyes locked onto mine for a scant beat before scanning the others. "Thank you for volunteering for the rotation. Per the treaty, we will only take as much blood as we need." He zeroed in on one of the male vamps to his left. The guy was average in height, build, and looks. Olive skin, dark hair, light blue eyes. It was a strange combination, but it was his mannerisms that frightened me. He was sizing us up. Suddenly, I knew what the animals felt like before they were led to slaughter.

"Since you are new to the coven, you may choose first, Tage."

Tage smiled, revealing his fangs. "I choose the young female."

Saul inched in front of me slightly.

"Oh, shit. Why do I *not* have a good feeling about this?" I whispered to his back.

The other vampires, only one female among them, chose from among the rest of us. Saul was chosen by the beautiful girl, with hair that was so blonde it was nearly white and lips the color of rubies. I couldn't help but feel inadequate and jealous that her mouth would be on his neck. I assumed that was where they would bite. That was where Mercedes had been bitten. Two tiny pin-prick holes that healed each night, only for new ones to be inflicted in the morning.

The others paired off, walking to separate benches with the vamp that chose them. Victor's, a tall, lanky man with skin so pale it was almost translucent, had already bitten his neck and was taking deep draws. James watched, trying to mask the horror on his face.

My view was suddenly blocked by a thick chest. "Hello, kitten," Tage cooed.

"I'm not a kitten."

"If you let me feed you back, you could be a queen. *My* queen." *Feed me back? Not even slightly tempting.*

"Eww. No, thank you. Can we just get this over with?"

Roman was with Mary on the bench next to us, sitting behind her. I watched him move her hair out of the way, brushing it back and holding it in place. His eyes never left mine as he licked the line of the artery that ran up her neck and waited.

Tage moved me backward until the backs of my knees found the concrete bench behind them. I sat stiffly, every inch of me trembling – not from the cold – from him, from what he was about to do to me. He straddled the bench behind me, the two of us facing Roman and Mary. Roman had begun to feed, but still watched us with hawk-like eyes that darted from Tage to me and back again. Tage's thick arm slithered around my stomach and clamped me tightly to him. He swept my long hair over my other shoulder to expose the skin of my neck, delicate and tender. My pulse raced. I could hear the thump-thump swooshing in my ears. I waited, but no lick came.

Instead I felt pinching, tearing pain, burning and relentless. I gasped for breath and then a high-pitched shriek filled the air. It was me.

Roman's eyes narrowed as Tage sucked greedily away. I could feel him draining me, my soul, and my life.

Dark spots swarmed my vision like a plague of locusts, hungry and frantic. I heard Roman swearing, and then more pain. My throat was ripped open. Tage had killed me.

I landed in a heap, one arm twisted behind me, but I couldn't move. "Shh." Strong arms pulled me into safety. "I've got you," Roman said softly.

"Give me a coat!" Roman screamed at the others. The night-walkers just smirked and walked away from the scene. Tage tsked his friend. "You interrupted my breakfast. What a rude host you are," he teased Roman.

"The treaty is important to our coven, and you just violated it." He bared his long fangs. "If she dies, I'll drain you myself."

At that threat, Tage's cold eyes locked onto mine, promising so many things: that I was his, that I'd better live, and that everything that just happened was my fault. He turned and strode away, following the others back to the few houses that were scattered across the square. Saul tucked his warm jacket over me. Raking his fingers over his hair, he paced and cursed. "Bastard. Please say she'll be okay."

Roman nodded. "Porschia, I need to numb your skin. I promise it will not hurt. Do you hear me?"

My teeth were chattering too violently to answer. I couldn't move. He moved my hair aside, exposing the wound. "It feels worse than it is. I'll take care of it." With a warm swipe of his tongue, the pain eased and my body's response began to calm.

When I could talk, I croaked, "Is it bad?"

Saul shook his head. "No, it's just two small puncture marks."

"It felt so much worse than that."

Roman spoke up. "Venom. You need to leave. I will deal with Tage when I get home, but I need you to keep quiet about this incident. The treaty is...let's just say that everything is already on shaky ground. If the treaty isn't in place the coven will have no choice but to feed, and volunteers will be a thing of the past. We, too, must survive."

Victor, James, Mary, and Tim stood quietly behind us. They assented with nods and murmurs and slowly retreated to their homes. Saul wouldn't leave my side. "I'll take her home," he vowed.

"She needs to eat. It'll replenish her energy and help build her blood. She needs meat, protein."

He swallowed. "I'll see to it."

Roman's arms loosened around me and he slowly stood up, placing my feet on the ground. My heart skipped and butterflies took flight, their wings tickling my stomach. I'd heard Mercedes talk about swooning over boys our whole lives, but never dead ones, or undead ones, for that matter. Why wasn't I feeling those wings for Saul?

EIGHT

Saul offered to carry me home but I wouldn't let him, so he walked slowly with me. My legs quivered and I felt weak, but he walked at my pace, side by side, his arm at my lower back ready to swoop in if I stumbled. (Which I did a few times.) "Do you have any chicken left over?" Glancing up at him, I could tell he knew the answer.

"I'll be fine. We just have to stop for the rations this morning."

"You need to eat."

I laughed mirthlessly. "I need the rations in order to eat, Saul."

His jaw worked back and forth, but he led us to Town Hall, ran in, and grabbed both his sack and mine and came right back to me like a boomerang. The burlap bags were half full of something, I hoped meat or cheese, but anything was better than nothing.

About a block from my house, Saul stopped and told me to hold on a sec. He rifled through one of the sacs gently. "Cheese, bread, and two eggs, so be careful. Here." He extended a hand with a wedge of cheddar. "It's not meat, but it'll help. Cook the eggs when you get inside."

I nodded, nibbling at the exquisite orange triangle, trying to savor every morsel. With cheeks stuffed with cheese, I accepted the sack he gave me. "Dinner this evening before we go back?" he asked hopefully.

"Sure. Where do you want to meet?"

"What about under the big maple near the river?"

"I'll meet you there."

He nodded and I shrugged out of his coat for the second time that morning. "I'll get Mercedes' for tonight," I promised. Saul sat his sack down and pulled his coat on, buttoning it against the cold. The sun had risen during our long trek home. Roman would already be inside by now.

"Take care of yourself, Porsch."

"You too."

I watched him walk away, one hand clutching the extra rations and the other on the cold metal handle of our front door. When I pushed it open, Father was standing there. I breathed a sigh of relief. "You look pale," he said in a concerned voice.

"It was my first time. It freaked me out a little bit."

"Let's cook some breakfast." He ushered me inside. "Your mother and Ford are still asleep."

"You haven't woken her?"

Father grinned. "Not yet."

Father stoked the fire while I broke the two eggs into a pan. I would split the ration with Father and Ford, but if Mother thought she was taking more food out of my mouth, she was sorely mistaken. "I have to work the soil in the back garden this morning so it can rest for spring, but I want you to come back from Mrs. Dillinger's at midday. I'll teach you what I can."

"Thank you."

He smiled slightly and told me to cook my eggs. "They're *our* eggs," I corrected.

Father placed his hand over mine on the pan. "They are yours. You are giving so that the entire Colony can have meat."

"What if the hunt isn't successful?"

"The risk you take is still appreciated, Porschia. And you will eat every bite of both eggs this morning."

"Fine, but we split the other rations." That would be bread, because I'd stuffed my face full of all the cheese on the way here.

"The bread and cheese will be wonderful. Thank you."

"Cheese?"

Father rifled into the bag on the counter, pulling out an orange triangle identical to the one I ate on the journey home. Saul took the wrong bag…or he gave me his on purpose.

Heat flooded my cheeks and my head sank in shame. What he must think of me. The reason he proposed was obvious. Pity. He felt sorry for me. And the reason I even told him that I needed a husband or the rotation's rations? Desperation. Weakness. Everything a man wouldn't want in a woman.

Mother made her appearance just as I swallowed the last steaming chunk of egg. She scowled, screeching "What is this? You're eating all of the extra food we have?"

Father stopped her rant. "She needed the energy! She's hunting so we can all eat this week or next."

Mother's eyes narrowed. "You'd better hope the hunt is successful, you pig of a girl!"

"Enough, Miranda!" Father shouted at her. My fork clattered to the floor and I stood abruptly to go wash my dish and find Ford. "And she needs Mercedes' coat!"

"She will *not* touch her things."

"She *will.* I'll not lose another daughter because you're hell bent on placing blame in the wrong place. Your bitterness is suffocating us all. Now allow her into Mercedes' room, or I'll remove the door from the hinges and let her in myself."

Screw the dish, I thought, abandoning it in the kitchen. I jogged up the steps and took an immediate left, barging into Ford's room. He was snoring, one arm thrown over his eyes. I shuffled through his drawers, pulling out one of the few pairs of pants he had clean and one of his button down shirts. I'd have to hem the pant legs to make it work, but I could make it temporary. "Just use darts to secure it," Mrs. Dillinger's voice said in my mind.

I slipped from Ford's room without him even stirring and turned to meet Mother in the hallway. With a scowl, she used an old key to turn the lock on Mercedes' door. "If you ruin it..." she threatened.

"Mercedes is gone, Mother. She won't need it anymore." My voice sounded as tired as I felt. Without a word, Mother retreated to her room and slammed the door behind her. Sighing, I opened the door to Mercedes' room. Her bed was exactly as she'd left it that day, down to the quilt perfectly in place on the bed. She always made her bed so neatly, even though everything else was a mess. Her dresser was strewn with things she and I found during our childhood: jewelry boxes and trinkets that went in them, books and paper, pencils. Her sketches, intricately blurry, of the townspeople, the falls at the river, me and Ford, hung on her walls. When she would sketch, she got the most serious expression on her face. She would bite her lip and her hands would fly over the paper in a frenzy. From that flurry of lead and paper emerged beauty, a moment of life captured by a young girl's raw talent.

As responsibilities grew in number she had less and less time to draw, but every so often I would catch her scribbling furiously over the paper. My hand drifted over the drawing near her dresser. It was of a man in a long coat, walking along the pavilion at night. Could she have seen a night-walker? Mercedes saw the world differently. She taught me to consider the goodness in everything. Since she fell, I'd forgotten that. I was letting Mother's bitterness seep in and steal that joy away from me. I needed to cling tightly to it. And to do that, I would need to leave home soon.

From her closet, I grabbed everything that looked like it might fit, which wasn't much. A spare dress, some underthings, and most importantly, Mercedes' double-breasted, black woolen coat. Catching a glimpse of a pair of sturdier boots tucked neatly into the corner, I snatched them up and walked quickly to my room. Mother would lock her memory away again soon.

Although Mrs. Dillinger wasn't feeling well, we continued to work on the dress I began yesterday. She instructed me on the types of stitches to use in various places to make the fabric hold together strongly. I made her tea and she insisted that I take some with her.

"How did it go this morning?"

Awful. Horrific. Terrifying. I almost died.

"Not as bad as I expected," I lied.

She made a non-committal noise and glanced at my neck where the wounds were beginning to ache before averting her eyes to the contents of her tea cup. It was almost midday. "My father wants to show me a few things before I have to try to sleep this afternoon."

"The tea will help you rest."

"It will?"

"Mm. It'll calm your nerves, too."

"Will it make me a good hunter?" I teased with a grin.

She smiled back, blowing the surface of the hot, golden liquid. "I certainly hope so. Go on home. I'll see you for a few hours tomorrow morning."

I stood and gathered my teacup and saucer, but her voice stopped me. "My door is always open if you need a place to stay, Porschia." I swallowed thickly. "I live here. That's my room across the hall," she said, motioning to it. "There are several rooms in this old house, and most of them are empty. One holds the bolts of fabric and other supplies, but there is plenty of room for you here if you need or want it."

"Thank you," I whispered and left her behind me.

My feet carried me home and by midday, it was warm enough to relax without a coat on. Mercedes' scent still clung to it. Every time I put it on, took it off, or simply looked down, I could smell her sweetness. I could remember her delicate fingers working over the buttons. It made my heart hurt, but in the best way when that happened. It was like a part of her still lived.

Father was waiting on the porch in a rocking chair when I arrived. Sweat dampened his hair and his fingers curled around the edges of the arm rests, turning his knuckles white. "What's wrong?"

"Nothing." He pasted on a fake smile. "Let's go around back."

He took out a large knife and handed it to me before retrieving another for himself. He gripped it tightly and showed me how to slash, stab at things. I was confused. "Father, if I'm hunting deer and bear, why would I need a knife? I wouldn't be fighting them so closely, would I?" *Please say no.*

Father let out a heavy sigh. "There are other things in the woods that are far more dangerous. I want you to be able to defend yourself if you..." He stopped, his voice shaking.

"The Infected?"

He nodded and swiped the wetness pooling beneath his eyes. "There's more. And you cannot breathe a word of this to anyone. Only a few people in town know about this. We're working with the leader of the night-walkers to handle the situation."

"Okay. I promise not to say anything."

Staring at the trees that stood beyond our back yard, which was basically a huge vegetable garden, Father told me something that shook me to the core. "A night-walker attacked someone last night. I found a body in a shallow section of the river this morning."

"Dead?"

He pursed his lips. "Bitten and then tossed out like garbage. They weren't even drained of blood." Tage's face immediately came to mind. But then Father said, "It's probably a new vampire. I understand they get overwhelmed with hunger and emotion and are very difficult to control. The night-walkers call it 'frenzy'." Was Tage a new vampire? I didn't get that impression from him at all. And if it wasn't Tage, who was it?

"I want you to be careful tonight. Stay with Saul. He knows how to bring down the game. You just worry about watching his back and staying alive. No matter what, you run if you get in trouble. I don't care if you have to leave everyone behind. *You. Run*," he said, emphasizing each word with a jab of his finger. "I can't lose you, too."

Father's lip trembled and mine began to wobble. I nodded my understanding and watched as he walked toward the house, unable to withstand the weight of the emotions swirling in the air around us.

NINE

Mother either stayed in her room all day or else she wasn't home. Her absence allowed me to swipe a pint jar of corn and two biscuits that she made yesterday and was saving for tonight. I would have felt guilty had my ration bag not contained fresher bread. Walking through the sunshine and grass toward the river, I hoisted the burlap sack onto my shoulder. Ford's clothes, which I temporarily altered to work for me, and to my knowledge he didn't yet realize were gone, were tucked inside, along with the food. I didn't want to go back home after dinner and after we *became* dinner.

My stomach knotted. Saul was hoping to get to know me because I suggested it, but what if he didn't like me? What if the gossips found out and smeared our names? I knew that if we were to ever get married he would have to ask Father for permission, and would likely receive it. Father would respect him as much as I did.

Mrs. Dillinger loved company and she loved to talk, though not idly. I replayed our conversation in my mind. "Why are our clothes like this? Old-timey? The vampires wear modern clothes."

Roman had worn denim pants, a snug-fitting cotton shirt, and a leather jacket.

She pursed her lips upon hearing the word 'vampire'. "They come and go into the city, taking whatever they want. Most of the homes and buildings were burned after the Great Infection to kill the germs, but what most young folks don't know is that the infection killed probably ninety-five percent of the people it touched. The rest were changed. It was like they reverted to a more primitive version of human beings. The bacteria might have affected their brains and their ability to think clearly and make decisions, it was said."

"Who burned the city?" With a haunted look in her eyes, she answered, "The only ones who escaped. Though not at first. Running was first. When things settled, people snuck back in to... well, to destroy the infection." *As well as the people who were Infected,* she didn't say. Wasn't that murder? What if those people could have been cured somehow, even if in the future?

"I see the question in your eyes and the same one's been running through my mind for years." She paused, folding her hands into her lap. "To answer your question, the Elders were afraid of using clothes from the city. They thought the infection had contaminated everything and were afraid to expose survivors to the germs. There was one factory on the outskirts of town with bolts of fabric and everything needed to make clothing inside: needles, thread, enormous machines that would sew the garments for you. The Elders took what they could from that place, including the few patterns we have, thinking it was better to make our own. The patterns are costumes."

"I saw that on the package," I giggled.

"They wanted women to look like women and to be modest. Girls from before were very bold in their clothing choices." She raised her brow and smiled.

"I borrowed clothes from Ford. Can you tell me how to dart them so that they fit me?"

"Absolutely," she immediately agreed. "A girl can't hunt in skirts, now can she?"

Saul was standing beneath the Oak waiting for me, a grin on his cleanly-shaven face. He smelled of pine soap. "Hi."

"Hi." I waved with my free hand. *Let the awkwardness begin.*

He motioned behind him where a blanket was spread over a nearby log. He must have dragged the heavy wood over, because I didn't notice it there the other day. "This is nice, thank you." I settled onto the blanket and took the food from my bag. He brought two boiled eggs and a jar of green beans. We would eat well tonight, and the company here would be much better than at home. Thank goodness he remembered forks and a jar of boiled water for drinking.

"How was the beginning of your apprenticeship?"

He smiled for a quick second. "They aren't happy that I'm in the rotation; something about losing me before I even get started. They think it's too risky. That's why many from town aren't volunteering at all anymore."

"The problem with that is that if no one volunteers..."

"Exactly. They will feed, one way or another."

The river water was gently tickling the rocks in its bed. A few buzzards circled overhead. Normally I wouldn't have given them a second thought, but Mercedes was somewhere across the creek bank, slowly dying, unless an animal had gotten to her first.

My appetite left in a rush. "Tell me something about yourself," I asked Saul. It was more of a plea.

He finished chewing and then took a swallow of water. "I don't like how that vampire looks at you."

"Tage? The one who--"

"I don't like him either, but I was talking about Roman, the leader."

My heart fluttered like hummingbird wings. "I think Tage is the one to be worried about. He seems intense."

Saul growled, grasping his fork until his fingers turned white. "He's psychotic. He almost killed you."

"That's what they do though, right? I mean, if the treaty wasn't in place, they would kill us."

"They could try," Saul bit out. "I want you to stick close to me tonight. We're splitting up, but we don't have to put distance between the two of us – just the other pairs."

"I agree. I'll stay close. My father taught me a few things this afternoon."

Saul smiled, looking up at the evening sky. The sun was inching slower toward the Western hills. "It's almost time."

"I know." Dread oozed into my veins and crawled through my body. I didn't want to ever see Tage again, but I would have to face him soon.

"They shouldn't even let him feed from you tonight."

I swallowed my fear. "They will. They don't care about us."

We packed up our dinner and the blanket. "Can we swing by my porch and get rid of this stuff?"

"Sure." I'd forgotten that he lived along the fastest route to the pavilion. We made tracks toward his house, Mercedes' sturdy boots carrying me forward beside Saul. His house, a brick Colonial that looked a lot like mine but with a beautiful new porch that spanned the length of the front, was lit up from within. Candles burned inside the windows, flickering like the stars above. I waited near the sidewalk while he quickly jogged to the porch and laid his blanket and bag down.

He hurried to me. "If my mom sees you, we'll be here till midnight."

"She doesn't know about your hasty proposal?"

Saul smirked, clasping my hand and pulling me toward the pavilion. "Not yet. I haven't gotten a yes from you. We'll tell her after you agree."

I smiled over at him. We walked quickly, arriving just as the sun set. But this time, we were the last ones to arrive. Roman looked irritated at our tardiness and at our locked hands. "Change of partners," he announced brusquely. Tage's eyes tore through me as he stalked toward Mary. Roman watched him like a hawk.

I squeezed Saul's hand once before he left to sit on his own bench. I sat on mine and waited. Roman stood and watched as Tage numbed Mary's skin with a disgustingly slimy lick and then sank his teeth into her neck. He groaned as he drawled deeply three times and then pulled away, licking the wound to seal it. Her blood tinged his fangs a pink-red as he sneered at me.

I felt a warm body slide behind me and then Roman's voice slid over my ear. "I won't hurt you."

I knew he wouldn't. He didn't let Tage kill me this morning, and he made sure he didn't hurt Mary this evening. "Why did you sic him on *her?*"

"It's a form of punishment. He likes your blood. Hers? Not so much."

Punishment I could accept, but what *wasn't* acceptable was making that monster hurt someone else.

"I'll be quick." His warm breath fanned my ear as he pushed an errant strand of hair out of the way. I'd worn it up this evening for the hunt. Twisted braids were pinned into place at the nape of my neck, but none of it ever stayed in place. My stomach tightened when his hand pulled me backward, his chest against my back. I glanced at Saul, who was holding his neck. The girl who'd fed from him had already stood and was waiting with Tage by the fountain.

Mary's eyes fell on mine and then she looked away. Was she angry with me? Tim, Victor, and James were also finished.

Roman's tongue traced a path up my neck, cooled by the breeze, and then I felt two tiny pinches, simultaneous and barely there. A deep rumble from his chest made me whimper. He pulled his fangs out and quickly licked the wounds, and then Roman jumped away from me as if he'd been burned and strode away, instructing the other night-walkers to provide the rings.

As each vamp found their dinner, Roman paused in front of me with a small, but ornate ring of silver on his forefinger. "Let's see if it fits," he suggested with a slight smile.

I held my right hand out, fingers extended.

"Are you left or right-handed?" he asked.

"Right."

"Then I think you should wear it on your left. If you need to use it, you might be fighting with your dominant hand."

I extended the other hand. "Do you think I'll need it?"

Roman shook his head. "Dara is going out with you. She's fierce and very good at guarding the hunt."

At least it wasn't Tage. Roman tried the ring on my pinky and then on my ring finger where it fit best, and he settled it. "Do you know how this works?"

I shook my head. "No. This is my first rotation."

"I know," he replied.

He flipped a tiny clasp that opened a compartment which lay beneath the stone. "These are poison rings. They were used in ancient times as a means to kill, to slip poison into the drink of your enemy."

"Don't you use them now for the same thing?" He stuck his fang into his finger and drew blood, squeezing it into the ring's tiny compartment, filling it and then closing the compartment and clasp. "Won't it dry up or leak out?"

"Vampire blood is thicker than human blood and it never dries."

"Oh."

He closed the clasp and sure enough, nothing leaked, even when I turned it to the side. Roman smiled. "Oh, ye of little faith."

I snorted and drew my hand away from him. The ring had black, swirling patterns along the sides until it tapered into the band. The stone at the top wasn't quite red, and neither was it purple. It was a strange mixture of both.

"Do not ingest the blood unless you plan to become one of us. One drop will turn you."

My toes curled. I didn't want to be a night-walker. "I wouldn't unless I had to."

"The alternative is worse, in case you're wondering. As an Infected, you slowly die. It's a curse, but being a vampire is also a curse. As a night-walker, you can never die."

"I thought that garlic or stakes could kill you."

He chuckled. "Garlic, no, and a stake through the heart would only piss a vampire off. Remove their head and they die, but that's extremely hard to do."

A snarl from behind revealed the other coven members. Roman nodded and turned his back to me, leaving with the others.

One drop.

One drop was all it took to turn a person.

Potent venom filled the ring on my left hand; the finger that should carry a wedding band.

TEN

SAUL FOUND ME AFTER ROMAN TURNED HIS BACK AND QUICKLY WALKED away, talking to Dara, the girl who had fed on Saul and was taking us on the hunt tonight. She was the one Roman said was good at guarding us.

"How often have you seen an Infected? You've been on several hunts."

He didn't hesitate. "Three. I've seen three of them. One was old and so badly decayed, it just stood there and moaned. I think it used to be a woman. All that was left of her hair was a few long strands that came out of her scalp. Her skin was falling off and you could see muscle underneath. You could see tendon. It was... awful. It was as if she was begging us to kill her."

"Did you?"

"I didn't, no. But another member of the group put an arrow through her head. It was a mercy, Porschia."

My pulse thumped. Would someone try to kill Mercedes? Would I let them? If she still looked like herself, there was no way I could stand by and let someone shoot her. But what if she didn't? What if she was rotting, starving, falling apart and begging for death?

A shiver rolled up my spine beneath her coat. "I need to change."

Saul nodded. "Town Hall?"

"Yeah, that'll work."

"No one should be there. I'm going to run home and grab my bow, then I can wait outside for you."

We walked toward the old church. It reminded me that everything in this God forsaken place was rotting.

"If we all die, if we all become Infected, how long will it be until the vamps die?" I asked.

Saul shook his head, stuffing his hands in his pockets. "I don't know. Roman made it sound like it was really hard for them to die. He never mentioned starvation, but it makes sense."

"It's hard not to think about all of this stuff. Sorry."

On the steps of Town Hall, Saul sat down heavily. "Don't be. I've wondered the same thing myself. I was just never brave enough to voice it."

"I'm not brave."

His eyes found mine. "You're the bravest person I've ever met. It's one of the reasons I want to marry you. Not because you asked me or because of your situation at home, but because I admire you. I respect you, Porschia."

"Thank you. I admire you, too." It wasn't a lie. I'd come to realize that Saul was a good man and a hard worker. He had many admirable qualities, and I respected him, too. It was a good start. I climbed the steps with my bag in hand and pulled the door closed behind me, watching him stand and jog toward his house.

Behind a small door beyond the foyer was an old bathroom. How I wished indoor plumbing was still available. Or lights, for that matter. I quickly pulled the items out of my bag, pulled Ford's pants on and then removed my dress, pulling his shirt on over the top. I had to roll the sleeves up, but it worked. Ford was taller than me and skinnier, so the pants were tight around my hips. On the hem, the darting was strong. Mrs. Dillinger supervised my efforts and made sure they would hold for the week. She also promised that once the week was up, I could cut the thread and it would be like they'd never been altered at all.

Stuffing my dress into the bag, I looked at myself in the mirror. The glass was fading along the edges but I could still see my reflection. In these clothes, I wasn't Porschia. I was a badass huntress and no Infected was going to come near me tonight.

I TUCKED MY BAG BENEATH ONE OF THE PEWS. AFTER TOMORROW'S morning rotation I would have to stop by for my rations and could grab it then. Saul stood when he heard the door open, but I wasn't prepared for his mouth to gape open at me. My skin warmed.

"They should let women wear pants all the time."

I giggled. "I take it they don't look stupid?"

"Definitely not."

"Are you ready to go meet the others?" I fitted my knife sheath along my right hip and made sure I could reach it easily.

Saul held out a hand. "Ready as I'll ever be." He looked up at me and then at the ring on my hand.

"Let me see yours," I asked. His was silver and larger, with a shiny black stone on top. "I wonder how they got these, and how they choose them."

"They reuse the rings with every rotation," Saul explained.

"Makes me wonder which one Mercedes wore." The words slipped out before I could stop them. "I'm sorry."

"Don't apologize for thinking about her. She's your sister."

"She is, you know? Everyone acts like she's dead, but she's not. We might even see her tonight."

Saul put his hands on my shoulders. "Listen, Porsch. If we do see her, you can't go near her. It's not safe."

I nodded my head, tears filling my eyes. Silently, I prayed that I wouldn't see her again, though everything within me wanted to so badly.

"I know," I croaked.

He pulled me in for a hug. When I let go of him, we walked toward the river. There was a log that had fallen across the gurgling water years ago. It was broad enough to walk across, but rumored to be slick with moisture and algae. It was the only crossing safe enough for all of us.

Tim, Mary, Vincent, and James were already waiting for us, and everyone was obviously amped up. The Freemans held several long strands of twine and rope. Vincent was reminding James of the importance of tying the knots so they would slip, snaring the animals and tightening more and more as they struggled to get free.

Tim and Mary were nearest the tree. "As soon as our tour guide arrives, we'll cross," Tim joked.

Dara appeared a second later, small and graceful in her movements. "I was merely waiting for all of you to arrive. Just so you know, it's never a good idea to split up like you're planning to do. It divides my attention and the rotters might take advantage of the situation. Maybe not tonight, but if they catch on..."

Dara's platinum-blonde, silky hair made her look ethereal in the moonlight. With a curled upper lip, she all but growled at Mary, who was still wearing her dress. When she found me, Dara smiled. "At least one of you has brains. You might want to wear something like her tomorrow. Easier to run in."

Mary huffed and crossed her arms. "This is all I have, and I can run in this as easily as pants. Deal with it," she bit back.

Dara smiled, revealing her fangs. "I won't have to beyond tonight. You'll have another watchdog tomorrow."

My stomach roiled. Would it be Tage? *Saul is thinking the same thing,* I thought. He pursed his lips and when Dara took off across the trunk, he followed behind her, motioning for me to join him. The trunk *was* slippery. The soles of my boots were sliding all over the place, but in the end, I stayed upright and made it across. We all did.

At the other side, we all agreed on the same plan. The Freemans would set snares up the middle. The Browns would take the forest to the east, and Saul and I would set off to the west. Dara said she would stay centered and would go where needed. "Just scream like you're dying if you need me. I'll be right there." She flashed her fangs and took off after the Freemans.

I bet she'd be there…to suck us dry.

ELEVEN

Although we tiptoed through the forest, the leaves crunched noisily beneath our feet. Harsh puffs of visible breath escaped my mouth as we reached the top of the first hill. "We have to go further away from the Colony, so we'll be walking for a while," Saul whispered.

"Sounds good."

I followed his footsteps, careful to stay close. Night descended like a thick blanket, but the sky was clear. The moonlight was bright and though I couldn't see perfectly, visibility was better than expected. My other senses were heightened. From above us came the hooting of an owl, while nearby, small creatures scurried through the dried undergrowth.

Saul's feet stilled and he raised his crossbow. "Stay with me. No matter what."

"No matter what," I mouthed back. Was it an Infected? I peered around his shoulder to get a good look, but saw nothing. Saul took aim.

From just ahead, there was movement. A large buck raised its rack high, its eyes and muscles tense and alert. Saul eased the bow into position, aimed, and squeezed the trigger. The animal reared when the arrow hit its flank but took off, frantically trying to get away from us. Saul sprinted after it. "Come on!" he yelled.

I ran after the two of them, keeping Saul in sight until a loud thump from behind me stopped me in my tracks. The hilt of my knife was cold in my hand as I eased it from the sheath. Footsteps. "Dara?"

No answer.

"Saul?" It couldn't have been him. My pulse throbbed in my ears. That sound and the autumnal song of crickets was all I heard. I faced the sound and backed in the direction that Saul had taken off in. My heart was about to explode.

From behind, crunching leaves. Louder. Closer.

"Who's there?"

From the valley beyond me, too far away to help, came Saul's voice. "Porschia?"

Another crunch, closer this time. The pines were blocking the moonlight, making it even more difficult to see. I reached into the darkness in front of me. "Mercedes?" I whispered. Could it be her?

"Porschia?!" yelled Saul.

"Here." My voice was raw. Shaking, I held my knife up in front of me. The dark blade glinted as I moved backward, trying to put distance between myself and whatever was approaching.

I could hear Saul running to me. When he was close, I turned toward him. "Hey!" he beamed, but then his smile was replaced by an all too serious look. He put two hands out in front of him. "Easy."

I was still holding the knife, my hand trembling with fear. "Sorry. I heard something and got scared."

His eyes scanned the area. "I don't see anything," he said, pushing my hand down. "You can put it away."

"Did you take him down?"

Saul smiled. "Bet your ass I did. Let's go get him."

Relief loosened my taut muscles. We had food. One deer wouldn't feed the entire Colony, but it was something. And something was better than nothing, any day of the week.

Dara caught up with us at the bottom of the valley where the buck lay bleeding out, another arrow piercing its neck. Every part of Dara shook violently. Her eyes flashed in warning. "GO!" she roared, pointing for us to make tracks.

"We have to carry it back," Saul protested. We couldn't just leave it there. The Colony needed the food.

Dara bared her fangs and sank to her knees. Her lower lip quivered, raking against her long, delicate fangs. "I'm starving. I'll bring it to the river, I swear, but I need this."

She pierced the deer carefully to avoid the arrow wound and drank greedily, kneading its fur and flesh, digging her long nails into its hide.

She gulped and moaned, pulling the animal against her body. Saul backed away from the sight and grabbed my arm. "Let's go."

We ran.

CLIMBING ONTO A LOW TREE LIMB, SAUL AND I WAITED AND WATCHED FOR more game. We stayed silent until the ebony cloak of night lifted and turned gently, fading the sky from black to royal to pale blue. Golden-edged wisps streaked the sky merrily.

"We need to get to the pavilion."

Saul nodded. Purple circles ringed the skin beneath his eyes. "Yeah."

He climbed down first and then grabbed me as I jumped. "I've never seen them feed like that," he confided.

"Me either."

"It seemed like she was desperate."

"That's a bad thing. Desperation usually equals bad decisions." For me it did. Because if I wasn't desperate, if Mother hadn't made her ultimatum, I would never have applied for the rotation or stepped one foot across the river. But then I wouldn't have met Saul, either.

We trekked out of the forest, ignoring the birds that chirped in the canopy above. Slipping and sliding over the tree trunk, our feet found Colony soil. "We need to run," Saul said. The others had left us.

"Let's go."

It was almost daylight. We were late. The others were probably worried about why we hadn't emerged from the forest. The night-walkers were probably irritated. Roman was probably the most volatile. I got the impression that he didn't like to wait, but at least Dara had taken her fill last night. She wasn't starving for Saul's blood.

When we got to the pavilion, every head turned toward us. On the faces of our teammates was relief. Roman stalked toward us. "Where have you been?"

Saul moved in front of me. "We heard something strange and had to hide until it was safe."

Roman turned to Dara, who picked at her cuticles as though she were bored. "Did you sense anything last night?"

"Nothing of urgency," she deadpanned.

Roman let out a pent up breath. "Fine. Let's get this over with." He grasped my elbow from around Saul and pulled me toward our bench. "Sit."

I sank onto the gritty concrete slab and brushed away the tendrils of hair that had escaped my braids. Roman wasted no time numbing my neck and then sinking his fangs in. A few quick draws, his arm possessively snaking around my abdomen and between my breasts to hold the front of my neck, and he was licking my wounds again. I was reeling. Between the morning's sprint, the feeling of Roman's hands on me, and Saul's eyes cutting into us both, it was too much.

I tried to sit up straighter, but Roman refused to let me go. His warm breath fanned my ear as he whispered, "Don't be late tonight."

"Why? Will you turn to dust if the sun hits you?"

I could hear his smile and small puff of laughter. "You wish. I do, however, worry about you."

"You mean your next meal."

With his free hand, he tilted my head toward him. "No. Just about you."

I swallowed and he released me, standing up and silently calling for the others to follow him.

Saul and I stopped for our rations at Town Hall. I was able to grab the dress I stashed, slip into the bathroom and change back into it before many saw me in Ford's pants. Most people probably had the manners and couth not to say anything, but my mother was not like most people. She would have a fit.

I didn't check my ration bag; I just hurried to Mrs. Dillinger's, promising to meet Saul for dinner before the evening rotation. She was working upstairs, as usual. "How did the hunt go?" she asked hopefully.

"We got a few things. Saul took down a huge buck and the Browns were able to kill a raccoon. The Freemans set snares, so hopefully those will be full tonight."

"Sounds like you all have a plan. You split up?"

"Yeah."

She looked up at me. "Could be more dangerous that way."

"Sometimes you have to take the risk to get the reward."

Mrs. Dillinger smiled. "You're exhausted."

There was no point lying to her. "I am."

"Go home and rest. Come tomorrow only if you feel that you can. I understand your burden."

I thanked her and gave her an awkward hug before heading toward my house. The sun was peeking out from behind thin bands of clouds. The concrete was warming. Steam wafted up from its surface. Smoke rose from the kitchen chimney.

Steeling my spine, I stepped onto the walk, crossed the porch, and pushed my way inside, keeping Mercedes' coat pulled tight. Mother was busy in the kitchen. I peeked into the ration bag and saw a pint of cooked apples, more bread, more cheese, and an egg. I tucked the cheese and apples into my pockets. Mother's eyes narrowed when I stepped into the kitchen and laid the bag on the counter. Before venom could begin to spew from her mouth, I walked away, up the steps and to my room, locking the door behind me.

From under my arm, I pulled the bag containing Ford's clothes and from the pockets, I took the food. I chewed quickly and then sank into my mattress, pulling the covers over me in a cocoon of warmth.

TWELVE

I DIDN'T WANT TO MOVE. MY MUSCLES WERE SORE. I WAS TUCKED INSIDE the warm bed clothes. My feet weren't freezing. My hands weren't shaking or numb. Nestled inside the blankets, I could stay in a tiny world where my mother didn't hate me, my sister was across the hall asleep, my father was brave enough to handle my mom's crazy, and my baby brother didn't have to steal food.

Peeking out of the dark cavern, I saw the sun, too much of it. The acrid smell of smoke filled the air. "What's burning?" I mumbled to myself, throwing the covers back and slipping my feet into my boots.

From the window, I could see Mother outside, stoking a fire—a fire that was built way too close to the house. The laundry on the line thrashed in the blustery wind. She was going to burn the house down!

I laced my boots quickly, grabbed my coat, and ran down the steps to the back door. Just beyond lay a huge burn pile. "What are you doing? You're going to catch the house on fire!"

A mirthless laugh bubbled from her throat.

"You won't take anything from her again," she taunted.

"What are you talking about?" I asked, pushing my hair out of my face. Then I took a good look at what she was burning.

Drawers full of clothes and Mercedes' things were thrown into the inferno. Her drawings. Everything from my sister's bedroom was being destroyed. "NO!" I screamed and launched myself to the base of the pile.

The skin of my fingers boiled but I managed to pull one of her drawings out of the flames, one of her summer dresses, and her brush.

"Why would you do this?"

"She's gone and it's all your fault. You shouldn't have anything of hers!" she roared.

"You're crazy! I didn't kill her. She isn't even *dead*. She's just across the river. I didn't go out on the hunt. I didn't volunteer for her. I wasn't *supposed* to protect her! If you want to blame someone, Mother, blame Mercedes! Blame the night-walker who was supposed to be guarding her. Blame yourself for not teaching her never to volunteer for the rotation, but this is NOT MY FAULT!"

The pride in her face crumbled and she ran into the house, wailing, slamming doors behind her in a fit of insanity and rage. Glass shattered. Thumps. More screaming.

I heaped dirt onto the edges of the blaze, smothering it before it could consume any more of my sister's life. There came a point in everyone's life where they came to a crossroads. This was mine. I couldn't live here anymore. Mother was going to smother me, one way or another, and I couldn't be an accomplice to her malice anymore.

Ford jogged around the side of the house and pulled me to my feet. "What did you do?"

I shook my head as tears carved paths through the soot that felt thick on my face. "Mother?" he asked, already knowing the answer.

"I'm done," I rasped.

He scanned the burn pile. "I understand."

"I'm sorry, Ford."

"Don't be. I won't be far behind you."

I rushed upstairs and grabbed only what I could carry: my dresses, shoes, Ford's clothes, and food. I knew Father deserved to hear from me that I was leaving. Mrs. Dillinger had offered a room at her house, and I decided I would take her up on the offer for the time being.

Ford silently stood guard around my things as I made sure to get all that I could. When I was finished, he asked me where I would go.

"Mrs. Dillinger has a spare room."

"I'll check on you tomorrow," he promised.

The sun sank further to the west. It was already evening. I needed to meet Saul at our spot, but I needed to move my things. "I'll take them to Mrs. Dillinger's shop, if you want. You can go."

I grabbed the sack of his clothes, half a loaf of bread, and a jar of beets. "Thank you. I'll tell Father tomorrow."

He stacked everything into the barrel of our wheelbarrow and pushed it down the walk and into the street. "Be safe, Porschia."

"I will."

ANGER PULSED THROUGH MY VEINS AND I WONDERED WHETHER ROMAN would taste its bitterness tonight. Carving a path through neighbor's yards, I walked quickly toward the river. The clouds, which were mere wisps this morning, were dark gray and roiling, clamoring for dominance in the sky.

I could hear the roar of the falls in the distance. Even the dryness of autumn hadn't stopped their ferocity. The river barely seemed affected at all. I wanted to see Mercedes' pool, the site of her false farewell. I wanted to let it and her know that I hadn't forgotten, hadn't given up on her. She needed to know it, too. Or, I needed her to know that I still loved her and I was sorry.

The water on my bare feet would calm me. It would connect me with my sister. And I needed that connection now more than ever. The bank wasn't steep here. I made my way to the water's edge and bent to unlace my boot. That was when I saw her.

She was in my sister's pool, the water tinged red around her, coating the smooth rocks. Her red hair was spread in a wide halo around the eyes that stared into forever. Bite marks, spaced very far apart, were on her neck on both sides. Meg. White linens filled with air pockets hovered in the water around her. Her arms stretched wide, welcoming eternity.

I couldn't breathe. Sliding down the river bank, I couldn't catch my breath. No.

My heart sank. "Meg?!" I screamed, wading into the water. "Meg, please. *No.*"

I grabbed her arm and pulled her heavy, soaked body to the edge of the shore. She was gone. She was dead before I even came here. Meg was gone. Meg was dead. Meg wasn't Infected. She wouldn't be Jonas's wife. She wouldn't be my friend and make tea for us and...

My skirt was heavy as I stepped out of the water and climbed the bank. Her blood was in the water. Her blood was on my dress, seeping into the fabric, staining it.

I ran for help. I ran for Saul.

SAUL'S EASY SMILE FADED WHEN HE SAW ME RUNNING, SLINGING WATER AND blood and crazy everywhere. "What's wrong?" His hands clamped onto my upper arms.

"M-Meg. She's dead. She's dead in the river," I sobbed uncontrollably. My friend was gone. My friend was dead. Someone killed her. A vampire.

His eyes widened. "Let's get someone."

Saul kept his cool and tugged me toward the closest house, which was much too far away. "Mr. Bateman?"

Mr. Bateman, a man who had long been friends with my father, stepped out his back door. "What's the matter?"

"There's been an accident at the river. Meg Sanford is dead."

His mouth formed an O. "How far up?"

"Near the falls," I croaked. "The farewell pool."

He grabbed a coat from inside the door. "I'll get your father and we'll take care of everything, Porschia. Thanks for getting me, son," he said to Saul.

"You're welcome."

"Don't go near the river. We'll take care of everything."

We watched him jog away and Saul rubbed his hands up my arms. "You need to get changed. Is your bag near the falls, too?"

"Y-yes," I said, my teeth chattering.

"I'll go get it and our food. Meet me at Town Hall. Go inside to stay warm," he said, pointing in the direction he wanted me to walk.

I followed my feet, numb.

THIRTEEN

Before I reached the Hall, the sky began to cry. Fat droplets of rain splattered over the land, soaking into my hair and running down my scalp. Saul was no doubt getting soaked. I picked up my pace and jogged the rest of the way to Town Hall. The door groaned as I entered it, as if God himself didn't want me in his space. My dress dripped onto the floorboards of the foyer. I couldn't see Meg's blood, but I knew it was there.

Tucking myself into the bathroom, I draped my coat over the sink and stripped my dress off. Maybe I would burn it, just like Mother burned Mercedes' clothes. Banging my palm against the mirror, I watched the glass shatter and sprinkle to the ground. It fell all over, but even the brokenness of the mirror wasn't enough to calm me.

Screaming at the top of my lungs, I cursed the one who took her from me. My only friend. The girl who was kind enough to look past the prejudices that influenced everyone else in this God-forsaken place.

Closing my eyes, I tried to repeat the words, "Meg is alive," "Meg isn't dead," "Meg is alive," "Meg isn't dead." Mother always said people could tell a lie so often that even they began to believe it. The truth would become muddied and difficult to discern.

Meg was alive.

Meg wasn't dead.

Meg hadn't been attacked.

A night-walker didn't feed from her.

Didn't throw her into the river like garbage.

Meg wasn't garbage.

Meg wasn't gone.

Meg would make tea.

Meg would marry in the spring. She and Jonah would be happy.

Meg was alive.

Meg wasn't dead.

Meg was… A sound pulled me from the chanting inside my head. Freezing, my body shook violently. Saul's heavy footsteps fell on the floor outside. Two soft taps on the door and I cracked it open, but it wasn't Saul's face who smiled back at me; it was Tage's. He was too strong. I couldn't close the door, though I tried with all my strength. I would have settled with smashing his fingers in the jamb. Pushing my weight against it and grinding my teeth together didn't work.

"Are you finished?" he teased.

"Not on your life," I huffed out.

"I just came to offer you a friendly piece of advice."

"What's that?" I pushed again, harder.

"Don't tell anyone about the girl at the river."

I finally gave up pushing and just held the door closed, but with a small gap. His eyes raked down my flesh. "Is *that* what you're hiding under those dresses?" Tage's eyes narrowed. "Keep quiet. If you care about Roman at all—"

"I don't, and I won't keep any dirty secrets for someone like you, either."

He moved his hand and the wood slammed closed behind me. I heard his footsteps fade away and re-approach. "What now?" I screeched, throwing the door open.

Saul stood in front of me, mouth agape. "Uh, here." He thrust my bag of clothes toward me and averted his eyes.

"Sorry! Thanks." I took the bag, slammed the door, and dressed as quickly as I could.

When I opened it back up, Saul was still standing there. "What was that all about?"

"Tage."

"Tage?"

"Tage was here."

Saul's hands balled into fists. "Did he...did he hurt you? Is that why you weren't dressed?" Water sluiced off of his hair, down the sharp angles of his face.

"No. I took my dress off because I got caught in the downpour. I was freezing."

"He saw you without it?" Saul questioned.

"The door was only open a couple of inches."

"He was toying with you. What did he say?"

"He threatened me and told me not to say anything about Meg." My voice cracked. Saul took two enormous steps toward me and I threw myself into his arms, wrapping mine around his neck. "She was my friend, my only friend in this God-forsaken place."

"Not true," he murmured against my neck. "You have me."

In that moment, I couldn't have been more thankful for that fact.

"And you have me."

When his lips found mine, they were soft and searching. He lent me his warmth and I knew that we had taken a huge leap forward together. Saul pulled away first, leaving me breathless. "Your father needs to talk with you before we go, but we need to hurry."

I brushed my fingertips over my jaw, where his stubble had deliciously rubbed against my skin, bereft that the feeling was over with and wanting to capture it again. Instead, I captured his hand and we walked out of Town Hall back to the last place I wanted to see: the river.

Not only was Mercedes Infected, her favorite place was, too.

THE RAIN STEADIED, BUT THE EARTH WAS OVERWHELMED. IT ABSORBED THE moisture as fast as it could. Through the haze of rain drops, Father approached, holding his coat over his head. "Where did you say you saw Meg, Porschia?"

"She was in the pool that Mercedes loved, and the water around her was full of blood. She'd been doing laundry."

He shook his head. "There's nothing there now. Your mother said you took off after you woke."

"She burned everything," was all I could say. Meg was there! I saw her!

"I saw the pile, but Porschia, I don't see anything at the river. I'll keep looking, but you should go. It's already nightfall."

He was right. Somehow, the night had descended. We were late again. "She's in Mercedes' spot. I swear. I saw her, I swear."

Tage knew I had. If he moved her or took her, I would kill him.

"You have your knife?" Father asked.

"Yeah." I had it clipped onto the waistband of my pants.

Father nodded. "Keep safe, and remember what I told you earlier this week." He eyeballed Saul. "That stays between us." His brows raised.

"I understand."

Saul squeezed my hand. "We're late."

"Again."

He echoed my words. "Again."

The ring on my left hand was loose because of the rain, so I pushed it up again as we rounded the corner between streets and approached the pavilion. Everyone was there. The rain would make tonight unbearable. It was turning cold without the sun's warmth. We would all freeze before morning, but the sound was a blessing in disguise. It might mask the crunches of our footsteps and give us the upper hand over our prey.

———

"YOU CAN STAND," ROMAN SAID, STANDING IN FRONT OF ME WITH HIS HANDS in the pockets of his leather jacket. "You'll get soaked if you sit."

I laughed mirthlessly. "I'm already soaked." Shuddering, I thought about Meg's unfocused eyes, the weight and drag of her body through the dark water. Why wasn't Father able to find her? Did the rain swell the river so much that she'd floated away? No – I pulled her onto the river bank. It couldn't have swollen that much.

I glanced over at Tage as he drank from Mary, who still seemed aggravated at the change of partners. I didn't blame her. As Roman moved my heavy, wet hair to the side, Tage's eyes locked on mine while he drank what I knew was more than his fill.

"Mary," I whispered to Roman.

"That's enough, Tage," he warned.

With a grin, Tage released Mary's throat and gave it a slow lick. She clamped her hand over her throat and moved away immediately. Tage stalked toward us and I instinctively moved closer to Roman. "Tage. Back off," he warned.

"Want me to hold her still for you?" His hands clamped down on my arms. I twisted to get free, but couldn't fight him. And then in a flash, Roman was gone and Tage's hands were off of me.

Tage was on the ground, holding his nose, while blood gushed from between his fingers. "Never lay a finger on her again," Roman warned. By this time, Saul and Dara were finished and rushed over. Saul stood with me and Dara helped Tage up.

"Let's go," Dara told Tage.

Tage's eyes locked on mine. "Fine!" *This isn't over,* his eyes said.

Roman turned to find Saul by my side. "Are you her guard dog?" he barked.

Saul stood up straight, the same height as Roman. "I'll be more than that by this time next week."

Roman scoffed. Water dripped off his hair and into his eyes. "I don't have time for this. Porschia, come here."

I stepped forward and placed my hand in his. He jerked me flush to his body and snaked a hand around my back, holding me tight. I leaned my head to the left, baring my neck to him. His fangs carved delicate paths down my skin, stopping short of breaking the skin. He slid his tongue over my supple flesh. It was agony, a fire he ignited that only his fangs could cure. Was it true that vamps could manipulate people? Make them feel things they normally didn't or wouldn't? Because I shouldn't have been standing next to Saul enjoying Roman's tongue on my skin or his fangs in my flesh.

At Saul's growl, Roman chuckled and let me go before quickly sealing the wound. "You all have your rings?"

Everyone murmured in the affirmative.

"The blood is still good. Remember what I said: one drop will turn a human."

Words flew out before I could tuck them inside. "When is the last time a human changed into a night-walker this way?"

Roman stilled and turned to look at me over his shoulder, his eyes grazing Saul in the process. "It's been several years, but we don't want it to happen. It's merely a safeguard—part of the original treaty."

"Why don't you want it to happen?"

He shook his head. "Have you ever seen a vampire in frenzy?"

"No."

"You don't want to, especially a new vamp. They're uncontrollable. Feral."

Feral? That was terrifying. If it scared me seeing Dara, who was so in control most of the time, freak out over deer blood, I couldn't imagine a new vampire feeding.

FOURTEEN

Saul was amped up. He squeezed the handle of his crossbow, pacing back and forth like a caged animal while the others gathered their weapons. I didn't ask him what was wrong because I knew. He wanted to shoot Roman through the heart and rip his head off his shoulders. I felt the same way every time Dara touched him.

Saul was becoming very important to me. His lips were magic, able to set me ablaze or calm me. His hand was comforting when it cradled mine. Saul looked out for me, always considerate and caring. There was certainly no future between a night-walker who would likely live forever and a human who would die sooner rather than later in this diseased world.

A night-walker appeared through the sheets of rain. He was partnered with James. "My name is John Everson. I answer to 'Everson'. Let's get this over with."

His stony expression was typical, but he was young, or looked it. His skin was darker than the other vampires, bronze, and his hair was an odd shade of bright red, which didn't suit him. He wasn't tall, but stout and confident. With ease and nary a look back, he crossed the tree in front of us.

James shouted out, "Why can't the Infected cross this same tree?"

Everson stilled and smiled back at him. "They lose muscle tone rapidly. And it's a difficult tree to cross, don't you think?"

It was. I slipped the entire way over, nearly sliding into the river at the other side. Everson's hand grabbed my forearm before I fell and he jerked me onto the ground beside him. "Told you," he smirked.

I waited as the others crossed the tree. Saul was last. But before we split up, I heard my name. "Porschia!"

"Father?"

Everson sighed. "Go."

Each of my footsteps along the slick tree trunk slid off toward the water, but I kept my steps fast and light. He met me on the other side, rain pelting us both. "What's wrong?" I asked.

"I want you to be very careful tonight." Father lowered his voice. "We can't find her."

"What do you mean?"

"There's no trace of Meg…not in the river, not at home. Nowhere. It's like she vanished."

"That makes no sense." I shook my head violently. "I *saw* her! She was just floating there and then I...I pulled her to the bank."

"I believe you, I just don't know what's going on. I want you to be careful. Stay with Saul," Father said, staring down the vamp waiting across the river.

"You think it's the night-walkers?"

"I don't know what to think."

I SCUTTLED BACK ACROSS THE TRUNK, LEAVING FATHER STARING AT US FROM the opposite bank. Everson smiled and wiggled his fingers mockingly at him. "I'll take good care of her, *Sir*," he teased.

"Break the treaty, night-walker. I dare you," Father warned. My mouth dropped open. Father never even stood up to Mother, and I'd never heard him say anything cross to anyone in my life. However, Everson just laughed and clapped his hands after a particularly loud clap of thunder sounded nearby. I jumped closer to Saul.

"Fun times. Let's go hunting, children."

We split up the same way as the previous night. James raced ahead to check the snares, Mary and Tim disappeared into the forest to the east, and I tried my best to keep up with Saul's determined stride as we headed west. He was quiet, pissed, and soaked to the bone. The rain slanted and pelted our backs as we slipped up one slope and slid down the other side.

We repeated this dangerous dance, up and down hills until we were farther than we should have been and I worried we might be lost.

Saul stopped and turned to listen ahead of us. He readied his crossbow and motioned ahead of him while I waited and watched through the torrents of rain. When the deer lifted its head, he fired. And missed. We raced after the animal, Saul trying to get another shot off and me trying to keep up with him once again.

The doe ran off, blending in with the soaked brown trunks and bare foliage surrounding us. "God damn it!" Saul raged, throwing his crossbow on the ground. He paced, threading his fingers behind his head.

I picked the bow up and held it to my side, looking at the dangerous black metal. "If you could show me how, maybe I could borrow another bow and we'd have a better chance at taking them down tomorrow."

He stopped, lips parted. Water ran down his face and dripped off his top lip. He scoffed. "You think that's what this is about? I'm off my game, and it's because of that... that night-walking-fang-fucker!"

My eyes widened. It wasn't that I hadn't heard anything like that before or said it to Mercedes during one of our evening giggle fests, but hearing Saul say it was funny. I tried so hard not to smile, not to let out the giggle, but it had nowhere to go once the dam of my resolve broke.

I laughed out loud, head tilted into the rain, abdominals in cramps. His big hands wrapped around my waist. "What do you think you're laughing at?"

"You," I hiccupped.

He smiled in warning, eyes firmly hooked on my mouth, and then claimed my lips with his. This was no soft exploration. He lifted me, pinning my back against the bark of the pine behind me. His hands knotted in my wet hair, pulling my head back so he could reach me better. My hands knotted in his coat, pulling him closer to me, but it wasn't close enough. "Saul," I breathed into his jaw. His lips moved in again.

A high-pitched keening sound came from my left. Saul's eyes widened and he pulled away, his fingers digging into my upper arms. "Very slowly, move around the tree." My lips trembled, but I nodded, easing around the massive trunk I prayed would hide us.

"The branches are low. Let's climb." He lifted me until I could reach the branch and pull myself up. I looked down to find him right on my heels. "Go!" he said, looking down below him. *Don't look down. Don't look down. It takes more effort to look down. Down impedes progress. We need progress. I don't want to be eaten.* I felt for my poison ring. It was still there despite the rain, and despite the fact that I didn't want to use it. It was there.

Sticky pine resin coated my fingers as I shimmied up the weeping pine, its needles hanging down like a willow. Saul tapped my ankle. I looked down to see him hold his hand out. He climbed onto the branch, settling beside me.

"Did you see it?" I whispered.

"No, but I heard it."

"Why do they scream like that?"

Saul pursed his lips. "Something about the rot on their vocal chords."

Another high-pitched screech tore into the night from just beneath us. I dug my fingernails into the bark of the limb across my chest, hoping the one beneath my thighs and Saul's was strong enough to hold us. "What does it want?" I whispered into his ear.

"Us."

FIFTEEN

I SAW HER THROUGH THE DARKNESS, THROUGH THE RAIN THAT WAS ONLY beginning to taper off. Her once-red hair was flattened and thin. Soaked tendrils clung to her flaking scalp, dull and lifeless. Her eyes were sunken in. Cheek bones protruded where plumpness had been only a few days ago.

"It's Meg," I whimpered. My warm tears met the cold mist now falling. Saul's hand on my low back steadied me. I wanted to climb down, jump from the lowest branch and throw my arms around her.

How did she get Infected? I saw her in the water. I saw her blood. It coated my dress and skin and hands.

My eyes questioned Saul's, but they held no answers. Meg kept walking, sniffing the air periodically and letting out those soul-stealing screams. She wore only her white slip, and it was torn from the briars she walked through. She moved past us slowly and then a male chuckle filled the air.

Everson moved toward her. "Must be my lucky night. I get to hunt, too." Meg stiffened and screamed, her mouth stretching longer than should be possible.

Before I could move, he closed the distance between them, grabbed her head, and twisted hard. The snap of her vertebrae echoed through the wood and Meg collapsed to the ground.

"NO!"

Damn gravity. I clambered down the tree limbs, slipping on the lichens, but I didn't care. "NO! Meg!"

Falling on my knees in front of her, I reached out to touch the red hair that was strewn across her forehead. A hand clamped down on mine before I could make contact. "Unless you want to be the one who dies tomorrow night, don't touch her."

I looked up at Everson. "Why did you kill her?"

"That's my job. It's in the treaty."

"The treaty?" I pulled my arm away from him. Saul was hovering over me, but grabbed my elbow and helped me up.

Everson rolled his eyes. "I'm to keep you safe, to act as a guard, and to eliminate any and all Infected found in the forest. It's for the good of the Colony, or so they say."

"She was my friend," I shoved his chest hard, but he never wavered.

Instead, he snorted. "You should be thanking me. I did your *friend* a favor. Now, either find food or go back to the Colony."

Saul crouched near Meg's body. "It's not her."

"What?" The word left me in a mixture of gasp and plea.

"It's not Meg," he affirmed. "This woman's been Infected for a while now. Meg had freckles and blue eyes. This one's eyes are green, or at least they were at one time."

Milky cataracts covered her corneas, but at the edges, I saw a vivid green.

I just assumed it was her. Why did I think it was Meg?

"The two do look alike. It's... I don't know. It's weird." Saul drew me away with him. "Let's go," he said, picking up the crossbow he left on the ground when he started climbing after me. A chill went through me. What if the Infected could still remember how to use those things?

Our roles were reversed. *I* was the one raging now. That might not have been Meg, but it very well could have been. It could have been Mercedes. Everson disappeared after I threatened to gut him if he touched my sister. She was still out there somewhere, I hoped. If someone... More hot tears carved their way down my face. Every inch of me trembled. It was a mixture of fear, anger, and bone-deep cold.

"Let's make our way back, but keep an ear out."

I was too pissed to hear anything.

Saul and I failed. We didn't kill anything. Luckily, the others were luckier. It wasn't much, but it was more than we had before. The Freemans snared two hares and the Browns were able to kill a coyote.

Saul spoke first. "Did you have any encounters last night?"

"With the Infected?" Tim asked. "We didn't." Mary shook her head.

Victor and James looked at one another. "What?" I asked.

Victor stretched his neck left then right. "We thought we heard something, but never saw anything."

"The screaming?"

He furrowed his brow. "No, more like shuffling."

Everson stepped up, bright and peppy. "Almost breakfast, kids. I'm starving." He smiled and his fangs shone brightly. "We had a little incident, didn't we?" He threw one arm around Saul's shoulders and one around mine. I shoved him off of me and Saul stepped away calmly.

The others asked what happened and Everson began to recount the entire gory event, omitting the fact that the 'monster' he slayed was a friend, a neighbor. I didn't wait for anyone, but walked quickly to the crossing, which was... missing.

"Where's the tree?" I muttered to myself. Looking up and down the river, I was positive this was the spot where we'd left it.

"Well, damn," Saul said. "Now what do we do?"

Everson chuckled from behind. "We find another way."

I smiled sweetly at him. The sun was almost up. "Guess breakfast will be late."

The smile fell from his face and I claimed sweet victory.

He sighed and waved for us to follow him. "I know another way. It's just along a more scenic route."

When we finally found the tree line, it had finally begun to clear. The sky was brightening and Father was waiting across the riverbank. I crossed first. "What is it?" His expression was tight and dark bags hung beneath his eyes.

"They found Meg last night."

The sound of the Infected woman's neck snapping filled my ears. "Where?"

"Downstream. Roman had a few night-walkers help search for her.

We're going to lay her to rest in the cemetery. I thought you'd want to know right away. Roman said you all can go straight to the pavilion."

I thanked him and rushed away, unable to stop the tears from flowing. Saul ran after me, catching me between two houses, just across from the square where the vamps were already waiting for us. "Stop," he said, grabbing my arms and turning me to face him. "Shhh." He pulled me to his chest and wrapped his arms around me. Saul didn't offer any other words. He must have known they were pointless. He held me against him, absorbing my grief and pain. When the others caught up with us, glancing at me with a mixture of pity and disappointment, we walked out of the yards and across the street, his arm wrapped around my shoulder.

Saul walked me to the concrete bench where I numbly sat down, my entire body spent from the exhaustion and sadness. I didn't look at Roman before he fed. I barely felt anything at all as he pulled me back to him and sank his fangs into my flesh.

I stood and began to walk away before he could seal the wounds he made. "Wait, Porschia. You have to let me heal the bite."

When his hand found my forearm, I tugged it away. "I don't need anything from you!" The blood. Meg was surrounded by blood. "Did you do it? Did *you* bite her?"

"The girl who was found in the river last night?"

"I found her yesterday evening further upstream. She had bite marks on her neck, Roman! Did you do it?" I looked behind him at the night-walkers now rising to their feet, hissing at me for speaking to their leader with such disrespect. It was so much more than that. They had no idea.

"None of us killed her. It would violate—"

"The treaty?" I scoffed. "Like any of you give a shit about the treaty, or about any of us. We're only good for one thing, right?"

Roman pushed his dark hair from his eyes and stared at me. "We don't kill humans, Porschia."

"Something did. Something with sharp fangs." And with that, I left him standing behind me.

Saul caught up with me and we walked in silence to Mrs. Dillinger's house, my temporary home. I hoped she was okay with the arrangement. Ford had no doubt explained the situation. "I'll meet you at the cemetery," he said, before turning and walking toward his house.

On the porch, I shrugged off my heavy, wet coat and wrung it out into the soil below. Floorboards creaked from within the house and Mrs. Dillinger opened the door for me. "You'll catch your death."

"It seems contagious," I deadpanned.

"I know you were friends with Meg."

"I was."

"I'm sorry, for what it's worth," she offered.

"Thanks. I'm sorry, too, for snapping at you."

Mrs. Dillinger waved me inside. "Bring your coat. We'll hang it by the fire to dry."

SIXTEEN

I FOUND MY BELONGINGS ON A BED UPSTAIRS, IN THE ROOM MRS. DILLINGER had told me was empty and available. When I told her this arrangement was only temporary, she rolled her eyes. "Stay as long as you'd like, child. Don't rush your life." When life was so fragile, and survival so difficult, rushing seemed like the thing to do. It only made sense.

Peeling my clothes off, I found a dress to pull on. It wasn't warm but it was dry, and that feeling alone was like heaven. Drying my hair, I quickly braided it and pinned it in place at my nape. Slipping my feet into my old, too-tight boots, I realized that they were a reflection of me. My emotions were spiraling out of control, like my body was too small to hold them in and I might explode at any moment.

Tears pricked my eyes. Between Mother's bitterness, the burning of my sister's memories, moving in with Mrs. Dillinger, Saul's sweetness, and finding Meg yesterday, not to mention being food for the night-walkers for the week, I was falling apart at the seams.

I took the poison ring off and sat it on the small wooden chest of drawers, the rounded metal teetering back and forth.

Mrs. Dillinger walked with a cane. She couldn't walk far, so she was one of the few exempt from farewells, funerals, and weddings. She met me at the bottom of the steps. "I wish I could go with you, Porschia," she said.

I swallowed thickly and nodded.

"I'll have some warm food waiting for you when you get home."

Home.

The tears flowed.

CLOUDS LINGERED IN THE MORNING SKY, HIGHLIGHTED GOLDEN BY THE SUN. The cemetery was near the river on the night-walker side of town. They kept watch over it. Precautions were always taken with the newly buried. Another part of the treaty.

People from all over the village milled around on the outskirts of the cemetery. Most would keep their distance, allowing those closest to Meg to say goodbye to her. Father was standing on the riverbank, staring into the dark water below. Mother didn't bother to show up. Ford found me.

"Hey," he said, hugging me tightly. "So sorry."

I answered with a sniffle. The Sanfords were standing beside a freshly-made mound of earth, watching the smiths pound the long legs of the cage onto the grave. The cage was literally that; bars of metal spaced a few inches apart, long enough to cover the mound and hold a newly changed night-walker. Meg had been bitten, and no one was taking chances. The use of the cage was almost unheard of in recent years, mostly because of the treaty.

With every inch that the metal sank into the earth, every pound of hammerhead against that cool steel, I jerked. It was as if the sound of the treaty breaking could be heard. If Meg had somehow consumed even a drop of the blood of the vamp who attacked her, if she bit him or her, she wouldn't stay beneath any amount of soil heaped on top of her.

That cage was control. It gave the night-walkers a way to stop the devastation of a new vamp in frenzy. I'd never seen a newly changed night-walker, and had barely seen the ones who've occupied our Colony for so long until now. Entering the rotation brought more questions about the vampires than it answered.

Why couldn't they control their own hunger? We were forced to tamp it down, to ignore the pangs and the growling of our stomachs.

Ford tucked his hands into his pockets. "I want you to watch your back. The treaty..."

"I know."

"They could hurt you."

I laughed. "I don't know that they could."

He tucked me beneath his arm until Saul approached and shook Ford's hand as an equal.

"Hey man, thanks for watching out for her," Ford's voice broke. Mercedes' fall was too new. Being here at Meg's grave with the smell of fresh earth lingering in the air, just solidified how delicately the treaty hung in the balance, if it hadn't already been rejected entirely by the Elders.

"No problem," Saul said.

I gave him a thankful glance and left the two men behind to pay my condolences to Meg's family. Mrs. Sanford, who had given Meg her red hair, was wringing her hands. Tears filled her brown eyes when she saw me. "Oh, Porschia. She loved you so much," she said, folding me into a tight hug. I gripped her just as tightly.

"I loved her back."

"We know," she sniffed. "We know. I just... I just don't understand. The treaty has been in place for so long."

My blood boiled. It was Tage. It had to have been. He was new to the coven and he lacked respect for Roman, for the Colony, for life. But Meg had just been doing her laundry at the river. In the daylight.

I hugged Mr. Sanford and told him how sorry I was. He had given Meg her eye color, and looking into his was like looking into hers. It was too much. Staring at my feet, I waited beside Meg's father until he walked over to his wife, holding her as she sobbed.

Jonah, her betrothed, stood and numbly watched the men finish hammering the cage into the ground. His long blond hair hung into his eyes.

"I'm sorry, Jonah," my voice broke.

He hugged me quickly. "Me too. I should've gone with her. Most days I met her there to spend time with her, but I had work to get done. I should've gone."

I shook my head. "It's not your fault."

"No it's not. It's theirs." He nodded toward Roman and the nightwalkers standing across the cemetery. In daylight. Apparently the nightwalkers were not affected by the sun after all. For the first time in years my hunger abated, replaced by the thirst for revenge, for Tage's head on a spike. Only, Tage was missing. He wasn't with the others.

SEVENTEEN

After the funeral, Saul said he would come to Mrs. Dillinger's to get me for dinner before we had to report. He wanted to rest and then head to the carpentry shop to work on a project. We picked up our rations and then he walked me home. "Listen," he said. "I'll show you how to use the crossbow this evening, if you'd like."

"I would."

His eyes pierced into mine. "I'll see you in a few hours."

"Okay."

Standing toe to toe, he tilted my chin up and placed a soft kiss on the skin just beside my lips. I watched him walk away, the empty void he filled gaping open again.

After stopping by Town Hall for our rations, I brought them in to Mrs. Dillinger. They would go a long way for only the two of us. As promised, she had two scrambled eggs and buttered bread waiting for me, steaming hot and delicious-smelling. It felt bad to enjoy food on such an awful day, but I had to keep my strength up. No one was impressed with the spoils of last night's hunt.

"You're tired. Go rest now," Mrs. Dillinger ordered, shooing me away from my dirty plate.

"I can wash this first," I argued.

She narrowed her eyes. "I said go rest."

I exhaled deeply, too tired to argue anymore. "Thank you. Saul is coming to get me before sundown for dinner. Is that okay?"

"Of course," she said, smiling over her shoulder as she took my plate to the sink. Someone had brought in a bucket of water. I knew it wasn't her and I hadn't been here, which made me wonder if Ford did it. Maybe he was atoning for the chicken theft. Maybe he was just a good fella. He always had been. You could always tell how a person really was by the way they treated children, their Elders, and animals. Ford was kind to all three.

She replied with a simple, "Mhmm," as I turned my back and climbed up the stairs.

SAUL CAME BY EARLIER THAN I EXPECTED. LUCKILY I WAS AWAKE, DRESSED IN my dried clothes and prepared with a sack full of dinner. Mrs. Dillinger answered his knock at the door and asked him to come in for a moment. She smiled at him. "I've heard a lot about you," she cooed. I could feel heat flood into my cheeks. I really hadn't spoken to her about him very much, but she heard me speak his name more than any other, simply because of circumstance. We found ourselves in an emotional and dangerous situation.

I gathered our food and hugged her. "Thank you for everything."

She nodded slightly. "Be careful tonight."

"I will."

Saul held the door for me and we stepped off the porch together, our steps in sync. "You ready for this?" He moved to a nearby tree where his crossbow and the extra he'd brought for me were leaning against the bark, waiting for us.

"I am." And I was. I wanted to learn, to be as helpful as I could. This might have been my first rotation, but it wouldn't be my last.

We walked through yards and side streets to the river. Between firing and retrieving my arrows that went tragically askew, we ate. Fresh bread, eggs, and even smoked deer jerky. We were already eating the buck we took down the other day.

"You're not bad," Saul said with a smile, retrieving my arrow.

"I'm not good."

"No." He smiled. "But you have the potential to be."

"Great," I deadpanned. "Because *potential* will take down a deer."

"There are more than just deer in the woods."

"Squirrels are too fast to catch."

He smiled. "Leave that to the Freemans. They're doing okay with the snares."

"They are, but small animals only go so far."

He stared at the blue sky like it held the answers to everything.

"So how did your secret project go?"

Saul smiled. "Good. You can see it soon."

"I can?" It was my turn to smile. The arrow's shaft felt smooth in my hand. It was just a piece of wood, but if fired fast and sure, it could kill. I would just have to imagine Tage's head on any game I saw.

"Yeah. Hey, I want to ask you something."

I lowered the crossbow and turned toward him. "My mom wants you to have dinner with us tomorrow."

"Tomorrow?" My eyes popped open. "Why?"

"She wants to meet you. She knows how I feel about you." His storm cloud, blue-gray eyes bored into me.

"How do you feel about me?"

He smiled and it was like the sun had no reason to shine anymore. He could light the world with a smile like that. "I'm... fond of you."

"You're fond of me?"

"Yes."

I giggled. "I'm fond of you too, Saul."

"Good." He erased my laughter with the strength of his hand on my back and the pressure of his lips on mine.

THE NIGHT-WALKERS WERE ON EDGE. TENSION FILLED THE PAVILION, squeezing out the stench of putrid water and rotting leaves. Roman stood with his kind, waiting for us all to gather. Mary, Tim, Victor, James, Saul, and I stood across from them. "There's been a change in plans for tonight," Roman announced.

Victor answered him. "What sort of change?"

"With the events that have unfolded, the Colony Elders are reconsidering the treaty. We're trying to persuade them to allow the treaty to remain in place, so we'll be helping in the hunt and sending a small party into the city to retrieve some goods that the Colony needs. Call it a show of good faith."

Victor snorted in derision. Tim whispered to him, "I don't like this."

"Me either," James said.

Tim and Mary exchanged a glance at the same time Saul's hand squeezed mine.

"All of you are helping tonight?" Saul questioned.

Roman's dark eyes found mine. "Yes."

Tage would be in the woods, or in the city, with us. That was not good. I could feel every muscle in my body tense, and then as if my thoughts brought my nightmare to life, Roman announced, "Mary and Porschia will be going into the city. Tage will guard them."

"No way in hell," Saul growled.

"They'll be safest there," Roman barked. "You care about her safety, don't you?"

"Of course I do, but you know he's a danger to her!" Saul and Roman crossed the square, standing toe-to-toe. Roman bared his fangs but Saul never flinched, never backed down. "Tage has had it out for Porschia from day one. He's the biggest threat you have. Hell, he's probably the one who killed Meg!"

The vamps behind Roman began to growl, low and deadly.

"It was no vampire who killed that girl." Roman turned to me. "You found her in the river, with blood in the water all around her. No?"

I nodded. "Yes."

"If one of us had killed her, we would have drained her. Completely."

EIGHTEEN

The feeding was quick and ferocious. The night-walkers numbed us but took more blood than usual. They needed energy to help with the hunt. Every time Roman gulped from me, I felt a tiny piece of my soul slip away. I hated him. I hated the feelings he evoked. I hated that I loved it when he drank from me. It had to be some sort of spell. I was too *fond* of Saul to have feelings about anyone else.

When Roman's warm tongue swiped my neck to seal the wounds he made, he whispered, so low I almost didn't hear him. "I'll be watching tonight. Don't worry."

My breath left in a rush. He was baiting Tage.

Saul rushed over to me after Dara was finished with him. "You take your crossbow. I don't like this. If he does anything, you shoot for his skull or his heart."

"I'd probably aim a little lower," I grumbled, hugging him tightly to me.

His deep chuckle rumbled through his chest beneath my ear. "I don't like this."

"What choice do we have?"

"There's always a choice, Porsch."

I swallowed. "I'll meet you tomorrow."

"The city is...it's still dangerous. It's just a different forest."

Nodding, I squeezed him one more time, hoping we both made it out of this situation alive, and that the night-walkers were genuine in their hopes to maintain the treaty. The entire situation was like an unraveled thread that was so taut it was straining apart.

Roman was telling some of the vampires I didn't know, the ones who fed on Victor and Tim, to go fast and far, to look for livestock that might still be milling around further than we could travel on foot for a night. He told them to bring back any and all animals they came across and stressed how important and tenuous the situation was. They nodded. Both of them were male and looked like little more than teenagers. One had white-blonde, spiked hair and the other had hair that was longer than mine and dark as midnight. They took off running and I felt the wind in their wake, my hair thrashing around in the dusky evening that descended around us.

Tage approached with a cocky grin and Mary moved to stand beside me. "Looks like it's you and me, sweetheart." Mary tried to smile but it faltered, weighed down by the apprehension covering us all.

"Yep."

Tage threw two large duffle bags at us. "Tonight we'll pillage and plunder." A slow smile spread over his face, sending a shiver up my spine. "There is a cache of oil lanterns just inside the city. We'll have to stop for those."

Mary whispered, "I have a bad feeling about this."

"The city?"

"Not just the city, but what's in it," she whispered.

"The Infected," I mouthed more than spoke.

She motioned toward Tage. "And him."

———

ON ONE END OF THE FLOOD WALL, NOT FAR FROM MY HOUSE—OR WHAT *used* to be my house—

was a steel ladder. It was sturdy and tall and led to the top and over the other side into the city below. Mercedes and I had sat atop that wall more times than I could remember. The city inside didn't look enormous. I'd seen pictures of larger ones in books that Mercedes had hidden in her closet. No doubt Mother burned those, too.

Taller buildings were across town, but close to the wall were homes that looked the same as ours. The only difference was that they had been burned. Houses of brick and stone still stood, though they were gutted.

Most of the others were gone; charred bones of rotting wooden spires delicately balanced on concrete slabs. Mary climbed up the ladder and I followed her. Tage climbed behind me.

When we descended and stepped onto the ground again, Tage dropped down beside us with a thud. "Let's see what we can find, ladies." He'd cut his dark hair short, making his blue eyes more visible. It didn't make me feel better. Those icy orbs took in far more than they ever revealed.

Tage led us into the city, where the only sounds were the soles of our boots slapping against the concrete street. The light of day was fading into purple and orange. We would need those lanterns soon.

Mary tugged her bag onto her shoulder. "What are we looking for, and how are we going to find it here?" I was thinking the same thing. It looked like everything was already burned out.

Tage smiled at us as if we were children. "Some of the taller buildings didn't burn all the way. The top floors are preserved, and there are some stores with things we can loot, too."

"You don't have to be so condescending," Mary grumbled.

"Yes I do," he tossed over his shoulder, never slowing his stride, and we had to jog to keep up with him.

Houses turned into townhomes, townhomes into apartment buildings, and with each block, the buildings grew taller. The glass that surrounded the facades was broken and soot-covered. The scent of burned wood still lingered, even after all of these years. Weeds and vines were growing in between sidewalk slabs and creeping up the walls of some of the buildings. The city truly was a different forest. Nature was reclaiming what was hers. Small animals scurried in alleyways and inside the remnants of buildings. It was their underbrush.

We jogged until my breath came out in puffs. I had to slow down. Clasping my left side, I asked, "Are we almost there?"

Tage pouted. "Having trouble, kitten?" I didn't dignify his comment with a response. "I can give you a piggyback ride? Now that you're not wearing that hideous dress," he said, eyeballing Mary for a second, who scowled at him, "you can do *so* much more." Tage licked his lips lasciviously.

"Could you either just not speak to me, or not call me kitten when you do?" I asked him. With a chuckle, he led us to an old shed in the back yard of a nearby home. In the shed, as he promised, were lanterns and small containers of oil.

We quickly filled them and continued into the city in silence. Sometimes silence was a magnificent thing, especially when Tage was involved. I was wondering where Roman was and how he was watching us without Tage knowing, and in my reverie, I didn't see Tage stop until I bumped into his back. "Let's go in here."

The building beside us was at least ten stories tall—a concrete shell. While the bottom three or four stories were burned, the top floors still looked okay. I just hoped the bottom levels would support the top ones long enough for us to get the hell out of there.

Stepping inside the building was easy; we just stepped wide into what used to be a window, our feet crunching on shards of sooty glass and leaves. Mary looked at me as I held my hand out for her. I clutched my crossbow tightly. It was awfully heavy to have to carry this far, but Saul was right. I needed it.

He'd been in the city before and said that although he never saw the Infected inside, they definitely had access to it. "Are there Infected here?" I asked Tage.

"Some small pockets, according to Roman, but I've never seen any."

His eyes found my hand and narrowed. "Where's your ring?" he growled.

I held my hand up and my heart dropped. "I took it off earlier. I must have forgotten to put it back on." Oh, my God. Oh, my God. I was going to die if they caught me. I would be like Mercedes. I would rot.

"Roman usually makes sure, but with the treaty and all of this bullshit going on, he must have forgotten." Tage shook his head. "You've got yours?" he asked Mary. She nodded.

"You stay close," he ordered me.

"I'm fine. I'm sure we'll be fine."

"What'd I say? Roman will rip my head off if something happens to you."

"To either of us," I challenged, following him into the darkness.

"Bingo!" Tage said, pointing to a door that was hanging askew. "Stairwell," he said as if it explained his bizarre personality. "And he probably wouldn't kill me over Mrs. Mary. *You're* his favorite."

"That's ridiculous."

Tage snorted. "You have no idea, do you?"

I climbed step after step, crossed landing after landing. Tage never tired, but Mary and I collapsed at the top of the eleventh floor. The building was taller than I'd estimated from the ground. "You both need to work on your physical fitness," Tage teased. "We'll look on this floor. I'd hate to see the old lady keel over."

He opened a door that led to a long hallway, lined with doors on either side. Mary huffed beside me. "If I weren't so out of breath, I'd kick him."

I smiled and nodded, sucking in oxygen. "Ready?"

"Ready."

NINETEEN

THE FIRST DOOR WE CAME TO WAS UNLOCKED, AND IT LOOKED LIKE someone had already ransacked the place. Furniture was overturned. Curtains and blinds were torn down. Cobwebs covered absolutely everything, a delicate lace. "What happened here?" I whispered to Mary. Tage was rifling around in the kitchen.

"I don't know."

"What are we supposed to look for?" Overwhelmed was an understatement.

"The Colony needs metal, but beyond that, maybe books, tools? Look for anything that could be helpful. Come on." She tugged me further into the room.

I didn't find much; a few screwdrivers, a hammer and some nails, some coins. There was a leather bag in the corner with a long strap, so I emptied the papers out of it and threw it over my shoulder. There were men's dress shirts in the closet. "Clothes?" I yelled.

"Leave them unless *you* want them," Tage answered. "You need them," he said, lowering his voice but saying it loud enough that I could still hear him. The entire room smelled awful. It wasn't mold or the stench of the smoke from the floors below, it was a pungent musk that permeated everything. The windows of the rooms had exploded and the elements had been working on this place for a long time. Birds built nests on lamps and on the upturned furniture. There were droppings everywhere we stepped.

Mary was rifling through a closet in the next room. "I'm going across the hall."

She stood up and looked at me. "Be careful." Her eyes flicked in Tage's direction and my hand tightened reflexively on my crossbow.

"I will."

I didn't bother to tell Tage where I was going, though I knew he could hear me leave. The hallway was cloaked in shadow. I tried to imagine the luminescence of the lights that ran in large rectangles across the ceiling, but couldn't picture electricity. Would it hurt your eyes? I shouldered the door across the hall open. It wasn't in disarray, but dust and cobwebs had taken over. The windows in this place weren't broken.

Holding the lantern up, I saw a couch in a colorful red floral, matching arm chairs, and an end table that still held drinking glasses on it. The kitchen cabinets were shut. If I didn't know better, if the layers of dust weren't there, I'd think someone just stepped out and would be coming back home any minute. That almost made it worse.

The hallway walls were lined with pictures, so I swiped the dusty glass surfaces in order to see them more clearly. Two children, a young girl and her older brother, it looked like. They were smiling, looking up from a crystal-blue pool of water. I'd never seen water so blue. The image was so clear, you could see tiny water droplets separating their eyelashes.

Another picture, another swipe. This time the children were posed on chairs with their parents behind them. They had their mother's golden hair and their father's strong nose. The first room I found was the washroom. I could imagine the running water in the sink. One knob had an H and the other a C. Hot and Cold. *Hot water.*

I remembered Mary saying there was a shower indoors and a cabinet behind the mirrors. *Check the cabinets.* I eased one side open and inside were assorted brushes, bottles, and tubes. One label said "Parfum." I squeezed it and sprayed my face with the most foul-tasting liquid I'd ever tasted. I raked my tongue over the end of my shirt to get rid of the flavor. Yuck.

When the shock of the taste wore off, I realized how nice I smelled. I decided I liked Parfum, so I slipped it in my bag's outer pocket where it was least likely to get crushed. The razors were rusted, but there were a few bars of soap in boxes, so I grabbed them. Soap didn't expire. Bypassing the children's room, I made my way to the back of the apartment. A large rectangular bed rested against the wall, and chests of drawers were on either side. The tallest chest held men's clothes. I grabbed the plain undershirts. Someone might be able to use those. The other dresser held women's clothes and undergarments. They looked like they might fit me, so I stuffed bras and panties into my bag as quickly as possible. They were lacy and delicate, like nothing I'd ever seen before.

"That's better," Tage said, making me jump out of my skin. "You'll look amazing in those."

I swallowed. "Where's Mary?"

"She's in the other apartment."

"Why did you leave her there?"

"Why did you take off without telling me where you were going?" he countered.

"Do I *have* to check in with you?"

He chuckled. "I'm responsible for you. You were stupid enough to forget your ring at home, so it would be in your best interest to let your guard know where you're going."

"I think we need a new guard."

Tage laughed, throwing his head back. "You have no idea how right you are. Do you know that your blood tastes sweet? Sweeter than anything I've ever had."

"Why would that be? I don't eat sugar."

His eyes narrowed. "I have no idea why you taste so good. I almost fought Roman for you. He let me choose you, and then took my choice away."

"You *bit* me!"

"You entered the rotation. You knew you'd be bitten." His eyes danced with laughter.

"You know what I mean. You didn't numb me first."

"Ah, yes. That was an oversight."

"An oversight? Haven't you ever bitten someone before?"

"Not in a controlled way, no," he admitted, glancing away. "Look, I didn't realize that our saliva contained numbing agents. I didn't mean to hurt you, but I didn't know there was another way."

"You act like you're new to all of this."

His eyes darkened. "I'd love to have another taste of you."

"I just gave Roman my blood. It wouldn't be wise to let you feed so soon. I might get weak." My heart was beating out of control. I'd set the lantern on the dresser earlier, and my crossbow was leaning against the wall beside it. My hand felt for its grip as Tage stalked closer.

"Just a little taste wouldn't hurt." He noticed my hand inching along the wall and stepped up, snatching my wrists in his hands. "That's not nice. You were planning to shoot me."

"I was *planning* to defend myself."

He slammed my hands against the wall above my head. "I'm hurt," he feigned. "You know," Tage said, running one finger down my cheek, jaw, and neck. "There are places I can bite you that no one else will ever see. No one will have to know about it." His hard body pinned me to the wall. "I almost wish you were wearing your dress. Easier access." His hand stroked my outer thigh.

"Saul will kill you," I ground out.

"The little boy you run around with? I don't think so."

He began to unbutton my pants and a tear streaked down my face despite me. Squeezing my eyes shut, I debated screaming for Mary, but I knew there was no way she would be able to fight him. There was no way we could fight him together and win.

All at once, I fell to the floor in a shaking mess as a growl tore through the room. Roman had Tage pinned to the opposite wall by the neck, his feet dangling a foot off the floor. "What part of *Do not touch the humans* did you not understand?" Roman enunciated every word.

Tage just smiled, blood leaking from his lip. "I just wanted a taste."

"She is *mine* now." Roman lowered him to the floor. "Go home. If you ever touch anyone else, I'll end you myself."

Tage straightened his jacket. "Fine. 'Night, ladies!" he called merrily, brushing by Mary, who stood in the doorway covering her mouth.

Roman composed himself and turned to help me up. I was bracing against the wall, halfway there. "Are you okay?"

"Yeah," I turned to button my pants and then brushed the errant strands of hair from my face. My fingers wouldn't stop trembling. Tage would have bitten me, but there was no way he would have stopped at just a taste. He would have drained me. Ford would have lost both of his sisters in the span of a month.

"I'm sorry I was late. There's trouble. We have to cut the trip short."

"What sort of trouble?" Mary asked.

"There's a nest of Infected nearby. They're looking for something, probably us."

"A nest?" I asked, gripping my crossbow tightly.

"Leave the lantern. It might buy us some time if they think we're still in here. And to escape, we'll need the darkness." Roman led us out of the apartment, into the hallway and down the steps. "Quiet," he warned as we crossed over the glass shards in the area labeled 'Lobby'. My duffle wasn't heavy at all. I should have taken everything and sorted it later. This supply run would be a bust, which meant someone else would have to be sent in. I never even knew there were "nests" of Infected, though I figured some were in the city. Most inside died from the virus, and the ones who did survive became shells of the people they used to be. Maybe they were clinging to the lives they once lived, to the places they remembered.

"We take the alleys," Roman said, pointing to the dark void between two brick buildings that were at least four stories high. He led us into the darkness right as high-pitched shrieks came from the direction of the building we just left. My heart pumped faster and I got a new burst of energy. Mary did, too.

At every cross road, Roman would have us wait while he watched the area for movement. His hearing and vision seemed much sharper than our own, so we relied on him. I was waiting, glancing to the right, watching for motion when I saw a flash of long, golden hair.

She turned to face me and then waved me to her. "Mercedes?" I wasn't even sure I'd said it out loud.

I started walking toward her and then broke into a sprint. "Mercedes?"

"Porschia, no! It's a trap!"

"It's my sister!"

I pumped my arms, running as fast as I could down the street. Roman was on my heels and Mary was on his. "Stop, Porschia!" she pled.

"I can't!"

By the time I reached the intersection, there was nothing. Mercedes was gone. I spun around, arms out. "Where are you?"

"Shut up!" Roman hissed.

"Mercedes!" I screamed, ignoring him. "She's still alive. She's *here*."

Roman grabbed my arm. "She is Infected! Get a hold of yourself! If she touches you, you'll never see the Colony, Saul, your parents, or Mrs. Dillinger ever again. It'll be over with. You – your life – will be over, Porschia. Is that what you want? To die?"

I shook my head and tears burst from my eyes. "I just want my sister back. I want my life back!"

"This isn't the way," he said, pulling me to his chest almost tenderly.

"Uh, guys," Mary interrupted. "We're in trouble."

TWENTY

"Arm your crossbow," Roman told me, his dark eyes colliding with mine. I pulled away from him, my fingers finding their target, and nodded to him.

"Mary, stay with Porschia," he ordered.

Looking around, his eyes ticked by, stopping here and there on something we couldn't see. But the shrieks and shuffling could be heard through the sound of blood whooshing through our ears, through the sound of our erratic breaths and frantic pulses.

"I'm so angry with you, Porschia. We better make it out of this alive!" Mary hissed scathingly.

"I'm sorry." It was all I could say and it wasn't enough. Even if we made it out of this mess, it wouldn't be nearly enough.

Roman was tearing something he'd pulled from his inner jacket pocket. A bright red flame burst from a stick in his hand, burning hot and fast. He threw it on the ground nearby and it gave us light. It gave us the ability to see them. I almost wished it hadn't.

Mercedes was standing with a guy who looked to be about her age. His hair was gone and his flesh was gray, but Mercedes looked unchanged. Her hair was still beautiful and bright. Her skin was still tan and perfect. She looked like she'd just left the house, with the exception of her clothing. She was wearing tight jeans and a bulky, green sweater. The pair was grinning at us, just like Saul described. It was creepy as hell.

This wasn't my sister. My sister would never hurt me.

I raised my crossbow and took aim. "Wait," Roman said.

More shrieks came from behind us and then from either side. "Son of a bitch," Roman cursed. "They're surrounding us."

"What do they want?" Mary was glued to my side. She had no weapon other than the butcher knife she pulled from her bag.

"They're hungry," Roman answered.

"Are you kidding me?" Mary shrilled, sounding like one of them.

"No, and they're coming. We have to make a path and run like hell."

"How do we do it? Make a path?"

"Take some of them out and run like the Devil is on your heels...because he will be." Roman raked his eyes over the encroaching throng. Young, old, children. Some with no hair, some with strands, some with full heads. Some with sagging skin, some mottled and rotting. The smell of decay and rot permeated the air.

It wasn't this place; it was them. It was Mercedes, because she was one of them. She might be trying to survive, but so was I.

"If we cut out the strongest among them, the others won't catch us," Roman plotted.

I nodded.

"That means—"

"I know what it means. Fine."

"On three."

I aimed for my sister. If I could hit her, Roman would at least let her live. If he got a hold of her, he'd kill her. And this time, it truly would be the end of Mercedes.

"One."

"Two," he paused.

"Three."

I squeezed the trigger and somehow the arrow found its target, striking Mercedes in her side. It wasn't a deathblow by any means, but it would stop her in her tracks. She shrieked uncontrollably, shaking hands clasping the skin around the arrow. She looked at me incredulously. "You were trying to eat me, Mercedes!" I screamed as we ran for it. Roman was running toward the man beside her, his body beginning to blur with speed. The man shifted at the last minute and took Mercedes with him, avoiding the blow from Roman, but we made a hole, one large enough to slip out of. And we *did* run like the Devil was on our heels. Their shrieks, though a ways back, followed us all the way to the wall. Roman sent us over first and then stayed on top. "I'll watch. They're riled up. I wouldn't want them to try something stupid."

"What is their problem?"

"Just because they're different doesn't mean they don't have the same problem you and I do. They're starving."

MARY SCOWLED AT ME AND THEN CROSSED MY PARENTS' YARD, LEAVING ME to stare at the shells of the three rusting cars in the back yard.

Mercedes. Ford. Porsche.

Neglected. Starved. Forgotten.

I stayed there, sinking to the ground beneath a crabapple tree, my back against the familiar curve of its bark. I finally stopped shivering, letting the adrenaline pumping through me wear off. The rest of the hunt wouldn't be over. I didn't want to wake Mrs. Dillinger, and if I fell asleep, no one would be able to wake me. So I sat there, watching the house the way Roman was watching the Infested on the other side of the wall.

Leaning my head back, I watched clouds streak across the bright moonlight and the stars peek from between it all when they had the chance. It was beautiful and peaceful in a world full of chaos and danger.

The back door creaked open and two steps came from the boards of the back porch. What was Father doing out at this time of night?

When the door closed, more footsteps sounded and Ford's lanky figure stepped into the back yard. I stayed still, watching him as he crossed the yard, heading toward the tree line. The only thing behind the small thicket of trees was the flood wall. What was he doing?

I kept my steps light. When he crossed through the saplings and grabbed the metal rungs of the ladder, I finally spoke. "What in the hell do you think you're doing?"

He jumped back like the rung was white-hot. "Porschia?" he asked in a high pitch.

"Don't 'Porschia' me! What are you doing near the wall?"

"I heard something."

"You *heard* something?"

He nodded. "Something was screaming over there, and I knew you guys went to the city tonight. I was coming to help you." Guilt furrowed his brow. "I'm sorry. I just thought I could help if you were..."

"You didn't want me to end up like her."

Ford nodded, stared down at his feet, and shoved his fists into his pockets. "Sorry."

"I'm the one who's sorry, but you can never go over there, Ford. Promise me."

He wouldn't look me in the eye.

"Ford!"

"I promise, okay?"

"Okay. Now go back inside." I watched him until he disappeared back into the safety of the house. Dust from above sprinkled my hair and nose. When I looked up, Roman was standing atop the wall, standing over me. "You heard that, huh?"

"I did."

I shook my head. "He's going to do something stupid, isn't he?"

"He almost did tonight."

For the first time since I left, I wished I were back home. At least that way I could keep a closer eye on him.

"Porschia?"

"Yeah."

"He wasn't the only one who did something foolish tonight. Wear your ring tomorrow."

I swallowed. "I will."

TWENTY-ONE

Roman stayed on the wall as the sky began to lighten. He said he would be at the pavilion before sunrise, so I set out to find Saul. My feet couldn't carry me fast enough. I walked, then jogged, and then ran to the crossing. No one was there. I waited until it was almost sunrise before running to the pavilion.

Saul and the others were there with the night-walkers. Seeing him, it was like my chest could expand, I could breathe again. Saul was okay. I ran to him and threw my arms around his neck. His strong arms wrapped around me and I held him tightly before kissing his mouth, his cheeks, his jaw. Frantic.

A low growl came from behind us. We parted to find Roman, fists clenching and fangs bared, staring at us. Tage laughed from just behind him and put his hand on Roman's shoulder. "Easy. Wouldn't want to break the treaty."

Tage must have had a death wish. His teasing was too much for Roman in that moment, and I barely saw him move before he was grabbing Tage by the throat and launching him across the square. The ground shook from the impact of his body slamming into the concrete. Saul pulled me behind him and watched Roman stalk toward Tage, who was chuckling as he lay on the ground, staring up at the sky.

"Long time coming," he teased.

Roman's eyes darkened and I knew his intent. The other vamps started to line up behind Roman. He was their leader. As awful as Tage was, there was still something he was hiding. I didn't want to see him torn apart. There had already been too much death, too much loss lately. "Roman!" My voice was shrill.

"Roman, it's almost sunrise. If you don't feed now while it's still dark, the colonists will see you. It will scare them," I pleaded. "If they're frightened, the treaty won't matter. There will be no volunteers for the rotation, and you can't feed on us indefinitely."

He stopped stalking toward Tage and spun around, walking intently to me instead. *I did this,* I reminded myself, wringing my hands. Saul moved to stand in front of me, but Dara pulled him away. He struggled, but she whispered something to him that calmed him down somewhat. I could still see his jaw ticking, the dangerous look in his eyes and how he aimed it at Roman.

Roman quickly licked my neck and sank in, pulling me tightly against him, and I had to hold onto his biceps to steady myself. He was taking much more than was necessary. He was teaching me a lesson. I could feel my body weakening. "Roman, stop," I whispered.

He didn't stop.

Tage must have gotten loose. His growl, just a foot away, was what made Roman stop gulping from me. He didn't seal the wound. It stung. I winced, holding my hand over the dripping wound.

"You were draining her," Tage said with a shrug as Roman shouldered by him, walking toward the houses across the square.

Was he going to leave me like this?

"I'll help you," Tage offered.

"You just want a taste, you freak!"

He laughed. "Guilty, but you need me to seal those."

Warm blood oozed down my chest. "Fine."

Saul was beside me, warning Tage to seal it and get the hell away from me. I felt the earth spin. "Uh-oh!" Tage said, catching me as I fell. "He took more than I thought. Lucky bastard."

I felt his warm tongue on my neck and the world went dark.

When I came to, I was in bed at my room in Mrs. Dillinger's house. "Hey," Saul said quietly, perking up. He'd been sleeping in the chair beside me.

"What are you doing here?"

"I wanted to make sure you were okay."

My mouth was like cotton, but I seemed to be all right. "I'm fine. Thank you for helping me."

"Dara explained a few things to me last night. I want to talk to you, but we both need some rest."

"How did the hunt go?"

Saul smiled. "Amazing. We don't have to go out any more this rotation."

"Seriously?" I sat up, smiling.

"Seriously. The vamps were...it was insane. They're so fast and fierce. They took down seven deer including a twenty-point buck, a large black bear and a boar, and the Freemans' snares caught two hares and a squirrel."

"That's...wow."

"Yeah." He smiled. "If you're okay, do you care if I get some rest?"

"Absolutely. Your mom is probably expecting you home."

He shook his head. "Ford stopped by to see you. He said he'd come again later, but he was going to stop by my house and tell them I was with you." He looked down at me, a guarded but hopeful expression lifting his brows. "Can I lay with you? Just lay and sleep?"

My heart leaped. "Yeah. Of course."

I scooted to the edge of the bed. He toed his boots off and sank into the mattress beside me, letting out a deep sigh. "Long night."

"Yeah."

"How was the city?"

"It was weird. I'll tell you about it when we wake up."

"The Elders have called a town meeting at five o'clock, but Mrs. Dillinger promised to wake us in time. I can go get you something to eat if you want. You're probably starving."

I wasn't. I was tired to the marrow. "I just want to sleep. We'll eat when we wake up."

He stroked my cheek. "Goodnight, Porschia."

"Night, Saul."

When Saul stretched beside me, I realized I was using his chest as a pillow. Quickly checking for drool, I was glad to find his shirt still dry.

That would have been embarrassing. Saul grinned, his hair flattened on the right side of his head. He was cute when he was sleepy.

"Mrs. Dillinger just knocked."

"I hope she was okay with you staying. I should've asked."

"She knew we were sleeping."

"How do you know?" I asked.

"Your snoring could wake the dead," he said with a wink.

I slapped him and sat up, stretching my back. My neck still stung. Roman numbed me to begin with, so I didn't know why it still hurt so badly and why it didn't heal with sleep. Gently touching my skin, I felt two large scabs on my neck. *Ouch.* "Why haven't I healed?"

"It's the venom in their fangs. There's enough of it in their saliva to numb human skin, but the fangs have more. When they just take enough, the wound heals. But Dara said that if a vampire drinks for long enough, if they don't drain the person, the wound won't heal for days. Him drinking from you wasn't about hunger or thirst. He was marking you for everyone to see."

"That's disgusting." I stood up and noticed the blood that had oozed down my chest was dry, forming a hard, brownish-red crust on my shirt. "Gross! I'm changing."

Saul's eyes lit up.

"Not in front of you. Can you give me a few minutes?"

He laughed and stood up, grabbing his boots. "Can't blame a guy for trying. I'll see what that delicious smell is."

"Do men always follow their noses?"

"The way to a man's heart is through his stomach."

My duffle was in the corner. I hoped Saul didn't peek inside, or else he would have found scraps of delicate fabric in every color imaginable. I wished I had time to look in the woman's closet. I pulled one of Mercedes' dresses from the chest of drawers and laid it on the bed. A small basin of water sat on a tiny wooden table in the corner. I needed to get the blood off of me.

Freshly dressed and feeling somewhat cleaner, I made my way downstairs. The smell of chicken hit my nose and my mouth began to water. Saul was talking with Mrs. Dillinger. "I think it's wonderful that your parents want to meet her," she said. I stopped and listened.

"They're excited."

"Are you nervous?" she asked.

"Not at all," he answered confidently. "She's what I want. I just hope she knows it."

"I think she's beginning to, but you haven't known her well for long. Are things going too quickly?"

Saul chuckled. "No, and life's too short to waste time. If you find something like what we have, you take it."

Mrs. Dillinger's hearty laugh filled the kitchen. "I couldn't agree more. I didn't even meet my husband until the day we were married. Things were different back then, though."

"How long has the Colony been here?" I asked, stepping into the conversation and the room.

Both heads turned toward me. Mrs. Dillinger was turning chicken in the pan. "My mother was one of the first settlers."

"Oh my goodness. Really?"

"Yes. Her husband and children were killed by the virus. She was immune somehow, and one of the only survivors. They lived in the hills and she walked for days to get to the city. When she got here, everyone was either sick or dead. Within days, there were only a handful of people remaining. The Infected began to attack people, but couldn't climb the wall or cross the river, so the survivors huddled here until things died down. But things didn't really end. The people decided to stay, thinking this was the safest place. It took years to build the Colony up to what it is today. People trickled in through the year, looking for shelter in the city and never finding it. Those who weren't attacked were taken in by the Colony. A city of more than a million was reduced to less than one hundred. It's a miracle in itself that we have over two hundred people now."

The gravity of the situation caused me to blink. "When was the last time someone found the Colony?"

"I don't remember anyone, so it must have been before I was born," she answered. "Let's eat before the meeting starts."

"Are you going?" Saul asked her.

"If you will help me get there. The last meeting was held before I was born, so whatever the Elders have to say is important."

Before she was born? I assumed that the Elders called meetings once in a while, maybe to keep in touch with residents. I assumed wrong.

The chicken was mouthwatering. "Where'd we get the chicken?"

"Ford delivered it and our extra rations."

Damn it, Ford.

I chewed the chicken, savoring the cooked potatoes and apples and vowing to try to talk sense into Ford after the meeting. We left our plates for later and set out early enough to get Mrs. Dillinger there. Arthritis in her back and legs stiffened her movements and limited her range of motion, but step by step, she fought. Residents were gathered outside of Town Hall. The small church wouldn't hold everyone, and it looked like absolutely everyone was there.

A gentleman on a log offered Mrs. Dillinger his seat and we stood behind her. Father stood with Ford near the front steps of the building. They must have gotten there early. Mother didn't come. I scanned the crowd for her again, but she wasn't there.

The Elders were nothing if not prompt. At five o'clock, an hour before the sun would set in the western hills, they called the meeting to order.

Elder Beckett spoke, the other two Elders flanking him in support. "The treaty we've had with the night-walkers is in jeopardy. People are dying. Two people in less than one week have been attacked and killed. We've heard of your concern, and we wanted you to know that your safety is our top priority. Therefore, we need to implement a few changes until a proper investigation can be made."

"Number one: No resident is allowed out of their homes after dark. The only exception are those in the rotation." A low murmur rumbled through the residents.

"Number two: The rotation will remain. We will start again next week, as we have plenty of meat from the current hunt." Beckett paused. "However, no one has volunteered for next week. The night-walkers are. . . upset by this, and feel that the safety measures we are implementing implicate them in the recent deaths."

"Damn right it does!" someone yelled.

"Alright, alright," Beckett said, motioning for everyone to simmer down. "Emotions are running high. What we need is time. The rotation will stay in place for now. Those on the current rotation will remain on rotation until further notice."

Victor Freeman stood up at the front. "Indefinitely? Is that safe, or even possible for us? I wouldn't care if it was just me, but my boy is in the rotation for the first time. He's young."

"Dad," James grumbled beside him.

Elder Beckett pursed his lips. "The night-walkers assure us that as long as you have extra rations, you will not be harmed by staying on the rotation indefinitely. It is actually a custom in other settlements for a vampire to select a companion of sorts for long-term feeding."

Victor scoffed, curling his lips in disgust.

Elder Beckett spoke gruffly. "You will remain in the rotation. The treaty will remain in force for the time being, but mark my words. . . if the night-walkers are violating the terms, I will make sure they know that they won't be welcome in Blackwater anymore."

Nodding heads and arms crossed over chests, the citizens assented. "Curfew is at dusk, so I suggest that you return home and finish whatever outdoor chores you need to complete."

I pulled my jacket together and huffed out a pent-up breath. Saul was angry. His jaw ticked and his hand held my side tight, pulling me closer to him. "This is ridiculous," he fumed.

"Let's just hope they can figure out what's going on quickly," I added.

"We're immune from the curfew. Maybe we can help," Saul said decisively.

TWENTY-TWO

As our neighbors filed out of the yard, their eyes found the wounds on my neck. I should have worn my hair down, should have covered them. Saul and I helped Mrs. Dillinger up and escorted her back to the house, each of us acting as a crutch, but her breathing was labored by the time we got back to her house. "Are you going to be okay?" I asked.

"I'm fine, but you're going to be late." Her eyes found my neck and she pursed her lips together.

"We'll be fine," Saul assured her, helping her inside. I wished I could be as confident as he was.

"After the evening rotation, I need to find my brother," I told Saul.

"Okay," he said, his eyes searching me.

We rushed to the pavilion to find only Dara, Tage and Roman waiting. Victor Freeman had his arms crossed over his chest. James stood beside him. Saul spoke first. "Where are Tim and Mary?"

"It seems that they are refusing to come back," Roman replied.

"Where are the other night-walkers?" I asked, feeling Saul's hand grab hold of mine.

"They left in search of greener pastures," Roman spat.

"It's just you three left?" I asked.

Tage stood up from the concrete bench he sat on, stretching his arms into the air over his head. "Yep. The two we sent scouting last night never came back. Probably made plans with the others to skip town."

"Where will they go?" Saul asked.

"Who knows? Who cares? I'm hungry," Tage drawled.

Roman's eyes bored into me. "We only need three in the rotation now."

Victor said, "I'll stay," and then told James to go home.

James protested for a moment but followed his father's instructions, walking into the darkness toward his house. Victor called out, "Straight home, son." The only reply from James came in the toss of his hand into the air.

Saul squeezed my hand and then stepped toward Dara. I hated that she would feed from him, or touch or even look at him. Tage muttered something to Roman and for the first time since I approached the pavilion, Roman turned his attention from me. "No," he spat at Tage.

Tage shrugged and winked at me. "Can't hurt to ask." He motioned to Victor, who walked to a nearby bench with him. Tage moved quicker than my eyes could keep up with. In a blur, he was feeding from Victor and then pulling away again.

Roman's hands snaked around my stomach, reeling me in to him. "Do you prefer to stand, Porschia?"

"It doesn't matter to me."

His heart beat slowly against my back. "You're concerned for my comfort?"

I didn't know how to reply. I didn't care about him at all, but didn't want to make him angry again. When he licked my neck, a whimper came from the back of my throat. "I love the little noises you make," he whispered on a warm breath.

Then he sank his long fangs into my throat on the opposite side from where he marked me. He only drank for a moment before pulling them out of me and sealing the wound. At least *it* would be gone in the morning. "Why did you do it?" I asked softly. I should have kept my mouth shut.

He walked around to the front of me and smiled. "Mark you?"

"Yes."

Roman grinned like a little boy. "I wanted the others to know that you were spoken for." His eyes flicked to Tage and then Saul.

"Spoken for? What exactly do you mean by that, Roman? Because I'm with Saul."

Roman's eyes darkened. "You aren't married to him."

"Not yet," I said, tipping up my chin in defiance.

A growl rumbled in his chest. "You will *not* marry him."

"Don't tell me what I will and will not do. You don't own me."

Roman's face was an inch from mine when Saul intervened, pulling me away from him. "She's right. You don't own her."

Tage laughed from behind him and Dara looked distractedly at her fingernails. "Can we go now?" she whined. "Come on, Roman. Leave the girl alone."

Roman growled at Saul as Tage and Dara urged him to leave us behind. Begrudgingly, he did. Saul grabbed my hand and pulled me back into the human part of the Colony, back to safety. After the first rotation, I thought Tage was the night-walker to be concerned about. I was wrong. It was Roman.

"I need to stop at home for a few minutes. Are you still coming to dinner tomorrow?" Saul asked carefully. The hopefulness in his voice was laced with residual anger.

"As long as you want me to."

"I do."

I squeezed his hand in reassurance. "Then I look forward to it."

He stopped, pulled me into his chest with a thud, and wrapped his fingers around my neck before pulling my lips to his. I was dizzy when he let go. Roman might have marked me with his fangs, but Saul claimed me with his kiss.

"What was *that* for?" I asked, my voice still breathy and trying to recover.

Saul smiled. "I just needed to know you still felt the same."

"I don't like Roman at all, Saul."

His brows furrowed. "He sure likes you."

"It doesn't mean that the feeling is mutual."

"I know. I just... never mind. It's stupid."

I grabbed his arm as he started to walk away. "It isn't stupid. What's on your mind?"

"He can give you more than I can, more than I'll ever be able to." He pulled away, pacing back and forth.

"What are you talking about? He can't give me anything. Roman only takes, Saul. He takes what he wants, uses it up, and then tosses it away. Why would any woman want to subject herself to that?"

"I guess I just see the draw. Most girls in the Colony have started swooning over the night-walkers now that they're more visible. I hear the whispers."

"They don't come from my lips."

He smiled slightly. "Not yet."

"Not ever. I hate him. I hate them all. Even though I'm afraid of the repercussions, part of me hopes the treaty will end and the night-walkers will be forced to leave."

"They won't leave. They'll just take what they want, like you said."

WE WALKED TOWARD SAUL'S HOUSE, THE SKY DARKENING WITH EACH STEP we took. From the corner of my eye, I saw Ford walking between two nearby houses. "Ford!"

He didn't stop. "Saul, I'm going after him."

"But, I—"

"No! I'll be safe. He's my brother. Just talk to your mom and then find me, if you want."

"Fine. I'll be right behind you," his voice echoed behind me.

Running into the darkness, I called out for Ford again. "Ford?"

The only sound was the wind rattling the dried leaves and the sound of the black water to the north. I stumbled over exposed tree roots, between the last rows of homes, toward the river. Ford's white shirt should have been visible, but I didn't see him anywhere. The river bank was steep, so I stepped carefully. Meg's death was no accident, and neither was the other man's. But accidents could still happen, and I didn't want them to happen to me.

"Ford?"

Nothing. A frigid wind blew through my coat. I wrapped it tighter around my body, wishing I wasn't too afraid to wear Ford's pants in public. The material of the dress was too thin. Either Ford vanished into thin air or he entered one of the homes. Either way, he wasn't here.

An acorn landed beside my foot. Then another. I looked up, expecting a squirrel, but found Tage grinning down at me instead. He was perched on a branch half-way up a maple tree. "What are you doing out here?" I asked loudly.

My heart thundered in my chest. Was he hunting? Waiting to feed on someone and dump their body in the river?

"I can hear your heart beating wildly."

He grabbed the limb above him and swung himself down, landing beside me gracefully. If I attempted the same, no doubt I would break something. Tage smiled, his fangs glowing white in the moonlight.

I swallowed and took a step away from him. "Saul will be here in just a few minutes."

He smiled. "Oh, I don't think he will."

"He just stopped at his house for a second."

"Then why were you calling out for your brother?"

I saw red. "What do you know about my brother? You leave him alone." Poking my finger in his chest, I enunciated every threatening word.

"What are you going to do to me if I don't?" Tage said, toying with me.

I ignored him. I didn't know what I'd do to him, but I would figure out how to end him if he touched my baby brother.

"Why are you out here? Searching for dessert?"

He clutched his chest as if hurt. "You wound me."

"I'm sure."

Tage blew out a breath and stared at the swirling water beneath us. "I didn't kill that man, or your friend either, Porschia. I know you don't believe me. Hell, even Dara and Roman think I might have done it. But I didn't. And I'm out here..." he stepped closer to me, "to watch the river. This seems to be where the bodies end up, so if I can stop it or catch the person in the act, I can exonerate myself."

"You're trying to defend the Colony?"

He chuckled. "Nothing as honorable as all that. I'm just trying to save my own neck."

"Have you seen anything?"

"Not tonight."

"How many nights have you been watching?" I asked.

"Since the day you found Meg."

He was too close to me, so I stepped back to put space between us. "Have you ever heard of personal space, Tage?"

"Once or twice." He invaded that sacred space again with another step, which made me roll my eyes.

"Why don't I ever see you during the daylight hours?"

Tage laughed. "I'm a night-walker." He flipped his fang and blood trickled from the pad of his finger. "Cut myself," he said with a wink. "Do you have your ring?"

I held my hand out to show him that yes, I was wearing the ring. I had slipped it back on as soon as I got home the morning after I forgot it, the morning after Mercedes and her new friends cornered us. "Yeah, why?"

He flipped the compartment of the ring open and dripped some of his blood into it. I tried to pull my hand away, but he held it tight and then locked the tiny hinge again. "Why did you do that?" I screeched.

I pulled my hand away from him, feeling the bones of my finger pull apart. He finally let go. "Just making sure you were still covered."

"I don't even need this thing until next week."

"Don't take it off, ever," he ordered.

"Whatever, Tage. Look, Ford's not here, so I need to go back home."

"You mean to Saul's, right? You could just stay here and wait for him. He'll be along in a second." Tage. Even his name was aggravating. "Oh, you mean he's not really coming?"

He toyed with an errant strand of my hair. "I'm here," Saul said, stepping toward us. "Now get away from her."

Tage put his hands up in surrender. "Just making sure no one tries to hurt her."

"Like I buy that."

"Believe what you want," Tage said quietly.

Saul's hand clasped onto mine and he tugged me away from the river. "I leave you alone for five minutes and the night-walkers descend."

"I followed Ford, but I couldn't find him. Tage was up in a tree. He threw an acorn at me."

"And he was touching you because?"

"He's annoying. He was fiddling with my hair. He has a complete lack of respect for personal space."

"Just yours."

"He was probably hungry," I mumbled.

"For more than your sweet blood, I'll swear it," Saul said.

"Not everyone is interested in me, Saul." No one was but him, actually. The vamps would corner anyone with a viable vein. I wasn't special at all.

"You have the attention of two-thirds of the remaining night-walkers, both of whom are male, Porschia. It's not a safe or enviable position to be in, and not one you should take lightly. I think you're in danger—more from Roman than Tage, but both could tear you apart in a second."

"I know."

He slowed his steps. "Dinner is at four thirty tomorrow evening. Mom's excited."

"So am I," I promised, only half lying. I was terrified. Meeting his family scared me to death. What if they didn't like me or didn't approve? What if they didn't want us to marry? What if they did?

TWENTY-THREE

I WOKE BEFORE DAWN, HAVING GONE TO SLEEP EARLIER THAN I HAD IN almost a week. I gathered the laundry, twisted it into a bundle, and took off toward the river. I set up further downstream than Mercedes and I ever did because I couldn't bear to look at the pool where the flowers of her farewell sank into the water, where I found Meg floating peacefully just a couple days earlier.

In this section of the river the water was angry. It tore over rocks and foamed and churned. The sun was out and I felt its blissful warmth on my back. I couldn't help but long for the spring and summer days when my fingers wouldn't numb and mottle.

Mrs. Dillinger and I didn't have very much laundry between us--nothing like at home where five of us constantly soiled our clothes. Laundry was a daily chore then. Now, I could wash for the two of us just twice a week, a welcome respite in the bitter winter.

Lost in my own world, I didn't hear it when he stepped up behind me. "Porschia."

I screamed and turned around to find Roman standing to my right. "What are you doing here?"

"It isn't safe near the river right now."

"Well, some of us still have laundry, Roman."

He smiled. "I see that. I like the sight of you like this." His eyes raked over me.

"Like what? Wet and half-frozen?"

"No, I like to see you on your knees."

I gulped. "Don't worry," he soothed. "I'm only kidding." But he certainly didn't look like he was kidding.

"I need to finish washing," I said awkwardly, and turned back to the task at hand. He didn't leave. "Why are you still here?"

"I protect what's mine."

"I'm not yours, Roman. We've been over this before."

Roman chuckled. "We'll see."

All of a sudden, the anger and agitation I felt toward him melted away. The heavy feelings of hurt and sadness lifted. I was just a girl washing clothing in a stream filled with dark silt and secrets. Letting out a sigh, I leaned back and took in the beauty of the day. Birds perched on bare branches and twittered back and forth with one another. There wasn't a cloud to be found in the blue sky. All was well in the world.

Tage's voice came booming from behind us. "Roman!"

I almost collapsed to the ground, shaking, the scared and anxious feelings coming back full force and crushing me under their heavy weight. "What's going on?" I struggled to say, fighting to even breathe.

"What, Tage?" Roman growled.

"It's Dara – something's wrong. She's back at the house."

Roman looked at me and then back at Tage. "You stay and guard her. Touch her and I end you."

"Yeah, man. I'll stay until you come back or she wants to go home."

"You walk her home," Roman ordered. He turned to me. "I have to go."

I watched him silently until his dark eyes turned away from me and he strode quickly toward the cemetery.

Once he was out of sight, Tage shook his head, pinching the bridge of his nose. "You felt it that time, right?"

"I felt *something*."

"He's compelling you. He has the power of compulsion. Roman can even compel our kind, but he uses it on you any time you're near him."

"Humans aren't immune?"

He laughed. "Humans are the easiest to compel. We can all do it to a degree, but Roman is exceptional; a true master."

"Why does it hurt so much?" I asked, rubbing my chest.

"Heartache always does." Tage looked into the forest beyond. "I know about your sister, and about your family."

My tears fell into the dark water at my knees. I nodded weakly.

"Mercedes wasn't your fault, no matter what they say," he said softly, crouching down beside me.

"Why are you being so nice to me, and why are you out in the daylight?"

He squinted his eyes. "It's getting easier. Every day it gets a little better."

"What does?" I asked.

"The sensitivity to light."

"How new are you?"

"New enough."

New enough. "But not in the state of frenzy people keep talking about?"

Tage looked at me. Dark strands of hair curled toward his sky-blue eyes. "Not now."

I sat back. "When were you in frenzy?"

"Before I came here. I got it under control before I found the Colony, but Roman doesn't know that. No one does," he admitted.

"And you didn't kill Meg, or the other man? Could you have done it and not been aware of it?"

He shook his head. "Porschia Ray, I did not kill your best friend. I swear that much to you."

Tage wasn't lying, or else he was using his powers of compulsion on me. Either way, he seemed to believe what he was telling me. I knew he was a new vampire.

"What happened to you, Tage?"

"How'd I turn?"

"Yeah," I said, sitting down on a nearby rock. I wrapped my arms around my knees, shivering from the cold. He pulled his dark sweater over his head, revealing a soft gray t-shirt underneath. Sitting on the rock beside mine, he threw the soft fabric at me. "Put that on and I'll tell you."

I hesitated just long enough for him to smile and grab a hand full of walnut-sized pebbles. I pulled it on and the warmth wrapped around me instantly. So did his scent. It was woodsy, masculine, and unexpected. Tucking my hands into the sleeves, I folded the fabric over my quivering hands. "It's on. Spill."

"Bossy," he said before nudging my knee with his. Tage threw a pebble across the water's surface, making it hop twice before it sank into the churning water. I always thought the surface had to be still to skip rocks across it.

"I have skills," he boasted.

"Whatever. Tell me, Tage."

He sighed dramatically. "Fine," he began. "I lived in a tiny community of survivors in Florida. It's south of here, several days' travel on foot. And it's warm there, just so you know—

year round."

"Great. Thanks for that."

"You're most welcome. So anyway, there was no treaty in place there. Obviously vamps lived nearby, and I got caught alone one day. A female vamp found me and attacked before I could defend myself—not that it was likely I could do much—but I'd heard about their blood. I really didn't want to die, so I bit her back."

"You bit *her* back, or you bit her *back*?"

"I bit her arm. The venom changed me faster than she could drain me, and the rest, as they say, is history."

"What happened to her – the vamp that bit you?"

He shrugged. "I killed her."

"You tore her head off?" I asked.

"No, there's another way to kill a vampire." Interesting.

I stared at the water. "How?"

"Drain them."

My eyes widened and locked on his. "You drained her? And then she died?"

"That's pretty much it. Most of it was sort of hazy. I think I tore her apart afterward, but her heart had already stopped by that time."

I gasped. "I always heard that vampires didn't have a heartbeat, but I've felt it."

"Do you know why a vampire feeds on human blood?"

"No, but I know they can feed on animals. Why don't they just do that – live off the blood of animals?"

"Because they would die. It's part of the curse."

"Curse?" I didn't understand.

Tage hesitated. I looked behind us, up onto the river bank above our heads. "There's no one there. I'd hear them."

I reveled in the warmth of his sweater. "Your hearing is more acute?"

"Much. And I stay warm as long as I feed. We just wear warm clothes to blend in. Hot and cold don't really affect us at all."

"Why are you telling me all of this? Isn't it forbidden or something?"

He smiled. "Probably. Don't really know. Don't really care." Tage tilted his head and looked at me.

"Oh! I get it. It's pity, right? Well." I straightened myself. "You can save it for someone else. I'm fine."

He shook his head. "No you're not, but one day you will be. You need to steer clear of Roman and stick close to Saul."

"I know, but how?"

"Haven't figured that out yet," he admitted.

We both agreed, then. I was screwed.

TWENTY-FOUR

When I finished washing the last dress, Tage volunteered to wring them out for me. It took one minute to finish his part, where it would have taken me twenty. I shook my head and gathered the damp fabric into my arms. "Oh, I need to give you back your sweater."

"Keep it. Looks good on you."

I narrowed my eyes. "Who are you goading, Tage? Saul or Roman?"

He laughed. "Roman."

"That's not smart, Tage."

"Never claimed to be. I'll walk you home. Give me the clothes. You're already soaked."

"I'm fine."

He held his arms out petulantly. Grumbling, I relented and handed the pile to him. "If you want to freeze, that's fine by me."

Tage grinned at me. "You're welcome, kitten."

"Why do you call me that?"

"Because you're tame and cute, but seem to be hiding some sharp claws beneath the furry paws."

I rolled my eyes. "Whatever," I muttered. I wasn't tame and I sure as hell wasn't a kitty cat.

The colonists were up and about when we started toward Mrs. Dillinger's house. They stopped their chores and stared at Tage and me, at the bite marks still marring my neck. That was when the whispers began.

"Night-walker." "Get inside." And, "What's that girl thinking, bringing him onto our side?"

The Elders were mentioned. The treaty was mentioned. Tage was visibly tense. "Maybe I should go."

He wasn't even doing anything. Actually, he was. Tage was helping to carry my wet laundry, and if they couldn't see past their fear, then it was their problem. "Too weak to carry a woman's load?" I teased, wagging my eyebrows at him. Frigid gusts of wind plastered the wet fabric of my skirts to my legs. I really didn't want to carry the wet stuff home, and I honestly thought my neighbors would have been more understanding.

"I'm not afraid, I just don't want you to get in trouble."

"From whom?"

"The Elders," he replied.

I laughed. "What more could they possibly do to me?"

"Kick you out of the Colony," he whispered.

"They won't."

"Tensions are high. You don't know what they would do." Tage stopped, handing the soggy bundle over. Part of me hated that he was giving up, but the other part of me appreciated his concern.

"Thank you…for everything." He was the most confusing creature I'd ever met. I watched him walk quickly back to his side of town, head down in defeat, and part of my heart broke with him.

He hadn't been a night-walker for long at all. He wasn't used to this life, and he didn't ask for it. I wondered if he regretted biting the vamp. Now that he'd tasted eternal life, did he crave the empty solace of death?

The concrete of the road was settling and slipping into the soft earth in places, looking like rippling rivers of flowing stone. I stepped carefully over the bumps, making my way to Mrs. Dillinger's. She was on the porch waiting for me when I stepped onto her walk. "Oh, thank God you're okay!" Wringing her hands, she hugged me so tightly I dropped the clothes. I responded by awkwardly patted her back.

"I did the wash," I told her as she strangled me.

"Please tell me when you leave. Things in the Colony are dangerous, and I..." she pled.

"Okay."

"You haven't heard?" She steadied herself with my arms. "Two people are dead. An elderly man and his wife. Murdered in their home this morning. Their necks, oh Porschia. They had bite marks. The Elders are telling everyone to stay inside, but we aren't even safe in our own homes now."

"They had wounds? But I watched the night-walkers go back home this morning. It doesn't make sense, Mrs. Dillinger."

"Maggie, dear. We're beyond formalities."

"Maggie, I watched them go home." I shook my head. Something wasn't right. It couldn't have been the night-walkers that were left. Could it be someone new, or one of the ones they thought had fled?

"Couldn't they come back? Aren't they fast?"

I nodded. "They are fast, but something isn't right about this."

From the street came the pounding of footprints. "Porschia?"

Ford came running up the walk. He almost tackled me, but I stepped away from Mrs...Maggie in time. He didn't hit her. His momentum alone would have knocked her over. "I hate this! I never know if you're okay or not."

"I'm fine, Ford, but you can't keep doing the things you're doing." He knew what I meant, and though Maggie narrowed her eyes at him, she didn't pry.

"It's nothing."

"Don't tell me it's nothing. If you're caught you'll be banished, and you wouldn't survive, Ford—not out there."

I stared him down until he looked away. I wasn't exaggerating or playing games. Mercedes wasn't in the Colony anymore. I didn't want to lose Ford, too.

"Maggie, can I walk with Ford for a few minutes?"

"You don't have to ask permission, dear. I was just worried," she said.

"We'll be back soon."

Maggie shooed us away and I shut the door behind him. My dress was still wet and although normally I would have changed, something in Ford's eyes told me he needed me. "What's wrong?"

He scrubbed the back of his neck. "I have to help dig the graves."

"Okay."

"Listen," he said. "Don't go near the river alone."

"The people today were killed in their homes. What does the river have to do with it?"

He hesitated, pursing his lips until they were thin slices of flesh. "Just stay away from it!" Ford never yelled at me, not since he'd grown taller than I had.

I grabbed his elbow. "What is *wrong* with you?"

"Just for once in your life, listen to me, Porschia. I don't want you near the water."

My baby brother stepped off the porch and stalked away. He would be digging deep holes in the earth, helping lower the bodies of our fallen neighbors. But what secrets were eating away at him, weighing down the skin beneath his eyes?

TWENTY-FIVE

Mr. White, the elderly man who lived nearest to Mrs. Dillinger—Maggie—knocked on our door a few hours later. Worrying the edges of his hat, he shifted his feet on the porch planks, making them creak and groan. "Burials will begin within the hour. I was sent to tell everyone on the street."

Maggie thanked him and told me to start bundling up. It was frigid. The air that swirled into the room when I opened the door for Mr. White was marrow-chilling. "It's going to snow. I can feel it in my knees."

I didn't know what knees had to do with the weather, but it was certainly cold enough to flurry. Upstairs, I pulled on Mercedes' coat and then Ford's pants beneath my skirts. Another layer would help. I wore both pairs of my socks and laced my boots up tight to keep the warmth in.

"Let your hair down. It'll help guard your ears," Maggie said as she waited at the bottom of the step. "I don't think I can make it to the cemetery."

"I know. No one will think anything of it."

"They will, but there's nothing they can do about it. My body is giving out. Simple as that."

I wished she was wrong. Feeling her arms wrap around me in a warm hug, I patted her shoulder and pulled away. "I'll be back as soon as I can."

She smiled. "I'll start supper, but I know you'll be eating with Saul tonight."

Butterflies flapped wildly in my stomach. I was going to meet his family.

"They'll love you, Porschia. Don't worry yourself over that."

Easier said than done. I stepped onto the porch and pulled the door closed, locking myself and the cold outside. People were already leaving their homes or walking toward the cemetery. Most nodded, a few waved, but no one spoke to me. Some refused to even look in my direction. I tucked my hands into the silk-lined pockets of my coat and balled my fists. Flurries of snow swirled in the air. Tiny crystalline flakes got caught in my web of dark hair and slowly melted away, replaced by new ones.

When I was close, Saul found me, his hand wrapping around mine. "Hey," he greeted, giving a comforting squeeze.

"Hi."

"My mom is excited about dinner."

I smiled. "I'm scared."

His brows furrowed. "Why? They'll love you."

"Why would they? I have absolutely nothing to offer you." It was true.

"They'll love you because you're amazing, funny, and smart. But if you were none of those things, they would simply love you because I do."

A tiny gasp flew from my lips.

Saul loved me. Was that possible in such a short amount of time? My heart thumped as though it had morphed into one of those insane butterflies in my stomach. "I thought you were just *fond* of me," I teased with a grin.

"Oh, I am." He threaded his fingers through my hair and leaned down toward my face. "Tell me you don't feel the same way."

"I do."

"Oh, thank God." He placed a chaste kiss on my lips and pulled away, but his sparkling blue-gray eyes promised that there was much more to come later. There was a storm in them that I hadn't seen before now.

He toyed with my ring. "Soon, you won't need this. You'll wear mine."

"Okay."

He grinned. "Okay." Saul paused. "For someone who talks a lot, you certainly get quiet when you're nervous."

I did. Smiling up at him, we walked toward the gravestones. My father was standing with the Elders and seemed to be in deep conversation with them. Mother was missing, as usual, but so was Ford. He was supposed to have been here, helping to dig the new graves.

Nearby, leaning against a bare oak tree, was Jonah. He stared at Meg's grave blankly. "Jonah?"

Focusing his attention on me and Saul, he nodded. "Hey."

"Have you seen Ford?"

He shook his head. "Not for a long time. He helped Noah and I dig for a while, and then said he needed a drink. I haven't seen him since."

A shiver crawled up my spine and I swallowed the bile that bit at the back of my throat. "Saul, I need to find my brother. *Now*."

"Okay." His hand tightened around mine. "Thanks, man," Saul yelled back to Jonas as he ran to keep up with me. I was going to the river. I was going to find my brother. I just prayed I wasn't too late.

"He tried to warn me! Ford?" I yelled frantically.

I ran between houses and around bushes and trees, jumping over their roots, stumbling over dips in the earth. "Ford?"

"He's probably fine," Saul said soothingly.

"He isn't. He tried to warn me. Today he came over and told me to stay away from the river," I said, my voice breaking at the end.

The sound of surging water came closer and closer. We were almost there. That was when I heard the sound of voices. Saul slowed and motioned for me to keep quiet, one finger over his lips. I nodded.

We crept toward the riverbank.

"Mother, you can't. Please don't do this," Ford begged.

Mother?

"I have to. She's my daughter."

Tip-toeing toward the bank, we crouched low until we saw the pair of them. "She's not herself. You can't help her now. She's Infected, and there isn't a cure."

"She's hungry."

"How do you even know that she is?" Ford tugged his hair in frustration. "She doesn't speak anymore."

Mother's hands and dress were coated in crimson. There were streaks and blood splatter on her forehead and cheeks. My stomach turned. *What did she do?*

From behind her came a soft bleating noise. A lamb with a noose around its neck was tied to a nearby stump. "Shhh," she cooed. "It'll all be over in a minute, sweetling." When she stepped toward the lamb, I saw another lamb, blood soaking into its wool in the place where she'd stood.

Silver glinted in her hand. Ford backed away from her slowly, his boots crunching the soft pebbles coating the mud alongside the swirling black water, tinged red.

Instantly, the image of Meg's body floating in the water came to mind.

Wildflowers floating, then sinking.

Mother grabbed the tiny animal by the wool at the back of its neck. It screamed. "No! Mother, don't hurt it!" I screamed.

I scrambled down the steep, muddy embankment toward her. She held the lamb beneath her arm and with her other hand, she pointed the butcher knife at me. "This is all your fault!" she ground out.

"No it's not," Saul countered, placing himself protectively between me and my mother before I even knew he'd climbed down. "Life isn't always fair, but Mercedes' fall had nothing to do with Porschia."

"You were supposed to be in the rotation, you, you, you," she muttered, backing toward the water.

Ford eased toward her, his eyes flicking between Saul, me, and Mother. Rustling from the other side of the river drew our attention. Mercedes stood across the bank, her dress tattered, torn, and dirty. Her hair was matted and snarled. Her once vibrant skin was dull and her arms hung lifelessly at her sides, but her eyes were full of life and full of malice.

She saw me and let loose an evil screech that had me, Saul, and Ford clasping our hands over our ears to keep them from bursting. Mercedes clutched her side—where my arrow's tip embedded just a night ago.

Mother's feet sloshed across the freezing water. Her teeth chattered, but she held the lamb tight and somehow made it across without falling on her own knife. Ford yelled after her, "NO! Mother, she'll kill you!"

Slipping up the opposite embankment, Mother just smiled. "She won't. She hasn't hurt me yet." To Mercedes, she turned and held the lamb out. "Brought you something new."

New?

Ford looked from the horrifying scene back to me, and set his jaw. "No. Ford, no."

"She's our mother."

Before Saul could reach him, Ford was running across the shallowest section, following Mother's footsteps up the slippery, dark mud. He took the lamb from Mother with force and set it down on the ground, pushing it toward Mercedes. But even animals can sense predators. The lamb wouldn't move. Its legs quaked as it backed away toward the river. The tiny animal would rather drown than be eaten.

However, Mercedes wasn't looking at the lamb. She wasn't looking at Mother. She smiled, a terrifying, satisfied smile and walked toward Ford.

"NO!" I roared. The water stung my legs like a million tiny needles. "Don't touch him!"

Saul splashed behind me, screaming at me to stop.

Mercedes might have looked like hell, but damn, she was fast. She grabbed Ford by the throat and lifted his feet off the ground.

"Holy shit, she's strong!" Saul yelled from behind me.

I was on her in an instant. "Don't you dare touch him!" Breaking her hold on him, I shoved her down. From my periphery, I could see Saul shoving Ford toward the river. Mother was backing away. That tiny slip in my attention was all my sister needed. With all her might, she rolled me over and straddled my hips. Grinning like the devil, she bared her teeth and bit at my face. "Don't bite me!" I gritted out every word, trying like hell to push her off me. "I'm Porschia! I'm your sister!"

Mercedes growled low in her chest. Finally, I bucked hard enough that she fell off of me and rolled to the side.

Mother was still on my side of the river. "Saul, get her across!" I screamed. Ford was sloshing through the water and I could see that he wanted to come back. Saul wouldn't let him. I would make sure of that.

Saul picked my mother up and carried her over the rocks. I started crawling as fast as I could away from Mercedes, but she grabbed my ankle and tore my pant leg away. "No!"

She yanked both pairs of long socks down. Time slowed. My head throbbed, blood pulsing through my temples.

Saul screamed, "The ring!"

The ring? I looked to my finger. The poison ring. She was going to bite me. I would be like her...or else I could turn.

I unclasped the ring, trying to kick at my sister's face with my free boot, trying to roll away from her, but it was no use. She was too determined. When her teeth tore into my shin, I screamed. She bit me.

"The ring! Use the fucking ring, Porschia!"

The clasp broke free and I tipped the thick blood into my mouth. It disintegrated, coppery on my tongue, and then it began to burn. My throat burned like someone was scorching it from within. "AAHHHHHHHH!"

My scream must have hit the gray clouds roiling above. Mercedes bit into my leg again, but it was too late. I could feel the change. I'd gotten to the vampire blood in time.

Hot.

Hot.

My blood.

Hot.

My skin.

Hot.

My eyes.

Hot.

My fingertips.

Hot. My feet. Hot. My ears. Hot. My... Fucking fire. I was on fire. I was on fire. I was dying. I was being eaten. By my sister. My sister. My sister was eating. Me. My leg. Fire.

A guttural scream tore through the air. Birds were scared from their perches, from their nests. I was frozen and dipped in hot water. Steam. Cold. Hot. Hot. Hot.

"NO!" Ford. My brother. My brother who was not eating me. My brother who was not Infected. Thief. Protector. Brother.

"Porschia!" Saul. Love. Fondness. I looked to him. He was so close. No. He was in the water. He was coming toward me, coming for me.

"NOOOOO!"

Hot. Fire. I was on fire. Mercedes. Sister. Infected. Bitch.

"You bitch!" I roared before I felt my teeth tear apart. Blood dripped down my face. Warm. Not hot. Why was blood cooler than I was?

Shaking fingers.

I felt my mouth.

Blood.

Sharp.

Fangs.

I had fangs.

I had fucking fangs.

"You'll pay for this, Mercedes," I told her in a low, growling voice. She backed away. My blood was on her face, on her chin, on her dress.

She bit me.

"My turn," I said, stalking toward her. Everything hurt. It was her fault.

In a split-second I was on her, my fangs in her neck. She bit me. She fucking bit me. Now, I was biting her. But the blood in her...

I tore my fangs from her neck, sat back, and vomited into the grass. Bile. Black bile.

Her eyes wide, she clasped her neck.

Thump-thump. Thump-thump. Thump-thump-thump-thump-thump-thump. Rapid. She was scared. I thought the Infected had no heartbeat.

Did I?

Yes. It echoed through me.

My stomach. Oh, no. I vomited into the grass again.

Mercedes pushed at the grass and mud as she scuttled away from me. Run, you bitch. "I will end you if you come near the Colony again, Mercedes!" She pushed to her feet and tried to run away.

"Do you hear me?"

Power. It surged through me.

No. Something stronger.

Hunger.

I'm so hungry.

My eyeballs. Fire. They're on fire. My stomach on fire. My thighs on fire. My bones. On fire.

Saul ran back across the river. "We'll get Roman!"

I smiled. *Ouch.* My smile faded. *My fangs hurt. My gums hurt.*

It's too late. He already knows, I think.

The lamb bleated from the riverbank, raising its head to the sky, screaming for its mother. I looked at my mother. She cowered, her hand covering her mouth.

"You." That's all I say. It's all I have to say.

It was her fault.

Now both of her daughters are monsters. Now one is dead and one can't die.

Now I am on fire and Mercedes is cold death.

Fire.

Hunger.

Bleating.

The lamb didn't know what hit him. I sank my teeth into his neck and drawled, then groaned. It was so good. So good. Mercedes was not good. Raven wings flapped overhead. They circled. I heard the wind sluicing off its wings. I heard the movement of its necks. I saw the down tucked under its feathers.

I drank.

I drank until the animal was dry, but it wasn't enough. The hunger didn't fade at all. I turned toward Saul, toward Mother and Ford.

Hungry.

Something had to stop it. Fire.

I was on fire.

Frenzy.

I was in frenzy.

Throwing the lamb to the side, I stood up and launched myself at them.

FRANTIC

ONE

TAGE

Porschia.

Porschia's in trouble. The urge to run burst over me like a wave against the shore. *She's in the forest. Why is she in the forest? She used the ring. Did the Infected attack her? Why would she leave the Colony? Did Roman know?* If I knew she was in trouble, he would too.

Roman was going to kill me, but if I didn't reach her before he did, he would claim Porschia first. The moment she changed, the instant my blood was absorbed into her, I felt her. It was a new awareness, something that reached all the way into the marrow and took root. She was out of control. My kitten wasn't tame now. Kitty had claws, and if I was right, she was about to claw my face off.

My feet pounded the pavement and loose strings flopped from the boots I hadn't laced, threatening to fall off with each step forward, but I was still faster than Roman. Being a newer vampire had its perks. Brick and white blurred as I raced through town, leaving a wake of wind that kicked dead leaves into the air. It was daylight and colonists were out and about. Their gasps meant they saw me, which meant trouble for our kind.

The Elders wouldn't be happy.

Wait until they find out about Porschia.

She is hurt. She hurts. I need to help her.

From ahead came the sound of rushing water from the river. I focused on it, trying to sharpen my senses further. She was close. Her scent floated to me on the slight breeze. I inhaled her deeply and pushed harder. She was *mine*.

ROMAN

Town Hall was my least favorite place. The Elders, three old men who had the nerve to think they could threaten to banish us from the Colony, coolly stared at me. Although they didn't believe my assurances that it hadn't been one of my coven who killed the colonists of late, I *knew* it wasn't. "The bite marks are spaced too far apart. Measure our fangs and you'll see. But that isn't the most compelling argument in our defense." I crossed my arms over my chest. "I explained the same thing to those in the rotation who were worried about their safety. If a vampire attacked a human being – if they drank from them with the intent to kill – the humans would have been drained almost entirely."

"You say it isn't a night-walker? Then explain the wounds on the victims' necks," said Elder Beckett, the alpha male in the room; the unequivocal leader, despite their proclamations of this being a council-style democracy. He was fast becoming a thorn in my side.

"I can't," I replied in frustration. "Perhaps someone or something is trying to make you believe it was us, but I'll say it again: It was not a night-walker who killed those people. My—"

I grunted, holding onto the edge of the pew beside me. A deep, wrenching feeling filled my abdomen and tugged me toward the river. It was either Mary or Porschia. One of them had consumed my blood. One of them had changed.

Clutching my stomach, I stood up clumsily. "We will make ourselves available and help in any way we can, but I am not feeling well. I need to go," I explained, fighting through the pain of the binding. I could feel her, but I wouldn't be able to claim her unless she fed from me first.

The sharp pangs were hard to breathe through, but even stronger was the pull to her. *Porschia*. She was near the river. I jumped down the steps and landed with a loud thud, drawing the eyes of every human milling around.

My senses were dulling. My reflexes, too. Something was very wrong with her.

Hot. Cold. Pain.

Tripping over tree roots, I ran toward the river. A cool sheen of sweat coated my body and I shivered. I hadn't shivered since I first changed, and that was thousands of years ago.

Since the first time I met her, I knew she was mine. She just didn't know it. Then the human, Saul, got in my way. Now nothing would keep us apart. She was one of us. And I didn't even have to turn her myself.

PORSCHIA

Saul was closest, standing between me, Ford, and Mother. Mother clawed at the mud of the steep river bank, trying to get away from me. *Coward.* White-hot rage flooded my tissues, burning my ears, my tongue, and my eyes. "Going somewhere, Mother?" I asked mockingly. She was the one who had been feeding Mercedes, seeking her out, and yet now she ran from *me*?

Saul took a sloshing step forward and closed the distance between us, angry water swirling around his thighs. He kept his eyes on me, but shouted back to Ford. "Help her up."

Ford's wide eyes took me in as he backed toward Mother and clasped his hands together for her to use as a makeshift step. She took his help and didn't even bother to turn around and pull her only son to safety. From deep in my chest, a growl escaped and my fangs scraped across my bottom teeth. Coppery blood filled my mouth. *Mmmmm.*

"Ford, go!" Saul screamed.

Ford's legs were long, so using the twisted tree roots as a foothold, he easily climbed up and away from me. My brother yelled over his shoulder, "Saul, come on! We have to get Roman!"

"What's Roman going to do, Saul?" I asked breathily. *Roman? Roman isn't going to do shit.*

My heart thumped wildly, echoing in my ears, louder with each beat, each whoosh. I covered them with my hands, trying to make the noise go away. The light. I kept my eyes on Saul, but the sunlight was blinding me. Everything was white-yellow and intense, like I'd stared at sunlit snow for too long. I squinted. It didn't help.

To myself, I muttered, "What *will* he do?" Would Roman attack me? I had to be ready for that. I had to be ready for anything. Would I be able to stay in Blackwater? Would I kill someone? Feed from them? Make them a husk? Dead and unwanted? Could I hurt someone I loved?

My stomach rolled, growling and angry. Hungry. I looked at Saul. "What have I done?" He was too light, like an avenging angel sent to rid the world of me. He stepped through the water and planted his feet until he was on the bank just a few feet from me. He smelled divine, but he always did. However, this was a different scent. I could smell his blood, his soul.

"You're hungry, Porschia."

I shook my head. It was so much more than that. He didn't understand. No one did. No one would. "Listen to me," he demanded. "You're going to be okay. You're not Infected. We'll figure this out."

I crouched down, balance coming so naturally to me now. My fingers were on fire. Now my cheek was, too. A bloody tear splashed onto the fabric covering my thigh, soaking in and burning the flesh of my leg.

"I promise we're going to fix this," he said. But the confidence he was trying to infuse his voice with wasn't working and his voice faltered. I wouldn't have heard it if I were still human, but with my heightened senses I could hear every distinction. I heard every intonation, whisper and nuance, every thread of hopelessness.

"There's no 'fixing' this, Saul. Don't you get it? And there's no *us* anymore, either."

"Yes there is," he said gently, stepping toward me.

"Stay back!" I warned. "There's no us. You have to let them get rid of me."

"I will *never*—"

I squeezed more hot tears from my eyes. "You *have* to, because all I can think about right now is draining you. It's taking all I have to keep from tearing you apart. It's what I need."

"Not what you want."

I bared my fangs and my fingers shook with primal need. I wanted his blood. I wanted to erase Dara's lips from his neck and replace the delicate swipes of her tongue with my own. My thighs quivered, not struggling to hold me up, but desperately trying not to propel me forward at him. I coiled into a ball, squeezing my ankles tight.

I tried to control myself, to stop the hunger and accept my fate. *Roman*. He needed to kill me. He would tear my head off or drain me and that would be the end of it.

No more Saul.

No more Ford.

No more Maggie.

No more Father.

No more Mother.

No more Mercedes.

No more Colony.

No more rotation, ring, feeding, pain.

No more hunger.

No more heat. No more fire. No more. No more. *No more...*

My legs could no longer obey. They needed blood. They launched me across the scant space that separated us and I sprang at Saul like a jungle cat, arms extended, fangs bared. The sound of the pulse at his neck was manna.

Saul jumped backward into the water and somehow managed to stay on his feet. Steel arms suddenly wrapped around my waist to stop my flight and I sniffed the air. *Tage*. His intrusion made my feet swing out and into the water. Frigid. Cold. The fire. It was there, but it wasn't in my legs. My teeth chattered. "Let me go."

"Do you really want to eat your boyfriend?" He paused. "On second thought, don't answer that. I know you do."

Saul had tried to run when I leapt at him, and he made it to the steep mud bank. Now he hovered over us, unable to make himself leave.

"Go!" I roared at him.

His lips pressed into thin lines and he stared, his gaze swinging between Tage and me and then back again. "Does Roman know?" Saul asked.

"He does. He's on the way," Tage replied with a shrug, pulling me to the opposite bank.

"Why are you stronger than me?" I gritted out.

"You haven't fed. You're weak."

I scoffed. "I drained the lamb."

"Not big enough to sate you though, right? But it did buy pretty-boy some time. You tried so long and so hard." His baby talk was followed by a ruffle of my hair, which enabled me to escape his hand. I whipped around and dragged my nails down his jaw.

"Ouch, dammit! What was *that* for?" He blotted his face.

"For...for stopping me!"

"You'll thank me later." Tage winked and then pulled me away from Saul and into the forest. "Let me guess – you had a run-in with an Infected."

"My sister."

"Ouch," he said, rubbing his chest.

"She bit me, and Saul yelled for me to use the ring."

Tage's feet stilled. "She bit you and *then* you used the ring? And it worked?"

I nipped at his face, baring my fangs, and a slow smile spread over his lips. "Your fangs are tiny." He reached out to touch them, but I smacked his hand away.

"Don't touch." I ran the pad of my thumb over the sharp points. "And they aren't tiny. They feel huge."

"Your gums are just sore. It'll ease when you feed, *if* you can get blood out of something with those itty bitty fangs."

"I ate the lamb."

"Psh. It was a baby. You need a real meal. Something big. I might have to bite it for you," he laughed, slapping his leg.

"If you don't help me find something soon, I might eat yo—"

From the valley, a bellow. A bear.

The wind kicked up.

Southeast.

I ran.

TWO

PORSCHIA

Tree trunks blurred. I pushed harder, despite the pain at the back of my eyes, despite my bleeding gums and bottom lip. Hunger propelled me. Like a banshee streaking through the woods, I barely registered my feet touching the forest floor. Maybe they didn't.

"Porschia, wait!" Tage yelled from behind me. He wasn't far behind. I could hear his arms pumping to keep up with me.

Its scent hit me from my left. I tried to glance in that direction, but the brightness of the sun through the bare trees burned and I squeezed my lids tight, moisture seeping out of them.

That way.

Run.

"Stop!" Tage screamed. I glanced back at him and then wham!

I hit a tree. Or a brick wall, I wasn't sure. Looking up woozily, I saw it was a pine. The bark had scraped the right side of my head and ear, tearing and burning my skin. I grasped the tree to keep from falling over until Tage caught up with me and grabbed my shoulders. "You okay?" He looked me over.

"No," I whimpered. I almost knocked myself unconscious! Could night-walkers do that?

Another bellow came from just yards away. "I *need* it. Help me?"

He nodded. "Yeah."

Tage moved like lightning. I followed him, keeping a hand pressed against my tender scalp. He reached the animal and wrapped his thick forearm around the black bear's throat, squeezing. As the animal struggled, he held tight. "Come on," he gritted out.

I ran toward him, unsure of what to do. The animal stilled and Tage eased it to the ground. With the lamb I had been overly confident, but a bear was intimidating. "Is it dead?"

Panting, Tage shook his head. "Unconscious. He won't wake up any time soon. Go ahead and feed."

"You make it sound so simple." I stared at the bear, focusing on the rhythmic rise and fall of its chest. I could hear its heartbeat now. A gust of wind scattered dry leaves across the ground. Tage held the bear's neck up and I crouched down, putting my arms around its neck.

I knew what to do.

My fangs pierced the layers of hair, hide, and meat. I pushed harder, pain shooting into my gums, but I couldn't reach its artery no matter how hard I tried. I pushed again. Coarse hair tickled the inside of my nostril, but still nothing.

I pulled away in frustration. "I can't. I can't reach it!"

Tage stared at me with his crystal blue eyes. "This might be a problem."

My stupid tiny fangs. I covered my eyes with my hands where the tears burned. My stomach growled loudly. "I'm going to die if I can't feed, aren't I?"

"There are lambs," he said with a small smile.

"Not enough to sate *this* feeling!" Frustrated, I stood and paced, clasping my stomach. *This* was torture. *This* was hell on earth. It truly was a curse to exist like *this.*

"I have an idea," he said, turning to the animal.

Tage bared his fangs and sank them in deep, drinking deeply. When he raised his head, he motioned for me to come back. "Try to drink now that I've opened the vein."

Again I sank my teeth in, and although I was able to get a few swallows of blood, I couldn't get anything substantial.

"Well, that didn't work," Tage said, sitting back on his haunches. "Let's try something different."

He filled himself on the blood of the bear, whose heartbeat slowed and then stopped altogether. My fingers shook with jealousy. I wanted to tear him apart. The bear was *mine*. I heard it, tracked it, and nearly knocked myself unconscious trying to get to it. And now *he* was taking it.

My upper lip curled in warning and Tage's eyes widened. He held up his forefinger, gulping like the greedy bastard he was.

My hands balled into fists. I was about to knock him away, to try to feed from the bear again; maybe a different vein. A shallower one would work if I could find it. Tage tore his fangs from the bear's neck and smiled, blood coating his teeth and lips. It dripped down his chin before he swiped it away.

"Easy, tiger," he teased, laughing and pushing himself up.

"I thought I was a kitten?"

"That was when you were human. You're definitely a tiger now." I raised an irritated eyebrow, to which he replied, "A tigress, pardon me."

I bared my fangs. I would show him what kind of a tiger – or tigress – I was. The only thing that stopped me were his next words. "Feed from *me* now."

"What?" I whispered.

"Feed from me. Humans have veins and arteries close to the skin's surface. You should be able to feed from me."

I stepped back from him. "You're not human. What if I drain you? You said night-walkers could die if they were drained by another one."

"I *was* human, and in theory you could, but you won't."

"How can you be so sure?" I wasn't confident that I could ever stop once I got started. The only reason I'd tossed the lamb away was because it was dry.

"I'll make sure of it. Just," he rolled his eyes, "come here." His fingers urged me to come to him. He knew what he was asking. He knew the risk, but he wanted to feed me. He wanted to stop the pain. The pain. The hunger. The pain. The fire in me.

I stepped toward him, snaking one hand into his hair and pulling his head to the side. "Make me stop," I breathed.

I felt him tense beneath the hand on his chest. "What if I don't want you to?" Who was this Tage—the one who insinuated that he wasn't only talking about feeding me?

I tensed, too. "You have to. I need your help. I can't survive this without you."

Tage had been through this change recently, which meant he would know how to help me. He could show me how to control the urges and sensations, since that was all this was. My emotions were running away with me.

His body was warm and hard against mine as I groaned and licked the flesh of his neck. "You don't have to numb me. I'm not human." His voice was scratchy, despite the fact that he just drank my dinner.

"Hmm." He tasted good. The pulsing of blood beneath the skin, my fangs piercing him, driving them deeper, slicing through layer after layer of him until at last, they punctured him. The blood in him flooded my mouth and tasted like divinity. *This* was heaven--exactly what I needed and had been missing. I groaned and gathered him to me. Drinking and drinking and...Tage began to slump.

"That's enough, Porschia," he whispered, trying to push me away.

I pulled him close, still gulping. My fingers were steel. I was so strong.

"Porschia, you're draining me."

From above us on the ridge came Roman's voice. "I should let her finish you off."

That made me do it. That made me ease my fangs out of Tage's throat and turn my attention to Roman. He stood tall as he looked down at us, like he thought he was some sort of king, some sort of god. But he was nothing. Anger blazed beneath my fingertips, searing me from the inside out. This was *his* fault. Tage tried to help me. He fed me. But Roman wanted to remove my head. I could see it in his dark, empty eyes.

He was a void and I would pour all of my anger into him.

Tage weakly crawled over to the bear's prone body and began to drink more blood. He hadn't drained it after all, although I wasn't sure if five night-walkers could. It was easily six-hundred pounds of animal, but it *was* dead, so what did I know?

Bouncing back and forth on the balls of my feet, I clenched and unclenched my fists before launching myself at Roman. Too preoccupied with shooting daggers at Tage, he never even saw me coming. Pinning him to the ground with one hand gripping his throat, he struggled and panted, trying to buck me off of him the way I did with Mercedes just a short while ago.

"Get off me!" he seethed.

"No!" I shouted. His head fit nicely between my hands. One quick twist...

Hands clamped around my waist from behind and pulled me off and away from Roman. I kicked and thrashed until I broke the hold and then saw Tage standing beside me, eyes and arms stretched wide. "She's strong!" he yelled to Roman.

"No kidding," Roman muttered, finding the strength to pull his own sorry ass up from the ground.

I started toward him again, when all of a sudden a strange sound caught my attention. Rustling, from the right. Then, a high-pitched keening.

Hands over my ears, I tried to shut it out, rocking back and forth. They were so close. They were coming. Mercedes wasn't finished with me. She was coming back and I would kill her. I wouldn't be able to stop myself if she started another fight, but I didn't want to kill my sister.

No.

No.

No.

"Hey," Tage whispered, gently wrapping an arm around my shoulders. "They aren't here. It came from several valleys away. They're making their way around toward the city."

I looked up and eased my palms from my ears, making sure the sound wasn't waiting for me. "It did?" The noise had sounded so close. I pressed fingers to my ears to make sure they weren't bleeding. "None of this makes any sense," I said, my voice breaking. "The noise, the light, the hunger, the sick feeling, the pain."

"What sick feeling?"

"I feel so sick right now." Cool beads of sweat formed on my brow, on my chest.

Tage looked from me to Roman, his brows bowed. "Why would she feel sick? That makes no sense."

Roman shook his head and answered, "I'm not sure. We need to get her home."

I muttered to myself, "Don't have a home."

Tage pursed his lips and looked back to Roman. "What if someone sees her?"

"Then we go downstream and cross somewhere else—beyond the cemetery. We can avoid the humans from that side."

Tage pushed up to his feet and hooked his arms beneath mine, lifting me. My legs quivered. Roman approached, pushing damp strands of hair from my forehead. "She's ill."

I was about to tell him *duh* when a wave of nausea crashed over me, pulling me under and refusing to let me up for air. I vomited all over him. The bear's blood burned a fiery path up my nose and throat, but I couldn't stop. Waves of crimson spewed from me, over and over, barely letting me catch a breath in between. Tage steadied me while Roman tried to clean himself off. Bastard.

When the puking stopped, I was weak—too weak to make it out of the forest. "I'll stay here," I told them, grabbing onto the rough bark of a pine to steady myself. The dark green that I'd always loved in winter, the only thing strong and stubborn enough to survive the frigid temperatures and heavy snow, loomed above me. My focus drifted in and out until it was more out than in. The canopy blurred.

THREE

PORSCHIA

STRONG ARMS HELD ME UP, BRUISING MY SKIN, BUT I COULDN'T MOVE. I couldn't talk. My head flopped around as though it was no longer filled with bone. Did Roman kill me? I felt like death. Maybe he did.

Then, from the buzzing in my ears, voices came through the static.

"Her fangs are too small for her to feed off of anything but humans and small animals," said Tage from right above me. I could feel his breath on my face, punctuating his words.

"That makes no sense," Roman replied.

"No shit, Sherlock," Tage rebutted. Was Roman's last name Sherlock?

"There's the crossing. Do you want me to take her?" Roman asked.

Tage scoffed. "I can handle it. She weighs nothing." Mother would disagree. *Mother.* Mother got me into this mess. My stomach growled, reminding me to try to eat her later. She deserved it. She fed Mercedes, so it was only fair that she feed me too, right?

The sound of rushing river water swirled around me. Tage's footsteps became labored, heavy, and he tried to hold me higher on his body. Water soaked into my dress. Cold, frigid water. I began to shiver. "Almost across, Porschia," Tage whispered, tension lacing his words. "This is the shallowest way through on this side of Blackwater, but it's not easy to cross. The water's strong."

"Easy," Roman warned from ahead. I heard the sound of mud sucking on Tage's boots; of water over rock, wearing it down speck by speck. Of Tage's rapid heartbeat. Of his panting. Of his muscles straining. I could hear it all, feel it all. Tage was frightened. Tage was worried. *Tage.*

I wanted to help, but I couldn't even open my eyes. Why couldn't I open them? Why couldn't I move?

Then suddenly, Tage repositioned his grip and his steps became lighter and faster. His tension eased. The sound of water wasn't as close. He began climbing up and then lifted me, where Roman's long, bony fingers wrapped around me. "I've got her."

"What did you do to her?" came a low voice of warning. Saul.

"You've *got* to be kidding me," muttered Tage. "You're like a lost dog. Go home, boy!"

"Is she dead?" Saul asked, undeterred.

"No, but she just turned. She's exhausted. It happens during Frenzy. Everything about her will be extreme now, especially her moods. She'll alternate between having loads of energy and strength and intense exhaustion," Roman explained. "She's completely worn out, and we have to get her home and contain her before the Elders find out that she turned."

Tage spoke up. "Or did you already tell them, golden boy?" *What was it with his nicknames for everyone?*

"No, but you can be sure that Mrs. Dillinger will notice, and her father will probably know by now. Her mother and brother already know."

Roman's feet shifted and Tage's hands lifted me once more as I was transferred between the two night-walkers. Footsteps. The tone of red—anger. "You keep your mouth shut," Roman hissed.

"Or what?" challenged Saul.

"Or I'll tear your mother's throat out. Your father's, too."

I could hear Saul swallow slowly, as if he were trying to hide the motion from Roman. Roman was intimidating, even to me when I wasn't manic. So internally, I swallowed too, but then something kicked in. It felt like the lock that had been holding my lips closed had become disengaged. I parted my lips and found my voice, albeit weak. "Touch Saul or his family and I will end you, Roman."

"You couldn't," he argued, staring down at me with emotionless eyes. I blinked in the bright sunshine, confused by the light. It should be nearly dark by now. Why was it still so bright?

"Try me," I grunted, trying to push myself up, trying to get Tage to set me down, to let me go. Saul walked over, completely un-phased by the two massive night-walkers flanking me.

"Why are you covered in blood?" Saul asked softly.

"I overfed. Lesson learned." The lie came so easily.

He scrubbed his hands over his handsome face. I was really going to miss that face. Something inside me broke all over again. It felt distinctly like my heart.

"Don't look at me like that, Porsch. I told you I'd fix this," he said, stepping toward me as Tage set my feet back on the dark soil.

"And I told you it couldn't be fixed. I'm sorry, Saul," I sniffed. "I don't want to see you again." It was the hardest truth I'd ever spoken—a lie to both of us, but what needed to be done to keep him safe, to keep him away from me.

"That's not true. You're just afraid, but we can work through this. I love you."

I shook my head in denial and swiped crimson tears from my cheeks. "I can't love you. I can't love anyone now." Turning to leave him, I stumbled, fell to my knees and began vomiting all over again.

When I regained control, I looked up to see Saul standing a few feet away. Tage was helping me back up while Roman stood between me and the human. My thighs and calves shook violently. He was protecting Saul from me because my stomach was almost empty and I needed to feed again. I was just too sick to do it. I was too weak.

But I want it.

Saul's mouth was parted and his fingers were intertwined, clasped onto the back of his head. "Tell me what I can do," he said.

Roman answered, "Keep this a secret for as long as you can. The Elders know what Frenzy is. They'll come for her."

"You'll have to stop them," Saul said.

Roman shook his head. "We have to maintain the treaty."

"Screw the treaty!" Saul roared. "She isn't *dying* – teach her how to control it!" He pointed at Tage. "You – you're new, aren't you? When you bit Porschia during the rotation, you didn't numb her. You didn't, because you didn't know you could. Teach her. Please."

Tage stiffened, but nodded.

Roman's eyes zeroed in on Tage suspiciously. "What's he talking about? How long ago did you turn?"

TAGE HELPED ME WALK AWAY FROM SAUL. WE FOLLOWED ROMAN TO A large Victorian home, one that fit in well with the others in the Colony, but was slightly bigger and better maintained. Dara was waiting for us on the porch.

"Where have you been? It's time for the evening rotation," she said. Glancing behind Roman to me and Tage, she gasped. "What's *she* doing here?" She sniffed the air.

"She turned," Roman answered matter-of-factly.

Dara's mouth gaped open, but she covered it with her delicate hands. I hated those hands. Those hands had touched Saul. *My* Saul. Mustering the energy I had left, I ran up the steps at her and knocked her down. She stared up at me with her mouth agape; half-angry, half-shocked. "Don't ever touch Saul again."

Roman and Tage were immediately behind me, pulling me away from her, but Dara's eyes were wide. "You have to lock her up. She's a loose cannon. The Elders are going to freak out."

"We know," Roman gritted out between his teeth, his hands bruising my arm. "Get the cell ready," he ordered.

Dara opened the door and the three of them wrestled me down a wide set of steps into a dank, musty-smelling basement. Scents of mildew and the scurrying of mice had my head spinning; spiders, their legs tapping surfaces and working silk. Roaches skittered. It was dark. My eyes focused on it all, especially the floor-to-ceiling bars arranged in a large rectangle across the room. Inside the cell? A rusted cot with a bumpy mattress, stained with blood. That was it. Floor. Ceiling. Bars. Cot. Mattress. Stains.

I fought them with all my might, pulling my arm from Tage, pushing Roman away, kicking, clawing, and biting at Dara. But in the end, they were stronger than I was in my weakened state. I was sick. The bars slammed behind me with a loud clang and I covered my ears as they secured the locks. So many locks.

Then they left.

"Tage?"

"Rotation," was all he said. They had to eat. They had to feed. I wanted to feed.

"I'm hungry! I need to feed, too," I screamed. "Let me out!"

Roman pulled the basement door shut. "We can't do that right now, Porschia."

"When, then? When can I feed?"

No one answered.

"I'm hungry! Please! Let me go with you."

"Please," I repeated in a choked whisper.

Please. Please. Please.

Hungry.

The pain.

Please.

Don't leave me down here alone.

FOUR

TAGE

Saul was the only one waiting at the pavilion, leaning up against the fountain like he'd been waiting there for hours and we were wasting his time. "Where are the others?" Roman growled.

With a shrug, Saul answered, "Guess they made a choice." He stood up straight, pushing away from the fountain.

"The treaty says—"

"The treaty is void. *You* voided it."

Roman was in front of him in a flash. "We didn't turn her. She used the ring."

"What about the recent deaths? The victims all had fang marks on their necks," Saul goaded. What an idiot.

"Not. A. Vampire," Roman growled in exasperation.

"So you say, but it looks like no one believes you. Anyway, I'm here. Do you want to feed or not?"

"Why are you doing this?" I asked. "What's in it for you?"

"To keep her safe for as long as I can. If you all tear through the Colony to find someone to feed on, the colonists you feed on will tell the Elders. The Elders will call a meeting, and if Porschia's not there, they'll want to know why." He obviously loved her, and it was no wonder. She was exceptional: strong, beautiful, and sarcastically funny, and now that she'd turned and I had claimed her, the sexiest thing I'd seen since I left Florida and stumbled into the freaky time-warped Blackwater Colony.

Roman's dark eyes bored into me, promising that we were going to have a legit man-to-man about me running interference.

I ignored him, turning to Saul instead. "You can't marry her now. You can't be with her. You can't even be her friend. If she approaches, you need to run in the other direction as fast as your legs will carry you. Because even if she seems like your Porschia, she's not. She's a huntress. She wants nothing more than to drink from you, and if she feeds, she will not be able to stop herself. Not right now, and maybe never."

Saul stiffened and tipped his chin up. "I know. So…let's get this over with."

There was a saying that 'curiosity killed the cat', but stubbornness might kill Saul. He was going to try to rescue her, and the only possible conclusion was that Porschia would drain him, after which she would fly into a rage that none of us would be able to contain. There weren't bars powerful enough to hold that sort of heartache; that despair. It was why Roman was such a cold-hearted bastard. And if Porschia killed Saul, or anyone else she loved, she would lose herself. She might slaughter the whole Colony.

Roman might try to kill her before she managed it, which meant I would have to try to kill Roman. And Dara. And anyone else who tried to hurt Porschia. I didn't want her to die. There was something in her green-gray eyes that understood what it was to be human, and that still saw humanity in me. It was something I could no longer see in myself when I glanced in the mirror. I would help her through this, right after we figured out how to make her well.

Roman fed from Saul first and then Dara took her turn, but they were careful not to take too much. When it was my turn, I declined. I already fed from the bear and was good for now. I might still be good in the morning, but wouldn't push it. My control was a tight string that could easily be snapped. One vamp in Frenzy was frightening as hell, but something that could be dealt with, given the proper guidance. Two? Two would be a blood bath. And nothing under the heavens could stop a pair.

Not only would they feed on everything living they could capture, they would feed off of one another's heightened emotions. They would bask in the glory of their kills, high on competition and blood, drowning out the sorrows that always followed behind; a constant roller coaster of ups, downs, twists and turns. Happiness. Sadness. Contentment. Despair. Longing. Anger. Frustration. Hopelessness. Giddiness. Desolation. Confusion. Fear. Annoyance. *Feed.*

Before I left, I turned to Saul and said, "Don't do it."

"What?"

"Try to be the hero. There are no heroes in this story. She's cursed now."

I could hear his teeth grinding against one another. Upper versus lower.

"I'll be here in the morning," Saul replied dryly, ignoring my warning completely.

"I'll get food for you and your family," I vowed.

He nodded and so did I. Walking quickly through the darkness, the three of us returned to Roman's house. There was room for all of us to live there, now that the other vamps were gone – wherever they'd gone. I had my own place, but someone needed to stay and keep an eye on Roman. No matter what, I was going to stay close to Porschia. And 'close' tonight meant standing guard in the basement, watching her sleep. Her chest rose and fell so softly, one might think she wasn't breathing at all. But I could hear it. Every puff, every sigh.

I WAS THERE WHEN SHE WOKE UP, ROLLING IN DISCOMFORT ON THE MOLD-spotted mattress, clutching her stomach. I was there when she begged me for something to sate her thirst, and I offered my neck to her. I was also there when she began rejecting the blood, spewing red fountains onto the dirty mattress, across the white peeling paint curling down the wall.

Roman still hadn't said anything about me claiming her. My blood was already inside her from the ring, and now the fact that she'd bitten into me made her mine and me hers. However, she didn't know that tiny fact.

So I stayed with her. Watched her. Because we were so tightly linked, I was able to feel her every emotion. Seeing them, seeing her pain, was hard. This went on for another day. She would wake, so hungry she couldn't sit still, in pain from it. She would feed, vomit, and then she would sleep. The cycle was even worrying Roman.

"We need to try something different," I announced, easing the legs of my metal chair onto the cracked concrete floor with a bang.

"What?" she rasped from her new mattress, clutching the blanket that covered her body. I could hear her trembling shaking the fabric.

"I'll be back."

She didn't make a noise in response. I jogged up the basement steps, meeting the others on the landing. It was evening rotation time and they were ready to eat. So was Porschia. Saul could help me with that.

Roman, Dara, and I each took turns feeding from Saul at the pavilion. He never complained, he just asked for an update on Porschia. "Actually, I think you should come and see her, Saul."

Roman stared at me, head tilted in question.

"You're the only one who knows about her situation, besides her mother and brother. They haven't said anything to anyone that you know of, right?"

"Right."

"Seems odd, but whatever. Well, she's having trouble feeding from us, and we thought that maybe if she gets it straight from the source, she'll be able to hold it down."

Roman's jaw worked back and forth. If Saul wouldn't come, I'd drag him by force. At this point, someone had to do something or she was going to die.

There was no need for doubt, because Saul answered immediately. "I'm in."

The four of us walked toward Roman's house in the dark. The days were getting much shorter now, and darkness came faster and faster each evening. Flurries of snow hit us in the face. "Thought you said she'd kill me," Saul said, nudging my arm. His hands were tucked into the pockets of his coat.

"She'll want to, but we'll be there. Plus, she's . . . contained."

"Contained?"

Roman butted in. "She's locked up. It's the only way to keep her and the Colony safe."

Saul stopped abruptly. "You're serious?" His eyes searched ours, person by person. "Jesus, is that necessary?"

Roman laughed. "Let her feed from you, and then you can answer your own question."

Saul stared at Roman's house from the yard. "This is nice, man." With a pinched look, Roman thanked him. "She's in there?"

"In the basement, yes. Are you ready for this? She's not the same."

"I know. And, yes, I'm ready." I almost believed him.

FIVE

PORSCHIA

The door upstairs opened. Voices: Dara, Roman, Saul, Tage. *Saul?* I leapt to my feet and rushed to the bars, grasping the metal despite the peeling white-gray paint. "Saul?"

"She knows I'm here?" he asked. The familiar, deep timbre of his voice sent waves of goosebumps over my flesh. My mouth began to water.

"She can smell and hear you," Tage explained.

Footsteps on the stairs. *Saul.* Saul was coming. *My Saul.*

As he approached, his scent wrapped around me like a comforting blanket. With each step it became stronger, and yet weakened me by the same measure. I gripped the metal bars that separated us, sending paint flecks sprinkling to the ground, soft as ash. My hands wrung the barrier between us, strangling and suffocating it.

Tage came into the room first. His eyes were alert, his muscles taut. He was ready for a fight. Then Saul stepped onto the half-painted concrete slab of a floor. Dara and Roman appeared behind him, flanking Saul.

"Saul?" *Why is he here?* "Why are you here?"

My stomach growled. It pinched and hurt. I gasped the bars tighter. *His heartbeat.* His scent: hard work, wood, pine soap, *Saul.* The swoosh-swoosh of the blood in his veins. The sound of his Adam's apple bobbing.

The unsure looks he shot Tage and Roman. The sweat forming on his brow despite the cold.

"Tage said you can't eat from animals or from them, and I came to see if I could help."

My heart was bursting I was so happy to see him. I needed...needed to touch him. "Come closer," I said, smiling so widely I felt that my face was splitting in two. "I've had some trouble, but I'm okay now that you're here. It's been so long since I saw you."

"I saw you yesterday."

"Has it only been a day?" It seemed so long ago. Letting go of the bars, I waved him toward me. "Come here. Please?"

He smiled lightly and stepped forward. *The swishing sound of the wool pants he wore. The crack of his knuckles against his thigh.* He removed his fists from his pockets and slowly eased toward me. The vampires circled him, Tage staying between us.

"Move, Tage," I said in a low whisper.

"I'm good, tiger," he said with a smirk.

"Move," I commanded, louder.

"Nah, I think it's probably in Saul's best interest if I—"

"Fucking *move*!" I roared, climbing the bars to the ceiling, trying to find a weak spot. I wanted out!

I jerked hard, plaster falling down like a white rock slide, tumbling, falling, and raining down.

"She's tearing the cell apart!" Dara screamed.

Pulling harder, I could hear the metal weakening and bending. I wanted out. I wanted Saul. I wanted to touch him. I wanted to feed from him. Would his blood taste sweet? Could I hold it down? He was a part of me. Surely, this would work. Surely this awful feeling, this hunger would end. He would end it.

At the sound of metal meeting metal, I stopped and dropped to the ground in a crouch. Tage stood outside the door to my cell, keys in his hand. "What are you doing?"

Tage rolled his eyes. "Well, since you're hell bent on getting at Saul, and I'm pretty sure you're about to rip the bars out of the wall—the ones *cemented* into place—I figured that opening the door might be the best option." He jiggled the key in the final lock.

When it gave way, the door swung open and Tage motioned for me to come out, but put his hands up to calm me. It didn't work. I bared my fangs at him, stepping toward the door and easing out, the flesh of my back scraping against the outside of the bars I'd been trying to break. My shoulder blades struck each bar as I slinked across the cell.

Saul's eyes were wide and I could hear him trembling. I smelled his fear; sour and acrid as smoke. "Porsch? What are you wearing?" he asked.

It was my slip. I'd been cold, hiding under a cover, but then I was scorching hot and took the dress off again. Crisp blood stains marred the white fabric.

"I was hot," I replied sheepishly.

He nodded, palms out as I circled him, easing away from the bars. "I get that."

"You don't. You don't understand."

No one understands. No one knows. Hot. So hot. Fire. Flame. Burning. Flesh burning from the inside out. Charred. Singed. *It hurt so much.*

He shook his head. "I don't know how you feel, but if you feel hot, I can see why you're only in your slip. Though I'd prefer you in more clothing while we're in the presence of mixed company," he muttered. "Especially when you decide to start climbing the walls."

I snorted. Climbing the bars was easy.

My eyes darted over to the night-walkers. Now *I* was a night-walker. My pulse beat rapidly. "I'm one of them," I whispered in disbelief. A sob bubbled up from my throat.

"It's okay," Saul said.

"It isn't."

"No, but it will be."

A hunger pang suddenly rolled through my core, and I sprang forward and sank my teeth into his throat, drinking and holding him tight to me. His warmth, his blood...I took him in. I had part of his heart. *Mmmmm.* I moaned. Now I was consuming part of his soul. I felt this when Roman fed from me, but not as a night-walker. It was addictive... until Saul's scream sliced into my eardrums. I pulled away and covered my ears, shielding them from the sound.

Rocking on the floor, I screamed. "What? Why?"

Tage helped me up while Roman quickly licked Saul's wound. "You didn't numb him first," Tage replied.

My lip quivered. Saul's blood slicked the delicate flesh and I could still taste him on my tongue. More. I needed more, so much more. I clamped a hand over my mouth. "I'm so sorry," I said, shaking my head rapidly.

But the urge wouldn't leave. The hunger continued to gnaw at the bottom of my stomach. Saul could help me. He *came* here to help me, right? "Can I have more?" I was weak; too weak to ask that of him. I knew how much it hurt to be fed from without being numbed first, but hunger was selfish and so was I. These were desperate times.

Saul's eyes locked onto mine. Gray-blue, wide, roiling. He spoke first. "I'm fine. I just want to help you." Easing forward with as much restraint as I could muster, I wrapped my arms around him and sank my fangs in as deep as I could. Feeding from Saul was ecstasy. I loved him, he loved me, and this felt right. Deeply gulping, drawing him into me, I barely had time to get a sip...

"Let go," Tage gritted, tearing me away from Saul. I loved Saul! Why were they taking him away?

Roman shoved his body between mine and Saul's, and Dara helped Tage pull me backward. Once we were separated, she licked Saul's neck to seal the wounds. "I told you not to touch him," I growled; my voice, not my own. It was low, predatory, and deadly.

Her eyes flicked from mine to Roman's and then back again. Tage helped Saul to the side of the room, where his back hit the cinder block wall and he slid down to sit on the cold floor. He held his head in his hands.

"What's wrong with Saul?" I screamed.

Tage grabbed my shoulders. "You took a little too much, tiger. Now, I think you need to go back inside until we get him out of here."

"No! I want to talk to him."

"Hey," Tage said abruptly, snapping a finger in front of my face to get my attention. "You'll kill him. If you feed from him again, he'll die. You took too much. Are you *hearing* me right now?"

Roman helped Saul move across the room and toward the door.

"Yeah." I backed away, slinking back into my cage. "I'm sorry. I'm...so sorry, Saul. I'm sorry."

He nodded. "It's okay, Porsch," he replied weakly.

"Saul?" I asked tentatively. Tage locked the cell door with the key and slid it back into his pocket. Roman and Dara helped Saul stand, and as his eyes met mine, I said, "Thank you."

Saul nodded, adding, "Of course," and started walking toward the basement door.

"Don't come back."

Saul's feet stopped and he turned to look at me, his hand clasping his neck and his brows furrowed in confusion. "Why?"

"I don't want to hurt you. Please don't come back until Tage tells you it's okay. Please. I...I couldn't live with myself if I hurt you, and I will. I'll hurt you and not even mean to." My voice splintered. He started toward me, ignoring the fact that I nearly drained him just moments before. "No! You have to stay away from me."

I sat on the floor, on a spot that wasn't covered in blood, and rocked my body. I held my head and rocked back and forth. Back and forth. Saul's sacrifice churned in my stomach.

Roman and Dara urged him out the basement door and I listened to his footsteps tap up the steps, out the front door of Roman's home and toward the human side of the Colony. His footsteps had a different tone. They were usually so strong and sure, but now they were weak. I weakened him.

Looking at Tage, I sniffed and wiped my eyes. Blood was smeared all over me. "Can I have a wet cloth and some clothes?"

For once, he had no smart remark. "Sure. Be right back."

SIX

PORSCHIA

Last night, I washed and changed into a pair of Dara's jeans and a long-sleeved shirt, but I was still freezing. Shivers shook my body until I curled onto the mattress, covered myself with a thin blanket, and fell asleep. An hour later, the vomiting started.

Tage helped me while Roman stared at us from outside the bars and Dara was simply pissed off. "So let me get this straight," Dara fumed. "She took all of this from Saul, we get nothing to eat for two days, and now it's being vomited all over the basement? This is just great!" She threw her hands up in frustration. Tage rubbed my back as I vomited into a bucket.

"Why can't you feed?" I asked, wiping my mouth on my forearm.

"Because no one but Saul showed up for the rotation," Tage answered softly.

Roman growled, placing the heels of his hands against his eyes. "I'll talk with the Elders. Someone needs to help us, or else we'll have to feed on our own. Period."

"Diplomacy is dead here. We should just feed. Maybe they would understand how good they had it with the treaty," Dara suggested. Her silky blonde hair was braided around her head like a crown and not a strand was out of place.

Rapid knocking came from the front door. My stomach was cramping. "You okay?" Tage whispered.

"No," I answered. He handed me a wet rag and I wiped around my mouth. "Thanks."

Dara ran to get the door. "Roman!" she yelled.

"My hearing isn't so great right now. I can't tell who it is," I said to Tage. "I'm dying, aren't I?" When I first turned, I was able to hear everything so acutely!

He scowled. "No, you'll be fine. We have to figure this out is all."

"I'm a vampire who can't drink from animals, other vampires, or even humans without puking the blood back up. I'll die."

He shook his head. "We won't let you."

"I hope I die fast. I should just have Roman twist my head off. I can't do this for years and years, let alone an eternity."

Tage shook his head. "Without blood you won't last that long, so we have to figure it out fast. And we will."

I smiled. "My hearing sucks, but I hear the tone of doubt in your voice."

Tage looked toward the basement door, where three sets of feet were coming back down the stairs.

"Porschia?" Ford asked tentatively when he looked into the cell.

"No! I don't want him to see me like this," I whispered, trying desperately not to cry. Bloody tears would surely freak him out.

Tage slid the blood-filled bucket beneath the cot, keeping it accessible, but not drawing attention to it. Around my shoulders, he wrapped the knitted blanket he'd brought me earlier.

"Hey, Ford."

My brother's eyes took in all of the blood. The walls, the mattress, the floor and the blood. Then he looked at me. I expected him to say how I deserved to be in there, but he didn't.

"You don't look any different. Maybe a little pale." He took in my clothes; modern, or as modern as they were the day the infection killed their original owner.

Ford didn't look like a teenager pretending to fill adult shoes. He looked like my baby brother. "I'm fine. How's Mother?"

With everything going on, I'd almost forgotten about her. He wasn't safe with her in the house. Mother had obviously lost the final piece of her mind when Mercedes fell.

Ford cleared his throat. "Father has her locked away right now. He's been giving her herbs to help keep her calm."

"Is it working?"

"Sometimes it seems like it. Other times it doesn't."

"Ford, go stay with Mrs. Dillinger. Maggie will give you a safe place to stay. You can have my room."

He shifted on his feet, shoving his fists into his pockets. "I check on her for you, you know. Make sure she has split wood by the back steps and plenty inside, too. I go get her water. She's a good cook."

I smiled. "She is."

"She wants to know where you are, but I don't know what to tell her. Father, and of course Mother know what happened, but no one else in the Colony knows yet. But Mrs. Dillinger is getting worried."

"Tell her I'm sick." It wouldn't be a lie.

"She knows you aren't home."

"Tell her I'm at Saul's. Send him over to her if he'll go."

Ford nodded. "You know he will."

"I don't know if he'll want to do anything for me now. I almost killed him last night." Admitting that out loud was one of the hardest things I had ever done.

"Why?"

"He came to see me and I attacked him."

Tage interrupted. "Not true. He offered to let her feed from him and she just took a little too much." He pinched his fingers together to show just how much I took over the amount I should have. "There was no *attack*," he emphasized, using air quotations. But who knew how much was too much? Tage continued talking to my brother as if I wasn't beside him. "Porschia has tiny fangs. It's hard for her to feed on anything but humans, and right now she can't go outside. She has to learn to control her urges first."

"Frenzy, right?"

"Exactly." Tage smiled. "So Saul came here to help, and Porschia, being a brand new night-walker, took a little too much. That's all."

Ford tore his eyes from Tage and looked around the room. His eyes took in the cell, the cold, bare floor, the cot with its new and old stains, and the bucket beneath it. "Is that why you're in the cage, Porsch?"

"Yeah. When I get hungry, I can't control myself."

Tage interrupted again. "But we're working on that."

Dara rolled her eyes and then marched upstairs. Roman turned to

Ford and brusquely said, "You've seen that she's fine. Now talk to Saul and see if he'll help with Mrs. Dillinger."

"Sure. Uh, I'll be back soon, Porschia."

"Bye, Ford."

As Roman saw Ford out, Tage eased out of the cell and locked the door behind him.

"How did *you* do it?" I asked, curious.

Tage blew out a long breath and rested his forehead between two bars. "Honestly?" He looked at me with a very serious expression on his face.

"Please."

"It wasn't easy, but I had this friend. He helped show me how to curb the cravings before going around people. At first it was almost impossible to control myself, even if I was full. The sights, the light, sounds, and smells – everything was too much. It was overwhelming and I wanted to kill everything and run away, all at the same time."

He pursed his lips. "But each time got a little easier. My eyes adjusted to the light. My ears to the sound, my nose to the smells. And then I could finally walk around without wanting to tear everything apart and eat it."

I let out a quick laugh. "That's how I feel. Everything is just too much, and my emotions are all over the place, too."

"I wasn't very emotional before I turned, so while mine were heightened somewhat, it was nothing like..." he added, motioning to the ceiling above me. I'd almost brought the house down. Literally.

"Can you help me with the rest of it?"

Tage's icy blues burned into me. He pressed his lips into a thin line and pushed off the bars. "If we can figure out how to feed you properly, it'll help. And when we go out, we'll go at night. Less temptation that way."

I nodded. "Thank you."

"Don't thank me yet. I have no idea how to help you feed."

SEVEN

FORD

I STEPPED IN THE FRONT DOOR, SHRUGGING MY COAT OFF. SNOWFLAKES sprinkled onto the hardwood, melting on contact. Father was stoking the fire and the whole house was warm. My cheeks stung from the temperature difference. He turned to me, asking, "Is she okay?"

"As okay as she can be, I think," I said, lying through my teeth. Tage had tried to tuck her chuck bucket under the cot, but I saw the blood and smelled the bile. She was sick, but then again, so was Mother. Only she was a different kind of sick than Porschia and Mercedes. Father had no idea how to fix Mother. The herbs were only taking the manic edge off, but she was still restless. Boom. Boom. Boom. Boom.

From overhead I heard her pace the floor, turn, and pace back. Four steps. Turn. Four steps. Turn.

Father swallowed, letting go of the handle of the poker he'd been using. The glowing end brightened in the fire. "She has turned, then?"

"Sort of."

"What does that mean?" He stood up and crossed the room.

"They said her fangs are shorter than normal and she's having trouble feeding from large animals."

"What's she eating?"

"They're still trying to figure that out, but for now she's staying in the house. Porschia wants to keep away from everyone until she is confident she can control her urge to feed."

"She was always concerned with the welfare of others."

I shoved my fists in my pockets, clenching them tightly. "She isn't dead. Don't talk about her in the past tense."

Father braced himself against the door frame. "No, she's far worse off than that. I'm not sure who's better off – her for living eternally, or Mercedes for dying, albeit slowly."

"Jesus, Father. They're still alive, just different."

"They're damned. Both of them." He left out the part about he and I being Hell's newest residents, and the fact that he looked like he'd aged twenty years in the last two days was a testament to that. Father looked up to where the repetitive noise was still making its way back and forth across the ceiling above us. "And now, so is she."

That, I agreed with. Mother had lost her mind. It began even before Mercedes fell, but when Mercedes never came home, a piece of my Mother's mind went with her. And now Porschia had changed. To Mother, she was as gone as Mercedes was. But why had she been feeding, or even communicating, with Mercedes?

I climbed the steps, my legs heavy from seeing my sister in such a state. Sleep sounded like the best option.

I heard Father trying to calm Mother down from behind their closed and locked bedroom door. "She's one of them!" Mother ranted. "Porschia. She killed Mercedes, and now she's one of the blood sucking night-walkers. She'll eat us all!"

Mother chanted the words, "eat us all," over and over and over again.

I leaned my head and shoulders against the wall and stared up at the textured, swirled ceiling plaster, wishing that someone could help Mother; wishing someone could keep her quiet. Father wasn't able to, and sooner or later someone was bound to hear her. We had neighbors just a yard away and across the street, but for once I felt lucky that we weren't close with anyone in town. Father always said there was too much work to do to have friends of any kind, and that we needed to keep our noses in our own business. I just hoped the neighbors felt the same way.

I tossed and turned all night. Mother didn't calm down until it was almost dawn, and then only because she'd worn herself out. From her room came the sounds of sobbing and screams, glass breaking against the wall and more screaming. She begged to leave her room, crying and pleading. Again and again, Father would try to talk to her like she would finally be able to understand his words. The man was part saint, or at the very least, as patient as one. I would have locked her up and walked away.

Dressing quickly, I pulled on my boots, tugged on my coat, and set off toward Saul's. It was dark and so cold I could see my breath, but I needed to talk to him. Porschia's precarious safety hinged on his ability to tell an old lady a lie.

Some people had tells. For Mercedes, it was a crinkling of her nose. Porschia worried her hands. Father stuttered. Mother didn't lie. She was unflinchingly honest, but sometimes that was a bad thing. Sometimes people needed to hear that they looked good, that their garden looked healthy or that everyone was fine. However, Mother wouldn't give anyone an inkling of kindness. She enjoyed making people miserable and used honesty as her weapon. Because sometimes, honesty was brutal.

Saul's house was several streets over, beyond Town Hall and close to the river. I saw movement in the window to the left of the front door and tapped lightly on it. Saul's mom answered the door.

"Sorry to bother you so early, ma'am, but I need to speak with Saul if he's awake."

His mother was pretty, with crinkles fanning out from her eyes like she laughed a lot. "I'll get him. Do you want to come in from the cold?" She was already dressed for the day, but sleep still made her voice deeper than normal.

"Nah. I'll wait here, but thanks."

"He'll be right down." She eased the door closed but left a crack, the warmth from inside escaping out just enough to warm me. She was kind. She didn't scream or insult. She didn't scowl or criticize. Saul appeared a moment later, just as she'd promised.

His hair was matted on one side, but he was dressed. He pulled on his coat and stepped outside, folding his hands and blowing into them. "It's freezing."

"Well below it."

"Is she okay?"

"We both know she's not." I looked toward the pavilion, where this god-awful mess got started, first with Mercedes and then with Porschia. "She needs a favor."

"Name it."

"I've been helping Mrs. Dillinger, but she is starting to ask questions. Porschia hasn't been there to do some of the things, but even when she was, I used to help bring water and wood. She knows Porschia and Mother were on the outs, so she knows Porschia isn't staying back at home. Now she's getting suspicious, asking questions."

"You want me to tell her?"

"Not about that. Just tell her she's sick and that your mother is taking care of her."

Saul blew out a visible cloud of breath that disappeared into the night. "She might not believe me. Mom visits her sometimes. Not often, but what if she did and then Mrs. Dillinger questioned her?"

I swallowed. "I don't know. I mean, the Elders will eventually find out, but if she can get control of herself by the time they do, maybe they won't freak out."

"There's no guarantee of that. Tensions are already high between them and the night-walkers, but it's the best plan. I'll talk to her." He paused a moment and rocked back on his heels. "I need to talk to my parents first. It's a risk, but if I ask them not to tell anyone, they won't. *And* they'll back up my stories."

"If you're sure," I replied uncertainly. I sure as hell wasn't sure. What if they ran straight to the Elders?

"You want to come in so you can see their reaction for yourself?" he asked.

"Yeah." If they were going to be able to keep the lie, I'd be able to tell it. I could at least warn Roman.

Saul crossed the porch and opened the door. "Mom?" He waved me inside right as she reappeared from the kitchen area. "Is Dad up?"

"Yeah. Everything okay?" Her eyes bounced nervously from her son to me.

"No. I need to tell you both something, and I need you to promise that it'll stay in this house."

EIGHT

SAUL

DAD CAME DOWN THE STEPS AT THE SOUND OF MOM'S VOICE. "WHAT'S wrong?"

"Saul needs to speak with us."

I have never asked to sit down and talk with them, and I've never asked them to keep a secret. But for Porschia, I'd do both.

Ford and I sat at the kitchen table and Mom and Dad settled across from us. I steadied myself by rubbing my calloused fingers along the edge of the table. Worn smooth by both time and oiled hands, it grounded me. Ford looked young, too young to hold such a burden. I wasn't referring to Porschia, although she was definitely part of the equation. I was talking about his mother. She had completely lost it at the river, and I felt sure she wouldn't regain her wits any time soon.

He lost Mercedes, probably felt like Porschia was gone, and now his mother had mentally checked out. Poor kid.

Dad looked at me expectantly and I cleared my throat. "This can't leave our house," I stated.

"Agreed," Dad said. Mother nodded her assent, and that was all the encouragement I needed.

"Porschia has turned into a night-walker."

Mom's gasp filled the room before she clasped her hand over her mouth. Tears filled her eyes and spilled over as I gagged on the tears clogging my own; looking away at the walls, the windows, anything. If I looked at her or Ford, I knew I would lose it.

"Did the night-walkers turn her, son?" Dad asked after a moment.

"No. She was across the river, and—"

"Without the protection of a vampire?" Mom asked, wiping her cheeks. "What was she *thinking?*"

Ford spoke up. "She was trying to save me and our mother." He paused. "Mother changed after Mercedes fell. She'd always been hateful and angry at the world, but something in her snapped when Mercedes became an Infected. She took it out on Porschia more than anyone, and I know I shouldn't have let it happen. I found out that Mother had been sneaking to the barn and taking animals. She would slaughter them, wade across the river, and throw them over to Mercedes. I assume she'd been doing it since my sister fell, but I don't know for sure. I caught her sneaking out of our house in the middle of the night and tried to follow her. One time, I lost her. But the next time, I was able to figure out what she was doing."

"She became bolder, and even started feeding Mercedes during the daylight. I was trying to stop her on the afternoon Porschia found us. I'd been digging graves and was thirsty, so I went to the river. She had been muttering all morning about feeding her eldest, so I knew she'd be there at some point, but until then, she'd only approached Mercedes at night. I heard Mother singing and saw two lambs tied up on the branch of an old fallen stump. That's when I noticed she had a butcher knife.

"Mercedes came, but I don't know if Porschia saw her at first. Porsch was entirely focused on Mother, who was covered in lamb's blood at that point. She made sure I was okay, and then tried to stop Mother from going across the river. She'd never tried to cross the water before, but the river was lower than normal and Mother was strong. She made it across. When I waded in after her, Porschia came after me. Mercedes and Porschia had always gotten along, but for some reason, Mercedes attacked Porschia."

I cut in to add my side of the story. "I followed Porschia to the river. She yelled at me to help her mother, so I dragged Mrs. Grant back across the water and went back for Ford. Mercedes and Porschia were fighting by that point, and I saw Mercedes bite Porschia on the leg. I knew I couldn't get to her, so I yelled at her to use her ring. My only thought was that I didn't want her to become infected. Luckily, she was able to get the blood from the ring into her mouth in time. She turned."

Father steepled his fingers while my mother swiped tears away. "You could have been infected, Saul," she cried.

I shook my head. "Porschia told me to get Ford. She kept me safe." And that killed me. I should have protected her first. Their mother didn't deserve to be saved first. She had created the whole damn mess in the first place.

Father took in a deep breath. "We won't tell the Elders, but you know they're going to find out, Saul. I know how you feel about her, but when they learn that she's changed, they'll order the night-walkers to kill her. Have you seen her? Is she in Frenzy?"

Ford and I nodded affirmatively. The left side of my neck still throbbed with the memory of her feeding from me. Part of her was damn near feral at this point. And the other part? It was like she hadn't changed at all. Porschia, my Porschia was still in there.

"There is a night-walker in the Colony who is relatively new, who just came out of Frenzy. He's promised to help her learn to control herself."

Father's kind gray eyes bored into mine. "I hope he can, son. I hope he can."

"I have to tell Mrs. Dillinger something, and I was hoping I could tell her that Porschia is ill and staying with us for the time being. It might buy her some time."

"Of course you can," Mom said. "We will stand behind you one hundred percent, Saul. But if she puts you in danger, I will kill her myself."

"Mom!"

"You are my son. Now, I know you love her – though it happened faster than I would have liked, I know it's true. I know you'll try to help her. I just ask that you be smart about it. Don't put yourself in danger. And please understand that if she's in Frenzy, she *is* dangerous. It's as simple as that."

Father grunted his agreement and pushed his chair away from the table, the legs scraping across the wooden planks underfoot.

"Don't you have to get to the rotation?"

I raked my hands through my hair. "I don't think there will be one today."

"Why is that?" Dad asked.

"The others are refusing to come. I can't do it alone."

"Hell no, you can't!" Dad's voice boomed. He stood up. "The Elders won't be happy about this."

"You can't say anything! Let the night-walkers handle it, Dad. *Please.*"

"What if they *handle* it by feeding on us all?"

It was a valid question, and one I didn't have an answer to. If the Elders couldn't convince the colonists to volunteer, the night-walkers would find a way to feed, willing or not. And the citizens would live in terror. Because while the Infected threatened from afar, the vamps had no physical limitations whatsoever. I had seen pissed off vampires, and no one wanted to mess with that.

NINE

TAGE

Dara and I followed Roman to the pavilion—the very empty pavilion—this morning, and now we were making tracks toward Town Hall. The sun was rising. The wind was blowing. It seemed like a great day to either pick a fight or issue an ultimatum, and this impromptu meeting could go either way. Give the Elders time to talk some sense into the dumb humans, or else we tear their throats out. We were hungry, and none of us had eaten anything since yesterday morning.

"I'm going hunting after this," Dara whined. Dara always whined. "I don't see why you keep giving Porschia all of our food. It just comes back up. It's such a waste."

Roman groaned, obviously sick of her constant complaining. "She has to eat."

"No she doesn't," Dara argued. "Let her waste away. She obviously wasn't cut out for this. She's a freak! Those tiny fangs? It's nature's way of telling you she should die. She can't even feed herself."

I growled low in my chest.

Dara giggled. "Aww, Tage. We all know you have a soft spot for her, but Porschia is still hung up on her human lover, Saul. She doesn't want you, does she?" she added with a baby-like pout.

"I don't want her either. Not like that, anyway. She's my friend. But then you wouldn't know anything about friendship, would you? You get on everyone's nerves with your constant bitching and moaning."

"You'd love my moaning," she teased, ignoring the insult. "Roman does."

Unfortunately, I knew he did. I'm sure half the Colony had heard the two of them rutting. Roman wasn't really into her, but he had needs and Dara offered to scratch his itch. Often. Humans were too fragile for intimacy with a vampire, so the walls in Roman's house banged a lot.

However, their noisy lovemaking was nothing compared to the sound of Porschia trying to tear the cell bars out of the ceilings and floor. That made me really damn proud of her for some reason. But since I didn't want the house to land on my head, I opened the cell. It was a win for everyone—everyone but Saul.

Poor guy. She would've killed him. The look in his eyes when he realized his Porschia was about to kill him, and that a large part of her was gone forever? Misery. I'd seen it time and time again. They said that misery loved company, and I could attest to that fact. Because misery was a real hateful bitch – a bitch I'd like to throat punch almost as much as Dara. I didn't hit women, never had, but Dara pushed that boundary. Hard.

She thought Roman would protect her, but she thought wrong. I *knew* Roman. Oh, I hadn't known him long, but I knew his type. He liked power. He liked being the alpha and he would stomp anything in his way, even his current plaything. He'd toss her away and keep right on walking, not even bothering to look back at her.

A few people had already ventured out of their homes this fine morning, but one glance at us and they felt the need to revisit the sanctuary they'd just left.

"Will the old men be awake at this hour?" I asked.

"They'll be at Town Hall, or else we will go find them at their homes and invite them there."

Well okay, then.

We turned toward the Hall, which was an old church, climbed its steps and entered inside. Most thought vampires were unable to step foot in churches, but that was a myth. There were a lot of those surrounding our kind. People tended to make stuff up about things they didn't know or understand, and unless you were a night-walker, you didn't get it. Believe me.

Sure enough, the three old men were in the building. Roman wasted no time.

"To what do we owe the pleasure of your company, Roman?" One of them stood up, his chair legs scooting across the floor boards. I think his name was Yankee.

"Only one person, Saul Daniels, showed up for the rotation yesterday. We asked Saul not to come today, because he allowed each of us to feed from him yesterday. However, would you care to guess how many colonists showed up this morning?" Roman paused for dramatic effect before continuing. "Zero. So here's the deal, and you can take it or leave it. We *will* feed tonight. The three of us will show up at the pavilion after sunset. If none of the colonists show up on their own, we will be forced to find food…and it will be from the veins of your citizens. We are not responsible for the recent murders, but we must eat. I know you can understand that."

Roman turned and walked away, leaving the old men to gape and gasp. Dara giggled.

"Oh!" Roman threw his finger up and turned to the men with a sinister smile on his face. "And the treaty will be nullified if no one shows. That means no more help from us in the forest. If you hunt, you'll go it alone. Good luck with the Infected."

To us, he said, "Let's go. I'm done with their games. They know the rules."

"And I look forward to breaking them." Dara smiled, showing off her long, delicate fangs. "Right after I pay Saul a little visit. Rumor has it that the carpenters need wood."

I shook my head. "You're playing with fire."

"Consider me a pyro, Tage. I'm not afraid of Porschia Grant."

TEN

PORSCHIA

"I HAVE TO GET OUT OF HERE," I SAID ON A GRUNT. I WAS WEAK, BUT WAS still a million times stronger than my human self. Muscles teemed with energy as I eased metal apart, prying and lengthening the space between them. The bars groaned again, bowing under the pressure. "Just. A. Little. More." Sniffing at the air, I sensed that it was still there. Just outside the house, maybe?

Another wince and the hole in the door was just big enough. I squeezed through, the metal taut against the sides of my head, followed by my chest and shoulder blades as I eased out.

The smell. There it was again. My mouth watered. This was no human. What was it? I ran up the steps, out the door, not even bothering to close it. I only stopped when the sunlight assaulted my eyes. Using my forearm as a shield, I ran toward the scent. The cold earth should have stopped me, but I didn't feel it on my bare feet. Not now. Now, I was hot. So hot. Burning from the inside out. Dara's clothes fit like a second skin. I ran faster than I'd ever run, blurring through the vampire section of town, past the pavilion, toward the barn. It was coming from there.

When I got close, I stopped and took in my surroundings. Beyond the barn, there was an oak tree. *There.* I ran again, pumping my arms, forgetting the light that burned my corneas.

"Porschia?"

"Ford?" I held my hands over my eyes, blinking away the pain.

"What are you doing here? I thought you were...sick."

"What are you doing? What am I smelling?" It was warm, earthy, gamey, and bloody.

"I'm slaughtering a cow. The Elders ordered it this morning. They're planning some sort of celebration in Town Hall, though I don't know what in the world there is to celebrate in this place."

I walked further around the large trunk of the sycamore. There hung the carcass, stripped of its hide. Ford had already gutted it and was using a bucket of water to clean the bile from the meat. The meat, muscle and sinew, so fresh. "Can I have a bite?" I asked tentatively. I didn't want to tear it away from him, but my fingers twitched toward the swinging carcass.

"It's not cooked," he said in horror, stepping back from the animal and holding the knife down. I heard his fingers tighten on the hilt.

"I won't hurt you, Ford."

"How can you be sure? Does Tage know you're out?"

"Tage is *not* my keeper," I growled back at him. *I have no keeper.*

"No, but you were the one who said it was safer. You know what? Never mind. Eat some if you want it."

I wasted no time. My fingers shredded the meat from the bone of the thigh and my teeth sank into it. I chewed, swallowed, groaned. It was so good. When that piece was finished, I tore more away, ate it, and then licked my fingers clean.

Ford stood back, wearing a bewildered, terrified, wide-eyed look that I hated to see on his face. I hated it because I knew I'd scared him. I scared my brother. "I'm so sorry, Ford." When I reached out to him, he flinched.

"I know you wouldn't hurt me, Porsch, but that was insane. You just ate a raw cow."

"Not all of it," I mumbled sheepishly, looking down at my shoes. I felt like I could eat all of it, but thought better of it. Someone would definitely notice a missing cow or two from the small herd the Colony had. Ford had already taken enough chickens to get his hind end kicked out of this place. No need to stir the pot.

"Thanks, Ford. I'll go back to Roman's now."

He nodded, easing his grip on the knife. "If you can hold it down, let me know."

"How'd you know I was having trouble eating?"

"I'm your brother."

I smiled. "And I'm still your sister."

He laughed. "Always will be."

I hoped he was right. On an unrelated note, sunlight was a real bitch. I decided I needed to only walk around at night, because this was for the birds. I shielded my eyes and ran back to Roman's house as fast as I could go. On the porch stood Roman and Tage with their arms crossed over their chests.

"Where have you been?" Roman demanded.

I wanted to tell him that I'd eaten and so far my stomach wasn't forcing the food out of my body. That was a call for celebration all on its own, but something – or someone – was missing. "Where is Dara?"

My eyes narrowed and I sniffed the air. She wasn't there. She wasn't inside. I couldn't hear her.

"Where is she?" Tage looked away pointedly, toward town.

Roman just stared at me like he didn't owe me an explanation. Molten fire coursed through my veins. "She better not be sniffing around Saul," I growled, clenching my fists.

Roman was in front of me in a split second. "She is assisting the carpenters in the forest. They need wood. She isn't making a play for your human pet."

"He is *not* a pet."

"But he *is* human. *You* are not."

It was like a knife to the chest. "I know that."

He shook his head. "But I don't think you've accepted it."

I didn't, although my body *did* feel different. My senses were on overload all the time, but I didn't feel like I was a new person. I was still me. My personality, the worries I had before changing, they were the same.

Pushing past Roman, I made my way up the steps and walked past Tage. "I ate. Just so you know."

Roman grabbed me by the scruff of the neck, his warm breath fanning my cheek. "Who did you drain?" His fingers dug painfully into my skin.

"I... I didn't drain anyone! I ate a cow."

"You ate a *cow*?"

"Yeah. A dead one."

"Its blood?"

"Nope. Its meat."

Tage huffed out a laugh. "You ate a dead cow? In a field, or...?"

I nodded as much as Roman's death grip would allow. "Ford was slaughtering a cow and I ate part of it. It was delicious." I sighed in relief. "It's been over half an hour and I haven't puked, so..."

"What the hell?" Roman breathed.

"Exactly."

"How did you happen to find the cow? You just happened to come upon your brother while strolling about the Colony?" Roman asked.

"No," I replied indignantly. "I smelled it from the basement, I guess. Though I didn't know exactly what I was smelling when it first hit me. I just knew I wanted it."

"You wanted it?" Roman confirmed. Again. He was getting very repetitive, like one of those parrots I'd read about. Talking birds. I would have thought them a myth, but at one time who would have imagined vampires were real? Roman and Tage were straight-up vampires, and now I was a night-walker myself.

"Can I go inside?" The sun was terrible, and I blinked until tears slid down my face. Roman finally released me.

"Yeah."

Tage followed me into the house. I knew it was him, because I could hear his footsteps. His were lighter than anyone else's. He was nimble, like a cat, yet he called *me* tiger.

I trudged down the steps, loathing the dreadful bars I knew Roman would make me fix. "What's wrong?" Tage asked.

"I'll have to go back into the cage."

His lips formed a pout. "Oh, kitten doesn't like her cage?"

"How did I go from kitten to tiger, and then back to kitten again?"

"You aren't all psychotic right now. You ate, and so far you're holding it down. I'd say you're ready to curl up and take a nap."

"Did you sleep a lot after you turned?"

He shook his head. "No, I barely slept at all and barely do now. But each person is different."

"Roman says I'm not a person."

"Roman's a dick," was his quick response.

"Shh. He can hear you!" His eyes flicked from the metal cage and back to me.

"He knows I think he's a dick," he whisper-yelled. I rolled my eyes. "Don't bother with those." Tage flicked his head toward the bowed bars.

"Why?"

"What's the point in fixing them if you're just going to break them again? We know you can do it, and it's no longer an effective means of controlling your crazy. You'll have to learn to rein it in, but I actually think you can do this pretty easily as long as you aren't provoked. You bypassed thirty or so colonists on your way to bovine breakfast this morning, and no one lost their throats."

I smiled. "I did?"

"Yep. Colonists, colonists everywhere. And you didn't have a drink."

"No, I certainly didn't." I puffed my shoulders out. "Maybe I *can* do this."

"You don't have a choice, so suck it up, buttercup."

Roman came down the steps and entered the door. "You're a dick, too, Tage. And don't bother with the bars. We need to hunt tonight. If you hold down the cow today, you can have more fresh meat later."

Fresh meat. *Mmmm.* My mouth began to salivate.

"Shit!" Tage jumped away from me.

"What?"

"Your eyes just got like, eight shades darker somehow. What were you thinking about?"

"Food."

"Have you ever seen anything like that?" Tage asked Roman over his shoulder.

"Not like that. That was... different."

I giggled. I was definitely different, and for once in my life, it looked like it might actually be a good thing.

ELEVEN

SAUL

I didn't bother going to the pavilion. I knew the night-walkers wouldn't bother feeding from me, and no one else was likely to show up. I didn't know what they would do, but one thing was certain: they would have to eventually feed. I hoped they at least talked to the Elders and gave them a chance to fix this mess before they went to find breakfast on their own.

Mrs. Dillinger's house was dark, but I could hear an occasional thump from upstairs as I walked toward the door. Some of the planks on her porch were spongey and needed replacing. I tested my weight and shook my head. Poor woman didn't go out much, so people tended to forget about her.

I knocked twice and waited. "It's open," she yelled from what sounded like upstairs. Her voice was muffled, yet it carried.

"Mrs. Dillinger? It's Saul," I said, my head stuck in the front door just enough to holler.

"Come on up."

Stepping inside, I eased the door closed behind me. To the left was the kitchen. There was a fire, but it needed wood. I'd fix that on the way out.

She needed more wood. I'd fix that later today, or send word to Ford later.

The steps creaked underfoot, but I climbed them fast and found her in an old recliner, fabric draped over her lap, brows drawn in concentration. She moved the needle, quickly stitching the two pieces of fabric together. I cleared my throat, breaking her concentration. "Good morning, Saul. I suppose it's your turn to try and feed me some crap about Porschia. Seems her brother couldn't tell a lie. Can you?"

I laughed. The woman had me. "She's sick, but my mom's taking care of her. She didn't want to go home, but she didn't want to get you sick either."

"Bullshit."

"Pardon?" My face heated with embarrassment and I pulled my coat away from my neck.

"I said bullshit. That's a lie. Did she get bitten? Was it by her sister or another Infected?" The woman tried to sound tough, but I heard the waver in her voice.

"No. She isn't Infected."

"Well, at least *that* was the truth. Is she a night-walker, then?" My heart thundered. "Oh, no," she said, dropping her work and using the arm rests to help herself to her feet. I grabbed her elbow and eased her up. "I knew something was going to happen. I had the worst feeling about her being in the rotation. And that mother of hers, if she can even call herself that. Why, I ought to wring her neck..."

I let her rant for a while before interrupting. "Mrs. Dillinger?"

"What is it?" she snapped.

"The Elders don't know."

She stared at me for a long moment before adding, "That's good. Let's keep it a secret for as long as we can." Motioning toward my neck, she asked, "She do that to ya?"

"Yeah, but I told her to. I was trying to help."

"With what, exactly?"

I swallowed. "She's having trouble feeding."

"I've never heard of that before. Night-walkers have always fed from us."

A strand of sunlight peeked across the floor, the shutters unable to hold it back. "You were in the rotation?" I asked tentatively.

She shook her head, silver hair flying this way and that. "There wasn't always a rotation," she replied shakily.

"If the colonists don't uphold their end of the treaty, it will be that way again."

"That's the most frightening thing I've heard all day. Listen – about Porschia? She'll be okay. Just give her some time. But you need to keep away from her right now."

"I want to help her." I did. I'd trade places with her if I could.

She smiled softly, her wrinkles becoming shallow. "I know you do, but Porschia has feelings for you. And feelings, emotions, can make a person spiral and make poor choices. Imagine what it would do to a new vampire."

She pursed her lips, having said her peace.

"I understand. It'll be hard-"

She finished my thought, "But it's what's best for Porschia."

TOSSING TWO PIECES OF SPLIT WOOD INTO THE FIREPLACE, I STOKED MRS. Dillinger's fire before heading back to the wood shop. Brian Yankee, Elder Yankee's son, was waiting for me there. "You've been through the forest, Saul. We need wood, and I need your help."

The man had barely spoken four sentences to me before this morning. Now he made it six and stunned me at the same time. "How can *I* go into the forest?"

"With my help," came a sultry voice from the shadows on the right side of the shop. I knew that voice. Dara walked boldly into the sunlight. "You fell the trees and I'll drag them across the river."

"Won't they be too heavy?"

She slapped my arm playfully and gave me a bright smile. "No, silly. It's no trouble at all. When I overheard Brian talking the other day about needing new material, I volunteered to help."

Maybe it was that her hair was perfectly styled, with not a strand out of place. Maybe it was the fact that she wore make-up, jeans that were painted on, and a low-cut top. Maybe it was her smile: too perky. Whatever it was, she wasn't in this for the lumber. And I doubted nothing Dara did was ever altruistic.

"Okay. Let's go now so we can get back as soon as possible."

Dara pouted her lips. "You make it sound like this will be a chore, Saul. We'll have fun. I promise."

I doubted that, but whatever. *Part of being an apprentice.* I turned back to Brian, who was already back to work shaping a chair leg. He looked up at me. "Can you send word to Ford Grant that Mrs. Dillinger needs firewood and water?"

"I will," he answered, and turned back to his work. He would probably need a break in a little while and would tell Ford himself. The man worked hard from sun up until sun down, taking small walking breaks between projects. The cycle repeated itself until late at night, when he finally gave in and went home.

Dara threaded her arm through mine, and it took everything in me to remain a gentleman. I bit my tongue, careful not to draw blood. The last thing I needed was to tempt another hungry night-walker.

I snagged my coat from a hook behind the door, successfully getting rid of her arm in the process, and found an ax embedded in a chopping stump outside. The ax's handle was worn, but in the right spots you could still see its red paint. At least I had a weapon and my ring. The combination made me a little more at ease about leaving the Colony with Dara.

We walked into the sunlight together. Clouds raced across the bright blue sky to hide the sun, and then as if it couldn't contain it any longer, the rays would burst out again. Dara and I walked through town, drawing glances from my neighbors like metal to magnets.

My jaw muscle ached from clenching my teeth so tight. Dara gracefully crossed the tree that led to the forest while I slipped my way clumsily across. It had been a few days since I'd left the Colony. My legs were still weak. Hell, all of me was. No one said it out loud, but I think Porschia crossed whatever invisible line there was. She almost drained me completely, or at the very least took too much for me to be able to recover like normal.

I'd eaten as much as I could, but there was never enough. With all the commotion lately the Elders had forgotten about providing extra rations, even though I was the only one who had shown up to the rotation. I would've taken all of it and fed my family well.

We made our way over the hills and into the wood where the trees were thicker and more varied. I knew we needed cedar and oak at the wood shed. "That cedar looks like it's thick enough." I shrugged off my coat and rolled my sleeves up. The cold wind bit into my arms, but after a few swings of the ax, I didn't feel it.

Chop.

Chop.

Chop.

Soon, the wedge was large enough that I could start on the opposite side of the trunk. "Stand back."

Dara listened, standing behind me to the left, a little too close for comfort. Sweat beaded on my forehead and neck. "What are you doing?"

"Standing back," she smirked.

I dragged my forearm across my head. "I mean, what are you *really* up to? Why'd you volunteer for this?"

"To help the Colony, of course," she said with a sly smile.

I shook my head. "Whatever." I lifted the ax and gave a couple more swings before hammering wedges into the space. Slowly, the tree began to lean. A cracking sound echoed through the hills and the cedar leaned and then fell, splitting the air in a whoosh and landing with an earth-shaking crash.

At the first sign of movement I moved back, throwing my arm out and protecting Dara instinctively. "Sorry," I mumbled.

She rubbed my arm as I lowered it, answering, "Don't be."

After a beat of awkward silence and her standing too close for comfort, she moved toward the tree. "Do you want to chop the limbs off here or across the bank?" she asked.

"Here is fine."

"The more you chop, the more attention you'll garner."

"From the Infected?"

"Bingo."

"Fine. Across the river, then."

She winked. "Be right back." Dara lifted the enormous trunk and dragged the tree down the hill so fast, its branches slapped loudly against the trunks on either side of it. I'd never seen anything like it. For a moment, I wondered if Porschia had the same ability. If she could get herself under control, she would be a force to be reckoned with.

TWELVE

PORSCHIA

"Will you go check on him?" I whispered, barely audible. Tage looked up from the book he was reading. He was sprawled on the couch, one leg over the arm.

"He's fine."

"He might *not* be fine." I paced, wringing my hands and pretending they were cinched around Dara's neck. "Please? I'll go if you don't."

"Threats don't work on me," Tage said, his eyes moving over the pages. A low growl came from deep within my chest and he finally sat the book on the coffee table, upside down. "Fine. I'll go. But you have to leave me alone the rest of the day. I know you want me, Porschia, but it's getting pathetic."

I grabbed the closest thing to me, which happened to be a white glass vase, and threw it at his head. He ducked and glass shards and plastic flowers exploded, ricocheting across the floor and slamming into furniture.

"Not pathetic. Not you. Nope," Tage teased, walking past me with way too much swagger. "Back in a flash," he taunted, and was gone.

I blew out a frustrated breath and started looking around for a broom. Off the kitchen was a utility room, and I found the broom and dust pan there. I grabbed the broom handle and turned to face the mess, running into a solid chest instead.

I bounced off of Roman and stepped back a foot to put distance between us. "He claimed you. Did he bother to tell you that?"

"Who claimed me?"

"Tage."

"Tage claimed me?"

"That's what I said." Roman folded his arms over his chest.

"What's *that* supposed to mean? Some vampire mating ritual or something? Didn't happen, Roman," I scoffed.

"You're bound to him."

"From the change? Your blood was in the ring, too. Does that mean I'm bound to *you*?"

Roman's eyes darkened. "In a sense, yes. I can feel your emotions if they're heightened. But you can't feel me, can you?"

I searched my brain and tried to sense him somehow. Nothing. "Now try to connect with Tage."

"I don't know how—"

Wait. Tage was frustrated. Angry.

Roman smiled like the cat who caught the canary. "You feel him."

"I do. Why do I feel him?"

"You took in my blood and his, but feeding from a vampire is a very intimate act, Porschia."

I swallowed, my hands twisting around the broom handle. "It is?"

"When I saw you in Town Hall, I knew you were special. I wanted to turn you then, but that's frowned upon in this Colony."

He wanted to turn me? "Why would you want to turn me?"

"You remind me of someone."

I smiled fast, trying to break the tension. "Someone good or someone bad?"

"Yes."

"That's not good." There went my smile.

Reaching out, he took the broom from my hand and removed the dust pan from its handle. "I'll help you clean up."

"Thank you."

Roman nodded, turned, and began sweeping tiny pieces of shrapnel away from our feet. The silence was maddening. "Are you trying to work your mojo on me?"

"Excuse me?" Roman looked up from the floor, his neck craning.

"Your mojo. Are you making me happy, or at least, not sad?"

"Are you sad?"

I thought about it. "No, I'm not sad right now."

He smiled. "Good."

I marched over to him in a huff. "Do *not* use that mess on me, Roman. I want to feel what I feel."

He shook his head. "Frenzy is overwhelming, especially to women. Their emotions—" Now I knew he was manipulating me, and I'd had enough of that to last a million lifetimes. Circling him, I bared my fangs. "See? You're overreacting," he said smugly.

"I am *not* overreacting."

We danced around the furniture, not bothering to avoid the splintered glass, our eyes locked in a dangerous competition.

I sensed Tage closing in and he burst through the door in a rush. "What's going on? Porschia?"

"He's compelling me, and I want him to stop."

"Uh, well, that's a bad idea, Porsch. I asked him to help you out."

I wheeled around to face him. "You *what*?"

Tage closed the door behind him and stepped inside the foyer. "You wanted my help to get yourself under control? Well, this will help. Your emotions will spiral if Roman doesn't calm you down."

"Do I *look* calm?" I screeched.

"No, and *this* is with him helping, so just imagine what would happen if he wasn't smoothing the rough edges." Tage and his talking in circles. I didn't have any rough edges!

"Saul is fine, by the way. He said to tell you hello."

Wait, what? "He said hello? That's it?"

"He was chopping wood, shirtless, while Dara watched, so he was pretty busy."

I leaped across the room at him, fangs bared, ready to sink them into his flesh. Luckily Roman caught my hair, holding me back from his jugular. "Shit," Tage grunted, clutching his chest. "I think she cracked something."

My rage-filled scream echoed throughout the house.

I couldn't stand it.

She didn't belong with Saul. Saul was *mine*.

I would kill her.

I would eat her, and not just her blood. I'd eat her flesh.

Tage. He was hurt.

I looked down to find him wincing in pain beneath my thighs, which straddled his hips in a bone-crushing vise. He coughed and leaned up. "Are you okay? I'm so sorry!"

I sat up on my haunches and backed off his legs. He needed room to breathe. "Hyde to Jekyll in three-point-oh," he wheezed out.

"What?"

Tage laughed, followed by Roman as he released my hair and helped me stand up. "It means you need Roman." A smug smile slid over Roman's face. "For now," Tage added quickly, effectively erasing that arrogant smirk. Mine fell away, too. I had a lot to learn on the road to self-control. This wasn't going to be painless for anyone. *Especially Dara.*

Clutching his sore ribcage, Tage showed me to a real bedroom on the second floor. There were no moldy spots on the mattress; instead, it was covered by a deep red blanket that was thick and soft. Other than a chest of drawers, the room was bare. "You can stay here. The cell isn't going to hold you anyway."

I smiled. "Nope."

"It held everyone before you, you know."

My mouth opened wide. "Did they try to escape?"

He shrugged. "Probably."

"Was he really shirtless?" I asked, biting my thumbnail. I walked over to the window and eased back the lacy white curtains, peering outside. More empty houses. Beyond, I could see the fountain that sat in the center of the pavilion square.

Tage snorted. "No. I was just messing with you."

"Why do you do that?" I turned to face him.

"Do what?"

"Push people. I saw you do it to Roman during the rotation. You do it to everyone."

Tage looked at me and leaned back against the wall. "I don't know. I guess I like to see reactions."

"That might not be the smartest thing to do."

He shrugged and looked up at the ceiling. "I've never been accused of being smart. Now get some rest." He stood and tugged the door open. "We hunt tonight."

"In the forest?"

Tage bared his fangs in a wide smile. "Depends on the Elders."

I LAID AWAKE STARING AT THE PEELING, SILVERY DAMASK WALLPAPER UNTIL my eyes blurred and sleep came. I woke to the mouth-watering scent of fresh meat. "Breakfast in bed," cooed Tage in a falsetto.

Stretching and yawning, I smiled. "Oh, honey. You take such good care of me." His pupil took over his iris, dilating as he approached. "Kidding, Tage."

"I know." Someone was grumpy.

"What's for breakfast?"

He smiled like a proud little boy, puffing his chest out. "I drained it and cleaned it for you."

From behind his back, he produced a silver charger plate. The animal had been skinned and my God, did it smell delicious. "What is it?"

"Groundhog. He was digging along the river bank. Never even saw me coming until it was too late for him."

"That's his problem." I tore off a leg and began tearing away the meat, chewing. Blood and sinew filled my mouth in a medley that would have made me vomit as a human, but somehow was a delicacy now.

Tage watched me in awe. "What?" I asked around a mouth full of food.

He shook his head and sat down on the bottom of the mattress. "I don't get it."

"Me either."

I noticed suddenly that I didn't hear Roman or Dara in the house. "Where are the others?"

"Carrying the trees to the carpentry shop."

My teeth hit animal bone and snapped it in two. I hated her being near Saul. I hated her, period. Whatever she was doing, it wasn't because she was trying to be helpful. No night-walker ever volunteered to help a colonist do anything before. At least, I didn't think so.

"Your brows are touching. What are you thinking about?"

"Why'd you bring me food?"

"We're going for a walk, and I thought it would be best for everyone if you went on a full stomach."

Good thinking on his part. "What about you? Did you get enough blood? I can share some."

"I'm good."

I devoured the rest of the groundhog in no time and while I cleaned up, Tage found my boots. Sitting in the chair, my fingers shook as I fumbled with the strings I'd tied a hundred times before. Looking up from the laces, I smiled; nerves trembling my lips. "Ready?"

"It's sunset. You'll be okay."

"Does Roman know?"

Tage's smile fell. "He's not my keeper."

"Well he sure seems to think he's mine." Leaping up from the bed, I looked at Tage. "Don't let me hurt anyone," I said softly.

He shook his head. "Never." Tage held his hand out, waiting for mine, and watched me with a guarded expression. When I slipped my hand into his, he smiled slightly. "I'll take care of you."

"Since you claimed me and all?"

Tage's mouth opened and then closed abruptly. "Roman?" he guessed.

"For the record, I'm glad it wasn't him. He's really intense."

Clutching his heart, he whined, "And I'm not?"

"Not in the same way, no. Roman's very possessive and entitled. You're more intensely emotional, but I trust you. I trust you with me."

Tage squeezed my hand. "I won't let you down."

I smiled.

"Ready?" he asked.

"I hope so."

THIRTEEN

SAUL

Chopping down the trees was easy. With Dara helping, it took no effort at all to get them across the river. Roman came to help in the late afternoon, and Ford joined us on the Colony's river bank to help. I think he was trying to avoid going home. He'd already finished his chores at the barn. Ford and I removed limbs while Roman tossed them into a pile, and then Dara would take the trunk to the shop. An awkward tension filled the air. No one spoke. No one laughed. Nothing.

When evening came and the sun began to graze the tops of the western hills, I finally asked Roman, "How is she?"

"Better."

"Can she feed?"

His dark eyes narrowed. "She isn't your concern anymore, Saul."

"What's that supposed to mean?"

"It means she is a night-walker. You can't be with her. You need to do your best to pretend she doesn't exist anymore. She will do the same."

I swung the axe, embedding it into the trunk of the tree I'd finished working on. "She won't just forget about me. She loves me and I love her. You can't stop that, Roman."

He smirked. "I can and I will. Stand in my way, and I'll let her drain you, just like she wants to."

"It would destroy her, and then she would hate you for letting it happen."

"Wrong. It would take time, but I would build her back exactly the way I want her."

"She isn't a *thing*. She's a person," I spat.

"She isn't a person anymore. She's cursed, just like the rest of us. And she's mine... or she will be once Tage is removed from the equation."

"Tage? He likes her?"

He snorted. "He claimed her and she is bound to him, but I intend to break that bond as soon as possible."

My fingers balled into fists. "How did he claim her? What does that even mean?"

Roman smiled. "It doesn't mean what you imagine it does." He walked toward me slowly. "It means that she fed from his vein. She can feel his emotions and he can feel hers. It's an intimacy very few night-walkers ever get to experience. She was supposed to bind to me, but I'll take care of the problem."

"You'll have worse problems than that if you don't take care of Porschia."

Roman stepped back. "You should get ready for your feast. The Elders are providing the meat in the Fellowship Hall tonight."

"What about the rotation? Did they find anyone?"

"I'm about to find out." He hefted the giant tree trunk and sped away toward the shop. Chips of wood covered my clothes and most of the grass underfoot. I laced my hands behind my head and looked up to the darkening sky with no idea of how to fix any of this.

From across the swirling water came a shrill keening, and my eyes were riveted to the source. Blonde hair, matted and tangled. Torn jeans and a dark sweater. She clutched her side. It was Mercedes, Porschia's sister. "What do *you* want? Haven't you done enough?"

She smiled, turned, and slowly walked away. I wanted to throw something at her, but she was still freshly Infected and faster than most of the rotters. She was up to something.

———

Roman and Dara made it very clear that I wasn't to go to the pavilion for the evening rotation. Maybe I should have listened, gone home, and changed into clothes that weren't glued to my skin with sap. The only thing I knew when I walked closer to the square was that I wasn't prepared to see *her*.

"Porschia?" The words barely tumbled from my lips in a whisper, but she turned to face me. Her hand was wrapped tightly around Tage's. He was her anchor, keeping her from floating away on the current that was consuming her. Frenzy was a beast, and I couldn't help but wonder if I did the wrong thing by telling her to use the ring. I'd wondered it almost every waking moment since that day.

Her hair was glossy, dark, and smooth. It hung long over her shoulders like a curtain of silk. Her skin was the same, not paled at all, and her eyes…God, how I missed them. Streaks of green mixed with dark and pale gray, bursting from the center.

"Saul? You aren't supposed to be here." She stepped backward and hid behind the night-walker. *Does she not want me here?* I pushed that thought as far down as it would go. She was still my Porschia and deep down, I knew she wanted to see me as much as I needed to see her. That alone was a gift. She was okay. Better than okay, by the way it looked. Another thing I tried to shove down? Jealousy. Green as moss in spring time. Her hand in his. It was wrong. My hand should be the only one holding hers.

Mary, Tim, and Victor were present and very angry. "Hey," I said with a nod. They nodded and Mary's eyes questioned me. *Did you know*? I moved toward their group. Apparently I had no poker face. She clenched her jaw after reading my answer.

Victor ticked his head toward Porschia. "How long?"

"A few days."

"Did they turn her?" he asked, crossing his arms over his chest.

"No, she used the ring. She tried to stop someone from crossing the river bank and an Infected attacked her. She had no other choice." I didn't tell them that it was my fault she used the ring. I screamed at her and told her to use it; to turn. To change. I did this, and yet she was the one who would pay. She would pay for that mistake for an eternity, but her wasting away as an Infected was an even worse option. I wouldn't have survived it.

Victor huffed. "You were there?"

"Yes."

I looked at her. She wore dark jeans that hugged her every curve, a baby blue sweater, and her dark hair was braided at the nape of her neck like she used to wear it. Her skin was luminous and she almost seemed to glow from within, almost ethereal. She seemed more alive than she ever had. Her sister wasn't as fortunate.

Porschia's cheeks flushed and she stared at me, her eyes darkening somehow. I blinked. Did I just imagine it?

Roman stepped forward. "Thank you for coming. I know you have a celebration to attend, so we won't keep you."

Tim nodded toward Porschia. "Is she feeding tonight?"

"No."

I looked to her for confirmation and she smiled and shook her head slightly. Did she already feed from something, or someone? I needed to talk to her. Roman paired with Victor, Dara with Tim, and Tage with Mary, who looked scared and pissed all at once. No love lost between those two. But Tim and Victor were obviously not happy about being there either. What did the Elders do to persuade them to return?

I walked over to Porschia. "You okay?"

She took a step back, putting an uncomfortable amount of distance between us. If my discomfort made her feel better, so be it. "I'm fine," she whispered, glancing at Tage, who was feeding from Mary's neck. He kept his eyes trained on her, too.

"Why are you looking at him like that?" My face heated. I wanted to pummel him.

"He's helping me." She shifted her feet like she was ready to run away.

"He claimed you – is that it? That bond that makes you think only *he* can help you?"

Her mouth parted. "It's not like that, Saul." Her eyes sought him, and then she looked toward the night-walker dwellings.

"What's it like then? Do you like him the way you like me?

"God, no," she breathed. "I love you, Saul. But I can't...I feel like I'll lose control when you're around. My emotions are all over the board." The more she spoke, the higher pitched her voice became. She panted, stepping back gracefully, but moving as if her legs were too heavy to lift at all.

Tage licked Mary's wounds and was beside Porschia in an instant. His hand was on her back, rubbing circles. Roman was quick to follow, leaving Victor on the bench. The pair of vamps flanked her. With them at either side, Porschia began to visibly calm down.

"Are you doing something to her?" I growled.

Tage looked at me. "Do you want her to feel normal, to feel like Porschia again?"

"Of course."

"She *cannot* control herself. We have to help, or she'll do one of two things. One, she'll run away, because that's what she does. Or two, she'll lose control and hurt someone. The more her emotions are heightened, the more dangerous she is. We have to help her, Saul."

I swallowed. *Fuck*. I knew they had to help, but also hated that she seemed to need them so much. The question was hanging in my mind. If they had the power to make her calm down, could they make her do other things as well?

Dara stared between Porschia and me, a scowl on her face. She hated Porschia. I didn't think Dara gave Porschia a second thought when she was still human, but now, her envious expression mirrored mine. Envy was a dangerous thing. Memories of Dara eating the deer during the hunt flooded my mind. Dara was dangerous.

They all were. Roman, Dara, Porschia, and especially Tage. He was closest to Porschia, had bonded to her.

Dara sauntered over to me. "Let me know if you need more help in the forest. I loved spending time with you," she said, raking her nails over my forearm.

A low growl came from Porschia, which made me smile for the first time since she'd turned. When I looked in her direction, her fangs were bared and her eyes were dark again, almost black. I took a step back, silencing my girl. Turning toward Dara, I offered, "Thanks anyway, but Porschia's doing better. Maybe *she* can help me next time." Winking at Porschia, I grinned and walked over to the huddle of humans at the edge of the square, throwing back over my shoulder, "You're doing good, Porsch."

She smiled and nodded slightly.

Victor's voice sliced through the air, again separating us from them. "We need to get to the feast."

Everything in me, my feet, eyes and hands, wanted to stay, even if only to watch her walk away and disappear into the darkness. One more glimpse. But Victor stormed off and Tim and Mary made sure that I followed.

Mary muttered, "You're going to get yourself killed, Saul."

The Fellowship Hall was situated behind Town Hall, and a breezeway, once covered with a metal archway, connected the two buildings. What was left of it looked skeletal, metal beams attached to shriveled rusted sheets or none at all. Some of them had been stripped away during wind storms over the years.

The din of laughter and two hundred people talking seeped out of the old building. It was hollow, just one large room. Tables lined one of the walls, stuffed with all sorts of food. Mom and Dad waved me over to where they stood.

"You okay, son?" Dad asked.

"Yeah. The others showed up. We should be good." He wasn't surprised by that fact. *What did he know?*

"What about *her*?"

"She was there. She's doing remarkably well." *With help from two vamps I am growing to hate.*

Mom slid an arm around my back. At five foot-two, she was on the short side. "No one knows."

"They will. The others saw her," I whispered.

I could feel her arm tense behind me. I felt the same way.

FOURTEEN

PORSCHIA

WALKING AWAY AND LEAVING HIM AT THE EDGE OF THE SQUARE WAS THE hardest thing I'd ever done. Bloody tears poured from my eyes and my chest heaved. Sobbing, I found myself wrapped up in Tage's arms as we sat on the front steps of Roman's house. Not surprisingly, Roman and Dara had scattered like cockroaches blinded by light.

"I can't be with him."

Tage shushed me gently, but kept his arm around my shoulders and waited patiently as my feelings ebbed and flowed. "No, you can't," he answered. "Not like you were planning to before."

"We were going to get married, I think."

"I know," Tage rasped as we sat in silence and the darkness wrapped itself around us. "And it'll never get easier. That kind of hurt is deep. Love doesn't just stop. But no, you can't be with him. He's human, you aren't. It's that simple."

I sniffed. "It sounds like you lost someone, too."

His arm tensed on my shoulders. "I did."

"Were you going to marry her?"

Tage groaned. "I don't know. Honestly, we weren't at that point yet when...you know. But I did care for her."

"Did you love her?"

"Yes. I didn't know it at the time, though. But I feel the loss every day now."

Thin, silver-lined clouds streaked across the sky, blurring the moon, and that was as good a metaphor as any for how this was going to be. Different things – people, events – might dull the pain for a moment, but it would never go away. Not entirely.

There would always be reminders of my former life, like wounds that were torn open again and again. They would never heal, but I had an eternity to bleed. "This really is a curse. I believe you now."

"At least we weren't there at the beginning," Tage replied, stretching his arms above him.

"What do you mean?"

"They have bible study in the Colony. Did you not attend?"

"If my father made me, I did. But he hasn't made us for years."

Tage took a deep breath and began to explain. "In Exodus, regarding the plagues of Egypt. Have you heard of them?"

I stiffened, hugging my legs. "Of course I have."

"The water ran red for a reason. That is when vampires were first created and unleashed. The first Frenzy took place in Egypt, all because Pharaoh refused to free his slaves. And they had a particular appetite for the blood of the first-born. The flies and gnats, the boils and sores? They created a plague, too. It was the source of the Infection itself. Two curses on the houses of the Egyptians were unleashed, and those curses continue today in one form or another. Night and day. Vampires and Infected."

"Vamps have always been around, though, right? The Infected haven't. They're new."

Tage shook his head. "Medicine found a way to tamp down the Infection for a long time. There were drugs that would keep it at bay, but it always lurked, dormant. However, curses always find a way. They bubble to the surface, unhappy to be tamped down for long. Throughout history, there were many times it reared its head, killing millions of people at a time."

"The livestock that died?"

"Drained, and then they rotted, causing more disease," he supplied.

"My God."

"Yes."

I STOOD UP TOO FAST AND CLUTCHED MY HEAD TO WARD OFF THE spinning. "This is impossible. I...I can't even wrap my head around it! We can't get out. We'll never get out of this. There's no cure. There's no hope!"

Tage stood and reached out to calm me, but I batted his hand away angrily. "Don't touch me!"

"Porschia, you're getting upset."

"No SHIT!"

"Roman!" Tage yelled.

The door flew open and Roman appeared in the doorway wearing only a pair of jeans slung low on his hips. The zipper was undone. Dara appeared a second later, wiping her plump bottom lip. Roman looked murderous. "Sorry to interrupt," Tage started, "but I need you to calm her down."

"Calm me down? I will *not* calm down!"

Roman zipped the fly of his jeans and casually strode down the steps, his eyes intent on me. "Don't touch me," I warned.

"I won't if you don't want me to," he replied with a smirk.

I ticked my head toward Dara. "You have *her* for that. I'm no one's plaything."

Roman growled, the smile slipping from his face. "You'll be whatever I *want* you to be."

"I'll never be yours."

Tage maneuvered himself between the two of us. "Easy," he warned, but I wasn't sure which one of us he was talking to.

"You treat us like property!"

"I'm the leader, Porschia. Deal with that or leave."

"Who made you leader?"

Roman bared his fangs, and with the back of his hand swatted Tage away. He landed hard on the steps. "*I* did."

Coming toe-to-toe with me, Roman growled, fisted my hair, and held my neck to the side. He dragged the sharp tips of his fangs down my throat. "Roman?" I whimpered.

"That's better," he breathed.

"What are you doing to me?" My knees buckled.

Dara's voice cut through the fog. "He's making sure you behave. Now do you see why I'm addicted?"

Because he wants you to be.

Tage recovered enough to pull me away from Roman, and in that moment, I was angry for his intrusion. In the next, I was thankful for it. What was that?

Compulsion.

"We're going for a walk," Tage announced. Roman walked back up the steps, the muscles rippling through his perfectly chiseled body. He didn't reply; he just threw a hand up in dismissal. Dara grinned as he prowled toward her.

The door slammed behind the pair of them and then Dara's body hit the back side of the wood. Her moans were both deep and theatrically loud. "I'm ready for that walk," I admitted, staring uncomfortably at the door.

Tage pulled my arm and we walked toward the cemetery. The further I was from Roman, the more my mind cleared. He certainly didn't touch me like a leader; he touched me like a lover. I shook my head to get rid of the image. Scenes from even before I turned filled my mind – like during the feedings when he would sit behind me on the bench, wrap his arm around my body, and pull me toward him. Was he compelling me even then?

Tage's demeanor also changed the further we walked away from Roman's house. He balled his fists and paced back and forth down the rows of graves, each marked with a simple wooden cross at the head. "What's wrong?"

He huffed and stopped pacing. "Roman's the problem."

"Not *your* problem. I'm pretty sure he doesn't want to eat you."

"He doesn't want to eat you, Porschia. He wants to consume you. And that, back there?" He pointed toward the house. "That was a warning to me, too."

"How is this about you?"

"You're mine."

I shook my head. "I'm Saul's."

"Never mind Saul. *I* know you're Saul's, but I also know that I claimed you, and what he just did crossed a line that can't be uncrossed. I want to rip him apart and feed you chunks of him." Okay, so that was hot, and I was hungry, so just the thought of Tage feeding me hot, warm meat....*mmmmm*.

"Stop it, Porschia," he warned, his eyes dilating.

"Tage, I know we're bonded or something, and you probably have to help me anyway, but I really appreciate you helping me," I said haltingly as I worried the hem of Dara's shirt.

"Save it. I know how you feel, but I won't let Roman compel you into bed."

"I'd never sleep with him!"

"No? Did you see yourself a minute ago? You practically melted into a Porschia puddle with just one whisper from him." Tage raked his fingers through his hair. "I swear if he touches you, I'll kill him."

"What if you can't kill him?"

"I'll die trying if he lays one finger on you, Porschia. I swear it."

Are you kidding me? I strode over to him and poked my finger in his chest. "Don't you dare use me as an excuse to make yourself some sort of martyr. If anyone dies here, it'll be me. Got it?"

"You really want to die?" Tage asked, his voice soft as he tucked my hair behind my ear.

"Most of the time," I admitted.

His hands found my waist and reeled me in until my body was flush with his. "No, baby. Don't ever give up." Warm breath fanned my forehead and weaved through the strands of my hair.

"Are you compelling me right now?" I whispered when his lips ghosted my cheek and grazed my jaw.

"No. Why?"

"What is this, then?"

"You know what it is." His lips paused over mine, his fingers digging into my skin.

"The bond?" I looked into his clear blue eyes. If ice could burn, his would be an inferno.

He shook his head, the soft, supple skin of his lips brushing across my own. "It's more, even if you aren't ready to admit it. You and I could be together. You can't hurt me, Porschia."

"I can't, Tage. It would hurt *me*." Using everything inside me, I pushed him away, my lips immediately angry and bereft. They wanted to taste him. Traitorous bastards.

FIFTEEN

SAUL

Elder Beckett asked everyone for their attention. The building quieted and all eyes were focused on the three men standing at the front of the building on a small raised platform. "Thank you for your contribution to the Colony. This feast is in your honor. Each of you worked tirelessly to grow and harvest from your gardens, and many of you also work in various other capacities. It is this work, this dedication to the greater good, that makes the Colony thrive."

Elder Beckett, flanked by Elders Yankee and Brown, continued. "A wise person once said that it takes a village to raise a child. Well, I tell you now that it takes a village to survive. And survive we will. It's come to our attention that the Infected have been drawing closer to our haven. We will not let them in. We will fight as one. The night-walkers and the treaty is still in place. They will help us." Murmurs rumbled throughout the crowd.

"As one united front, we will keep Blackwater Colony and her citizens safe from this threat."

Victor Freeman stood up, followed by Tim and Mary Brown. "How can you trust the night-walkers?" Victor defiantly asked the black-robed men.

"They've given us no reason not to trust them," Elder Beckett answered.

"What about the fact that Porschia Grant is now one of them?" Victor questioned.

Elder Beckett, flustered, shook his head and his wobbly jowls flapped back and forth with the motion. "Is this true?" His rheumy eyes searched the room for Porschia's father, Carson, or Ford for confirmation.

Carson stepped forward with his head down and his fists jammed in his pockets, and Ford pushed through the crowd to stand beside his father. The citizens whispered loudly behind covered hands.

"Porschia was not turned by a night-walker. She was attacked in the forest by an Infected and forced to use her ring as a last resort. She chose to consume the night-walker blood instead of becoming Infected, and I'm proud of her for making that decision."

Ford nodded his assent. "So am I."

"Is she in Frenzy?" Elder Beckett asked.

Ford shook his head. "She's doing great. The transition wasn't as hard as everyone expected."

Elder Beckett's eyes narrowed. "If she just turned, then she is a danger to everyone. Though we don't fault her choice, we must protect ourselves from it. Porschia needs to be removed from Blackwater."

"The hell she does!" I shouted, pushing forward. "She hasn't hurt anyone since turning. Not one person. She isn't a threat."

Elder Beckett opened his mouth to argue, but Elder Yankee tugged on his elbow and stepped forward. "We appreciate your concern for the Colony, but until she is out of Frenzy, she is banished. That is final."

Citizens crammed leftover food into their pockets: crusts, meat, cooked vegetables, and fruit wrapped in small towels. Carson, Ford, and I met outside the hall, beneath the walkway. "We can't let them banish her," Ford whispered.

"I agree."

Carson spoke up. "She'll have to prove herself. I hope she's ready."

I prayed she was too.

Looking at Ford, their father said, "I have to see to your mother. Find Porschia."

"I will," he promised.

"*We* will," I corrected.

Ford rushed down the pathway, nudging people and children out of his way. "Excuse us," I said, trying to smooth things over. We rushed into the night, the moon cloaked in thin clouds. The warm light that spilled from the Fellowship Hall was blocked by the shadows of too many people.

Ford wheeled around and stuck his finger in my face. "Don't apologize to them!" he panted. "Don't ever apologize to those bastards. They're trying to banish her. She's fine!"

"I know." *Mostly.* "Now let's go find her before they do."

Ford was so angry that his lips shook. "Damn right." He took off running and I stayed on his heels. His family could haul ass when they needed to, that was for sure. I thought Porschia was fast, but Ford was ridiculous. He was tall, and his stride was lengthened by determination and fueled by anger.

We crossed yards, streets, and the paved slab of the pavilion, followed by more streets and houses. The night-walker portion of town was dark and creepy as hell. I felt like prey again, similar to what I felt in the woods with the Infected. Now that I knew how dangerous the night-walkers could be, I was terrified. Not that I'd tell Ford that. I ran beside him until we reached Roman's doorstep.

He took the steps two at a time and didn't pause on the landing; he just burst through the door. "Porsch?"

Looking through the darkness, we heard shuffling overhead. "Seriously? Is everyone going to interrupt us tonight?" we heard Roman complain.

He and Dara appeared at the top of the steps. He was naked, except for a tight pair of dark undergarments that hugged his legs, and Dara wore nothing but a white silk sheet. Her hair was a tangled mess, and it was obvious what they had been doing. The tension in my stomach eased. I was so glad it wasn't her…not my Porschia with him. He could have Dara, but I would kill him if he touched Porschia.

"Where's my sister?" Ford yelled, louder than necessary. His voice echoed through the tall foyer, bouncing off mirrors and a crystal chandelier that glistened in the dark overhead.

Roman narrowed his eyes and focused them at me. "She's out with Tage."

"Where?" I growled.

"Who cares?" he said, shrugging his shoulders.

Ford grabbed a book from the ledge next to him and launched it at the pair of vamps. The spine of the book slapped Roman in the chest before bouncing off, flopping page over page down the steps. The sound of crinkling paper echoed around us. "*I* care. The Elders just banished her. Was that your doing? Did you have her thrown out? Because if you did—"

Ford stopped mid-sentence, staring at the vampire that was slowly descending the steps toward us. "I had nothing to do with this, but I will handle it. You have my word. Now *leave*."

"No," Ford gritted out. Beads of sweat formed on his forehead and lip and I heard his teeth grinding against each other.

Enough. I stepped between Roman and Ford. "What the hell are you doing to him?"

Roman smiled. "Telling him to go home where it's safe, like a good little boy."

"Why wouldn't we be safe? You love the treaty, right?"

"It's not me who poses a threat to him; it's his sister. She's a little emotional tonight."

I had seen her 'emotional', and that wasn't a good thing for her to be right now. "Where is she?" I asked.

"She's with Tage, as I said earlier. He's taking *real* good care of her." That was it. I'd had enough. I launched myself at Roman and there were fists and grunts, and then one of us tackled the other to the ground in a blur of blood and hissing.

Roman was on top of me, hand positioned to knock me into oblivion, when we heard the noise. He and I turned our attention to the door behind us.

"Porschia?" Roman asked breathlessly.

Her eyes darkened menacingly and her fangs raked her plump bottom lip. She bounced on the bottoms of her feet, ready to do battle.

"Told you it wasn't safe," Roman said, hovering above me with a smirk.

Tage grabbed her arms from behind. "You're okay," he reassured her.

She shook her head. "I'm not. I'm not. I'mnotnotnotnot. Not. NOT! I'm *NOT* okay. Not OKAY!"

"You just ate. You're not even hungry. Focus. You aren't hungry. You know what the blood will do to you. You can't hold it." She sniffed the air, her eyes closing and a moan of pleasure pouring from her mouth.

"I *want* it. I want it so bad, Tage." She turned in slightly to him and he eased his grip as Porschia breathed against his neck. "Can I just have a taste?"

"What the hell is this?" I boomed out. I was going to have to kill Tage, too. Roman laughed, rolling off me so I could stand. "Are you with Tage now?" I asked incredulously.

Porschia began laughing, softly at first and then louder, which wasn't quite the reaction I expected. Her laughter bubbled out as if she just heard the funniest joke in the world. "We," she motioned between her and Tage, "are definitely not together. He's like my brother. He's like Ford. Right, Ford?" She looked at Ford for confirmation, but Tage was looking at Porschia, mouth agape. He definitely didn't have brotherly feelings toward her.

Ford looked at me and shrugged. "Sure. I guess."

"And *he* isn't bleeding," she added. "You are." The happiness was gone. Only accusation punctuated her tone.

I motioned to Roman. "Blame him for the blood, but I wasn't going to let him talk about you like that."

"Like what?"

"He insinuated that you and Tage were more than friends or...siblings."

She shook her head. "You don't trust me." Crimson tears filled her eyes. "You'll never trust me, and you can't love me if you don't trust me. Love can't breathe without trust. It dies without it."

Red streaks ran down her face. Thick bloody tears. So much sadness.

She was losing it. We'd gone from thoughts of eating me to laughing hysterically to crying in one minute flat. I stepped toward her. "Porsch, it'll be okay."

"Like hell it will!" Annnd, now we were back to anger. "Why are you even here?"

Ford cleared his throat. "The Elders know that you've turned. At the feast tonight, they announced that you are to be banished from Blackwater."

"They can't tell me where to go," she warned.

"I know, but we just thought you should hear it from us."

She turned to Roman and glanced at Tage. "They can't really banish me, right?"

Roman swore under his breath. "Let me get dressed."

SIXTEEN

PORSCHIA

SAUL WAS HERE. SAUL BLED. SAUL WAS HERE. THE SCENT OF HIM. THE scent of his blood. The scent. I needed it. I had nowhere to run, except to him. At war with myself, I wanted to pounce on him. I wanted to feed from him. I wanted to run away from him, from this place. I wanted.

Tage held my arms back, but I wanted to tear them away, to hurl him down the steps. He was interfering. No one interfered with Saul. *My* Saul.

Ford. My brother, my baby brother. He brought him. Why was Roman hurting him? I would tear Roman limb from limb. Dara watched passively from above. I would tear her apart along with him.

Banished. I was banished.

They didn't want me here. I wasn't welcome.

I didn't fit in.

This wasn't my home anymore. It never was.

What was wrong with me?

Why did no one want me?

They thought I cried for no reason, but I had reasons. I had loneliness, despair, greed, selfishness. I wanted to stay. With Saul. I wanted to stay with Saul.

I needed him. I wanted to be with him.

I couldn't be with him.

Hot tears.

Blood.

Crying blood. My life leaked.

If I pulled Saul to me, I would hurt him. If I hugged my brother, I would hurt him. I would hurt them. I would kill them. I would kill. I killed.

Dead. Death. Despair. Danger.

I was danger.

I was despair.

I was death.

I was undead.

I was cursed.

Cursed. Cursed. Cursed.

Where will I go? my eyes asked Tage. He had no answer, only a vow. He would go with me. He would help me. He promised to help me get myself under control.

There was no control. It didn't exist. It was a ghost. You couldn't touch it. It was a vapor. It was complete bullshit!

Roman was almost naked as he went back upstairs. Dara was naked save for a sheet. They were relentless. They were passion. They were not death.

"Calm down," Tage whispered into my ear. His body pressed into mine from behind and a fire ignited. The same fire I found in the forest. He had sparked it then, and he sparked it now. I hated that fire. Saul could see its smoke, feel its warmth.

Saul stared at the fire behind me and clenched his jaw. Hate radiated out from his body and toward me. I would take it. I would take his hate.

I couldn't have his love, but I could absorb the bad. I was bad.

In the forest, I ate a raccoon. I was full. I was empty.

Empty. Void.

Nothing.

I was nothing. I wanted to be nothing.

I ran fast; fast as lightning to Roman. "End me. Don't send me away. Just...I want to die. I can't live like this. I can't. I don't *want* to live like this. Help me," I begged.

Beggar.

His eyes widened.

"Please, don't think. End me."

I grabbed hold of his forearms and placed his hands on my neck. We were at the top step, one from the landing. One snap was all it would take. I would land below. I would fall. I wouldn't hurt. Nothing.

No hunger.

No loneliness.

No death.

Nothing.

"What did you say?" Ford breathed.

I pled with Roman, tears streaming again. "End me."

Dara's sheet swished behind her as she retreated. "I wish you would, Roman. I mean, really. Could she *be* any more pathetic?"

A slamming door.

An ending.

His fingers squeezed my throat. One twist.

Tage breathed into our faces. "Do it and die, Roman. I will kill you."

"You aren't strong enough to kill me," he smirked.

Tage never wavered. "End her and find out exactly how strong I am."

Strong. Weak.

Crushing fingers.

Stretching skin and sinew.

"Please! Please, don't," Saul said from two steps down. "Porschia, there are other options. This isn't it."

"No there aren't."

I couldn't do this. I was weak. *Weak*. I wasn't strong. Undead, but not strong. Only the strong survived. The weak begged for death, unable to give it to themselves.

"Please," I whimpered. Roman pulled my face toward his, only a hair's breadth apart, he bared his fangs. He would drain me.

Drained.

Empty.

Nothing.

Tage fumed. "Enough!"

Roman looked at him, really looked at him, and for the first time, I saw fear. But it wasn't in my eyes. It was in Roman's.

He loosened his grasp, ghosting his fingers over the slender column of my throat. Up and down. Up. Down. Smoothing the shards. Calming me. Easing the fear. Removing the mania.

Slowly, I sank to the floor. My legs wouldn't hold me.

"She needs sleep," Roman announced nonchalantly. "Deal with her," he ordered Tage.

Saul and Ford both released a pent-up breath.

Roman continued, "She isn't going anywhere tonight. Go home."

Hesitation. They paused. Tage reassured them. "I'll watch over her. I swear it."

Saul nodded with warning in his eyes.

Tage met them head-on.

Tension.

Longing.

Anger.

Ford tugged Saul away. I slumped. Bereft. I missed them already. I missed Saul. I missed Ford. I missed life.

Real life. Living with the possibility of dying.

I, too, could die. I could never live again.

Hopeless.

Strong arms lifted me. Legs strode toward my room. My mattress and blankets cradled me. I shivered.

Cold.

So cold.

I lay awake, shivering. Staring at the window. I couldn't see the moon.

The sky was desolate.

Closing my eyes, I willed sleep to come.

It had abandoned me as well.

Morning came with no fanfare. The sun rose, the cocks crowed, but no one stirred inside Roman's home. Tage's shallow breathing came from behind me. His arm rested on my waist. He held me all night. I let him.

"Are you warm? Your teeth aren't chattering anymore." His voice was raspy in the morning.

"I'm comfortable now. Not too warm and not too cold."

"Goldilocks."

"Hmm?"

He smiled. I could hear it. "It's an old story about when something is just right."

"Yeah, I'm just right." *Why is your arm around me?*

As if sensing my unspoken question, he eased it away. I breathed and relaxed the muscles that had been stiffer than wooden planks. "Sorry. I didn't mean to make you uncomfortable."

"You didn't."

He grinned and rolled onto his back, folding his hands behind his head. "Liar."

"I'm not lying. I *was* comfortable."

"Pants on fire," he said. I looked down.

"They are not."

He chuckled.

SEVENTEEN

PORSCHIA

Tage suddenly growled and leapt from the bed, tugging a sweater over his bare chest. "You stay in this room, understood? Stay until I come for you."

I didn't hear anything, but Tage's reaction meant someone was here. Sniffing the air, I sat upright.

"Promise me," he demanded.

I crossed my arms. "Fine, but you should hurry. I'm not very patient right now."

He nodded and ducked outside my room, pulling the door closed behind him.

I stayed in the room for a long time, longer than I thought I had the willpower to. I heard voices. Sometimes I could pick out Tage or Roman's, although Dara's was easiest to discern. But one was deeper than the others. Foreign.

I pulled on my coat with quivering fingers; Goldilocks no more. I was freezing. And hungry. Always hungry.

Easing the door open, I listened.

"You can't stay here, Julian." *Roman.*

Julian?

"There are plenty of people from which to feed," he replied haughtily. His accent was strange, abrupt, and harsh.

"We have a treaty with the humans in Blackwater. We don't feed whenever or on whomever we would like," Roman explained.

"You barter with them for their blood?" Julian asked incredulously. "Why not just take it?" He didn't understand that the treaty was good for both parties. The humans wouldn't have to live in fear, and the night-walkers were guaranteed a meal in exchange for being the watchdogs of the forest. What was so wrong with that? However, Julian acted as if the entire scenario was absurd.

"We want to live peacefully," Roman said forcefully. He was angry. He smelled of it; all musk and blood and red.

"That doesn't mean you don't feed when you need to! That's ridiculous. We are superior to the humans."

Julian sniffed the air. I could hear his nose move now that I was closer. Why couldn't I hear it from behind my door?

"You have another."

I started to ease the door closed again, but it was forced open and I had to take a step backward to avoid being struck by the swinging wood. A large man with dark skin and hair, voice deep and smooth as velvet stood before me, taking me in. "Who are you? And why are they hiding you?"

"I'm Porschia."

He sniffed. "Mmmm. I love the scent of Frenzy."

"How can you tell?" My heart pounded against its iron cage.

Julian prowled forward. "It's very distinct, although I haven't smelled it in a very long time. How fresh are you, peach?" He stroked his forefinger along my cheekbone.

"Very."

"Why were you hiding her, Roman?"

I looked over Julian's shoulder and spoke before Roman could respond. "He wasn't hiding me. I was sleeping."

Julian's eyes widened. "So new. You still sleep." In the dark orbs, darker even than Roman's, was green jealousy. He wanted what I had. Why would anyone want this?

"So powerful," he muttered, stepping forward.

Tage growled. "She is mine. I claimed her."

Julian chuckled. "We'll see. I wouldn't mind sharing." His eyes raked over my bed, the sparse furnishings.

"I don't share," Tage threatened. "Get away from her."

Julian raised his hands, but kept his eyes trained on me. "It was nice to meet you, Porschia. Roman," he added, turning around to face him. "I think I'll stay for a while."

"Then you abide by *our* rules."

"Of course," Julian quickly agreed, never taking his eyes off of mine.

THAT EVENING, WE GATHERED AROUND THE FIREPLACE TO TALK. TAGE BUILT a fire for me and golden, flickering light filled the room as Roman filled Julian in on the Elders and their decision to banish me. Julian was dumbfounded. "Why do you bother with these humans? They are only here for one thing: our food. *We* say when we eat. *We* say where we live and how. They serve us, not the opposite."

Those were dangerous ideals, but I could understand how some nightwalkers might feel that way. We were the ones who were cursed, so why bend to a human's will – to someone who would only be alive for a fraction of your lifetime? Why allow them to dictate anything at all?

We sat on the velvet covered furniture. Dara was draped over Roman, who was seated beside Julian. Tage and I sat opposite them on a smaller matching couch. I raked my fingernails across the deep plum fabric, watching it lighten and darken depending on the stroke. Tage stared at Julian, Dara picked at her nails as if bored, and I watched the nail marks.

"Why is there a cell downstairs?" Julian asked. His eyes flicked from face to face until he landed on mine, and a slight smile formed on his lips. "And were you the one to tear it apart, love?"

"She's not your love," Tage barked, "and you'd be wise to stay away from her. We might just unleash her on you."

Julian laughed, his enormous shoulders heaving with delight. "I might enjoy that."

IT DIDN'T TAKE LONG FOR JULIAN TO MAKE HIMSELF AT HOME. HE TOOK THE bedroom next to mine, enraging Tage and annoying Roman. Dara left, claiming she needed fresh air. I tried to slip out of my room to follow her, but Tage caught me.

"Where do you think you're going?"

"I need fresh air, too," I asserted, standing up straighter.

Tage smiled. "You know, you don't actually need air at all."

"We breathe."

"It's a mechanical function only; not a requirement. Not breathing won't kill you, night-walker."

I smacked his chest, making him stumble back a step. "Don't call me that!"

"You have to accept it. It's called tough love, kitten."

He liked to play games. Fine. I gave him a sly smile and crept closer toward him. He looked behind him on both sides, but seeing nothing unusual, he backed into a wall covered in dingy floral wallpaper.

"What are you doing?" Tage gave a nervous smile, but watched as if fascinated. I rubbed my face along his, breathing him in, and heard him gasp. "Kitten?" Dragging my lips along the stubble of his jaw, I heard his lips part. "What's this?"

My hands found his waist, chest, shoulders.

"Kitten wants to play," I finally told him.

"Mmmm," he moaned deeply from his chest. His fingertips flexed. I could hear them lengthen.

As my lips ghosted over his, he opened his blue eyes. I took his bottom lip in my teeth, grazing it with my fangs.

His arms slipped around me, pulling me flush to him. As soon as his fingers dug into my flesh, I sank my fangs into the plump inside of his bottom lip. Tage froze, his eyes widening.

I gently eased the tips out, and blood trickled in their absence. Tage's eyes narrowed and he grasped his lip. "What the hell was that?"

"Call me kitten again, and I'll bite it off."

I left him there with his back against the wall. Before he could regale me with more factoids about why I didn't need air, I was gone. The door slamming behind me was the last thing I heard. I was a blur.

EIGHTEEN

PORSCHIA

THE SCENT OF DESPERATION WAS AN EASY ONE TO FOLLOW. I TRACKED DARA across yards and down the street as she weaved past the pavilion and made her way toward Saul's house. I picked up the pace. Was he in trouble? Would she hurt him? I could smell Tage behind me, tracking me like I was the danger. I wouldn't be a danger to Saul, but Dara was another story. She was poking her fangs in where they didn't belong, and I'd be happy to remove them for her. I'd love to rip them out of her nasty mouth.

Rounding the corner of Saul's neighbor's yellow house, I paused, hearing his voice and hers. My heart beat frantically. It was happy to hear him, angry that he was speaking with her, and angry with her for being there with him – all at the same time.

I listened.

"No, it's fine. Thanks for checking on us, though," he said.

"I'm just worried that she'll hurt you. They can't keep her in the cage anymore, and she almost tore the house down. I know she loves you, but if she can't control herself around you, she could kill you, Saul."

"She will control herself." Even I didn't believe his tone. "Porschia will be fine. She just needs...time and guidance."

"Tage is helping her. We're all trying, but she's manic. Tage is better with her than anyone else. He and Porschia have become very close." I bristled at her words. Tage and I weren't that close. Sure, we were closer than the others, but that was because the alternate options weren't very appealing. "Frenzy can drive some new vampires insane, and even ones who didn't have those issues in their human lives can be affected. But Porschia is in a different situation. Her mother has mental problems, and you never know… Porschia may have already been headed down the same road. Emotional control is a difficult thing to master, but as a night-walker in Frenzy, they're multiplied by thousands, even tens of thousands. Everything seems important, urgent, and all-consuming. The emotions, especially for a female, can be overwhelming." Was she telling the truth? Could Mother's mental state really have been passed down to me?

"I know," Saul answered, shifting on his feet. "But she'll be fine. And thanks for checking, but I have to go now." Saul looked at his upstairs window, where a curtain fluttered closed.

"Just yell if you need anything," she cooed, taking hold of his arm.

Saul shrugged her off and nodded as he turned and walked back to his porch. Dara quickly sped back toward the vamp side of town. I watched Saul as he stood there, running a hand through his hair and letting out a tense breath.

Without realizing I'd moved, I was in front of him. He gasped. "Porschia?"

"Hi." My palms began to sweat, but seeing him at his home felt almost normal.

"Hey…what are you doing here?" His voice was soft, pleading.

"I wanted to make sure you were okay. I followed Dara's scent."

His eyes widened. "She just left."

"I know."

"There's nothing between us, if that's what you're worried about. I don't know why she keeps coming around, but there's nothing on my end."

I nodded. "There is on hers, though."

"Doesn't matter. My heart belongs to a different night-walker."

I laughed and sobbed at the same time, and then the tears began to fall. "I was just playing around," he said softly as he pulled me close. "I'm sorry."

"It's not the joke; it's just that reality sucks sometimes."

He smiled and looked down at me. "It does."

A shuffling noise from inside the house startled both of us and we parted quickly. He hooked his thumb toward the door. "My mom."

"I'd love to meet her sometime." I wiped my tears away and gave him a smile.

His eyes dipped to focus on my fangs. "Yeah, maybe some other time. She's...busy."

I swallowed the thick lump of his lie. I was fooling myself if I thought he would want me to meet his mother or father now. This wouldn't work. "Look – no matter what, I'll keep an eye on you."

He shook his head. "You don't have to leave Blackwater."

I smiled. "Can't stay. The Elders want me out of here, and it's not wise to be seen."

"They can't force you out, either. No one can tell you what to do or where to live." He took a deep breath and then said, "Hey – thanks for taking the risk of coming to check on me."

My voice broke. "You're worth it. You're worth everything."

"I lov—"

But before he could finish the lie I ran away, leaving nothing but a whirlwind of dried leaves in my wake.

Near the pavilion, I almost ran over Ford. He was carrying a basket and barely kept the goods inside it. "I'm so sorry!" I said, steadying him.

"Nah. I got it," he said, settling everything back in his basket. "I was just heading to Mrs. Dillinger's house."

My heart swelled again before breaking.

"She'd love to see you, Porschia. She knows."

I nodded. "I think everyone knows now."

Ford's eyes narrowed. "They can't make you leave, and I think you should come and visit her for a few minutes. Unless you don't have time, or haven't eaten lately."

"I'm not hungry, and if we hurry, I can go. I'll run ahead and meet you there." Leaving him behind me, I pushed faster and harder. Trying to hide behind the porch posts, I waited for Ford.

"I hear you out there, Porschia," a scratchy voice called from within the house. "Come on in."

Easing the door open, I rushed upstairs. "How'd you know it was me?"

"No one else could run across the planks that fast."

"It's good to see you." She sat in her chair, needle in one hand and fabric in the other. I smiled until her eyes found my mouth.

"Don't hide yourself, child. I know what you've been through. It's a shame, but not the end of the world. In fact, for you it's just the beginning of a new adventure."

"It's hardly an adventure," I said, plopping onto the bed across from her.

"It will be exactly what you make it out to be. If you believe it to be the worst thing that ever happened to you, I'm sure it will be. But if you decide that it is something exciting and wonderful.... I'm sure it will be that instead."

"It isn't that simple."

"Saul still loves you. You just have to learn to accept yourself, calm and control yourself. You look amazing, even with fangs." Her head tilted to the side. "Hmm. I thought they'd be longer."

"Me too."

Ford yelled a greeting from downstairs. "Sit it on the kitchen counter, please," Maggie replied. He promised to be back in later with fresh water. He was giving me time with her.

"I'm glad you came today. I was just finishing this for you." She held the dark dress up, looking over the last stitches she'd made. "Remember starting this?"

"Is this the dress I worked on?"

"The very one. It's made to fit you, if you still choose to wear it." Maggie looked over my jeans. "Although I have to admit that those clothes look more comfortable."

"They aren't comfortable at all, but they are functional. I had to borrow them."

Maggie nodded, looking me over. "Roman? He's the leader, is he not?"

I sank into the mattress. "He is."

"You be careful with that one. I don't trust him." I didn't either, but didn't want to tell her that. She'd only worry. Plus, I had Dara to worry about when it came to Saul, and now had to figure out how Julian fit into the equation.

"I will. I should probably go. I don't want to cause trouble."

Maggie waved me off. "The Elders? I'm not worried about them."

"I am."

She nodded thoughtfully, folding the dress into a neat rectangle. "Have you voiced your concern to Roman?"

"He's been busy."

"Hmm. Maybe talk to another night-walker – the girl, perhaps?"

A low growl erupted from my chest and she chuckled. "And then again, perhaps not. What about the other boy; the one with the dark hair and light eyes?"

"Tage?"

"Yes. Can you speak with Tage about your concerns?"

"I can, I just don't know that there is anything he can do about it regardless of what happens."

Maggie's wrinkled hand covered mine. "You never know what will happen until it does, but talking things over is never a wrong decision."

She handed me the dress. "Thank you, Maggie."

"Please come back when you're able. I miss you, Porschia."

"I miss you, too."

I allowed myself a quick hug and then ran away. I needed to talk with Tage.

NINETEEN

PORSCHIA

I heard boisterous laughter coming from upstairs at Roman's. Dara, Roman, and Julian were obviously in good spirits, although Tage wasn't here yet. He was tailing me when I followed Dara to Saul's. He didn't follow me to Maggie's, but he didn't come back here, either.

I pulled the door open, only to be met with silence before Julian's voice echoed from above. "Come in, Porschia. We were just discussing you." Of course they were. I hid my dress in a small cabinet just inside the door, knowing that Dara would tear it just to spite me. I trudged up the steps and into the kitchen, where the three sat around the long, wooden kitchen table. "And what have you decided?" I asked haughtily. Would they make me leave?

Julian smiled. "You're lucky. It seems that Roman is siding with me instead of Dara regarding your immediate future."

I smiled slightly. "Dara sees me as a threat."

Julian nodded while Roman simply stared at me. "And are you?"

I shrugged. "Depends on her actions."

Roman chuckled. "At least she's honest."

Dara calmly stood up and brushed the strands of her golden hair back before launching her chair across the room. The wood splintered into a thousand pieces, denting the sheet rock. She grabbed a shard and was in front of me in a second, the sharp end of a chair leg raking against the hollow of my throat with every breath I took.

"Dara, don't," Roman warned.

Julian's hand stopped him. "Let them handle this. They need to get it out of their systems."

Dara's eye flicked to Julian for a split second, and while her attention was focused on him, I grabbed her wrist and twisted. A loud crack filled the room, followed by Dara's gasp. "You bitch!" She released the piece of wood and it clattered to the floor.

"Don't ever threaten me again, Dara. I may be a new vampire, but I'm strong. Do *not* underestimate me. Sniff around Saul again, and a broken wrist will be the least of your worries. This is the last time I'm warning you." I stared at her until she looked away toward Roman, her eyes beseeching him for help. She wouldn't find it. His lips were compressed in a tight line. He never said a word, never defended his lover.

I let go of her wrist and she rushed from the room, glancing back at Roman once, followed by the sound of her bedroom door slamming and more curses. Turning back to Roman and Julian, I found them smirking and Tage standing in the doorway looking bored. "So are you kicking me out?" I asked, uncertain.

"Not yet," Roman answered honestly. "Though you still need to work on your self-control."

"That *was* controlled. You have no idea what I wanted to do to her."

I RAN AND GOT MY DRESS BEFORE HEADING TO MY ROOM TO HIDE IT. MY legs were leaden and every part of my body ached. Tage followed me up the stairs. *Always following me.* "Why did you track me to Saul's?"

"To keep you out of trouble." He shouldered past me and stood in the middle of my room.

Well come on in, Tage. I closed the door behind us and leaned back against the wood. "Why do you care if I get in trouble or not?"

He stared at me, waiting for me to understand something I clearly wasn't comprehending. "What? Why do you even care? Is it the blood bond thing?" But he just kept staring. *Great.* Suddenly, I was so tired and wanted nothing more than to get to the bed. I stood up too fast and my vision began to fill with tiny black dots. I fell into the room, my head striking the wooden floor boards.

"What the hell?" Tage said, lifting my head with his hands.

My teeth chattered together. "So tired and c-cold."

He shook his head. "This doesn't make any sense."

I smiled, unable to hold my head up. "Maybe I'm dying."

Warm arms lifted me into a cool, soft cloud. They wrapped around me and pulled warmth overtop me, and I floated away.

WHEN I WOKE, TAGE WAS SITTING IN A CHAIR BESIDE MY BED, HIS FACE LIT from the warm light of a flickering candle as it dripped onto the bedside table. "What time is it?"

"After eight."

Trying to shake the cobwebs from my mind, I took a deep breath. "Wasn't the rotation tonight?"

He nodded.

I sat up, heart thundering. "The hunt?"

Tage nodded again.

"Who's going with them?"

"Roman, Dara, and Julian."

Julian? I threw the covers off and ran to my boots, shoving my sock-covered feet inside. Somehow the fact that Julian was in the woods with my loved ones and neighbors didn't sit well with me.

"You aren't in any shape to go into the forest, Porsch."

"The hell I'm not," I said, lacing one boot tight, then the other. I looked around the room for my jacket. My fingers were icicles.

"Roman said you are to stay here." Tage raised his voice as he stood, maneuvering between me and the door.

I narrowed my eyes at him. "Who's going to stop me?"

"Me."

"You can't." It was as simple as that.

"I can and I will."

I huffed out a laugh, shrugging on my coat, but when I tried to step around him, he blocked me with his body. "Move, Tage."

"No."

"Move."

He crossed his arms and planted his feet firmly. "Nope." The popping of the *p* was what enraged me.

"FUCKING MOVE!" I tried to shove him, but he wasn't budging.

"You're weak. *One* of us hasn't fed," he said in a sing-song voice.

I squeezed my eyes closed. "Is that why I feel this way?"

"Probably," he said on a shrug.

"Then I should go find something to eat. I need meat. And you know the best place to find meat?" I grinned, watching him silently curse me.

"Fine, but we can't let Roman know you're there. We go, we hunt, and we come home."

"Right." I nodded happily.

"We go. We hunt..."

"We come back here. It's not home, though – but we come back here – to this house." I nodded, watching him grab his leather jacket.

"Why isn't it home?"

"Home is where the heart is, and my heart isn't here."

Tage stared at me for a second. "It wasn't at your other house either."

"No it wasn't, but I'm hoping to make one someday."

"A home?"

"Yes. I want to make a home—somewhere I want to spend time at and can't wait to go to at the end of the day. A house is just made up of brick and wood, but a home is filled with the people you love the most."

Tage snorted. "You think the human boy can give you a home?"

The smile fell from my face, along with my mood. "No I don't. But if I give up hope, there isn't much left to live for."

"You begged Roman for death. What changed?"

"I have no idea." My mood swings were either going to get me killed or have me killing someone. I wasn't sure which would happen first, but I prayed neither would.

As we walked out the door, Tage paused. "There's something you should know."

"Why do I get the feeling that I'm about to get very pissed off?"

"Because you are, but don't shoot the messenger."

"Fine. What is it?"

He blew out a harsh breath. "Ford's hunting."

I.

SAW.

RED.

And then I ran.

"Porschia!" *Good luck keeping up, messenger.*

TWENTY

FORD

AT THE PAVILION, I WAS GLAD PORSCHIA DIDN'T SHOW. SHE'D FREAK OUT IF she knew I was in the rotation, and no one wanted that. Least of all me. I'd heard about Mary falling and hurting her ankle. The doc wasn't sure if it was broken or just badly sprained, but she wasn't in any shape to walk. Someone had to help, and I knew there wouldn't be any volunteers from the Colony.

Father was trying to rein Mother in when I left the house. If anyone was in real Frenzy it was her, not Porschia. Porschia was more human than Mother in a lot of ways. At least she could be brought back to normal, whereas Mother might never see normal again. And if she didn't, neither would Father.

I made up my mind. Once Porschia learned to control herself, I was going to see if I could live with her. There were plenty of houses on the vamp side of town that sat vacant. Hell, I could just go ahead and stay in one now. No one would have to know.

My neck didn't throb. The bite from Julian didn't hurt at all. "You're shaking like a leaf, boy. Calm down. I will not hurt you," he said with a chuckle. But something in the darkness of his eyes was cold. Something said he might enjoy hurting me. That was why I attached myself to Saul like a dog tick.

"You okay?" he asked as we climbed the steep hill.

Panting, I answered, "Yeah." I was pretty fit, but this climbing up and down wasn't something I was used to doing every day...or ever.

We both had crossbows, although it took me eight tries to pull the arrow back. My boot held the stirrup steady, but damn if I wasn't too weak to pull the string into place. "Keep trying," Saul said, his eyes telling me that I had to do it myself, but that he would stay until it was done. He was great. Saul never treated me like a boy, but like an equal.

A shrill scream split the night air and stilled my feet. *Infected.* Saul put his finger over his lips and we listened for it again. For several minutes, the only sounds in the forest were the shallow breaths we took, visibly puffing into the cold night air. My muscles were rigid.

Saul shook his head. "It wasn't close. Maybe they were moving away."

"Maybe," I said, nodding my head quickly.

"We need to keep going."

"Where's the night-walker?"

From the ridge above us came our answer. "Here." Dara, the blonde with an attitude, had been put in charge of the pair of us. Victor and Tim were on the other side of the forest with Julian, and Roman was on his own somewhere.

Dara turned her back to us, looking beyond for signs of the Infected. "What's her problem?" I whispered to Saul.

"She hates Porschia."

"Yep," Dara agreed. "And since you are her brother, it's hate by association."

"Awesome," I deadpanned.

Another scream, this time much closer. Dara jumped from the ridge and positioned herself in front of us. "Run! Back toward the others. I'll be right behind you."

Saul and I locked eyes right before the Infected screamed again. I turned to look at Dara and found my sister staring at me. "Mercedes?"

Her hair hung in thin strings, every part of her body hollow. She was a shell of what she was only weeks ago. I lowered my crossbow, the arrow pointing at the ground. "What happened to you?" My voice wobbled.

Mercedes opened her mouth, but only scratchy noises came from her throat. A tear carved a narrow track down her sallow skin. She reached a hand toward me.

Saul's grasp on my shoulder pulled me back. "Don't. She's dangerous."

"She's my sister." I shrugged Saul's hand off of me. Mercedes gave a faulty smile, clutching her side.

"Your sisters are losers. Both of them," Dara said, looking back toward me. When we looked back toward Mercedes, she was already limping away. Dara sprang forward.

"NO! She's leaving. She didn't hurt anyone!"

I scuttled to the edge of the hill and saw Dara closing in on Mercedes, fast as lightning. Raising my crossbow, I fired before I could consider the consequences. The arrow missed them both but did its job. It got Dara's attention. She slid to a stop. "What was *that*?"

"An arrow, dumbass! Leave my sister alone. She wouldn't hurt me!"

Wheeling around on me, Dara was in my face in a second. "She wouldn't hurt you, huh? What about how she bit Porschia, or how she tricked your mom into feeding her? Do you think that all she wanted was lamb? She was luring her over so she could feed from her, Ford. It's what they do. And if I hadn't been here, she would have hurt you. She would have bitten you, infected you, and ultimately killed you. You stupid little boy," she spat.

"She showed no hostility!"

"She *embodies* hostility!" Dara screamed. "Holy shit, you people are thick. We've probably scared all of the game away."

Dara paced while Saul and I watched the forest for more Infected. Mercedes didn't try to harm us, but Dara was right. She did manipulate Mother into helping her, and she did bite Porschia.

I twisted the silver ring on my finger, filled with Julian's blood.

A whoosh of air blew past us, followed by a hiss. Porschia, her hair swirling in the wake she made, positioned herself between us and Dara. "Why is my brother in the woods?" I didn't recognize her voice. It was low and lethal, like she was now.

She and Dara slowly danced in a circle.

Saul cupped his hands to his mouth. "Roman!"

"You shut your mouth!" Dara warned him with a flick of her eyes, and then bared her fangs at Porschia. "You think you can tell everyone in this Colony what to do. 'Roman do this.' 'Tage do this.' 'Saul do that.' 'Ford can't go on the hunt.' But you know what? You are *nothing*. You were nothing as a human; an unwanted piece of trash so easily discarded by those who should have loved you. You were unlovable then, but you are unwanted now. If Roman wants Ford on the hunt or in the rotation, that's *his* choice. You don't get a say."

Porschia's eyes darkened. Her fangs may have been tiny, but they were sharp as needles and almost glowed in the bright moonlight. "You think you have any influence on Roman just because you spread your legs for him? He could have any woman he wanted in this settlement. He doesn't need you. You are expendable, Dara. Have you ever considered that? And I may get no say in anything, but I will protect my brother—in and outside of the Colony."

"You're too late! Your rotting sister just strolled up here to have a sisterly chat."

"You lie." Porschia looked back to me for confirmation, then to Saul, and that was all the lapse Dara needed. Dara tackled Porschia to the ground, the entire earth shaking from the impact. Cackling, Dara held Porschia to the ground with one hand on her neck.

"Only one of us has fed tonight. I think it's time to end this," Dara bent down low with her fangs out.

I stepped forward, crossbow poised, and only then realized there was no arrow. The string was loose and it would take me ten minutes to get another one ready to fire, but I could damn sure knock the bitch off my sister with it.

Or I could have, if Saul didn't beat me to it. Wham!

Dara never saw him. *I* didn't even see him. His bow landed hard across Dara's cheek and she released her hand from around Porschia's throat and fell over, rolling to a crouching position. She growled at Saul.

"Dara," Roman said, appearing at the top of the hill above us. "Stand down."

"Fuck you, Roman," she spat.

His eyes focused on her until she let out a whimper and fell to the forest floor, her blonde hair splayed over the damp leaves. "I said," Roman enunciated as he stepped down the hill, "Stand down."

Tears of blood fell from her eyes, staining the hair beyond her temples. "Let me up. I won't hurt her."

"You won't hurt anyone unless I say so. Now go home."

Dara nodded and sniffled, sitting up and then slowly standing, her entire body shaking. The look she gave Porschia and Saul was murderous, but in the end, she left us there in the darkness.

Roman clapped his hands once. "Now that we've frightened away every living thing within twenty miles, we'll need to go in further. Tage, find Porschia something to eat. If she's guarding the hunt, she needs strength."

I turned to find Tage standing behind me. Holy shit, these people were stealthy. "Got it," he answered, sprinting into the forest.

Roman stayed with us until Tage returned with a gutted, skinned squirrel. "Din-din, love." He held the animal out for Porschia, who wasted no time stripping its flesh from the bone and devouring every ounce.

I could see her transformation with each bite. Her skin brightened and her hair became glossy, shining almost black in the moonlight. Her movements were no longer sloppy, but purposeful and sharp.

When nothing remained of her meal but a scattering of tiny bones at her feet, she smiled. "Thank you, Tage."

He gave a deep, courtly bow. If Saul had been a vampire, he would have growled. I could feel him tense at the familiarity of the exchange. "We should get going," Saul interrupted. "We have a Colony to feed."

Porschia nodded, turning her head from side to side. "This way," she said, pointing to the North. "Deer."

"Can she really do that?" I asked Saul as we ran after her.

"She just did," was all he could answer. And she was right. It took us a lot of running up hill, sliding and flopping downhill and trudging back up, sneaking around trees and rocks, but with screaming muscles and pounding hearts, we found them near a stream. They sipped on the water as Saul easily pulled back the string to my bow, engaging the arrow. His was ready. "On three," he whispered. "One....two.......three."

We fired, both striking a deer. The animals tumbled to the ground as the younger deer sprang away into the cover of darkness. His buck had at least twenty points on the rack, and my doe was healthy and strong. Tage gave a slow clap as Porschia gave me a quick hug. "I'll get it for you, Ford."

The pair of night-walkers easily lifted the deer as if they were kittens and carried them up to us. "We should get them across the river," Tage said. "I'll take the deer; you lead the humans back."

Porschia smiled. "Sounds great."

TWENTY-ONE

PORSCHIA

"How's your throat?" Ford asked as we strolled up the hill, back to the Colony. The hard work was done. I didn't hear anything else nearby, and two deer was a phenomenal result. The Elders would be pleased, as would the colonists.

"My throat?"

"Yeah, where Dara had you..."

I waved him off. "She didn't hurt me." She did at the time, but food was healing to a night-walker. It was regenerative.

Saul grumbled something about Dara, making me happy. I hated that they seemed close somehow.

Ford grinned. "At least Tage is gone and we can talk to you for a while."

"Tage?"

"Yeah, he's always around you now." Ford shrugged, repositioning the crossbow on his shoulder.

"I can carry that."

"Nah. I've got it."

A shrill scream from far away caught our attention. "It's close to the city," I commented. "Sometimes things echo out here."

"Your hearing is amazing, Porschia! And you're so fast and strong." Ford chattered on, like me being a vampire was the best thing in the world. "I bet you could take her now that you've eaten."

Ugh. My brother and Saul almost saw me get beaten down by vampire Barbie. And that was exactly what Dara looked like: beautiful danger in a pretty package. Mercedes and Dara actually looked a little alike. They were both blonde, curvy, and had attitude. Mercedes had never turned that weapon on me until recently, though. When we were children, Mercedes found a box with a Barbie doll in it. I teased her and said that someone thought she was so beautiful, they must have made a plastic miniature of her and shoved her into their closet for safe-keeping. Mother found the doll and took it away.

"She wouldn't have killed me," I told the guys, puffing up my shoulders. "I was just a little slow. I hadn't fed yet."

Saul's eyes watched me. "Why squirrel? Why meat?"

"I don't know. I... Roman doesn't even understand it. But I can hold it down, whereas any time I take blood it comes back up. I get so sick on the thing that I crave. It makes absolutely no sense."

"You crave blood?" he asked.

My mouth began to water. "I do."

"All the time?"

"Not *all* the time," I replied, curling my fingers into balls. "Can we talk about something else?"

"Your eyes." His voice was a whisper.

"Yeah. They're weird too. Everything about me is wrong."

Saul shook his head. "Just different. Not wrong, Porsch."

I wanted to kiss him, throw my arms around his neck and rake my fingers through his hair. I wanted to run my palms up the ridges of his stomach and make him moan. Make him mine.

But Ford was here. "How did you get involved in the rotation?"

"Simple. I volunteered."

"Why?"

"Mary sprained her ankle. It may be broken, so the Elders asked for more volunteers. And, because I wanted to."

"Ford, that's crazy. You see what happened to Mercedes and me."

He nodded. "I want to help the Colony, and I'm of no help to anyone sitting at home listening to Mother."

"She's still...?"

"Crazy?" he supplied. "Yep. All day and all night. She only sleeps for short spurts before starting all over again. Fun times."

Ford stumbled over a tree root. "You need a break?" I asked, sensing his exhaustion.

"Yeah." He plopped down on a flat stone that jutted out from the hillside and Saul leaned his back against the trunk of a large oak.

"I'm doing better," I told them, watching their eyes lock onto me. "Actually, I plan to ask Roman for my own place."

"You sure you're doing that well?" Saul asked.

"I think so. But I also think that putting some distance between me and Dara would be wise. Most of the time, I just want to tear her throat out."

"There's nothing between us, Porsch," Saul said, pinching the bridge of his nose.

"I know, just like there's nothing between me and Tage." And there really wasn't…most of the time. When I could control my emotions and contain myself, there was absolutely nothing there.

"His feelings are not brotherly, Porschia," Saul spat.

"And Dara's aren't sisterly. So where does that leave us?"

"Right here," he swept his hand across the air. "We're right here. We just need to remember that. It's you and me, not us and them."

"I know." *Except when I lose myself.*

And with perfectly screwed-up timing, Tage stopped in front of us. "Where have you been?" he asked.

"Enjoying the brisk night air," I replied, trying to smile. It wasn't Tage and Dara driving a wedge between Saul and me; it was the change. He was human. He was prey. He was *my* prey.

Tage's shrewd eyes narrowed on mine. "Let's get out of the forest."

He left out the part about 'before you do something stupid or that you will regret for the rest of your life'. "Yeah."

Ford and Tage chatted amiably as they walked in front of me and Saul. I reached for Saul's hand, only to have him squeeze it once and let go.

I built another layer of stone around my heart. When the two ahead were at a considerable distance, Saul asked, "Are you really thinking about moving out?"

"Yes."

"Could I move in with you?"

My brows shot up. "What?"

"If you're really doing so well, maybe we could give this a shot?"

I wasn't doing that well. Okay, I wasn't doing well at all, but he didn't need to know that, and if he was with me all the time, he would see. I didn't want him to see me for what I was.

"Maybe so," I offered with a smile that I prayed looked genuine.

"You still crave me?"

My feet stilled. "What?"

"My blood," he replied, a challenge in his eyes.

"Of course. I crave you in every way, Saul." His hand tightened around mine.

"Then take some."

"What?" My heart skipped a beat before it began to gallop.

He nodded. "I want you to take a sip and then stop."

I shook my head. "No, I don't want blood."

"You do."

"It makes me sick."

He nodded slowly. "But you need some. Not much, just a drink."

Tage and Ford stopped a few hundred feet ahead along the trail on which we were walking. With the slightest shake of his head, Tage urged me not to drink from Saul. But I wanted it so badly. I wanted him. I wanted to taste him, to taste normal. Just for a moment.

"Maybe just one drink?"

His fingers sank into my hips as he jerked me toward him, my chest hitting his, my heart matching the rhythm of his own. "Can you do it?"

"Mmmmm," I could smell what I wanted. Coppery, tangy, sweet.

He leaned his head toward his shoulder, offering himself to me. One slow, agonizing drag of my tongue over his pulsating flesh was all it took. "NO!" Tage yelled as I sank my fangs into Saul's neck.

One sip and then...ecstasy.

My God.

Mmmm.

Right after I eased my fangs out of his throat and swiped the wounds with my tongue, my shoulder was yanked backward and I stumbled to the ground, only to look up at the angriest Tage I'd ever seen. "You fed from him!" It was an accusation.

"Only a sip, and why does it matter?" *What the hell?*

Ford jogged over and helped me up while Tage pointed at Saul meaningfully. "You'll kill him!"

I shook my head. Ford steadied me. "I didn't hurt him. I only took one drink and then I stopped myself. I *stopped*."

Tage looked from me to Saul, who was shaking with rage. Saul bumped Tage's chest with his own and said, "Don't you ever touch her again!"

"You tempted her. You wanted her to fail!" Tage was wrong. No – Saul wouldn't have tried to test me like that.

A shadow of guilt fell across Saul's face. "No," I argued. "He wanted to help me, to show me I could do it. Right, Saul?"

Tage laughed bitterly. "He was baiting you. He wanted to see you fail so you wouldn't leave Roman."

"That's not true," I said, looking at Ford, but his eyes were focused intently on Tage. Ford's Adam's apple bobbed up and down.

"Did you want me to hurt you?" I asked Saul.

His eyes flicked to mine. "No, but you aren't ready, Porschia. You need Roman's help, and—"

"I do *not* need Roman's help. As you can see, I am able to feed from a person without killing them."

Tage smiled and put his hands on his hips. "Wait, did the Elders put you up to this? Did they ask you to test her?"

I gasped when Saul's eyes widened guiltily. "They did?"

Saul shook his head and reached around Tage toward me. "Don't touch me!" I hissed angrily. "Who put you up to this?"

"My father," he replied. "But listen, it's not like you think."

It was exactly like I thought. "Why?"

"He thinks you'll kill me. He said you couldn't control yourself, but you did! You did – don't you get it? This proves them all wrong!" Saul pleaded, but Tage resolutely stayed between us. Smart thing, too, because I didn't know whether to tear his head off or cry. His father might have told him that, but he was the one who decided to test me. He fell headlong into his Dad's trap and if I'd have lost it, the Elders would have...they would kill me.

The water of the river roared ahead of us; the only sound other than betrayal. I wasn't even sure if he realized what he'd done. "Go home, Saul."

"What?"

"Go report back to Daddy about how I'm doing. I'm done with you."

"No, Porsch, I love you. I was just proving them wrong! I was on *your* side. Not theirs."

"You were testing me. You were just a tool for them – for the Elders – whether you realize it or not."

He reached for me. "Porschia?"

The divide between the two of us was no longer a fissure, it was a chasm.

"Just go," I said, turning my back to Saul. "You need to get some rest too, Ford."

Ford pressed his lips together and gave me a quick hug. "I'll see you tomorrow," he whispered before walking toward the river. I listened as his boots slid across the fallen tree, but refused to watch as Saul walked away.

Tage's arm stretched out, warm around me. "I'm sorry."

"No you aren't," I sniffled, swiping the tears away.

"Anything that makes you hurt, makes me hurt. And it isn't the damn bond, Porschia. I care about you," he said, frustrated, pulling me tightly against him.

"He didn't know what he was doing," I told him, excusing Saul. I really didn't think he realized that his father's challenge was a test. What kind of person did that? He knew Saul was stubborn, he knew he would test the boundary, and he sent him anyway. His own father knew he was putting himself in grave danger, and he sent him anyway. Anger poured from my eyes. It seemed all I did lately was scream or cry!

What kind of father planted seeds of doubt into their son's mind and led them into a potentially deadly situation? The kind of father who was like my mother, I realized. Only, Saul's dad wasn't insane in the same way Mother was. But maybe being sane and indifferent was more frightening.

Did the Elders make him do it? All the times I saw them together as father and son, they seemed to have a healthy and loving relationship, something I craved and coveted.

"They're across," Tage said. Roman and Julian, Tim and Victor, Saul and Ford. They spoke across the swirling torrent.

I turned to Tage. "Thank yo—" I started to say, but Tage's mouth met mine. Lips, soft but strong, explored and melted. One hand wound into my hair and pulled me closer as his other hand found the small of my back and reeled me in. It felt good, and for once since becoming a monster, I felt like a girl; a normal girl. So I let him kiss me. I moved my lips in turn and took out all of my frustration and confusion on his.

His body wasn't as tall and lean as Saul's. He didn't feel the same. Though it physically felt amazing, my heart wasn't in it. My heart knew it wasn't right. And it wasn't fair for me to treat Tage that way. Despite the rocky start we'd gotten off to, he was my friend. I eased my body from his, pinching my lower lip and stepping away.

"That was wrong," I whispered.

"That...was the only right thing that's happened to you in days. You just don't realize it yet."

And with those words, Tage stalked away, leaving me alone in the forest. For a long moment, I considered leaving the Colony on my own. It would be so hard, yet so easy. Behind me, I'd leave Mother, Father, and Ford. Maybe someone would find a way to help Mother, and then maybe Father and Ford would find happiness. I would be leaving Maggie, the most positive influence in my life. Saul could be free to find a wife who would make him happy, who wouldn't want to drink him dry. He could have children and keep them safely tucked inside the Colony; tiny versions of him running around, digging in the mud and making mischief. One day they might even help him in the carpentry shop.

I would leave the other night-walkers. I would leave Mercedes and the Infected behind.

But out there were legions of other Infected, other night-walkers to contend with. And I wouldn't be free because my heart was here, even if it was torn to shreds. It was here, with these people and this place. Somehow, Blackwater itself had become my home.

I climbed a tree and draped myself between two branches.

TWENTY-TWO

SAUL

STALKING TOWARD THE HOUSE, I LEFT THE NIGHT-WALKERS AND THE OTHER volunteers behind. Ford yelled after me, "It's almost sun-up!" but I ignored him and kept walking. He was the one who needed to stay with Porschia.

Just hours ago, I'd spoken to Dad and Mom over dinner.

"Has Porschia left the Colony, son?" Dad asked.

"No. They can't make her leave."

"She's dangerous," he said, stabbing at his potatoes. Mom um-hmm'd in agreement. "The Elders banished her. I know that both you and her family have told her about their decision, so why does she not respect it?"

I sat my fork down. "She does, but this is her home. She doesn't want to leave. And where would she go?"

Mother took a drink from her glass of water. "That really isn't our concern. Until she's out of Frenzy, the Elders have made it clear that she's a threat to everyone. She isn't welcome here."

"And what about when she's no longer in Frenzy? You'll just welcome her back with open arms, huh?" I wiped my mouth with my napkin. Staring at Dad across the lit candle, I waited as he pinched his lips tight. I knew I wasn't going to like his answer.

Father's fork and knife clattered across his plate. "Perhaps she won't be. Perhaps *none* of them will be welcome before long."

"Are you kidding me right now? Do you really think you can make any of them leave if they don't want to?"

He scooted his chair back. "I think we can, and I think we will. Look, Porschia is dangerous. She couldn't take one gulp from you right now without losing control and trying to kill you. That's what the Elders say, and I believe them. They've always been right about these things. They've never led us astray. And I'll be damned if I'm going to stop listening to them because my teenage son naively thinks he's in love with a night-walker."

"Honey—" Mom tried to interrupt.

"No!" He slammed his fist on the table, knocking his glass over and spilling water over the wood. He wagged his finger at me. "Think you know it all, huh? Well, I'll tell you what. You get her to drink from you. If she can restrain herself and only take one sip, I'll tell the Elders she's safe, that she's gotten herself under control and they should lift the banishment. But if she hurts you, if she can't stop herself, then *you* go to them and tell them that she's still in Frenzy and refuses to leave."

"No!" Mom yelled. "I will *not* have you put my only son in danger just because you're trying to prove a point!"

"I accept," I replied calmly. "She won't hurt me."

Dad scoffed. "She will. One way or another, son. But maybe this will open your eyes. Just do it when another night-walker is around so they can pull her off before she drains you."

Memories of her drinking from me in the basement flooded my mind. She couldn't control herself then. Could she now?

She sure as hell could, and I couldn't wait to tell Dad. He could come to the Elders with me and watch this shit. Crossing through yards, I jogged to my house, ran up the steps, and pushed through the door. "Dad!"

Mom tackled me, her arms around my neck. "Please tell me you didn't do it," she said breathlessly. The familiar scent of wood smoke clung to her hair.

I broke free of her hold. "I did, and she took one sip before stopping herself. Where's Dad?"

"Here," he said from the top of the staircase.

"I'm going to talk to the Elders. Porschia just passed your little test and I'm going to tell them she's fine. And you're coming with me."

He nodded slowly, his eyes raking over the pair of fang marks on either side of my neck, one from Porschia and the other from the evening rotation the night before, if they were even still apparent. They healed quickly. "Fair enough, son."

THE ELDERS WERE WAITING FOR US AT TOWN HALL. "YOU PLAYED ME," I accused my father as we walked down the aisle toward the three fickle old bastards who had no clue what the night-walkers were all about. Even the papers they had the old women print were wrong. They had no clue.

Dad stayed quiet beside me, hands in his jacket pocket. We had matching gaits and builds, but that was where our similarities ended, it seemed. I'd grown up wanting to be just like him. Now, I wanted exactly the opposite.

"Why don't they fix the damn roof?"

"Watch your mouth, Saul," Dad warned.

"Well, why?"

"I don't know. It's always looked like this."

We had carpenters and could build homes if we needed to, so surely we could patch some roofing holes and rebuild the bell tower. I looked up through the skeletal hole to see snow flurries leaking into the building, fluttering down to the pews.

"You've spoken with Porschia, Saul?" Elder Beckett's voice echoed through the dark, empty room. The candles in the windows had melted into wax puddles overnight. Had they been waiting here all night?

I looked at my Dad, a man who was fast becoming a stranger. "I'm sure you've heard of our little bet, but Dad's sorry to tell you that he lost. Porschia Grant is in control of herself. I told her to take one drink and that's all she did. She's been eating meat – uncooked meat – and somehow it's calming her cravings. I don't know why or how. The other night-walkers don't even understand it, but it's working. She's fine, and you have no right to banish her."

Elder Brown scoffed, nudging Elder Yankee and whispering something to him. "Pardon?" I asked challengingly. "Care to share your thoughts?"

Elder Brown huffed. "I said, we have the right to banish whomever we see fit."

"Well, perhaps you should take the time to actually see and speak to Porschia yourself before ordering her to leave in front of the entire Colony. She wasn't turned; she was bitten by an Infected. She used the only defense she had, one that was given to her for that very purpose, and did what anyone in her position would have done. She didn't ask for this. Now, I'm asking only that you stand beside your citizen in her time of need, not turn your back on her. What you do now will show everyone what kind of men you truly are. Do you have a backbone or not?"

Dad tensed beside me with my closing remarks and I searched the faces of the Elders seated before me. What did I see? Not just wrinkled versions of their younger selves; I saw reluctance and stubbornness. They didn't want to rescind their decree, but they were backed into a corner. I just hoped this worked.

"We'll see her. Go find her and tell her to come here right away."

"What?"

"You think we'd just reverse the banishment without seeing her, questioning her? Testing her? I don't think so." Elder Yankee stood up and wrapped his robe tightly around his paunchy middle.

Testing her? What exactly were they planning?

Dad led me out of Town Hall, anger fueling his footsteps. Once we were out of the building, he turned to me. "Did you think that speaking to them like that would make them sympathetic to Porschia's plight?"

"Did you think that tricking me into testing her willpower was the best way to figure out if she's really okay?"

"She may have been okay earlier, during the night, but the daytime is different. And believe it or not, son, I didn't have much of a choice. I'd heard they were about to assemble a team to capture her. There are ways to end a vampire. Not many, but there are a couple. The Elders aren't above murdering her if they think she poses a threat. They aren't above anything."

"I've got to find her," I said, walking away.

"Saul?"

"What?" I turned around to face him.

"Be safe."

I turned and jogged toward the pavilion. It was almost sunrise. They either rose early or...they'd been waiting all night. I remembered Dad's eyes, and Mom's. Heavy, dark bags draped beneath them.

TWENTY-THREE

PORSCHIA

JULIAN CLIMBED THE TREE AND SETTLED ACROSS FROM ME. HIS BROAD FORM looked ridiculous on the tiny tree limbs. I waited for them to break so I could laugh when his big butt hit the ground. "What do you want?"

"Nothing, poppet." He stared out at the forest below us. Squirrels and mice scurried in the almost-frozen leaves, quickly jumping across them.

"What's a poppet?"

"A doll."

"I'm no doll, Julian."

"I know that."

We sat in silence for at least ten minutes. "Why are you here?"

"I don't know. Something about you draws me to you. Have you seen a moth fly to a flame?" I nodded, watching him stare at me. "It's the same thing. It's very much like the human boy you and Dara seem to pine for."

I tensed at the very mention of her name and Julian chuckled, his body shaking the entire tree. Gripping the bark, I stared at him until he stopped trying to kill us.

"What is it about him? Hmm? His scent, perhaps?"

Scent. I snorted. "I loved Saul long before I became a night-walker."

"Long before? Or a week before?"

Okay, so not that long before, but definitely pre-vampire. "What does it matter? I gave him my heart before I turned. Dara only wants him to get at me."

Julian's lips pursed together. "Are you sure about that? Could she not have the same emotional connection to Saul that you claim to have?"

"She barely knows him."

"Perhaps she knows him better than you think."

I swallowed, drawing his eyes to my throat. Maybe they did know each other better than I realized. He'd been in the rotation before. Were they paired up then? "I envy you," he said.

"Why would you possibly envy me?"

"You're in Frenzy," he said, as though it was the simplest explanation in the world.

Frenzy. I hated it. The loss of control. The mood swings. The hunger. The cravings. The feelings that couldn't be real, but felt exactly that. Anguish. Torment. The knowledge that everything you once had was gone and you would live an eternity without the things you wanted the most: love, a family, true friends.

"It's the worst curse imaginable," I told him, my chin quivering.

"No, poppet. You're looking at it all wrong. You can have anything you want. You're stronger than you'll ever be as long as you feed. Nothing can stop you now."

"I can't have Saul."

"Saul isn't a thing. He's a human, and humans can change into vampires. Change him."

Curling my lip in disgust, I jumped from the limb, landing on my feet. Looking up at his smirking face, I told him, "That isn't love. You don't turn someone you love into something you hate, just so you can keep them with you."

"What if he asks you to turn him? Have you ever thought about it? Dara would do it. In a heartbeat, she would turn him, bond to him. And he would feel a pull to her for an eternity. Food for thought, poppet."

"I'm not your doll. Why does everyone give me weird nicknames?" I stomped off toward the river. The sun was rising, painting the sky with strokes of pale pink and blue. Clouds to the west meant snow and they were thick, butting up against the eastern sky. Later today, a storm would hit. Was anyone ready? Tiny flakes swirled around me as I crossed the trunk and stepped foot into the Colony.

Saul met me as I crossed the boundary into Blackwater, his long stride infused with determination. "What's wrong?" I asked, stopping just shy of the trunk's roots.

"The Elders want to talk to you this morning," he replied resolutely.

What? "Why?" Would they officially tell me to leave?

"My Dad, or the Elders – it doesn't even matter. But I told them this morning. I told them you can control yourself; that you just took one drink and let me go."

A game. It was all a big game to them. "My life is not a figure on a board, Saul. You had no right to test me! Your dad had no right."

I tried to push past him, but he caught my elbow. "I know this isn't a game to us." He pointed toward town. "But *they* are the ones playing it!"

I shook my head. "Then you are their pawn. You know what? I really can't deal with this right now."

"What can't you deal with?"

"You!"

His head ticked back as if I'd backhanded him. "You can't deal with *me*?" The muscle in his jaw worked back and forth angrily. "But you can deal with him, huh?" His eyes fixated on something over my shoulder. Looking back, a fuming-mad Tage was standing a few feet behind me.

This dance was exasperating, around and around and around, never going anywhere but in circles. "He's helping me, and if you can't deal with that, I don't know what else to say. I cannot get through this alone. And now, because you played in to their plan, because you took a bet from your own father, I'm going to be fed to the wolves!"

Saul pulled me forward, the heat from his hand searing my skin through the long sleeves of my shirt. "Just remember that I never doubted you for a second. I knew you could handle it."

Pulling my arm away, I blew out a tense breath, my upper lip ballooning outward. "Tage, I need to feed before I go."

"Why do you think I'm here?" he rasped, holding out the flesh of a small bird. "It's not much, but it'll help take the edge off."

"Thank you." I held my hand out and accepted his offering. "We should start walking." Tage nodded and fell into step beside me, shoving his hands into the pockets of his leather jacket.

"I'm coming, too," Saul said, following us.

Tage stopped. "What if she doesn't want you?"

Uh oh. Boy drama. I maneuvered between the men, sandwiching myself between Tage's and Saul's chests. "She wants me," Saul answered defiantly.

"There," I inserted.

Saul's eyes flicked to me. "What?"

"She wants me *there.* That's what you meant to say, right?"

"Not what I mean, Porsch. He said, 'What if she doesn't want you?' and I'm informing him that you still do. You still want me, don't you? One little fight can't ruin what we have, right?"

"No, it can't ruin it. And of course I still do."

A low growl rumbled against my chest from Tage. "She wants *me,* too," Tage inserted.

"Because you claimed her? It's not real!"

Tage shoved Saul's chest from around me. "It is! It *is* real!"

"Enough," a voice boomed. From the side, Roman approached and Tage stepped back, immediately relaxing. Roman was compelling him, but I knew he wasn't working his magic on me. Every muscle in my body was tense, some shaking, and I backed away from Saul nervously to chew the bones of the tiny bird I'd forgotten about during the argument.

"We'll all go." Roman motioned for us to follow him and we did.

"Roman, I need to go to my room and get something really fast."

"What do you need?" he asked.

I glanced at the three men surrounding me. "Something that will make me seem more like...me."

"Go. Come straight back here."

I ran away, tossing the bones of the bird behind me in my wake.

TWENTY-FOUR

PORSCHIA

Climbing the steps of Town Hall was like climbing the steps of the gallows. I felt the noose being tucked tighter around my neck with each step. Behind Roman and flanked by Saul and Tage, I walked down the center aisle, the dingy, once-red carpet underfoot. The Elders were waiting, their black robes making them look regal and frightening. I'd grown up knowing that their word was the law. Now, I hoped that Roman had some sort of say in this matter.

Saul's dad was nowhere to be seen. *Thank God.* To think that at one point I wanted Saul to introduce me to his family.

The Elders rose from their seats around the rectangular table behind the podium and raked their eyes over me. Hopefully I made the right decision in running home to change. The dress that I started and Maggie had finished for me fit perfectly. The sleeves fell at my wrists, and there was plenty of material at the waist to keep the empire seam from riding up the way Mercedes' dresses had. I even plaited my hair and pinned it back the way I'd always worn it. I looked like me, before I became a night-walker. Just a week ago. Time flew. Had any vampire in the history of the curse beaten Frenzy in only one week? *No. They hadn't. And I am nothing special. I'm a mess. I can't do this.* My palms began to dampen. *I'm losing it. I'm going to snap, like a twig bent just a millimeter too much.*

Elder Beckett spoke first. "We see you are well, Porschia. Please step forward." *I'm not well. I feel like I'm going to explode. I feel like I'm dying. I feel like I can't die. I feel like...* Tage nudged my side at the same time Saul did.

Roman eased to the side but stayed close, letting me step up beside him. His eyes never wavered from the trio of men in front of us. It was like a battle of wills. Old versus young. A traditional school of thought being challenged as much men's stubborn pride.

Elder Beckett began, "You were forced into this situation, so please know that we understand there was no other choice for you. Infected or night-walker? That is no choice at all. Given the situation, you did what any prudent person would have done. You used the ring given to you and chose life over death. In changing though, you've put the Colony's citizens at risk. Do you understand our concern?"

"I do," my voice cracked. I cleared my throat and tried again. "I do."

"Blackwater has only seen a night-walker in Frenzy once, and she killed several before we were able to contain her. I'm sure you recall the details, Roman," Elder Yankee said snidely.

I glanced over at Roman, watching his upper lip shake with barely restrained fury.

"It hasn't been long at all since the transformation, yet I'm told that you can restrain yourself," Elder Brown said. "That when tempted, you will not falter. You won't harm a human being. Is this true?"

Roman spoke for me. "She is in control of herself."

"Completely?" Elder Brown questioned.

"She is," Roman answered.

Elder Yankee smiled unpleasantly. "Then you wouldn't mind a small test."

I swallowed. Roman's hand moved to the small of my back, his thumb drawing tiny calming circles into the fabric of my dress. It was working. I felt okay. A little nervous, but okay.

Elder Yankee motioned to the back of the room. I turned to see who he was signaling to, but only saw someone's back disappear into the foyer. The doors slammed open and morning light spilled into the back of the room, mingling with that from the unfortunate hole in the ceiling. "Bring her in."

Tage and Saul gasped. Thrashing legs were the first things I could see, and then her voice cut through the small space. "Let go of me!"

"Mother?"

Roman's hand clamped down on my hip, holding me in place. She kicked and clawed, even though her hands were bound together with twine in front of her skirts. "Don't look at me, Porschia! This is all your fault!" She spat at the two men bringing her in. I recognized them but didn't know them well.

If the Elders thought Mother could upset me, they were wrong. I'd been down this road with her for far too long. Her words, her hatred? They couldn't hurt me anymore. She fought the two men all the way down the hall.

Her dress was drenched, but it wasn't raining. The dark fabric looked soggy and darker than normal. "What's all over her?"

"Blood," Roman answered, still holding my hip.

I smelled it. The scent hit me when she kicked her leg up again, as the wind stirred behind her and the odor wafted toward me.

The blood wasn't hers. I could smell hers, and the smell of it was rancid. "Whose blood is that?"

Elder Beckett cleared his throat. "Your mother escaped your father's care last night. She was caught inside someone's house, attacking them." The scent swirled through the air again. Familiar. Something was familiar about the scent. "She was attempting to stab them in the neck with a small, sharp metal instrument."

"What?" I gasped. "*You* did this? You killed Meg and those people? They were our neighbors! How could you? Meg was my friend—my only friend." Tears leaked from my eyes, the crimson splashing to the red carpet beneath my feet. Roman's fingers dug into me, but couldn't hold. "Why would you do that?"

Father burst through the door, followed by a worn-out, wild-eyed Ford. "Because she's insane," Father expelled in one breath, leaning a hand against the door facing, exhausted.

"You *are* insane," I said to her. "You are absolutely out of your mind. I should have let you cross the river and let Mercedes have you. I shouldn't have saved you."

"You didn't save me! I *wanted* to go to her. I love her. Mercedes needs me! She *needs* me. I feed her. I still do. Or at least I did before you locked me away!" She turned to Father, kicking at him like a feral animal. "You locked me away and now Mercedes is starving. I hear her at night. I can hear her now. She needs me."

I stepped forward, giving Roman a nod. I had this. "You'll be put to death or banished. Banishment is the same as death, Mother. Mercedes can certainly help speed things long, but you've done this to yourself. You've brought it all on yourself. Why the wounds in the neck? Why would you try to frame the night-walkers?"

She blew a crinkled strand of gray-streaked hair from her face. "They were supposed to protect her, but they let her get bitten. Where were they? Hmmm? Was it you?" She craned her neck to look at Roman. "Or you?" she asked Tage. "Who was with her? Why won't you tell us, you cowards? Own up to what you've done! You *let* her get bitten. You *wanted* her get Infected. You were supposed to protect her. The treaty...the treaty said so. You said the treaty was there to protect our citizens," she muttered, pointing her two index fingers at the Elders. "You all lied. YOU LIED!" she screamed, thrashing and biting at the two men who tried to keep her still. "You still lie! All of the colonists should know that nothing you say is truth."

Father's eyes were emotionless, dead. Ford's glistened. We were losing Mother today, one way or another.

The Elders looked to me. "You've handled this well."

"She can't hurt me anymore," I replied simply. I wouldn't let her.

"You'll escort her across the river, then?" Elder Yankee asked.

"I will."

"Alone," Elder Beckett added. "You'll go alone. Just you and her."

"Fine." The men backed away from Mother and she stilled, her eyes tracking my movements. "You got what you wanted, Mother. Let's go."

A mad laugh burst from her lips along with spittle. "Let's go for a walk, Porschia. It'll be like when you were little."

That was a lie. She never took us for walks, never did anything with us at all. Not like the other parents who made time for their children, who played games and sang songs with them. Mother led the way out of Town Hall, stopping to spit on my father and then walking out the door. Ford handed him a handkerchief and father blotted her hatred away. Only the soaked remnant remained.

The further away from Roman I got, the more agitated with her I became. "They want you to lose too, you know," Mother taunted. I ignored her. "They want you to attack me. They want to be rid of both of us. You kill me, and you'll be banished. It's all a trap."

"I won't attack you."

She smiled, wrinkles bursting from the outside of her eyes. "You will."

"You aren't worth it."

She cackled. "Not worth it. Not worth it. Not worth it." Mother repeated those three words with each step we took toward the river. Citizens watched us pass, peering curiously from porches or pulled-back curtains. The remaining Grant women. The crazy Grant women.

TWENTY-FIVE

PORSCHIA

ANGER CRACKLED THROUGH MY VEINS LIKE LIGHTNING. SHE'D KILLED people. She killed my best friend. "Why Meg?"

Not worth it. Not worth it. Not worth... Those two words stopped her chanting. "Because you loved her."

"Why would you destroy everything I love?"

"Because I *hate* you and didn't want you to have anything left to love. You took everything away from me."

I looked at her, took her in. Her torn clothes stank like she'd worn them for three weeks. They were drenched in someone else's blood. "I didn't take anything from you! You had me. You had Ford. Even with Mercedes gone, you still had us and Father. You just didn't see it!"

Mother smiled. "There she is. There's my little girl."

Narrowing her eyes at me, Mother took off running toward the river. I kept pace easily. "You're just making this easier on me," I taunted.

The snow began to pour around us in thick, wet plops. It clung to the grass, and within minutes, a thin, white blanket stretched over the earth. Mother pulled at the ropes binding her hands in front of her. She wasn't paying attention and tripped over an exposed tree root, falling onto her chest and scraping her face over a sandy, rocky patch of earth. Dark, gritty soil stuck to her cheek and forehead. I helped her up, but she screeched, “Mercedes!”

Urging her toward the sound of the river, I knew she’d never make it across the trunk with bound hands. I’d have to carry her.

Should I carry her across? She’ll die, probably before Mercedes can even find her to Infect her. She won’t last the day.

“You killed Meg to hurt me. You killed the others to hurt the vampires. You hurt everyone you touch, Mother.” With a simple tug, the knotted rope came undone, pooling at her feet. “You can’t hurt anyone anymore.”

“Mercedes!” she yelled, cupping her hands to amplify her voice.

Pathetic. I laughed. “You think she’ll actually come?”

“She will. Mercedes needs me.”

“Mercedes wants to eat you! Wake up!”

She shook her head vehemently, strands of now-damp hair clinging to her face. Her body began to tremble. “Jesus, where is your coat?” I asked impatiently.

“Don’t need it,” she said, lifting her chin.

I shrugged mine off. “Here.” I held it out to her and she eyeballed the black woolen fabric. “It belonged to Mercedes. You didn’t even want me to have it.”

“You’ve already contaminated it with your filth,” she muttered, eyes darting between the river bank and the coat. I rolled my eyes.

“Vampirism isn’t contagious, Mother. But what Mercedes has? What you’re hollering so loudly for? That will kill you....slowly.”

She snatched the coat from my outstretched hand and shrugged it on, quickly buttoning it. It was slightly too small across the chest and waist, but it would keep her warm until she… became Infected.

I helped her toward the river bank. “Step on the roots, nice and slow.”

“I know how to get down there! I’ve lived here a lot longer than you’ve even been alive!” I took a deep breath, trying to suck in some of the fresh snow. It was better than the poison that spewed from her mouth. But the thing about poison? You didn’t know you’d consumed too much until it was too late. A little bit and you got sick. A little bit too much and you died.

“You know, I asked for you to be the one to take me here. I told them you were a danger, a weapon for the night-walkers to unleash on the community. I told them you would snap. Like a twig,” she enunciated hatefully.

“Sorry to disappoint you, Mother.”

She cackled, slapping her leg as if she'd heard the funniest joke in the world. She eased down the bank and stood at the side. The snow coated her shoulders and crowned our heads. "You never asked me," she said with a smile.

"Asked you what? Why you asked them to let me escort you to your death?"

She stopped laughing suddenly, growing serious, and her dark eyes met mine. "You never asked me whose blood soaks my dress."

My upper lip twitched. "Whose blood soaks your dress?" My teeth wouldn't come apart, even though I spoke.

"Margaret Dillinger's."

I crouched, baring my fangs, feeling the heat flood my veins and the wrath flood every cell in my body. She smiled, a slow, steady thing full of malice, and watched me become the thing that I hated. She took pleasure in my pain. Mother truly hated me, and I hated her. I would end her. I would fucking end her. She wanted to die? Fine. Let her die by my hands.

I launched myself at her, arms outstretched, and her eyes widened when she realized that the monster she asked for was about to get her. *There she is.*

TWENTY-SIX

Tage

The swishing of Porschia's skirt filled my ears, along with the sound of my pulse. Swoosh. Swoosh. Swoosh. She was aggravated, overwhelmed, stressed, and trying to hold herself together. She had been since Saul approached her with the news that the Elders had requested her presence. Roman was able to steady her, but she was still in Frenzy and that meant she was hanging on by a thread even when she felt in control. It meant she could break, fast and hard.

She did better than I had. I killed more people than I could count before someone showed me how to ease the cravings and control the impulses. Sometimes, like now, it was still hard.

I turned to follow her.

"No one leaves this room," said Elder Beckett. He was rubbing me wrong.

Roman flexed his biceps. He was probably thinking the same thing I was: maybe we should just eat the old men and get on with it.

"How will we know if Porschia passes your little test?"

"We have someone watching," he retorted haughtily. Well, hadn't they just thought of everything?

Saul's eyes met mine grimly, and even though I hated the asshole, we both had a mutual respect for one another. Neither one of us would intentionally hurt Porschia, nor want to see her hurt. If she escorted her mother across the river, her mother would die and Porschia would hurt. If she snapped and drained her mother, Porschia would hurt and she would break. She wouldn't come back from that.

Roman's voice filled the space. "You have a human watching?"

"Of course," replied Elder Brown.

Roman smiled and nudged me. "Good thing we have balance, then. I have a night-walker watching as well."

Dara? my eyes asked. He shook his head. Julian was there.

TWENTY-SEVEN

PORSCHIA

I WAS JERKED BACKWARDS BY MY HAIR SO HARD, TEARS SPRANG TO MY EYES. That stung. The fist still held me tightly, but the arm it was attached to eased me around so I could see who stopped me. Mother's loud laughter hit my ear and I lunged toward her again. However, Julian wouldn't let me go.

"Julian."

"Poppet."

"Let. Me. *Go*."

He smiled, his plump lips stretching wide. "Can't do that."

"Who says?"

"Roman."

"Roman? Is he your keeper?"

His mocha eyes hardened. "For now, but," he pulled my head to him until my ear was beside his lips, "I'm working on that."

"I'm sure he'd be interested in that piece of information."

"He'll never hear it from you," he growled.

A high-pitched squeal came from across the river. Mercedes stood there, a guy about her age standing next to her. His skin was gray, and I remembered seeing him in the city with her. Mother clapped her hands excitedly and waded into the icy water. Her skirts billowed and then plastered to her thighs.

"Mother, don't! The current's too swift."

The dark liquid swirled around her knees, thighs, hips. It clung to her skirts and relentlessly shoved against her body. We all saw the moment she lost her footing. Mercedes raised her hand out toward her and started to walk down the river bank on the forest side, as mother fought the white-capped water churning around her.

"Let me go!" I pleaded.

"You'll save her?"

"Yes!" And just like that, Julian released his grip on my pinned back hair. I ran down the side of the bank, pushing off rocks until I was right across from her. As she went under, I jumped in. Tage said that temperature didn't affect a night-walker, but Tage was wrong. Or was it Roman? The water cut into my skin like a thousand knife-points, a thousand splinters of wood fired into my flesh at once.

I gasped, grasping at the water, "Mother?"

Her head popped up and she gulped in another breath before the water pulled her under again. It was just enough to tell me where she was and would be. I found her upper arm and jerked hard. Her shoulder dislocated with a pop that reverberated through my hand, but I planted my feet and pulled hard toward the forest side. I helped her up onto a rock. Her dress and jacket wouldn't keep her warm now. Mercedes descended toward us slowly.

Teeth chattering, I watched her jerky movements. "You look like death, Mercedes," I taunted.

She opened her mouth with a scowl and pointed at her side. "Oh! How's the wound? Healing up nicely? Oh! I forgot. You don't heal. You rot!"

Mercedes made a guttural sound that sounded like a snarl.

"You wanted Mother? Well here she is – take care of her. And stay away from the colonists. If I see you on a hunt again, in the forest or in the city, it won't be a flesh wound you have to worry about. I'll tear you apart, limb from limb."

She opened her mouth and reached for Mother, who was scuttling up the bank toward her favorite daughter.

Good riddance.

Julian helped pull me up the muddy bank, my forearm locked with his. His eyes raked over me and I became aware that even though I was freezing to death, my wet dress was plastered to my body, leaving nothing to the imagination.

"Why...?" he asked.

"W-w-why w-w-what?"

"You're cold."

"I think I have hypothermia."

"Your lips are blue."

Mother screamed as Mercedes pulled her dislocated arm. "AAAAAH! I want to go back!" she shrieked, using her feet to kick the ground and push herself away from Mercedes and her boyfriend. Mercedes just smiled at her with a mouth full of receding gums, exposing more of the roots of her teeth. She'd lost more hair in the short time since I last saw her, too. She tugged on Mother again, but Mother was strong. She pulled Mercedes hard and my sister stumbled.

Enraged, Mercedes bared her teeth and made an awful howling noise. I covered my ears. She sounded like she was right beside me. Looking up, I saw her boyfriend approach the pair; patchy scalp with skin peeling away from the top. He had little hair left now, and hollow cheeks and eyes. The only thing he did look was sharp, intelligent. He approached Mother, who began to sob. "I want to go back. Come and get me, Porschia, please. I'm so sorry, Porschia, please."

My fingers bent toward her, but I didn't move my feet. The Elders would kill her rather than let her return to the Colony. I couldn't swallow the ball of emotion building in my throat. "Mother, run! Get up and run," I screamed, a hot tear warming a path down my frozen cheek. "Get. Up! You're faster than they are."

But it was too late. Mercedes locked eyes with the Infected guy and he ticked his head up. As she bit Mother on the collarbone, her screams startled the crows and pigeons from their perches above us. A flurry of snow and dark feathers rained down over the swirling water. "Porschia!" Mother screamed, trying to get away. Other Infected appeared on the ridge above them; young and old, male and female. Tattered. Torn. Rotting and dangerous.

"You have to go with them now." My voice cracked.

Julian locked his meaty palm around my upper arm. "Time to go check in."

"Porschia! Porschia, save me! Only you can help me now! I'm sorry, Porschia!" She screamed for what seemed like hours, and I just wanted to sit on the ground that now held a few inches of snow. I wanted to rock back and forth, cover my ears, and squeeze my eyes shut. I wanted to stop crying. I wanted it to stop. Stop. Stop. Stop.

"STOP!"

But Julian wouldn't stop. He pulled me forward. So instead of stopping, I put one foot in front of the other. That was the only way to meet adversity. Keep walking. Keep talking. Keep hearing. *I'll take care of her, Porschia. But this isn't over between us.* "Mercedes?" We were near the first row of houses when I heard her. It *was* her! It was her voice; the voice she had before she had no voice. It was Mercedes. It was my sister. It was her voice. In my head. Her voice was in my head.

And then more voices. So many voices, I couldn't discern male from female. Tattered from torn. Dying from dead. Living from...Was I dying?

Was I dead?

No. My feet kept walking. Julian's hand hurt. My arm hurt. My head hurt. It was splitting. I was cold. I was ice. I was nothing. I was. Nothing.

My teeth. They crashed together. Again. Again. Again.

I couldn't feel my feet. They moved me. I couldn't feel my toes. I couldn't feel anything but numb.

Numb.

The pain was not numb.

My body was numb.

I was dying.

I was living.

This wasn't living.

"Julian?"

"Hmm?" Even he was affected by the entire scene, it seemed.

"Are you g-g-going to k-kill Roman?"

"No."

He seemed honest. "I'm going to usurp him. Someone else will kill him."

"Who?"

He smiled. "You, poppet."

My feet stopped. Were they frozen to the ground?

"W-why would I?"

"Because he was on watch the night your sister became Infected. He let it happen." My breath came in quick bursts of steam and I couldn't breathe. I hurt. My chest hurt. I couldn't get air. Tage said I didn't need air, but he lied. I needed it. I needed it badly. I clutched my chest, above my heart. My palm rubbed the skin. It hurt. I couldn't reach the pain.

"Why would he do that?" My tears burned.

"He set this entire ball of shite in motion just so he could have you for himself."

"Why not just turn me?"

"Politics, poppet. Politics are a bitch. That's why I plan to eradicate them. We are at the top of the food chain, or we will be again soon. There is no need for silly games and manipulation."

From a few yards away came Roman's voice. "Julian? What happened? You need to go speak with the Elders."

Hate. Anger. Wrath. Hate. Ice. Fire. Freeze. Burn.

My feet melted. They carried me toward him.

TWENTY-EIGHT

TAGE

I RAN AFTER ROMAN RIGHT AFTER HE TOLD THE ELDERS IT HAD BEEN LONG enough. I felt the moment she was in trouble. A tightness formed in my chest and I couldn't breathe. She was in danger, and was cold and scared. It wasn't hunger; she was frightened, torn between anger and disgust. The old men looked to me. "Roman's right. Porschia's in trouble."

The Elders motioned for us to go, but followed as quickly as their bowed legs would carry them across the Colony. Roman and I sped ahead, with Saul and Ford running after us. A flock of birds took flight from the forest and flew away together, passing overhead.

I could hear Miranda Grant's screams, followed by Porschia's erratic rambling. "I'm dead. I'm dying. I'm dead. This isn't living. Mercedes is dead. Mother is dead."

"Roman," I said softly. He stopped and turned to look at me, holding his hand up. I stopped. "Help her."

Julian was hauling Porschia back into the Colony, his hand tight around her arm. My fists flexed at the same time my fangs raked against my bottom lip. He was either helping her or looking for a fight, but I couldn't tell which was true. Observing Porschia's state was no help. She was freaking out.

Smiling, Julian whispered something to Porschia. I didn't hear it because Saul nudged me at the same time and asked, "What the hell is going on?" He panted, his heart beat was high.

"I don't know, but it's not good."

Saul swallowed the truth, taking in Porschia. Her hair and dress were dripping with what I'd bet was ice-cold river water. Did Julian throw her in? Did her mother? "Roman," I warned. He needed to help her. Her teeth chattered violently and her breaths were short and labored. Ice clung to strands of her hair. She was freezing. Literally.

"Where's her coat?" Ford whispered, stepping up beside me.

"I don't know." She'd left Town Hall with it on.

"Mother. She gave it to Mother," he swore, shaking his head.

"Of course she did." If Mercedes wasn't already killing that woman, I would have crossed the river and done it myself.

Roman's eyes met mine. He looked to Porschia and back to me. I nodded and eased forward. "Stay here," I warned Ford and Saul. "Something's wrong."

"Get my sister away from him," Ford whispered, eyes clamped on Julian.

"Not a problem." Roman and I stepped carefully toward them. Porschia was clutching her chest, rubbing it with the heel of her palm. We stopped in front of them. By that point the Elders had caught up and stood with Saul and Ford, taking in the scene.

"Did you do it?" Porschia asked, focused on Roman.

"What are you asking, Porschia?"

"Did you kill my sister? Did you let those sick bastards eat her, infect and kill her? Did you do it on purpose?"

Faster than I've ever seen him move, Roman struck Porschia in the neck and she went down, eyes rolled back in her head. His eyes dared us to defy him. "She's delirious. The cold water is affecting her. Julian, run to my house. Start a fire and start warming water. Tell Dara to help."

Roman scooped Porschia up like a flimsy doll and sped away with her. Julian was already gone. Saul caught up to me. "What the hell was that?"

I shook my head in disgust. "Roman's manipulation."

The Elders were flabbergasted. I turned to them. "Miranda's across the river, and Porschia didn't bite her. She controlled herself."

"You call that 'control', young man?" Elder Beckett asked, his finger pointing to the spot in the grass where Porschia and Roman had just confronted one another.

"I do." Stepping toward him, I asked, "Have you ever seen a vampire in Frenzy?"

The old man swallowed. "Not personally."

"They wouldn't have left any of you alive. You would all be dead if she was a threat to you. All of you. Don't you get it? Somehow, she's handling this better than any vamp I've ever seen turn. Give her a break!"

Mr. Grant hugged Ford, who was trying not to cry. His chin quivered and he looked to the sky. "It'll be okay, son."

"The hell it will!" Ford yelled. "It will *not* be okay!" He pulled away from his father and stomped away in the direction of his house. His sisters were gone. His mother was gone. His father stood stone-faced beside me.

Mr. Grant and I stood together as a united front across from the Elders, who were quiet, hands folded across their middles. Finally, a boy ran across the field.

"Garrett, what did you see?" Elder Yankee asked. The kid couldn't have been more than nine. They put him in danger and didn't care. These men just kept giving me reasons to end them. It would be so easy.

Warmth flooded my skin, reminding me of Porschia and how frigid she looked.

"Porschia and Mrs. Grant argued and then Porschia let her go. She loosened the rope around Mrs. Grant's hands, and then Mrs. Grant tried to wade across the river. Mercedes was there and she tried to get to her," Garrett said, not pausing to take a breath in between his words. "Porschia warned Mrs. Grant that the water was too strong, and that's when a big night-walker showed up. I'd never seen him before today. When Mrs. Grant slipped on a rock and went under the water, Porschia went in after her. She saved her! Then her mom went across to Mercedes and she got bitten and started yelling for Porschia to save her, but it was too late. Porschia cried. She was really cold, too."

"That's it?"

"Mm-hmm." The light-haired boy nodded vehemently. "That's all."

"Porschia did not bite or attack her mother?"

"No, she never even tried," he said, sounding disappointed.

"Thank you, son. Go on home and get warm," Elder Yankee instructed. The kid ran toward the houses on the human section of town.

Mr. Grant looked at the Elders. "I trust that this little experiment is the last time you'll test my daughter. If I hear of you bothering her again, I'll ask Roman to end you myself."

Their harrumphs and gasps echoed through the air and snow fell in thick clumps. "Go home," I told Mr. Grant. "Ford needs you."

"Take care of my daughter, Tage."

"I will," I replied solemnly.

Saul butted into the conversation, adding, "So will I."

"Guess you're coming over uninvited," I replied dryly.

"I think you should stop trying to pick a fight with me and go check on Porschia before Roman kills her," Saul added.

"Or Julian. I can't figure him out."

"Or Dara," Saul added.

"Shit." I sped away, knowing that the pest that was Saul would be close behind, and not knowing what lay ahead of me. Roman had some fucking explaining to do, and if what she said was right – if he failed to protect Porschia's sister in the woods to propel some sick plan of his into action – I would let Porschia tear him apart. Hell, I'd help.

TWENTY-NINE

PORSCHIA

I blinked awake. Logs crackled and shifted in the fireplace, burning hot and fast. Kettles and pots of water were sitting overtop the flames and in the embers themselves. Steam rose from each, swirling together with the wood smoke. My body hurt. I was stiff. The place where my arm met my shoulder was incredibly tender. *Roman.* He hit me.

I tried to speak. "Shhh," Roman said, crouching beside me. I was on one of his couches, pulled close to the fire. When I opened my mouth again, he shook his head. "Don't speak." I couldn't. I couldn't get words to come out of my mouth at all. No matter how hard I tried to ask him, I couldn't. I was weak. I needed to feed.

"The frigid water weakened you. Now, my compulsion finally works on you the way it should. I just have to keep you in this state somehow."

I swallowed, trying to lift my head from the pillow beneath it. "Still," he commanded. That was all it took and I was paralyzed. He warm fingers ghosted over my hair. "You look so much like her. Sometimes, now that you're in Frenzy, you act like her, too."

Who?

"I loved her, you know. She was human like you when we met during the rotation, a few decades ago. But she was interested in me—not just because I was forbidden fruit, but genuinely interested in me. We fell in love and she asked me to change her. She wanted to be with me forever. I'd been alone for thousands of years, but I'd finally found someone. So I did it."

He took a deep breath before continuing, "She went into Frenzy. We expected it, of course, but we never expected that she'd be so feral. She began tearing through people, just for sport. She'd hunt them instead of game. She didn't want to control herself. The out of control feeling gave her the high she craved."

"The Elders, not the current ones of course, banished her. She laughed and told them to go to hell. She held her chin up, walked out of the Colony, and never looked back. She didn't really love me, after all."

Roman stared into the fire. It was daylight, but so overcast it looked dark. Through the slight slice in the curtains, I could see the snow falling hard and fast. How long was I out? "So I tracked her," he said, standing up to his full height. "And I drained her myself."

He earned the Colony's trust by killing the only girl he'd allowed himself to love. Roman smiled when he saw I'd worked it out.

"You don't look exactly like her or anything; it's more of a feeling I get when you're talking, sometimes in the way you tuck the loose strands of hair behind your head or the way you kissed Saul—like he was the oxygen you needed to breathe. She looked at me like that."

If it had ended so tragically, why would he want that again? Why ask for more pain? And why me? I wasn't her. Obviously, he saw that I felt for Saul the way the girl had felt about him at one time.

"I decided that if love wasn't real, I'd make myself happy at any cost. You made me feel things for the first time since her, so I wanted you with me. I decided to turn you, but I needed you to come to me. I didn't turn Mercedes, but didn't stop the Infected from attacking her, either. I knew you'd join the rotation. I didn't know she'd attack you and force you to use the ring."

He bent down again, toying with the circle of metal on my finger. Why I still wore it, I wasn't sure. "I wanted to turn you, to claim you and have the bond that you and Tage have. But he beat me to it.

"Julian wants to either force me out or end me. Either serves his purpose, and using you to do it was a stroke of genius on his part. Kill two birds with one stone." Sighing, he looked toward the door, dark hair falling to his lashes. "Speak of the devil."

The door banged against the wall behind it, ricocheting with a shake. "Porschia?" Tage called.

Roman stood up. "Now you understand it all, except for Tage's role, right? *Speak*," he ordered.

"Tage's role?"

Roman smiled and walked away. "Water's ready," he told Tage in passing.

Tage rushed to my side with long strides. "Hey," he said softly. "Let's get you to the bath."

I nodded. I'd learn what his role was later. Right now, I needed to thaw and gain my strength. I couldn't do anything in the shape I was in. Weak. Manipulated.

Hooking one arm under my knees and the other around my back, Tage lifted me and carried me up the stairs to the bath. I clung onto his neck, shaking against his warm chest, trying to absorb it. The tub had a few inches of cold water in it. "I'll be right back."

It took five trips, but soon the tub was full of warm, steamy water. Tage sat the metal pot aside and said, "This is going to hurt."

Pain. This life was pain. Mother's screams echoed through my mind. My chest hurt again.

"Help me?" My fingers were numb. I couldn't unbutton the dress. Maggie. "Maggie? How is Maggie?" My eyes went wide. I'd forgotten. How could I forget? It was like my brain could only handle one emotion at a time.

"She's fine. Resting. Your mother stabbed her in the neck, but someone was able to heal her."

"Who?"

He shook his head. "I'm not sure, but she'll be fine. Let's get you warmed up and maybe you can go see her later."

"O-k-kay."

"Porschia!" Saul yelled from downstairs.

"Up here!" I squeaked. Tage's eyes stayed locked on mine as he backed away, his hands falling from their outstretched position. He was going to help me undress.

Saul's footsteps were heavy as he rushed down the hallway. "Hey," he breathed out. "What's this?"

"I need to get w-warm," I told him. "Help me get warm."

His brows furrowed. "Yeah, of course. Excuse us." He stepped around

Tage and waited while he left. I flinched at the sound of his bedroom door slamming closed. "You okay?" Saul asked.

"N-n-no."

"Let me help you." Saul stepped forward, shrugging off his coat. His fingers unbuttoned each button that led from my neck down my chest, stopping high at my waist. "The fabric is freezing."

I just stared at him blankly. "Let's get it off. Raise your arms, okay?"

This wasn't how I pictured him seeing me for the first time. A warm tear fell from my eye as I slowly raised my arms, wincing from the pain. "It's okay," he whispered, pulling the stiff skirt up and dragging it over my head. It wasn't okay, but Roman was right. I was too weak to argue.

More tears.

Gently as a feather, Saul eased my panties down and dragged my cotton bra overhead. He never looked away from my eyes as he pulled me to him. "The warm water is going to burn your skin. You're like an ice cube."

"I know," I said, chin quivering from sadness instead of cold.

"I've got you, Porschia. I love you."

I loved him, too. I just couldn't say the words. The knot in my throat gagged me. He picked me up and eased my feet into the water, then sank me in to my calves, then to my thighs. A burst of steam came from my flesh as it met heat. "Tage?" Saul asked softly.

In an instant Tage was at the door. "What?"

"We need more hot water. She's cooling it down too quickly."

"On it." He grabbed the pots he'd emptied and ran down the steps and outside. He would refill them at the well in the back yard of the house next door. If only he could make water boil.

"Just put me in. All the way," I pleaded. Saul's muscles strained as he held my weight above the surface of the water.

"No," he said calmly.

"Do it!"

"NO!"

Saul eased me in the water to my waist, and then when my buttocks settled against the cold porcelain beneath me, he let me go. Searching the linen closet, he brought out a navy blue towel. "Drape this over you," he said, holding it out for me.

Another tear. Saul crouched down. "Porschia, I don't want him to see you. Please cover up."

"Who, Tage?"

He nodded. "I thought *you* didn't want to see me," I answered shakily.

"No," he said, his face contorted in pain. "No, baby. I love you, and believe me when I say I want to explore every inch of you, but not like this. And I don't want him to see you. I have my own reasons for that."

I swallowed and draped the towel over my body. The water soaked into it, plastering the terry cloth to me. When Tage returned, the midnight cover was the first thing he noticed. But he didn't say anything. Not to me. Not to Saul. He simply motioned for me to tuck my feet in and poured in steaming water. We repeated this process until the water stopped cooling as soon as it was poured in, until my body slowly thawed, until the water was tinged crimson by my tears.

"Can you check on Maggie for me? Tell her I'll come as soon as I can?" I begged Saul.

He nodded. "Anything for you."

"Tell her I'm sorry."

"None of this was your fault, Porschia."

I shook my head. "Yes, but it was my mother. Just tell her. Please."

Sobs wracked my body. He stepped toward me but I turned my head, clutching the towel tightly to my chest. "I need to dress and feed, and you can't be around me until I do. The craving is too strong." But it wasn't; not really. I felt dead, not hungry. Not out of control. Numb. Still frozen.

"Feed from me."

"No." I stood up from the water, wrapping the sopping wet towel around me.

"Feed. From. Me." Saul enunciated each word.

"NO!" Damn him. I didn't want his blood. I didn't want to hurt him, or to hurt anyone ever again. I just wanted to know how Maggie was doing.

"Why not? I'm here. Feed from me, Porschia."

"No!" I didn't want it. I didn't want to feed. I didn't want to feed from him. Or anyone. Or anything. I didn't want it. "Just go see about Maggie!"

His lips formed a thin line. "Fine. But I'll be right back." I watched the muscles of his shoulders flex as he shrugged his coat on. He gave me another look to punctuate his words and then walked out the door.

THIRTY

PORSCHIA

TAGE CAME IN AFTER SAUL LEFT. I WAS STILL STANDING OUTSIDE THE TUB with water sluicing from every inch of me. Water from the towel dripped heavily onto the tile floor, pooling at my feet. Tage swallowed, guardedly watching me as he spoke. "I laid some clothes out for you. They're on your bed. The fire's stoked."

"Thanks."

"Julian is working downstairs. I'm sure you hear it." I did, I just didn't know what it was. Bang. Bang. Boom.

"What's he doing?"

"Reinforcing the cell."

"Why?"

"Roman wants you in it."

I closed my eyes. He was going to keep me, even if it was against my will. I walked by Tage, squeezing past him and out the bathroom door. On my bed was a pair of black fleece pants and a cable-knit sweater in a soft baby blue. There were fuzzy socks and a robe laid out beside the clothes.

Tage startled me from behind. "I didn't pick your under...things."

I smiled. Under...things?

"I can handle that."

"Yeah." He cleared his throat. "I'm supposed to escort you downstairs after you're dressed."

"Fine. Give me a few," I said, slowly padding to the pile of soft, warm things.

The door clicked shut behind me.

Why was he helping Roman? Was he being compelled? Was I? I still felt numb. Maybe it was Roman's doing.

I dressed slowly and opened my door once I was cloaked in fuzz. "Thank you for the warm clothes, Tage," I said, looking up. But it wasn't Tage staring back at me.

"I wish I could take credit for them, poppet."

TAGE WAS NOWHERE. I COULDN'T HEAR HIM. I COULD FEEL HIS ANGER, BUT where was he and why wasn't he the one escorting me down there? As I stepped into the cell, I noted that it was definitely better. Julian had used some fast drying cement-like stuff on the ceiling. I could break it, but I wouldn't. He bent the bars back into place, too.

Now Julian stood guard outside, slouched in a chair that was too small for his large body. "Plan didn't go as you hoped?" I teased with a grin. The small amount of light from the candle he brought down with him struggled to illuminate the large room.

"Not yet," he countered with a shrug, a confident smirk on his face.

"I won't kill him to help you."

"I know."

"He won't let you kill him now that he knows you told me about Mercedes."

Julian sighed. "I know, but have you ever heard the phrase, 'If you can't beat them, join them?"

"I haven't. It's a stupid phrase."

"Maybe not," he mused, staring at me through the bars. "But there's still an inkling of hope for you to do it."

"I can't kill anyone from in here. Nice job on my cage, by the way."

"Thank you. The job seemed to appease Roman for the time being. Of course, he'll make me pay for a while, but I'll act like a good boy. He'll get comfortable again."

"Then you'll try to kill him?" I asked.

He sniffed. "Might not have to."

"Where are the others?" The house was still.

"Evening rotation."

I leaped toward the bars. "Are they hunting?"

"Not tonight. Too much snow, too fast."

"How much?"

"Three feet and counting."

DARA TOOK THE NIGHT WATCH, AND SURPRISINGLY, SHE STARED OUT THE tiny window and left me alone for most of the night. The morning was a different story. I wasn't able to sleep well, despite needing it desperately.

She ran up the stairs and brought back down a bag. "Time to get ready!"

"For what?"

"To see Saul. Oops, I mean morning rotation."

I jumped from my bed, grasping the bars. "Stay away from him."

"Funny thing – he said you told him you didn't want to feed from him. I think you hurt his feelings. But I made it all better yesterday evening. And I'll help again this morning." Why was he confiding in her?

Jerking the bars, I realized I wasn't as strong as I had been when I nearly ripped them down. "Now, now. I promise to tell him you said hi." She brushed her long blonde hair into a silk curtain and applied red lipstick, pursing her lips and watching the movement in a small handheld mirror.

"Tage is coming to do... whatever you two do. I told Saul that Tage is *super* helpful in dealing with you."

When Tage came down the steps, she snapped her compact closed and pranced away. Tage saw me straining against the cage bars and looked concerned. "What's going on?"

"Her."

"Ignore her. She's just trying to get you mad."

"She does a good job of it."

Tage stuffed his hands in his pockets and slowly walked toward me. "Want to play a game?" He looked up and smiled.

"A game?" I released the bars and sat on my bed. Tage had disassembled the entire thing, brought it down here, and set it up before Julian locked me in it. How he did it so fast, I didn't know, but it was better than the cot and blood-stained, moldy mattress. "Okay. How do I play?"

"Easy. You just answer questions."

"Okay. Shoot."

Tage smiled. "Pretend you're Julian. How do you take Roman out of the equation?"

I sighed, flopping back onto the mattress. "Get someone else to do it for you."

"I think he's going to the Elders behind Roman's back. I just need proof."

"So get it."

"It's not that simple." Guilt filled his eyes.

"Don't worry about me. I'm fine. Just hanging out. Living the dream of mostly-eternal life."

He snorted, crossed his arms over his chest, and sat in the chair across from my cell. "Dara's been sneaking out, too. Maybe she's helping him."

"Maybe she's seeing Saul."

He shook his head. "I doubt that."

"Why?"

"Saul doesn't want her. He wants you."

I lifted my head, rolling onto my side. "Doesn't matter. She isn't easily deterred."

Tage's smile fell. "I checked on Maggie for you."

Sitting up, I looked at him. "You did?"

"Yeah. Saul did too, but I checked again this morning. She's doing great. She'll be back to normal in a few days, not that she was able to get around well before."

"Did you tell her I was sorry?"

"She doesn't blame you for the actions of your mother, Porschia. Maggie's a great person. We had a long talk."

I swallowed. "I want to see her."

"I told her about your... current situation."

"Permanent situation. Roman admitted everything to me. He was going to turn me himself, but I beat him to it. He said I reminded him of a girl he once loved, that he turned. She went into Frenzy and went crazy, so the Colony banished her. Unfortunately for her, she decided to leave without him."

"What did he do?"

"He killed her – drained her. Then he told the Elders that he did it to protect the village from her, but he actually did it because she broke his heart. She was leaving him."

"He said you remind him of her?"

"Yep."

"That is a very bad thing."

"For me, it is," I whispered.

"I won't let him hurt you."

"He already has." The cell bars seemed to lengthen. He couldn't do much more to me. He could drain me and end me, but life would go on for everyone else. The world would keep turning and Roman would still be a cold, heartless bastard who loved control more than anything in the world. He'd find someone else who reminded him of her or of me and terrorize them, too. He'd play politics to make himself feel important. It would be a repetitive cycle. It was hard to tell how often it had repeated itself over the years he'd been a night-walker. He said the girl he drained was the first he loved, but I doubted that. Any word that came from his mouth was probably a lie.

"What are you thinking about?" Tage asked.

"Nothing." My stomach growled.

"You're hungry."

I just nodded.

"I can't get you anything right now. I'm sorry. Roman will be back any time. He said not to feed you."

"He wants to keep me in here and I'm too weak to bust out this time."

"Dara?"

"Yep."

The front door opened and several sets of footsteps filed into the house. Roman came downstairs. "Your time's up. I've got the day shift."

I looked at Roman. "I can't leave, Roman, and I don't need a babysitter."

He snorted. "Maybe I just want to spend time with you."

Great. Just...great. Tage left. I didn't know what to think of him at all. Why was he listening to Roman all of the sudden? Taking orders? He hated Roman. He always fed me. Something was definitely off.

THIRTY-ONE

TAGE

I FOLLOWED JULIAN AND DARA'S SCENT TOWARD THE CEMETERY, CREEPING close enough to hear their conversation, yet staying downwind. The snow had finally stopped pouring, and now only tiny flurries fell from the sky. The dark clouds had thinned and an end to the storm was in sight.

I could hear them kissing, their hands searching one another. Grunts and moans, his and hers. Rolling my eyes, I stayed tucked behind a pine. Was *this* what all the secrecy was for? An affair? I was pretty sure Roman didn't care who Dara slept with, especially now that he had Porschia in a cage in his basement.

"We're going tonight," she panted against his lips. "The snow stopped. The Elders said the colonists are desperate for meat again. Sporadic supply isn't good enough for them, apparently."

He groaned. "So you'll do it, then?"

"I will, and I'll love every second of it."

Julian chuckled. "You're so cold. You feel nothing for the human at all?"

"Not a thing. Turning him, claiming him? That'll kill her. And I want her dead."

Shit.

"Plus, you can tell the Elders that Roman let me turn the human. The treaty will end and we can terrorize the Colony together. Tage will leave. He'll tuck tail and run when Porschia's gone. He won't have a reason to stay."

I sped away before they said anything else, before they could smell or sense me. Roman was going to walk into a trap tonight, but it wasn't him I was worried about. Porschia would give up if her precious Saul or little brother was turned. I knew Dara was talking about Saul, but she'd turn Ford in an instant if given the opportunity.

I needed to get home, and I needed the key to the damn cell. But first, Porschia needed to be fed.

PORSCHIA

I SAT ON THE BED WITH MY BACK AGAINST THE WALL AND MY FEET outstretched, refusing to look at Roman. He'd been talking, asking questions, and then answering them himself since I wouldn't and he thought he knew best.

We heard Tage burst through the front door and run downstairs. "We have a problem," he said breathlessly.

Roman stood up and crossed his arms, instantly on alert. "What?"

"Julian and Dara. They're talking about turning a human during the hunt tonight and pinning it on you."

Roman leaned his head to the side. "Which human?"

"Saul."

I was off the mattress and jerking at the bars before they even had time to swivel their heads in my direction. "Let me out!" From afar, I could hear Julian and Dara returning to the house. "They're coming!" I whispered. "Let me out, Roman. Please."

He put a finger to his lips and walked upstairs, acting as if nothing happened. The scent of raw flesh filled the air and my mouth watered uncontrollably.

"Please," I whispered. Tage pulled a rabbit from behind his back, already prepared for me. And I wanted it. "I need it."

"Shhh." He walked over to the cell and shoved it between two bars. I began to shred the meat with my fangs, but heard the shrill sound of

Dara's voice approaching. I stuffed the hare beneath my pillow and sat down on my bed, looking bored. Tage was already in the chair, flipping through some sort of hardcover book.

"Saul said to tell you hello and he hopes you're well enough to rejoin society soon. Blah. Blah."

I ignored her. "Aww, is little Porschia pouting?" she asked condescendingly.

She wouldn't stop until she got a rise out of me, so I gave it to her. When she stepped within arm's reach, I launched myself against the bars and grabbed her by the hair near her scalp. I could hear strands of her golden mane tearing and snapping.

"Cat fight!" Tage yelled.

Slamming her head against the cell bars was easy. The hard part was stopping myself from beating her skull against the metal repeatedly. *Rein it in.* I stopped in an instant and acted worn out after that. I could explain away a short burst of energy, but if I kept it up, she'd know I had eaten. She'd suspect something and would call the whole plan off. We would no longer have the element of surprise.

"I'll kill you!" She clawed at me, but oops – I was just out of her reach.

Roman pulled her away from the cell. "Go upstairs!" he screamed in her face. She looked genuinely taken aback and so was I, since I'd never seen him so much as raise his voice at his little pet. "NOW!"

She rubbed her head and cheek. "Aww, is little Dara pouting?" I sing-songed.

Dara hissed, "Bitch!" over her shoulder, her chest heaving as she retreated, staring daggers at me.

"Slut," I enunciated.

"You'll pay for this."

I stood up and brushed myself off. "No, *you* will pay for this."

"Let her out, Roman, and I promise I'll take care of your little problem for you," she said sweetly.

What problem?

"You'll never have to be reminded of that back-stabbing bitch again. I know you see her in Porschia. Let me end her for you." She put her hand on his forearm and Roman snapped, backhanding her so hard, she smacked against the wall with a loud thud before falling to the floor. She picked herself up, mouth agape.

"You hit me," she whispered, using the wall to get back up. Instantly, her rage for me turned to Roman. "Well don't come looking to me to satisfy your cravings. Maybe Porschia can help you scratch your itch. I'm *done*!"

Her heels clicked all the way to her room. Roman was visibly furious. He turned those sharp, dark eyes to me, and then looked to Tage. Roman flicked something shiny through the air and began to walk away. Tage's palm caught the item and he smiled, looking at his prize. Dangling from his forefinger was the key to my cell.

Tage made motions like he was tearing an animal leg apart and pointed to my pillow. I smiled and so did he. It looked like we were going hunting tonight, after all. Only this time, I was hunting jealous bitch.

THIRTY-TWO

PORSCHIA

I ATE MOST OF THE RABBIT. OKAY, I ATE IT ALL EXCEPT FOR THE BONES. They lay in a tiny pile in the corner. And I felt amazing. I wasn't cold anymore, I wasn't hot…I was just right. Goldilocks. "I need to get out of here," I whispered to Tage. Pulling on my boots, I laced them tightly. Tage had snuck them down to me earlier and I'd shoved them under my bed until now.

He shook his head, pointing upstairs. Dara and Julian were still here. "Fine, but when they go, I want to see Maggie."

He nodded. We waited in silence while Roman, Julian, and Dara got ready for the evening rotation. The sky darkened early, and after what felt like an eternity, they finally stepped outside onto the crunching snow. The sun must have melted it during the day, but it was re-freezing into a thick, slippery crust. How would Ford, Saul, and the others cross the tree trunk if it was frozen?

Tage waited for a few minutes and when we heard nothing, he walked over to my cell and stuck the key in the lock. *Click.*

Best.

Sound.

Ever.

I gave him a quick hug and whispered in his ear, "I'm going to Maggie's."

In a mocking tone, he answered, "I'm going with you."

"Let's go, then. They'll be feeding now, and then will head into the forest." I didn't know how she would do it. Would she just pounce on him after the group split up? It was stupid to go along with that plan. They should stay together.

We ran to Maggie's house, avoiding the pavilion and blurring past houses along the wall and then doubling back. Her door was unlocked. "Who's there?" a voice called out. It wasn't Maggie, but it made me stop in place. At the top of the steps stood Saul's mother. "Porschia?" she asked incredulously.

"I just wanted to see her," I answered warily.

"Let her in," Maggie yelled from her upstairs bedroom.

Mrs. Daniels – Ella – motioned us forward. Tage stayed with me. Ella eyeballed him, letting out a quick breath as we passed. "Thank you," I said softly as I passed her on the step.

I peeked into Maggie's room. Her neck was bandaged, but no blood was seeping onto the cloth. Covering my mouth, I tried to choke back the tears. "I'm so glad you're okay," I blubbered, running into her outstretched arms.

"None of this was your doing, Porschia. Your mother has a touch of the devil in her."

"She does."

"Saul and Ella filled me in on what happened to her, to you. I'm the one who is sorry for your loss. You've suffered so much in such a short amount of time. You're too young for this shit."

I laughed a little. "You look good. Someone came to help heal the wound?"

"The dark-headed vampire that I don't care for," she huffed, crossing her arms and pursing her lips.

"Roman?"

"That's him. He came and said it would hurt you if I died, so he wanted to help." Maggie looked to Tage as he stood in the doorway.

"He's up to something. You could see it in his eyes. You keep clear of that one, you hear me?"

"I'll try," I promised, taking hold of her hand. The blanket was one she'd sewn. It was a patchwork of different fabrics, but looked like it fit together perfectly. Vivid and spunky. Very Maggie. I imagined she had been quite a handful in her prime.

"Who are you?" she asked candidly.

"Tage," he replied.

"You're the one helping her?" Maggie grinned. "Oh, ho! Saul does *not* like you, fella."

He smiled, leaning against the frame of the door. "I know."

Ella cleared her throat behind him and Tage stood up straight, his cheeks turning pink. A blushing night-walker. And Tage, to boot! HA!

"Sorry. It's just...never mind," Tage fumbled.

Maggie nodded her head. "A wise man knows when he is outnumbered."

"I have to go, Maggie," I said quickly. "I just wanted to check on you. I don't know when I'll be able to come back. I don't know when they'll let me."

She nodded, squeezing my hand. "Don't you worry about me. I'm fit as a fiddle. Your brother and father have both been by today. Thank them for the company if you see them before I do." I would be seeing Ford. Very soon.

I hugged her again, kissed her softly on the cheek, and stood up. Tage said goodbye and the other customary things like, nice to finally meet you, hope you get better soon, etcetera, and we walked out the door. As we stepped toward the front door, Ella called out, "Come back anytime, Porschia." She smiled, her eyes filling with understanding.

"Thank you." It meant everything to me. Somehow she finally saw the same girl I'd always been. She saw me as me, as *human* me, and someone who would never hurt Maggie. She saw me as someone capable of love, maybe even someone who could love her son. Or at least I hoped Ella was saying that. It sure seemed that way.

We sped across the land, between houses and outbuildings, down sidewalks and through yards. "Let's cross near the barn," Tage said, trying his best to keep up with me.

"Sounds good."

There was another fallen tree there, but it was close to the water. When we got to the crossing, it was almost covered. Dark, frothy water lapped at the wood, sometimes bursting overtop. "Snow melt," Tage said. "It's not the best idea."

"It would give us the element of surprise."

"If you fall in..."

"I won't. I'm strong. Are you afraid?" I teased.

"Hell, no. Let's do this. Ladies first," he said with a bow, sweeping his hand toward the log. My bravado disappeared in a second. Mother fell in. I might fall in. *What if I fell in? What if something happened and I didn't make it across? What if Dara was already draining Saul?* With that thought spurring me on, I sprang across, foot finding the log once, just enough to propel me forward, and Tage was right behind. We sniffed the air. Northwest. Saul was northwest and Ford was with him. So was Dara. Lightning struck through my veins.

"Wait up!" Tage yelled. I was already gone, but I wasn't stupid. I would let him catch up, and then I'd stop to assess the situation before pouncing.

THIRTY-THREE

SAUL

THE SNOW HAD MELTED AND FROZEN BACK OVER AGAIN. FORD WAS WALKING to my left, with Dara to my right. We took it slow. The terrain was slick, which made hunting nearly impossible since the animals could hear our boots crunching from half a mile away. Walking along the ridgeline, we saw nothing. No movement. Other than old animal prints that were half-melted, it seemed like the forest was empty except for us and the wind.

"I can't even hear anything," Ford whispered.

There was no sound. No rustling. Nothing in the trees.

"Let's keep walking," I answered. "Eventually we'll have to find something, right?"

Ford nodded half-heartedly, readjusting his grip on the crossbow. It was the lightest I could find, but it was still too heavy for him. Though he acted like an adult, Ford was just a teenage kid. He was like the brother I didn't have, and I promised myself and Porschia that I'd look after him.

Dara had been quiet. She usually was during the hunts, but more so tonight. Maybe it was just that everything else was so still. I glanced over at Dara to see her sniffing the air.

"What is it?" I whispered. I knew she could smell the animals before we could see them.

"A complication."

Ford huffed, his breath coming out in a big cloud of white steam. "What's that supposed to mean?"

"Nothing," Dara said. "Look, there's nothing here. Let's just walk toward the others. Maybe we'll scare something toward them."

Ford looked to me for the final say. "Yeah. There's nothing here." His eyes flashed with concern. He must have also felt the strangeness in the air. There was nothing here, nothing we could do, but if we could find the others, there was strength in numbers.

Unease made me tighten the hold on my crossbow. Our boots crunched over the ridge as we began our descent. Nothing stirred around us but the bitter wind.

FORD

DARA SMELLED SOMETHING, BUT SHE WASN'T SAYING WHAT. A complication? More like a rotter. Were they in the forest? I sure as heck couldn't see anything other than a thick blanket of crunchy snow that was more ice than anything, trees, and the dark sky above us. Our breath was visible, too. I was more than happy to keep moving. At this rate, I wouldn't be able to feel my toes by morning. Plus, if we could get to Roman, I would feel better.

I wished Porschia was here. Roman said she was sick, too sick to go into the cold. When she went into the river after Mother, something happened. I asked Roman about it. "I thought night-walkers could withstand water and any temperature, even freezing ones?" I asked him.

His eyes narrowed. "Normally they can, but Porschia is different."

SEVERAL SLIPS, FALLS, AND FREEZING MILES LATER, WE FOUND VICTOR, TIM, Julian, and Roman. Tage had stayed behind at the house to guard Porschia, which meant they had her locked in the cell again. Everyone was tight-lipped about it and I didn't know if she was going nuts again, or if the Elders made them lock her up.

She didn't hurt Mother, so why would they punish her for anything that had happened?

Roman waved as we approached. "Nothing?" he asked.

"Nothing at all, man," Saul said, shaking his head and looking out into the forest.

"Do you want to return to the Colony and try again tomorrow?" Dara asked. She really rubbed me the wrong way, the way she was always looking at Saul even though she knew he and Porschia were together...sort of.

Victor and Tim spoke up at the same time. "Yes." Tim blew into his gloved hands. Victor shifted on his feet.

"Agreed," Roman said. "Let's get out of here."

He led the way down the hill and toward Blackwater. It would be a long walk back, but at least we could get home soon and get warm!

THIRTY-FOUR

PORSCHIA

I PRESSED THE HEELS OF MY PALMS AGAINST MY HEAD. THE WHISPERS. THE voices wouldn't stop. Different voices.

How much longer until they come back?

It's freezing.

Do you think they smell us?

"What's wrong?" Tage asked, brow furrowed.

"Don't you hear them?"

"Hear who?" He looked around. We'd just crossed the river, and no one was around that we could see on either side.

Here come two more night-walkers. We didn't plan on this many.

Stick to the plan. It doesn't matter how many there are.

Your sister's here.

Porschia?

Mercedes? That was Mercedes' voice. "Cede?" I asked incredulously.

In a whisper, my sister responded: *Can she hear me? How is that possible?*

"Tage," I hissed, grabbing his hand. "I can hear my sister. She's close, and I think she has some friends with her."

"She could be a mile away. Your hearing is acute."

"I'm not hearing her with my ears; I'm hearing her in my head!" I whisper-yelled.

Tage shook his head. "That's not possible. You're just confused. Sometimes things sound louder, like they're closer than they really are. You know the cars? The ones in your back yard?"

"Yeah."

"The mirrors on the side say: 'Objects may be closer than they appear.' It's the same thing. You're hearing her because you've fed. Everything is heightened. Amplified."

She can hear us. Mercedes. *I can hear her.*

Go silent, a male voice ordered.

I swallowed. "Then why can she hear me?"

Ford yelled from the hilltop. "Porschia!"

He and Saul slid down the hill more than they walked, but they made it to us first. Roman was furious. "Why are you here?" He turned to Tage, playing the part well. "What the hell is going on?"

The bitter cold wind bit through my borrowed coat. Tage had stolen one of Dara's for me. I grinned as her eyes narrowed in on the familiar puffy white fabric, but then I caught the whiff of a different smell; one that overpowered even the flowery perfume that Dara poured on every day. Decay. Rot. Death.

My eyes darted around. I didn't see them. They weren't on the hilltop.

"What is it?" Saul asked, grabbing my arm.

"The Infected."

Everyone wheeled around, backing toward the river that was only yards away. "I don't see anything," Ford squeaked.

"Do you smell them?" I asked the other night-walkers. Julian, Roman, Tage, Dara, and I sniffed the air, and everyone nodded. It was them, and they were close.

"I do. Help them get across," Roman ordered me. "Tage, help her." Roman bared his fangs and yelled, "Come out, come out wherever you are..."

Square patches of ground rose up from the forest floor in a semi-circle around us. They must have dug holes and hidden inside, covered by small doors covered with dirt, leaves, and then snow.

"Ford," I said, grabbing my brother. "Go! Careful, though. The log is icy." I looked pleadingly at Tage. "Please help him."

Tage gritted his teeth, but agreed and led Ford to the tree, Victor and Timothy right behind them. The Infected began to slowly, jerkily close in.

Vampires were immune to their germs. They couldn't harm us, but if they caught one of the humans, we were in big trouble.

Saul stood beside me with his crossbow aimed at the guy who stood next to my sister. "Go, Saul."

"No."

"GO!"

"I'm not leaving you here. Not with them."

"I'm immune to them!"

"Like you are to the cold? Like you can eat your fill of blood like the others? Something isn't right with you, and I'll be damned if I let the rotters get ahold of you!"

I swallowed. "I stand a better chance than you do, Saul," I said quietly, easing in front of him.

His bow was over my right shoulder.

Looking back, I saw Ford slip on the trunk. His stomach hit the wood and he began to slide toward the water. "No!"

I ran toward him but Tage stopped me. "I've got him."

"You haven't fed!"

Tage looked at me, blue eyes churning like a summer storm. "I'll take care of that now. You help Ford."

I grabbed my brother's hand and tugged him back to me as Tage approached Tim. "I need to feed. I won't take much, but I need it." Tim's chest heaved in distress, but he nodded and let Tage feed from him for a moment. When Tage was finished, he smiled, teeth coated in a bloody film. "We need a new tree."

He sped away, knocking two Infected down as he went. They groaned and struggled to get back up. I had no idea if they were male or female, old or young. They'd been sick for a long time. No hair, just skin and bone, with eyes sunken in. They looked skeletal, and their shrieking hurt my ears. I shoved my palms against them for relief, but the voices started back up.

Get one of the humans before the night-walker comes back with a better way across.

Get the old ones. They can't run.

Any will do.

I want Saul. The boy next to Porschia. My sister. Damn her.

He has a crossbow, a male argued.

I don't care. I want that one. Mercedes.

A short distance away, a loud crack came from the forest in the direction Tage had run. He must have found a suitable crossing tree. I shook my head as the voices grew frantic.

He's coming.

Attack!

Something stung my neck. I clasped it, finding a dart with tiny feathers sticking out of the end. My skin burned, but that wasn't the worst of it. More darts whizzed through the air, striking Roman and Tage. Saul used his bow to deflect them, but another hit my thigh. Julian and Dara were nowhere to be seen. "Where are Julian and Dara?" I screamed, holding my arms up in front of my face.

Enough of this. I walked straight up to the Infected asshole who was shooting the darts at me and grabbed him by the throat. His vertebrae snapped apart and he gasped, a puff of steam signaling his death.

She killed Amon!

Get the young man now! Saul. Get him.

More darts. It stung! Something was on the tips. *Aaaah!* I eased another from my thigh and shoulder. Stumbling, I couldn't see straight. There were two of everything. Two Infected. Two of Ford, two of Victor, and two Tims near the two rivers.

"Porschia!" Ford yelled.

I held a finger out to him. "No! I'm fine! Tage, hurry!"

Another loud noise near the river. Tage had thrown the two trees across and was helping Tim scurry across, slipping out of fear and not because of ice.

"You're next, Ford!" Tage yelled, motioning for him to come forward.

"GO!" I screamed. Another dart hit me in the back, between my shoulder blades. I reached back for it and couldn't...quite. . .reach...it.

Saul began to fire his crossbow, but something jammed. He tugged, grunting and straining. Then he was gone. "Saul?" My vision blurred.

"Saul!"

I looked to Roman, who was tearing the head off of one of the Infected. Julian was still gone, and so was Dara. "No!"

Tage sped over to me. "Everyone's across but Saul. Where is he?" he asked quickly. I shook my head, disoriented.

A dart hit Tage in the bicep. "What the hell is on these? God, it burns!"

"I don't.... know. Saul is gonewhereisDaraTage?

"You've been hit?" He grabbed my upper arms. "How many times?"

I pointed to my back. He eased the dart out and narrowed his eyes on the remaining Infected. There were only seven or so left. Where was Mercedes?

"Saul?"

Roman stopped what he was doing and turned to me. "Saul is missing?"

"Dara has him. Doesn't she?"

I shook my head, trying to clear the fog away.

The night-walker has the one I want. We have to get him from her before she turns him.

Tage sniffed the air. "Let's go," he said, easing my arm over his shoulders; the sounds of cracking bones and shrieking filled the air. "Roman's dealing with the other Infected. He can handle them. I don't see your sister, or her little friend."

Saul yelled. "Get off me!"

Tage sped through the forest, all but carrying me. "Porschia?" Saul said, looking over to us.

Dara held her finger up, slicing it with a small, knife. The blade glinted in the moonlight, showing the blood on the tip. She eased the bleeding flesh toward his mouth. "NO!"

No. She couldn't turn him. He couldn't live like this. No, not this curse. Not Saul. Not my Saul. Not my heart. NO! I launched myself at her, knocking her to the ground.

She roared, grabbed a handful of icy snow, and threw it in my eyes. It stung like a bitch! I swung at her but she was already on the move. Saul had gotten up and stood behind Tage, who just nodded at me. Julian, standing nearby and watching the scene, just turned away.

I stalked menacingly toward Dara. "Julian?" she whimpered. "Help me."

"Sorry, love," he said, walking past us both, back toward the Infected and Roman, who sounded like he was almost finished ending them. "This isn't my fight." My heart clenched. *Mercedes. No. Yes. NO, don't kill my sister.*

"You tried to turn him!"

Dara eased her hands out in front of her. "You can't hurt me, Porschia."

"I will fucking *end* you! I told you to stay away from him. I told you. I *told* you!"

"He isn't yours!" she shrieked, balling her fists up.

"He isn't yours either!"

Dara turned to run and made it half way up the hill before I caught her. Somewhere in Saul's distress, I'd come out of the fog. I knocked her to the ground, her chin clamping shut with a snap. She let out a groan and rolled over, ready to spring back up, but it was too late. I was on top of her.

No.

No turning Saul.

No hurting him.

No hurting me.

No more.

No lies.

No plans.

No biting him.

No licking him.

No changing him into a monster.

I was a monster.

I was biting her.

I was drawing from her neck in thick, hot gulps. She grasped my neck, trying to pull me away, but I fed. I fed. I was strong. I was feeding.

I drained. I gulped. I ended.

I could feel her hands weaken and slip away from my neck.

A struggle behind me. What was that noise?

I couldn't stop.

More blood.

I needed more.

I needed it all.

I wanted it to stop.

I needed it to end.

When I could drink no more, I eased my fangs from her neck. Dara stared blankly up at the stars glittering above, her golden hair an outspread halo. Blood oozed from her neck. Thick droplets splashed onto the stark white snow beneath her.

We've got him.

"Porschia!" Tage yelled. "It's Saul!"

I ran. I ran as fast as I could. I blurred through the trees, vision sharp. Hearing sharp. Voices loud in my ears. There were only a few now. Loud. Insistent.

Get him to the river.

"Mercedes, no! Please, no! Please Mercedes, I'll do anything. Don't hurt him. Please!"

At the river, Roman and Tage panted, watching the scene unfold. The Infected had actually made a raft. The rotters already had Saul on the raft and Mercedes' boyfriend held him down, sticking little darts into his skin with a sickening grin on his face. The poison on the darts immobilized Saul immediately. The Infected man's dark, golden eyes burned into mine. *You're too late,* he said.

"Please, Mercedes. Take me. I'll do whatever you want. I'll leave. I'll leave Blackwater!"

She shook her head.

He's ours now.

I love him, I thought.

I know, she answered.

She sank her teeth into his shoulder as her boyfriend cut the rope that held the raft steady on the river bank, and Saul screamed as the infection entered his body. The raft floated over the water, bumping against boulders and barely holding together against the force of the water.

"Saul!" I ran after them along the bank. "NO!"

Tage was behind me. "Porschia, stop!"

"No! SAUL!"

Saul yelled for me; he cried out for me in anguish. "Porschia!"

"I'm coming."

"Porschia, you can't help me now!"

"Saul!" I pushed harder, I could see them just ahead.

"Porschia, stop!" Tage yelled. "He's Infected! There's no coming back from that!"

Faster. I needed more speed. The only thing faster than a nightwalker? An angry, snow-swollen river.

"I'll kill you, Mercedes! I will kill you, I will kill your little boyfriend, and then I will kill every last one of you!"

The raft disappeared around the river bend, swallowed by the darkness.

He was Infected now; he wasn't turned. I should have just let Dara turn him, but now he would rot. He would die. Saul would die. For all intents and purposes, Saul was already gone.

I grasped my head and let out a guttural scream that echoed throughout the valley. Tage's feet slowed beside me, and I knew Roman was close behind.

He would calm me.

I didn't want to calm down.

I wanted blood.

I wanted to end them all.

"Where would they go?" I asked Roman.

"To the city. There's a way in on the other side."

I needed weapons.

I needed a plan.

Julian jogged up with a concerned look on his face. "You're a force to be reckoned with, poppet."

Damn straight, I thought, just before I started vomiting. Dara's blood burned a path up my throat and out my nose. Tage grabbed my back, steadying me. "It's okay," he said soothingly.

But it wasn't okay and it would *never* be okay. I wouldn't be okay. I wasn't okay. This wasn't okay. None of this was okay. *Damn it!*

"I should have just let Dara turn him," I sobbed between heaves. Tage rubbed my back and tried to comfort me as best as he could.

"No, Porsch. You couldn't let her hurt him. You only tried to protect the one you love. It's what anyone would have done."

Hands on my shaking knees, I looked up at Julian. "Why were you helping her? And why are you trying to double-cross Roman by playing the Elders against him?"

The muscle in Julian's jaw worked back and forth in anger. "Is that right?" Roman asked, walking toward Julian with deadly intent. Dara wasn't the only one who died that night, and it looked like Roman would get to flex his precious compulsion muscle. I was certain that nothing could fill the gaping hole in my chest now; nothing but revenge.

Vengeance. Such a sweet word. It tempted those who sought it, like a siren into dangerous waters.

FREQUENCY

ONE

SAUL

There are moments in a person's life that happen at a slower speed. Time slows, and so do you. Then there are other moments that fly by so fast you're powerless. You become overtaken by their current, only able to ride out the momentum until something stops either it or you. Most moments fit into neither category. Time is just time; neither fast nor slow, but steady and predictable.

But there is fourth kind of moment: the kind that seems as though it's happening at a snail's pace, but in reality is a building wave, ready to crash over you and speed you into a new phase of your life. I was trapped in the fourth kind of moment. Slow but fast. Agonizing but all-consuming.

The frigid dark water was damning and comforting at the same time. My shoulder was on fire. It sizzled, bubbled, and burned. I was done being bitten by creatures who assumed they had the right to do as they pleased; creatures that weren't human anymore and had forgotten what it meant to be. Humans didn't do this to other human beings. I'd been bitten by vampire fangs until I felt like a piece of Swiss cheese, holes and all, and now an Infected had bitten me? And not just any Infected...Porschia's crazy sister. I could feel my skin blistering where each of her teeth cut through my skin, like their enamel was infused with hellfire. Maybe the

Infection was made up of exactly that – hellfire. In any event I was about to find out, and powerless to stop the change coursing through me.

Icy cold water splashed onto the makeshift raft as the angry current carried us away from the forest crossing and Blackwater. The sound of Porschia's frantic voice echoed through the valley. "Saul!" She cried out for me, but she had already seen what her sister did. "Use your ring!" She knew I couldn't go back now. It was pointless. The ring wouldn't help me now. Mercedes bit me and now I was as good as dead. I was Infected. Now I would rot like the others. Eventually I'd roam the forest, desperate to find my next meal, regardless of what that meal was; dead or alive.

Mercedes held onto my shoulders as we curved around the city. The guy with us was using a long piece of wood to try and guide the raft, but the river had its own agenda. He growled as the muscles along his back and arms began to shake.

Motioning to me, he held the wooden pole out. *Take it,* he said in my mind. What the hell? *We need to stop in the calm stretch of river, but we won't make it if the raft gets torn apart by those rocks, and even you can't survive the rapids now. The Infection is weakening you quickly.* He pointed ahead to a row of jagged rocks that dammed the river slightly. If we hit those, we'd all be swimming in the glacially cold river. Cold chills crawled up my spine.

Standing and moving toward him, I reached out for the pole. If I let the raft smash apart, it would take him and Mercedes both out. It would end the misery I knew would be waiting for me in the city. I wouldn't rot. Drowning sounded better than wasting away. The stench from his skin and hair almost knocked me back down. *Rot.*

"Saul!" Porschia's voice faded the faster the river took us. The water was the only thing faster than her, and it was just as deadly. The guy's eyes zeroed in on my face and he threw the long stick at me. I caught it easily, holding it level at my waist. *We're close to finding a cure. Don't be stupid,* he said. The sloshing of the water on the raft rocked us and the row of rock spires was getting closer by the second. Digging the wooden pole into the river bottom, I gritted my teeth and hoped the raft would slow. It finally relented and we passed between the widest gap between two of the sharp rocks, only scraping the right side a bit as we slid through. When we reached a wide stretch of the river and the water calmed, I eased the raft over to the bank.

The guy jumped off the raft and onto the bank. Mercedes struggled to stay upright as she jumped off behind him, slipping and sliding on the wet earth. My pants were soaked and I was freezing as I leapt off behind her. "Do you have fire?" I asked softly.

She nodded and motioned toward the flood wall. In one of the wall joints, the metal had corroded and one could squeeze through the small barrier. Once we were inside the concrete barrier, I grabbed Mercedes' bicep. "Why did you do it?"

Her brows touched one another in confusion.

"Why did you attack? Why the hell did you target *me?*"

She looked at the guy who was walking ahead of us and then back to me; silent, but swallowing thickly.

"He made you?"

The slightest nod of her head said I was right.

"Who is he?" I jutted my chin toward him.

Mercedes parted her lips and tried to speak, but small screeches from her throat were all she could muster. In my mind, she spoke. *He is the leader of the Infected. Pierce is well-respected here. No one questions his orders. And if you're smart, neither will you. Trust me on that one.*

Trust her? She just fucking killed me! One bite and I was already dying. I could already feel the virus spreading quicker than should be possible. My head began to pound. I clutched my temples and steadied myself with the gritty flood wall stretching tall beside me. Had it always been so tall? My vision blurred and then cleared before blurring again. *We need to get you indoors and warm, Saul.*

Warm was a good idea.

Pierce walked ahead, his long, dark hair swishing back and forth. It was stringy and as weak as he looked now. The fight in the forest had obviously taken the wind out of his sails. I watched as he disappeared between two tall buildings. I'd been in the city before on hunts for supplies and food, but this walk was different. This walk had no retraceable steps. I was never going home to Blackwater. I couldn't go back to Porschia, and I would never see my parents again. I was completely screwed.

My legs shook so violently, I didn't think I would make it to wherever Mercedes was leading me. After passing a few more buildings, she led me into a brick four-story. *We live here. Pierce wants you to stay with us – not in his room, but in his apartment. You'll need someone to stay with you for the first few days. I volunteered.*

Well how nice, considering you *were the one who bit me,* I thought. Apparently she heard me, because she looked back at me with wide eyes full of pain. She had been through the change recently, and I wondered how someone so small was able to survive this. I was strong and much bigger than her; I towered over her, yet I could barely stay upright. "Who helped you?" I asked. Did Pierce help her after she was bitten? Was he the one who infected her?

Her eyes were big in her face and her cheeks were sunken in. She shook her head and kept walking slowly to a stairwell. Pointing up, she motioned for me to follow her. On the next floor, she stopped and led me down a hallway. The scent of mold was thick in the air, and dark spots crept up the walls from the floor boards to eye-level. I followed her, trying to keep my legs from breaking in two. Halfway down the hall, she opened a door on the right and stepped inside, grabbing a bucket and pushing it toward me.

The dingy yellow plastic pail might as well have been a crystal ball. I didn't make it one foot inside the door before the vomiting began, and when it started, I couldn't stop it. For days. I suddenly knew what Porschia felt like after changing.

TAGE

Nothing helped her. She couldn't stomach meat. She couldn't hold down blood. She couldn't do anything but lie around or scream from the pain. The fluctuation between the two extremes was enough to drive a sane person mad. Ford stopped by during a particularly terrible episode, and she told him to leave and let her die alone. He came back that night with their father and a pot of chicken soup. She refused to take her dress off; the one Maggie made her. She said she still wanted to feel like herself when she died. When I tried to tell her this storm would pass, she would scream that it wouldn't.

She was calm when her father visited, or as calm as she could get, simply lying in the bed crying. He sat at her bedside and brushed the flyaway strands of hair from her face. "You'll be okay. You're the strongest night-walker I know," he told her with gentle confidence.

She just shook her head. She'd been sick often since turning, but this was something entirely different. Ford stood at her door watching the exchange while I sat in the window sill. I didn't want to intrude, but didn't want her to hurt someone she loved, either. She didn't seem to be hungry at all, which was a very good thing, but her heart was completely broken. Saul was gone and she blamed herself. Even worse than that was the fact that she was sick and she couldn't garner enough energy to leave her bed, let alone go into the city after him.

But what would she do if she could? She couldn't bring him back into the Colony, but I wasn't sure if she realized that or not at this point.

Her family didn't stay long. "I need to rest," she lied. I could see the sheen of sweat breaking out on her forehead. Her father kissed her temple and stood up, the bed bouncing back into shape. Ford waved at his sister from the doorway. *Take care of him*, she mouthed. Ford nodded and disappeared behind their father, giving her one long, last look.

That night she tossed and turned, rolling from side to side, moaning from the pain and screaming from hallucinations. She swatted at imaginary wasps and looked at me in terror as she called me Mercedes and scooted away like I was the one who hurt her.

"Get back! I don't want you to Infect me!" She clutched her sheets and pulled at the headboard.

"Porschia, I'm Tage. I'm not Mercedes. You're safe."

She shook her head vehemently.

"Listen to my voice. I am Tage. Mercedes isn't here. She's in the city. You're at Roman's house."

"You're my sister. I know my own sister! You're here to bite me and kill me! You killed Mother. You killed Saul. You ruin everything you touch and I hate you! I. HATE. YOU!"

Porschia clawed at her face until I held my hands up and backed away. "I'm leaving. I won't hurt you, Porschia."

"You always hurt me. You always kill," she sobbed.

Her wails filled the air as I closed the door and pressed my shoulder blades against the wall. Roman appeared in front of me. "She's not getting better."

"No shit."

"It was the darts – whatever it was on the darts poisoned her. I haven't felt well since then either," he admitted. His dark eyes searched me for weakness.

"I got hit and I feel fine," I argued. I'd thought about the darts, but the couple I took didn't take me down; then again, the tips barely touched me because of my jacket. They didn't faze me at all. But maybe they had used something else on her...

"How many times did you get hit?" Roman asked. "Once? Twice? Porschia looked like a well-used pin cushion."

I beat the back of my head against the wall once. Porschia's cries and whimpers came from behind me, soaking through wood and wallpaper, soaking into my flesh and bone. "What can we do?"

Roman smiled. He'd been waiting for me to offer. He looked out the hallway window, saying, "We find out what poisons a vampire."

"And how do you propose we do that?"

With a wide smile, he ticked his head toward the city. "We destroy every one of them until they tell us what we need to know."

I pushed away from the wall, cracking my knuckles. "I'm down with that."

"Thought you would be," he said, walking toward the stairs. "We need to find someone to stay with her. And she'll have to go into the cell until we get back so she doesn't hurt anyone."

"Ford will do it."

Roman paused at the bottom of the steps. "I'll go ask him. You stay with her. She's happy to see you when she's lucid."

"She isn't lucid often now."

He looked at his feet and then up at me. "Then let's change that."

TWO

PORSCHIA

Mercedes stepped into my room. This had been my room since childhood, while hers was just across the wall. She didn't knock and she didn't even ask to come in from outside the door. She just barged in there like she had the right to speak to me and invade my privacy. "Get out!" I yelled. "I'm still angry at you."

"What for?" she asked breezily, easing the door closed behind her with a soft click. "I didn't do anything to you." Mercedes tried to look innocent, but she knew she was guilty. She knew it. She. Knew. It.

She knew.

She knew.

She knew.

"You did. You got Infected. You hurt Mother. You took Saul and I saw you bite him. I love him!"

Mercedes smoothed her dress over her stomach and sighed sadly. "I didn't hurt Mother and I'm not Infected. *You* are. That's why you're locked up in this place, that's why they're all afraid of you, and that's why they sent the mosquitoes. They'll eat your blood and rid you of this affliction. Don't you hear them buzzing?" Mercedes smiled. "They're coming now."

A high-pitched squeal sounded near my ear and I swatted clumsily at the air. More buzzing. More tiny shadows. She was right. Mosquitoes, first a few, then an entire army of them, flew into my room from the open window. I leapt from the bed, trying to get to the window to close it. It was open, just a few inches, but enough to let them in.

Pushing harder and harder, gritting my teeth, I tried to close the window. Finally the wooden frame gave way, but I'd pushed too hard and it slammed shut with a bang. The glass pane fractured, splintering slowly up the middle with the tiniest pinging sound at each start and stop. A thousand tiny buzzing sounds swirled around me and I realized the mosquitoes were pushing on the outside of the glass. They saw the weakness in the barrier separating us and were using it to their advantage. Acting as one, they landed on the pane and pushed the glass in until it shattered, spraying me with shards and splinters.

Tiny cuts spread across my skin until I looked as though I was made of lava, like something primordial and deadly. But I knew their plan. The blood was what they wanted, and the splintered glass brought it to the surface for them. They were coming for my blood, my life.

The bugs swirled through the air and came for me; a black, seething mass. I ran, slicing the tender soles of my feet on the discarded glass shards and shredding them into slivers of flesh and sinew. With one last cry, I lunged and finally reached my bed. I covered myself with the blankets but the mosquitoes were too strong. They tore the fabric from me, landing on me and drawing from my skin. Mercedes' laughter echoed through the room as I fell to the floor and they fed from every exposed piece of flesh.

They fed.

I fell.

I died.

Mercedes laughed.

Mercedes killed.

Mercedes ruined.

A lifetime later, strong hands lifted me from the floor. Had the mosquitoes cleansed my blood? Did they really take the Infection from me? Was I really a rotter or was my sister, whom I'd loved so much, a liar?

My eyelids were heavy, filled with dead mosquitoes and tainted blood. My ears were filled with the same. "This is only temporary, Porschia," a voice called out.

What was only temporary? Death? Life? Infection? Cleansing?

"PORSCHIA?" FORD ASKED TENTATIVELY. I BLINKED MY EYES OPEN AND SAW my brother peering cautiously at me from between two metal bars. The cell. I was back in Roman's basement.

"Why am I here?" I rasped. "What did I do?"

He shook his head. "You didn't do anything, Porsch. This is just a precaution. I have to stay with you for a little while today." The tiny window let sunlight spill into the room, just enough to illuminate my baby brother's concerned face.

"You aren't little anymore," I said, trying to smile.

"Definitely not." He laughed, but it was true. He looked more man than boy now. I guessed that was how I looked to Mercedes, too, at one point. My heart hurt just thinking about her. She was attacked and that wasn't her fault, but attacking other people? Who else could be to blame but her? She was dangerous.

"What are you thinking about?" Ford asked.

I debated on whether to be honest, but in the end I decided I couldn't lie to him. "Mercedes."

His face fell. "What about her?" He crossed his arms over his chest.

"She's the most dangerous of them all, I think."

Ford sat in a metal chair and placed his elbows on his knees. "How is that even possible? You and I both know she wouldn't have hurt a fly when she was alive. She'd catch them and throw them out the back door so Mother wouldn't swat and kill them."

"It has to be the Infection. Maybe it messed with her brain or her personality. Whatever the reason is, she's a danger to everyone in Blackwater. If I see her again, Ford…I have to get rid of her." My voice cracked and the tears began to flow. I knew in my heart that it would kill me, but in the end I would have to kill my sister. I couldn't let her hurt anyone else, because I also knew she would never stop. Killing was as much a part of her as it should be a part of me as a night-walker.

"Nothing makes sense. Why can't I feed on anything now? Why have I never been able to hold down blood, and why does everything seem so extreme? Hunger, energy, moods, strength, sadness. It's all just a mess, Ford. I'm such a mess." A blubbering mess.

Ford stood up and moved to the cell bars, squatting down in front of them. "Sit with me?"

I eased off the cot, thankful to be in a pair of soft pants and sweater, but unsure of how I had changed my clothes or who'd helped me. I didn't want to think about it; I just hoped it was Tage and not Roman. My limbs shook as I sank to the floor, sitting next to him through the bars. Although a row of metal separated us, his hand found mine. "You'll always be my sister, Porsh."

"Mercedes should be, too. This shouldn't have happened."

"We just got caught up in the game."

"The Elders' game?" I asked.

He shrugged, raking his hands through his too-long hair. "Maybe. I don't know. I was talking about the game between the night-walkers and the Infected, but I think the Elders play a much bigger part in all of it somehow."

"It's been going on since the two breeds of monsters were created," I agreed. Ford leaned his head against the bars between us. "And it will go on for an eternity. The Infected will keep spreading the disease, and the night-walkers will keep feeding on humans. Some of them will turn or be turned. It's a cycle that's doomed to repeat itself, and everyone involved is damned." That was the absolute truth.

"Father was right," Ford said softly. "Everyone who isn't one or the other is damned, too, simply because we're caught in the crossfire."

Silence stretched thick between us. My baby brother's warm hand made my cold, clammy one feel normal for a few moments. "Where did Tage and Roman go?"

Ford stiffened and tried to pull his hand from my grasp, but I tightened my hold on him. He wasn't going anywhere. Not until he told me.

"Where are they?" I asked again and sat up straight.

He swallowed thickly, but told me, "They went to the city."

"To find Saul?" I jumped up, hope and blood pumping through my veins.

"To find out how to make you better," he replied. "They went to find out what was on those darts they shot at you."

"The darts are what made me sick?"

Ford stood up and looked in my eyes. "Roman thinks so, but do you know what I think?"

"What?"

"I think that I don't trust Roman as far as I can throw him." I didn't either. Not at all. He was too intense and manipulative. He used his powers of persuasion to get his way, just like a petulant child.

"Me either. When did they leave?" I tried to listen for any noises in or around the house but couldn't hear anything except for Ford's pulse, the growling of his stomach, and his even breathing.

"About an hour ago."

"You should search the house. See if there's anything you can dig up on Roman." Something wasn't right. Roman admitted that he wanted me, and that he let Mercedes get Infected and fall in the forest just to bring me closer to him. But what was he hiding? How did he become leader of the night-walkers in the first place? There had to be some kind of proof that would give us real answers. We needed to find a hint of truth in a pile of lies.

"What am I looking for?"

I shook my head. "I don't know, but I *do* know he was responsible for Mercedes being turned. I might not be able to kill him now, but it will eventually happen. He will pay for what he did to our family, and it will hurt him worse if I'm able to figure out his game before he can see it being played out. Roman loves to control the board and all the pieces on it."

"What if he isn't playing at anything?" Ford asked.

"But what if he is?" I countered.

FORD RUMMAGED THROUGH ROMAN'S ROOM, SEARCHING FOR ANSWERS TO questions we didn't know. I could hear the wooden drawers sliding against their metal frames. "Hear anything?" he called out. I was listening intently, pushing my body to work and function like a night-walker should. My fingers curled into balls as I strained to hear any noises near or far. Colonists were milling around outside the house. The sound of someone chopping firewood echoed in the air; the thwack of the axe and splintering of the wooden wedge ringing in my ear. Birds chirped. Animals at the barn rustled around, chewing and snuffling. Chatter from farther away...but nothing of Roman or Tage. No scent or sound.

"Not yet." If they went into the city, it might take a while for them to find who or what they were looking for. Guilt filled every cell in my body when I realized I was putting Ford in danger. If Roman found him snooping around, if he smelled his scent later...

Ford went silent, his heart skipping in his chest wildly. "Porschia, I found something."

"What is it?"

His boots clapped down the stairs and he strode across the room, showing me a rectangular cardboard box that read "Cigars," across the top in bright red lettering. Holding it closed, he slid it through the bars to me. I flipped the lid open and gasped.

Inside was a small portrait, only as big as my palm. "Is that a picture of him and the Infected guy that was with Mercedes?" I asked incredulously. "Or am I hallucinating again?"

Ford shook his head. "That's the same guy. I mean, his hair is long now and he's rotting, but that's him. But *how* is that him? Look at their outfits!"

Roman and the dark-haired man were clad in matching uniforms that were covered with sand-colored splotches in varying shades and identical black caps on their heads. Their arms were slung companionably across one another's shoulders, and they wore large smiles on their faces. They were *smiling*. They were happy. And if my eyes didn't deceive me, they were brothers. A patch on each man's chest read: Nelson. Their straight rows of pearly-white teeth had no points whatsoever. There were no sores on their skin. They were human.

I always thought Roman the night-walker was much older than the date printed on the back of the picture: 04-14-2004.

THREE

TAGE

FORD WAS CONFIDENT ABOUT HIS ABILITY TO WATCH HIS SISTER. ME? NOT so much. I wanted to tear into the city, remove a few Infected heads, get the information we needed, and get back to Porschia. She was lucid when we left her. While she was mentally weak, she was physically strong. Even not having fed in days, she was still stronger than any human would ever be, even at the peak of their fitness and health.

Her brother? He was young, and young guys did stupid things. If she begged enough he might cave and let her out, and Roman was crazy enough to leave one of the two keys of her cell with him.

When I asked him why he did it, he answered, "It just made sense." The hell it did.

As we made tracks toward the flood wall, a male voice called out behind us. "Roman?" The sunlight was already directly overhead, and we didn't have time for a distraction. It might take hours to find an Infected who could communicate at all. It had to be someone fresh and still sound of mind, like Saul. But he might not know what was on the darts.

Roman had been jittery, fidgeting the whole walk, like he was amped up and trying to calm down, or calm and trying to get amped up. I wasn't sure which. We turned to face none other than Elder Yankee.

"May I have a word with you?"

"We're in a hurry," Roman hedged, glancing at me for backup.

"It shouldn't take long. I have a few questions about Porschia Grant and the attack from the Infected. Everyone in Blackwater is concerned that the Infected may now be stronger than they have been in the past. We are nothing more than sitting ducks if that's true." How did he know already? Damn it. These old men were like flies on shit.

Roman sighed and looked at me. "Go. Find someone who can help us. I'll catch up as soon as I can."

I nodded, watching his unblinking eyes as they stared back at me. Then I ran. Roman could deal with the Elders. I had no use for them anyway. They actually thought they ruled the Colony. What a joke. Roman ruled it. There was no question about that now that I'd been around him long enough. I scaled the wall and leaped down to the other side with a thud, crouching low. The air was cold and still, but the sun warmed the earth. I couldn't smell the rotters at all. Cold air hit my face.

Each house, building, and store I passed was empty. The city's taller buildings were clustered together in the center, and I knew that was where I'd find them. I would just have to take it one building at a time. *No time like the present.* Reaching the first building, I stepped onto a pile of crushed glass and snow, through the frame that once housed double panes of shiny glass. The structure had a stale, musty odor and the lobby's furniture was shredded; upholstery and foam on every surface. Desks were overturned, with deep scratches gouged into the wood. Rat droppings littered the floor, along with some substances I couldn't identify and didn't want to *try* to identify.

Glass crunched under the soles of my boots as I walked around the inside of the building. I came to the empty stairwell and paused at each floor to smell the air. Nothing putrid stirred. Building after building, floor after floor, I searched. Where the hell was Roman? He should have been able to lose Yankee and join me by now.

I stepped outside of yet another empty building, getting aggravated. If I wasn't able to find them before sundown, I could follow the light of the fires they would light to keep themselves warm. Why didn't they have them lit during the day? Looking around, I found a single swirl of smoke slithering into the blue sky. *Bingo.*

Turning the corner, I ran past a red stoplight and abruptly came to a stop. I didn't have to look any further for a rotter. In the middle of the road stood Mercedes.

"Just the girl I was looking for."

Mercedes' upper lip curled. She let out a snarl and then pointed at me, her finger ram-rod straight.

I ticked my head back. "You were looking for me, too?"

She shook her head, pointing at me again.

"Oh, you want to know why *I'm* here?"

Mercedes nodded.

"I need help. You're in tight with the asshole leader of the Infected, so you are *just* the person with the information I need."

She crossed her arms. Her greasy hair hung limply over her shoulder. Why didn't they just cut it off? Suppressing a shudder, I took the rest of her in. Her thin body swam in a dingy white t-shirt, four sizes too big. Her jeans were torn, and any exposed skin was mottled or scabbed. There wasn't much on her that wasn't scraped or bruised, from the look of it. Visibly shaking from her knees to her lips, her eyes held the same stubbornness as her sister. That was where the resemblance between the two young women ended.

But something was off. A single tear slid from her eye, crystal clear. It splashed onto her arm, soaking into her scaled skin like rain on a serpent's back. Why the hell was she crying?

"Can he hear me?" I asked, trying not to move my lips.

She shook her head once.

"Did he send you to fight me?"

She gritted her teeth.

"Alone?"

Blinking up at the sky, liquid frustration fell down her soot-covered cheek.

"Why would he do that?"

She opened her mouth to try to speak and a made a tiny screech. Her mouth pinched closed.

"You want to come with me?" I whispered.

She looked to the building behind her, full of crumbling red bricks, and a shadow moved inside the third-floor window.

"Who's that? Is that him?"

She shook her head and more tears fell. Lady tears tore me up. Always had. Mercedes' weren't as terrible as Porschia's, but damn. "No? Then who?"

Her lips moved, silently forming the word *Saul.*

Saul. Great. "Is he alone?"

She shook her head ever so slightly.

"Damn. Look," I whispered. "I'm going to come at you. Fight, but come with me, okay?" I took a step forward and then sprang at her lightning fast. She fought, clawing at me for all she was worth, even getting a few chunks of skin under her nails. *Damn it! These feline sisters.* Once I felt we had put on a good enough show, I picked her up and carried her off toward the wall. When I was sure we weren't being followed – not that the rotters could run, anyway – I sat Mercedes down.

"Do you think we fooled them?"

She shrugged through her labored breaths.

"Did we need to fool them, Mercedes?" She pointed toward the spine of metal rungs on the concrete wall in front of us. I didn't miss the way she looked behind her like everything was about to go to shit at any moment. I half expected it to. The merry band of rotters had been prepared for the attack in the forest, so why weren't they defending their own nest now? Why weren't they defending Mercedes? And why in the hell was I taking her into Blackwater?

"Climb onto my back and hold on tight."

Mercedes did as she was told, almost too well. "Not that tight," I eeked out. She loosened her elbows around my neck. "Just hold on."

What the hell was I doing? If she thought she would feast on anyone there, she had another thing coming. I scaled the wall and eased her down the other side. A jump might have split her bones. Her teeth chattered in my ear as I stepped foot onto the soil again. The sun was still up, even if only barely.

Roman was in front of us in an instant, teeth bared. "Are you insane? Bringing her in here? I told you to get information, not capture Porschia's Infected sister and bring her into the Colony!" he spat.

"She has information. Anyway, something weird is going on with the rotters. They pretty much sent her to die. Why would they want Mercedes dead?" I jutted my chin at Mercedes. "Didn't she attack for them? Kill for them?"

Mercedes bit her lip until I smelled blood, which wasn't a tempting smell at all; tar-like and putrid. "Where's your mother? Why didn't they send Saul? He's stronger than you are. He's freshly Infected, right?"

She clamped her teeth together.

Roman growled. "Take her to the cell, but take her the long way around. Avoid the colonists if you can, though most are inside by now. There's a storm coming. It's going to be bad, but probably the last one of the winter season."

To my right, an oak tree stirred, its branches already tipped with buds. The leaves would appear soon, the grass would brighten, and the snow would turn to rain. We'd had several snows since Porschia fell ill, but I was afraid this might be the last snow she would ever see. If Mercedes didn't help us get her better, it would certainly be the last Mercedes saw. I'd see to that.

FOUR

PORSCHIA

ROMAN BURST THROUGH THE FRONT DOOR AND RUSHED DOWNSTAIRS. I'D heard him outside talking with Tage; the deep timbre of their voices mingling together. The wood frame of the door splintered, echoing through my ears. He was a blur of speed as he raced down the steps, and like an angry bull, he backed Ford into the wall. Ford's shoulder blades made a thump against the cinder blocks. My brother's fear was palpable. "Get away from my brother, Roman," I warned.

"The key," Roman ordered impatiently, holding his palm out. His nostrils flared rapidly. Ford slid the cell key into Roman's hand, wide-eyed. Roman raced to the cell door, slid the key in the lock, and opened it. He moved my cot to one side of the rectangle and pointed. "Get on the bed."

"And if I don't?" I challenged.

He stalked slowly toward me. "Don't make me repeat myself. We have a problem and it involves *you*."

I didn't even *do* anything. How could whatever problem he was alluding to involve me? I sat on the edge of my cot and stared at him. He moved back across the room, grabbed something off a chair, and returned to my cell. A chain with shackles clinked in his hand. "Hell no! No, Roman. I didn't *do* anything! I haven't been *able* to do anything."

"This might come as a shock to you, Porschia, but not everything that affects us is all about you. Now give me your wrist."

"Only one of them?" I looked at the cool metal.

"Yes. One of them."

I held my left wrist out to him. It was my non-dominant hand, and I might need the other. He clamped the steel around my skin and the other end around one of the bars behind me. "Stay put."

I snorted. "Like I can go anywhere now."

With a satisfied look on his face, Roman left the basement, his footsteps trailing up the steps and overhead. I looked across the room to my brother. "Ford, go."

He shook his head vehemently. "I'm not leaving you with him. Where's Tage?"

"I don't know, but if Roman finds out about…" I whispered, gesturing to my pillow. The cigar box lay beneath it. Roman wouldn't like people going through his things. I just prayed he didn't notice Ford's scent in his room before he made it out of the house.

"Go. I can handle myself. I promise."

He shifted on his feet.

"Ford?"

"Yeah."

"Go home. I know you don't want to, but I promise I can defend myself."

He nodded. "You can right now, but what if…." I silenced him with one look. "I'll check back later," he relented, backing out of the basement.

I smiled. "I hope so."

MERCEDES

TAGE GREW MORE AND MORE IRRITATED WITH MY SLOW SPEED UNTIL HE growled, hunched down, and told me to climb onto his back. I was hesitant to be that close to a night-walker again. After all, Roman was the one who was responsible for feeding me to the Infected. If my vocal chords were still working, I'd have asked him why I should trust him. He was smart, I would give him that. I was surprised he figured out that I'd been sent out to meet him. He just didn't know why. Yet.

Pierce was angry at Roman. Roman had been giving him vials of night-walker blood, which Pierce drank until not even a drop was left behind. They didn't stop the Infection, but rather seemed to revitalize him somehow. He was decaying more slowly than any other Infected in the nest, even though he contracted the virus years ago, near the same time that Roman was turned.

Much of the time, Pierce was able to throw up a mental screen to keep me and others out of his mind and thoughts. But when he slept, I listened to his dreams. Most of them were of him and Roman during a great war. When he heard the explosions in his memories, he would awaken, skin slick with sweat and stare at me hatefully, as though I'd conjured the apparition just to haunt him.

I couldn't see what he envisioned in his unconscious thoughts, but the conversations between him and his brother – imagined or remembered – were disturbing. Pierce and Roman had demons to spare. Pierce had more than most others, but I understood why now.

As the night-walker sped over grass and rock, my stomach churned. The last few times I'd seen Porschia hadn't gone so well. She shot me, she bit me, she sent Mother to me when she was banished from the Colony. *And Saul.* She'd never forgive me for that. Saul was in torment in the city. His every thought was to get back to her, but he couldn't and he knew it.

We did crave meat, raw and bloody, but our hunger wasn't as terrifying as the night-walkers'. It wasn't all-consuming either. Once we were fed, it was a long time before we had to feed again. An Infected's digestive system was about as fast as a turtle in molasses. My arms began to ache and I clutched Tage's shoulders tighter.

"Hold on," he shouted back at me.

My knuckles began to lose their grip, so I opened my mouth and screamed as well as I could. A screeching noise was the only sound I could make. Tage finally stopped at the base of a staircase. The stairs led to a door and the door was attached to a beautiful brick home; stately and well-cared for. We were in the night-walker section of town.

Tage sat me down, although I could barely stand. Tage had shouldered my burden but it was still too tiring for me. My calves alternated between cramping and quivering, and my breath puffed in front of me as I braced my hands on my knees. "We're at Roman's."

I stood up straight, shaking my head, mouthing the word *Porschia*.

His brows furrowed. "She lives here. Porschia is here."

Screeching at him, I backed away. No. She couldn't be with Roman. Not him. She couldn't fall for him. She liked Saul. Why was she living with Roman? She should hate him!

Tage watched me back away slowly. "Hey, it's no big deal. We're all staying here right now."

My body relaxed. Thank God. Clutching my chest, I looked back toward the door where movement caught my eye. Roman stood in the door frame, between me and my sister. I snarled at him and in a flash, he was in my face growling right back. Tage eased a hand between us, pushing Roman away from me. "Back off, Roman. She feels threatened."

"Good. Because I'm laying it on really thick," he replied.

I shoved at his shoulder, not able to budge him an inch.

Roman laughed. "I felt a breeze. Did you feel that, Tage?" He turned and smiled over his shoulder, but Tage didn't join him in laughing at me.

Instead, he took my elbow and said, "Mercedes, let me take you to your sister."

I nodded and let him lead me up the stairs, into the foyer and back down another set of steps. The stairs opened into a large basement where the room was separated, half of it made into a makeshift jail cell. Inside the bars that stretched from floor to ceiling, their white paint peeling off in curling tendrils, was my sister. Porschia was shackled to the bars, sitting on a bed and sniffing the air. Her body was smaller than I ever remembered seeing it; a shell of her former self.

A noise involuntarily flew out of my throat, calling her attention to me. Tage stood between us, but Roman was on our heels.

"You'll be staying here. We've set up a second cot for you, just across the cell from your sister. I trust you'll be comfortable and won't cause trouble," Roman said with a sly smirk as Tage motioned to the small bed across from Porschia. She watched me with her green eyes, a brighter shade than I'd ever seen on her. The gray was somehow lit from within, making the green pop. Every step I took, she watched. Every sloppy, weak movement, she tracked with precision.

Tage stepped into the cell and motioned for me to follow. "You'll have to be shackled, too, Mercedes. It's just a precaution, given your history of attacking Porschia. If I had it my way, she'd be out of this cell and it would be all yours, but..."

I opened my mouth to argue, but a whoosh of air hit me. Porschia was within arm's reach before I even knew she'd moved. "Why?!" she screamed, spittle spraying my face.

Tears of blood leaked down her cheeks. "Why did you attack me?"

I pointed toward my side. She shot *me* with an arrow, and *she* was mad at *me*? Whatever!

"Before! Why did you attack me before?"

In the forest the first time? Is that what she means?

Yes, she answered. Her eyes bored into me, waiting for an answer.

I had to.

"You were going to kill Mother! She'd been feeding you and you were going to infect her, weren't you?"

I shook my head. *Mother was never the target.*

Who was the target? Porschia asked.

You were.

"Said who?" she asked aloud. I looked away from my sister, back to Tage and then Roman, whose eyes dared me to cross him. They were the same as his brother's; empty, manipulative, and dangerous.

I'll tell you everything. Just let me rest.

No.

Porschia, please. Please, I'm begging you.

Slowly, she backed away to her side of the cage and Tage blew out a relieved breath. I walked the few steps to my cot and offered my wrist. Pierce's shackle had always been invisible. I preferred to see the metal that bound me.

FIVE

SAUL

Pierce wouldn't let me out of his sight. The first chance I had I would run, and he knew it. He didn't trust many people, if anyone. I'd heard how he treated Mercedes. He barked orders at her, told her she was worthless, sent her out into the streets so Tage would attack her. Only, he didn't at first. I watched from the apartment window. He talked to her. They stared at each other and then he pounced, but he didn't bite. I'd seen Tage mad, and this wasn't him. This was a front to fool Pierce. Stupid night-walker was smarter than I gave him credit for. Tage scooped Mercedes up somehow and rushed away from the city, toward Blackwater and the wall that protected it. He wouldn't take her into the Colony, would he?

I could still make it over that wall.

But what then? I wouldn't risk infecting anyone. My mom and dad would take me in, but they couldn't protect themselves from this. This ran deep. My bones hurt. My muscles ached. My head pounded from all the constant chatter. Being in the city with the others, I could hear them all at varying volumes. It was deafening and was making me insane.

My voice was hoarse and almost gone. I asked Pierce, "How do I shut their voices out?"

Pierce brushed his long hair out of his face and smirked. He looked just like his brother. Roman had the same self-assured, arrogant look when he thought he knew more than anyone else. *You don't,* he answered.

Pierce took pleasure in the pain of others. He had minions who reported on everything, from the comings and goings of the colonists, the hunts and who was on them, and the night-walkers' activity. Not all of his information about Roman and Porschia was correct, but I wasn't sure how he was getting his intelligence. He ran everything in the city and was responsible for the Infected who roamed the forest, mentally shouting orders and gesticulating wildly.

Where Roman ruled through coercion and compulsion, Pierce ruled through fear. He made examples of anyone who dared to challenge his orders. Particularly deft with a long-bladed knife, he had gutted two of the Infected who were accused of stealing from the nest and left their remains outside on the fire escape. Vultures circled high in the sky, scenting the decay, before swooping down to remove the man's eyeballs and then what flesh hadn't rotted away yet. Pierce watched me as I took in the scene; detached, like one of those birds overhead. Only Pierce wasn't scenting a meal, he was sniffing to identify my fear or any hint of rebellion. I wouldn't give him the satisfaction.

Pierce's apartment was nice compared to everything else around here. There was a living room with decent furniture, all mis-matched but comfortable. The kitchen was full of jarred food. No one was offering information on where it came from, but it looked suspiciously like Colony food. There were two bedrooms. Pierce stayed in one and he locked me in the other most of the day. I didn't mind the solitude. At all.

If a quiet place was to be found, it was here. Here, the voices from all over the city were ambient, soft, and constant; muted at a tolerable level. What I couldn't figure out was how to keep my head from splitting apart when someone in the same room started having a conversation and the background noise became too loud.

Mercedes tried to help me when she first brought me to her place. Her apartment barely looked lived in, and I soon figured out why. Pierce had her on a short leash. She stayed with him most of the time, and now I would, too.

Why did you bite me? I asked as she tended the wound on my shoulder between bouts of vomiting and cold sweat. My stomach heaved and my arms shook as she considered whether or not to answer my question.

Steeling her shoulders, she pursed her lips together, answering, *He would have done worse if I didn't. I did it as a kindness, though I'm sure you don't see it that way right now,* she replied. Could there really be kindness in a death sentence? Mercy in a bite?

She cleaned the wound, bandaged it, and tucked me into a soft bed in Pierce's spare bedroom. As she eased the door closed behind her, I eavesdropped.

How is he? Pierce asked, his voice devoid of all emotion.

Sick. There was a thud against the wall, followed by a whimpering sound, high-pitched as hell.

Are you sweet on him? Like your sister?

No! Another thud.

Pierce growled. *Maybe it's time I found a fresh, more willing female to play with.*

She didn't respond. Holy shit! I thought Mercedes *wanted* to be with him. Porschia thought so, too.

Mercedes helped me through the first days of the infection, which were the worst. Take the sickest you've ever been in your life and multiply it by one hundred – that was how sick I was. I couldn't even stand or walk on my own. She carried some small containers of water from the river and then stepped onto the fire escape, where she'd set up a small area to build a fire. She boiled the water and somehow made a broth from animal bones. I didn't ask what happened to the meat. I knew.

She fed me, easing a spoon to my mouth and urging me to sip slowly. The warm broth burned a path down my throat and heated my stomach, and it was the first normal thing I'd felt since she bit me. Her eyes battled mine as she helped me sip.

Mercedes smelled better than the other Infected that came in and out of Pierce's apartment, and she tried to keep her room tidy. I didn't even know why I was there. Why was I in her space?

You're angry with me.

I'm trying to figure this all out...trying to deal with the fact that I can't go home, I told her. *Why are you helping me?* What was her angle?

She shrugged and held the spoon of broth to my mouth, easing my head up with her hand. *No one helped me.*

Pierce didn't?

She shook her head. *Pierce doesn't help anyone but himself.*

Why'd he want me? I asked.

To get back at Roman. Roman has a thing for Porschia. Pierce knew he couldn't hurt Porschia or Roman without them killing him, so he hurt Porschia by taking you and making you a monster. Now that Porschia hurts, Roman hurts. It's a really round, fucked-up circle – a spat between brothers that has dire consequences for those of us who are pawns. Mercedes dipped the spoon back into the small white bowl and blew over the surface of the broth, rippling it. *I'm glad Porschia had you. I know you helped her.*

My throat burned uncomfortably. *How do you hear anything at all about Blackwater? I can't hear anything but chatter. How can you possibly hear all the way into the Colony?*

Mercedes made a raspy sound in her throat. *We have people hiding in the forest. During the hunts, we learn a lot. Until recently, Pierce and Roman were on good terms and Roman told Pierce everything that happened in the Colony. I was so upset to learn that she volunteered for the rotation.*

What did that even mean? Roman was helping Pierce? To what end?

Footsteps outside the room halted our conversation. No doubt they could hear us. Mercedes fed me another sip of broth. She took a piece of paper and pencil from the bedside table and scrawled across the page. **There's a way to block others from hearing your thoughts. I'll teach you. But not tonight. You need to rest.**

Taking deep breath, I closed my eyes, sank back into the pillows, and tumbled into a deep sleep.

SIX

SAUL

Pierce circled like a vulture, raking his bony fingers through long strands of hair the guy should have cut off a long damn time ago. He stilled his steps and looked at me.

Mercedes isn't here to protect you now, he warned.

She didn't protect me before.

She helped make you as healthy as you'll ever be again. After she bit you, of course. Women. Fickle creatures.

His skin was mottled and looked worse than it had the day before. *How fast did the infection speed the decay of the body?* I asked.

It varies depending on the person, prior ailments and such, Pierce answered. *I was virile, healthy, and young when I was bitten, so I've lasted longer than most. You'll last a long time, too, as long as you don't get injured irreparably somehow.*

Porschia shot Mercedes with a crossbow. Did the injury shorten her life even more? I questioned.

It wasn't a mortal wound. We patched it as we do any flesh wound.

I had to know. *Why did you send Mercedes out there alone? Tage will kill her.*

I'm counting on it, Pierce answered, and started pacing again before continuing. *I hope he delivers her head to Porschia, too; perhaps on a silver platter. Tage is barely out of Frenzy, from what I've overheard. He loves Porschia, and is miffed at Mercedes for attacking his beloved.*

She is not *his beloved,* I answered indignantly, standing up.

He smiled, looking exactly like Roman in that moment. Then his eyes narrowed.

I know he's your brother, asshole.

He clapped his hands together slowly. *My guess is that Mercedes told you. But no one in that pathetic Colony has figured it out yet. Save the Elders, of course.*

What did the Elders have to do with this, and what else did they know? *How are you alive? I thought Roman was really old.*

He smiled. *He's not as old as he lets on, but he's pretty old. And I'm alive because of him.*

He keeps you young?

Yes.

It either had to be his blood or his venom. *His blood?*

Just a drop keeps me feeling decent, but any more than that would kill me. We've learned the hard way during our experimentation.

How'd you even figure that out?

His eyes hardened as he shrugged a thick tan coat on. *Someone lied to us. We found out the hard way.*

Who turned first, you or Roman?

He swallowed. *Me. End of conversation.* And with that, he strode out of the apartment and barked at two of his cronies to guard the door.

Where was he going?

To find out if Tage did what I hope he did, he yelled into my head. I grabbed my skull, a palm at each temple.

LATER THAT DAY PIERCE ENTERED THE ROOM WITH A PLATE THAT WAS covered with a towel, although the very thought of eating made my stomach turn and knot. When he stepped close to my bed and removed the cloth, a thick slab of raw, red meat stared back at me. A circle of blood swished on the plate as he held it out to me. It should have made me sick. As a human, I might have vomited to think about eating something so vile. It should have seemed disgusting and foreign. Instead, it made my mouth water.

I sat up as quickly as I could and lunged for it, but Pierce laughed and held the plate just out of reach, high above his head. *Someone's finally hungry. Good. You'll need your strength.*

For what?

To go see the rest of our community, of course, he replied.

He lowered the plate and I snatched it out of his hand, sloshing the bloody pool onto the bed. Backing up onto the mattress, my shoulder blades hit the headboard behind me. The meat was cold, but I didn't care. I tore into it like a ravenous animal, like Dara had gulped from the deer in the woods, like Porschia in frenzy. This was a frenzy of a different kind; the common thread of desperation weaving the two together.

Get dressed – wear a lot of layers and meet me at the door in ten.

I nodded, continuing to grind up my food, gristle and all. I finished eating and crossed the room to search the closet, layering on multiple sweaters and then a jacket. The only gloves I could find had holes chewed in them, but they were better than nothing. My boots felt a size too big. All of my clothes were stretched.

Pierce was waiting by the apartment door. He ticked his head and I followed him down the hallway, passing the doors that were shut; the occupants behind them growing quiet as we passed. There was a constant humming chatter. How many Infected lived here?

Forty-two, counting you.

That was more than I expected. That number must be hard to sustain, given the lack of provisions.

In my mind, Pierce laughed mirthlessly. *It is. We compete with the Colony for animals. Their population grows and ours dwindles, though we occasionally get a freshie.* He eyeballed me. Great.

Walking down the flights of stairs, I tried not to stumble. My legs were stiff and I felt like an eighty year-old man, skin too taut, muscles too weak. The hand rails were all that kept me from tumbling head over foot.

We aren't in a race. Take your time, Pierce said.

I slowed my steps and never felt so thankful to make it to the bottom of a building in one piece in my life. Before I was Infected, I came into the city for supplies. Climbing ten stories barely made me break a sweat back then. Now, I was drenched after just going down a few flights.

I heard a lot of chatter in your building. Do most of them live there? I asked.

Most, not all.

Outside, it was snowing on the dandelions that had blossomed early. Had it really been so long since that night? Time blurred when you were sick. Days ran into weeks and weeks into months. The question bit at the back of my mind: What did he learn about Mercedes' fate?

Pierce answered me immediately, leading me down the sidewalk. *She's alive. For now. But my brother won't let her live very long.*

Because of the treaty with the Colony?

No, he smirked. *Because she knows too much, and he doesn't want his pet to be informed about his involvement with what I'm about to show you.*

Two blocks later I was panting and had to stop for breath, but Pierce assured me our secret destination was only around the corner. I pushed away from the crumbling brick facade and shuffled toward the journey's end. A tall metal building loomed ahead, every windowed side slick with algae and grime. It wasn't the tallest building around, only four stories, but it was still impressive. There weren't four simple corners that made a square; rather, there were facets to each side, each building upon the last, making the entire thing look as though it was a diamond carved from the coal it was formed in.

I opened my mouth and tried to talk, but only a screech came out. It was easy to forget and hard to accept I would never speak again. Pierce stopped and looked over at me.

Use your words, he teased.

Asshole.

He smiled. *Since you're going to be with us for a while and you're now the new freshie on the block, I'll need your help with a few things. Tell anyone about what you see here and you'll be housed here as well.*

Staring him down, I waited until he moved to the door and pushed. It whirred in a circle, revolving around a central post. Following him around and into the lobby, the scent of rotting flesh hit me. I covered my nose.

Sorry, I forget how it is when you're not used to the odor.

Odor? That's what you call it? My eyes watered from it. *What is that?*

Let me show you. He smiled and waved for me to follow him.

I pulled the hem of my sweater over my nose and mouth and traced his steps down a long hallway. There were doors on either side that didn't look like they belonged to the rest of the building; steel, with a row of thin bars over a tiny rectangular window that sat at eye level. The smell came from within the rooms.

Pierce produced a flashlight. The Elders had a cache of them for emergencies, but over the years we eventually ran out of batteries. He pointed the beam up and the light cast shadows across his face. *Welcome to the freak show.*

He took a step toward one of the doors and a moan came from just inside. *Step away from the door,* he warned.

A shuffling sound from the other side had every hair on my body standing on end. Pierce eased a key from his pocket, long and oddly shaped. He inserted the key, twisted it, and the locking mechanism gave way. Even through the sweater, I could smell the stench even worse than before. He pushed the door open and I retched, bracing my hands against my thighs. Oh, damn. What was that?

Not what...who.

Pardon me?

Who is that, you mean.

Shining the light into the room, I pushed myself up and looked into the darkness. In the far corner a figure huddled in the fetal position, hands over its ears, a shrill keening coming from it. It stood – I now saw that it was a woman – looked at Pierce and then at me, with milky white irises and crusted blood all over from scratches. She peeled at her skin, raking trails into her own flesh, screaming at us, mouth wide. One of her upper teeth fell out and skittered across the floor. She had no hair on her head and her naked body was covered in wounds and blood, fresh and dried layering one over the other. Into my mind she screamed, *Out! Out! Out!* over and over. She wanted us the hell out of her space, or so I initially thought. But as Pierce closed her into the dark room and locked the door, she begged, *Let me out. Please.*

Clanging came from down the hallway, like something hard being raked across the bars of the door. Back and forth. Clack. Clack. Clack. Clack. Clink. Clink. Clink. Clink. And again. *I know him. I smell him. Where is Mercedes? Where is Porschia? If he's here, she's with him.* Holy shit! Porschia's mom was in this place.

Pierce answered matter-of-factly, *We tried to let her stay with the general populace, but she's crazy as hell. She attacked someone with a knife. It didn't kill them, but her mental state makes her unstable and she's a threat. So she has to stay in here.*

What do you mean I didn't kill him? Why didn't he die? They all die. We're all dying. Is Porschia dead yet? He said he was going to kill her. He said belladonna and infection was all it would take. He was going to poison her. Did it work? Is she dead? Where is Mercedes? I haven't seen her in days, weeks. Where is she? Miranda Grant was worse now than when the Elders first banished her from Blackwater.

Pierce stepped up to her door and slid two leaves through the hole. *Thank you,* she cooed. *This always makes me feel better.*

What is that? What did you give her?

The same thing she told you about – belladonna. It's poisonous, but better than that, it can cause hallucinations. Everyone in this building would rather be anywhere but here. This gives them that option. He strode to the next door and ordered the occupant to move.

Why did you give it to Porschia?

Pierce shrugged. *Just an experiment. It didn't seem to hurt the vampire who waltzed into town and took Mercedes away. I wonder how Porschia fared.*

I swallowed. What if it hurt her?

Ancients said it could kill a vampire with a large enough dose. I know Porschia looked like a porcupine with all of the darts she took that night. And we both know she isn't entirely a night-walker, don't we?

Bastard. *Why would you say that?*

Because I've been watching her. He unlocked the door and the sight of the next Infected made me vomit across the hallway floor, splattering onto the tile and Pierce's shoe. He looked up at me in anger, but then turned to the woman inside. Her lower jaw bone was sticking out of her mouth and she was somehow chewing on it with her upper teeth. Her skin was peeling away from the muscle beneath it, but instead of being a bloody mess, she was dry, like her body had no water. Flakes of skin peeled up from her scalp. She stood and stared blankly in our direction. Nothing came from her mind. Was it gone entirely?

She isn't there anymore. She hasn't spoken in months. He shook his head. *This one used to be beautiful. Such a pity. I tried to help her, but nothing I did stopped the decay.* He locked the door, enshrouding her in darkness once again.

What did you do to try to stop it? Did it make it worse? Passing another door, Pierce's light beam shone on a door and I jumped back at the sight. A man with thick pus running out of his eye socket, the eye shriveled and hanging like an over-sized limp raisin on his cheek, was groaning. His scalp was a patchwork of hair and bloody, seeping squares where hair had once been. Pierce urged me along.

Roman helped for a while, but then Porschia caught his eye, he began. *She distracted him. Now he refuses to help me. It was his idea, you know. Mercedes? He gave her to me. He was on watch that night. He wanted Porschia to be left all alone so she would come to him willingly. He knew of her family history with her mother, of course. It seems Porschia fancied a human boy, so Roman decided to turn her. If she was a vampire, she couldn't very well be with the human. But then her Mother got in the way again and Mercedes bit her, infecting Porschia just before she turned. Sure, she has fangs, but she can't stomach blood and she can't feed the normal way. She likes raw meat; craves it. She isn't one creature or the other, she's both. And if it takes killing her to get my brother back, I'll do it. I need him to help me here. Nothing else is more important than finding a cure!*

Stunned by the revelation, I countered, *What gives you the right to test your 'theories' on another person? These are still people, as cursed as they are.*

Sacrifices must be made, and most of the ones in here aren't people anymore. They don't think. They barely move. They tear their own bodies apart. Hell, some of them eat themselves. Why NOT test on them? And with that simple statement, he turned and walked out the door. Men's voices shouted in my head. *Let me out! Is there food?* Women's shrieks and banging on the doors echoed down the hall and followed me outside onto the sidewalk.

SEVEN

MERCEDES

PORSCHIA'S BREATH WAS ERRATIC AND SHE MADE A HIGH-PITCHED SQUEAL, thrashing back and forth on her bed in a panic. I tried to ease closer to her, but the chain attached to my arm held me back. Salty, uneven lines stood out on the dark fabric beneath her. Was she ill? She cried out, "Help me! NO! Mother, don't go into the water!"

Opening my mouth, I tried to call out to her, to calm her, but it was no use and the sounds I made just sent Porschia into a deeper spiral. She panted, twisting the blankets around her. I stood up and banged on the bars until Tage ran down the steps. Pointing at Porschia, I waited as he searched his pocket for the cell key. Where was Roman? It wasn't like I wanted him down here, but he was the leader of the night-walkers and might know how to help. Tage unlocked the bars and eased toward Porschia.

"Easy, Porsch," he said softly, sitting on the cot beside her. He brushed her hair out of her face and she came to, sitting up straight and staring at him. "Help me! Mother is going to get bitten! Mercedes is over there," she pleaded earnestly, her eyes searching his. Her fingers dug into his biceps. "We have to help her." She looked to the left, her eyes widening. "Ford! NO!" Tage approached her with his hands outstretched, but she looked beyond his shoulder as if the scene was playing out in front of her all over again. Her face was tight, her eyes wide and frightened. "No!"

She lurched forward, her shackle stopping her from moving far. "Help them, Tage. Please, help them!" Porschia pointed toward the wall only a few feet away where only cinder block was stacked tall, but where her mind told her the river bed was – just out of reach.

"I will," he said, pulling her back. "You're burning up, Porsch. Jesus." Tage looked over at me. "I let you rest, so now why don't you tell me what in the hell is doing this to her. Now! What was on the fucking darts?"

The darts were what caused this? I stood up and gestured as though I was writing. He sped away upstairs and was back down in a flash with a pad of paper and a pencil, shoving them at me. My fingers shook as I spelled the words: **Belladonna, also called Nightshade. And Pierce's blood.**

Tage's brows pinched together. "Why?"

I shook my head and wrote: **She's getting in his way, stealing Roman from him.**

"How so?"

Tears filled my eyes. I was dead for telling him this, but it was my sister: **Pierce is looking for a cure. Roman was helping him before Porschia came into the picture. Not directly helping, but he was giving him things to help his testing.**

"Pierce is jealous?"

Scribbling fast, I answered: **Yes. He's jealous. Roman and Pierce had a falling out. Roman isn't helping him anymore. Pierce was using Roman's blood to see if it might cure the disease. He was also harvesting natural things from deep in the forest. Pierce is too atrophied to walk there now. Roman won't give him anymore, so he's trying to hurt Porschia so Roman will come to him for help.**

With a final word, I wrote: **Desperate.** I underlined it twice.

Tage growled and slapped the paper out of my hand. "Doesn't he get it? There *is* no cure!"

I shook my head. Pierce *didn't* get it, and he would never give up. Even if it meant killing Porschia. He'd done much worse to other Infected persons. The things he'd tried were unfathomable: drilling into the brain, leeches, bleeding them out, feeding them various herbs, feeding them other Infected, letting snakes bite them... My God, who knew what else he'd done? Killing Porschia using a few darts was actually pretty low on his long list of atrocities. Pierce was stark-raving mad. He just concealed it with a handsome smile.

That was the ugly truth about the Infection and what Pierce felt gave him the right to experiment in the first place. The Infection eventually ate the brain of its victim, as much as it made them want to eat anything raw, brains included. It ruined them – body, mind, and soul – in that order.

That was where I was headed, where all of those who'd succumbed to the virus were headed. And the fact that Pierce thought Porschia's blood might be a better option than Roman's was a secret I would keep close to the chest. If they knew I was originally sent to retrieve her, they would never leave me alone with her.

Tage paced the cell. "What can help her?" His eyes roiled in anger, anger that was being turned on me.

I shook my head. I didn't know if there was anything that could reverse the effects of the toxic flower. It was just one of Pierce's theories. He'd heard that belladonna was poisonous to night-walkers, and he knew it was poisonous to humans and to Infected. That was why we shot darts at everyone. It was another of his sick tests. Porschia just happened to be hit with more of them. The fact that she wasn't entirely a night-walker doomed her. *I* had doomed her with one bite. What no one understood was that when a human was Infected, it set off a Frenzy of its own. We wanted to eat. After the initial sickness wore off, there was an insatiable hunger that only raw meat could provide. We didn't have to eat often, but we did have to eat when the pangs arrived.

The day Porschia turned, when she crossed the river, I was starving. My instincts and hers kicked in. She lost, but there were no winners in that game.

Someone knocked at the front door, and Tage cursed and marched up the stairs. "Look, it's really not a good time."

"I know what I saw. I want to see her again." Ford?

"Not now, kid."

Ford screamed. "I'm not a kid! I want to see both of my sisters!" There were sounds of a scuffle and I looked to Porschia, who sat up stock straight and turned her ear to the commotion.

"Ford?" she called out.

"It's me, Porschia! He won't let me in!"

Muttering over and over, she repeated, "Who? Who won't let him in? Who won't let him in? Who won't let him in?"

So I answered her. *Tage is blocking him.*

She opened her mouth, baring her fangs at me. They weren't nearly as large as Roman's or Tage's. "Tage! Let my brother down here now!"

How in the hell was she lucid now? I thought she'd fallen asleep. Or did she?

"Fuck," Tage groaned. "Five minutes, Ford. That's it. You see them, you leave. Got it?"

Two sets of boots clomped down the steps. *Ford.* I'd only seen him for a fraction of a second when he left Roman's earlier. Tage had thrown me up against some bushes and warned me not to screech a word as Ford jogged toward home, never glancing in our direction. Seeing him was more joyous than I could have imagined. He was so tall, taller than I remembered just a few months ago. And he was much more mature. Life had a tendency to do that; rob the young of magic and childhood.

Now he stood in front of me, staring between me and Porschia, who was sitting straight up on the bed.

"Mercedes?" His voice had even changed. It was deep and full of hesitation.

I nodded to him, wishing I could speak out loud. Just one sentence, one word to him. His hands shook as he reached through the bars to me. I lifted my hand and extended it toward his outstretched hand. The clanking sound of metal stole my attention from him. I looked over to see Porschia's shackle dangling and bouncing off the cell bars below it. Her breath was on my ear. Shaking, I turned in a slow circle.

"I. Won't. Let. You. Infect. My. Brother."

Before I could tell her I wouldn't hurt my brother either, she pounced on me, knocking me to the ground. My breath exited my lungs in a sharp puff and I couldn't take in enough air. In any event it didn't matter, because Porschia had other plans. She pierced my throat with her teeth and drank deeply. The pain was intense.

Burning.

Fire.

Stinging.

Stabbing.

Angry.

Full of rage.

Hate.

I pushed but she wouldn't budge, I bucked but it didn't matter. Nothing dislodged her. From somewhere far away I heard metal on metal, Ford shouting at Porschia to stop, Tage screaming curse words at the entire scene. Tage pushed his way in and removed her from me, but it was too late. My neck throbbed, the pain growing more and more intense by the second. I opened my mouth and released a shriek that made all of them cover their ears. My heart slowed, barely pumping. I was dying. My sister killed me and I pushed her to it.

Her eyes were satisfied as she looked down on me, but then she did something unexpected. She whimpered and covered her mouth with her hands. "What did I do? What have I done? Oh, God. Help her!" she screamed. "Where's Roman? Tage, you have to help her."

Tage crouched beside me and lifted me onto the cot. His tongue sealed the wound, but he looked at Porschia and shook his head slightly. It was too late. She'd taken too much.

Porschia's keening filled the air as she tried to climb the bars of the cell. Tage retreated and made Ford lock the door behind them. Good. Ford was safe from Porschia.

And I was...cold.

EIGHT

SAUL

WREN WAS A THIRTY-SOMETHING ROTTER WITH DARK SKIN AND TIRED EYES that wrinkled deeply at the corners. His hands were cracked open in several places, bandaged with once-white cloth that hung loose and threatened to fall off at any minute. It didn't seem to bother him, though. Before this moment, Wren seemed more like Pierce's bitch than anything else. It had been two days since I saw the building with all of the test subjects and I still wasn't able to sleep at night. Pierce was watching something in Blackwater and hadn't been home much, thank goodness. Whatever game he was playing was far too complicated for me to decipher.

It turned out that Wren was more than just a servant. On the morning Pierce left for the forest, he walked quietly through the apartment to my bedroom and brought a small piece of meat to me. *I can teach you how to block your thoughts. Right now, you're an open book.*

Yeah. Sorry about that.

He tried to smile and shrugged. *You have to find the frequency someone is using. It's different than the background noise. It's clear, no static. Can you hear me clearly?*

I could. Everyone else sounded muffled, their voices distorted.

Wren nodded. *When you hear someone loud and clear, focus on that sound. Each person's tone of voice is different. When we were human, the tone and inflections, even the accents were different. It's like that. You have to focus on the one in front of you, or the one you want to hear.*

Okay. I think I have it. The other voices that had prattled on non-stop since I became Infected finally stopped. There was only blissful silence, except for Wren's occasional thoughts.

Now, in your mind, build a wall. It can be metal, stone, or brick; anything solid and impenetrable. Build it around your words, only letting those you want the other person to hear float up and over the wall. I closed my eyes and built a concrete wall, taller than the flood wall, stronger and without weakness.

Try to block something from me.

I hid my worry for Porschia behind it. Her mother was in that place. Those people, we'd seen them in the forest. They were just another piece in Pierce's game. He would turn them loose to roam the forest and scare the colonists. They didn't have the cognitive ability to find their way out or for basic survival skills. It was a death sentence, inflicted twice over: once when he damaged them irreparably, and once when he unleashed them in the forest without the ability to get out or save themselves.

I can't hear you. Good. Now send something to me.

Can you really not hear me?

Wren smiled. *I heard that. Nothing else.* After a long pause, Wren spoke again. *I understand his intent. I don't agree with his methods, but Pierce started out by looking for an end to this curse. I'm not sure that if I were in his position, I'd do any differently. Especially with the vampires.*

Over my mental wall, I eased the words, *What vampires? His brother?*

His brother stopped helping him and stopped giving him vials of blood, so Pierce took the others. They were in the building you saw for a long time. But one by one, he ended them. It wasn't easy. One large male almost killed Pierce. Everson was his name? Now he has no one to play with.

Everson was here? The other vamps that Roman said ran off…they were here?

He kept them bound in intricate knots, starved and half-crazed, and would take their blood when he needed it. If they got violent, he killed them. He couldn't risk them getting free and coming after him. None of us are strong enough to fight off a well-fed night-walker. Wren paused before continuing. *Pierce didn't want Roman to know what he had done. Roman honestly may not have known – no – he couldn't have. Pierce was frustrated that Roman cut him off so quickly and definitively.*

Wren circled the bed that I sat upon. I eased more words toward him. *Why would vampire blood preserve him?*

He shrugged. *One drop can change a human, so Pierce thought that more than a drop might cure the disease. For a long time it kept him feeling better than the rest of us, but between you and me, I think he's grown immune. He had a steady source of blood from the captive night-walkers, but he's deteriorating rapidly now. Nothing helps him, and he is growing more agitated with each hour that passes.*

He was growing more dangerous.

Exactly, Wren answered. Oops, I didn't block my words.

Wren?

Yeah?

How far away can you tune in to a frequency? Do you have to be close to the person, or can you – could I reach someone in the Colony, in theory?

He shifted on his feet, reaching for the handle of my bedroom door. *In theory,* he answered with a smile. *Some can hear others from several miles away. You just have to focus and project your thoughts. It might take a while to reach them if they aren't expecting a message. If they know you're reaching out, it should be easier.*

How could I get word to her? How could I get her to listen?

I can help, Wren offered. *Write a message. I'll see that it gets to a colonist, but you can't let Roman know.*

I won't.

PORSCHIA

WHAT DID I DO?

What have I done?

What did I do?

What have I done?

I rocked back and forth, clamping my ears with my palms to try and close off the sound. Mercedes' screams were enough to drive me insane.

I am just like my mother. I am insane. I'm crazy. I killed my sister. My sister is dying. I shot her. I bit her. Twice. This time, she won't stop yelling. She's in pain. Doubled over. I can hear her clawing at the sheets beneath her. The fabric grates together like nails on a chalkboard. No one's safe. Ford's not safe. Father isn't safe. Mercedes is really dead now. Mother isn't safe. Maggie isn't safe. Tage isn't safe. No one's safe. I'm evil. I'm danger. I'm deadly. I'm death. Rock. Rock. Rock. Thump. Thump. Thump. Scream. Scream. Scream.

A cold hand clamped around my wrist. "Porsch!"

"Go away!"

But Tage refused to leave. He pulled me to my feet and held me up by the small of my back. "Look at me. Look!"

"She's dying, isn't she?"

His blue eyes bored into mine. "I think she might be. Do you want to talk to her, before...?"

"NO!" I shrieked.

He pulled me closer. "This might be your only chance to say goodbye. Do you understand?"

I nodded as bloody tears poured from my eyes. He helped me from my bed, in my room upstairs. He guided me, half-lifted and carried me to the basement where the screams grew so loud that I felt my eardrums would bust. Mercedes shook violently on the mattress as if she were having a seizure. I'd seen them before. Meg had them when we were kids. We would have to get something to wedge in between her teeth, lest she bite her tongue off or swallow it.

Mercedes' eyes widened when she saw me step into the cell. She whimpered, trying to move her body away but unable to do so. My sister was a prisoner in her own body.

"Do you need blankets?" I asked softly.

She nodded, but her watchful eyes tracked my every motion. She thought I was going to hurt her…again.

Tage reluctantly left the two of us alone. He probably figured that if I killed her now it would be a mercy. After she first became Infected I felt unmerciful and selfish, and I wanted to keep her with me as long as I could. Those same feelings washed over me like the water over the falls, only this water didn't cleanse. It damned.

NINE

PORSCHIA

Mercedes slept. Soft snores from the back of her throat used to annoy me, but now they were a reminder that she was hanging on, that she was alive. Tage had locked me out of her cell, which used to be my cell. He never said it outright, but I was a danger to her. Watching her chest rise and fall, I wondered how we got here. How and why did everything in our already crappy lives fall completely apart? Tage left to look for Roman. He still hadn't come back home, which wasn't like him. It had been almost two days.

Neither of us thought he would go into the city to confront his brother, but I didn't still know what Roman's ultimate goal was. There was always an end in his mind, and he was ever-striding toward it. No one else could figure it out, though. The man was exhausting.

Cold metal from the chair seeped into my legs and I pushed myself up and climbed the steps to find another blanket. I'd stripped my bed clean to make Mercedes comfortable, but Roman had other blankets. Rifling through one of the hallway closets, Tage called out to me, "Porsch?"

"Up here. Did you find him?"

"No," Tage answered, now standing beside me. "You cold?"

"It's chilly down there."

"No one's seen him. But something weird happened while I was out checking the forest."

"What?" I asked, grabbing a quilt and closing the door.

Tage held up a piece of paper. "You got mail."

"Mail?"

"News from Saul."

My heart thundered. I dropped the quilt and opened the letter that bore my name.

Porschia,

I'm okay. The most difficult part of the change for me is over. God, I hope you're better. Pierce told me what was on the darts: belladonna, also called nightshade. It's poisonous. Maybe not to a night-walker, but he was betting on it hurting you. There's a cure, though. You have to find willow bark. Chew it. It may take a few days, but you'll feel better.

Tage grinned and held up a handful of dull, gray bark, freshly torn from a tree trunk. I would have grumbled about him reading my mail, but he did the right thing. I could recognize that now. I took one of the strips from him and began to chew. Disgusting and bitter. Woodsy and too tart. However, if it helped, I'd chew horse manure at this point.

Listen, I've learned to block my thoughts, to erect a mental wall. It seems to be working, but there's more. There are different frequencies when we communicate with people. Those who are close by are clear, and those farther away are fuzzy and sound like static. However, if I project my thoughts to you, we might be able to communicate. So I need you to focus on getting better. Focus on my voice. It will find you. I'll repeat your name in my mind until you hear me. Every person, every sound, has a distinct frequency. We just have to find ours.

Don't give up on me. I know Mercedes is with you. Red clouded my vision and I blinked up at the sky, praying for this agony to stop. **Don't give up on her. Pierce, Roman's brother, leads the Infected. He's insane, but he's trying to find a cure. Maybe there is one. I have to believe there is. If anyone can find it, you and I can.**

Listen for me,

Saul

Tage shoved the leftover bark in his pocket.

"How did you get this?" I asked, my voice cracking.

"Rotter in the forest gave it to me. He was waiting in some sort of makeshift shelter made up of sticks and logs. There pine needles on the roof and on the floor, covering it like a thick carpet. He was just sitting there. Stood up when he saw me and extended the paper, holding his other arm up to tell me he wouldn't hurt me. As if he could have."

"You never know." The sting from each dart I received was still fresh in my memory.

"Chew the bark, champ. You need to get better."

"Why does it matter?"

"Roman's missing. I have a feeling that he's in the city, but I can't go in there without you being one hundred percent better. We'll need speed, strength, and maybe weapons. Roman probably has some stashed around here. Now, we need to handle the rest."

I nodded. I wanted to help, and if the bark or anything else in this world would help my sister, I would tear the earth apart to get it for her. "I'm going back down with her."

His lips pursed into a concerned, thin line, a look I saw a lot lately. That line meant he wanted to help; to comfort me and say it would all be okay. He wanted to tell me that Mercedes would be fine and so would I. And I wanted him to tell me this entire fucked up mess was just a dream. I would wake up in my bed across the wall from Mercedes, and then we'd race each other down the stairs to the gardens and throw soil at Ford every time he passed by with water. We'd laugh and giggle, and I'd listen as she talked about the Colony boys and fueled the inextinguishable fire of teenage gossip.

Tage bent down and gathered the quilt in his hands. "I'll be here. I'm here. I just want you to know that."

I did. "I know. Thanks, Tage."

He wrapped the blanket around my shoulders and pulled me to him using the pillowed fabric. I sank into him, reveling in the comforting warmth of his chest. Tage sighed, stroking my long hair with his palm. How was it possible to be so close to someone, yet feel so far away from everyone?

I pulled away and grabbed the edges of the blanket. "Will you check on Maggie for me?"

"I will."

"Tell her I'll come over if I get better."

He smiled. "*When* you get better. Yes. I'll tell her. And I'll be back soon." Lifting his finger up like a parent scolding a child, he ordered, "Chew your bark."

"Yes, Dad."

"Daddy likes to spank. Be careful, kitten."

Rolling my eyes, I couldn't help but smile. *Damn it, Tage.* With each step to the basement, I reminded myself that I needed to focus on Mercedes and on hearing Saul's voice – his frequency. Maybe he *could* communicate with me. If we found the right frequency...

SAUL SAID THAT EVERY SOUND, EVERY PERSON'S VOICE, HAD A FREQUENCY. He was right. There was a distinct, clear sound for everything: desperation, fear, sadness, hunger, bone-crushing grief. I once thought that the death of someone you loved was the worst thing in the world, but now I knew it wasn't. The worst sound in the universe was that of a parent losing a child. My father clung to the bars, dropping to his knees when he saw Mercedes locked inside, the blankets over her chest barely rising and falling now. Ford stood beside him trying to be strong, but even his chin trembled as he looked from me to my sister. There was no accusation in them like there should be; only sadness swam in the depths of his eyes, in the downward slope of his frown.

Father cried. Deep, heaving, soul-emptying sobs that filled the room with a sadness so thick, it could swallow a person whole like quicksand and fill them up with all of its pain. I pulled the blanket around me, trying to keep it together. I couldn't lose it again. Chewing the bitter bark, I blinked toward the ceiling and hoped Tage would be back soon. Father had come to the door only minutes ago, saying he went to visit Maggie and found Tage there helping her. He asked if he could come in and visit me.

I met him at the door and told him it wasn't me he should visit.

"What happened?" he cried.

Hot tears fell into my mouth as I bit off more bark from the strip and chewed in earnest. Copper tang met bitter pulp. Ford spoke up first. "It was an accident."

"An accident? What is Mercedes even doing here?" Father looked at me for an answer.

"She was sent to fight Tage. We think the Infected leader wanted to be rid of her, but we don't know why. Now she's fighting for her life because I attacked her like a wild animal. It's no excuse, but I thought she was going to hurt Ford. I wasn't in my right mind." Honestly, I haven't been in my right mind in a long time. I bit her. I almost took too much. I might have taken too much. She teetered on that razor-thin precipice.

Father shook his head in disbelief, staring between the pair of us. His eyes zeroed in on my mouth. "What are you eating?"

"Willow bark."

"Why?" He pushed himself to his feet, staring at Mercedes.

"The Infected attacked us in the woods the night Saul fell. They shot darts at me and I've been sick ever since. Mercedes said the darts' tips were dipped in poison – belladonna and blood from an Infected."

Father looked at me closely. "You are so thin, Porschia." Tears filled his eyes. "I don't think I'll survive losing either of you. Despite your mother's problems, I did love her. That love may have changed as she did, but there's a part of me that will always love her."

"I know. I loved her, too." It didn't make sense to anyone, let alone me, but I did. I loved my mother.

"She was awful to you. I'd understand if you didn't." He wiped his eyes, pinching the bridge of his nose tightly and muttering a curse. "I tried to keep her away from you, but I failed."

I shook my head and stepped toward him. "You didn't. You are an amazing father and we're all blessed to have you."

Ford agreed and Mercedes, still hanging on by a hair's breadth, lulled her head to the side. Her eyelids were slightly parted, although seeing her eyes was disturbing. The whites were bluish and the vibrant blue of her irises had faded somehow, like her breath.

Tage opened the door and slammed it behind him as he made his way down the steps. "Hey," he breathed, moving to stand beside me. His warmth was instantly comforting in a situation where there was none to be found.

"Hey," I answered.

"Thank you for letting me see my daughters and for helping Mrs. Dillinger, Tage." My father offered Tage his hand and Tage accepted it with a shake and a nod of his head.

"No problem. She's doing well. Misses you, Porschia."

Tage looked at my mouth and grinned. I was chewing and he was like a proud peacock, strutting his willow bark plume. He pointed to his pocket where I was sure a fresh batch awaited me. Oh joy.

"Tage," Ford asked.

"Yeah?"

"Do you need to feed?"

I watched as Tage's Adam's apple bobbed up and down. "I'm okay. But thanks, buddy."

Ford shook his head. "No. You need to be strong right now, for both of my sisters. I can help."

Father agreed. "I agree, and I can help, too. It's been a while since I've done this, but you can feed from me."

Tage's eyes met mine and I nodded. "Go ahead. They're right."

"What about you?" Tage asked. "You have to feed at some point, Porschia."

"I'll get sick," I whispered, reveling in the feel of his strong fingers lacing through mine.

"You're already sick. You need strength. We don't know where Roman is, and I bumped into the friendly Elder Yankee on the way here. I agreed to go into the forest tonight and bring back meat. The Colony is desperate."

"I can go with you," I argued.

Tage raked his hand through his head. "Someone needs to stay with her." I looked over at Mercedes, her steady breaths raising and lowering her blankets rhythmically. He didn't believe I could hunt anymore. And what about the treaty? I guessed it was as good as gone now. They weren't asking for help; they were *telling* us to get food, and they weren't willing to feed us to get it, either. And where in the hell was Roman to fix this mess?

"I'll do it," Father volunteered. "I'll stay here. You two feed and take the two in the rotation on the hunt. She'll be fine," Father said.

"I'll stay, too." Ford ticked his head toward Mercedes. "In case he needs backup."

Everyone in the room knew that his staying with Father had nothing to do with backup. If Mercedes passed away, Father would lose it. Plain and simple. And so would I.

My fingers shook. "Okay. We'll feed, help with the hunt, and then hurry back here."

Feeding from my brother's throat, I only took a few sips. It was all I thought I could stomach and more than I ever wanted to take from him. Ford shuddered as I sealed the wound.

"Gross," he said disgustedly.

Amen to that, Ford. Amen to that.

TEN

MERCEDES

VOICES FLOATED ALL AROUND ME, HOVERING LIKE CLOUDS IN THE CLEAR blue sky when no wind pushed them. Father's. Ford's. Porschia's. Where was Mother? I felt warm, wrapped in a cocoon of blankets and familiar scents. Wood burning, rich soil, the dark water swirling around in my spot of the river.

I dip the toes of my foot in the warm water, the rock beneath my bare feet warming my heels. The sky is blue and billowing clouds float happily across the sky. The trees are thick and full and the sunshine...my God, does it feel amazing. It feels like heaven; perfection and contentment.

Warm hands on my waist startle me. I crane my neck, brushing my cheek against Noah's jaw. His tiny shadow of hair scrapes against my skin and I melt into him. "Just think, 'Cedes, just five more months and we'll be married."

"I can't wait."

Mischief in his eyes, he answers, "We don't have to, you know."

I turn in his arms. "We do. I don't want to get pregnant yet."

That admission startles him. "I don't know if I ever want to have kids."

"Why on earth wouldn't we?"

The wind ran her fingers through his dark hair, ruffling it deliciously. "Because of them," he said, looking across the river. "Not to mention the night-

walkers. Now that you've been on the rotation, you know what they're like. Do you really want our kids to be in the same situation? Do you want to put them in danger?"

"I want to give them life and protect them from danger. And you know what?"

"What?" he said, pulling me tighter.

"I want to do that with you. We'll be the most amazing parents in the world, and no night-walker or Infected piece of garbage will ever mess with us or our family."

He smiled, the tension releasing from his chest on a deep exhale. "I want that, too. I'm just afraid. Stupid to say, huh?"

I shook my head. "No. It isn't. We'll be raising our kids in a dangerous world, but we can protect them. I believe that. I know I'd never let an Infected catch me. I'm fast," I sassed, grinning up at him.

"Oh yeah?"

"Yeah." I twisted in his arms and was gone before he knew I'd left. The thing about Noah? He was fast, too. He caught me as I was almost up the dry, dirty bank.

"Not as fast as I am," he said, a smile playing on his lips.

"Then I guess we make a great pair."

"We do," he answered softly.

"Good. Now kiss me, Noah."

He smirked, pushing my back into the bank. "With pleasure." And did Noah ever know how to deliver that.

ELEVEN

SAUL

Pierce invited me to go back to the "freak show." I made sure to block my true feelings about that place and told him I would try to help him find a cure. Truthfully the guy was crazy, but if he found a cure it would benefit me. I could go back to normal. I could have my life back. There was nothing to lose, but everything to gain. So...why the hell not?

Upstairs is something interesting, if you want to see.

Sure. I panted as I walked up the stairs, trying to get oxygen to my cramping calves. It took me longer to walk the few blocks from the apartment, and longer still to walk up the two flights of stairs. At the top landing, I rested against a wall and caught my breath.

Pierce smirked. From behind the wall in my mind, I released, *Asshole.*

He just smiled. At least he knew it. Handing me a flashlight, he led the way down the hall. The doors that lined this hallway were solid and had no bars. They were metal and looked damned near impenetrable.

What's in here?

Pierce walked to the farthest door on the left and removed a set of keys from his pocket. I made a mental note to find out where he kept them, but thanks to Wren, Pierce didn't hear my plan. Metal clanged from the other side, angry and aggressive, absolutely pissed off. The door's lock released and Pierce slowly eased it open, a wry smile on his face. *You've already met my brother. Did he feed from you, Saul?*

Roman sat in a chair, his nostrils flaring, dried blood caked to his brow and forehead. A strange, thick metal circle was clamped around his neck.

What is that? I asked. *How are you holding him? I know he's strong.*

If he moves too much, it's off with his head. Do you like the gadget I designed?

Roman's dark stare fixated on me and he bared his fangs. "Get me out of here, Saul," he commanded.

I shook my head, flicking my eyes toward his brother. He and I both knew I couldn't get by Pierce if I wanted to. Plus, I wasn't so sure that Roman being away from Porschia, and Blackwater, was necessarily a bad thing.

"Coward. She'll never want you now. You're a rotter. She's eternal."

Only she isn't, is she? Pierce said. *She might not live long at all. In fact, I'm surprised she's still here. How are the hallucinations? Is she able to eat?*

What the fuck did you do to Porschia? I stepped up to Pierce, every muscle in my body taut. For the first time since turning, I felt like I could win a fight against him.

Settle down. I just had to teach my brother a lesson. See, it's supposed to be bros before hoes, but when Porschia sashayed into the picture Roman forgot all about loyalty. It was simply time to remind him.

That was the problem with those two – they thought they were the only two players on the board at any given time. They were wrong. And I would show them just how wrong they were. I just needed time.

PORSCHIA

"I FED FROM HIM, TAGE." THE THOUGHT MADE MY STOMACH TWIST uncomfortably.

"And now he needs you to keep it together because *he* needs to be fed, kitten. Did you see how hollow his cheeks are now? The winter has been harsh on him. He needs us to bring meat. We'll hunt for a few extra things for your family, but you have to chew your willow bark and hold down Ford's blood or he'll starve another night. We don't want that, now do we?"

"No. We don't." Tage had a unique way of calming me and putting things in perspective. Most of the time I loved him for his candor.

Tage headed to the river as I started toward the pavilion. Noticing his departure, I stopped. "Aren't we meeting the volunteers?"

He shook his head. "Not this time. There were no volunteers. We're just doing this out of the goodness of our hearts."

No volunteers? No rotation? No treaty? No Roman?

We walked side by side toward the river, the sound of the rushing water growing louder with each step. I hadn't heard it from this distance in far too long. I hadn't felt it. I appreciated its darkness; its unsettling, unwavering fury. It wasn't afraid of anything. No obstacle would impede it. The river would conquer, and so would I.

"How do you feel now that you fed?" he asked.

For the first time since I was turned into a pin cushion, I felt well. Energy coursed through my veins. "Why do I always feel this way after I feed? When I drink blood, even though I can only handle a little, I feel like it truly is possible to live forever."

Tage put his arm around me and squeezed once. "That's because it is. If you feed, that is."

"How do you mean?"

"Every time you feed from a human, you take part of the time they have. The more you feed, the more years you take. Just a swallow gives you months."

"Isn't that robbing them of their years? Is that what I just did to my brother?"

"Slow your roll."

"Pardon?" I clutched my chest. "Did I just take part of my brother's life?"

"Not exactly. I don't completely understand it, but that's how it works on our end. Maybe on theirs too, but you just took a couple of swallows, so don't worry. And you mostly eat raw meat – or at least you did before those Infected fucks poisoned you. Oh! And you won't have to worry about them tonight."

"Why?"

"We're making a diversion," he answered, smirking playfully.

I hoped it was a good one.

Tage stiffened as we neared the two trees that now spanned from river bank to river bank. Old and fresh, but both were reminders of nights we would rather have been tucked away safely at home, and of what could be lost in the forest beyond.

"Is my sister going to die tonight?" I asked, watching the water swirl beneath the slickened trunks.

Tage sighed. "I don't think so. Not tonight. If you're asking if she will die, the answer is that she was already dying."

"I hastened the process."

Tage took my hand. "You were protecting your brother, and the only reason you thought she was a threat was because until I found her in the city, she acted like one. Even if she gets well, if she is somehow able to pull out of this and remain Infected for years, I still wouldn't trust her. I wouldn't trust her not to hurt you. So in my mind, and in the minds of your family, you did what you had to. You did what anyone in your position would have done, given your history with her. She has repeatedly attacked you and those you love and you had to protect them, even if it was against her."

I nodded and he pulled me into his chest. "You did the right thing, kitten."

If he was right, if I really did do the right thing, then why did it feel so wrong?

"Where is Roman?"

Tage blew out a breath, white mist forming a cloud between us as he pushed away slightly. "I honestly don't know, but I don't think Roman would leave Blackwater without a fight…which means we might be in for one."

TWELVE

MERCEDES

Bouncing onto Porschia's mattress, she popped into the air. She might be taller than me, but she was thinner. She was tiny. "Brought you something!" I whispered excitedly.

"What is it?" Her eyes glittered. She loved the thought of surprises more than the thing itself.

"Hold your hand out and close your eyes."

"'Cedes, come on. I'm too old for that."

I tsked her. "You'll never get too old for fun. Now, hand out, eyes closed."

With a huff and half a smile, she gave in, holding her right hand out and closing her eyes. I caught her peeking, but didn't call her out on it.

Releasing the hand full of blackberries into her palm, I watched as her smile lifted her cheeks. She'd been sick, though it was late summer, and I found them while I was out on the hunt. Blackberries were her favorite. Somehow they survived the trip through the woods and back home without being smashed. Mother would have cursed me for having a stained pocket full of smooshed berries, though I did my own wash and had since I was seven.

Porschia opened her eyes. "From the forest? Oh, I want to go with you!"

"No you don't. It's boring. Besides, the Infected roam the woods."

"Everyone says that just to keep children from wandering, but I know they aren't real. I've never seen one. Ever."

I steeled my shoulders. I didn't want her to wander, it was true, but that was because the monsters we thought were only ploys used by our parents were actually real. They did roam the woods. The night-walker overseeing our hunt last night had torn one's head off. It was the first Infected I'd seen up close. He was tall, thin, and his skin was mottled and purple. His eyes were clouded over and he moaned as he stumbled through the woods. Instead of seeing a monstrous creature, I saw *him. I saw him as he might have been during his life before he became this. Perhaps he was a father, perhaps he held an important job. He was someone's son, someone's friend. And now, as if the disease hadn't robbed him of enough, he was dead.*

The night-walker acted like it was normal to walk up to a person and extinguish them. Of course, I didn't want to be Infected, but what the vamp did wasn't necessary. He didn't even see us to hurt us. The man wasn't fast. He couldn't have caught us.

But maybe it was for the best.

The Infection had one more victim to add to its tally, hastened by the night-walkers.

The forest might be slightly safer.

The vampire warned us of the freshly diseased. "They're faster and they still think and problem-solve. They're dangerous, so the Elders told us to kill any that come near. If it can make it that close to us, it's a threat. Simple as that."

That was the first time I met Roman, and I hoped it would be the last.

As my baby sister chewed her berries and offered to share those that remained, I took only a single one. Tartness and sweetness exploded in a symphony of sadness, on what should have been a great moment of sisterly bonding. I couldn't get the cursed man's face out of my mind. I couldn't erase his moans from my memories. I couldn't help him and I couldn't shake the fact that I didn't trust the night-walkers.

"Listen, Porsch," I said. "The Infected are real. I've seen one. They were dangerous and disgusting and..." I grabbed her upper arms and stared in her eyes. "No matter what, you have to promise me never to go into the forest alone. NEVER. No matter what. No matter if someone else is across there and in trouble. You stay put. Get help. But never cross the tree. Okay?"

Porschia nodded, her eyes wide and solemn. "Okay, I promise," she said earnestly, purple berry skins still stuck in her teeth.

THIRTEEN

PORSCHIA

Tage paused at the crossing as he noted that the tree he'd felled was askew. The recent snow falls had melted, swelling the river. The only viable option was to use the old trunk that had served us for so long. He pursed his lips and asked, "Can you make it across?"

"Of course," I said, rolling my eyes. "I actually feel okay."

He shoved his hands into the front pocket of his jeans. "You have no idea how relieved I am, Porsch."

I swallowed. "Me too." I thought I'd lost everything.

"I thought I'd lost you," he continued, his brows pinching together. "And that would have killed me."

My chest tightened and dragonfly wings tickled the inside of my stomach. I smiled, unable to tear my eyes away from his somber gaze.

"I know how you feel," he continued. "You've made it clear. But you mean everything to me, and I want you to know that in case something happens."

"What would happen?"

He shook his head. "I don't know, but crazy shit keeps going down and I'm afraid we're going to get caught in the crossfire again. Who knows how it'll end? So I just needed you to know that before we went any further."

I nodded, my throat clamping shut.

Tage nodded back and made his way across the new trunk laying across the river. "Less slippery," he called back to me.

My boots felt too loose. Feet didn't shrink, did they? I crossed carefully, one foot in front of the other, listening to the water churn and feeling the wind comb my hair over my shoulder. Tage waited on the other side with his hand stretched out to me. I took hold of his and let him help me the last few steps.

Grinning at him, I said, "I made it."

"You doubted it?"

"You didn't?" I teased.

"Not for a second," he returned. "Or I would've carried you across. I won't let you fall. I'll do everything in my power to make sure you survive whatever storm is coming, Porsch."

"I'll protect you, too, Tage."

He snorted. "Like I need it. I'm the most amazing vampire ever."

"And so humble," I added with a giggle.

"Always. You ready to find some innocent, unsuspecting animals?"

"I'm ready to feed my family," I answered honestly. Killing anything bothered me, but they had to eat and protein was important. I would fill the hollow of my brother's cheeks if it meant slaughtering a thousand deer.

"Can I ask you a question?"

He chuckled. "Of course, kitten."

"Why did you come here? There must be other surviving communities. Why Blackwater?"

"When I left home, I just started walking. I did pass by other settlements and cities that managed to survive the Infection, but I didn't stop until Blackwater. My mind and gut said to keep walking. I approached from the south and went straight through the city. I could see smoke rising from behind the wall, so I decided to have a look."

"When did it tell you to stop?"

"When I saw your face."

Said face began to feel hot. "Stop joking around."

"I'm not. I was going to stay a week, maybe two. I'd been walking for weeks and thought I'd take a break. Plus, the weird outfits everyone wore in the Colony sort of threw me for a loop. I thought I'd stepped back in time. I never meant to stay. I thought the treaty was stupid, but I respected the rules everyone set up and I came to the rotation. That's when I saw you."

"That's when you bit me without numbing me."

He squinted one eye and winced. "Yeah, sorry about that."

"You said my blood was sweet. What does that mean?"

Tage looked at the budding trees above us. Life was ready to begin anew once more. "It's not a *diet* thing. Like, what you eat doesn't determine how your blood tastes."

"What is it, then?"

"It's more that the taste of you matched your face. You were so innocent, but trying to be fearless. I could hear your heart pounding, see your muscles straining to keep you from crumbling. You should have tasted like steel, but you tasted like the sweetest sugar imaginable. It's how I knew you were good, all the way to the marrow. You *are* good, Porschia. Regardless of what's happened, you always do what's best for everyone else."

"It doesn't seem that way. I always mess everything up."

He shook his head. "That's your mother talking through you; that's not you. That's not what everyone around you sees."

I doubted anyone saw good in me now. Ask any of my former neighbors. They would assume I was a blood-thirsty, crazed creature, always dangerous, never to be trusted. And I might agree. After all... "I couldn't save her."

He huffed. "Your mother? People have to want to be saved before anyone or anything can help them, Porsch. You aren't responsible for her kind of crazy. Some people just have problems that are too big for them or others to overcome. She was one of those people. Her problems consumed her, and then she consumed everyone around her."

"Not anymore," I countered.

"You don't know that. I'm sure she's a stellar Infected," he teased, pretending to eat his own forearm.

I smacked his chest. Hard. "Let's go."

"Yes, ma'am. You know, an aggressive woman is very attractive."

"Tage," I warned, a smile tugging at my lips.

My senses were in overdrive. We had already taken down two does and were stalking a pack of either wild dogs or coyotes; it was hard to tell which. Once man's best friend, dogs had become wild again, traveling in packs and living together in old homes or abandoned dens. They weren't immune to the Infected who craved raw meat, or to the humans who needed it. And then there was me. I craved meat, too. And being in the woods, having killed two does, the craving was insatiable. I needed it. My body needed it.

I tamped down those feelings.

My brother needed it.

My father needed it.

Maggie needed it.

The Elders were desperate, according to Tage. Yankee told him that the colonists refused to hunt with the night-walkers. Somehow they knew that Tage had brought Mercedes into Blackwater. "How do they know that?"

"It was daylight," Tage whispered. "Someone probably saw me. He said that he told them Roman had broken the law by bringing an Infected over the border, and that Roman had been banished. But you and I both know that is complete bullshit. Roman wouldn't go down without a fight. He wouldn't tuck tail and run into the woods just because the Elders said so."

"You still think he's in the city?"

"I do," he answered matter-of-factly. "Especially now that you told me about his brother."

"What do we do?"

"I'm not sure yet. We need to know if he's there before we go charging in."

"I'm trying to reach Saul."

Tage frowned disgustedly. "I know."

"How do you know?" I asked curiously. I hadn't said anything aloud.

"You keep looking toward the city, you're quiet, and I can tell you're concentrating."

Why did I feel so guilty? "I have to try, Tage. And it's quiet here. Here I'm not worrying about Mercedes. I mean, I am, but she isn't right in front of me. There aren't any distractions."

"I know, but I don't have to like it. Especially the fact that I'm not distracting you enough."

It was quiet in the forest. Other than the occasional animal, I didn't hear much at all. The wind stirred the branches, clacking them against each other. There wasn't constant chopping or rolling or hammering like in Blackwater. In the Colony, everyone worked until dark. They stayed busy because they had to. This time of year, the residents were preparing the land for spring planting. Everyone pitched in. It was deafening during the times that my hearing was more acute.

Tage handed me a piece of willow bark. "Chew."

"Ugh. I hate this stuff."

"Well it likes you, kitten. You're feeling better, holding down food. I'm proud of you. We need to strip some more bark while we're out here tonight. I won't let you forget. Don't worry."

Putting the bitter strip of bark in my mouth, I began to chew, grumbling, "Gee, thanks."

Tage smiled, but it was fake. It didn't reach his eyes. "Chew, try to tune in to Loverboy, and I'll keep tracking those mangy mutts."

Something on the wind, from the west. "Forget the dogs. Let's go."

"What is it?" he asked.

My eyes lit up. "Bear." I remembered the taste of bear's blood. It was the first thing I drank after becoming a night-walker, and Tage had helped me then, too.

Tage tossed his head back and laughed. "Your itty bitty fangs can't bring it down."

"No, but yours can."

"You look excited, kitten." I was. It was exhilarating to watch an enormous animal being brought down. "*Very* excited," he continued, a twinkle in his eye. "We'll have to find bears more often."

"Let's go!" I took his hand and tugged.

The bear didn't know what hit her. I rammed into her side, knocking her over while Tage pierced her throat. She bellowed and clawed, but it was too late. Tage drank fast, his eyes growing dark as he fed from her.

When she faded and stopped fighting, he pulled his fangs out. "Hungry?"

I shook my head. I wanted the blood. I wanted the meat. I was hungry, but I felt good and didn't want to ruin that feeling. It was so rare.

"Just a little will help you, Porschia. Just take a few sips."

I walked toward him where he held the giant animal's head and neck for me. I tried to ease my fangs in the holes he made, but no matter how hard I pushed, they were too small to puncture her hide and find a vein.

"Drink from me," he ordered in a gravelly voice.

"I might hurt you." My voice was shaking as violently as my lips.

"Drink. From. Me."

He didn't have to ask twice. I tackled him, straddling his hips and pulling his throat to me. Night-walkers didn't have to numb other night-walkers in order to feed, but I dragged my tongue down his throat out of habit or some deeper need I didn't want to name.

He moaned and clasped my waist hard. I sank my teeth into him and slowly took some of the blood from his body. His scent, masculine and dangerous, filled my nose along with the coppery scent of the blood filling my mouth. After a few gulps I eased my fangs out of his flesh, but couldn't bring myself to let go of him just yet.

He had the same problem. Our erratic breaths visibly danced in the cold air, intertwining and coexisting as one. "Porschia," he breathed, as though I was the answer to his problems.

"Tage," I said, as though he were the answer to my prayers.

Drunk on blood and the feeling of wellness, I let him reel me toward him. I let his lips touch mine, soft and strong and filled with longing.

It was in that moment when I let go and lost myself, that I heard a voice calling out to me.

Porschia?

I pulled away from Tage, my eyes growing wide. "Don't run from me," he pleaded.

I shook my head. "It's not that. I hear him." I stood up, dusting the damp leaves from my knees.

"Saul?" he asked, swallowing.

Nodding, I parroted, "Saul."

Saul? I answered.

I hear you! he replied instantly.

I hear you, too.

Tage's stormy eyes held mine captive as he stood up and hefted the bear's body. "Be right back," he mumbled, running toward the Colony as fast as he could, blurring through the trees.

FOURTEEN

SAUL

I HEARD HER! I FINALLY HEARD HER. WE FOUND THE FREQUENCY. FOR DAYS I called out for her, putting up a wall around Pierce and hoping he didn't know what I was doing. I prayed he couldn't hear me. Wren promised that he heard nothing, and for some reason, probably because we were in the same desolate situation, I trusted him.

Tonight was different. We spoke. I stared into the mirror atop the dresser in the spare room at Pierce's, the one that had become mine. The blue shirt I wore was stained with blood and God knew what else from helping Pierce today. He was twisted as all hell, but his theories could work. One of them might work.

Where are you? Are you still sick?

In the woods hunting with Tage. I feel much better. The willow bark really does help. I can stomach small amounts of blood.

She was with Tage. I didn't like it, but it was better than her being with Roman. Of course, he was still locked upstairs in the experimentation building.

Who's in the rotation?

She took a long time answering. *No one.*

No one? *What do you mean, no one is in the rotation? No human is hunting?*

No. The Elders said they're desperate, but the treaty is as good as dissolved. Tage and I are getting as much meat for the colonists as we can. They're starving. My brother looks terrible. My father looks worse. Have you seen Mother? Do you know if Roman is in the city? We haven't seen him in a couple of days, which is weird.

I didn't know what to tell her about Roman, so I kept silent. What to tell her about her mom? *The treaty shouldn't be nullified. It puts the humans in danger. And I've seen your mom. She's as well as she was when she left Blackwater.*

When she was banished, you mean, Porschia corrected.

Yeah.

And Roman? Have you seen or heard from him?

I hated to do it, but I lied. *No.*

Could you look around for him? Just in case he's there with Pierce? You probably already know by now, but they're brothers.

I do know. I'll keep my eyes peeled. I knew I would see Roman in the morning. Pierce wanted me to help him draw blood from him.

She was silent. *Are you there?* I asked.

I am. I'm afraid to move. My feet feel like they're cemented to the ground.

Why, Porschia?

If I move, I might lose you. I'm afraid I won't be able to find the frequency again. I think I found you because the forest is so quiet at night.

I smiled. I didn't want to let her go either, but my head was pounding just trying to keep up the blocks while letting my words filter only toward her. *Find me there. Go back to the woods, to the quiet, if you need to talk. Just keep me in mind.*

I will.

How is Mercedes? I assume she's with you since you're with Tage.

Porschia answered, but it wasn't what I expected. *I attacked her. She's not doing well.*

Did she hurt you? That was what Pierce wanted. He sent her as a weapon, one he assumed he could wield against her.

No. The poison made me hallucinate and I thought she was going to hurt Ford, so I...

It's okay. She'll be fine.

Nothing will ever be fine or normal again, Saul.

I love you. That won't change. I wished I was with her to hold her close and kiss away her tears. I knew she was breaking down. She was crumbling. Her entire world was imploding. First her sister and then Meg. Her mother's insanity. Being turned. My fall to the Infected. Her brother and dad starving. She was losing it, and I was afraid that if she did, I would lose her forever.

We need to go. It's almost dawn. The Elders will be waiting for the meat. Everything is changing.

Not everything. *It's still the same in some ways, too.*

Goodnight, Saul. I hope you're feeling okay.

Better than I expected to.

Good, she said.

Goodnight, Porschia.

Silence.

MERCEDES

A HEAVY SHROUD LAY OVER ME. I TRIED TO MOVE MY ARMS BUT COULDN'T. My toes. I couldn't wiggle them or my fingers. My breathing was steady. I could feel my ribs expand with each breath. I was warm, so warm. It was like I was inside a cocoon. My eyelids were heavy and my tongue felt too big for my mouth and far too dry.

With every ounce of strength I could muster, I raised my head. It was only for a second, but I did it. The back of my skull thumped against something soft as it crashed back down. Gravity was a bastard. So was cotton mouth.

Finally, I managed to move my right forefinger and thumb. Then the big toe on my left foot. Slowly, I managed to move them all. Every digit awakened. I opened one eyelid and then the other, rolling my head to the side. A small shaft of sunlight spilled into the room, dust motes swimming through the warm rays like a happy school of fish.

The bars that caged me reminded me where I was. Roman's basement. But the snores from across the room weren't foreign. It wasn't Roman who guarded me. It was my baby brother.

Ford looked too long for the chair he had somehow gotten comfortable in – too long by a mile. He was tall and lanky and far too skinny. This spring and summer would help matters, but not soon enough. I wanted to tell him how sorry I was. I shouldn't have volunteered for the rotation. If I'd stayed at home, put my pride away and offered to do chores or simply ask neighbors for help, none of this would have happened. I wouldn't have fallen. Mother wouldn't be in the city with Pierce, and Porschia wouldn't be half Infected and half night-walker. She wouldn't have shot or bit me. She would still love me.

I tried to raise up but couldn't find the strength. I tried to cry but my tears were dried up. Like so much of me, there was nothing good left.

Someone was rustling around upstairs. Porschia maybe? My muscles felt tight and I was hot and uncomfortable. Frustration poured from my throat in an agitated groan; a groan that sounded more human than I had in months. I opened my mouth and tilted my head toward Ford, who was startled awake at the sound. He rushed to the cell, fumbling with the key in the lock. Dropping them on the ground, he tried again. "Was that you?"

I nodded.

"That sound came from you?"

I nodded again, my mouth wide in disbelief.

He threw the door open and rushed to help me sit up. "Make it again!"

"F---"

"Holy shit! Father, get down here! Fast!"

"F-f-f--" I tried. Oh my God. I was actually forming sounds.

Father ran down the steps, his hands sliding down the drywall. "What is it? Is she okay?" His eyes widened when he found me sitting up, Ford supporting my back.

"Fo-r--d" I said, a huge smile splitting my face.

I motioned like I was drinking something. "Father, sit with her. I'll get her some water from the well."

Father sat next to me, helping me sit up. His mouth was so wide, flies could go in and out at their leisure. "How is this possible?" he asked himself in a whisper. "I thought Porschia's bite had killed you."

Ford rushed back in the house and down the steps. There was more water soaking his wool pants than in the cup, but it was perfect. Cold and fresh. I gulped greedily. "S-sa--ved m-me."

"What saved you?" Ford asked, out of breath.

"Porschia," Dad replied in awe. He pulled my head to his chest and cried. "The bite of a night-walker can heal the Infected. My God."

FIFTEEN

PORSCHIA

Tage carried the bear across the tree trunk, then the two deer, one on each shoulder. I kept the squirrels hidden beneath my jacket. Just as Tage suspected, Elders Beckett and Yankee were waiting on the opposite bank, flanked by six strong young men. Jonah, Meg's fiancé, and Noah, whom Mercedes loved, were among them. The others were their friends, but I didn't know them by name. I'd never spoken to them. Mercedes would know. She would know them by name, family, and home. She would know their siblings and gossip about them. She would know what to say. I said nothing.

They watched me and I watched back, all of us afraid to cross the invisible, incredibly fragile line that lay between us. "Is this all you could get?" Yankee asked.

Tage put his hands on his hips and smiled, a telltale sign that he was about to punch the old man in the face. "Seriously? We did this without your help and you still complain?"

"With two night-walkers in the forest, you would have thought we'd have a feast," Yankee continued.

"You no longer have famine. You should be thankful," I retorted, rushing across the tree trunk to stand beside Tage.

Beckett's eyes narrowed. "I see you're doing well, Miss Grant."

"I am, thank you." His rheumy eyes raked down my modern clothes and I watched as his lip curled in distaste. It was probably the exact mirror image of my own. I didn't like what I saw when I looked at him, either.

"I trust that we can count on the pair of you to provide us with meat for the next month, until the early spring plants can produce," Yankee butted in.

Tage snorted. "What about your precious treaty?"

"The treaty was broken by your kind. We will not honor it."

"Then we will not feed you," I told him. Tage grabbed my hand and squeezed like a proud papa.

Yankee smiled. "Then we will not return Roman to you."

Tage's eyes narrowed. "Good. Keep him," he smarted.

The flab of flesh beneath Beckett's chin began to quiver. "Well, I never."

"No!" I shouted. "You never! You order people around like slaves, but you NEVER hunt. You never help garden. You never *provide*."

Yankee's face turned bright red as he pointed his finger at me. "We provide everything! Food, shelter, sanctuary. And we even provide it to *your* kind."

"I was 'your kind' just months ago! I turned because I had no other choice. You would have done the same thing. Given the choice between becoming Infected or becoming a night-walker, you would have used the ring!"

Jonah stepped forward and Noah followed. "She's right," Noah said. "She did what any one of us would have done. It's what those in the rotation were told to do. And if anyone in the Colony feeds us and keeps us safe, it's the night-walkers."

With that, Noah grabbed the doe's feet, front and back, in his hands and hefted it into a wheelbarrow that I didn't even notice was sitting to the side of the mob. Anger blurred my vision. They threw the other doe's carcass on top and Jonah wheeled it away, muscles straining and teeth grinding together.

I turned back to Yankee. "And *you* provide me nothing. I am still a part of this community, regardless of my lifespan. And yes, I'm a night-walker. If you cross me, I will take what I need."

"Don't threaten us, young lady!" Beckett growled, pulling Yankee backward and away from me.

"It is no threat. You don't keep me. You aren't responsible for me. *I* am. And I will survive this and you. Oh! And I will find out what has happened to Roman. If you have him, if you're holding him against his will, there will be repercussions."

Beckett pulled Yankee's blubbering ass away from me. At least one of them had the sense to know when they were about to push a girl too far.

Tage and I watched as the guys took a paw of the bear and half-lifted, half-dragged it across the grass toward town. Either of us could have carried it for them, but it was obvious that they wanted to prove a point: they were in control. But they couldn't even hunt without becoming Infected. What they thought was control was only an illusion; a mirage of pride and stubborn foolishness.

I sniffed the air. Roman's scent wasn't on them. I would have picked it up. "They don't have him," Tage affirmed. "If they do, they haven't been around him."

"You still think he's in the city?"

Tage threaded his fingers together and laid them on the back of his head. His shirt and jacket rode up, exposing his taut stomach. I had to look away. "I do."

"Why do you think that? Saul hasn't seen him."

"And you trust Saul, huh?"

I did. "Of course."

"What if he hasn't been allowed to see him, Porsch? Roman could tear the Elders apart, but Pierce is clever. He's been trying to find a cure for this disease for years. What if he thinks Roman is the key? He poisoned you! What if he figured out a way to bring a night-walker down without killing him? You know what? The next time Loverboy calls out to you, tell him that I know about their little secret, the one they keep locked up tight. I stumbled across it during a supply run one night. I'm not the only one in Blackwater who knows about it, either."

"What secret?"

"You trust him? Well then have him tell you what they keep locked behind the doors of the silver building." Tage stormed off toward Roman's house, angrier than I'd ever seen him. I waited, looking at the water, at Blackwater, at the grass path trampled by Tage's feet. Why would the Elders want Roman? How could they hold him, and what secrets were the Infected keeping locked away in the city?

SIXTEEN

PORSCHIA

WHEN MY BROTHER'S FRANTIC VOICE CUT THROUGH THE SOLITUDE, I RAN TO him, my heart a palpitating, quivering mess. "Is it 'Cedes?"

He huffed and puffed, nodding his head, bracing his hands just above his knees.

"Oh, God. Oh, no!" I cried, my chest heaving with sobs. The cemetery loomed in the distance, a thin strand of fog weaving its way a few feet above the wooden markers. The cage was still laying on top of Meg's grave.

Mercedes was dead.

Meg was dead.

Mother was dead.

Everyone was dead.

Saul was dead.

I was dead.

I was crying. I was screaming. Tearing at the roots of my hair, listening to them pull from their follicles one at a time, then in a large clump.

"Chew your bark!" Tage's voice called into my ear. My eyes snapped to his and I clawed at his face.

"Don't tell me to chew the fucking bark! My sister is dead! I killed her! Fuck the bark. Fuck every fucking thing in this fucking place! I've had it!"

Ford's eyes widened and he shook his head as Tage held me at arm's length. I wanted him to hurt. Chew my fucking bark? I'd stuff the bark in his fucking eyeball!

"No!" Ford screamed. "Mercedes is fine! She's awake and she..."

I stopped fighting Tage and turned to my brother. "What?" I asked in disbelief.

"She said my name, Porschia."

"What?" I cried, tackling him in a hug.

Muffled by the fabric of my jacket and shoulder shoved into his mouth, he spoke. "She said my name."

"She spoke? How can she speak?"

Tage's hand appeared in front of me. "You healed her. You drove the infection from her body, or so we think."

"How?"

"It's the venom in your fangs."

My heart felt like it had snapped in two again. "I thought I killed her." I dug my palm into my chest, trying to keep it together.

Tage pulled me up and into a hug. "You saved her, kitten. Holy shit. You've saved them all."

"I didn't mean to." The implications from my bite still hung heavy around my neck. I almost killed her, the one who'd always loved me.

Tage picked me up and swung me around, my feet flying outward in a long arcing motion. "You....I could kiss you!"

Ford cleared his throat and looked away from us toward Roman's house. "Wanna go see 'Cedes or what?"

"Yes!" I chirped. Ford took the tails of the four squirrels I'd hidden away. "You just try and keep up, little brother!"

"Little?" he barked, running after me.

THE FRONT DOOR HANDLE EMBEDDED DEEP INTO THE DRYWALL AND PLASTER behind it as I slammed the door open. I leaped down the flight of steps and bolted into the basement. Father was sitting with Mercedes inside the cell, the two of them perched on the hard-as-rocks cot. Father was helping my sister take slow sips from a cup.

"Mercedes?" I asked softly, tears dropping like red paint splatters all over the concrete floor.

"P-por-schhhia," she said quietly. It was her voice, only scratchier; weaker, but it was her. It was my sister. She was speaking. She was crying. She was alive.

"Oh my God. You're actually okay." I sat on the bed next to her and threw caution to the wind, gathering her in my arms and holding her body and hair as I cried against her and she cried against me.

For the first time since she fell, these weren't tears of anguish. These were tears of unbelievable joy – the kind that fills up your heart until it might burst from being too full of happiness. These were the kind of tears that sisters *should* share.

Father stood up, brushing moisture from his own cheeks. "I'll give you girls a minute."

I could hear him stop Ford and Tage at the door. "Squirrels? Let's go cook dinner, son."

"But, 'Cedes-" Ford argued.

"...isn't going anywhere right now," Father finished for him.

We laughed and I held her face tenderly in my hands. "I am so sorry for attacking you."

Snorting, she giggled. "I'm pretty sure I forgive you."

"We need to tell Saul! We have to get Mother. Maybe a bite would make her...better."

Mercedes' smile fell away. "Saul will tell Pierce."

"That's okay. We can cure Pierce, too."

She shook her head. "I can hear them. Saul is helping Pierce."

"Helping him what?" I searched her face and found that the answer was something I wouldn't like to hear. Was this the secret Tage alluded to? "Tell me, Mercedes."

"Pierce is obsessed with finding a cure, but it's more than that. The disease eats away at brain tissue, very slowly. Eventually, the Infected lose their ability to think and reason. They're shells of their former selves. You've seen them in the forest – not the ones with us – the ones that roam."

"I have." Thinking back, I remembered the red-haired girl that Everson killed. She was little more than a husk, a walking body with no purpose and no soul.

"Roman's blood stopped Pierce from deteriorating as quickly, but he's been preserved for a very long time. I think the disease has finally begun to take its toll on his mind. He... God, this is hard to say. He takes the ones who can't think anymore, or the 'defects', as some call them, and experiments on them."

Gasping, I grabbed ahold of her hand. "What would he do with Mother?" We both knew she wasn't mentally sound even before she was banished.

Mercedes shook her head, sparkling liquid running down her face. "The question is, what has he already done?"

"Saul wouldn't help him. There's no way. He would never hurt another human being." He wouldn't do it. He was a good man.

"That's the thing, though," she said sadly. "No one considers them to be human anymore."

I knew the feeling. The moment I turned, I could feel the judgment, the stares and the separation from my human life and this one. The expanse of the rift between worlds was too great to overcome for some people. It wasn't for me. Once my emotions settled down and I was in control, I could see me living in a cozy house nestled between Ford and Mercedes. With Mercedes feeling better, if she truly was cured, maybe she would have a chance with Noah for a normal life. And if we could find a cure for the Infection, maybe there was a cure for vampirism. Maybe we could all be saved.

I understood Pierce in a visceral way. He wanted his life back. Part of me hated him for what he was doing, but a darker part of me understood why he did it.

SEVENTEEN

SAUL

Roman's forearms were tight as Pierce approached him with a syringe. "You've probably used that a hundred times," he spat. An interesting fact I'd learned: when Roman was given a drop of Infected blood to drink, he could hear us.

Pierce laughed. *Probably more. But who gives a shit about hygiene and disease when you're already Infected with the ultimate killer?*

"I care. They're my veins."

Pierce blew him off, tying a strip of cloth around his bicep. *Like anything can hurt you. You're immortal.*

"Vampires can be killed. You know that, or else you wouldn't have bothered with the dog collar. And, I'm fucking starving," Roman said. I half expected he would take his chances with the mechanism that choked him. Pierce said it would take his head clean off, but Pierce wasn't the most honest of persons. Roman was impatient; a leader, not a follower. There was only so much time and abuse he would take before he snapped, even if the mistreatment came at the hand of his brother.

Pierce looked at me. *You see the vein swelling?*

I do, I answered. It bulged, raising up angrily from the skin.

He smirked and held the syringe up for me to take. *Aim for that. With the needle in the vein, pull this bottom part backward to fill it full of blood.* Pierce demonstrated the motion of the bottom piece.

You want me *to do it?* My palms began to sweat. It was one thing to see someone else get poked and prodded, but it was another for me to be the one doing the poking and prodding.

Pierce grabbed my hand and opened my palm, placing the syringe in it. *If you want to learn, you have to get your hands dirty, Saul. With your help, maybe we can finally find a cure.*

Roman chuckled. "You've been searching for decades, brother. Others have searched for thousands of years. No one has found a solution because there isn't one. It doesn't exist. Like unicorns and fairies. There were smarter people than you Infected. No one's found a remedy because curses weren't meant to be cured. Using Saul Daniels won't change that. He's just another unfortunate person who's fallen victim to you, Pierce."

I could hear Pierce grinding his teeth in protest. Roman's words cut him deeper than me, but they did smart. And suddenly, wielding the syringe, shoving it into his vein and drawing blood from him wasn't so off-putting. It felt good.

Crimson liquid spurted into the small vial portion, ebbing and flowing until it could hold no more. I eased the needle from his vein and smiled at him. *It's not so fun to have your blood taken by someone else, is it?*

"You volunteered, Saul."

I volunteered so someone less fit than me didn't have to. Choices like that aren't really choices at all.

Cackling filtered into the room from a vent in the floor. Roman's room was directly above Mrs. Grant's. *Roman's in this hell hole?* she laughed. *How'd they catch you, Roman? Not fast enough for your undead brother?*

"Make her stop," Roman groaned. "She realized I was here yesterday morning, and again last night and here we go again. Her jokes are exactly the same lame ones each time."

Pierce grinned and clutched his heart. *Aww. You made a friend.*

I can still hear you, asshole! Miranda yelled, her voice like nails on a blackboard.

Never thought you couldn't, Miranda, Pierce called back to her.

You'll burn for what you've done. I'll tell them all. I've been trying to tell them for years, but no one would listen. Not even my own husband. Everyone just assumed I was insane.

You are insane, the brothers said simultaneously.

Well I wasn't then. They're all going to know what you've done. The colonists, or should I call them sheep, just follow the Elders like good little lambs, never questioning, never wondering why people fall or disappear or lose their minds. They don't know about the treaty at all, do they? Mrs. Grant's voice trailed away. What did we not know?

Saul, have you put it all together now that you're on this side of the flood wall? Is it all crystal clear to you now? You see, the treaty –

Miranda, Pierce warned.

Fuck you, Pierce. What else can you do to me? Anyway, as I was saying, the treaty isn't just for the Colony's protection. It's not just about the hunt and cooperation between night-walkers and the citizens of Blackwater. The Elders are behind everything. They're the ones who control Pierce and Roman. They are the ones who came up with the idea to experiment on people. For the greater good, for humanity, they said. If they found a cure for the incurable, they would make themselves into gods on earth. They wanted power and fame. Governing a couple hundred people wasn't enough. Roman and Pierce were merely the first to take the bait. Before they came, we rarely had anyone fall. The Infected weren't clustered in the city. The night-walkers didn't live in town. We knew of the Infection, but it hadn't touched us. We remained safe, tucked into what everyone believed was a sanctuary provided by God to protect his people. The Elders told everyone they were prophets, that there was a new order from above. That we should trust the night-walkers to take care of us, to watch over us. They only needed one thing.

Roman growled. His eyes grew black. *Hungry.*

Did you know Roman sent his own friends to Pierce? The night-walkers didn't just skip off to the next town, not that there's anyone close by. Roman incapacitated them and dragged them here, to this place, so that Pierce could perform tests and use them up. He killed them all. Some more swiftly than others.

Again, Roman growled. *Shut up, Miranda Grant.*

She continued, undaunted by Roman's threats. Pierce stood tall, watching my reaction, which I tucked behind the wall that was growing taller by the minute. *And they didn't stop there. They performed experiments on colonists, too. Tell Saul what you did to me, Roman.*

Roman fought against the restraints holding his arms to the rests, to those holding his legs to the chair legs. His throat swelled with rapid breaths. "Let me out of this chair!" he screamed.

I was pregnant. The Elders called for Carson to help that night because someone's house was on fire. Did you set the fire, Roman, before you came to my house and invaded my home? Mercedes was almost two. She was asleep. My screams woke her and then hers mingled with mine, but you still hurt me.

What the hell did you do to her, Roman? My stomach turned. She must have been pregnant with Porschia.

Roman, is the needle they just used on you the same you used on me?

Roman thrashed violently.

Pierce shoved me out of the room and locked the door. *Calm down. I'll deal with her,* he told Roman as he limped down the hallway to the stairwell. I followed, but slower.

They injected her! When she was in my womb, they put Infected blood and God knows what else into my body! They hurt me. They made her into a monster! She was a monster before she was born because they made her one!

No way. Porschia wasn't a monster. She was as human as anyone.

The needle didn't pierce the fetus. It poisoned Miranda, not Porschia, Pierce said quietly.

How could they do that? What else did they do? Did they hurt my family? How would I even know? Is that why everyone followed the Elders' orders without question? Did they know the consequences of dissension and were too afraid for their own families?

Roman was finally quiet. In an exhausted, gravelly voice he called out, "That's why she tastes different. That's why she smells different. It was like her body somehow fought the virus. It had to have been in the womb, but neither she nor Miranda became Infected. We only put a tiny drop into the syringe, but we thought that it would either Infect the fetus, or the baby would develop antibodies to fight the disease."

But something had gone wrong. Miranda Grant lost her mind, a side effect of the Infection, and Porschia became the object of her disdain. She blamed her unborn child for what Roman and Pierce did, what the Elders had sanctioned. And they waited, setting a new plan into motion. Both brothers wanted her, but for very different reasons. Roman was in awe because of her strength, and Pierce was in awe because she somehow beat the Infection. But what if it was just a fluke? What if no blood had been pushed into Miranda Grant's swollen stomach? What if Porschia was just normal, and Miranda was pushed over some sort of invisible edge that she couldn't cross again?

She was different! Pierce yelled at the both of us. *She was the key. I told you not to turn her. I told you she was ours – not mine or yours, but OURS! I told you not to let her get Infected, not to let her into the woods at all. I told you to keep her safe and not let her turn into a fucking night-walker! But you couldn't stay away! You couldn't leave her alone for a minute. And fucking Mercedes. She was hungry. That was her excuse. Though in the end, it may prove to be helpful. I think Porschia's blood...*

A low humming filled my ears before a loud thump silenced Miranda's sobs. Roman's voice came into my mind loud and clear. He was blocking his words, so I was careful too. I tucked his words behind my wall.

My brother has lost his mind. You see that, don't you? He wanted to test on her. He would have killed her to dissect her. He thought she had the solution he's been searching for so long. For years I watched her grow from a distance. I watched how Miranda treated her, compared to Mercedes and Ford. I watched as the Elders kept an eye on her. And I saw how hungry and desperate she was when she entered the rotation just after Mercedes fell. I knew she would be, of course. I knew she'd be at rock bottom. I wanted to be the one to pick her up.

You fell for her, I accused.

I did. But there were two things I didn't count on.

What?

You....and Tage. You both love her.

We did. I knew how Tage felt about her. *You don't love her, Roman. You wouldn't have done what you did to Mercedes if you did.*

That's not true. I love her, just not the way that you do. It's been a long time since I've felt human, let alone processed things as I did when I was one. I saw her as someone I could love, or someone to have companionship with.

You saw her as a possession.

Don't you? You wanted to be the girl's savior! She was starving and you offered to feed her. She needed to get married, so you offered to marry her. And you didn't even know her. You saw her pretty face, but didn't know Porschia Grant because you'd never taken the time to do so until that morning. In fact, if Noah hadn't gotten in the way, you would have been interested in Mercedes' hand. Isn't that right?

I swallowed. It was true that I had noticed Mercedes in the Colony before, but I knew of both sisters. Mercedes was happy with Noah. They were going to be married. Meg was taken, and Porschia was right in front of me, needing something that I could provide. She was strong and beautiful. And I did fall for her.

But now she was a night-walker and I was in this forsaken city helping some asshole test people for a cure that didn't exist and never would. I'd had enough. This shit was going to end. Tonight.

EIGHTEEN

PORSCHIA

Mercedes was sleeping and Father and Ford had gone home for the night when the acrid scent of smoke filled the basement. "Tage?" I called out as I stepped toward the front door.

"Yeah?"

"Do you smell that?"

I heard him sniffing the air and then he was in front of me in an instant. "Smoke. But from where?"

"I'm not sure, but-" I began, but as he eased the door open, the sight stunned me into silence. "What is going on?"

Elders Yankee, Brown, and Beckett stood at the bottom of the steps leading to the doorstep that we stepped onto. Colonists, all dressed in their cotton and wool, black and white, stood behind them holding torches and pitchforks, hoes and axes. "How nice of you to pay us a visit," Tage said, wrapping his arm around my waist and tugging me to his side. "We'd have cooked something if we knew you were coming."

Beckett snarled, "We know you harbor an Infected in this house."

Tage pursed his lips and tapped his chin with his forefinger. "Infected, Infected... Now, to what Infected are you referring?" He turned to me. "Do *you* know of any Infected in this house behind us?"

"I do not," I growled, baring my fangs. The colonists, some whom were former friends and neighbors, gasped and took a measured step back.

The smoke was increasingly thick and I realized it wasn't coming from their puny torches alone. Smelling for the source, Tage nodded. He knew it wasn't them either.

"Bring her out or we'll burn it down."

Tage laughed. "You see, this isn't our house; it's Roman's, and we're merely house-sitting for him while he's away on business. It would be incredibly rude for us to harbor an Infected inside, but it would be even ruder to let you burn his home to the ground. So I'm going to have to say no, because there is no Infected inside. And if you set this house on fire, I'll tear your fucking head off your shoulders." He grinned. I think he'd like that.

Yankee stepped forward. "Mercedes Grant is not in this house?"

"I am," came a weak voice from behind me. I pressed my eyes closed, my heart dropping for a split second. Why did she do this? We could handle them. "But I'm not Infected. Porschia has found a cure."

The collective gasp was deafening. Then came the chatter from the crowd.

"Truly?"

"Is it possible?"

"She's one of them now, maybe it's a lie."

"How can we know for sure?"

Brown and Beckett whispered to Yankee, who spoke for the trio. "How do we know this isn't a trick?"

"Because I am not dead. I can speak again and I feel better with each passing moment. Whether I'll completely heal or not remains to be seen. Time will be the only judge of that. But I can tell you that she took away the Infection. I can tell you that my sister saved my life."

Mercedes clasped my hand.

"And just how did she manage that?" Brown said, his eyes narrowing.

"She bit me, asshole."

Voices, what sounded like a hundred of them, flooded my ears. I clutched them, crouching low. Tage's hand was on my shoulder, squeezing, and Mercedes laid a concerned hand on my head.

Pierce is coming.

He has the night-walker.

Testing...

Saul is with him...

Serves them right.

It's not right.

Suddenly crystal clear, everything else – even what was happening right in front of me – was tuned out. I found him: Saul. But he wasn't talking to me; he was talking to my mother. I could hear her, too.

She was farther away...

They don't know about the treaty at all, do they? Mother asked. *The Elders are behind everything. They're the ones who control Pierce and Roman. They are the ones who came up with the idea to experiment on people.*

No, it wasn't her speaking to him. It was him remembering their conversation, followed by a remembered conversation with Roman... *The needle didn't pierce the fetus. It poisoned Miranda, not Porschia... My brother has lost his mind. You see that, don't you? He would have killed her to dissect her...*

You...and Tage. You both love her.

Saul? I reached out to him.

Porschia?

Is it all true?

Is what true? he asked, sounding as confused as I felt clear.

I took a breath and let Tage pull me up, releasing my temples. *I just heard your memories, or what I think were memories.*

He was silent for a beat. *I'm not strong enough to block all of this.* His voice cracked and I heard him whimper. *It has to stop. He has to be stopped. He can't keep doing this to people. But they aren't people. Not anymore. The virus killed them. They're hollow, like dead trees in the woods.*

Who was he talking about? *Who's hollow?*

But I took care of them. For the Colony. For you. They can't hurt you or your family or mine. Not anymore. I ended it.

Who's hollow, Saul? What did you end? My palms began to sweat and my heart clenched. I couldn't control it. The smell.

"Tage?"

He raked a hand through his dark hair and turned his light blue eyes on the Elders. "What is it?" He glanced at me, keeping the mob in his periphery.

"Do you smell it?" I sniffed again to be sure. Yes, it was there. Burning human flesh.

"I do. Holy shit. Saul?"

I nodded.

"What did he do?"

Mercedes whimpered. "Mother?"

"Where was she?" Tage asked my sister. "In the main apartments or the special housing?"

"She was locked away," Mercedes cried. "They call it the 'freak show'!"

Tage jumped down the staircase, landing in front of the Elders. "Listen up. We are going into the city. If you so much as set fire to a blade of dry grass in this yard, I will personally hunt you down and drain you dry. Got me?"

Flabbergasted, the old men backed away from him, enveloped by the crowd, who had been watching with rapt attention. Most couldn't peel their eyes away from Mercedes. I couldn't blame them. For hours after I came home, I couldn't stop looking at her either. I was afraid it was a dream or another hallucination, and that I would wake up and she would still be behind the flood wall or roaming the forest. I worried that she would still be my enemy and not my sister.

"Porschia?" Mercedes called.

We needed to go, but I couldn't leave her behind with the colonists in an uproar and the Elders on a rampage. "Tage, we need to take her somewhere safe," I whispered.

His breath fanned my ear. "Maggie's?"

"She couldn't defend them. We need to take her home."

He nodded, gathering Mercedes into his arms. "Let's run," he said before speeding away. I watched the torch fire flicker in his wake before running after him.

NINETEEN

PORSCHIA

Father and Ford had no idea that the Elders had rallied the colonists into a mob or that they tried to come after Mercedes, but both vowed to keep her safe while we went into the city. Tage sat Mercedes' bare feet down on the worn planks of our porch. "I need to tell you something," Mercedes said desperately, grabbing hold of my forearm.

"I really need to go."

"I know, but it's important. You know how Frenzy makes a vampire go crazy with hunger?"

"Yes," I replied, trying to hurry her along and wishing she'd get to the point.

"The Infected experience hunger as well, but more than that, it's a different type of hunger. It's a craving for normalcy, to have one's life back and to do anything at all to get it. I was sent here by Pierce, but it was my idea as well. I wanted to trick you; to make you think I was still me and that you could trust me. Then I was going to poison you and drag you back to the river. They were going to bring the rafts. I just had to signal them."

Jerking my arm away, I stared her down; Father and Ford both watching the scene with slack jaws. "Why are you telling me this now?"

"I was using Mother to get to you, too. I knew you would protect her. I knew you would do the right thing, regardless of how horrific she was to you. You loved her. Pierce wanted you. He still does. He wants to test on you, and I'm afraid this might be a trap. I'm actually sure it is. I don't want you to go into the city."

"I have to! I need to see if I can save her. And damn you, Mercedes! If you were supposed to bring me to Pierce, why'd you bite me?"

"I was hungry and scared and I just did, okay?" She composed herself, smoothing her shirt. She was still wearing the clothes she'd left the city in the day she was brought back into the Colony. They were hideous and smelly. She looked longingly at my dress. I had put it back on when we returned from the forest. I never wanted to take it off. "You look good, Porschia. Fierce, actually. Just be careful. The Infection changes a person. It makes them focused on only one thing: finding a cure. Now that we've found it – which is so incredibly wonderful – you still need to be aware that some won't be able to be saved. The damage is too significant, too consuming. Some, though technically alive and functioning, are already dead."

Tears fell onto the porch from both of us, clear innocence mixing with crimson cruelty. She whispered, "I wanted to either kill you or Infect you and give you to Pierce. I wasn't sure which I wanted more. He told me about what he and Roman did to Mother."

I looked to my father. "And did you know about it as well?"

"There was nothing I could do," he replied, his voice breaking. "The Elders ordered it. I fought it, but they had me beaten to within an inch of my life and thrown in a cellar for a month. Your mother had a hard time dealing with it afterward. I tried to refocus her on you, to get her to understand that you and she were both fine."

"What did they do?" Ford asked, wide-eyed. Father's eyes darted to him and back to me.

"Never mind. Tage, let's go." I reached for his hand and found his already reaching out. "We need to hurry."

"Please forgive me," Mercedes cried.

With Tage by my side, I ran toward the back yard. We scaled the ladder and jumped to the ground. Tage pulled me up and together, we ran toward the fire.

SAUL

Pierce always scurried away at night like the rodent he was. I waited until he left, until he went to sleep and then I went for supplies. He kept those locked away in the basements of buildings all over town, in rooms that no one wanted. He had fuel. He had matches. I took both. And I had to work fast. Pierce would suspect I was up to something if I waited too long, so I handled everything that night.

The accelerants made the fire travel fast through the building. Fire was hungry, too. It consumed without discriminating. It fed without ceasing. It ended what Pierce began. His pets…some of them didn't even scream when the flames came for them. They sat in the smoke, unaware that they were going to be burned. I limped away, avoiding the liquid trails of fire starter fluid. I found the cans stored in a room in the main apartment building the night Pierce snipped two fingers off one of the older Infected shells, ground them up into dust and gristle, mixed them with Roman's blood and then fed them to another Infected. He planned to try an eyeball next. I couldn't take it anymore.

And I couldn't listen to Miranda Grant anymore. She ranted night and day about Porschia, Roman, and Pierce. The woman was a loose cannon. She would make Porschia's life a living hell if she ever found her frequency. I couldn't let that happen. I had to protect Porschia from her mother, from the toxins she spewed.

The flames lapped at her room, warping the door, bowing it. The paint on the metal door bubbled and boiled. She laughed and cackled at the fire right up until it reached the corner she was huddled in.

You're burning, Roman! she called out to him. *I told you! I told you that you would burn for what you've done. Now you will. Now you'll burn with me. You'll burn with us all! I bet fire can kill a night-walker. Burn. Burn. Burn...*

I limped out of the door and into the night air, gasping for freshness, and found Pierce waiting. He grabbed my shoulders and squeezed, his spittle flying into my face. *What have you done?* he asked angrily.

I smiled. *I saved them from you.*

You killed them all!

Still smiling, I spat in his face. *You killed them long before I came around,* I answered smugly. *You know what?* I pulled back from him. *You picked the wrong human to turn into a monster.* I slammed my fist into his jaw, the crack reverberating up my arm. When he grabbed his face, I reared back and hit him again. His cheek shattered and he fell to the ground, his skull striking the concrete with a dull thud. Wren appeared silently from the shadows.

Don't kill him. You'll be no better than him if you do.

I'm already worse, Wren.

You aren't. Leave him. You need to get away from the smoke.

I leaned over with my hands on my knees, completely spent. *I could walk a thousand miles and never be rid of it.*

Why'd you do it?

I couldn't watch it another second.

You've only been here a short time. It couldn't have been that bad.

I looked at Wren, really looked at him. His wrinkled skin. His tired eyes. His dull, torn clothing. And he looked at me. The soot, the sweat, the sin. I killed them all. He never expected that. None of them did. But I did them a favor! I saved them from him. From Pierce. From more tests and experiments, from mutilations and manipulations. I. Saved. Them.

Wren waved his hand for me to follow him. I stepped away from Pierce, his scratchy moans filling the cool night air. And I followed him; away from the fire, from the screaming, from the smoke and the flame. Away from the insanity.

PORSCHIA

We found Pierce lying on the sidewalk outside of the burning building. Actually, the building was worse than burning, which I didn't even know was possible. The structure was completely engulfed; every orifice being lapped at by the flames that ate away at it. The glass windows that were still intact overhead finally exploded, littering our heads and backs with tiny shards as we covered our faces and ducked. The shrill shrieking from within was more than I could stand. I didn't know if they were in my mind, if I was hearing them with my ears, or both. But it was too much.

The flames.

The smoke.

The smell of burning flesh and hair.

The crumbling building.

The glass.

The screams.

The cries for help.

Pierce's moaning.

The yelling.

One voice was familiar: Mother's.

She was being burned alive.

I ran toward the door. The flames wouldn't hurt me, right? Tage's arm on my bicep stopped me. "Don't. She's already gone."

I shook my head. "I hear her. She's in there!" Gesturing toward the building, I cried, chest heaving.

"It's too late!"

"It might not be!"

Tage ground his teeth together. "Let me go instead. You stay here."

"NO! She's my mother!"

"I'm stronger than you are right now. If anyone can save her, it's me!"

I swallowed the harsh truth, angrily swiping the tears from my cheeks. "Hurry, Tage. Please come back to me."

"Always," he said, kissing my lips lightly before running into the burning building to save my mother. Some would argue that she didn't deserve saving, but I would argue that none of us deserved mercy. This entire mess began with a curse; one that would have ended as quickly as it began if humans had the ability to see past differences and work together. But humans were evil. Night-walkers and Infected were once normal people. It wasn't the virus that addled their minds, it was the nature of humanity. It was the inherent evil, selfishness, and short-sightedness that lived within us all. And I just sent Tage into danger because of it.

My stomach turned. Pierce rolled over to his side, pushing up onto his elbow. I watched him flail and flop like a fish out of water. Did I offer him a hand? No. Because I, too, was evil. I didn't know if I wanted him to live, let alone stand up again.

TWENTY

TAGE

My eyes watered from the heat radiating off the flaming mess around me, waves distorting my vision. Door after door was easy to kick in. The metal had already begun to melt from the heat, but Miranda was hard to find in the smoky mess. And when I did find her, my heart broke. It didn't break for her; it broke for Porschia. I was too late. Huddled in a ball in the corner of an empty shell of a room was her charred body, still smoldering and being licked by flames. Above her room, a familiar voice raged above the din of the inferno.

"Get. Me. OUT of here!"

"Roman?"

"Tage? Tage! Get me out of this room!"

"What the hell?" I yelled, fighting my way past the support beams that were crashing down one by one. "I can't get to you. Kick the door down!"

"You think I haven't tried? I haven't fed in too long."

I should just let the asshole burn. I jumped over one metal beam, so hot that all but the center of it glowed orange. The stairwell door was missing. I found it across the lobby. My boots melted on each concrete step, despite the fact that they were probably the coolest thing in this place. I could smell gasoline or kerosene. Some kind of accelerant… I couldn't place it and didn't know where they'd even gotten it from. It wasn't like the gas station pumps worked anymore.

The door that led to the second floor was also off the hinges, but it was lying in a molten puddle at the entrance to the second floor. "Where are you?" I called out. The flames roared in my ears. The walls were on fire. The drop ceiling was falling, also consumed by flame.

"Here!" came Roman's voice from all the way down the hall. Of course. He would naturally be in the most difficult place to reach. I pulled my jacket over my head and ran through the gauntlet of falling and already fallen debris and holes in the floor, past the people who had been shrieking and were now silenced forever.

I kicked his door in and Roman stepped into the hallway, a glowing metal collar falling from his neck. The building groaned and the walls began to bow inward. "Shit. Let's go!" he screamed, the skin on his hands and face bubbling angrily.

Roman was going to tear whomever did this apart.

PORSCHIA

I CUPPED MY HANDS OVER MY FACE. TAGE WASN'T COMING OUT. I COULDN'T see anything but fire, flame, and smoke. Oh, but the noise. Metal on metal, crumbling, groaning from the structure itself. It was going to fall. "Tage! Get out of there!" I wanted him to bring Mother, but I couldn't lose him, too. "Leave her and get out! Tage!"

Porschia?

I turned to find Saul standing behind me. His clothes were torn, he smelled like the burning building, soot was streaked and smeared all over his face, and his light brown hair was black and singed. Only his blue-gray eyes were the same. They reflected the burning building, reminding me of what horrors lay inside.

"What happened here?"

You have no idea what happened in there, Porschia.

"Did you do this?" I screamed. "Was my mother in there?"

His eyes hardened. *She hated you. She would have killed you. She would have made your life a living hell.*

"We found a cure, Saul! We could have helped her! But she wasn't alone in there, was she? How many were there?"

He stepped toward me, putting his face in mine. *She can't hurt you now!*

No. She can't, I answered.

I turned my back on him, focusing on the one who might still be saved. "Tage!"

Saul laughed mirthlessly. *Always comes back to him, huh?* He opened his mouth and let out a screech, making me cover my ears and look at him. He'd lost it.

"What the hell happened to you, Saul?"

Pierce happened. The Infection happened. You happened. If I'd just left you alone the day you showed up to volunteer, I wouldn't be here! I would be safely in the carpentry shop, learning a trade. I would be alive instead of this walking death. He clawed at his clothing, pulling it away from his sweat-soaked skin.

I backed away from him toward the fire. Looking into the flames, I closed my eyes and willed Tage to come out of the inferno, to come back to me. When I opened them again, I saw movement from within. Tage nearly knocked me down when he sped out of the fire with Roman on his heels. Roman caught his breath, looking from me, to Pierce, and then to Saul. He bared his fangs and pounced on Saul, knocking him to the ground. Saul's breath left him in an oomph, but it was too late. Roman sank his teeth into his neck and gulped.

"Roman!" I tried to pull him off of Saul but he pushed me away.

Tage pulled me back from the two men.

"Don't kill him! Please!"

Tage's grip on me relaxed. "After what he did, you still love him?"

I shook my head no. "It's not that. I just think that every Infected with a chance deserves it. Just like every night-walker does. They deserve their lives back. Everyone has a chance to be rid of this curse, and so does he."

Roman pulled his fangs from Saul's lifeless body. With shaking fingers, I reached for him, easing away from Tage. "Is he dead?"

I fell to my knees, my skin shredding from the impact. I watched Saul's breathing, shallow but there. And I cried.

"Thank you, Roman."

Roman sat back on his haunches and wiped his chin. "Thank me for what?" he spat.

"For saving him. I couldn't have done it."

Tage crouched next to me. "You said he deserved a chance."

I nodded. "I did say that, but I couldn't have mustered the strength to give it to him. Not after this." I stared at the flames. When the walls finally buckled and caved into the center in a molten heap, Tage shielded me with his body, holding me when the ground shook violently beneath us.

I looked over Tage's shoulder at Roman, who stared blankly at the two of us. His skin was angry and red, blistered and peeling, but he would heal. "Saul didn't think this through very well. Fire won't kill a night-walker. It'll only piss them off."

"What about your brother?" I asked.

"What about him?" Roman stared at Pierce, who was unconscious now.

"Are you going to bite him? The vampire venom can heal the Infection."

Roman threw his head back and stared at the stars that blanketed the earth. He squeezed his eyes shut.

"What is it?" I said, cocking my head to the side.

"I always wondered about that."

"About what?"

He opened his dark eyes and fixed them on me. "About you. It wasn't just Infected blood that was injected into your mother while she was pregnant with you."

"Venom?"

"I never told Pierce. The two probably cancelled each other out."

"But how did that explain Mother's mental state? If neither toxin affected her, then why…?" I began incredulously. "Why did Tage's venom sting me so badly when he first bit me? How did I become a night-walker if my body fought the venom? How could I become Infected, too? *How?*"

Roman blew out an exhausted breath. "I don't know. I don't understand what happened with your mother. Some people are just born crazy, Porschia. There is no reason. Maybe the contents of the syringe did nothing. Maybe it never touched you. We have no way to know. But I do know that I've regretted that night since it happened. And if you ever need anything from me – need me to bite another person that you can't, or anything else – it's yours. Just name it. I'm truly sorry."

The three of us sat in silence, watching the flames, flanked by the unmoving bodies of Saul and Pierce. Part of me wondered if Mercedes could be tricking us. Could she be attacking Father and Ford right now?

"Roman, go check on Porschia's family," Tage ordered, reading my mind.

"Why?"

"Porschia's worried. You said anything, now go."

Roman pushed himself up. His skin was already looking paler and the blisters were receding. "I'll never live that moment of weakness down, will I?"

"Not on your life," I answered.

He smiled slightly. "Be right back." As Roman sped away he blended with the darkness. He was part of it, or it was part of him. I wondered when that metamorphosis had happened. When he turned, or before? Was he always this version of Roman?

I wasn't always this version of Porschia. Most of me was glad. Frenzy seemed to be over, for the most part. Since I woke up from the poisoned daydreams, I felt more like me than I ever had. I felt like the me I wanted to be, no longer wanting to escape my own life or reality. I just wanted to be whatever I was. A freak? A hybrid? Doubly cursed? Whatever.

Tage slung an arm around my shoulders and pulled me into him, and then reached into the pocket of his jeans and pulled out a piece of willow bark. It was warm to the touch. I laughed. "You have *got* to be kidding."

"Nope. Chew your bark. We don't know if you're out of the woods yet."

"I think I'm out of Frenzy."

Tage scoffed. "You're a woman. Should one little thing piss you off, you'll go back into it again."

I smacked him and popped the piece of bark into my mouth, chewing dramatically. It wasn't as bad warm as it was fresh and cool. The bitterness was replaced with a sweetness.

"You know you like the bark," Tage crooned. "All women like my wood."

Giggling, I shook my head. "You're awful."

"I'm sexy."

"You *think* you're sexy."

Tage smiled and pulled me closer. "Admit it. Me running into that building was hot."

"You were definitely hot, Tage. You still are." I nodded toward the steaming pieces of leather on his shoulders. With a proud grin he patted the battle scars lovingly, like old friends reacquainted.

Saul moaned and grabbed his throat.

"Great. And... Loverboy's back."

"Please don't call him that again."

"Kitten, don't patronize me. If you're gonna run back to him the second he loses the sick gray pallor and gets the raspy voice back, I'm going to be pissed. I'm warning you now."

"I won't. I can barely stand to look at him." It was true. I stared at Tage, at the sky and the flame, but couldn't bring myself to look at Saul. Or Pierce, for that matter. They were two of the same kind of evil in my eyes now.

"I'm a hypocrite. I killed Dara. Why do I feel so angry with him?"

"Because you were protecting others – namely him – from Dara. He just ignited an entire building of people for a cause he claimed was just, but what he did can't be justified. It's not right, regardless of the reasoning behind it."

"The fact that he reasoned it at all proves I didn't know him very well."

Tage sighed. "It could be the Infection."

"He hasn't been Infected for very long."

"It could affect him differently than the others."

I pushed myself up off the ground. "Why are you defending him?" I shouted before throwing my hands up and walking toward Blackwater.

"Why aren't you?" he yelled back. Tage jogged to catch up, grabbing my arm and turning me around. "Hey, I'm not defending him. I just want to make sure you think this through."

"Why do you even care?"

His eyes bored into mine. "Because I care about *you*. Now come on. The Infected will handle Saul and Pierce."

He stalked away toward Blackwater, leaving me to stand in his wake. I could smell the smoke that still clung to his jacket all the way back to the flood wall. My hands pulled my tired body up each frigid rung until I stood on top of the wall, at the divide between two worlds. In the distance, the falls thundered. The normal citizens of Blackwater were asleep. All windows were dark and there was no motion except for one house: my childhood home.

Roman climbed up the opposite side of the wall and I moved over to give him room. "She's fine. Your father and brother are fine. She's eating, talking, and her coloring is getting better. For what it's worth, she smells different. I know only time will tell, but I think she's fine now. She's human."

"Isn't it weird that the venom of a night-walker can heal an Infected person?"

Roman squeezed his head and began to teeter. "Roman?" I stepped toward him. He swayed and almost fell backward off the wall, city-side. "What's wrong?"

"I feel weird."

"Tage?" I called out. "I need you!" I didn't know if he would come. I'd upset him. Steadying Roman's weight, I noticed he was feeling heavier and heavier. "Tage," I croaked.

"Move him over," he replied from the ground. "I'm coming up."

Roman's eyes lolled back into his head. "Something's really wrong!" His body went slack and I tried to balance us both.

Tage took Roman from me, gathering him onto his shoulders like he was carrying a bear carcass. He scaled down the wall slowly but stealthily. "You need to eat," he yelled up at me.

"Bark?"

"Smartass."

I climbed down, meeting Tage at the ground. The soil smelled rich and softly squished underfoot. The tiny trails of the last snowfall of Winter still clung to the edge of the wall's bottom. "Meet me at the house. I'll get him situated."

I nodded and watched him run away before slowly walking to the back of my house, to the kitchen window. A candle flickered in the window, warming the scene. Mercedes, Father, and Ford sat around the kitchen table, talking and laughing. Mercedes swiped tears from her cheeks. She looked up and saw me.

"Porschia?"

I raised a hand. Father stood up, followed by Ford. They came to the back door, but I was already gone.

TWENTY-ONE

PORSCHIA

Back at Roman's, Tage had already laid Roman in his huge four-poster bed by the time I arrived. "I'll get something for you to eat. Be right back. Stay with him."

I nodded.

Grabbing a blanket from the hall closet, I spread it over Roman. He was shaking like a leaf, yet his forehead was hot to the back of my fingers. Whether it was from the fire or a fever, I didn't know. I grabbed a towel and some leftover snow from outside, and he sighed when I laid it on his feverish head. I could've sworn I saw steam rise from his skin; a slow-moving, quickly-dissipating tendril of relief.

"Roman?"

He muttered something that sounded like, "Sorry, Porschia," before his lips parted. I swallowed and moved closer. Roman's fangs were long, longer than any other night-walker I'd ever seen. But I didn't see them.

I eased the soft, poufy flesh of his upper lip up and quickly let it go with a choking sound. His fangs were receding. They were smaller than mine.

Tage rushed up the stairs and into the room, holding a rabbit out for me. "How is he?" He ticked his head toward Roman as I took the hare. Tage used his forefinger to close my mouth. "What's wrong?"

"He's healing."

"Fire won't kill a vamp, Porsch."

"No." I shook my head in disbelief. "But look at his fangs."

Tage curled his lip, but did as I asked. "I'll be damned," he added softly. "The answer was there the whole time. The cure was one another." Tage shook his head in disbelief and looked at Roman in wonder. "Vampire venom cures the Infection, and the Infection cures vampirism. It's genius," he marveled, a smile creeping up on his face. "Brilliant."

"Night-walkers didn't want to bite the Infected."

Tage shuddered. "Who'd want to bite a rotter? You've smelled them!" He laughed, raking his fingers through his hair. "This is gonna change everything."

"It already is." I looked at Roman's shivering form.

Tage looked at me and the brown hare in my hand. "Eat your bunny."

"Damn it, Tage."

SAUL

I CAME TO, LYING ON THE CONCRETE SIDEWALK OUTSIDE THE BUILDING THAT I'd torched, the one that once housed Pierce's freaks. My palms dug into the gritty pavement as I pushed myself up to look around. The blue sky was streaked with pinks, oranges, and golds. The only cloud in the sky was a remnant of the plume I created.

The building couldn't even be called that anymore. It was just twisted metal and crushed block. The facets had crumbled, leaving behind a heaping mess, gnarled like the Infection had gotten hold of it. The way it was contorted was how I felt right after the virus first worked its way through my system.

Flexing my palms and stretching my legs, I stood up. The familiar ache of pulled-taut muscles and atrophy wasn't there. My back didn't hurt. My legs didn't hurt. Nothing but my head and neck hurt at all. I clutched my throat. Roman. He bit me.

Wren?

Pierce?

Porschia?

I threw each over my wall at their different frequencies. No one answered. The two-block walk was still tiring, but I didn't feel like I was going to fall over. The stairwells of the apartment building were empty, but there was shuffling and movement behind the doors that lined the hallways.

Pierce burst through the door, Wren on his heels. He screeched at me, gesturing for me to leave.

Where am I supposed to go? I threw back at him. He acted like he never heard me. Wren pointed to his hears and shook his head. They couldn't hear me. Why couldn't they hear me? Did I hit my head? I slid my fingertips over the back of my skull. No bumps or gashes. I opened my mouth. "P-pier-ce." *What the hell?* My mouth hung open and so did theirs. While they couldn't speak, they could still hear, and they heard me form Pierce's name. "H-how?"

Pierce shook his head and pointed for me to leave again. Wren pushed past him, standing beside me in solidarity, and we left together. I just didn't know where to go. I wasn't welcome in the city. Pierce…there was something in his eyes back there. Relief? Guilt? Anger? Maybe it was a mixture of all three.

We wouldn't be welcome in Blackwater. The only option was to see if we could cross the river into the forest, although with the snow melt, it might be difficult. I motioned toward the break in the wall on the far side of the city, the same one that I'd entered the city by. Wren nodded.

Walking was easier for me. The further I walked, the better my legs began to feel. They were more elastic. The tightness that had plagued me was gone. Wren wasn't so lucky.

He hobbled past buildings and through streets until we began to pass houses and homes. The outskirts had long been abandoned, but if we squatted in one of these homes, Pierce wouldn't have to know. It would just be until the river receded again.

I volunteered to go to the river and check it out, just in case it was low enough to cross at some point. Wren volunteered to hold up the wall of an old shed just inside the wall. Huffing for air, he leaned against the building and panted, motioning for me to go ahead.

"Wait here," I rasped.

He nodded, still trying to catch his breath.

The river was high, but our salvation would end up being what damned me in the first place: there were rafts tied to stumps. We could push ourselves across. I knew there were still houses in the forest. They were deeper in, farther away from Blackwater, though remnants of some could still be found, reclaimed by nature. We could stay in one of those, safe from Pierce and his insanity and safe from the Elders and colonists who would kill us before they'd welcome us back inside the sanctity of the Colony.

I walked back inside the flood wall to find Wren, but he was gone. I checked the house and all around the shed and outbuildings nearby, finally realizing that he'd left. Probably thought it was safer staying in the city.

Most people were comfortable with the familiar. Anything else was too frightening to try. But comfort zones could become cages if you weren't careful. They could hold you back and pen you in, and before you knew it, you were terrified of trying anything else.

Porschia, I called out in my mind. She didn't respond. Either I couldn't communicate telepathically anymore, or she was done with me. Maybe both. I had to do it! I had to, and I refused to apologize. Seeing Pierce torture them was more than I could stand for another minute. And whether Porschia knew it or not, she was better off without her mother.

The long raft poles were leaned up against the bottom of the wall. I grabbed one, testing its weight. It was twelve-feet long at least. I could do this. I could push the raft across the water. The muddy river lapped at the rafts, although that term was probably too kind. The rafts were made of small tree trunks haphazardly lashed together. One good knock against a rock would break them apart for good.

I eased the rope off the stump it was tethered to on the bank and stepped onto the raft's center, testing my weight. My boots filled with icy water, but I was determined to do this. It was holding me up enough. I just had to get across before the raft hit the jagged rocks ahead. Pushing with all my might and widening my stance, I let the current take hold and shoved the pole into the river bottom, guiding it as best I could.

The swirling liquid spun me around, but I managed to lift the pole and reposition it, shoving hard toward the opposite bank. The rocks were getting closer, but I kept shoving until I was across. The tether was underwater. With one leg on the raft and one on the shore, I fumbled for the rope, but it was no use. The water was too strong and I wasn't strong enough to fight it. Stepping both feet back onto the muddy bank, my feet sunk in while the raft succumbed to the angry water. It spun around in a circle once and then was dashed against the rocks, breaking apart; the individual parts swept away by the furious current.

Fatigue was setting in and I needed to find shelter. This was going to be a long day.

TWENTY-TWO

PORSCHIA

WITH THE BIRDS CHIRPING AND SUNBEAMS FILTERING DOWN FROM THE heavens, Tage and I helped Roman emerge from his bedroom and then his house. He said he was weak, but maybe he'd been incredibly strong for so long that he forgot what it meant to feel human, to feel mortal. Each step down the staircase that led to the sidewalk in his front yard was careful and deliberate. "You're not made of glass, Roman. You won't break."

He gave a shaky smile. "I'm afraid I might." Pausing, he looked at me. "I'm still afraid this is all a dream."

"It isn't," I reassured him again. "This is real. You feel the pain, the difference." It was the fiftieth time I'd said it in the last twenty-four hours. He'd woken in a cold sweat, panicked and afraid. I'd never seen Roman show fear before that moment. I wondered if he was happy to have his human life back, or if he already regretted having drank from Saul.

Tage was quiet. Too quiet.

"What's wrong with you?"

"Nothing," he replied tersely.

Roman snorted. "Saul must be human now. That's what's wrong with him."

"And...?"

"*And* he thinks you'll go running back to him the first chance you get," Roman completed.

I shook my head. "I won't." It was a vow, an absolute certainty. Saul was human now. If his blood cured Roman, then Roman's venom must have healed him from the Infection. But it wasn't the Infection that made him burn those people to death. He wasn't sick that long. Maybe something made him crack, or maybe it was a sickness deep inside him. However, I couldn't love someone who didn't see others as human beings. I just couldn't.

"Want to know what I think?" Roman grunted as he walked down the sidewalk stiffly.

Tage rolled his eyes. "No, but I bet you're going to tell us anyway."

"You know me so well. I think…" He paused dramatically. "You talked yourself *into* Saul – into the idea of him, anyway. I heard you talking to him the morning you volunteered. You were given a choice: either enter the rotation or find a husband. Your mother was being your mother. For some reason he offered to marry you, just like that. And when you made it into the rotation, you put the brakes on. But I think that you made yourself fall in love with the idea of him; someone who would rescue you from the hell you were living in. The idea of someone who wanted you was more than you could resist."

I swallowed. Honestly, I'd thought the same things a few times. Why would he say he would marry me? Why wouldn't I just say yes? Giving it time was prudent. Yes, I grew to respect him, and yes, my hormones were a crazy mess. But did I really love him? I think I did, but maybe Roman was right. Maybe I just loved the idea of him. Or maybe I loved the idea of leaving home with him.

Tage muttered something under his breath before saying, "Look, if you've got him, I'll go get Mercedes. Meet us at the pavilion."

"We're good," I replied. Roman walked like a sixty-year old man, but in reality he was older than that. So we walked slowly while Tage sped away. The plan was for him to get my family and gather the colonists in the pavilion square. They needed to see Mercedes and Roman. With their own eyes, they needed to see that there was a cure, that it worked fast, and that they were safe. They also needed to know about the Elders and the role they played in the experimentation, if they didn't already know. Some did. Some had experienced their depravity first-hand.

Roman was sweating and smiling, no trace of a fang in his far-too-handsome face. He leaned against the tiered fountain. I moved to a bench, unable to stand the stench of rotten leaves in the water, of dead bugs and algae that were trapped in its basins until they flooded out. No one had bothered to clean it in years. Maybe they never had. It was nauseating.

I ate the hare Tage brought me. Eating smaller, more frequent meals seemed to agree with my stomach. Even small amounts of blood were tolerable and gave me the energy that raw meat couldn't. I was part of both curses and had to feed each one's craving.

Roman brushed a piece of dark hair out of his eyes and I took him in; his dark jeans, white t-shirt, and leather jacket. The slight smile he couldn't wipe off his face entirely. "What are you going to do about Pierce?" I asked suddenly.

He gripped the edge of the fountain with his palms. "I don't know. There isn't an easy answer to that. I truly think he's lost his mind. The venom may cure him, but would it bring my brother back?"

"You have to try."

"No one will be happy about it. Where will he live?"

I smoothed the creases from my skirts. Maggie had finished stitching the dress I started and I wanted to wear it today, to show the colonists that in some small way, I was still part of them.

"The dress might not help, you know," Roman said softly, intuitively.

"I know."

"I hope it does."

I did too.

Roman ticked his head toward the human section of Blackwater. The pavilion had long since divided the night-walkers from the colonists, but now that divide was about to be erased. "Not everyone will want to change. Have you thought of that?"

"Yes," I answered simply. "Did you *want* to be human?"

He blew out a breath and stood up straight. "If you'd have asked me that a few days ago, I would have said no."

"But..."

"But I'm relieved. I'm happy. It feels good to feel normal."

It looked good on him, too. He smirked. "It's okay to check me out. You've been eyeing the goods since you first saw me standing in Town Hall."

"You're so full of it, Roman."

"Full of truth. Speaking of which, here they come."

Men, women, and children walked together in tight family groups.

The girls' dresses swished as loudly as the gray woolen pants the men and boys wore. Everyone's clothing matched. Everyone's facial expressions did, too. They were curious and afraid. Concern hung on the faces of the adults, and wonder on the faces of the children circling their legs.

In the distance, Tage walked toward us with Father, Ford, and Mercedes. The four of them kept perfect stride, by-passing any group moving too slowly. Whispers and murmurs accompanied the crowd. Word spread quickly throughout the village, even to the trio of Elders, who approached from the direction of Town Hall.

"What is the meaning of this?" Yankee blubbered as he stalked angrily toward us.

I ignored him. So did Roman.

Standing up, I climbed onto the bench so everyone could see and hear me. "Thank you all for coming today. I know you're working hard right now and every minute of daylight counts, but the light of day is good for more than just gardens and planting. Revelations can be brought to light."

Elder Brown stepped forward, but I stopped him with a gesture.

"A cure for the Infection has been found." The crowd of people began to talk loudly, questioning the statement I'd made. "And a cure for vampirism has also been found."

I motioned for Mercedes to step forward and helped her up onto the bench. Her dress was freshly pressed and she smelled of bread and butter. Her hair was combed and tucked into a knot at the base of her neck. She looked healthier than she did before the fall. "Mercedes is fine...and so is Roman."

The colonists turned their attention from Mercedes to Roman and he smiled brightly, waving and basking in the attention.

"He has no fangs!" someone shouted. They all knew Roman. He was the face of the night-walkers in our community, the leader; the one they feared for so long.

"She isn't rotting!" came another yell. They also knew that my sister fell in the forest, that she had become a monster.

"We are going to spread the news far and wide, but there is another matter that as citizens you need to address."

Father stepped up to me. "May I tell them?"

I nodded and accepted his hand as he helped me down. "The Elders should be banished from Blackwater," he began with no preamble. A collective gasp came from the colonists, who quieted immediately.

"Now you wait just a minute!" Beckett shouted, waving his hand in front of Father's face.

Tage grabbed the old man's wrist, instructing, "Let him speak."

"Some of you know about the experiments, and some don't. The Elders told you about the treaty with the night-walkers, but what they didn't tell you was that it was more than just protection in exchange for time in the forest. What they didn't tell you was that they also had a treaty with the Infected in our area. And in this treaty, they promised to cooperate with each cursed creature to find a cure. In this treaty, they vowed to use any means at their disposal to heal the Infected. They used some of us as guinea pigs. They used my wife and child."

"And my husband," came the raised voice of a widow.

Father nodded at Widow Tanner.

"They used my son," cried a man from the back of the crowd. He broke down into sobs, comforted by those around him, and by the blessed relief of the crushing weight of such a secret lifting from his shoulders.

"The night-walkers performed the tests at the instruction of the Infected," Father continued. "My wife hated them for it. I can't say for sure that what they did to her – what they did to our unborn child – affected her mind, but I can't say that it didn't," he said, his voice cracking.

Roman walked across the pavilion pavers, parting the crowd like the sea. "Some of the Infected may be too far gone to save. My brother is their leader. I would understand if you didn't want to invite them back into Blackwater. I couldn't blame you one bit. However, I would ask that you consider the situation. If you stood in their shoes, you may have been as desperate for a cure as they were." He cleared his throat, shoving his fists in his pockets. "Thank you."

"What was in it for the Elders?" someone shouted. "Did you work with them for our protection?"

Yankee began spouting lies first. "The Colony had no choice, you see. We were stuck between the night-walkers who threatened to eat us, and the Infected who threatened to either eat or contaminate us. We. Had. No. Choice."

Roman laughed, holding up a piece of paper that was yellowed and curling at all ends. "And the clause that says you get to take credit for finding the cure meant nothing to you?"

Brown threw his hands up and began to walk away, but Yankee and Beckett walked toward Roman, trying to snatch the original treaty from his hands. Tage and I positioned ourselves between them, fangs exposed.

"They *should* be banished," a man shouted.

Murmurs of agreement came from every direction, male and female alike.

Yankee was outraged. "We didn't *make* the treaty! We weren't Elders when it was drawn up."

"You enforced it!" Roman yelled back at him. "You encouraged my brother!"

"And *you* did his bidding, Roman." To the crowd, Beckett shouted, "You can't do this! You have no right!" Wisps of his white hair flapped gently in the soft breeze. The sun made the spots on his head darker and his scowl deeper.

"They just did," I growled. "Gather your things. We'll help you across the river or over the wall. Your choice."

Father called for a group of men to accompany each Elder while they packed what belongings they could carry. The citizens of Blackwater slowly dispersed, each taking in Mercedes and Roman again and again before they went back to their chores.

I settled on a bench, spent from the emotions of the morning, and Tage flopped down next to me. "That went better than I expected," I commented dryly. "After they have a few minutes to gather their things, I'll take them wherever they choose to go. Then I guess we need to go see who we can save in the city."

Tage's brows scrunched together. "I can help you with the Elders."

"No, I need to do it," I answered decisively. "There are still a lot of emotions running high and this needs to be done quietly. I'll see them across the river or the wall. We can meet here afterward."

Roman chuckled. "Have fun with that. I'll hang with Tage until you get back. And then when you leave, I'll make myself busy humaning at my house."

"You mean sleeping," Tage teased.

"Guy's gotta get his beauty sleep. Don't be jealous, Tage. Green isn't your color."

The Elders were indignant, huffing and puffing as we escorted them from Blackwater. They chose the forest. The carpenters, led by Brian Yankee, son of Elder Yankee, had gotten busy after the meeting, making a long, wide bridge of sorts for the old men to walk easily across.

The rungs were close together and made of strong, fresh wood. I positioned it, escorted them slowly across one by one, and then pulled the entire wooden platform back up and over into the Colony. Brian thanked me for allowing them to use the walkway. "Of course. Wish we'd have had this for the rotation," I teased.

Brian watched his father walk across the boards, his thin frame hunched in shame and his salt and pepper hair flapping in the spring wind. The water swirled beneath us, having receded in the last couple of days. It was clear. The mud that clouded it had settled. Colonists gathered a family at a time to watch the men who had led them for so long leave the village.

I understood Brian Yankee. His father was misguided. He had done bad things. Those things weren't his own sins, but he still felt them. Deep in his marrow they resided, scarring him from the inside. Yet he still wanted his father to have a safe trip across the water. Not on a slippery log that even the most fit of men and women struggled with, and not through the cold water or over the algae-ribboned rocks. He loved his father.

As I loved my mother.

As sick as it seemed, I missed her.

The entire scene was solemn. No one clapped or cheered or shamed the men. Everyone watched as the once-mighty quietly fell from power and grace.

To Brian, I whispered, "There are homes. It's a far walk through the forest, but there are homes to the north." I'd seen the clearing, the rooftops glistening with snow. It would take a lot of work to get them cleaned up, but it was shelter.

He nodded once. "I'll help them find one. Thank you."

"Will you stay here?"

"My family and life are here, so I will stay. But I'll help them get established, too."

"I understand."

He looked at me, lip quivering. "I know you do. Thank you for sparing them at all, Porschia."

"It wasn't my choice."

"They banished your mother. Any other person would want revenge."

I sighed as I watched the trio slowly follow the hunting trail that led up the first hill, the one that my feet had helped tramp down. "There's too much revenge and not enough mercy in this world."

"That's the truth. Thank you again." He made the trek easily across the old log and jogged to catch up with his father, telling them there were homes north of Blackwater, and that he would help them all.

TWENTY-THREE

TAGE

I STAYED WITH ROMAN AT THE PAVILION, SIMPLY RESTING ON THE BENCHES, while Porschia took the banished Elders across the creek. She asked us not to be present, fearing that we might incite emotions that shouldn't be brought to a farewell. And that was what the Elders' walk of shame was: a farewell. In many ways, it was an end to a regime. It was also a new beginning for the colonists, one that we would gladly step forward into with them.

When Porschia returned, her mood was somber and reflective. I could almost see the wheels in her brain turning. I wasn't sure why Roman stayed while she went, but his company was welcome. When he saw Porschia walk to where I was standing waiting for her, Roman smiled, waved, and slowly walked away from the pavilion; whistling happily as he took in the clear blue sky.

According to Porschia, the colonists took the news better than I expected. They were an emotional bunch. Overall, I think they felt the same way most did when they heard the news. They felt relief, a weight lifted off their shoulders. They could relax. Almost. We just had to go into the city. Porschia hadn't said a word about herself. She was smart, so I knew she understood that she couldn't be healed. She'd bitten and drank from Mercedes, but while her sister healed, Porschia didn't change at all.

Whatever happened when she changed into both creatures prevented her from becoming anything but that. Would she eventually decay like the Infected, or would the vampirism allow her to live forever? Would her lifespan be like that of a human as the two battled and cancelled each other out? No one knew. No one had dealt with this before, but I was damn sure not going to let her face the uncertainty alone. And she was about to get really pissed at me.

I followed her toward the wall, watching her hips sway the fabric of her pilgrim dress. I liked her in dresses. Maybe in ones that were a little shorter...

At the wall, she and I stared at the rungs that would lead to the top and over the other side. "You first," she insisted.

"Nah. Ladies first," I said with a sly smile.

"I'm wearing a dress, so..."

"Exactly, kitten."

She slapped me on the chest. Hard. I rubbed the spot. Kitten was strong. Dang. "What was that for? Chivalry isn't dead."

She cocked her hip out, fists at her waist. "You and I both know that I'll stand here all damn day."

"You're totally stubborn like that."

She harrumphed indignantly. But she was. Stubborn kitty.

"Fine," I sighed dramatically. "I'll go first, if only because you're a girl."

"Not gonna work. Get moving." I loved that she always called my bluffs. I laughed and started climbing. At the top I waited for her, looking over at the city beyond. The building that Saul burnt still smoldered, one long, gray plume of smoke stretching into the clear sky. We'd smelled it, smelled *them* since the day it happened. Porschia didn't mention it and neither did her family when I was around them. But they all felt it. Regardless of how crazy Miranda Grant had been, regardless of what she did, part of them loved her and always would. Love didn't always make sense. It just was.

I reached for her and though she didn't need any help from me, she took my hand. "You know I can't help you with them, right?" I asked.

"Not until the last one."

I shook my head. "Not even then."

"If you heal the last one, you can turn back into a human, Tage."

"I don't want to be human again." Not while she wasn't. Not while this whole thing was so new. And not while she might need someone to have her back.

She forced me to look at her. "You have to turn back."

"Nah," I said, easing my tongue over the tip of one of my fangs. "I kind of like the sexy night-walker status. Really helps with the ladies."

The narrowing of her eyes said she didn't buy it. "I can't believe you." Her voice wobbled between anger and sadness. "I'd give anything to have my life back."

I pulled her into a hug. "I know, and I'm so sorry, Porsch." Stroking her hair, I let her hold tightly to me, calming herself until the storm passed. She swiped the bloody tears from beneath her eyes.

"Sorry. I just...it's hard to cope with."

"I know. But I want you to know that I'll be here for and with you the whole way. I don't want to be human if you aren't. I'll be here to help you…because I love you, Porschia Grant. Friends don't leave when the going gets tough. Besides, you're my favorite kitten in the world."

She laughed through her bloody tears. "I love you, too, goofy." I caught her limp hand as she tried to swat me. "And thank you. I understand if you change your mind, though."

"I won't. I can be just as stubborn as you."

Porschia groaned and ticked her head toward the city. "We should get going. I'm sure they would like to hear the good news."

"You're scary when you cry, Porsch," I told her. It was more than just the crimson tears; it was the fact that I didn't know if I'd ever be able to put her pieces back together. When you loved someone, you wanted them to be happy. It might be a long time before she felt that emotion again, but I would damn sure try to bring it to her.

TWENTY-FOUR

PORSCHIA

The Infected were quick to listen when Tage cupped his hands and began screaming through the city, "We have a cure for the Infection!" Their screeches mainly came from one building, but soon they came filing out of several. There were fewer than I'd imagined, though. Pierce even bothered to show his face.

Where's my brother? he asked.

"He's human now. He can't help you. Only I can. And if you want my help, we do this my way, Pierce."

Tage spoke up and explained how we'd found the cure and how the colonists were aware of it and welcomed them…with the exception of Pierce and Saul. Pierce wasn't happy about their decision, but the other Infected weren't concerned with his wants anymore. Tage asked them to form a line.

The first was an older Asian man with graying thatches of hair on his scabbed scalp. I didn't recognize him from the Colony. While most of those in line came from Blackwater, falling over the years to the Infection, some were from worlds away, it seemed. Where did the outsiders come from?

Some of us wandered from place to place until we found one that fit, at least for the time being, Ma'am. Thank you for telling us about a cure. I'll be forever grateful.

I smiled. "No need to thank me. You'd have done the same."

Not sure if I'm a good enough person for that, Ma'am.

I wasn't sure if I still counted as a person either. I motioned him forward. "I can't numb you. I don't think it will release enough venom if I do."

He nodded and braced his hands on his knees. His beard was long and surprisingly soft. I tilted his head to the side and bit down, sinking a small piece of my soul into his vein. He shrieked over my shoulder and I held him tightly as he tried to push me away. It was instinct. Fight or flight. He fought. I won.

I fed.

I poisoned.

I healed.

I cried. A lot.

Tage stood beside me.

His blood tasted strange. Not rancid, exactly, but not fresh or healthy. It was like meat that had sat out for too long, or bread that was about to mold.

When I eased my fangs out of his neck he thanked me again, tears flowing down the ridges of raised skin on his face, scarred and peeling. *Thank you. I can never repay you.*

"You'll feel worse before you feel better," I warned.

One by one, I fed from them.

One by one they thrashed and screamed.

One by one they cried.

One by one they thanked me.

One by one they broke me.

One by one they put me back together.

Pierce was last in line, but accepted the gift of healing without protest. His tears bore testament to the ordeal that he'd both endured and caused.

Tage stood beside me.

AFTER A LONG AFTERNOON IN THE CITY AND FILLING MYSELF FULL OF TOO much blood, I was sick. Tage helped me back over the wall. "Let's get you home."

"No. I need a few minutes if you don't mind."

"Sure. We can take a breather."

I shook my head. "I need to go to the cemetery. Alone."

"Can I take you there? I'll leave if you want after that. I'm...I just want to make sure you're okay."

Nodding, I squeezed his hand. "Okay."

He picked me up and ran across the Colony. The cemetery grass was overgrown now that spring had arrived. Tage eased my feet to the ground. "You need me, you yell. Okay?"

"Got it. Thanks, Tage. For everything today."

He pressed his lips together tightly and one side of his mouth turned up. With a quick wave, he was gone.

I watched the grass rebound from the weight of his feet, blade by blade until they stood tall again. The cage still hovered over Meg's grave. I let my fingers fall over the warm metal and sat beside it.

"I'm so sorry. I never knew that you were in danger, that being a friend to me would get you killed. My mother –" I swallowed. "My mother is gone now. She can't hurt you. Neither can I."

Lambs bleated from the direction of the barn. Horses whinnied. From the homes beyond, children laughed. A small blue jay perched on the side of the cage, tilting its head back and forth to assess me. Was I a threat? Yes. To everything.

"If I could go back in time, I would have turned her in. I didn't know she was killing people. I never imagined that her hatred for me could have..." My chest heaved and I sobbed until there was nothing left. Looking up to the beautiful sky, I closed my eyes and whispered, "I'm sorry, Meg."

The river was beautiful. It wasn't the swirling, angry deluge it normally was. The dark water was calm and serene, as if it, too, was relieved. We'd carried our burdens across it for longer than I'd been alive. At times it muddied us and at others it cleansed. The river was the heart of this place; the only reason Blackwater remained a sanctuary despite those who manipulated her. Sliding my boots and socks off, I stepped onto the rocks. Those that were dry were warm, while those that were wet as I walked on them were cooled from the river spray. The rhythm of the falls was erratic but soothing. This was our song, our anthem.

"Porschia?"

I gasped, looking up to the opposite bank. Saul Daniels stared back at me, his hands in the pockets of his pants.

"What are you doing here?" My heart threatened to run away and my feet eased to the dry rocks, threatening the same. Saul was no longer Infected. He couldn't physically hurt me. But the wound he caused was an insurmountable chasm in me. It was deep and angry and filled with sorrow. It also needed to be filled up with answers to the questions I wanted to ask.

"Why did you do it?"

"Set the fire?" he said softly, sitting on the bank, dangling his boots.

I shook my head. "The morning I volunteered. Why did you say you would marry me?"

"You needed help."

"That's it? You would help someone, just like that?" I snapped my fingers.

He shook his head. "I wouldn't have volunteered to wed just anyone. I'd seen you and Mercedes. I watched you from a distance."

"Mercedes already had Jonas, so you figured, why not?"

He blew out a breath. "It wasn't that. I just – I don't know why I offered. I don't know. I could say that it was love at first sight, but it wasn't. I thought we could grow to love one another. I *did* love you."

"No you didn't." The hell he did. You couldn't hurt someone you loved so badly. If you loved someone, you put them first. You honored their friends and family. You stood beside them.

"I'm sorry, Porschia. I'm sorry that I hurt you so much."

"Would you have done anything differently?" I sat to put my socks back on, angrily lacing my boots because I already knew his answer.

His stare pierced me. He ground his teeth together, but finally said exactly what I expected. "No." Saul Daniels was nothing if not honest.

"That's how I know you don't love me and never did, Saul." I stood up and took one last look at him before walking away, at human pace. I wanted him to feel each step, every inch and centimeter of distance I placed between us. Truthfully, there wasn't enough space on earth to fill the space I needed between him and me.

When I crested the small knoll near the barn, Tage joined me. "I'm sorry about him."

"You aren't," I said pointedly.

"I am."

"Why would you care about how I feel about Saul? And how did you know to come to the river?"

"Because you hurt, and because I can't stand for you to feel pain." That damned bond. He stopped and looked at me. "I want to eat him now. Damn it, Porsch. You attract such losers."

"He's the only one I've attracted, so please."

"Roman?" he asked, eyebrows lifting.

"Ugh. Fine. Him and Roman."

"And me," he added softly.

I stopped walking again and looked at him. "I'm just your favorite kitten, Tage. Isn't that what you said at the wall?" Admitting to myself that his words stung was hard enough. Admitting that to him was excruciating, worse than when he first bit me at the rotation without numbing me first.

He tilted my face up to him and caressed my jaw with his thumb. "I only call pretty girls 'kitten', kitten."

I rolled my eyes. Of course he did. Mercedes would be kitten, too, I supposed. I pulled away from him and started toward Roman's. "Stop, Porschia."

My feet obeyed and I turned to look at him. His face was already in mine. My hands found his chest. "Stop running from me. For once, just stop running."

His warm breath fanned across my lips. "If you want to be my only kitten, you better say so. Now."

I swallowed. "Fine."

"Say it."

"It." I smiled against his lips.

"Kitten...say it."

He was infuriating. "I'm reconsidering."

Tage pressed his lips against mine, silencing any further smart remarks and stealing my breath. He kissed me like a man who'd been gone from home for so long he'd forgotten what his love tasted like. He kissed me like I was the only girl left on the planet. Pulling away, he stared into my eyes. His eyes? They said... say it. So I did.

"I don't know what this is or how to handle it. My feelings are all over the board. What I *do* know is that I don't think I could stand it if you called someone else kitten. I want to be your only kitten. "

He smiled. "I know."

I slapped his chest. "Asshole."

"I like it when my kitty talks all dirty to me." He wagged his eyebrows.

"I like it when my Tage kisses me." I liked that a lot. And I didn't have to say that part twice. He was happy to offer another. And another.

When we walked toward Roman's, he held my hand. "Why the sudden change in heart?"

"You never left me."

"Hmm?"

"Through all of this. The turning, the sickness, the meat eating..." He barely suppressed a shudder as I continued, "Mother's banishment, the hunts, the cure, today... You stayed there. You never left me."

"Never will, Porsch." He threw an arm over my shoulders and we walked together toward Roman's house.

TWENTY-FIVE

PORSCHIA

Several weeks went by. Trees blossomed, flowers fell, and leaves grew wide and green. Flowers and vegetables sprouted from the rich soil. I appreciated it now, the dark earth. It gave life to everything in Blackwater. My sister was completely well and so was Roman. Father and Ford worked beside them both in their gardens. Roman helped everyone in the Colony, hell-bent on paying for the misdeeds he'd taken part in and thanking them for not banishing him along with his brother. No one ever brought that up and I was glad. Human Roman was someone I would have liked as a young girl. He joked, smiled, and threw mud like the best of them.

Kneeling in the freshly turned earth in front of my own house, I smiled. Tage and I had gathered our things and moved almost immediately after I saw Saul at the river. We needed space. So did Roman. But we wouldn't be welcome across the invisible line of the pavilion. Roman wouldn't either. I thought time would erase such boundaries, but maybe it would take more time than I imagined.

Tage was helping set snares in the forest. He'd learned the technique from the Freeman's and perfected it over time. Small animals fell into his traps each day. Teams and families hunted freely for larger game now, but everyone still shared, splitting the bounty as they always had.

"You need a hand?" Roman called out as he approached. "Place looks good. You've done a lot to it."

"I'm just planting some beans and cabbage."

"I'll help." Roman dropped to the ground beside me and began using his fingers to gouge holes into the soil. He dropped a few seeds in each one before making new holes. I mirrored him to his right.

"I'm sorry, Porschia."

"I know. You've said it a thousand times."

He sat back on his knees. "I'm sorry that it wasn't me. You're being punished for something I did. You'll never stop being punished for it."

It was true. He'd set a lot of stuff into motion and many more people than me had been caught in the webs. But that was water under the bridge.

"It's fine." Turning my attention back to the beans, I kept working.

"It isn't."

"Fine!" I yelled, taking a cleansing breath. "Fine. It sucks. It sucks being the only one who is both things she hates, and it sucks not being able to be healed. I was pissed off at you for so long, but Roman, life goes on. You can't dwell on this forever. I can't dwell on it. I have to accept this shit and move on. So if you could stop apologizing and start helping me accept what I am, that would be great."

He nodded determinedly. "I can do that."

"Awesome," I huffed.

"I want to go with you to spread the word. Some of the night-walkers nearby know me. It'll help prove that what you're claiming is true."

"How far away are the next survivors?"

He squinted at the sun. "For a human, maybe a week of walking, shorter on horseback."

"Mercedes is coming."

Roman looked over at me. "I know. She told me that's what you'd been waiting for. She wants to help. So do I."

"What did Tage say?"

"He called me a cockblocker."

I laughed out loud. "That sounds about like him."

"Tell me a story and I'll let you go with us."

Roman narrowed his eyes. "Once upon a time..." he smarted.

"...there were two human brothers." I needed to know his story and Pierce's.

Swallowing, he sat down, stretching his legs out and looking up at the sun. "Once upon a time, there were two human brothers. They were best friends. When the entire world began fighting against itself, country against country, friend against friend, ally against ally, the brothers decided to help defend their own country. They wanted to do something important. So they joined the military, were assigned to the same unit and shipped out to the coast. Fighting was hard. Other countries tried to invade via a neighboring island. The brothers were tired and weary. So were the others who fought alongside them."

"One night they were given a reprieve, a night to rest and kick back. There were no sirens, no explosions, and no bombs. They took full advantage of that night with women and liquor. When they left the bar, Pierce – the far less handsome brother – got into an argument with a man who looked like he'd had way too much to drink. In the scuffle, the man bit Pierce. It turns out that he wasn't drunk at all. He was Infected, and now Pierce was, too."

"Pierce had to be quarantined. The virus was tearing through the populace quicker than the bombs could tear it apart. The far more handsome brother still fought for his country. One night, he was patrolling a section of beach by himself because his unit was so thin, there was no backup. A woman approached, claiming that she could help me and others win this war. She could give us all immense strength and make us damn-near invincible. The handsome brother was so tired that he asked to know more. She told him that if he wanted such power, he had to listen closely to what she had to say. She came close to him and he listened, her mouth to his ear. She bit him. The pain was worse than anything he'd ever felt in his life."

"The handsome brother woke on the beach, so hungry he was absolutely mad. A note was in his pocket. The words scrawled on that paper would change everything."

I looked at him, his dark eyes blurring from the tears they held back. "What did the note say, Roman?"

"It gave directions to Blackwater. It said there was a sanctuary for our kinds: mine and my brother's. It said: *Your blood can heal.* But that was a lie. My blood didn't heal anything. It damned those who took as much as a drop. Though it kept Pierce alive, it didn't heal him. She was a liar. Why wouldn't she say that the *venom* healed?"

I blew out a breath. "Maybe she didn't know. Maybe she meant for you to heal the battle-wounded. It's hard to say without asking her."

He swallowed, wiping the wetness from his eyes. "I know. I'm sorry. I know you don't want to hear it for the one thousand and first time, but I can't stop."

"I'm sorry, too. How old were you?"

"Eighteen. Both of us were."

"I'm sorry for you, Roman."

"You shouldn't be." There was a long moment of silence. "Can I go with you now?"

I smiled. "Yeah. You can go. You'll need a horse, though."

"The Colony said we can only take one, but Mercedes said I could ride with her." My eyebrows hit my hairline at that admission.

Lately I'd noticed the glances the two exchanged and how helpful Roman was when it came to my sister. He hauled water for her, split wood, carried it indoors. He lifted heavy pots from the hearth and doted over her as though she were his. Maybe he wanted her to be. Time would tell that, too.

Tage's footsteps, I knew them by heart, approached from the sidewalk. "You okay? Hey Roman." His blue eyes locked onto mine.

"I'm great. Roman's helping me plant."

"Maggie's ready for you."

"Okay." I stood up, dusting the mud from the knees of my skirt. "I should probably change."

Tage nodded, watching me walk inside.

EASING MAGGIE'S DOOR OPEN, I WAS GREETED WITH A HUG. "IT'S BEEN TOO long!"

I laughed. "I saw you just yesterday."

"We have a lot of catching up to do. And now that you're leaving, we have less time to do it in. I have a surprise for you!" She hugged me tightly and swayed us back and forth.

"You don't have to do anything for me, Maggie."

"I know I don't *have* to, Missy. I *want* to. Now help me up the steps."

Lying on the bed in the room where she first began to teach me to sew were dresses; four of them in different shades: purple, blue, green, and yellow, with small flowers sewn on the hems and collars. "They're amazing, Maggie," I said, stepping back to admire them. I didn't want to cry on them. Blood stains were a bitch to get out of light fabric. She handed me a rag and hugged me tightly again.

"I've been working on them all winter. Don't tell Mercedes. I know she needs some new dresses, but yours will always come first, Porschia. I love you like you were my own daughter. I've worried about you so much, but you're resilient. You're beautiful and fierce."

"I'm a freak," I blubbered.

"You are *not* a freak. You're perfect. And you can handle this. If anyone in this whole world can handle being something beautifully different, it's you. Your heart leads you. Make sure you let it."

I nodded, unable to form coherent words.

"I'll miss you. I know you have to go and how important the journey ahead of you is, but I wanted you to have a piece of me to carry with you... or wear on you, rather."

Smiling, I hugged her again. "Now, no more tears," she admonished. "They'll ruin the fabric."

"Yes, ma'am."

"You're coming for dinner tonight? I cleared it with Tage. Your Father, Ford, and Mercedes are coming, too."

"Can Roman come?"

She pursed her lips together.

"He's not so bad now, Maggie. Give him a chance?" A dark part of me understood Roman, his motives and actions. I understood his loyalty to his brother, because despite all she did to make my life hell, I loved my mother. She didn't deserve the punishment Saul handed down.

She took a deep breath, her wrinkles deepening. "I trust you. If you say he deserves a second chance, then that's exactly what I'll give him."

"Thank you. Let me help you back downstairs?"

"Of course, dear."

I helped her take each step, slowly but carefully. At the foyer, she paused. "See you in a few hours."

"In a few hours." We'd had dinner every day this week now that Mercedes was better and I'd had time to calm down from all the craziness that had happened.

Walking home, I was shocked that some neighbors actually waved at me as I passed by them, my arms full of pastel dresses. I wiggled my fingers back at them, making the children giggle and their parents smile.

Blackwater would survive because its people were strong. They worked and helped one another. They shared in tragedies and triumphs alike. They were a community. In the days that passed after the Elders were removed from power and banished from the Colony, a new council was formed. Comprised of nine men and women, they would make decisions based on the majority of votes among them.

There was no more manipulation, no hunger for power. Would it come to that again one day? Maybe, but for now things were good. There was no longer a need for a treaty. Most of the formerly Infected chose to move into the Colony. They claimed houses that were empty, most huddling in the night-walker part of town. As much as the colonists were afraid of them, they were afraid of the colonists. Circumstance and fear drove a wedge between the worlds. While that gap was being bridged, the small separation seemed to be a soothing balm on wounds inflicted a long time ago.

Pierce stayed in the city with a few others. I assumed Saul was still in the forest, as were the Elders. Brian Yankee and a few others trekked through the woods to help them every few days. No one faulted him for that, because he did as any child would do.

I asked Brian for a small favor and he granted it. Within a day, a small wooden marker was erected in the cemetery bearing my mother's name. He had taken his time carving it, giving her the respect she deserved, that anyone deceased deserved, because he understood that love was love. It was neither right nor wrong. It didn't have to make sense; it simply was. Father cried when he saw it. Ford and Mercedes placed bouquets of flowers at its base.

Soon, Brian had requests from other residents. He carved them for the fallen, the Infected and night-walkers alike, that fell victim to Pierce and time.

Tage said there'd always been a darkness in this world. He said that though some night-walkers might be reluctant to change, we had to give them the option. Now that we knew how to tamp out some of the darkness, it was our duty to bring the light.

The sun warmed my shoulders and face.

The fabric of the beautiful dresses fluttered happily in the warm breeze. No longer a symbol of control, I would wear them proudly because I wanted to. The decision was mine.

Children laughed.

Birds sang.

Puffy clouds floated over the clear blue sky.
An axe fell upon wood.
In the distance, the water cascaded over the falls.
Animals bleated.
And I smiled.

FRICTION

ONE

SAUL

More than my family, my few friends, Blackwater, or home, I missed her. I missed her voice in my head. I missed sharing a frequency that only she and I had. I missed her strength and the softness of her body. She had the fortitude of steel and a heart as beautiful and delicate as a spider web covered in dew, and just as easily broken lately. I wish I'd made time to know her sooner.

From afar, I'd seen her from time to time; she and her sister, Mercedes. Mercedes and her beau Noah were well known around the Colony. Both were outgoing and full of life individually, but together they shone. The entire Colony was present at funerals, farewells, weddings, and the occasional gathering that the Elders mandated, but Porschia would sit in the corner alone or stand on the fringe, sometimes flanked by Ford. When she went, her mother would stick close to her father and neither paid their children any attention at all. If one of the three was the favorite, it was definitely Mercedes. Porschia was hated and Ford forgotten.

She was convinced that what we had wasn't love, and for the briefest of moments I convinced myself of the same thing. She didn't love me; she merely needed me, and I was a convenient way out of her hellish home life. The friendship we had was only that. Maybe a hint of something more, but certainly not love.

Love was something too strong to break. Love was without condition; a foundation and a shelter. And we took shelter in one another, calling it love… calling it something it couldn't have been in such a short amount of time.

That was what I told myself.

Every day.

Over and over.

As if saying it often enough, forcefully enough, would make it true and would make my heart believe the logic of my mind.

Our minds were tethered, despite all I'd done and the cowardly way I refused to drink from my ring, assuming it was all over for me and selfishly giving up all hope. The fire itself. Killing her mother.

I still couldn't stop watching her, making sure she was okay, making sure she fed and was well. Hiding in the trees and thickets to get one glance of her wasn't enough. My heart missed her. It ached for her above all else, even as she hated me and her hatred grew stronger every time I came near. I wasn't bonded to her like Tage was, but I felt hate radiate from her like heat waves rising from the hot, crumbling asphalt that bisected Blackwater. However, my feelings for her—even if it wasn't called love—weren't gone. They didn't disappear.

Despite repeated attempts to reconnect and in spite of her open disgust for me, I still watched. But watching wouldn't make her feel the same way about me. I erased any chance for a future with Porschia Grant the moment I lit the flame that torched that building. It was why I decided to approach Mercedes. It was why I had to leave Blackwater.

Befriending someone who could help me achieve that goal, even if that someone was Porschia's sister, was step one. Fortunately, Mercedes was fast to forgive, fast to offer food, and open to helping in any way she could, in her own words.

I would ask her for that help very soon.

I climbed the oak as high as its branches would support me, bracing my back against its trunk, my feet stretching out along the strong wood. I waited for night to fall over me like a thick, dark shroud. Porschia was the collection of tiny lights that peeked through the tightly-woven fabric. Sometimes her light was missing, and soon it would be too far away for me to see. So every opportunity, every night, I waited for her.

PORSCHIA

CERTAIN MOMENTS ARE BIGGER THAN OTHERS. THEY HOLD MORE WEIGHT, more importance somehow. I remembered the first time I took a step onto the log that crossed the river, the step that took me out of the confines of the Colony and led me into the forest and into the unknown. Over time and with each hunt, the forest became less of a mystery. I learned her valleys and hills, her streams and rocks. Memorizing her paths with my feet, we became quick friends. She was simply a place covered with beautiful trees, providing life to the animals who lived there and food to those who hunted them. The forest saw everything, even the most feral parts of humanity. Because in the end, parts of every creature, Infected and night-walker alike, were human. And though I was neither and both at the same time, I was human too, beneath it all.

Venturing beyond the river and into the forest was a huge step. Traveling beyond the forest to tell other survivors about the cures? That would be an enormous leap, one taken in both fear and faith, but it was one that just might save the world and all the people left in it.

Mercedes burst through my front door, yelling my name. I looked up from the backpack I was stuffing. "Porschia?" she screamed again, her voice panicked and trembling.

I ran to her, the wind from my speed making her hair blow back away from her face. "Hey," she said, startled and blinking. "I don't know if I'll ever get used to that."

In the last few weeks, I'd found the balance of nutrition that seemed ideal for me: one part blood and three parts raw animal meat. With that ratio I was faster than I'd ever been, and stronger and more in control than I'd been since changing. I felt an intense power flow beneath my flesh, like tiny forked rivers of lightning sparking beneath the surface of me.

"What's the matter?" I asked. Things had changed between me and Mercedes, perhaps permanently, and I knew small talk wasn't going to happen now. It was pointless. She had a choice and chose to stand beside Saul instead of with me. I also had a choice, and it was to keep her at a distance.

She glanced up at me. "Roman is very sick."

"Sick? What kind of sick?" 'Sick' could mean a great many things. It could mean nothing more than a cold or it could mean death would follow.

She shook her head. "I need you to come and see him, and there's no way he can travel, despite his stubborn argument." She crossed her arms angrily.

Mercedes had been spending a lot of time at Roman's for the past two days and now I knew why. I noticed her coming and going, and at first I thought he'd worked his charm on her. He had no power of compulsion now, but I'd learned that his personality was still pretty charismatic. He didn't need to wield compulsion; he only needed to smirk and wink. Mercedes had visited Saul recently as well. I could smell his scent lingering in her hair. He was living in an abandoned home situated deep in the woods, far from the Elders and any other human being. I'd passed by it during the hunt one night and though he wasn't inside, his scent was strong there. So strong, I nearly lost my balance and fell to the forest floor. The familiarity and comfort that were once associated with the scent of his pine soap and skin now haunted me.

As far as my sister, I imagined that guilt fueled her steps to him. After all, she was the one who bit him, passing the infection knowingly, and made him a monster. Part of me still blamed her for the fire, even though his hands were the ones to set it and his conscience failed to tell him that such an act was wrong.

I knew it wasn't her. It was him. He may have chosen his own path, but blame didn't make sense. It simply was.

I'd seen Saul twice, staring from the forest as I passed through, hunting meat for the colonists and for us. Between the former Infected, the current night-walkers, and the humans who'd always been only that, there was still a distinct divide, possibly a deeper and more severe chasm than before the cures were discovered. From the cover of foliage, he stared but never spoke. Each time, a small slice of my heart hardened into something solid and impenetrable. I didn't tell Tage he was lurking for two reasons. One, he knew but didn't talk about it. If I could smell his scent, Tage certainly could. Two, Tage would tear his head off.

Between the infection and the vampirism, there had been enough victims, enough death. At some point it had to end. Perhaps we could spread peace via the cure instead of spreading more hatred and disdain.

Father and Ford stopped by early that morning with a basket of smoked meat, cans of food, and bread for Mercedes and Roman. Their horse was ready and we were supposed to leave within the hour, but now I hear that Roman is sick.

"I'll go check on him."

"Thank you," my sister said, awkward silence enveloping both of us. I left her behind and ran toward Roman's, where I found him upstairs in his bed. His breathing was deep and rhythmic, but his scent was different, medicinal. What did Mercedes give him?

I approached his bed. "Roman?"

He stirred slightly, his eyelashes fluttering. "Roman," I said more forcefully. This time, his eyes opened and he sucked in a sharp breath.

"What are you doing here?" he said weakly.

"My sister sent me. You're ill?"

He rolled his eyes. "It's just a cold."

His skin was flushed and he shook slightly, though he tried to mask it from me. It was definitely more than a cold. "Flu?"

"Maybe it is. I'm okay to ride, though."

"Did Mercedes give you something for the fever?" I could sense the heat rolling off his forehead and body.

"Yes. I think it made me drowsy."

He needed to stay home. "You aren't well enough to go."

"You won't survive without me." I stared at his dark, brown-black eyes. "You won't. Some places are safe, but others aren't. In those places, people will be mistrusting of you. God help you if they find out what you are."

Shivers ran up and down my spine. "They'd only see the fangs, but... Why would they care?"

"Because they'll either fear you or be fascinated by you, and neither option bodes well for Porschia Grant."

"And you'll keep them from knowing? Save me from all the bad in the world?"

He shook his head with a smile. "I'm only human."

I smiled. Roman was enjoying being human again, despite the fact that his brother had disappeared from the forest. He worried for him.

"But some of them knew me as a vampire. They'll see irrefutable proof of the cure."

Snorting, I scoffed. "They'll see that now you're a human and you feel like you're dying. I'm sure they'll all stand in line to be just like you."

His expression fell, growing serious as his brows folded together. "You already know some won't want to change. Well, all Infected will, but some vamps will be reluctant."

"I realize that, and I know we can't make them change; we can only give them the information. What they choose to do with it is their choice."

"If anything happens, do not approach The Manor without me." The only thing Roman would say in detail about The Manor was that it was a vampire stronghold. There were no Infected, but the vamps there didn't bow to humans. The human population feared them, and for good reason. Roman didn't give me details, but my imagination ran wild with that assertion.

It was my turn to frown. "We're only going to tell them about the cure…we don't go inside the walls. Right?"

He shook his head. "There aren't walls. There's a moat, but you don't cross it and no one goes inside the front door. If you take one step inside the building, you're not likely to leave."

"If your fever isn't gone by the time—"

"I'm going, Porschia. It's only a day's ride to Mountainside and it's safe there. I can rest for a day or so before we move on."

I gritted my teeth, a bad feeling in my gut telling me he shouldn't go, that he was too sick. Mercedes was right about that, but Roman was the only one who knew the way. He was also the only proof that might help persuade people of the cure easily, rather than demonstrating that it was real.

Familiar arms wrapped around my waist and a slow smile spread across my lips. "What's wrong?" Tage asked, warm breath fanning my hair. "I like this dress," he said in a barely audible voice.

Roman groaned, throwing his arm over his eyes and burrowing further back into his pillows. His hearing wasn't as acute anymore, but he was still a guy. He knew what Tage said and how he felt.

"Roman's sick."

Tage snorted. "Poor baby."

"No, look at him."

It took a few seconds, but Tage found the same thing that I did. Roman was too ill to travel. "He can't go. Not like this."

"I have to." Roman pushed himself up onto his pile of pillows.

I offered an alternative. "We could postpone it."

"We've postponed it twice already because of the spring storms," Roman argued. "Look – Mountainside is another haven, a lot like Blackwater, only...mountainous. They'll let us stay for a few days and I can recuperate there."

"What if they aren't as accommodating as they've been in the past?"

Roman winced, sitting up straighter. "They will be."

When we planned our first journey, Roman told us about the three places we would travel. The first, Mountainside, had no treaty but welcomed night-walkers as long as the vampires provided meat from game in the forest that they resided in. It was a poor system, Roman argued, secluding themselves on one mountain, securing it around the bottom with a tall, thick stone fence that kept the Infected out of their safe haven. A poor system, because even safe havens could become cages. Much like Blackwater, the people of Mountainside's separation became a weakness as much as a strength. They depended upon the night-walkers for food that they couldn't grow themselves on stepped gardens that striped the sides of the mountain. Their dwellings were basically caves, hand-hewn into the rocky hillside. They lived primitively, he said. But didn't we all to some degree?

Tage stepped back. "If Roman says he can make it, let's give him the benefit of the doubt."

I narrowed my eyes at him. Jerk. He was just thinking that if Roman died along the way, that would be one less thorn in his side. Tage's eyes twinkled, knowing I caught on to his game.

Roman groaned again. "Would you two go home for a little while? You're making me nauseous."

TWO

MERCEDES

I RAN ACROSS THE LOG, MY FEET SLIPPING. THE SOLES OF MY SHOES WERE worn slick and nearly all the way through the soles in spots. Normally, Tage or Porschia would ease the bridge that the carpenters made across the river when we needed to cross, but I didn't want them to know who I was meeting. Across the bank and over the hill, he waited. "Hey," I said, out of breath.

"Are they still traveling today?" Saul asked.

"I think so. Roman is too sick to go, but he's too stubborn to stay."

"You have the fabric?"

I patted my pocket where lumps of fabric were piled together. "I do. I'll leave a trail for you."

Saul craned his head toward the Colony. "No one knows you've been coming?"

"They haven't said anything, so I don't think they know."

"Porschia knows," he said. My body tensed. She couldn't know. She would be furious. She would snap.

"I don't think she—"

Saul smiled sympathetically and then said, "She's stronger than ever. She can probably smell me from here. She can probably smell you, too."

I hadn't thought of that. We were so far away. I handed him a bag of bread and cheese. Ford had brought extra for him, but only because I promised Saul would be led away from Blackwater and wouldn't return. Ford harbored mixed feelings but would be glad to see him go. So would Porschia, though I knew she warred with herself over residual feelings. Emotions that strong couldn't be erased by a single act, but her stubbornness ran deep. She could be judgmental of others without giving them the benefit of the doubt. It would take time, possibly a lifetime, before Porschia's forgiveness would even begin to show its head, unless a miracle or tragedy happened. Both were strong enough to spark change; catalysts of life-altering changes of perspective, as we'd all learned lately.

"Thank you for the food," he said, looking up but refusing to meet my eyes.

"You're welcome. What do you plan to do after you leave here?"

"If Mountainside will allow me to stay, I will do that and see if it's a fit. If not, I'll follow you to the next settlement and try there. I'll keep trying until I find somewhere to belong."

My chest tightened. "I'm sorry, Saul."

"No sorrier than I am, Mercedes."

The pieces of fabric were small but bright red-orange, and would be an effective trail of bread crumbs as long as Porschia or Tage didn't catch on. Hopefully Roman wouldn't feel well enough to pay close attention to anything. I was the one who bit Saul and turned him into a monster, so I was partially responsible for the monstrous things he did and would be responsible for making sure he survived. In another settlement, he could start anew. As a human, with a new life, new prospects and possibilities, he could live out his days in peace. Saul could become anyone he wanted to be. Hovering around Blackwater was torturous to him, as it was to the Elders. Although he didn't have much contact with them, he watched the forest closely and saw the ones who came to offer them help, his former boss included.

I jerked my thumb back toward Blackwater. "Keep a lookout. I need to get back in case they leave soon."

He shifted his feet. "I'm ready and I'll watch for you."

"Okay," I said with determination, already turning my back to him and jogging back toward the river. I firmly believed it wasn't a betrayal to my sister; it was simply helping someone who needed it. As I approached the swirling currents of the water, I saw that Porschia was waiting for me on the other side. "What are you doing, Mercedes?" Her voice wasn't angry, just exasperated and tired.

Pursing my lips together, I tried to think up a good lie but decided with her uncanny instincts, it was pointless. "Saul needs food so I took him some."

She inhaled deeply. "Was it some of what Father sent for you and Roman?"

"Ford packed extra."

"Did he know who was getting the extra rations?" she bit out crossly.

I straightened my shoulders. "He did."

"Why would Ford help Saul?" She was asking one question, as well as another unspoken one about why I was helping him. The answers were different and yet the same.

"Saul wants to leave Blackwater behind. He is going to follow us to Mountainside, where he plans to start a new life."

My sister's jaw tightened. "So Ford only helped so he could be rid of him?"

Mine tightened, too. "More than likely."

"And you? What's your excuse for visiting him so often? For bringing him food and helping him follow our trail?"

"Are you jealous or angry, Porschia?" She stared intently at me, and if her eyes could have burst into flames or lit me on fire, it wouldn't have surprised me at all. But I told her how I felt and for once she listened instead of getting angry and walking away. "I made him the monster he became, and I feel responsible for how everything happened."

"You feel responsible? Guilty? Good. You deserve it, Mercedes. You made many monsters and several enemies along the way."

"Porschia, I *know* that. I've said I'm sorry a thousand times, but I can't apologize forever."

"Then don't bother," she said as she sped away.

Porschia was right. I bit her, bit our mother, and bit Saul. Mother was gone, and although Saul was human again, he was an outcast because of me. And Porschia… she was damned because of my actions. I could say it was because of Pierce and how he frightened me, but the fact of the matter was that I had a choice and I chose to avoid his wrath by infecting others. I took the easy path and made the wrong choice. Porschia couldn't be helped, but Saul still could – and I was going to help him. Everyone else, including my sister, could just learn to deal with it.

When I caught up with her at her house, she and Tage were walking over to get Roman from his. "We need you to get the horse from the stable, Mercedes," Tage said.

"You want *me* to get it?" I didn't mind; I was just surprised they trusted me to do anything.

"Unfortunately," he smiled, exposing his long fangs, "I tend to spook them. My bet is that your sister would too, so that's why we need *you* to get the horse and come back for Roman as soon as possible."

Porschia narrowed her eyes at me in response.

"Hurry, we're going to bring him down."

I took off running as fast as my legs could carry me. They were infinitely better now that the Infection was gone, but weaker than I'd been before the illness took hold. Sometimes I envied Porschia. Once she fed she was so strong, even stronger than Tage and twice as strong as Roman had been as a night-walker.

Ford was already waiting at the stable, saddling a beautiful dark brown mare. He smiled as he saw me approaching. "Cedes, you're just in time. This girl is ready." He patted her back and stroked her mane.

"What's her name?" I looked at her, her eyes as dark as freshly turned soil.

"Her name's Lady. Take care of her, and –" He approached to whisper, looking around to make sure no one was listening to our conversation. Satisfied that no one was around, he continued, "Don't let Porschia get too close to her. Tage, either."

"They frighten you, Lady?" I said, stroking her mane. I wasn't scared of horses. I'd ridden before, although not nearly enough to be considered good at it, and a spooked horse might be more than I could handle.

"That…but also, Porschia likes meat and I like Lady—alive."

I swallowed. She wouldn't eat the horse. At least, I didn't think she would. I saw Porschia eat raw meat once, and it was enough to make me never want to see it again. Nodding to Ford, I took her reins and he eased a stool over to help me climb on. "There are apples and oats in the bags behind you. Feed her well and stop for water as often as you can."

"We will. I'll see to it that she returns to you in the same shape she's in now."

He looked away. "Take care of Porschia, too. I know no one thinks she needs help, but I think she needs it now more than she ever has."

My brows touched one another. Why would Porschia need anything from me or anyone else? She was the most powerful thing around here. She had nothing to fear because everyone feared her. That included me.

Most days I didn't know if she wanted to hug me or strangle my neck. I wouldn't have blamed her for either one. Once the dust settled and after the cure was found, things between the pair of us had changed irrevocably.

I thanked Ford again before Lady trotted out of the stable and I guided her toward Roman's house. When I approached, Tage was supporting Roman's weight, Roman's arm draped around his shoulder, but he was still standing in the sunlight, draped in a thick, woolen coat.

Porschia flanked his other side, her dress also hidden by dark wool, wearing the coat that used to be mine. Lady whinnied when we got too close to the pair of predators, but I kept her calm as Tage helped Roman onto the saddle behind me. It wasn't the most comfortable situation.

"I need to hold on to you," he said, wincing. He squinted his eyes against the bright sunlight.

"That's fine."

He groaned and held on tightly to my stomach as Porschia spoke up. "We'll meet you at the crossing downstream."

They sped away, setting Lady at ease once more. The thing about prey? They knew what to be frightened of. Perhaps we should *all* be wary of the night-walkers. Even Porschia could be dangerous if provoked, and provocation seemed to be my strong suit lately.

THREE

TAGE

"WHAT'S WRONG, KITTEN?" I STRAINED TO KEEP UP WITH HER.

Porschia growled as she ran harder and faster alongside the twisting, angry river. I was losing ground as she yelled, "My sister is an idiot."

"We know that already, but why are you so upset right now?" I knew she was glad Mercedes was healed, but their relationship might never be if Mercedes kept pushing Porschia away. Most people thought Porschia was the instigator, but Mercedes had picked fights lately to purposely distance herself from her sister.

"She's going to leave a trail so that Saul can follow us." That statement stopped me in my tracks. This might be the most brazen thing Mercedes has tried yet. Porschia slowed and then stopped ahead of me, hands on her hips.

"Why is she helping him?" I asked. The woman might be Porschia's sister, but sometimes she acted like their mother. And despite what Mercedes said, she didn't do anything purely out of the goodness of her heart. What was in it for her?

"Guilt." Porschia accepted the excuse her sister gave. Me? Not so much. I wasn't sure guilt was an emotion Mercedes was capable of feeling. As far as Saul, I had smelled his scent for the last few days but assumed Porschia was the one with the charitable heart. It should come as no surprise that a sense of relief washed over me. "She's been helping him lately?"

Porschia nodded. "She said he wants to start a new life somewhere else, maybe in Mountainside."

It made sense. He wasn't welcome here, and living like a hermit in the woods didn't seem to be Saul's cup of tea. Porschia was all he wanted, Blackwater be damned, and I couldn't help but wonder if he was using this as an excuse to get into her good graces again. If he got close enough to her along the journey... "You can't blame the guy."

"*You* want to help him?" she asked, one brow quirked.

"No, but if getting him to Mountainside gets him out of my hair, I'm good with that." Not to mention that it would get him away from Porschia. I'd just have to withstand him for this leg of the journey. If puppy stayed behind like a good dog and just followed along after us, it might not be so aggravating.

"She could have asked first," Porschia fumed, pacing back and forth.

"She could have," I agreed with her, smiling. Watching her get all worked up was hot.

"She shouldn't have been sneaking around behind our backs."

"Or behind yours. You're her sister," I said, grinning wider.

"Why are you... You're enjoying this!" She tackled me to the ground before I knew she'd even moved. Porsch was that fast *and* that strong.

I chuckled as she straddled me and then realized she was straddling me. Her body was warm and perfect and... "Kitten, if you wanted me for breakfast, all you had to do was ask." I made my voice gravelly, the way she liked it.

Her long, dark hair cascaded from either side of her face, tickling my neck and driving me up the wall. She pursed her lips, not in a pout, but in aggravation. "Kitten needs a kiss."

"What?" she scoffed, easing away from me.

"Don't play with me. You do. You need a kiss to erase all of this bullshit from your mind. Let me help for a minute. We've got plenty of time before they catch up, thanks to your super speedy self."

She wasted no time, melding her mouth with mine. Warm and wet and soft. She used her fangs to bite my bottom lip, making it bleed ever so slightly. The scent of iron filled my nose as she continued her assault. And I loved when she assaulted me. Pulling her waist closer, I couldn't get enough.

In the distance, the sound of hooves beating against the earth could be heard. She pulled away with a frustrated groan and believe me… I felt the same frustration. Everywhere.

PORSCHIA

MERCEDES GUIDED THE HORSE ALONG THE OPPOSITE BANK. ROMAN CLUNG to her as best he could, but his posture was slack and I wasn't sure he'd be able to hold on the entire way. "Is he okay?" I shouted over the roaring water.

"I'm okay," he slurred. "Just tired."

Mercedes nodded and yelled, "I gave him peppermint and catnip. I saw Maggie before we left and she said they'd take the fever down."

Groaning, I felt bad for the guy. Herbs in general were horribly bitter. Willow bark and I had an unfortunate history, one I wouldn't soon forget. The river crossing, which wouldn't be easy for the mare because the water never dropped too low, was only another mile ahead. "We'll meet you at the crossing," she yelled, kicking the horse gently to spur her on.

Tage's hand found my waist. "Ready?" he asked.

"Want to race?" I said with a grin.

"You're on." And with that, he ran ahead. I laughed and chased after him, easily overtaking him and smacking his butt as I passed by him.

At the crossing, he caught back up and looked at me with awe. "I can't even win when I cheat."

"Cheaters never prosper," I teased, but the sound of splashing and my sister's frantic voice caught my attention.

Mercedes eased the mare into the water. "Hold on, Roman. Tightly."

He sat up straighter behind her and tightened his grip, though he was paler in the sunlight and his dark hair flapped about in the breeze. Tage started toward the river. "He's faltering. He's going to slip into the water."

"Don't!" I whispered forcefully. "You'll spook the horse and then he'll definitely lose his grip."

Muscles tense, we watched as the mare navigated across the rocks on the riverbed, finally making it through the deepest part, soaking the legs of her riders. I watched as the bag of food Father and Ford sent for the journey came loose and sank into the churning water. Mercedes didn't know it yet, but we were now at Mountainside's mercy in more ways than one. With a nicker, Lady trudged forward, pulling them from the dark water where we stood back to give her a wide berth. "Good girl," I whispered. The horse's eyes snapped to me.

"Good girl, Lady," Mercedes cooed, stroking her mane.

Roman slid down and Tage ran to catch him. Looking back at me, Tage held him upright. "We have to hurry."

Roman's head lolled against Tage's chest.

"I'll carry him," I said. Running was easy for me, and Roman didn't weigh too much.

Tage began to protest in that manly way of his. "I've got him."

"I'm stronger."

"You're a girl."

I took Roman from him. "Girls are stronger," I said sweetly. This girl was going to show the guys exactly how strong a woman could be. Sweeping his legs off the ground, I held him against my chest tightly. "Roman?"

He blinked up at me with tired eyes and I asked, "Which way to Mountainside from the crossing?"

"To Mountainside from the crossing?" he mumbled and then answered, "Due east."

"Thank you. Hang on, Roman. I'll find help." Somehow, someone would help us, right? They had to be nice in Mountainside. It was the safest place to start, Roman had said adamantly, repeatedly.

"Porschia?" he asked. His dark eyes were like glass.

I smiled down at him, trying to hide my fear. "Yeah?"

"Compel them to let you in or they won't," he rasped, his lips sticking together like paste had been applied to them.

"I don't know how to use compulsion."

"You look in their eyes and tell them what you need. Don't look away. Be confident."

"You didn't look at me when you compelled me."

He tried to smirk. "That's because I was awesome at it."

And always so humble. "I'll try."

"Do it, or they won't open the gate." With those words, he finally lost his battle with consciousness and I envied him. I had to figure out how to compel someone, and I had thirty miles to learn. I'd also have to compel them to help him, heal him if they could. The humans would fear the illness and might not help willingly.

I took a deep breath, repeating to myself that I could do this. Turning to Tage and Mercedes, I said confidently, "We'll see you soon."

Tage nodded once. Carrying Roman was as easy as I thought. I raced through the forest, past stone and fallen tree trunks, over limbs and burrows. Roman needed help. He would die if he didn't get it. And Mountainside would give it to us—one way or another.

East would have been easier to navigate if we'd left Blackwater early, but I ran fast and hoped I'd find a giant stone wall at some point. In my mind, I pictured a waist-high wall of cobblestones cemented together. What I found when we did almost literally smack into the wall was an enormous structure; two stories tall and made of thick, rectangular slices of stone, mortared together to make it impenetrable and guarded closely. Within seconds, two guards with sharp, flint-tipped spears approached. "What business have you here?"

I stared at the closest one. "My friend needs help. We're asking for refuge until he is well."

One of the men, the tallest of the pair, grabbed his spear and cursed, "Night-walker."

Damn my fangs. Even if they were itty bitty.

I looked at the man. "I will hunt for you and provide meat, but you *will* let us in and you *will* ask someone to provide us shelter and medicine to help him." I looked intently into his eyes, and then I said the exact same words as I held onto the eyes of his shorter friend. Their jaws went slack.

"Let them enter!" the shorter one yelled up to the wall behind us. A gate began to raise just a few hundred feet away, and then we were led beneath the cross-hatched iron and into Mountainside.

The settlement was literally one enormous mountain. I looked up toward its summit and saw the sides sparsely dotted with pine trees and a few maples. The others had been cut down, probably for firewood and building materials. No doubt they were going into the forest for those needs now, and the rock for the wall had to have been quarried from somewhere nearby.

The men led us up a stepped path past several round doorways and paused at one half way up the hillside. Citizens stopped to watch our assent but otherwise didn't bother us. Their whispers were filled with concern, but who could blame them? It must have been a strange sight; a woman carrying a sick man into their stronghold, their safe haven. It was frightening.

The shorter man unlocked the door and waved us inside, where he pointed to a small straw mattress. "I'll fetch Garreth, our healer."

"Thank you. Please hurry."

The two left the door open and I listened as their boots crunched on the small shale pathway that led back down the hill. Easing Roman onto the mattress, his head lolled back. Eyes snapping open, his hands reached out for my neck, angry breaths puffing his cheeks in and out rapidly. "Who are you?"

He tried to bare his fangs, but had forgotten that they were gone.

I knocked his hands away easily and he stared at them as though they'd betrayed him before launching toward me again. Batting him away a second time, he focused on my face.

"Roman, it's Porschia."

His face relaxed as his eyes glazed over. "I watched you grow."

"Because you felt guilt, Roman?"

"No, because your strength was enviable. Because the experiment could have killed you, but you survived. It didn't affect you at all, did it? You're just strong. It's just you."

I rolled my eyes. "I'm not strong. Physically yes, but most of the time, I feel like I'm about to snap and I don't know if I can keep controlling this feeling much longer. You're barely lucid, so I'm glad I can talk to you about it."

"You're going to eat me, aren't you?" he said, crystal clear tear drops flooding his eyes and spilling onto his cheeks. Poor Roman. He looked like a petrified child.

"Not yet. I'm going to let Garreth help you first. I don't like my meat overly warm." I smiled and patted his leg. The others in our little rag-tag party would arrive soon, and I needed to compel the guards to let them in and bring them to me. Then Tage and I would need to make good on our promise to provide meat for them.

Roman laid down quietly and stared at the ceiling until his eyes grew too heavy. That was about the same time that a new set of footsteps, this one more determined than the last two, approached the dwelling. Garreth was a behemoth. I'd expected a woman, but got a giant man who barely fit through the door. "Before you try it, I can't be compelled. I'm here because I choose to be."

"In all honesty, today is the first time I've compelled anyone and I hated it. I wish I didn't need to do it at all, so I appreciate your willingness to help." Compulsion might have worked on the two guards, but I didn't have a full dose of anything vampire and wasn't sure that *three* vamps could have compelled a person this big if size were a factor in such a thing.

He removed a leather pouch from around his neck and held Roman's head up. "He looks like someone who passed by here a time or two—a night-walker."

"He's human. Check his teeth." There were things that didn't add up. I wasn't offering more information just yet. Garreth used his meaty fingers to lift Roman's upper lip, huffing when he saw only a row of straight, square teeth.

"Where are the Infected?" I smelled no rot – nothing – on the way here. Nothing surrounded Mountainside for miles.

"Some roam the forest, but most are huddled in a small city about sixty miles to the east. The wall keeps those who do find their way here, out of our settlement. It's a simple but effective layer of protection."

So why won't they hunt?

"I know what you're thinking, and there are greater dangers in these parts than rotters." He held his leather pouch of water to Roman's lips and let his mouth fill with a little bit of water. Roman gasped like a fish, sputtering water over his chest, clothing, and all over Garreth. The giant ignored him and dug his meaty fist into yet another leather satchel, pulling out two metal containers. He twisted the lid off one and then the other. Roman's body went taut as he began convulsing, his face turning scarlet. From a belt on his waist, Garreth grabbed a wooden spoon and then Roman's jaw. He wedged the spoon between Roman's upper and lower teeth, holding tight to him. I reached out to calm Roman, but his eyes were unfocused. "What can I do to help?"

"He's having a seizure. We wait for it to pass," the giant gritted out, holding Roman's head as still as he could. When the spell subsided, Garreth and I sank back onto bent legs. My chest loosened again and I made mental notes of what the healer did to my friend, in case I needed to know how to do it again.

Once Roman's muscles finally relaxed, Garreth applied greasy, white salve from one container onto the skin of Roman's inner cheek. The other substance, thicker and dark like tar, Garreth rubbed on Roman's forehead, chest, and the soles of his feet. "Why do you care about him?" he asked. "Since when does a night-walker care about a human? Is there a familial tie?"

"We aren't related. It's because part of me is still human, whether any of you believe it or not." And part of me was pure animal, waiting to be unleashed. I swallowed. "My friends will be here soon. They're a mix of night-walkers and humans."

"Traveling together? That's the first I've heard of such cooperation between the two. I'll yell to the guards to let them in, if you'd like."

"Why are you helping me? You obviously don't trust me."

"Not completely, no," he said honestly. "But part of me can see the humanity in you and wants to believe in it."

I swallowed as he stood up in the small space. "Thank you."

"Don't give me a reason to lose faith in you, night-walker."

Could I do that? Could I remain in control of myself long enough not to disappoint someone else? "I won't."

"I'll be back in a minute. Keep the spoon handy just in case."

FOUR

ROMAN

My body was ice, frigid and stiff. Had I been Infected like Pierce? Where was my brother? I couldn't lift my eyelids and my back and legs were being poked by something hard; spikes or sticks. Straw, maybe? It made the pain worse. This had to be it, what Pierce felt like.

I was going to rot along with him.

Voices swirled around me. Some familiar, some not. Identifying the speakers I did recognize was impossible because of the fog. Then, they disappeared into the black void with me. We were gone.

Floating away…

PORSCHIA

Garreth yelled down to the guards, who began to argue with him. I sighed and left Roman to walk outside and see if I could help. Garreth muttered a curse and told me to go work my mojo on them as he stepped back inside to attend to Roman. At the gate, I was able to convince the guards to allow Tage and Mercedes to enter Mountainside, though I had to repeat myself a few times. Tage tried to compel them too, but the men looked away and refused eye contact with him. They obviously knew how to avoid it; so why did it work differently with a woman?

We would be allowed entrance, but our horse would be held as collateral and it would be killed and eaten if we didn't provide meat for the people of the hill. Mercedes angrily handed Lady's reins to the taller guard and he strode away with her, skirting along the inside of the giant wall.

Tage grabbed my hand as I began to follow my sister beneath the gate. "We have a problem," he ground out from between clenched teeth.

"What's that?"

"Me," Saul answered, stepping out from behind a nearby tree. I hadn't even smelled him.

"How'd you get here so fast?" I asked.

"Mercedes let him ride with her," Tage said sweetly. How did he even catch up to us?

Saul stepped toward Tage in anger and I put myself between them because I could tell Tage was struggling to control himself. All the scents and sounds, the tension. It was getting to him. "One day my sister will hate you for what you did, so enjoy her charity while it lasts, Saul."

"She'll never hate me more than she hates herself. And one day Porschia, you'll forgive me." His eyes were hard, yet pleading, stormy, and angry.

"You underestimate the level of hatred I feel toward you, and that is a very dangerous thing. For *you*." Forget fangs, I wanted to stab him in the throat with a twig; a small twig that should never hurt a human being. Or maybe I would fight fire with fire. Set him ablaze and let him try to fight his way free of the flames. Did Mother try to free herself from her confines?

His blue-gray eyes swirled with emotion. His jaw ticked. My fingers twitched. Tage's arm on mine pulled me toward him. I looked toward the guard. "Is there another dwelling, a separate one that he can stay in, please?"

The guard looked down. "You all stay together if you want to shelter here."

Tage breathed into my hair. "We could leave him outside the wall."

"No!" Mercedes interjected, moving past me and Tage to stand with Saul. I'd honestly forgotten she was even there. "He stays with us."

With a growl, I turned to the guard and nodded, rushing off to check on Roman and leaving my sister with her sympathy and the monster who garnered it. Saul had probably turned his sights on her. He was probably preying on her guilt and kindness. If that was the case, he would find that she had the former in spades, the latter only sporadically. Maybe it was best to keep them close. I didn't fully trust either of them.

GARRETH HELD A DAMPENED CLOTH TO ROMAN'S HEAD. HE DIDN'T BOTHER acknowledging us when we came back into the home. "How is he?" I asked.

"Fever is drawing out."

That was good. "Do you know what's wrong with him?"

Garreth stood, his scalp almost touching the ceiling. "I'm not entirely sure, but it seems flu-like. We haven't had it here in years, but it's very much a human condition. It's caused by a virus, and he has an extreme case of it from the looks of him. But it's not usually deadly for young people. How long has he been sick?"

"Not long," Tage said from beside me.

Pursing his lips, Garreth looked over Roman again. "Early on, the flu makes you feel like you're dying. Body aches, chills, fever. His fever is causing the seizures because it spiked too high, but he's fighting hard and it's been a long time since I've heard of anyone passing from it. We'll watch it closely and in a few days, he should be better."

"Thank you," I said as my sister and Saul stepped into the room. Garreth looked them over. "They're human. Both of them," I answered his unanswered question.

Garreth shook his head with a slight smile while he stared at each one of us in turn.

"I told you."

"I guess seeing is believing," he mused. "You're an odd bunch. Nightwalkers and humans..." He paused, handing the water bag to me. "See that he drinks every half hour. He needs to stay hydrated. If something changes, send a human for me. It'd be best if you and he stayed inside this room," he said, motioning toward Tage. "I'll be back at dark and can stay with him if you'd like. The illness tends to worsen at night, and I know that the two of you will be hunting."

Motioning between me and Tage, I assured him, "We won't bother anyone, and we'd appreciate it if you'd help him tonight." We needed to find food for the people. Although I hadn't seen many of them, the guards, who were likely the strongest among the people other than Garreth, seemed gaunt and thin. There was a hollowness even in the giant's cheeks.

A smile split his face. "You let me focus on your friend. You focus on finding food. I look forward to the meat. Good luck tonight."

"Thank you," Tage and I said as he ducked out the doorway.

Mercedes looked around the place. There was a small wooden table with two chairs, Roman's bed, and a wooden chest at his feet. A few utensils hung on the wall next to an assortment of charred pans. "I can see if someone will let us have some food for today," she offered.

"You noticed the food was gone?"

"I did. Tage told me it sank in the river," she answered, looking down.

"I'll look for firewood. There's a pit outside." Saul shoved his hands in his pockets.

Tage smiled. "I'll go with you, Saul. We can look for animal trails while we're collecting wood."

I almost laughed out loud at Saul's expression; half surprised and half angry. Squeezing Tage's hand wasn't enough for him. He caught me by the waist and planted a gentle kiss on my lips. "Be back soon."

Saul glared at the two of us from beside the door before disappearing outside. Mercedes huffed, following him.

"Stay with Roman. Saul and I will get firewood from the forest," Tage added, kissing my temple.

"Be careful."

"Wild horses couldn't keep me away from this hill hole, kitten."

FIVE

TAGE

MERCEDES WAS AT ANOTHER DOOR THIRTY FEET AWAY, ASKING FOR anything our new neighbors could spare. There wouldn't be much, if anything. I hated to break that to her, but she was from Blackwater, where resources were richer and neighbors dutifully helped one another. She would understand soon enough. Saul was striding down the pathway that was carved up the mountainside. I jogged and caught up with him quickly. "Leaving without your chaperone? Not the smartest idea."

"I don't need a babysitter," he replied gruffly.

Laughing, I pointed toward the forest. "*Something* has these people scared enough to build a twenty-foot tall wall around their homes. I wouldn't take that lightly. You were Infected once. We wouldn't want that to happen again."

"We both know you wouldn't care if I was out of the picture for good."

I smiled. I would love it if he were gone – from Infection, a fall off a cliff, a tumble down the mountain...

"You rub me the wrong way, Saul. What can I say?"

"You think you don't do the same to me? I hate seeing her with you. You were always getting in the way, even from the beginning. The blood bond, holding her hand, telling her she could get through the transition, telling her that this entire thing was a blessing and not a curse. You've been waiting for this since you saw her!"

"I have. And you know what? You're not angry because I've wanted her all along. You're angry because you threw it all away. You had her and in one moment, lost everything."

He strode down the mountain in brooding silence. Poor guy. Had he even seen it before now? Did he know how much he hurt her?

"Scent is one of the most intense senses for a human being, but for a night-walker it's even more overwhelming. Do you know what she smells when she looks at you?" Saul stopped just inside the gate, waiting for the humans to lift it for us. Once outside, as we stepped into the forest he turned to me.

"What do you mean what she *smells* when she looks at me?"

Let me inform you, asshole. "A vampire can detect the slightest of scents even a mile away if we choose to focus intently enough."

"So?"

"So, the night you decided to singlehandedly burn the city down, the first thing she smelled was the burning bodies."

Saul inhaled sharply.

"Even more specifically, she knew her mother's scent and could smell when it...when *she* began to burn. She smelled the flesh of her mother being overtaken by smoke and flame."

I watched as the realization hit him in the gut. "She smelled her burn?" His voice was quiet and pensive.

"Yes."

He exhaled sharply. "No wonder she hates me."

"And yet *you* think you did nothing wrong," I said, looking out into the forest. "Let's go east."

"I didn't realize," he stammered. "I was trying to do the right thing, especially after Pierce had his way with most of them," he said quietly.

"You thought wrong—about her mother, at least. The others, Porschia could have forgiven you for." It was cold, but true. He needed to stop sniffing around Mercedes to get to Porschia. He needed to stop looking at her like he could still have a chance if only he bided his time. Saul needed to man up and accept what he did like a man—a man with no chance in hell of getting Porschia Grant to love him again.

PORSCHIA

I KNELT NEXT TO ROMAN. THE CLOTH ON HIS HEAD WAS DAMP AND WARM, having absorbed the warmth from his body, but it wasn't doing enough because the skin of his forehead was still hot to the touch. I remembered a time that Ford had a fever when he was small that was worse than all the other occasional ones he picked up here and there. He and Mercedes were always the social butterflies of our family, whereas I stayed home, had few friends other than Meg, and even then, she did most of the work in keeping our friendship going. I didn't want to hear the whispers about Mother and was too embarrassed to leave the house and yard except for when it was required.

But I left home for help when Ford got sick and Mother decided to lock herself in her bedroom. Father told me to ask Mrs. Bracker, who lived three streets over, if she had anything that would help him. And though I didn't know her well then, he also sent me to Mrs. Maggie Dillinger's. Both of the women arrived at our home minutes later and rushed to Ford's side. At their instruction, Father and I brought buckets of water in and Father laid my brother in the cool water. It was the only thing that saved him.

There must be a water source somewhere...

Roman groaned, his eyes blinking open. "Are you here to kill me?"

I shook my head, making sure he could see my face. "No."

"You will," he said. His voice was weak but his tone was adamant.

"I won't. I'm trying to help you."

"I wouldn't blame you. I did a lot of things that were wrong, even to your Mother. I'm no better than Saul, if you think about it."

I didn't want to think about it and I didn't know why. Maybe because right now I didn't want to think about Saul or Mother. "I'll be back. You need to cool down. You're way too hot, Roman."

"That's what all the ladies tell me."

"Still an arrogant ass, though."

"They say that, too." He closed his eyes. "I'll stay here and guard the place."

"Brilliant idea." I looked him over. Garreth said people didn't die from the flu very often; however, if we couldn't get his fever to break, Roman might be one of the rare few who succumbed to the ravages of this virus. If he died from the flu, it would be a huge blow to his ego. Someone had to do something and I was the only one around. I eased the door closed behind me and started down the pathway, meeting a woman who held the hand of her small, toddling son. "Hello, could you point me in the direction of your water source?"

She pulled the child close to her legs, where his chubby hands fisted the fabric of her overalls. "What does a night-walker need water for?" the woman asked crossly.

Looking into her eyes, I told her simply, "I need water."

She looked down the hill. "There is a well at the base of the mountain. Follow this path." She pointed to one path that led away from the others, the dusty trail wide and well worn. "There's also a creek in the forest to the south."

"Thank you," I said, passing her by. She blinked and woke up from whatever daze I'd put her in and hurried the child along, away from me.

"She doesn't look dangerous, Momma," the boy said, looking over his shoulder at me.

"All night-walkers are dangerous to humans, most especially the females. Never forget that," she whispered harshly.

Most especially the females?

Two women at the well scattered when I approached. Backing away but keeping me in their sights, one went left and the other right. They couldn't see my fangs. They were tiny. So how did they know? Constructed of a cobblestone base with a small wooden roof covered in moss, the well smelled fresh and clean. I had nothing to carry the water in, though. Looking around, I saw an old metal bucket with a rusted crack running down one side. It would have to do.

Easing the rope and pail down into the dark hole, I could see the water's surface far below; dark as ebony and placid until the pail's bottom disturbed it. A crow cawed close overhead, making me jump and lose my grip on the rope. I caught it before the end went into the well, but only barely.

The rope's coarse fibers sliced into my fingers, burning them. I gasped. "Are you okay?" A young woman rushed over. Her hair was a deep brown and was as beautiful as her skin and toffee-colored eyes. "Yes, thank you."

"Night-walker," she whispered, stopping quickly and then stepping backward. Her eyes flicked between my face and the tiny droplets of blood pooling in the swirls of my fingertips.

"How do you know?" I asked.

"How do I know what?"

"That I'm a night-walker?"

"Your skin. And when you spoke, I could see the tips of your fangs."

"My skin?" I looked at my forearms. They weren't different. Were they?

"They're so pale they nearly glow," she supplied. "Why do you need water?"

"For a friend—a human friend."

"I didn't know night-walkers befriended humans." She smiled slightly, looking at the broken bucket I was ready to fill.

"Perhaps you should leave Mountainside more often," I teased.

"We aren't allowed," she whispered, her eyes darting up and down the enormous hill above. "Here. Use mine."

She proffered her wooden bucket but I shook my head. "I can't accept it. You need it."

"Then borrow it. Leave it outside your door and I'll fetch it later. Help your human friend."

I nodded. "Thank you."

"You're welcome..." she paused, fishing for my name.

"Porschia. Porschia Grant."

She smiled. "I'm Amelia Lane."

"Nice to meet you, Amelia. I'll leave your bucket outside my door. Thank you again."

Amelia nodded and retraced her steps up the path and away from me, less frightened than before, but still watchful. I poured the pail of water into her bucket and sped up the hill. Since people already knew there was a new night-walker in town there was no further reason to hide it, and Roman needed to cool off.

SIX

TAGE

HUNTING AT NIGHT WHEN MOST ANIMALS WERE ALSO PROWLING WAS EASIER than finding them in the daylight hours, but to feed people who haven't been fed in months, it would help if we could find something to bring back with us in addition to firewood. Something was 'off' here. I couldn't put my finger on it, but the people were skittish. Something or someone made them that way.

After skirting yet another side of one of the seemingly infinite mountains in the region, I finally picked up a scent. Saul jogged to keep up. "What is it?" he asked between labored breaths.

"I smell puppies."

"Ahh," he groaned. "You aren't gonna kill puppies, are you?"

"Says the man who took two dozen human lives." His stare hardened and he stood up straighter. What the hell did he think he was going to do? Fight me? I'd eat him. Literally. Rolling my eyes, I shook my head. "Not puppy dogs, dumbass. Coyotes."

He nodded, sweat beading on his brow. "How far?"

"Having trouble keeping up?"

"Yes," he panted, hands on his knees.

I grinned. "Good."

And then, like the asshole I was, I ran as fast as I could to the den I scented in a rocky outcropping across the hillside. I drained all eight of the 'puppies' before Saul reached me. Some were feistier than others, yipping and clawing and snapping, but nothing I couldn't handle. When he finally caught up, Saul's eyes were wide. "What?" I asked innocently. "I told you they were coyotes."

"You killed them all!"

"Yeah."

"You killed them so fast."

I stood up from where I crouched over the last mutt's body and wiped the blood from my chin. Clapping him on the shoulder, I grinned, feeling the slimy coating of blood over my teeth. "Remember that. Mess with Porschia and I'll kill you before you even know I'm near."

Gathering all but two of the mutts by their tails, I ticked my head back toward Mountainside. "Let's get back."

"You feel it, too?" Saul asked quietly. "Something's weird about that place."

"Yeah. It is." I just couldn't figure out what *it* was.

SAUL

GRABBING THE PAIR OF COYOTES BY THEIR TAILS, I HEFTED THEM UP, ONE IN each hand. They were big and heavy, easily sixty pounds each. From my house and during my nights in the rotation, I'd heard their howls when they hunted, but never came this close to one. The musk of their hide hit my nose. How the pack didn't tear Tage apart was beyond me. *Too bad.*

He could threaten all he wanted; he didn't scare me. Porschia wouldn't let him kill me. No matter how much she tried to pretend I didn't exist or that she hated me, part of her never would. Part of her would remember me forever. You couldn't fake those kind of feelings, and what she and I shared was something special, even if only for a short time. Even if I ruined it all.

I didn't realize how I'd hurt her. The scent. Tage said she was able to smell her mother, and then smell her mother burning to death. When I lit the fire I thought I was doing right, but looking back, maybe I wasn't.

Her mother – who hated her own daughter and murdered several of our neighbors, including Porschia's best friend – could never hurt her again, and because of that I still couldn't rationalize feeling too much guilt over what I did. The others in the building? So many of those in the "freak show" were so far gone mentally that they couldn't recover despite the cure. Their brains were deteriorated too badly. Besides that, how could she hate me and still look Roman in the face? He performed experiments on her and her mother, all for his brother Pierce. Weren't his actions as damning as mine?

I didn't bother trying to keep up with Tage, but this time, I didn't have to worry about it. He hung back with me, casually striding like he was taking a pleasure stroll through the woods. Meanwhile, I had to keep adjusting my grip. Coyotes were heavy bastards. They got heavier with each step and harder to keep ahold of as my hands began to sweat.

Tage carried six of them and had yet to break a sweat.

It was times like these that I wished I were a night-walker.

THE GUARDS AT MOUNTAINSIDE WERE EAGER TO OPEN THE GATES AFTER Tage held up the canines and announced that dinner was served. One yelled for someone to come with a wheelbarrow, and fast. Wheelbarrow guy skirted the wall and happily accepted the animals, rushing away with them with a smile on his face. How long had it been since they had meat? Did they never go outside the wall?

Back at the temporary dwelling, Porschia was crouched beside Roman. His sleeves and pant legs were rolled up and with a swath of damp fabric, she rubbed his skin.

Tage growled, his eyes fixated on the sight of Porschia kneeling beside Roman. I didn't blame the guy.

"Shut up, Tage. His fever is way too high; I'm only trying to bring it down. It's what we used to do for Ford."

"Well I don't like it," Tage snapped. "You're touching him."

"You don't have to like it, but you *do* have to deal with it. I'm not going to let him die!"

What did she even care? Why would it matter if Roman died? He was human. Humans got sick, and some died from the illnesses that afflicted them. It was natural. Mostly. I mean, young people didn't often die, but he was a good deal older than he looked. Maybe time was finally catching up with him. Maybe after a night-walker turned back into a human, they aged quickly, catching back up to the place they would have been if they hadn't turned in the first place.

Two knocks at the door announced Garreth's arrival. "How's he doing?" he asked, ducking inside. "Is his fever rising again?" He knelt beside Porschia.

"He's cooling off now," she said softly. "Somewhat."

Garreth looked over Roman's body, his hand hovering a few inches above Roman's forehead. "The cool water helps the body, although in this overheated state it feels awful. If he were conscious he'd think you were killing him, but it's necessary. To be strengthened, we must all endure pain."

Indeed.

Garreth waited with us as Roman's temperature continued to normalize. Mercedes slipped back inside with a few small containers. She looked to me. "It was all they could spare."

"It'll be enough."

Garreth spoke up. "You'll get a ration of the meat you provided as well. Don't let them exclude you, because given the chance, they will."

And exactly who were we going to speak with about sharing the spoils of the hunt?

Tage stood up. "What's going on here? Why are there no vampires? I thought Roman said you had an agreement with some similar to Blackwater's treaty."

"There was never any treaty; only a handshake and a nod, but that wasn't enough, it seems."

"What do you mean?" I asked.

"There were two that lived here among us humans. One, a male, disappeared. The female stopped hunting, locked herself inside her dwelling, and refused to come out. No one knew what to think of her behavior, but then she disappeared altogether. When someone went to check on her, she was gone. Vanished."

"Is that why people are so distrusting of the female night-walkers?" Porschia asked.

Garreth turned to her, eyes narrowed. "Why would you say that?"

"At the well, some humans were visibly terrified by my presence. A woman even warned her child about how dangerous we were, especially the females."

Garreth dropped his large head onto his chest. "The vampire who lived here came back one night with some of her new friends."

"Friends?" Tage asked.

"All female. She and two others began tearing a bloody path around the mountain. They compelled their way inside. With beautiful faces and dresses to match, at first people invited them into their homes. That was until they began feeding and draining their children right in front of them. Apparently they preferred the blood of the young. In the end, no one was safe. They drained one third of our population in only a few hours."

"Frenzy?" Tage asked Porschia, who shrugged in response.

"How'd you stop them?" I asked.

"We couldn't. They fed as they pleased, took what they wanted, and then compelled seven more to leave with them. So you can see why we'd be frightened that you are here." He turned to Porschia. "Especially *you*."

Her lips parted. "I do understand." She clutched her chest and sat back on her legs. "I can't even imagine."

"It left a scar on the survivors. They will never forget watching the children die, the flames from our torches flickering wildly as the light in their wide, innocent eyes went out," Garreth said quietly as his eyes became unfocused.

"We need to help you set up a defense," Roman mumbled, his lips so dry they stuck together as he formed the words.

Porschia nodded to Tage, who asked Garreth, "Do you know the belladonna plant? It can help slow them down, but you need weaponry as well."

Garreth shook his head. "I don't think anything can save us if that happens again."

"Garreth, we came here for a reason," Porschia offered.

"What's that?"

"There's a cure for both the Infection and vampirism."

The behemoth's eyes widened. "Are you serious?"

Roman groaned. "She's serious."

Garreth's hands shook as he clasped his chest and I narrowed my eyes when the realization dawned on me. "Someone you know is cursed."

The giant nodded. "Someone very special to me. Please tell me everything you know."

So we did. We told him that the cure resided within each curse, and for the first time, I believed in inflicting that cure on someone without their permission. The female night-walkers who tore through this town without mercy deserved to have their power taken away. They deserved to feel what it was like to be utterly defenseless before we killed them. And if I figured out who they were, that was exactly what would happen. We just needed an Infected or three to provide some blood.

SEVEN

PORSCHIA

Garreth was as amazed as we were that there was a cure for both plagues upon humanity, but he soon realized the same thing we did: there would be some who wouldn't *want* to be made human again. Some people lost their humanity over time and with some humans, I questioned whether they had it to begin with.

I walked him outside and he turned to me. "You're only passing through, then?"

Nodding to him, I turned toward the door of the dwelling. "Some of them would like to stay."

"Temporarily?" Garreth asked, crossing his arms over his chest.

"Maybe longer," I replied with a smile.

"I'll speak with the council on their behalf, though they'll want to hear directly from those who wish to stay permanently. Where are you going next?"

"Roman said there was another settlement to the northeast."

Garreth nodded. "There is The Glen. The Manor is close to it." He whispered to me: "Even *you* should be careful on the next leg of your journey. I think that the women who were with the one who used to live among us, who attacked us, came from The Manor."

Roman had said the same thing. He said not to approach The Manor without him, but what good could he do? If the women at The Manor were so dangerous, we couldn't just sit back and do nothing. They would attack again. It was only a matter of time. They would get hungry. They enjoyed brutalizing Mountainside, tearing apart the families. They enjoyed pain. And they would soon know it themselves.

"I'll be careful. Thank you for everything, Garreth."

"You'll choose to be human again after you spread the word?" he asked.

I swallowed. Roman had also warned me not to tell anyone what I was. I smiled slightly. "Of course. It's just safer this way for now."

Garreth's sharp eyes fastened on my face and I felt my cheeks heat under his scrutiny. "I suppose it would be."

I thumbed toward the dwelling. "Tage and I will hunt again tonight. We'll bring larger animals back for Mountainside, and if the council would like, we can hunt again upon our return. Blackwater is your friend and we represent our Colony well."

"Thank you. I'll pass the word along. And good luck on your hunt. We haven't seen large game in quite some time."

I smiled. "You're on the council, aren't you?"

This time Garreth grinned. "I am."

THE DWELLING WAS WONDERFUL FOR ROMAN TO REST INSIDE, BUT FOR THE rest of us, the quarters were cramped. Saul and Mercedes were too much for me to deal with. His eyes were always pleading, and Mercedes' permanent scowl was annoying. Each of them had issues with and beyond me to work through. I was done.

After being cured of the Infection, Mercedes had been all sisterly for a time before becoming angry with me again. All I did was bite and save her from rotting into a thousand putrid pieces of herself. Her problem, I thought, was that she was angry because I wouldn't forgive Saul. He was no doubt telling her how awful I was to him, but they could both go straight to hell.

I watched as the sun set in shades of fire and ash. Mercedes stepped outside holding a frying pan, the bottom covered in slices of potatoes and carrots with beans scattered between the circles of vegetables. It wouldn't be enough for us three, though Roman likely wouldn't eat. Two would still feel hunger soon after eating it. "Garreth is going to bring your portions of meat, I think."

She nodded. "That would be good."

Silence wrapped around us as the spring wind whipped strands of our light and dark hair back and forth, interweaving them with tendrils of gray smoke. The burning wood was too much. I walked away down the path, leaving Mercedes behind, but I heard her call for Tage. After he stepped outside with her, she told him, "She's leaving."

"It's the fire," he said softly. He knew. I didn't know how, but he knew I couldn't stomach it. My stomach churned violently and when I came to the end of the lane, my head tingled and my vision was overtaken by a swarm of black dots. "Hands on your knees. It's behind you," Tage said, rubbing my low back. "Let it pass."

I tried to focus on the blades of grass, the smooth pebbles along the path and the rough ones just beyond it. He stayed with me, soothing and calming me until it was over.

"Let's get out of here," he said, lacing his fingers through mine.

Music to my ears.

WE WENT DEEP INTO THE UNFAMILIAR FOREST BEFORE THE SICKENING feeling subsided and before we found any wildlife worth taking down. Large game would feed Mountainside for days, so we searched for it far and wide. Tage was careful to strike fast and take down the buck before it used his antlers on us as spears.

"We can leave him here and come back," Tage said, wiping the blood from his chin, panting from exertion. My God, that sight would never get old. He was strong, virile, and bloody, and he smelled so good.

"I wish I had a camera for you," he said, snapping me out of my daze.

"What they used to take pictures with?"

"Yeah," he grinned. "If you took a picture of me, you might stop staring and drooling..."

I rolled my eyes.

"We need more meat. Where *is* everything?"

"Overhunting?" he asked.

"Not by Mountainside."

The smell of decay hit me as soon as his scream did. A shrill but masculine scream came from across a small creek. The Infected stumbled down the hill, righting himself as he splashed through the water. Tage stood up and moved in front of me.

"Can he be saved?" I asked, trying to move around him. Tage blocked me.

"Something's not right with him." The Infected man's shoulders twitched uncontrollably.

"Duh, he's Infected." And he smelled like rancid meat and sweat.

Tage shook his head. "He's also very pissed off. Stay behind me."

"I'm stronger—"

"I just fed, and you should take some of the buck's blood right now."

He was right. I hated when he was right. "Fine."

I sank to my knees and then tried to puncture the hide of the buck. The fur and pelt were too thick. Straining and pushing him into my mouth didn't help. "You okay, kitten?" Tage laughed.

"Asshole," I said around the mouth full of fur and hide.

"Get back!" he yelled suddenly. The rotter charged forward, his chest heaving like an angry bull. As he tackled Tage, he hit the earth so hard, I was sure the ground shook beneath my knees.

The Infected swung wildly at Tage, who managed to roll and tuck his head to the right to avoid his fists. I'd never seen an Infected so strong, but his burst of energy was short-lived. He began to pant and collapsed onto his side, but used what strength he had left to crawl toward me, or so I thought. He grabbed hold of the deer's leg and pulled it away from me.

Where is the other game? I surged from my mind toward him. He stopped and his pale brown irises focused on me.

How can you hear me, night-walker?

Answer the question.

Realization relaxed the features of his face. *He warned us about you.*

Who warned you about me? I watched as he tugged the deer closer. Tage growled and tore the leg from the carcass with a quick snapping and ripping noise. Blood sprayed across the man's face.

"There's your food!" Tage yelled at the rotter. He turned to me. "Now, tell me what you're talking about."

"He said someone warned him about me."

Tage bared his fangs. "And who was that someone?"

The rotter shrugged and began tearing into the meat of the leg. My mouth began to salivate. I couldn't take my eyes off of his mouth as it chewed the meat.

"Oh, kitten. Did I forget your snack, too?" he tore the other leg off and handed it to me gently.

As I tore meat from the bone and began to eat with the rotter, he stared at me. *It's true. You're both.*

Unfortunately, I answered. *So where are all the animals? Are there more Infected somewhere?*

Heal me and I'll tell you what I know.

I looked to Tage, who must've sensed how the conversation had turned. "Do it," he said. Gritting my teeth, I felt like screaming at him. Why didn't *he* do it? He should be able to live a normal life! There was a cure now. Why didn't he want it?

"Fine." Before the rotter knew what hit him, I bit his neck. He screamed, high-pitched into my ear, and tried to shove me away from him as every instinct that was still human kicked in. Thankfully those instincts wouldn't fuel his energy stores. He weakened, and as I eased my fangs out of his neck, he sank to the ground, utterly spent. As the venom entered his body and began obliterating the virus within, he stared at the night sky above us. It twinkled happily with stars that had no right to such a carefree feeling, not when they shone down on such terrible things.

I gave him as much time as I could, but I wanted to know who was spreading the word about me. Roman warned about the repercussions of the knowledge of my being an Infected / night-walker hybrid falling into the wrong hands, and though I couldn't see how the news would affect anyone else but me, people everywhere had lost their minds. Nothing made sense, so maybe it was completely logical for others to be curious or frightened. I frightened myself most of the time.

Who told you? I urged again.

I don't know his name, but there was a man with dark hair who walked through the forest days ago. He told me about the cure and about you, describing you perfectly. But when I saw your food, instinct took over. Sorry about your friend.

He's fine. Tage's jaw ticked impatiently as he crossed his arms over his chest. He hated not being able to hear what was being said. *How old was the man you spoke with?*

He shrugged. *I didn't get a good look at him. It was dark. He was human, though, and faster than I could keep up with. I was on his heels for a time, but couldn't catch him.*

He was probably going to try to eat him. "He didn't see who it was, only that he was male and a fast runner," I relayed to Tage, and then stood up and brushed my dress off. Damn it. Blood droplets stained the light blue fabric.

"Definitely from Blackwater or the city around it."

"Are there more of you somewhere?" I asked the young man.

Scattered here and there. Nothing organized for miles.

"Seek shelter. You're about to feel like you've fallen from a cliff."

He nodded, but didn't move. Perhaps he was already feeling that way.

"Where are all the animals?"

There aren't many left, he answered.

Overhunting?

The Manor took a lot of them, and the others fled.

No wonder he was so hungry.

EIGHT

SAUL

ROMAN• PASSED OUT BEFORE DINNER AND WHILE WE SAVED HIM SOME, Mercedes and I were starving. She was pensive, staring at the rock walls after we scarfed the meager vegetables down. "What is it?"

She stared at her hands, alternately picking at the cuticles around her thumbnails. "I'm worried."

"About Roman?" He seemed fine now that his fever had broken. He would recover.

She shook her head slightly. "I'm worried about Porschia."

"She'll be okay." She was strong now.

"Something feels wrong. I can't shake it. I have a bad feeling in the pit of my stomach, and everything in me says to go after her."

"Stay with Roman," I said, standing up and grabbing my coat. As I shrugged it on, she stood too.

"I should go. I'm her sister."

I shook my head. "Stay with him. He needs you. I don't know what to do for him." What I didn't say was that I wouldn't help him even if he needed it and I *did* know what to do. If Mercedes had a gut feeling about Porschia, I trusted it. Siblings were close, and the Grant girls had been thicker than thieves before Mercedes fell.

"I'll be back soon." I closed the door behind me and stepped into the cool night. It wasn't winter anymore, but the nights were still cold, especially when the sky was clear. The path from our dwelling led me down the mountain to the gate, and the man and woman guarding it let me pass without so much as a question. Would they let me back inside just as easily? Highly unlikely, unless Porschia could use her mind tricks on them.

Which way? From behind me, the woman spoke. "They went toward your right."

"Thank you."

I heard her grumble to the man beside her. "Thank me by bringing meat." While I didn't have my crossbow, I did have a large hunting knife, and while hand-to-hand combat with an Infected wasn't high on my list of fun things to do, I was glad to have the weapon with me.

Turning right, I walked into the darkness for several minutes, blindly searching the forest for any signs of Porschia or Tage. However, it wasn't *me* who found *them*. Without warning I felt two sharp fangs at my neck; warm breath fanning my skin, pebbling it.

"Tell me I can, kitten," Tage pleaded.

"Stop it, Tage. Help me with the deer."

Tage stepped away from my throat. Porschia held one of the animal's front legs and Tage grabbed the other. "Where are the hind legs?" I asked. Porschia glanced back into the darkness. "What is it?" I asked curiously.

She dropped the buck and began to pace. "We need to leave tonight. We need darkness and we can be at The Glen by daybreak."

"What about more meat?"

Tage chuckled. "Well, this is pretty much all we could find."

"This is it?"

"You know how far we walked to find the coyotes? Well quadruple that."

I did the math; my calves still burning from it.

Tage turned to Porschia. "Maybe you're right about traveling at night. Let's take the kill to the guards and then we can split."

Lightly grabbing Porschia's upper arm, I bent in to whisper to her. "Mercedes is worried about you. She has a bad feeling. Maybe you should wait."

Tage growled at me for touching her but I stood my ground. Porschia looked from my hand to my eyes. "Mercedes doesn't need to worry about me. Tell her to take care of Roman."

"His fever broke and he's resting. We saved him a few vegetables for when he wakes." I took a deep breath and let my hand fall away. "Have you fed?"

"I just ate part of the deer, so yes," she answered shortly.

Shaking my head, I asked her again but more directly. "Do you need to feed from me?" Looking to Tage, I added, "Both of you?"

Tage smiled. "How nice of you to offer." He stalked forward slowly.

Porschia placed herself slightly in front of me. "Numb him first."

Tage's smile fell away. "You don't trust me, kitten? I'm hurt." He stared at me. "Really, I am."

Tage did numb my neck before he drank, but wasn't easy about any of it. When Porschia told him it was enough, he jerked his fangs out and wiped the corners of his mouth where my blood was pooled. I clasped the wound tightly, and though it was already healing from the second swipe of his tongue, it felt like the blood might burst free at any moment.

He looked to Porschia and though I knew it killed him to do it, he said, "I'll take the deer. Feed yourself and I'll be right back." He probably wanted her to snap and drain me while he wasn't there to stop her, not that he would have if he were standing beside her. He'd probably cheer her on.

She nodded and watched as he lifted the carcass and sped away.

When she finally looked at me, she stared at the wound he'd made. "I'm sorry we have to feed from you."

"I'm not."

"You've always offered yourself. Why?"

"Because I care about you."

"Cared," she corrected. But she was wrong.

"No, Porschia. I still care for you. That never changed. It never will."

Her lips parted and she stepped forward slowly, lacing her fingers behind my neck and drawing me toward her. Before our lips could brush, she forced my head to the left and licked a warm path up the column of my throat. She drank slowly, fisting my shirt as I held her waist tightly to me. If she wasn't a night-walker, I'd have snapped her in two.

Tage's reappearance made her stop. I don't know if it occurred to her before that to stop, but I wouldn't have stopped her. If she needed it, it was hers. *I* was hers.

She sealed the wound and stepped backward quickly. "Thank you for feeding us."

My head tingled, but I nodded and steadied myself on the trunk of an old oak. "Are you okay? Did I take too much?" she asked, rushing to me as I teetered. I smiled. Porschia was still mine, to a point.

"I'm fine. Honestly. Go. I'll tell the others. Just come back as soon as you can and don't go near The Manor Roman keeps talking about."

She looked to Tage, who ticked his head in the opposite direction. "You have some blood on your lip, kitten. Let me get that for you," he said, smiling in my direction before kissing her long and deep. I wanted to be a night-walker in that moment. I wanted to launch myself at his throat and tear him apart, one chunk at a time.

NINE

TAGE

Perhaps there was a reason that I was called Tage. Like the fact that Tage rhymed with RAGE, because that was what coursed through every inch of my body—white, hot, tear-his-face-off rage.

"Can I feed you?" What an asshole. Surely Porschia knew his game by now. Right?

His blood on her lips. I had to remove it. Immediately. I wanted to drain him until his eyelashes fluttered and then stilled; until his heart sped in fear and stopped altogether. I wanted to end Saul Daniels. The next time we went hunting together, I wouldn't waste the opportunity.

"This way," I barked and sped into the night. Porschia kept up easily.

"I need to give you a nickname," she said, smiling as we ran together.

"Why is that?"

"You call me kitten. I need something to call you."

"Stallion works."

She smiled widely and shook her head. "Don't worry about Saul, Tage."

"I'm not." I was.

"Liar."

PORSCHIA

We slowed as the sun began to rise, pausing beside a small creek. We'd covered a lot of land already and I wasn't sure if we were even going in the right direction.

"How do we know we haven't passed it, or that we're even going the right way?"

Tage smiled, hands on his hips. "We don't. That's part of the fun, though. Right?"

"Right," I agreed, stepping over larger stones until I was across. The water trickled musically over them. There were no animal tracks in the mud.

"Let's walk up that hill," Tage said, pointing to a taller one ahead. "We'll have a good vantage point from the crest."

"Okay." My breath clouded in front of my face as we walked up until the hilltop became flat and we could see the valley beyond. In the distance was a cross work of houses encircled by a tall, wooden wall. We found it. The Glen was just that – a valley of flat land surrounded by rolling hills, and it was beautiful. A small pond sat just beyond the western wall of the town. Fog hovered above the cool water.

At our feet, the grass was thickening into dark green clumps. It swayed in the wind as we left the forest behind and entered the rectangular patches of earth that had obviously been farmed last season. Why hadn't they turned the soil yet?

Tage sniffed the air. He turned to me. "It's cold. There's no fire from any of the houses."

No smoke trails rose in the brightening morning sky, yet it was cold outside. It made no sense. How were they able to stay warm or cook?

Tage grabbed my hand. "We aren't staying. We tell them about the cure and then make our way back to Mountainside."

I nodded. "I know."

He watched my expression for a moment and then began walking down the hill. A vee of honking geese flew overhead opposite us, and a shiver crawled up my spine. It was almost as if something was warning us away from this place, no matter how peaceful it seemed on the outside.

I heard the hum of bugs, dancing grass, and the sound of mice and moles burrowing beneath the ground. Birds chirped overhead as they flittered here and there, bobbing up and down in the light westerly wind.

When the land flattened, we could see the wall much better. It was made of large tree trunks, sharpened into points along the top edge. They were almost as tall as the flood wall in Blackwater and had dried and cracked, bleaching in the sun for what looked like a very long time. Why didn't the Elders ever tell us about the existence of these other places?

It was stupid to think about now that I'd seen Mountainside, but growing up, I thought Blackwater was it; that we were the only survivors of the apocalyptic plagues that extinguished an entire nation, maybe the entire world. It never occurred to me that there were others out there, struggling just as we were and surviving under similar circumstances.

Tage stopped abruptly, his hand tightening on mine. I looked to him. "What is it?"

"We should leave. Now."

I followed his crystal blue eyes until I saw what concerned him. The enormous gate to the wall we'd been walking beside was wide open. "Maybe they always leave it open?" I said, not believing it myself.

"Why go to the trouble of building one at all if you don't plan to use it?"

"I was trying to see the bright side," I added softly.

Tage shook his head. "I don't think there is a bright side here, kitten."

"We came all this way. If someone is still here, maybe we can help them get to Mountainside." If I'd been left alone and someone came who could help, I would hope they would at least offer.

"I have a bad feeling about this."

So did I.

Squeezing his hand, I tugged him forward with me as we passed through the open door. A crow cawed from its perch on one of the pointed logs above us as we entered into The Glen.

Everything was destroyed. The homes had been ransacked. Furniture and plates and clothing littered what was left of the concrete streets. Windows were broken out and the doors were left wide open. A small whimper came from around the side of a painted-blue home and a small black nose peeked forward.

"Come here. I won't hurt you," I crooned, crouching down and holding out my hand. The dog whimpered again and backed away, letting out a bark that echoed against the two homes he was between.

"He thinks you're hungry."

No matter what I did, I would always be a monster to those who weren't. It didn't matter how I behaved, how kind I was or who I tried to help. People and animals alike would always see me as a predator. I swallowed thickly.

"Let's see if anyone's here so we can leave," Tage urged.

"Fine. You go left, I'll go right."

"Nope. We don't separate," he said adamantly.

Big baby. "It'll be faster if we do, Tage. Then we can leave and go back to Mountainside." I looked around at all the brokenness. Dishes and chairs, curtains blowing from busted windows on the second floor. A cat ran quickly across the lawn. "Besides," I added, "no one's here."

Reluctantly, he let go of my hand. "Meet me back here in ten minutes. If I have to come and find you, you won't like it." Then he shrugged and grinned. "Well, you might like it."

I rolled my eyes.

"Who am I kidding? You'll love it. But ten minutes," he warned.

I smiled and walked toward the right half of the city and he moved away from me toward the left. Running through the yards, I made my way to the back of the city. I'd work my way forward, fast. Ten minutes wasn't much time to comb through thirty homes. Stepping into the foyer of an enormous three-story white home, I called out, "Is anyone here?"

There was no answer. Glass crunched beneath my boots. In the living room, furniture had been scooted toward the windows and hearth. The center of the room was empty except for a tennis shoe that lay on its side.

Sniffing the air, I couldn't find anyone here. The kitchen was in similar shape, chairs and table overturned and pressed up against the back door. "They were trying to keep something out."

A slow clap sounded from behind me. I turned quickly, heart hammering, and expecting to slap Tage across the chest for scaring me. But I didn't find Tage. "They were trying to keep *me* out of here, I expect."

The woman was ethereal. Her skin was pale brown and her eyes were the color of wheat. Her short, rust-colored hair hung in ringlets around her ears. Everything in me screamed for me to run, but all I could think about was Tage. He would feel my distress and come straight there.

"We haven't been here in months," the woman offered. "But a little birdy said you'd be coming this way soon and we had to see the hybrid for ourselves." Her eyes raked up and down my body. "You don't look special. You certainly don't look as strong as he said you were."

The scent of another night-walker came from behind me. "She looks harmless," he said. "They're waiting. What about the other?"

The woman smiled, baring her fangs. "Drain him."

"NO! Tage, run! I'll meet you at the front gate!" I screamed as loud as I could, walking in a circle as the two vampires closed in, arms outstretched.

The woman smiled. "I thought you'd be more cooperative, or at the very least curious to see The Manor. It's so much nicer than Mountainside. I used to live there, you know," she whispered.

My eyes widened and my teeth ground together. She'd fed her own people to the wolves. There was a special place in hell for people like her, and I would be honored to send her straight there, given the chance.

From behind, the vampire clamped a metal belt around my stomach with spikes in the center. He warned me, "Try anything and I'll have it slice you in two. This will be a little uncomfortable, but nothing the all-mighty hybrid can't handle, right?" He smiled, nudging me ahead of them. We walked down the streets, the teeth of the device digging into my core, tearing flesh with each step. Tage panted from the gate, angry as hell and ready to fight.

"Run, Tage. Please," I said to him, motioning to my stomach. His eyes fastened on the metal wrapped around me. "They'll drain you and cut me in half." The male vamp tsked from behind, wrapping his palm across my mouth and with his other hand, slapping the belt at my back.

"Aaaah!" I let out around his fingers. "Manor!" I bit my captor's hand as hard as I could and looked down at the warmth spilling from my waist, blood oozing down from each tooth into my dress; macabre stripes of crimson dripping down the fabric.

The vampire fumed, his green eyes darkening. Soon his cheeks began to redden to match his hair, puffing in and out with rage. "You'll pay for that," he said menacingly.

Tage was in a war with himself. I watched his jaw tick, his hands clench into fists and then relax again. Urging him again, I pleaded, "Go!"

He gave a stare of warning to the assholes to the left and right of me and then looked to me. "I'll be back for you!"

Tears pricked my eyes. "I know. Go!"

He sped away and the male vamp behind me took off after him. They were under the cover of the forest before I could blink. The female vampire laughed. "Gregor is one of our fastest runners."

"Runners?"

"Yes," she said, urging me out of the gate and toward the left.

"If Gregor hurts Tage, I will eat him, and I don't mean drain him. I'll eat every single inch of him," I panted in anger.

The woman shrugged. "Do you feel like a jog?"

"With this thing on? Not really."

"Too bad. Stay behind me. You don't want the dogs to catch you."

I was going to ask what dogs she was talking about, but then she sped away. I had no choice but to run after her. Each step while walking was difficult, but moving much faster, it seemed that the teeth of the belt couldn't do their job. It wasn't nearly as painful.

We ran over hill and valley, past several miles until we came to a clearing. On a knoll ahead of us was an enormous house, several stories high with spires on the corners. It looked more like a castle than a house, and then I heard the growling. The night-walker smiled. "The hounds won't like you."

"Why not?"

"Because you're part rotter, and we taught them to tear those apart on sight."

Lovely. Two dogs whose backs were taller than my waist came from both the left and right, baring their teeth. The black fur on their backs was raised and foam collected at the corners of their mouths. They growled, easing forward. "Better follow me, hybrid." She blurred away and I wasted no time following her.

I could hear the animals' hearts beating faster and faster, the sound of their paws propelling them toward us on the grass. They were incredibly fast, but luckily, we were faster.

The vamp grabbed my arm and stopped me as we stepped onto a wooden bridge. The dogs stopped at the end of the trail, refusing to walk onto the wooden planks beneath our feet. They snapped and growled and barked angrily. The scent of stagnant water and old, rancid blood filled my nose. Rotten wood. Contaminated, dirty water. I covered my nose with my hand and looked for the source. It took me only a second to realize we were standing over it. Swarms of gnats curled into the air all around, buzzing around my ears and threatening to fly into the corners of our eyes, nostrils, and mouth.

Beneath the bridge and surrounding the castle-house was a moat. The water was still, but what made me gasp was what was in the water. The bodies of dead humans bobbed lazily at the surface. Some floated face down, while others had their eyes fixated on the sky. Flies sipped from the surface of the water, bracing their legs against the coating of film atop it. A vulture sat on the far bank pecking at a corpse, fanning its wings to get a better grip of the person's flesh; tearing at the man's face.

I turned away, my stomach in knots. "What's wrong, hybrid? Weak stomach? Everything must be fed. It's the cycle of life," she teased. "Let's go inside. The others are waiting and I want to get out of these awful clothes."

She motioned toward her jeans and shirt as she walked across the bridge to a pebbled pathway. We walked up a set of stairs to the entrance of the house. The Manor was a mansion, a castle of the most unimaginable wealth with the most unspeakable atrocities kept inside its stone walls.

Glossy tile and red carpet, paintings that were taller than the walls of my house, tapestries woven of intricate portraits, vases that could hold trees. Everything was bigger, grander, and shinier. The vampire who brought me here led me to a sitting room and told me to wait, and then she ran up a staircase we'd passed upon entering.

It wasn't long until the news of my arrival spread throughout The Manor. *The hybrid is here!* And it wasn't long until I knew exactly who'd been spreading the word about me around the neighboring settlements. It was no surprise. The women of The Manor craved power, and he wanted that above all else, no matter the price or who had to pay it.

Three women, including the one who captured me, entered the room. Two of them wore elaborate gowns, one gray and the other a deep, blood red. They were beautiful, with ruby lips and jewels dripping from their necks.

"I'm Marta," offered the one who wore gray. Her hair was as black as the night sky, straight and shiny as silk. Her skin was caramel and she somehow looked younger than I was. There was an innocence in her face that betrayed the coldness of her stare. She stepped toward me and extended her hand, but I took a defiant step back. She smiled, revealing long, pearlescent fangs. "And this is Elise," she added, gesturing to the one in red. Elise stared at me with a curled upper lip. I could smell her displeasure and the perfume she'd bathed in that morning. Her hair was like Mercedes' used to be; blonde as butter and hanging over one shoulder in soft waves.

My heart pounded. I couldn't stop worrying about Tage. Wringing my fingers in my skirts, I ignored the women and stared at the rich belongings that surrounded us. While the finery inside was opulent, on the other side of the walls was nothing but death and decay. The putridness that surrounded this place was nowhere inside The Manor itself. It smelled like fresh flowers and... live humans.

Where were they?

The woman who brought me here stepped forward, still clad in her jeans. "I'm Lydia. Pardon me for not introducing myself sooner, but we had no time for pleasantries this morning. Tell me something." She skirted the furniture and stood beside me. "Where is Roman? I hear he's human now." She grinned widely but I wasn't sure if she was happy about the news or wanted to feed from him. Probably the latter, knowing Roman.

My blood began to boil. "Why did you bring me here?"

She began to answer, opened her mouth to form a word and then stopped, her smirk falling from her lips. Lydia's eyes flashed and darkened with anger. "Gregor is dead," she told the other two women.

I smiled. Tage had ended him. He would get rewarded for that later. "But he's your best runner," I parroted. Lydia's claws scratched pathways across my cheek. I launched myself at her, forgetting the belt, overwhelmed by rage. It was only when I knocked her down and bent toward her, that the metal teeth reminded me of their presence.

Lydia screeched, "He *was* my favorite!"

"That's enough!" Elise said from behind me. Something sharp pierced my neck and I clasped my hand over it as things became fuzzy. I knew immediately what she'd done.

"Belladonna." I could smell it and feel the poison begin to filter into my blood. My heart pumped it faster through my body, spreading the poison evenly.

"Word on the street is that it has quite an effect on you. Right, Pierce?"

As Elise helped me stand, Pierce stepped into the room. His hair had been cut short, making him look too much like his brother. My vision swam and my head bobbed, too heavy for me to lift for long.

"Remove the belt," someone said, to which Pierce pushed something on the side and it unclamped. He eased each metal tooth from my waist, one by one. I could feel blood pour from each wound, soaking into my dress—the dress Maggie made for me.

"You ruined my dress," I slurred. "You'll pay for this."

He smirked. "I highly doubt it."

TEN

TAGE

I could sense her distress. She wanted me to leave, but didn't want to go with them. The asshole chasing me was a cocky bastard, but so was I. I led him through the woods, blurring through trees, up and down hills and across streams and outcroppings of rock, and that was where I got him – near the den of the coyotes Saul and I hunted for the people of Mountainside.

Dropping down over the hill onto the rocks, I ducked back into the den and waited as he jumped down after me. Then I pounced. I drained him as he kicked and thrashed, fighting to squeeze my hands, throat, and head tighter and tighter until he lost strength and stopped fighting. I kept drinking until I was beyond full, until there was nothing left of him but an empty husk.

I had to go back for her, but I knew I needed help. The vamps of The Manor were nothing to toy with. They wiped The Glen off the map, along with almost every creature in the entire area. Having depleted their food source, it wouldn't be long until the residents of The Manor ventured farther to find food. I couldn't take them on alone and had no idea how many we were up against to begin with, but Roman might.

Pumping my arms, gut full of fresh blood, I ran toward Mountainside.

I knew Roman would have the answers I needed, and we had to get her back.

Her emotions ranged from angry to worried, but at least she was okay. I just hoped the guy I just drained had no blood bond with anyone, or else they would quickly realize he was gone and Porschia would pay the price.

THE GUARDS DIDN'T HAVE TIME TO OPPOSE ME. THE GATE HAD ALREADY been opened up for a man pushing a small cart of wood, and I ran inside past them and straight to the rocky dwelling where Roman lay. Saul and Mercedes were outside but followed me in.

"Where's Porschia?" Saul yelled.

"What happened?" Mercedes asked.

Roman sat up. He still looked awful but was awake and alert. I crouched low in front of him. "Did you know about The Glen?"

He ticked his head back. "What about it?"

"It's empty. All of the people are gone and the only thing there besides some stray animals—which I'm surprised they haven't already eaten—were two of your lovely friends from The Manor."

"Oh, no," he cursed, holding his hand out for me to help him up. He groaned as I picked him up and sat him on his feet.

"You need to tell me everything you know about them. Now."

He shrugged a sweater on and quickly pulled it down before beginning, "After Pierce fell to the Infection, a woman approached me..."

"We know the story," I snapped.

"Not all of it!" he yelled back.

"The note gave me directions to Blackwater and I took Pierce with me. I carried him all the way. One night when we were very close, we came across The Manor. The woman who originally turned me, Veronica, was there."

"Why do I feel like this isn't going to be a happy story?"

"Because it isn't," he continued. "I was in Frenzy. I'd just carried my brother, who I couldn't even stand to smell, let alone feed from, about three hundred miles. Hungry and tired didn't begin to cover it. 'Insane' only skimmed the surface of how I was feeling. When I saw her, I snapped. That's what Porschia doesn't know. Porsch said to me... I wouldn't get answers to my questions about her note, about why she did this and what any of it meant, unless I asked the woman who turned me—the woman who wrote it. But I can't ask her…because I killed her."

"You drained her."

"Yeah, and her sister is still pissed about it."

Mercedes huffed. "Well no wonder! And now the sister has Porschia! Does this woman know that Porschia knows you?"

"I think so, yes."

"How do you know that? What the hell is going on? What aren't you telling us?"

"You told us about what Tage said, the Infected in the woods knowing about Porschia? Well, I think Pierce is the one spreading the word about 'the hybrid.' He may have left Blackwater, but living in the woods was never his style. I went to look for him after I was made human again. I found some of his things in an old shack, but he was long gone. When the people here said they were afraid, I wondered whether it was of Porschia or of the ladies of The Manor. They're old and strong as hell. They feed, but not off a drink or two a day; they drain two or three humans *each* per day, sometimes more."

"How long did you stay at The Manor after you killed the sister? How long before they knew it was you?" Saul yelled.

"I didn't stay. After I fed from her, I ran like hell. I did what I had to do in order to survive," Roman shouted, stepping into Saul's face. "Like you didn't!"

"How'd they know it was you?"

"They could follow my scent!"

"Why didn't they come after you?"

"They tried a few times, but for a long time, Blackwater had more vampires. They could attack, but they still couldn't overcome the fact that we were more powerful in number. Over time they gave up, but I knew that if I left they'd hunt me down."

"And now you're human. You're like bait for them. Even if they didn't have Porschia, they would come here for you and slaughter everyone in Mountainside just to get to you," I said, shaking my head.

Roman looked to the rocky roof, bracing himself against the wall. "I thought this would be a simple trip. The people of Mountainside and The Glen are good people, but distrusting. They had seen me before as a vampire, so I thought my presence here would help. I didn't mean for all of this to happen."

I laughed mirthlessly. "Well now that it has, what can we do to get Porschia back?"

"We destroy The Manor."

"And how do you propose we do that, Roman? Are you going to club them? Swing a shovel? You won't last a minute."

Roman smiled. "You're going to turn me again."

"No. No way. You were hell on wheels as a night-walker. I'd hate to see you in Frenzy."

Mercedes stepped forward. "Then turn me."

"And me," added Saul.

Roman smiled. "These women are incredibly strong, but smart too, Tage. They have hundreds of years of tricks up their sleeves. You can't win this battle alone."

"I can't handle three vamps in Frenzy, either."

Saul huffed. "Neither can the witches at The Manor."

I closed my eyes. Porschia always wore her poison ring, even now. "Does anyone have a ring?"

Saul nodded. "I do."

"I'll turn two of you, but only once we get close, and the third wears the ring just in case they need to turn."

Roman shook his head. "If they catch a human, the human dies. If they catch any of us, even if we're turned, we might die. And they have a special security system, if memory serves me right. You'll want to change us right before we get there."

"Fine. I'll turn you all, but as soon as we get Porschia back, we find a rotter and you change back. Got it?"

They all agreed easily, too easily, and I wasn't sure if any or all would fight me about becoming human again. Being a vampire was like a high for most; an addiction that wouldn't be easy to overcome.

Roman turned to me first and smiled. "If you turn us, we can run to her."

He was out of his mind. "I won't set you loose in Mountainside."

"Fine, but you'll have to turn me as soon as we're outside the wall or else I won't make it. I'm weak," he drawled.

I nodded. "Fine. But you can't feed from them."

He nodded and leaned against the earthen wall to keep himself from falling over. "Let's go get our girl."

"She isn't your girl!" I shouted, my words echoing around the small space. Let them all know it. She wasn't up for grabs. Saul stormed outside and Mercedes followed him.

"How many are we facing?" I asked once they were gone.

"Three of the most vicious women alive, although I'm not sure how many others they have doing their dirty work. When I was there they only had a few slaves, though none lasted long. Pierce is probably there if they haven't killed him already. He'll only live as long as he's useful to them."

Outside, the sun was high. It was midday and she'd been at The Manor too long already. The others were stopped just inside the gate where Garreth stood. He inhaled deeply, his large chest rising and falling again. "I can't let you come back if you'll be in Frenzy."

"We understand that," Roman said from behind me, "and I'd advise you to close the gate behind us and not reopen it – not for anyone or any reason. You have some meat to last you. If this goes well, we can hopefully bring more. But you need to think seriously about leaving Mountainside."

Garreth's mouth bobbed open, ready to respond, but Roman held his hand up. "Think about it – you have no reliable food source. It's been ruined and will take years for the animal populations to increase to the point where it could feed your people adequately. Blackwater has empty homes and there is still game in the forests surrounding the Colony. I'm sure they would welcome you all."

"That's a lot to ask of a group of people who are also struggling to survive."

I butted in, "Would you refuse the citizens of Blackwater help or shelter if they needed it?"

"No," Garreth asserted thoughtfully. "We would welcome them."

Point made.

Garreth shifted on his feet. "I'll take it into consideration."

Mercedes and Saul were the first to step around him and beneath the tall gate. Roman followed. "Seal them behind us."

Garreth nodded. "Good luck."

"Thank you for everything," Roman added. Saul had all but carried him to the gate, acting as a crutch. The doors closed behind us and wood scraped against wood as they slid the beam into place.

Roman turned to me and smiled. "Now change me."

ELEVEN

PORSCHIA

THIS FEELING WAS FAMILIAR. MY HEAD WAS CLOUDY, MY BODY ACHED, AND I woke up in a bed that wasn't my own. Stripes of burgundy and gold were papered down the walls of the room, and the bed covers matched. I threw them back and gingerly sat up before sliding my legs around. The soft hairs of a snow-white rug tickled my feet as I eased them to the floor.

The door rattled and my eyes snapped up to see Pierce enter the room carrying a silver tray. He stilled when he saw me sitting upright. "I thought you'd still be asleep."

"You thought wrong." A low growl erupted from deep within my chest.

He stuck his free hand out. "Easy. I need to explain a few things before you go crazy."

"I don't intend to go crazy," I said softly, venomously.

"What do you intend to do?"

I smiled. "I intend to eat you. I told your little friends downstairs I would, and they sent you in here anyway. You must not be very important to them."

He let out a sharp laugh and pulled the collar of his shirt away from his neck. Fresh fang marks and bruises circled his neck, which meant that he'd been fed from frequently. "I'm definitely not important to them now. I have no more information that they need."

"You're still alive, but on borrowed time. One of them would eat you anyway. Well, they would *drain* you. I plan to actually *eat* you. Your muscle, soft tissues. I can eat everything but your bones. They wouldn't float outside in the stagnant water. They would sink to the bottom and no one would ever think of you again."

"You're delusional. It's the effect of the belladonna."

"I'm not delusional at all. You didn't give me enough of the poison. Your mistake. I'm completely lucid." And I was. My left foot held my weight and I shifted the right down to share the load. My mind was clear and my body was quickly catching up. He hadn't put enough poison in the syringe, or I'd become more immune since the last attack. Either way: good for me, bad for Pierce.

He kept his eyes trained on me as he stepped farther into the room and sat the tray on a small glass table. "You wouldn't hurt Roman like that."

Laughing hysterically, I clutched my stomach. I would. I would hurt Roman. Because as much as I didn't want Roman to die from something as simple as the flu, I didn't owe him anything when it came to his brother. "I could always drain you and tell him that one of the others did it."

Pierce's face paled. "You would be sick. Roman told me you couldn't hold down large amounts of blood."

I shrugged, standing at full height. "I could live with that. The sickness passes quickly. You, however, wouldn't be able to hurt anyone ever again."

A strange scent filled the air and my brows furrowed as I took it in. An Infected was here. "Why do you have an Infected here?"

"The ladies of The Manor have cured themselves."

"What?" I searched the room for my coat. It was freezing in here. "If they're human, I can just leave."

He shook his head. "It's not that simple."

The smell became stronger the closer he stepped toward me. "Were you not cured?" I covered my nose and mouth.

"I was, but the lovely ladies of The Manor had me Infected again so that I could help them. They took turns feeding from me this morning so my body is healing from the disease. Again. It seems much slower this time, though."

I swallowed. "Why would they do that?"

"It weakened me immediately. I couldn't leave with information that might help them. That's reason number one."

"The second?"

"So that my blood could cure them when the time came for it."

"So why don't they let you go now? You're healing. They have 'the hybrid'."

"I feel like they've somehow Infected me again." He looked at the opposite wall, sticking his hands in his pockets. "They want me to die slowly."

I had no empathy for Pierce whatsoever. Maybe they *did* infect him again. Maybe he deserved to rot. "Why did you tell them about me?" I stepped closer.

"I came here because my brother and I had stopped here once before. The women were frightening, but they were also the most powerful in the land. I seek power; it's that simple. But I learned fast that they didn't want me here. They almost killed me, believing me to be Roman. They kept me as their 'guest' just to lure him here, and when that didn't happen quickly enough, they planned to kill me and throw me in the moat. If you have nothing to bargain with, you lose here. Period. Information about you was the only chip I had left to play. Now, I have none."

"You told others."

"I told other Infected, so that they could find a night-walker and end their pain." His dark eyes paused on mine. He looked a lot like Roman now that his hair was shorter and he looked healthier. As a human he must have healed before the sick bitches had him Infected again. What kind of person would do that?

They want me to collect your blood, he spoke urgently in my mind.

What for?

They want to be what you are. They think your blood will make them hybrids, too; that it will give them your strength.

I'm not always strong, Pierce. Sometimes I'm weaker than anyone knows.

He nodded. *If you're going to run for it now is the time, but they have night-walkers watching both of us. Only the three women healed themselves. They didn't allow their slaves to be healed, and they only healed themselves in order to transform into some stronger version of what they already were. They didn't think it through.*

I shook my head. *Why would anyone want this?*

As vampires, they're still vulnerable. Someone could still drain or heal them, tear them apart and end them. They think you are different; that you can't be killed.

That's crazy! Believe me, you almost killed me with the darts in the forest. I can be killed. Probably easier than they could.

They don't see it that way. It's a chance they're willing to take, and that's all that matters. They always get their way. He stepped forward.

How does anyone know what my blood will do, anyway? Maybe it won't do anything. Maybe they'll turn into night-walkers again. Maybe it will Infect them. It's not worth any of that. And if it does work, if they are somehow able to absorb both curses, I guarantee they'll wish it hadn't.

A large man stepped into the room, baring his fangs and flexing his pectoral muscles as he clenched his fists. "What's going on in here? Get on with it," he ordered Pierce.

"I need some blood." He held up a knife. "I can take it from your palm."

That's not going to happen. Give me the knife.

He hesitated for just a moment before stepping toward me. I held my hand out as the brute watched the exchange. When the cold handle of the knife hit my palm, I launched it at the vampire before rushing him, knocking him to the floor, and draining him. When I eased my fangs from his throat, his eyes were fixated on the ceiling, the knife protruding from between them.

"Holy shit," Pierce said, backing away from me and easing around the bed. As if a simple mattress and a few pieces of metal and wood would keep me from reaching him if I wanted to.

A slow clap came from the hallway. "That's *exactly* why we want to be like you, Porschia." Lydia, whose once-lustrous hair was now dry and her skin was flaking away, approached. She looked Infected, not human.

"The three of us are very old, and it finally seems as if time hasn't forgotten that fact. When we turned back into humans, it caught up with us rather quickly."

"Nothing is intended to live forever," I quipped. Maybe that was Roman's problem. Maybe time was catching up with him and he happened to catch the flu at the same time.

"No, that certainly wasn't the intention, but surely even you can appreciate its appeal. Staying youthful, vibrant, strong, and healthy. Who wouldn't want that?"

"You're making a mistake. One moment of my strength is backed by one hundred moments of weakness. Bearing both curses isn't what it might seem. It's painful; full of sadness, punctuated with moments of strength and glory. It's very human-like. And if you don't like being human—like what you are right now—being a hybrid will crush you."

She smiled, her fangs gone, but the threat in her tone said she didn't want to mince words. "I don't believe you."

TWELVE

SAUL

We ran from Mountainside toward The Glen until Tage got tired of carrying Roman, and Roman's incessant belly-aching about feeling weak and his pleas of being turned finally grated on Tage for long enough.

Tage did all the work but didn't break a sweat from carrying a man on his back. Roman, still recovering from his illness, was panting and weak. He could barely lift his arm to wipe the sweat from his brow. "Thank God."

He gave us each a small plant. "Nightshade. Belladonna. It took us down a notch when the darts hit. Not enough to stop us, but enough that it might ease the frenzy you're about to feel and maybe keep it under control until we can get Porschia out. As soon as you turn, eat it. It might help the pain. Garreth said he'd seen a vampire use it to ease their hunger before."

"Is the pain like the Infection?" I asked warily.

Tage laughed. Roman clapped me on the back and said, "You thought turning into a monster was going to be easy?"

"No, I just wondered if the pain was similar."

I'd experienced turning into one curse, and seen someone turn into the other. I knew there was pain, but would the pain be like when Mercedes bit me? Would it spread fast and feel bone deep?

Mercedes frowned. "Can we hurry up and get this over with?" she said in frustration. She was emotional, much more than her sister. I didn't look forward to her in Frenzy.

"I'm just worried," she shouted, brushing the hair from her face. "And we're wasting time. Porschia is in trouble."

Tage pulled a small knife from his pocket. "Who's first?"

"Me," I said, stepping forward.

Tage's brow popped up. "Always the hero, until you're not."

"Turn me, asshole." God, I hated him. And while the others were dealing with the turn, I would run as fast as I could to her. Something told me there was no time to waste.

He cut his index finger. "Drink up. But don't think about being a hero. We leave here together as a group."

"Yeah," I lied. "We go together." I opened my mouth and let him squeeze a drop onto my tongue. Immediately my eyes began to water. Sharp pain. Fucking. Everywhere. I was on the ground. I was... "Aaaaah!"

Tage was laughing and I wanted to kill him for it. Maybe I would. Later.

White. Hot. Pain.

Oh, God.

I wasn't strong enough for this.

Chewing the flower didn't help.

I rocked on the ground.

God. Stop this.

Make it stop.

Hunger. My stomach. I held it tightly to make it stop.

My mouth.

My gums.

Holy...

ROMAN

. . .

I laughed at Saul as he writhed on the ground, his cheeks puffing out violently with each sharp exhale. The pain was going to suck. I'd been through it before, but I was healthy the last time I turned.

"Just do it," I said, stepping forward. Tage winced but squeezed a drop into my mouth. The same fucking fire began to burn in me, and soon I was writhing on the ground beside Saul.

I shouldn't have laughed. Karma's a real bitch.

MERCEDES

Watching the two men scream and tear at the hairs of their head, thrashing on the ground almost made me back out. My hands shook so bad, I had to lace my fingers together in front of me. "It's okay if you change your mind," Tage said quietly.

"These women are really that bad?" How bad could they be? I'd always feared the male night-walkers. They seemed so intense, almost like they were stalking prey when their eyes found their way to a human too often.

"They're the worst. You heard Garreth. They're depraved. They don't value human life at all. My bet is that they won't hesitate to hurt Porschia if it benefits them."

"They'll hurt her?"

He nodded. "I think so." I could see stress settle in the lines of his face. He wanted nothing more than to run to The Manor and tear the place apart until he found my sister, but now he was going to have to take the time to rein us all in. He loved her. I could see it in the crinkles feathering from the corners of his eyes, in the way he kept looking past me as if she'd appear from the direction he'd last seen her.

"Female night-walkers are the most dangerous. That's what they said in Mountainside." And Garreth was always honest with us. He was helpful but wary; frightened. The man was as tall as an oak and scared to death of Porschia. It wasn't Tage that he feared.

Tage smiled. "All women are vicious." I could see why my sister liked him. If nothing more, I owed her and him more time together.

"Then I'll do it. Let's go get my sister and teach these bitches a lesson."

He held his finger up and cursed. I'd taken so long to decide, his finger had already healed, so he had to cut it again. I stared into the blue sky, my eyes watering as he squeezed the droplet onto my tongue. This wasn't forever, I told myself. I'd find an Infected and we could heal each other –

Oh. My. God.

Lightning. I'd been struck by lightning. It coursed through me. It burned me from the inside out.

Singe.

Burn.

Tear.

Rip.

My mouth. My stomach. My head. It was too much.

My legs.

Arms.

Face. It was on fire!

Mouth.

My mouth.

My mouth was ripping open.

Back.

Feet.

I couldn't take it.

"Help me!" I heard myself scream, shrill and inhuman.

Tage was in front of me. "Chew the plant."

"I can't. My mouth!" My lips shook violently as I said the words. I couldn't chew, but I was getting hungrier by the second. Insatiably so.

"I know, but you have to, Cede. If you want to help Porschia, you have to."

He shoved the plant – leaves, flower and all – into my mouth and told me to chew. "You're as stubborn as your sister."

We *had* to be stubborn. It was a survival response. We had to be strong to be able to survive Mother. And it was all Roman's fault. I'd make him pay for what he and his brother did…right after I figured out how to make the pain go away. I chewed, my head thumping back onto the earth with a dull thud. The plant seemed to help. It eased the pain. Slightly. And it made me hungrier. Was that possible?

"You okay?" Tage asked, crouching beside me. Saul and Roman had stopped transitioning. I was coming out of it, too.

I nodded, tears filling my eyes. This was horrible, but Porschia had to deal with this and so much more. I bit her and then she started feeling ill from the Infection. Then she used her ring and turned into this… I couldn't imagine the feeling of both because right now, I felt as though I'd been ripped apart and was slowly and painfully being stitched back together.

How would she ever feel whole again?

"Don't cry," Tage said gently.

"I'll cry if I want, damn it!" I tried to sit up but my stomach hurt. Tage grabbed my hand and pulled me until I was sitting up. "My stomach."

"You need to feed soon."

Easing my trembling fingers toward my mouth, I felt them for the first time. Pointed and sharp, much longer than Porschia's, my fangs punctured my bottom lip. Tage growled at the sight of the blood. "Your sister is going to kill me."

I smiled. "Not if we save her first."

He groaned and shook his head with a smile. "Nah, pretty sure I'm dead either way."

"Feels like it," Saul said, standing up from the ground. He gave Roman a hand and the two staggered for a moment, like baby deer after being born.

THIRTEEN

TAGE

Saul crouched across from us. "I'm so hungry," he growled.

Roman was almost beyond the transition, too. They were becoming more steady on their feet, regaining balance. Saul's eyes darted toward everything he heard. I remembered the acuteness. It was overwhelming to me, but he seemed to be handling it well—another reason to hate him, I decided. I pointed in the direction of The Glen. "There are strays inside the walls."

When Saul smiled, I noted that the bastard had longer fangs than any of us. "Not anymore," he said slyly, and took off running like he was meant to be a night-walker. Roman chased after him.

"Roman!"

"I'm okay. Sort of!"

Mercedes asked me to help steady her, so I did. She was shorter than Porschia and pretty in a conventional way, but nowhere near as beautiful as her sister. Not as feisty either.

"I need to eat," she said, panting and staring at the rapidly disappearing backs of Roman and Saul. "How do I run as fast as you and Porsch?"

"Just run. Speed will come sooner or later. There's not a magical switch to flip."

She flicked her eyes to me. "She loves you, Tage."

My heart stopped for a long moment. How would Mercedes know Porschia's feelings? The two weren't exactly besties right now. As if sensing my question, she huffed. "She watches you. Any time you're in the room, her eyes follow you. She doesn't bother with the others. And I wasn't around when she and Saul were... friends, but I don't imagine that it's something conscious on her part. She follows you because she cares about you; where you are and what you're doing."

"I hope you're right." Because I truly did love her and would give up everything for her.

"I am." She flexed her fists and then looked at me. "See you at The Glen. I'm starving." Then she took off running, and although it took her several yards, the girl was fast. She was right on Saul and Roman's heels as the three entered the open gate.

Roman found a dog and Saul found two cats. They fed until they couldn't draw any more blood from the animals, roaring in frustration, blood dripping from their lips and clinging to their teeth. Mercedes came out from around a building, holding a chicken in her arms. She cooed to it, smiling at the three of us guys, petting its feathers gently. And then she slowly brought it closer to her mouth. It was over before it could even cluck.

Mercedes smiled, teeth covered in blood, a dark feather stuck to her bottom lip. "I love chicken," she sighed.

It was a terrifying sight. Even Roman and Saul stiffened. Mercedes waved to them. "There are more. I hear them. Come on!"

She took off running through the tall grass between the abandoned homes, leaping over obstacles like they were put there for sport, just for her entertainment. I'd been worried about Roman in frenzy, but he and Saul seemed calmer than I was after the transition. Mercedes, on the other hand? Mercedes seemed to be enjoying every second of her new strength and stamina. I instinctively knew she was going to be the hardest to control.

I followed Saul and Roman as they chased after her, feeding from my own cat when I found one. It felt wrong. I started calling Porschia 'kitten' because she seemed so panicked and frightened after she first turned, innocence with claws, and now I was feeding from one.

Mercedes watched me, noting my discomfort. "They would die anyway. There is no food for them here."

"I know that," I said defensively. It was weird to feed from domestic animals but I wasn't above it, especially if it gave me strength. Because I was going to need it.

Roman stopped eating one of the stray chickens. "We'll get a bigger kill soon. We should start heading toward The Manor."

"What bigger game is there?" Mercedes smiled, her eyes twinkling in delight.

"You'll see," Roman said with a wink. "They'll be fun to take down, too. You'll love it, Cede."

Oh, joy. Roman had already told me about the guard dogs, and now it was time to feed the frenzied. On the menu this afternoon? Canine.

A shiver like the legs of a millipede crawled up my spine. Porschia. She was scared and angry and... I needed to get to her. Now.

"Porschia is in trouble!" I panted, feeling her panic.

Roman's smile dropped away and his face turned to stone. "Let's go." With that, he sped away; the three of us doing our best to keep up. Roman laughed as he ran. "I feel amazing! God, I missed this!"

Saul chuckled, running on his heels. "Feels better than being a rotter, that's for sure!"

"I second that," Mercedes yelled, laughing maniacally.

"Here they come!" yelled Roman, stopping fast and turning toward the smell of wet dog and blood. The dogs, if you could call them that, were enormous. The fur on their backs stood on end as they snarled, approaching slowly now that we'd all stopped. One came from the east and the other from the west. "Only two?" I yelled to Roman.

"Looks like it."

"So hungry," Mercedes muttered under her breath as she stared straight at the animal about to attack her. She showed no fear because she feared nothing in that moment. She was driven by something primal, something that fueled her confidence. Mercedes stepped forward, whispering to the canine.

"Sit down," she cooed. The animal whimpered and tried to back away, but was unable to do anything more than obey her.

Roman's eyes flicked to me. He mouthed, "She's compelling it."

I nodded.

Mouthing back, "Try it," I ticked my head toward the other mutt. Roman stared directly at it, trying to calm it and tell it to sit down. Unfortunately Roman's animal compulsion did not work, not like Mercedes'. She smiled and stepped forward to pet the animal under her spell before turning around and telling its twin to sit as well. The second animal went a step further, lying on the grass, eyes big and round and pleading. It whined and laid its head on its front paws.

To one and then the other, she commanded, "Stay."

Walking to the first one she'd compelled, she dropped to her knees beside the animal, cooing and petting his coat. Then, before he knew what hit him, she sank her teeth into his neck and drank so quickly that he fell limply in her arms. She held his large body close to her as she fed. When she finished and the dog was drained, she shoved his large body away, discarding him and dusting her fingers off as if they were soiled. "I hate the smell of wet dog. You guys can feed from the other one."

Roman, Saul, and I stood stock still for a moment, watching her as she bent to pick a daisy that had been spattered by the animal's blood. "Beautiful," she said to herself, smiling. And then she tucked it behind her ear, the blood smearing into her pale hair.

Saul and Roman fed from either side of the second dog, who never put up a fight thanks to Porschia's sister. Mercedes' blood high lasted for all of a second before crimson tears streamed down her face. "What's wrong?" I asked, careful not to provoke her.

"I always wanted a dog."

Holy shit. She was terrifying.

FOURTEEN

PORSCHIA

Lydia wasn't alone in the hallway, and even though Pierce helped me by giving me the knife, he wasn't an ally. Three enormous male vampires formed a triangle around their master, two at each side and one in front of her.

Pierce held his hands up in surrender and stepped forward, coming out from behind the bed and standing beside me.

"I need her blood, Pierce," Lydia said confidently. "If you can't provide it, you're of no further use to me."

The vampire trio snarled, smiling.

I shoved Pierce so hard, his body flew into the wall to our left, slicing through the drywall and then crashing onto the ground. Bits of crushed white board thumped to the floor as the hideous wallpaper flapped in the wake of the assault. He groaned from the floor as he tried to pick himself up and failed.

What was that for?

That...saved your life. You're welcome. Next time, I won't bother.

He let out another moan and let his head flop back onto the hardwood floor. *Thank you.*

"If you want something from me, you either ask me nicely or come and get it yourself, Lydia. You don't send people to take from me. Period."

"I'll do as I please. This is *my* house. You're only alive because we want you to be." She tucked herself behind her guard, a false sense of security lulling her into wagging her tongue at me.

Haughty bitch. I did *not* think so.

The first vampire entered the room and I leapt on him, knocking him to the floor and chewing a chunk of flesh from his neck. He started to bleed out. Fast. The second came at me and I tore his head from his body, grabbing his ears and using every ounce of strength in me to throw his weight across the room. His headless form crashed through the window, busting out glass and unleashing the long, sheer curtains into the daylight. They flapped; furling blood-spattered flags announcing my victory.

The last night-walker moved in slowly. He thought to catch me off guard, but I could feel every vibration his foot made on the floor boards, every inhalation and exhalation from his lungs. I could feel the reverberation of his heartbeat and even if I were blind, I would still know exactly where he was in proximity to me.

I ran to him, grabbing his throat and squeezing, lifting him until my forearms screamed with delight and his feet kicked and thrashed, dangling just off the ground. I fed from him, lowering him to me and smiling, holding him to me just to show him he could never overpower me.

And then I tossed his body outside with his friend's. They could float together until they were nothing more than bones, and then until those crumbled into brittle powder. Because we would all become dust again. Death was the only guarantee in life.

It was all over in less than a minute. Lydia's hands eased across the wall behind her as she tried to creep away. "What's wrong, Lydia? You wanted to see what I could do. Do I impress you now? The *hybrid*? You want to be just like me? You want power, right? You want to spill blood?" Blood stuck to my teeth and my stomach began to roil in protest of its contents.

Her hair, laying in soft ringlets against her shoulders, shook violently. "Please," she implored softly.

"Please what?"

Her thinned lips formed the words, "Please don't hurt me."

I walked toward her slowly. "Did the people of The Glen say the same thing to you right before you slaughtered them? Did they beg for a mercy you weren't capable of giving?"

"I'm human now!" she cried.

"But you don't want to be. It's a gift you take for granted. It's not good enough just to have a normal, human life. You want more." I listened for the others. Marta and Elise were listening from another bedroom nearby, probably huddled in a closet or hidden beneath a bed. I heard their pathetic whispers, their murmurings and cries.

"Since I turned, there's been this feeling under my skin," I told her, following her movements down the long hallway.

"What sort of feeling?" Her fingers gripped the walls.

"Sort of like a hum; a current just waiting to break through the surface. And guess what?" I smiled.

"What?" she asked, her eyes darting around me.

"It's free."

I ran to her, pushing her neck against the wall with my forearm. "You want to taste what it's like to be me?"

She shook her head vehemently. "No, n-no."

"Yes you do." My arm crushed her larynx. "You wanted this, remember. Always remember that."

I bit the finger of my free hand and brought it to her lips. "Maybe those who wish to be cursed, should be. Drink it."

She shook her head, clenching her lips tightly closed. "Drink. It!" I screamed into her face, shoving my finger into her mouth and prying her teeth apart. She bit me, but it was too late. My blood was changing her, making her into the monster she wanted to be.

While she screamed and writhed on the opulent carpet, I found the two women she considered to be her sisters. They were crouched in a closet, just as I'd pictured, quivering. The fabric of their dresses was wrinkled and tear-stained.

"What's the matter?" I asked, crouching down. "You wanted this, remember? Let's go see Lydia, shall we?"

I pulled them along with me, up the steps to the landing of the next floor where Lydia was still screaming and clawing at the skin of her neck. The other two tried to look for an escape, but I held tightly to each of their wrists. "It really burns," I said conversationally. "I thought it would hurt, but you can't even *begin* to imagine the pain. It's torture."

They tried to pull away, but I asked, "Which one of you wants to go next?"

Elise screamed for someone to come and help her. However, there was no one but Pierce, and he was still in the room where I'd left him, unless he had climbed out the window.

"Pierce? Do you want to help them?"

He didn't answer. I made a pout in Elise's direction. "I don't think he wants to help," I whispered.

Marta blubbered, "Please, just let us go. We like being human. We don't want that," she said. Her eyes were fixed on Lydia, whose kicks and flails were moving her down the hallway slowly, painfully.

"It's not normal. That's not what happened to us after we turned into vampires."

I smiled, throwing them forward toward Lydia. "But you didn't *want* normal. Normal wasn't good enough for you."

Elise fell to her knees. "Please, just let us go." Marta went quiet and the only sound in the hall was Elise's heavy breaths. "Oh, God," her lips shook. "She's behind me, isn't she?"

Lydia, whose change had been faster than anyone expected, smiled from just over Elise's shoulder; a chilling smile that revealed tiny fangs. Elise moved her head the slightest bit to get a look at her. "Boo," Lydia whispered. Elise wailed, scrambling forward toward me, but it was too late. Lydia was fast and hungry.

She sank her fangs into Elise's shoulder, drawling deeply and groaning from the satisfaction of quenched thirst, of a fire extinguished. Marta backed into me, but I wouldn't let her escape down the steps. "Please!" she shrieked, turning her head to see Lydia drop Elise's corpse carelessly on the ground; her neck folded at an unnatural angle as she stared out from behind a loose curl.

Lydia wasted no time in grabbing Marta and draining her, too. This was going to be difficult. She'd be strong, but Frenzy was overwhelming. Her senses would be in overdrive. I would just have to use them against her.

Marta's fine dress, stained with spurts of blood, fell over Elise's face as Lydia tossed her aside. I was already walking toward her. She let out a growl and jumped toward me. "Stop," I told her, looking directly at her and hoping the compulsion worked on frenzied night-walkers.

She clutched her ears. I'd forgotten about the sensitivity. "Are you still hungry?"

"Yes," she answered, her lips shaking, fists relaxing and then clenching again against her head.

"There's a human in the bedroom I was sleeping in. Pierce."

From down the hall, I heard the door slam and then furniture sliding across the floor behind it, followed by Pierce's shouted curses. Lydia smiled and scampered quickly to the door, barely pushing it. It opened forcefully, shoving everything he'd been sweating to brace it with back along the floor. He was near the window, and that was when I had my chance.

Lydia leaped onto Pierce, gnashing her teeth at his face and throat as he fought in vain to push her away. Moving imperceptibly fast, I caught her by the head as she removed her fangs from his neck. She gasped in surprise. Then I jerked hard.

And Lydia was no more.

The room erupted in a violent burst of crimson.

Pierce, covered in Lydia's blood, wiped his face and eyes, pushing through the sticky fluid to get away from me. But it was too late. "Not so fast, Pierce. I can't trust you not to keep causing problems for me."

Drink.

Gulp.

Drain.

They'd killed one another.

Lydia wanted it.

So did Marta.

Elise did, too.

They Infected Pierce. They fed from him to become human.

The women destroyed The Glen. The people. The elderly. The children. Everything.

The bodies.

The floating bodies.

Corpses.

The scent of fear, of blood, of monsters.

I was a monster.

I killed them all.

Dead.

Death.

Destruction.

That was all I was.

That was all I'd ever be.

I stared down at Pierce. I killed him. Lydia would have killed him.

I stopped him.

My fingers. My muscles. Shaking.

Trembling.

Terrible.

I held them up, watching the blood drip down.

Splatters on the carpet.

I looked to Pierce, a warm, crimson tear falling from my eye. "No. You deserved this," I told him.

His chest didn't rise. His heart wasn't beating. He was gone.

I took a step backward.

I stared out the broken window, stepping over Lydia, over her head and through the crunching broken glass, smeared with her blood. Outside it was late afternoon. The sun shone on the blanched bodies floating below. It shone on the flowers in the field, the daisies and violets. And it shone on the four people running toward The Manor: Tage, Saul, Roman, and my sister. *My sister.*

They can't see me like this.

They will see what I've done.

What I am.

What I'm capable of.

And it will break me.

Or I will break them...

Run.

FIFTEEN

SAUL

RUNNING WAS EFFORTLESS, LIKE BREATHING. IN. OUT. LEFT. RIGHT. BEING a night-walker felt amazing. Roman ran in front of our group. "The Manor is just ahead!" he shouted.

And it was. The flattened land gave way to a small knoll, and on it sat a stone home that was castle-like. The sun burned my eyes, but it didn't dull my sense of smell, and the stench that hit my nose almost knocked me down. I stopped. Cupping my face, I asked, "What *is* that?"

Mercedes was in the same shape. She eased the collar of her shirt over the bottom half of her face, her eyes squinting in the late afternoon sun. Roman wasn't affected by the light at all. Was it because he'd been a night-walker before?

He sniffed the rancid air and gagged. "It's coming from the bridge," he said, pointing ahead of us. Walking forward, we soon found what the scent was. It was rot and decay, but not from the Infected. There were human corpses littering a large ditch that surrounded the main house. The cloudy dark water had a film across its surface, only broken by the insects that skimmed across it. All shades of skin, all walks of life, all ages were made equal in the cruelty of their deaths and in the manner in which they were discarded. Like garbage tossed out of a house, they lay still in the water.

Mercedes' eyes began watering, blood flowing from the corners. "I need to get out of here," she breathed, stumbling across the wooden bridge.

Tage nodded and helped her across. Roman and I ran around them before stopping at the sight of the front door opening. A woman emerged, human and so dirty she didn't smell human at all.

She screamed, "I did what she said! Let me go!"

"What who said?" Roman asked.

"The night-walker who freed me. She said to let the other humans go."

"What humans?" I asked, but the answer to my question came before he could voice the words. Covered with anything they could find: curtains, towels, or pillowcases, people began pouring out from around both sides of the house, running on bare feet. Desperation filled the air.

Men, women, and children; old and young, starved and dirty. Mercedes growled, baring her fangs at them. The women pulled their children close and screamed, backing away from her. Tage held her back from them. "We need to get inside and away from them."

He stared at me. "Are you okay?"

"Yeah." But was I? I didn't feel hunger. A sense of sorrow filled me up. Watching the emaciated try to garner the strength to leave this place was too much. They needed help.

Roman opened the main door as Tage pulled Mercedes along. I followed them into The Manor. While Roman and Tage tried to calm Mercedes, I slipped away, walking up the steps. I could smell her.

Her scent was almost masked by the iron scent of blood, but it was there. She was near. At the landing, I stepped over the bodies of two women wearing enormous dresses. Following the trail of blood leading down the hallway, I found her in a bedroom, soaked in blood. The pale dress she'd worn was soaked through, the hem of it dripping and the droplets splashing the floor and the tops of her bare feet.

When she sensed me, she stilled, her eyes wild. I eased my hands up, palms out. "It's just me."

She began muttering something unintelligible.

"Porschia? It's Saul."

A shrill laugh bubbled up from her stomach. "I'm no better than you now. I killed them all."

She held her stomach, her teeth covered in blood. "I drained one of them and then threw him out with the others," she said, pointing out the window.

"Was he human?"

"No. He was a night-walker."

"What happened to her?" I said, motioning toward the body on the floor, the woman's head torn from her shoulders.

Porschia shook her head. "She wanted to be cursed. And so she was."

"Is that Pierce?" I asked, looking over the woman's prone and bleeding body.

"It is."

"And the two in the hallway?"

"Drained by the cursed one."

She backed toward the window and vomited out, blood pouring from her mouth.

"We met a girl outside. She said you freed her."

She panted, grasping the edge of the stone outside the window. "Did she set them all free?"

"Yes."

She nodded, wiping her mouth with the back of her hand. Her blood-soaked hair hung in wavy, wet strands, dripping onto the earth below her. I eased toward her. "Do you ever wish you had never volunteered for the rotation?" she asked.

"Every damn day."

Sniffing, she turned abruptly. "You've changed."

I closed in. "It's okay. I chose this."

"None of us *chose* this," she argued.

"I did choose this. For you. I wanted to help free you; to save you."

"You always try, Saul, but there's no saving me now." Her eyes searched mine. A sense of foreboding settled deep in my stomach. I changed so that we could save her from those at The Manor, but I had no idea we would need to save Porschia from herself. "I'm a monster," she whispered.

"We're all monsters."

"Some are worse than others."

I couldn't argue with that. Some were worse than others. And some were worse at certain times in their lives, in a heated moment where they made the wrong choice.

"I'm sorry," I whispered to her, reaching out to stroke her hair. "I was wrong. I see that now."

Her short inhalation said more than if she'd spoken for days, but I didn't need words or forgiveness, I just had to speak those words to her. Now she knew. Now, nothing else hung unresolved between us.

"Thank you," she whispered back, staring at my mouth. "Will you turn back now?"

"Soon. I think we should all wait to turn back until we get everyone out there to safety, maybe back to Blackwater."

"We have to stop at Mountainside and offer them the same shelter. Will the new council object?" she asked.

"I don't think so."

She turned to the window, watching the steady flow of human beings stumble away from this cursed place.

Tage burst into the room. "Hey," he said slowly, looking between the two of us. "There was an Infected downstairs. Mercedes elected to change back. If you want to, his blood will still probably work on you."

I shook my head. "No. I'll wait until everyone's safely in the Colony." Namely Porschia. Because as much as she could deny it, she had a wild look in her eyes and I wondered if she was going to run as far away from all of this as she could, the first chance she got.

Tage rushed to her side, whispering to her how he was so scared she would be hurt or worse. I went to look for water and a change of clothes for her before I was sick or decided to take my Frenzy out on Tage. He was an asshole. Roman told me about what he did to Porschia in the city, back when she was in the rotation. He was going to feed from her femoral artery, or so he suggested. Would he have tried something worse? He said Tage knew he was around, but did he? Was he goading Roman or was he going to hurt her? Feed from the vein in her leg? Assault her? The thoughts spun in my head like a top; around and around, teetering and wobbling until they might topple me over.

As much as the plant curbed the intensity of the emotion I was feeling, it was still there. I just had the option of thinking before acting now. And even though I was in Frenzy and even though I could snap, I wouldn't hurt her. I knew that, deep inside me. I would never hurt Porschia on purpose. Tage? I wasn't so sure of that, or of him. And what would he do if she decided he wasn't what she wanted? Would he let her go easily? Or would he tear her apart?

There was something in his eyes that said he would never let her go. I didn't know if he really loved her or if he only loved that he'd won her, that he'd taken her from me. Because as much as Roman thought he would have her, she wanted no part of him. And as much as Tage hated it, she cared about me. She still did.

SIXTEEN

TAGE

Saul was too close to her. I knew what he was doing, apologizing and acting like burning her Mother and the others to death had just been a misunderstanding. Coming to her first while I was busy dealing with Mercedes. Saul swooped in, pretending to be her savior once again.

Porschia shook. With crossed arms, she hugged herself. "It's okay, kitten. You did what you had to do to survive." I saw Pierce lying on the floor, dead. Roman didn't know yet. This was going to send him into a spiral, and I wanted Porschia away from him when it happened.

She took a step back from me. "I killed them all."

"Good. They were doing much worse. You saw the bodies floating out there," I said, ticking my head to the window. "You saw The Glen. You stopped them."

"I feel sick," she said. "I feel so sick."

"Can I hold you?"

She shook her head vehemently. "Don't touch me. I... I don't want anyone to touch me."

"Okay," I stepped back. "I won't. I promise."

Saul stepped back inside with a basin of water, a towel, and a dark green dress that was poufy and not Porschia at all. "It's all I could find. No jeans in any of the closets up here."

She nodded to him. "Thank you."

I eased away toward the door of the bedroom. She needed space to collect her thoughts and wash the remnants of the day away. Time would heal her. Eventually she would see that she managed to survive where others had succumbed. She stopped something so evil that the stink of it might never leave this place. But for now, she had to make peace with herself. She wouldn't be able to do that with me or Saul in her face.

I nodded toward the bodies lying in the hallway. "We can clean this mess while she cleans herself up."

Saul hesitated, looking back toward her with his hands in his pockets. "Sure."

We each carried one corpse outside and tossed the shrews into the moat with all of their victims. It was poetic justice; their stories had come full circle, much like the cycle of life itself. Predators preyed on the weak. They lived well until something stronger came along and ended them. Life. Vitality. Weakening. Death.

When we were finished, Saul stayed inside with Mercedes, who was in the process of changing back into a human. Her fangs were already gone and shivers continued to shake her body. She lay on the couch beneath blankets that Roman brought down from the bedrooms above.

I ran to Porschia's room to find the door locked. Tapping my knuckles against the door, I sniffed the air. Her scent was there. Lavender soap, blood, and fresh water. Hay and daisies from the fields below.

"Porschia?"

There was no answer.

I knocked again but still heard nothing. It took a fraction of a second to break the door in and half of that again to realize that she wasn't in the room. Running to the window, I saw her on the ground below, crouching low in the tall grass, but looking up at me. "No," I whispered. "Kitten, don't run."

As a bloody tear tracked a path on each cheek, she sniffed and shook her head. "I just need to get away from all of this; the smell and sounds. The almost-dead people we just freed. I'm not strong enough right now."

"Let me come with you," I yelled.

She shook her head. "No, I need to be alone. Just for a little while. I'll meet you at Mountainside. I promise."

Everything inside me screamed to stop her, to hold her close and never let her go, but if I did that, if I caged her, I knew I would lose her for good. "Okay," I said. "I'll meet you there as soon as I can. Go ahead. Let them know Blackwater will take them in."

She nodded. "I can do that."

It was a start. She was crumbling, but she still might find a new purpose in helping the residents of Mountainside find a new safe haven in the Colony of Blackwater.

PORSCHIA

My skin was finally clean. Using the tepid water, I rinsed the ends of my hair until the water was pink, tinged with Lydia's blood. The dark green dress was ridiculous, something a princess or queen would wear. Thick material billowed from the corseted waist and way too much chest showed for me to be comfortable. Making my way over the bridge and away from the trail of fleeing humans, I headed toward the only place I knew I would feel at home, toward the woods, tearing at my skirt to make it shorter and easier to travel in. I decided to take a different trail than those of the fleeing people. If they saw a female vampire in a dress like *they* wore—in one of their dresses, no less—it would terrify them. And that was what I was; no better than the monsters I killed. Terrifying. The thing that nightmares were made of.

Human nightmares.

Because night-walkers and Infected didn't dream.

They didn't rest.

They couldn't find peace.

And neither could I.

But I also felt a duty to these people. They were my neighbors. I would listen and watch from a distance, making sure they made it to The Glen and that those who chose to move on to Mountainside would make it there safely as well. All the way to Blackwater, I would protect them.

Hay-filled hills gave way to saplings, saplings to trees, and trees to the thick underbrush filling in the forest floor with each passing rain. Disturbing a mouse, he ran for a hollowed log.

I walked slowly, at the speed they travelled. I listened to them talk about what had happened, how frightened they'd been, and how the first girl I freed told them it was all over and to leave this place and never return. She told them that Mountainside would take them in until they all moved to Blackwater, a haven safe enough and big enough for them all.

Reflecting on the control of the Elders I could now see that they did wrong by keeping us sheltered, but we had it better than others. I never realized there were people out there like the three women I'd just witnessed. Geographically, we were so close that even Blackwater wouldn't have been safe from their wrath if they needed to extend their reach to find further victims.

After passing through several hills and valleys I came to an abrupt stop, much like the trail of rusted metal shells stretching east and west as far as the eye could see. Nature was showing her power through it all. Cars, trucks, vans, and enormous vehicles pulling towering boxes behind them. Three rows in opposite directions. Every vehicle bumper to bumper with only weeds and saplings separating them now. It was a sea of desperation. I stepped closer toward the closest car. Four doors, no windows, and two skeletons picked over inside, the bones strewn over the seats, floor and console, even spilling into the back.

The other cars would likely be filled with the same. Mother said that when the virus hit, people tried to flee the great city beyond Blackwater to outrun the disease, but it was already too late for most of them. Most of them didn't make it fifty miles.

I stepped back from the car and moved back up the hill into the trees. I smelled him before I saw him. "Roman."

"Tage is a mess," he started. "You just left him back there."

He still didn't know about Pierce. What had they told him?

"I'm fine." The heart beneath the millstone on my chest shouted that I was a liar. Did the same show on my face?

"You're not, but for the record, you didn't do anything wrong, Porschia. You need to accept this or you'll never find peace." He didn't know yet.

"Was acceptance instantaneous for you? Did you immediately fall in love with being in Frenzy, or being a night-walking creature that fed on your friends and family? Or did it take a while to sink in?"

He sighed, leaning back against a tree trunk and scrubbing his face with his hands. "It took years."

"Then expect it to take me years, too. Allow me the same time to adjust."

He nodded, looking down at me. "I have a feeling you won't have the same luxury of time."

I had the same feeling. Something big was going to happen. For years, I had no idea of what was going on around me. I lived in a bubble of fear, trying to avoid Mother's hatred and sequestering myself from everyone in the Colony. I didn't see the experimentation, the way the Elders truly ruled, or the way the night-walkers interacted with one another and with others in the Colony. I did what I was told. A lamb among lambs, surrounded by wolves. But there were larger predators than wolves to worry about and no one realized that beyond the forests and settlements beyond, there was a strange wind blowing. Dust was being stirred and I could feel the tiny stinging particles beginning to pepper my skin.

"Where is Tage, Saul, and my sister?"

"Mercedes is walking with the other humans, toward the end of the trail. Saul is across the mountain from us watching from that direction, and Tage is running toward the front to make sure we cover all angles."

"That's good." *Mercedes must be miserable.* I'd seen how weak Roman felt when he changed, how he got sick almost immediately, how he almost died. I didn't want that for her. We had to get her back to Blackwater quickly.

Descending into a valley, there was a strange metal structure with poles holding it up and a building beyond. Roman smiled, offering, "Gas station. It's how they fueled the cars."

Lettering on the building's small sign had faded away to nothing, but I couldn't help but stare at the vines and weeds and wonder what it must have been like to live during the time it was in use, to drive in one of the cars—maybe the sleek one in our backyard for which I was named—to blaze down the highway when it wasn't filled with rust and trees and bone.

"I know you're in pain, because of your brother."

Roman sucked in a sharp breath. Some wounds were sharper than others. "The women drained him. There were bite marks and bruises all over him."

I pursed my lips, holding back my confession.

He paced back and forth; looking to me and then back at the hill before us. Roman sat down hard on the ground and cried. His shoulders shook and the sound of heartbreak and anguish poured from his mouth. When the torrent cleared, he looked up at me, tracks of blood trailing down his face. "You know what I miss the most? I miss the good part of him. Something changed him. I don't know if it was the Infection or the way desperation twisted his mind, but he wasn't the same brother he was when we were young." He gave a sad smile. "Though I guess I'm not exactly that brother, either. It's the same with you and Mercedes. You each made decisions and chose your actions, and maybe you wouldn't have done what she did to survive or maybe you would have. Maybe she wouldn't have done what you just did back there. Maybe she would have. It's just that life throws things at you so fast that you have to decide how to deal with them in the blink of an eye, and sometimes we choose right and sometimes we choose the wrong way of handling a thing. But it's a split second decision; more instinct than deliberation, and those choices, those split second choices can completely alter our lives forever."

"And the lives of everyone around us," I finished for him.

He cleared his throat. "Do you regret killing those women? The slaves that did their bidding?"

"I do." Lying was almost second-nature to me now. I didn't regret killing Lydia, Marta, Elise or the monsters who worked for them. But I regretted killing Pierce. In the moment, I thought it wouldn't matter to me. Did Pierce deserve to live? Maybe not. But what right did I have to condemn him?

While it was true that I was sorry for hurting Roman, I wasn't sad that Pierce's warped mind couldn't hurt someone else. Just like I wasn't sorry that those evil women had gotten their comeuppance. I was just sorry to have hurt someone in the process. And I understood now more than ever that sometimes split-second decisions regarding good and evil, life and death, are necessary—even when they hurt someone you care about.

Roman told me he needed space so I walked away, leaving him to his thoughts.

SEVENTEEN

TAGE

The walk must have been exactly what she needed, because when she finally arrived, the last to enter the gates of the abandoned settlement, Porschia seemed and looked like a weight had been lifted from her shoulders. We stayed at the homes in The Glen overnight, Roman and I repairing and then guarding the wall to make sure all felt safe to sleep within it. He was quieter than normal, working and not talking. The loss of his brother hung heavily on his face.

The next morning, we yelled out to the gathered assembly that we would need to leave early since Mountainside was a farther walk. Most gathered just inside the fence a half hour later. A few people decided to stay at The Glen, against our advice, but we couldn't force anyone to do something they didn't want to do.

Porschia came out of one of the homes wearing jeans and a deep blue tank top that made her look like someone I'd follow to the edges of the earth, powerful and fierce. She crossed yards and streets and carved a path through the people waiting in front of the gate, lifting the bar easily and opening it for them. "We will protect you. Until you get to Blackwater we will keep you safe, but you have to stay together and listen to us. We mean you no harm and no harm will come to you in the Colony."

The people who had been so frightened and still after their ordeal in the cages at The Manor began to clap. They thanked her for what she'd done. The freed woman told them when they were released, and Roman explained it again last night. He told them that Porschia ended the women who made them blood slaves, that she was the only reason they were being released, and to follow her until she asked them not to. Then he told them to begin walking, and that she would follow and make sure all was well.

They didn't fear her like she thought they would. I saw the surprise in her face when she realized this, the way her brows lifted and she blinked, startled for such a reception. She didn't revel in it like most men would, just waved them out of the fence and pointed in the direction they should travel.

We followed them, flanking each side with Mercedes among the people, all the way to Mountainside. Most had found shoes and better clothing in The Glen so the walk, though longer, wasn't as difficult on them.

I squeezed her hand as I took off toward the front of those walking. She returned the squeeze with a smile and I could see that this wasn't going to break her. I didn't know if anything truly could at this point. She had survived more in a few short months than any one of us had in as many years.

It was dusk when Mercedes, the last of the humans, walked into Mountainside where they were all welcomed and invited into their homes. They made space when there was little of that left. Garreth met Porschia at the gate. She didn't have to compel him to open the doors.

We were going to try to hunt. The people needed food and I could see it in the strain of her forehead that Porschia needed meat, blood, and rest. Scuffing my boot on the rocky path, I waited for her just inside the woods beyond the stone wall. It didn't take her long.

She'd changed into one of the dresses she brought with her, one of Maggie's. A soft yellow, it looked too delicate and feminine for what lay ahead of us. The crunching of boots from behind her drew my attention away from the dark hair spilling over her shoulders.

Saul cracked his knuckles arrogantly, wearing a big grin I'd love to knock off his face. "Are we hunting alone or in groups?"

Roman answered from behind him. "Two groups of two?"

"Or one in each direction," Porschia offered, refusing to look up at me. "I'd like to hunt alone."

What the hell was going on?

I shoved my hands in my pockets and nodded. "Either way, we're going to have to run far to find anything at all, let alone enough to feed all of the people in Mountainside."

"True," Saul agreed.

"How's Mercedes?" I whispered to Porschia.

"Doing a little better this evening. I think she's just tired at this point. She's resting."

I nodded.

Roman clapped and talked loudly. "Let's hunt alone, then. Nothing's too small. Every bite will count."

Porschia offered a small smile and she tilted her head toward the south. She was gone in an instant, her scent lingering in the gentle breeze of her wake. Saul took off to the east and Roman clapped me on the back before heading north. With the shortest straw, I took the west.

PORSCHIA

It was selfish of me, but I ate the first thing I could find; a gray squirrel that was well fed despite the famine plaguing the area. Without his meat, I wouldn't have lasted the evening. I could feel my strength waning with each stride forward, but I had to find something to bring back.

Five squirrels, a feisty raccoon, and a fox were all I could come up with. I gathered as many edible mushrooms as I could find, as well as clovers and dandelion. They weren't the tastiest things in the forest, but they could help stave off the hunger until we could get to Blackwater. Someone would need to run ahead and ask the Colony to prepare for the people's arrival.

Hunting should be better closer to home, too.

I couldn't believe how different everything was. We weren't even that far away from home, yet the rotation had always provided a steady source of meat, at least one or two animals each night, even if they were small. Had the hunts provided much more in the past?

A branch snapped on the hill above me. I looked up, and in the darkness saw her holding tightly to the trunk of a Sycamore tree. The sound of her fingernails digging into the bark grated at my ears. Her deep red hair hung silky straight as she looked around the tree trunk at me. She was trembling. Sniffing the air, I could tell she was human, her heart thrumming through her neck, and for a split second I imagined feeding from her.

"What are you doing in the forest?" I yelled.

"Help me," she whispered, her voice hoarse and raw. "I've been trying to keep up but I got left behind at The Manor. My ankle is... I don't know if it's broken or just injured, but I can barely walk at this point."

"You were at The Manor?"

"Yes. A girl came to let us out of the awful cage they had us in and told us to follow a female night-walker toward The Glen. After what we'd seen at that place... everyone was afraid. We preferred staying in the cage to trusting them. In the panic to get away from the cage's door, my ankle twisted. It wasn't long before humans from another cage came to get us and reassure us that we were being set free and that no one would be harmed." Her voice broke, but after a moment, she continued. "I made it to The Glen and spent the night in one of the homes, but I decided to walk to Mountainside on my own. I didn't want to slow anyone down. I kept up for a long time, but then my ankle bent again and I couldn't keep pace with the others. It may be broken. It hurts so badly."

A silvery tear fell from first one and then the other eye. Her eyes were the strangest color of pale green, the color of lichen on a tree.

Why didn't Mercedes say anything? Mercedes was at the end of the trail of people. Maybe she didn't notice her. She had just changed, after all, and her mind was on other things.

I walked slowly toward her. The girl was younger than me, probably closer in age to Ford, with a face streaked with sweat and mud. "Will you help me get to Mountainside?"

"Where is your family?" I asked softly.

She blinked more tears, looking up at the sky or canopy above, I wasn't sure. "Floating in the sickening river surrounding The Manor. My mother, father, and sister. There's no one else left. I'm all alone now."

More tears. She tried to limp away as I stepped forward, wincing and crying out with a shrill scream, "Don't hurt me!"

"I won't. I'll help you, but you'll have to carry a few things."

She nodded. "I can carry them." She nodded toward the animals I'd killed and the edibles I harvested. She was wearing what looked like the remnant of a table cloth or curtain, knotted at the sides and as dirty as she was. "I fell a lot. The mud is pretty unforgiving."

"We've all fallen, but at least you chose to get up. What's your name?"

The girl took hold of my things, clutching them tightly as I picked her up. "Delilah."

"Let's get you to Mountainside, Delilah. I'm Porschia."

Her eyes widened along with her mouth. "You're the one."

"I'm a night-walker."

"You're a *good* night-walker. You set us free."

"I did, but there are no *good* night-walkers. There are no good humans, either. I don't trust you, and you'd be wise not to trust me either."

She pursed her lips, gulping silently. "Fair enough."

Something about her bothered me. I didn't know if it was her story or her tears, but I could see that she was in pain, both physically and emotionally. That part seemed true.

I should have felt empathy. She was hurt, alone in the forest, and her family had been killed, but something felt 'off' and I'd felt that same nagging feeling in the pit of my stomach before.

Above almost everyone I knew, I trusted Maggie – and Maggie always said to trust my gut instinct. My gut said that Delilah was bad.

EIGHTEEN

FORD

TWO SHARP KNOCKS AT THE DOOR IN THE MIDDLE OF THE NIGHT STARTLED me awake, although Father was still snoring loudly from his room. I grabbed my candle holder, used a match to light the wick, and jogged down the stairs while cupping the flame with my hand so it didn't blow out. When I opened the door Roman was standing there, looking like he was well again. Until I realized *why* he looked so well. Two pointed fangs appeared when he smiled.

"Where are my sisters and why are you a vampire?"

"They're fine. They're in Mountainside and will be here in the next day or so. I came early. We have a situation and I need your father's help. Yours too."

"What kind of help?"

"Wake him up. I'll wait in the kitchen."

I walked up the stairs, hearing him slide into a seat. "Make yourself at home, Roman," I grumbled.

"Don't mind if I do," he shouted. Night-walkers. They didn't need sleep, but we still did. I preferred Roman back when he was human and sick. He wasn't as cocky.

Dad woke with a start. His immediate reaction was to ask, "What's wrong?"

"We have a guest."

"Who is it?" he asked, throwing back the covers and reaching for his candle.

"I have my candle, just follow me. And it's Roman."

"Where are the girls? Are they okay? They haven't been gone long."

Before he could spew more questions, I held my hand out. "Let's just talk to Roman together."

He followed me down the stairs, his own steps stiff. I could tell he wanted to go faster, but his body was holding him back. Father was getting more and more tired each day. I'd seen a huge change in him in the past few weeks. Luckily the girls hadn't noticed yet.

Roman tapped his fingers impatiently on the table top. "Nice to see you, Mr. Grant."

Father growled, surprising us both. "Why are you in my house? Why are you a vampire? And where the hell are Mercedes and Porschia?" The candlelight illuminated the tension between the two men.

"I'll tell you everything. Just sit down and calm yourself. Your daughters are fine. Porschia asked me to come ahead. She needs the council's help."

"For what?"

"For the refugees."

Roman spelled it all out. How the people of Mountainside had been so afraid of Porschia, and how there were no night-walkers in their settlement, even though in the past vampires and humans in Mountainside had co-depended on one another, much like those in Blackwater. He told us what Porschia said about the emptiness of The Glen and how she was taken to The Manor by a female night-walker. How Tage had come to get him, Saul, and Mercedes, and then changed them in order to free her.

Roman raked his hands through his dark hair. "We didn't realize that she didn't need saving from those women. She needed saving from herself."

"What did she do?" Father asked tentatively, leaning his forearms on the scarred wood.

"She gave them what they wanted, and then she ended them."

Father's sharp inhalation echoed across the room. "She isn't cut out for this life. Mercedes maybe would be, but not Porschia."

"Mercedes was the first to volunteer to turn back into a human, but

Saul and I decided to stay night-walkers until all are here and safe, maybe longer to ensure their safety. Don't ever think that Mercedes is the stronger of your offspring." His eyes flicked to me. "No offense, Ford."

"None taken." And it wasn't. Mercedes wasn't a bad sister or person, but I wouldn't necessarily describe her as being strong in her own right. In a crowd, she would follow. She went with the flow, afraid to face the current in case it was too hard or swift. Porschia was always the stronger one. I knew it and deep down, so did Father.

"Now the refugees have made it safely to Mountainside, but the resources—namely food—in the forest have been depleted or driven away. The people will starve without Blackwater's help," Roman explained, leaning his chair onto the back legs. The wood strained while balancing his weight.

"How many people are we talking about?" Father asked.

"Eighty-seven."

Father leaned his head into his hands. "Where will we put them all? We have some houses open, but enough for so many?"

"The city," I offered. "There are still some who will choose to live there, and it can be easily defended."

"It may be the only option," Father muttered.

"We can help defend the city *and* the Colony," Roman added. "Now that there's a cure for both plagues, we can rest assured that—"

Father stopped him with a bang of his fist on the wooden table. "Don't think that just because a cure exists, there will be rainbows and unicorns, Roman. You of all people should know the truth of it after this week. It's foolish to think this is all over with. Most of the world still doesn't know about the cures."

The front chair legs of Roman's seat fell on the floor with a thud. "I know that, and I'm no fool."

I was too tired to mind my own mouth. "How are you even here? If you just changed back, aren't you in Frenzy?"

"Turns out that the same flower that caused Porschia so many problems was a simple solution to controlling a night-walker in Frenzy. It calms the...cravings and emotions."

Father's mouth gaped open. "You're kidding?"

"Nope. So," Roman said, slapping the table and standing up. "Think about what we should say to the council. I'll meet you back here just before dawn."

"Why didn't you just show up at dawn?" I grumbled as Father saw him out, making sure to lock the door, even though that tiny sliver of metal wouldn't stop Roman from busting in if he was motivated enough to breach it.

It wasn't possible to rest knowing what work needed to be done, so after an hour of tossing and turning, I finally got up and went outside. Father was already sitting on the porch waiting for me. "We have a lot of work to do," he said. "Not just in making room for those who seek shelter, but in feeding them as well. Did you show Brian your trap?"

"I did yesterday. He seemed impressed, but one trap won't be enough."

"The extra meat will help. Can you make more? Maybe teach some of your friends to build them, too?"

"I can." Not that there were a lot of friends around, but I could find a few to help me. Rats weren't the tastiest creatures in the world, but they were meat and we needed more than we had now. We'd need a lot more in the coming days, and if what Roman said about the animals being scarce so close to home was true, it may be our only option. Feeling the weight of the moment with unspoken words, I scuffed my boot on the wooden planks, feeling the rubber tread grab hold of the grain.

"Say it," Father instructed gently.

"I'm worried about all of this."

"Me too, son." That said, I sat next to him and silently watched the sky as it began to lighten, waiting for Roman. The night-walker was punctual, I'd give him that, but I still didn't trust him very far. I wanted to see my sisters with my own eyes. Until I did, I wouldn't rest at all. Neither would Father.

I wasn't privy to the conversation with the council, sitting outside of Town Hall as the men and women spoke. But in the end, Father emerged with a heavy smile and nodded his head once. They would allow the citizens of Mountainside to seek shelter in Blackwater where there was room, or in the city if there wasn't.

Life was a constant changing thing, and we just struggled to hold on as best we could lest it sweep us away. The moment Roman stepped out of Town Hall behind Father, I felt my fingers trembling, threatening to give up. But if I ever wanted to be as strong as Porschia, I knew I would have to dig in and man up. So I grabbed the night-walker's sleeve.

"Can you take me to my sisters?"

His face was blank as he considered my question. "What does your father say?"

"I haven't asked him."

"Well, go ask him. Let him know I'll take you there myself. Porschia wants to take things in waves; harvesting the plants they have in Mountainside so we can replant them here. Some of the frailest will need to recover for a few days before traveling again, and some of the strongest will have to stay and help work. She also said we'll need horses and the wagon."

"She may have asked for it, but the council won't give up the wagon."

Roman smiled. "She isn't asking them to give it up, she's asking to borrow it. And they *did* consent."

"Did you have to work your mind-mojo on them?"

He smiled and ruffled my hair like I was some kid. "Absolutely."

NINETEEN

PORSCHIA

THE SURVIVORS DIDN'T FEAR ME, AND THAT BOTHERED ME WORSE THAN anything. They should never let their guard down. They should never feel that a night-walker, an Infected, or even another human was one-hundred percent good. Evil was evil. It lived and breathed in men and the creatures that used to be men.

I worked alongside them, digging up the tender crops they'd planted, wrapping the roots gently with torn cloth, and tying them with twine. They were quiet, talking to their neighbors, their children, stealing glances at me occasionally. But I didn't talk and they didn't try to converse with me. It was better this way. The distance between us all was comfortable to me.

Tage kneeled to my left and Saul to my right. Like always, I was stuck in the middle of them, on the rope they pulled between them. And much like a rope, my nerves were fraying by the second. Roman would have already made it to Blackwater by now. He would have seen Father and asked for help. Did the council grant it? Would they provide the shelter that we had already promised? It was midday and there had been no word from Roman for three days. Did he make it at all?

I sat back on my heels and laid another cabbage plant in a small box we found after rifling around in our hole in the ground. Anything and everything would be used. Pans, bowls, boxes, and pitchers. Everything that would be useful was brought out in preparation for the move – a move I hoped was still taking place.

"He'll come," Tage said quietly. He'd given me much needed space over the past few days. It wasn't that I needed it from him, I just needed it for me. Maybe it was selfish or mean, and though I didn't intend for it to be either, it was necessary.

"I know. I just wonder what's taking so long."

Saul chuckled beneath his breath. "What's so funny?" I asked.

"Nothing at all...." he paused. "Patience, grasshopper."

"Ha. Ha. Very funny."

The simple exchange sparked Tage's anger and I watched as he stalked away, too aggravated to chase after him. Saul offered the metaphorical olive branch. "Sorry."

"Don't be," I growled, going back to the task at hand. "It was a simple joke."

"Among friends?" he asked hopefully.

"Exactly." Saul and I could be friends. We were friends before this whole mess started.

"Well that's what's wrong. Tage doesn't want you and me to be anything but enemies."

"Well, he'll have to get over it." I looked over at Saul, mud streaked across his face and caked on the tips of his fingers. "Won't he?"

He smiled slightly. "I hope so. I want to be friends again. If you'll let me in."

It was a slippery slope, but one I was willing to slide across. "Friends, then?"

"Definitely," he said, unearthing more plants. I couldn't deny that my heart leaped at the sight of his smile. His fangs were like him, long and lithe and... I stared at the ground. No wonder Tage was angry.

He could feel everything I did. I didn't want Saul as a husband or anything else, but I was still attracted to him. I couldn't imagine how it would be for me to feel Tage have a response to another girl.

Chat time was over. Time to ignore my friend and work.

TAGE

. . .

PORSCHIA WAS GOING TO BE THE DEATH OF ME. SAUL WANTED HER BACK; everyone knew it. But feeling her response, her reciprocal attraction to him? It was going to kill me. I couldn't watch them get back together. I wouldn't.

Maybe it was shallow and maybe it was immature, but I decided to walk away instead of witnessing their heated exchange. When I passed by the gate, I heard a far-off but very welcome sound: the clopping of hoofs and nickering of horses. The cavalry had come. Roman knocked into my shoulder. "Sorry I'm late."

"Who is that with you?"

"Ford Grant."

I groaned, throwing my head up at the sky. "Porschia's going to come undone."

"Porschia should put her big girl panties on and deal with it. He wanted to see her. For some reason, he just doesn't think I'm trustworthy."

"Hmm. I wonder why that is," I deadpanned.

"Like you're any better." He had me there. Roman scanned over the people, his eyes landing on Porschia, who narrowed her eyes at him. "Trouble in paradise?"

"A thorn in my side," I answered gruffly.

He chuckled. "Drain him and get it over with." I growled, watching Saul reach for Porschia's hand. She didn't take it. Good girl. "No one would have to know. You know you want to," Roman goaded.

I *did* want to, and that was the problem. If I drained Saul and ended him altogether, Porschia would hate me. She might even kill me for it.

"It's just because she's working this all out in her head, man. Give it time. She likes you." Roman was being nice and sincere, and my first thought was that he wanted something. He just hadn't asked for it yet. I should have counted it down. Three, two, one... "So, can you let Porschia know that her baby brother is here?"

"I'll tell her, but you'll deal with her as soon as I do, so get ready."

Walking quickly back to kitten, I crouched low, waiting for her eyes to meet with mine. When they did and the puzzled look scrunched her brows together, I told her, "Roman's back. And before you smell him, you should know that Ford is with him."

Her eyes widened for a second before she was gone.

TWENTY

PORSCHIA

I RAN TO ROMAN, KNOCKING HIM TO THE GROUND AND STANDING OVER HIM as he gasped for breath, clutching his chest. "What the hell? My brother should be safe back at the Colony! Not here in the forest!"

The pounding of hooves on gravel and movement from behind me caught my attention as Ford guided the horses and hay wagon into the gate. He smiled and waved, but his hand withered downward when he saw the look on my face.

Roman jumped up, rubbing his pectoral muscle like I'd permanently injured him. "What was *that* for? I was just helping."

"Helping? If this is your version of *helping*, Roman, I'd hate to see you try to *hinder* something."

Roman's dark eyes narrowed. "Yes, you would," he warned. "He wanted to see you and Mercedes, and help the people who are coming. I needed a human to guide the horses. I kept him safe," he enunciated.

"And put him at risk in the process," I countered.

"Agree to disagree." He snorted derisively. "He's not a little boy anymore, Porschia. Look at your brother. If your father would allow it and it was still ongoing, he could enter the rotation. He's not a child."

"He may not be a child, but he is still my baby brother. If anything happens to him, I will hold you personally accountable. Do you understand what I'm saying?"

Roman stared at me in disbelief, but he'd better believe it. If a single hair on Ford's head was harmed during this escapade, I would scalp Roman for it. And then he ended the stare-off in typical Roman fashion.

"I'm not sure what you mean by 'accountable', Porschia. You helped kill my brother, so what else could you possibly do to me other than kill me?" He fumed, and then composed himself with a smirk. "And for the record, you're really hot when you're mad. I can see why Saul and Tage are still fighting over you."

I smoothed my dress. "They aren't fighting."

"Not out loud, but they will. This isn't going to end well. Surely even you can see that coming from a mile away. Can you smell the blood yet? I wonder whose will be spilt over Porschia Grant?"

"Nobody's." I would see to it. If there was friction between the men, they would need to resolve it. I was with Tage. I was friends with Saul. Period.

"You can't blame him for being angry."

"Tage?"

He smiled. "Either of them, really. Tage has every right to be angry that you're forgiving Saul and letting him back in. Saul loves you, so Saul has every right to be angry that Tage made a move when he was off rotting in the city. No surprise that there's bad blood between them."

Roman's fangs scraped his bottom lip as he looked over my shoulder at the progression of refugees. "Who is *that*?" I'd forgotten that vampire Roman was horny Roman. Looking over my shoulder, I saw Delilah approaching, wearing a gray tank top and jeans that were a size too large for her small frame. Her flaming hair waved behind her in the wind, a flag of warning and fire.

"That," I said, clapping Roman on the shoulder, "is Delilah."

"Delilah?" he mused.

"Yeah. Better keep sharp objects away from her."

His lips made a pout. "I don't think I'm the one she's interested in."

I turned to see Delilah petting the horses and talking with Ford. My hackles, every single hair on the back of my neck and back, stood at attention. A low growl rolled through the hollow of my chest.

Roman's arm stopped me from moving.

"Easy. She's just saying hi and petting the animals. And why do you care what Ford does?"

"Because I don't trust that girl."

"Didn't you find her? Bring her here?" Roman and I watched as she combed her dark hair back from her face, draping it over her right shoulder and chest. On her neck was a tattoo.

"What is that?" I asked myself.

"A serpent climbing a tree or... something," Roman said, squinting. "It's intricate. The details are surprisingly clear, but she seems awfully young to have gotten a tattoo before all the world went to hell..."

"You don't trust her either?" I asked hopefully.

He shook his head. "I'm not nearly as mistrusting as you, Porschia. I like to see the good in everyone, in every situation: rainbows and hearts and..."

"Shut up, Roman."

He just laughed. Asshole.

FORD

Holy shit. Porschia looked like she was going to kill me, or Roman, or both. She was talking to him and he was rubbing his chest. She probably hit him. Being a night-walker made her mean. Or maybe it was the Infection in her. Something sure did. Porsch wasn't mean growing up, but she had teeth now. Literally and figuratively.

A small hand stroked the mane of the stallion I was driving. He was usually a stubborn bastard, but something had him under a spell. My eyes followed the line of the arm to the most beautiful face I'd ever seen, freckled skin and hair as dark as red as a rose. Her eyes were big and brown and her lips were pink and full. "Hey," I said. It was basic but all I could get to come out.

She peered up at me from beneath her dark lashes. "Hi."

I watched her with the horse. She was comforting him, or he was comforting her. I wasn't sure which.

"He's a beautiful animal."

"Thank you. His name is Boots," I offered, pointing at the stallion's white feet, a stark contrast against the black that covered the rest of him. I climbed down from the wagon, my eyes flitting between my pissed-off sister and the girl standing in front of me, more often sticking on her.

"I'm Ford," I said, extending a hand. She looked at it for a second and I thought she wasn't going to shake it, but then she slipped her hand into mine and all the breath in me left, or maybe my lungs forgot to work.

"My name is Delilah." Her voice was husky and as warm as her skin.

"It's nice to meet you," I said, finally letting her go.

"I can take him, if you want," she offered.

She brushed her hair from her shoulders. "Yeah. That would be great," I answered. "He needs water and grass, and a shady place to rest."

Unhitching him, I watched her take his reins and lead him away. Lucky horse.

My sister was beside me in a minute. "What did she want?"

"To help with the horse."

Porschia narrowed her eyes, watching Delilah lead Boots toward the well. "She sure recovered fast," she muttered.

"What's that?"

"Nothing. Just be careful around her."

"She's human, Porschia."

"I know."

"Then why should I worry about a tiny girl who's my age?"

"She's manipulative."

"And you know this how?" I crossed my arms, waiting for more paranoia to spew from my sister's mouth.

"I brought her here with a broken foot. It's healed nicely in the few days since."

"Maybe it wasn't broken? Maybe it was just sprained."

"You and I both know that even a sprain doesn't heal in a day or two, Ford. Don't be stupid over a pretty face."

I scoffed. "Oh, but it's okay for you to lead Tage and Saul around like dogs with their tongues hanging out after you?"

"I don't," she growled.

"You don't lead? Well, they sure follow. Both are watching and probably listening to my every word," I said, realizing that the brother card would only take me so far with those two. Saul chewed something as he continued cultivating the plants, but he stared at me angrily. Roman laughed. Tage was around here somewhere. I searched the area. "Where's Tage, anyway?"

Porschia swallowed. "I don't know."

TWENTY-ONE

PORSCHIA

Ford and Roman set off that afternoon with a wagon full of people, carrying baskets and containers of harvested plants on their laps. Some strapped containers to their backs as well. Roman would guard from a distance so the horses wouldn't spook, and before he left I thanked him for watching over my brother. Fortunately we were able to take Lady home. The people of Mountainside hadn't eaten her as threatened.

Roman's eyes became sad. "It's the least I can do," he answered. I knew he missed Pierce. There was just nothing I could do or say to take that ache away. When someone you loved died, they took a piece of you with them, a piece you couldn't get back. But it didn't matter, because you'd gladly give them any part of you, the best parts, just so they could keep you with them always.

I'd started to tell him a hundred times, but couldn't get the words off my tongue... I killed his brother. Eventually he would find out, and when he did, he would kill me or die trying. Roman was loyal to Pierce in a way that I understood all too well.

Tage had been distant, mostly avoiding me and it was my fault. Part of me ached because he did. I wondered if the bond was mutual now, that maybe I felt his emotions as much as he felt mine.

Ford would be back tomorrow for more people. We would keep gathering the plants and shuttling people to Blackwater until no one remained. But in the back of my mind, I wondered about Saul. What would happen to him? Would the council reconsider his banishment? Could they show mercy when the wounds were still so tender and swollen?

If they wouldn't let him stay, would he live in the forest, always on the outskirts? Would he leave?

That was probably what I would do. Why stay where you weren't wanted?

I walked toward the well. We needed water to keep the roots and soil around the plants moist. "Penny for your thoughts?" Saul said, falling into stride beside me.

"I was just thinking about how everything is about to change."

"It always does. Change is the only thing life guarantees."

It was so true. "What about you?" I said, giving voice to my inner fears.

He rubbed the back of his head. "I guess I'll make sure everyone gets to Blackwater safely. After that, I might drink some Infected blood and become human again. Funny how that sounds," he said, nudging my arm. "How simple the solution was."

"Yeah, but what then, Saul? What if you can't live in Blackwater?"

He shrugged. "Then I'll find somewhere else; somewhere there aren't freakish women who trap humans for food and throw their bodies in moats around their houses."

"If you're human, you'll be vulnerable."

He smiled, glancing my way. "We're all vulnerable. Even night-walkers can be killed. Even you, a hybrid, can be taken down by a simple plant toxin. We lie to ourselves, telling ourselves that we're stronger than everything else out there, but we aren't. It's an illusion. Control. Power. Strength. It's fleeting. All of it."

"Why don't you stay a night-walker if you leave? You'll be better able to protect yourself."

He slowed his steps. "I've thought of that, but I don't know."

"Just until you're safe," I urged.

"Maybe."

My legs began to quiver as I lowered the bucket down into the dark water, black and glassy and reflecting the light sky above me and the crows that flew overhead.

"Are you okay?" Saul asked, grabbing the rope from my hands.

"Yeah. I just need to feed."

"I can look for meat," he offered.

It wasn't meat that I needed. Not now. My body needed human blood, but thus far, I'd made it days without it. I didn't want to scare any of the people here. They had been through too much lately.

"Oh, I get it," he said. "Ford will be here soon."

I hated feeding from my brother, and he would need his strength to keep driving the horses back and forth. It wasn't a crazy long journey, but made often, it would seem like it after several days.

"Stop overthinking it. Either feed from him or ask someone else for help. You can't push it too far. You'll snap."

"You're handling Frenzy well."

"Am I?" he asked, pulling more leaves from his pocket and placing them on his tongue. "I feel like all I do is chew this stuff, and while it makes me not want to eat the entire town, I'm always hungry. It doesn't erase it or even hide it."

"That's why you want to change back so quickly? Mercedes did, too."

"I'm not your sister, and I want to change because I have no reason to stay a night-walker. When I leave, I'll leave alone. I'll be alone. And I'd rather be me, the real me, than be anything else when I go."

What could you say to that?

Garreth approached, his heavy steps displacing more gravel than those of non-giants. "Thank you for everything, Porschia. Saul, how are you?"

I nodded and Saul answered for me. "She needs blood."

Garreth's eyes widened. "You're hungry?"

"I'm okay." It was a lie. My fingers trembled, so I tucked them behind my back, lacing them together to steady them.

"She's lying. She thinks it'll scare everyone if she feeds."

Garreth shook his head. "I'll feed you. We can go into your dwelling if you're shy."

"I'm not shy, I just don't—"

Garreth held his meaty hand up to stop my mouth. "This is why you feeding wouldn't scare anyone. You don't feed for sport or to frighten people into submission. You simply satisfy a need. Like drinking water or eating food. Your body needs blood and you take only what you need."

I nodded. I didn't like blood, but had to consume it or else sickness would consume me. Taking too much made me just as ill.

"Thank you," I whispered, following him up the hillside toward my temporary dwelling.

"It's the least I can do," Garreth said sincerely. Saul stayed at the well. I knew his control was a fraying rope and the scent of blood could snap it entirely. He would stay and see that the plants got watered.

"Could I take a little more than I normally would, Garreth? Not too much, just enough to feed Saul?" I asked as I stepped into the room behind him. "You're a large person, so you won't feel strange from me taking a little extra."

"It's fine, Porschia. Do what you need to. You've earned my trust. And I'll help you – any time, for any reason. Understood?"

I nodded, swallowing back the tears that clogged my throat. "Thank you."

I drank fast and only took enough for both of us.

Garreth stood, ducking to avoid scraping his head on the ceiling. "Do you want me to go get him?"

"Please." I watched him duck outside, the light of day filtering into the room.

Tage was going to kill me, but Saul needed to be fed and Ford was gone. Mercedes left with Ford on the wagon at his side, clutching a basket in her hands and one between her ankles.

She thought I was angry with her for leaving.

"I'm sorry I couldn't remain a night-walker," she said as I handed the second basket to her.

"Why would you apologize for that, Cede? No one wants to be a monster."

"I didn't mean it that way. You're not a monster."

I smiled slightly. "I know you didn't, and I don't blame you for wanting to feel normal."

She swallowed. "I wish things were different and that you could be healed. I know you probably know that already, but it's true and I want you to hear the words directly from my mouth."

I inclined my head. "Thank you."

"I love you, Porsch."

I pursed my lips. "I love you, too. And you, Ford." My brother was staring forward, pretending not to hear our conversation. A blush crawled up his neck as he nodded.

"You too," he answered. "Take care while we're away."

Laughing, I told him, "I think I should warn you*, not the other way around."*

His eyes found someone behind me and he waved for a moment, offering a smile. When I looked over my shoulders, Delilah's hand was raised, waving back.

Ford stood. "I have to go and harness Boots. She's holding him so you can say goodbye."

"It's not goodbye," I growled.

"Not a final goodbye, but it's goodbye for today. I'll see you tomorrow. Everyone should be in Blackwater within the week. We'll all be together soon."

I knew it, but 'goodbye' was too final a word. "I'll see you tomorrow," I vowed; moving away before he could say the awful word again, so he could harness up Boots without me spooking the animal.

TWENTY-TWO

TAGE

I WATCHED GARRETH LEAVE THE HOUSE AND WALK STRAIGHT TO SAUL, leaning in to whisper something to him. The giggling children nearby were too loud for me to filter them out and let Garreth's words in. Saul, ever the Boy Scout, made a bee line to Porschia, who was still inside.

And then he closed the door behind him. I could only imagine how he felt being alone with her, and why she allowed it was beyond me. What could she possibly need him for? She had me. She had Roman. Her brother and Father. Mercedes. She didn't need Saul anymore.

Sure, he was convenient for a time, offering to save her from her mother and to marry her.

He was a distraction. That was it.

He wasn't even a friend, no matter how hard she tried to be friendly with him. The truth of what he did would always be thick between them, viscous and ugly.

I saw red, and then I blurred out of Mountainside and into the forest before I tore apart Saul, Porschia, and anyone else who got in my way.

Things were changing. I thought I could stop it. I was wrong.

SAUL

Garreth told me that Porschia needed me. She already felt pretty awful before she fed, and I thought maybe the feeding didn't calm her down or ease the pangs of hunger. I didn't understand what she went through until I experienced it firsthand, and even now I wasn't sure I fully grasped the pain she went through. Turning into a vampire hurt. The light hurt your eyes. Your stomach ached. Your joints ached. You felt like everything in you was melting, reforming, and warming up to melt again. But the change didn't last forever. The hunger? It did. It never left you.

That was what made a night-walker go insane, what caused the Frenzy – the hunger. Unquenchable thirst. A fire that no amount of water could extinguish. Pain and agony and constant fear.

When I knocked twice on the door, she called out for me to come in.

After I stepped inside, I saw that she was sitting on an overturned bucket with her hands folded in her lap. She stared at them like they were foreign to her, like they were about to harm her and she was frightened, waiting for it to happen but powerless to stop it.

"Are you okay?" I asked, quietly.

"I am now."

"Garreth said you needed me."

She played with the poison ring on her right hand, twisting it around and around in a circle. "You saved me that day. You told me to use my ring."

Swallowing back my words, I listened. I wanted to tell her that I'd damned her. I thought the vampire blood would save her by pushing the Infection from her body and be powerful enough to rid her of the virus. It wasn't. I was wrong and she was the one who paid the price.

After Mercedes bit me on the raft, Porschia ran after me, screaming for me to use the ring. But she didn't see me get bitten, and I was too afraid of becoming both monsters. I wasn't strong enough to handle both curses. Not like Porschia.

"I want to ask you for a favor," she said, her eyes flicking up to mine.

"Anything," I croaked. "I'll do anything for you."

Her eyes narrowed slightly. "Feed from me."

My heart stopped and then began to pound. I didn't expect that. "I can't."

"You can," she assured me. "I took enough from Garreth to feed us both, and I'll be sick if you don't take some away."

I shook my head. "You don't understand. I can't control it well. I might take too much."

"I'll risk it," she said, jutting her chin out stubbornly.

My fingers flexed. The scent of Garreth's blood lingered in the air between us. If I did this, it would change everything. "I know about the bond. If I did this, you would be bonded to me."

"I know that," she whispered.

"Why, then?"

"Honestly?" she asked.

"Yes."

Taking in a deep breath, she stood up and walked toward me slowly. "Two reasons. First, I know you need to feed and are afraid of hurting someone. You can't hurt me, Saul. And if you start to take more than I want you to, I will and can stop you."

"Secondly?"

"Secondly, I want to make sure you're okay until you aren't a vampire anymore. Until you change back, we'll be linked."

"And Tage has nothing to do with any of this? Do you know how angry this will make him?"

"I'll talk with him. There's a third reason."

"I already know what it is," I growled. "You want to know if your bond with him is responsible for his loving you. It isn't. He's looked at you, wanted you, since we were still in the rotation. But he was in Frenzy. Roman told me." I stepped back from her. "So the question is really, will I let you use me for a short time in order to quench this fucking thirst?"

"Yes," she said boldly. "That's the quest—"

I didn't let her finish the word, or her sentence. I took a stride, grabbed her waist, and buried my fangs into her neck. Her heart thundered. I could hear the drumming in my ears. Or was that my heart?

She smelled like fresh flowers and tasted like sugar.

So. Sweet.

I gathered her toward me but she pushed me back. Growling on her neck I pulled her to me again. She pushed harder. Then she kneed me. Right in the balls. Only aware of the pain that made me nauseous, I must have let Porschia go. Grabbing her neck, she backed away from me.

Glaring.

I was grunting in agony as she glared at me like she was going to kick my ass, and in my state, she'd be able to. "What the hell was *that* for, Porschia?!"

"You were taking too much!" she retorted. She released her neck and clutched her heart before balling her fingers into fists. "Why are you so angry with me? I told you what I'd do if you did it!"

"I'm angry because you hurt my testicles!"

"You were going to kill me!" she shouted.

"Don't be so overdramatic!" Both of us were screaming and I knew people had to be hearing it all. And the person I figured would come to her rescue first, did.

Tage threw open the door and ran to her side. "What happened?"

"Nothing," Porschia said sternly, her face made of stone. She wasn't going to tell him.

"She kneed me in the balls." I was still bent at the waist.

"Why would she do that?" He tilted his head at a weird angle and then sprang at my throat. The back of my head hit the earthen wall, shaking it. The ceiling began to crumble and dirt and dust rained down on all of us.

"You'll bury us alive!" Porschia shrieked.

"We're undead, kitten. We'd make our way out. Eventually."

She glared at me again as Tage tightened his fist around my neck. "Why. Did. She. Knee. You?"

"Because," I started.

But it was Porschia who grew a pair and told him herself. "Because I made him feed from me and he took too much."

Tage released me and my feet hit the floor faster than I expected. I caught hold of the wall to keep from falling on my face, or God help them, on the boys. She was strong as hell. They might never recover.

Tage's face contorted into a half-pained, half-angry, and all-hurt look. "You did *what?*"

Porschia squared her shoulders before answering, "He needed to feed. He was about to lose it."

"That's a flimsy fucking excuse. Why did you bond with him? Are you still in love with him?" he asked. I prayed she said yes, because hearing that come from her mouth would go a long way towards easing the pain.

"That isn't why and you know it," she said, stepping toward him and reaching for his hand. "You can feel it."

Tage recoiled. "Then why?"

"I wanted to make sure this is real," she said, barely above a whisper. "What you feel for me. I need to know it's not just about our bond."

"And if it is? If it's because of the bond, will you leave me for him?" Tage paced back and forth, effectively blocking my escape route, even though I knew they needed to talk privately. "What if it's not? Then will you believe me? But not NOW? Not when I'm standing in front of you, telling you that I love you? I would lay down my life for you, Porschia. God damn it all!" he roared. "What do I have to do to prove it to you?"

A crimson tear leaked from her left eye and then her right.

She shook her head, silently telling him she didn't know.

Tage threw his hands in the air instead of around her. "I don't know either." Then he walked out the door.

TWENTY-THREE

PORSCHIA

Lydia smiled at me. "Thank you for changing me. I feel electric, like I could shoot lightning from my fingertips."

"It's because you just changed. You'll need to feed to keep the feeling. There's someone in the bedroom."

"Pierce?" she asked with a smile.

"Go see." I nodded my head toward the door. She twisted the golden knob, easing it open and then squealing.

"He's so young. I love the innocent ones."

I followed her inside. Ford stood across the room, backed into the corner. "Thank God you're here, Porsch."

"Don't thank anyone," I told him.

He tried to figure me out, puzzled by my words, and then shook his head.

"You won't eat me," he told himself.

"I won't," I told him as Lydia approached.

She ran to him and smiled, easing his head to the side. "But I will," Lydia answered. "It's only fair, you know. A brother for a brother."

She sank her teeth into Ford's neck and I woke with a start, having fallen asleep sitting against the wall, my neck sore from being crooked too long. My forehead was covered in sweat, and my heart…my heart was scared to death. What if Ford had to pay for what I did? What if Roman was reeling us both in so he could go in for the kill, making it hurt even worse when he did it?

Tage didn't come back to Mountainside for two days, and when he did, he barely looked at me, quickly moving out of my sight. He stayed in the forest near the western side of the wall most of the time. I knew he felt the deep ache in my chest. The same pain was visible in the creases and lines showing on his face, the ones that usually weren't there but would become etched into his skin in years to come if he became human and began to age again.

Saul's hunger was getting harder for him to suppress. He was losing the battle and the war. When Ford came three afternoons later, I asked Saul to escort him back to Blackwater. When he asked why, I told him it was so he could feed properly. My family and his would help him. Imagining the looks on his parents' faces, I cringed. They hated night-walkers. They were terrified of them, but I didn't think they would be frightened of Saul. He was still their son.

He agreed to go without argument, the hunger having won out, and Roman quickly agreed to stay. He was bouncing with energy that no one else possessed and promised to put it to work finishing up the last of whatever needed to be done. The final group of people would be taken to Blackwater tomorrow. We only had one night remaining.

I finally told Mercedes what happened with Pierce. She didn't say a word for the longest time and when she did, the only thing she did say was "Thank you." I wondered what he'd done to her while she was Infected.

Every day Delilah orbited my brother, and every day he became more enamored with her. With each passing day, my anxiety over the pair of them increased. More often than not during the hours Ford was away, she was nowhere to be seen. I searched for her. Her scent was missing from Mountainside, so I decided to ask for help. Tage was too busy avoiding me, so Roman was the logical choice. I waited until the sky darkened, becoming an odd shade of green; when the wind began to howl around the mountain and the hail stones began to salt the earth. All of the humans covered their heads and took cover.

Roman worked steadily alone during the downpour.

I approached him slowly. Part of me wanted his help, but the other part was testing him. Rain sluiced down too-long strands of his hair and poured in rivulets down his face and neck. His clothes were soaked and in a matter of moments, I was too. He didn't bother looking up at me. He knew I was there.

"I can't heal your lovers' spat."

"I'm not asking you to."

He sat back on his haunches as thunder shook the earth; violent and demanding. "What do you want?"

"Do you know Delilah?"

A slow smile spread across his lips. "Of course I do. Are you jealous? Is she toying with Tage?"

White hot rage filtered through my veins. "Is she?"

He chuckled and stood up. "Not that I'm aware of. Seems she's more into your brother."

"Do you know her scent?"

He looked up at the angry sky. "I... I can't smell her. Could just be the storm, though."

"It could be, but the thing is, I never can pick up her scent when Ford isn't around, and she disappears as soon as he leaves."

"Strange things are afoot." He grinned. "I love the scent of a spring thunderstorm."

I looked all around me at the thrashing tree limbs in the forest beyond the wall, water falling down the stones of the wall itself, and the thunderous torrents running down the mountain. Rain fell sideways, pelting both of us until it stung, but it wasn't uncomfortable. It was perfect. Gritty and angry and everything I was feeling on the inside.

"If it's bothering you, let's see if we can find the little minx. I'll go left."

I smiled. "I'll go right. Meet me at the top?"

"*Beat* you to the top!" he yelled, leaving me standing alone in the rain, watching his rapidly retreating back.

ROMAN DIDN'T FIND HER SCENT AND NEITHER DID I. IT WAS LIKE SHE HAD vanished, but she had to be here somewhere. Anger and frustration leaked from Saul. I could feel it pouring from him. No doubt he was sitting in the forest watching everyone get comfortable in the Colony and city.

Evening fell, leaving me wet and cold. Tage was still being stubborn. He was in his usual spot, which left only me and Roman, and we didn't need a fire to cook things. I could eat raw meat, if there was any to be had, and Roman only needed blood. It was still storming and the rain would extinguish a fire faster than we could fight to keep it lit. Drying out wasn't an option.

"You're shivering," Roman said from his chair as I laid on the makeshift bed he'd lain so ill in when we first arrived.

"I'm fine."

"You're stubborn." *So was Tage.*

"Ford said he would start at dawn instead of mid-morning," I continued, ignoring his statement. "That means he'll arrive sooner and we can get home, and then hopefully Saul can find meat for the Colony."

"And for you – when is the last time you had anything other than Garreth's blood the other day?"

"It's been awhile." The earthen walls were closing in on me. The space seemed smaller and smaller with each passing breath.

"Tage told me what happened."

I sat up. "He did?"

Roman nodded. "Can't blame him for being angry. Any guy would get pissed."

"I didn't mean it the way he's taking it."

"Does it matter whether you meant it a different way than he interpreted it? He's angry and has a right to be. You don't trust him."

"I don't trust anyone."

"You trust Saul."

"I do not." I didn't. I might be okay with having him in my presence and was trying to be friends again, but I still didn't trust him for the important things. I would never again trust him with my heart, and maybe that was why I didn't trust Tage completely with it. It had been battered, bruised, torn out, and put back in. Everything was so new.

Or maybe it was Mother's words constantly resounding in my head as though she were haunting me. *Who could ever bring themselves to love you, Porschia?*

Did I even know what love looked like? Felt like?

At one time I thought Saul loved me and that I loved him back, even through all of the muddled mess of the rotation, Tage's strong come-ons, and Roman's confusion. I thought Saul was *it* for me. Or at least I convinced myself he was.

Maybe it wasn't Tage I didn't trust.

Maybe it was me.

But how did I tell him that?

"I can see steam pouring from your ears. You're overthinking this."

"Maybe, but I think I just had an epiphany."

"Big words for such a small girl."

I groaned, wishing I knew a way to mend everything with Tage. Roman watched from his chair, his dark eyes taking in too much of everything around him. I preferred him human.

Then he muttered the strangest thing. "Though she be but little, she is fierce."

"What's that?"

"Shakespeare." Seeing the blank look on my face, he added, "Never mind."

"It's beautiful."

He picked at his cuticles. "It is. But ferocity doesn't always win the fight, Porschia."

My heart sank. Did he know?

TWENTY-FOUR

ROMAN

Porschia's body was trembling, so she laid back down and folded herself into the fetal position. It was going to be a long night. I let out a sigh. The wind howled outside the door. The wood clattered violently against its metal lock, making Porschia jump a foot into the air. She sat up and we watched as it was torn open and stood straight out on its hinges, the rain pouring over it in small rivers.

Gusts blew Porschia's hair everywhere. She'd been wearing it down more since the incident at The Manor. She wasn't cut out for this, for killing, but she damn sure was a survivor. I'd give her that.

"How is it just standing open?"

"The wind? Or maybe it's broken," I stood and walked toward it, catching the most delectable aroma. It was earthy and rich; spices and maybe myrrh? I'd only smelled it once, but maybe it was enough to remember it. I stood still, trying to inhale as much of the scent as I could, to commit it to memory.

"What's wrong, Roman?"

"Nothing at all. Do you smell that?"

She sniffed the air and stood up, moving toward me. "What *is* that? It's...amazing."

Suddenly the scent was gone. Faster than it had wafted in, it was gone. Porschia looked at me, her lip curled in disgust. I couldn't see the irises of her eyes at all. The ashy green color was gone. Just black remained.

She growled. "I should kill you right now."

"For what?" Fire licked its way through my veins, my heart supplying its oxygen, fueling the flames. "All I've ever done is help you!"

"Did you help me when you used my mother as a test subject? When you followed me around like a sad fucking puppy all year? Was that helping me, Roman?"

"We needed a cure, and I don't have to defend my actions to you. You aren't judge and jury over everyone, Porschia, but you sure as hell act like it. I'm beneath you because of what I did to your Mom, okay? I'm sorry! I'm fucking sorry. If I could go back in time and make another choice, I would. And at the manor, how you failed to keep my brother safe from those witches, I'm sure you'd erase that shit, too. I see how it eats at you. You say you're fine, that you've made peace with the situation, with yourself and with Saul, but I say bullshit! You are hanging on by a very fine, very frayed thread. And if you don't watch out, I'll bite the fucker in half!"

"I don't think you can," she teased, a half-crazed smile on her face. "You're not stronger than me anymore. You aren't stronger than anyone. You're just a night-walker. And if nothing else, we've all learned that there are much worse things out there." She pointed angrily toward the black storm raging outside the door, which still stood open.

Where did this anger come from all of a sudden?

I didn't have a chance to think of anything else before she plowed into me, her shoulder into my stomach. My head and back hit the wall just as a clap of thunder vibrated through the earth and sky. Porschia tried to sink her tiny fangs into my throat, but hell no. That wasn't happening. I used everything in me to push her back, my biceps and shoulders straining from the effort. Everything in me was holding her away from me, but I was weaker than her. She was right.

Thank God Tage wasn't a complete asshole. He blurred into the room and pulled her off me. She kicked and thrashed against him, but he held tight until the storm in her calmed. It took over an hour of both of us trying to subdue her until she finally relaxed and fell asleep on Tage's chest.

I finally breathed out, the tension ebbing from my body. "What was *that*? One minute she was cold and resting, and the next she was insane."

Tage shook his head. "I felt the anger swell and I've never felt her get that angry before."

"She was going to kill me, and the crazy thing was, I was almost as angry as she was. I felt like throttling her."

"Over what?"

I shook my head. All I knew was that she was laying there, the door flew open, and then Porschia attacked. Nothing about it made sense.

"I have no idea."

Tage stroked Porschia's hair gently and leaned back against the dirt wall. I collapsed into the only chair in the place.

"I'm not saying this to piss you off," I started, "but could she be overwhelmed with Saul's emotions?"

Tage's lips thinned into a tight line. "Could be."

"It's just weird, that's all. We were fine! She was going to sleep, and then the storm kicked up and the door flew open. That's when she attacked me, unprovoked and out of nowhere."

Tage shook his head. "I don't know. Nothing makes sense anymore."

TWENTY-FIVE

DELILAH

Ford guided the horse and wagon back into Mountainside's gates for the final time. The people were ready. They had packed everything they could carry, and that included the last of the plants everyone had been digging up. I met him and offered a bucket of water to his horse, Boots, stroking his mane and cooing at him. He was a beautiful creature.

Smiling brightly, Ford jumped down from the wagon. "Hey, Delilah. He needs to rest before we make the trip back."

"I'll care for him," I said sweetly.

"I'd appreciate that. I know *he* would, too." Ford cared for Boots so it was important for me to show that I shared the same sentiment. For now.

I pushed my hair behind my ears, drawing attention to the beautiful face I'd created. "What is Blackwater like?"

"Are you worried?" he asked sincerely.

"Yes. It's silly, I know. But it's different, and I think everyone fears change once they've become comfortable." He smiled with his eyes and lips. Brushing his fingers through his short, wheat-colored hair, he looked up at me.

"There's no shame in being worried. Blackwater has changed lately, too, but for the better. We're governed by a council. The Colony itself is really a suburb of a larger city, one that once thrived. We survived because of a simple concrete flood wall that the Infected couldn't climb over and a strong river they couldn't cross. But with the cure, a lot of people are choosing to live in the city. The housing in Blackwater is full now, so the city is the only option for you." He looked at me apologetically.

"That's fine. Any shelter is better than nothing, which is what I currently have. I can't go home. It's not safe."

"What about The Glen? Tell me about it."

"It was also made safe by a wall. You know, I really should get Boots something to eat."

"Yeah." Ford shook his head. "Let me unharness him real fast." He was young and worked fast to free the great horse. I gave him a demure smile as I led his stallion away.

This wouldn't take nearly as long as I thought.

PORSCHIA

When I woke, Tage was lying beside me, watching me. "Hey," I said, slowly blinking awake. My arms and legs felt like lead.

"Hey," he answered softly, with no anger lacing his voice. I wanted to ask him why he was there, why he wasn't mad anymore. What changed? But I held my tongue.

The nickering of a horse in the distance caught my attention and I sat up fast. "Ford is here? Already?"

Tage sat up, too. "Do you remember anything about last night?"

I tried to remember. "The storm?"

"Yes, there was a storm. You also attacked Roman."

My eyes widened and I sucked in a sharp breath. Roman wasn't there. "Is he okay?"

Tage nodded. "He's fine. I intervened in time."

An awful thought flittered into my mind, delicate as falling ash and just like it, a remnant of what burned within me. "What if you hadn't?"

"Let's not worry about the what ifs. Do you know why you snapped?" he asked cautiously.

I shook my head. "I don't remember anything but being cold and laying here, and then the sound of the thunder and wind."

"You don't remember me holding you away from Roman? Or Roman and I both holding you down?"

I swallowed thickly. "I don't." Why didn't I remember? Did I really attack him?

"It *did* happen, Porschia. It wasn't a dream or a hallucination."

"No, I... I don't remember a dream or anything about it at all."

Roman swung the door open from the outside. "Morning, sunshine. Feeling homicidal?"

"Not particularly," I answered honestly.

Tage looked at Roman. "She doesn't remember anything."

"You don't remember any of what happened last night?" he asked, brows raised.

Tage just shook his head.

"Seriously?" Roman asked, crouching down in front of me.

"I swear, Roman. I didn't mean to try and hurt you, and I don't remember anything but laying here, being freezing cold, and the violence of the storm outside."

He pinned me with a look, one I returned. Something was happening here, and it wasn't good.

Then Roman opened his mouth. "Saul's back."

TAGE

"Is Ford okay?" Porschia asked, leaping to her feet in a panic. "Is my brother okay? Why didn't you tell me if he was here and safe?"

"Yeah," Roman said slowly. "He's good. And he literally *just* arrived. Why are you so panicked about Ford?"

Porschia clawed at her throat absently. "I'm not sure."

"Are you okay?" I asked, leaning in to watch her movements.

"Yeah," she said absently. "I'm fine."

Her pale blue dress was wrinkled and her hair lay in tangles down her back. Porschia didn't look like herself. Even in the rotation, she took great care to braid and pin her hair back. And she sure as hell wasn't acting right.

Before she reached the door, she clutched her stomach. "Oh, God."

"What's wrong?" I yelled, running to her and looking her over.

With wide, terrified eyes and trembling lips she asked, "What if my blood turns him into a monster?"

"Who?"

"Saul," Roman answered for her.

"What if he's like me now?" she asked fearfully.

"What if he is?" I growled. "It was his choice!"

"I asked him to feed from me! It was my doing!" Palms to her temples, she paced, gritting her teeth and letting out a sorrowful, frustrated keening sound I'd never heard. "I may have damned him."

Roman smiled and eased toward her, palms outstretched. "If he were human, your blood would have done something to him, like with Lydia. But Saul had already changed. It wouldn't affect him at all, other than to nourish and satisfy a base need."

She gasped and held her heart. Crimson tears flowed from her face, splashing onto the dirt floor underfoot. "I thought I'd killed him. I don't want to kill anyone ever again. Ever again. Ever again," she muttered, staring at the door as if the wood were strong enough to contain her should she want out. "Ever again," she said brokenly.

I hoped she wouldn't have to. Porschia was disintegrating, and it wouldn't take much to wash the remnants of her completely away.

TWENTY-SIX

SAUL

Roman approached me before I even stepped out of the gate. He refused to elaborate when I tried to question him, but said to watch out for Porschia and that something was 'off' with her today. She wasn't feeling well or something. And he asked me twice if I felt sick or strange. I didn't – I felt fine, but worried for Porschia, obviously.

Tage was sticking close to her side on the opposite hill as we walked along, guarding the wagon and the last people fleeing Mountainside. I vowed to guard them, but didn't know what I'd do with myself after they crossed into Blackwater.

Roman and Ford said they would go to the council and ask them to reconsider, but I knew they wouldn't reverse their decision—not so soon after making it. Doing so would show weakness and they couldn't afford that right now, not with the chaos of taking in so many new residents at one time and the pressures that came with feeding and housing them all. Would these people want to be governed in the same way as our citizens?

There would be growing pains. It was inevitable.

The wagon rumbled through the valley, staying low. Ford took them through the flattest trail he could, one he'd tramped down himself. He was a good kid and looked awfully comfortable with Delilah sitting on the bench beside him. Porschia felt uneasy about her, but she hadn't done anything bad that I could tell. Porschia looked out for Ford as best she could after Mercedes fell. I hated to tell her, but he was almost a man. He could take care of himself. If he liked Delilah, there was nothing she could do about it.

I walked alone the majority of the way until the wagon came to the river crossing. The storm last night had swollen it, but not so much that it couldn't be crossed if the people were off the wagon. So they unloaded, leaving their baskets and belongings. Women held onto their children and old men held the hands of their wives, placing each step carefully along the riverbed.

Ford guided the horse across the current, its muscles straining to free the wagon wheels from the rocks and muck. I was about to offer a push when Roman splashed into the water. The horse bent his head to look at what was behind him and then found that he would rather pull the wagon than face a night-walker. I chuckled and watched as the horse won the battle, Ford stopping him on the far side of the river. Roman helped the stragglers across, but the horse never let the vampire out of his sight, pawing at the ground and flaring his nostrils.

"Easy," Ford said with authority. The horse knew who his master was. He knew Ford would take care of him. There was a trust between them.

"Do you feel okay?" Porschia asked as she stepped up beside me. Tage wasn't with her.

"I do, but why does everyone keep asking me that? Are *you* okay?" She looked well. She looked beautiful, actually. Her dark hair was braided down her back and she wore a white dress, fitted to her body's curves. Those were becoming more pronounced, and I wasn't sure if it was nature or if being changed suited her.

"I need to apologize to you. I didn't think."

"About?"

"I was worried that you might be hurt from...feeding from me. My blood."

I shook my head. "I feel fine."

"You're sure?" she asked, studying my face.

"I'm positive. The hunger abated for a little while." That was it. And I didn't tell her this, but I knew the risk and took it anyway, simply because she asked. I didn't think anything would happen and nothing did. If I had been human and drank a drop of her blood? Well, that may have ended badly, but fortunately I was already changed.

She turned her attention to the people in the valley below. "Almost home."

"*You* are."

Her eyes closed tightly. "I'll see if my father can help."

"We both know he can't."

She smiled slightly. "Maybe I'll leave, too."

I shook my head. "You're needed there. You're *wanted*."

"I don't know if I want to be," she said honestly. There was a long pause between us. "Most of the time, I feel like a threat. They aren't afraid of us now, but they should be."

"I didn't know how bad the hunger was. I felt hunger as an Infected, but it was more pain and a desperation to ease it. It wasn't this," I gestured to my stomach, "all-consuming, damned feeling you can't get rid of."

"Are you going to turn back? We should find an Infected as soon as possible."

"Not yet," I answered, shoving my fists in my pocket. "I will one day, but not yet."

"You don't have to stay a night-walker. Not for anyone or anything. I shouldn't have asked you to stay one until you got somewhere safe. I had no right," she said.

"You have every right," I said, grabbing her elbow and turning her to face me. "You have every right in the world."

She shook her head. "It was selfish. If you want to ease the hunger, you should change back."

"But that's the thing, Porschia. There's hunger no matter what you are. The humans have enough to eat, too. And... there are worse types of hunger than what I'm experiencing right now. This is bad, but it's nothing in the grand scheme of things."

I saw her swallow. She pulled her arm away from me slowly.

"You should come with us. No one will notice if you ride in the wagon and then run to Roman's or our house."

"You're living with Tage?" I asked incredulously. *This* was the hunger. I wanted her, but I couldn't have her. He was always in the way.

"Next to Roman. If our house is still ours," she added softly.

"And you want me to what? Live with the two of you? I couldn't stand it. I don't know if I could stand hearing you two even from the forest." My hearing was acute. I would be able to hear them if I wanted to, and I don't think I could stop myself from searching her out. And him with her? It would kill me.

"It doesn't have to be like this," she pleaded, tears clogging her throat.

"Doesn't it? You made a choice."

"So did you," she raised her voice, exasperated.

"And here we go again, stuck in a never-ending spiral, and the only way we can go is down. Well, I can't do this. I'll stay around until the dust settles and then I'm gone. I'm not crossing the boundary, either."

"Will you let me know when you're going?"

The tips of my fangs ground into my bottom lip, piercing it. "Fine."

TWENTY-SEVEN

TAGE

I WASN'T ABOVE EAVESDROPPING, ESPECIALLY WHEN IT CAME TO SAUL Daniels. Porschia didn't trust Delilah. I didn't trust Saul. Simple as that. When I heard him say he would leave after the dust settled, I wanted to give him a slow clap. Best judgment call ever. And add my kudos for not moving in with us against the council's wishes. That, too, deserved applause.

He'd be out of my hair soon enough, and with him gone, Porschia could fully move on and heal. I'd help her with that. The day he left couldn't come quickly enough.

She came back to me, never mentioning her conversation with him, and I didn't ask. "Feeling okay?" I tried to smile.

"Yeah, I'm looking forward to going home. I want to see Father and Maggie and Mercedes." Today she looked like she had herself together. I wondered how long it would last.

Ford called out, "I guess I'm chopped liver?"

"And you, dear brother," she added with a giggle. "How could I leave you out?"

He grumbled along playfully, and it seemed like a heavy fog had finally lifted from over everyone's heads the closer we drew to Blackwater.

People laughed. Children played. The cloudy remnants of last night's storm were emptied from the sky and only vibrant blue remained overhead.

PORSCHIA

THE CARPENTERS HAD MADE A CROSSING LARGE ENOUGH AND STRONG enough to hold the full wagon. Roman and Tage lowered it into place and tested its weight. Saul was in the forest, watching us from above. Sadness and anger wafted from him. When we crossed over, Mercedes and Father found Ford and me, enveloping us in hugs. "You look great," I told my sister.

"You do, too," she lied.

Father brushed the "mist" from his eyes after greeting me. "It's been too long. I was worried."

True to my word, I would talk with him. "Father, there's something I need to discuss with you."

"Ford already mentioned Saul. I've taken it to the council and we are waiting for their decision. Until it's made, he has to stay out of the Colony."

I nodded. "I understand."

"Regardless," he whispered, "his parents will go see him this evening."

"Do they know he's changed?"

He blew out a breath. "Yes, so perhaps they'll offer to feed him as well."

"I want to go with him. His control is wavering."

Father nodded. "That would be wise. For now, though, I think you need to visit Maggie."

"Why?" my heart thundered in warning.

"She's ill and even *she* doesn't think her body will recover from this." Hearing his words was like taking a hard blow to the back. All breath left my body.

"I need to go now," I choked out. Father nodded knowingly. Mercedes called out for me but I was already running, leaving them behind to make sure the people arrived safely. Avoiding people as best I could, I ran so fast the surroundings blurred, or maybe it was the red tears clouding my vision. I couldn't lose Maggie. I hadn't been gone that long. How could she get so sick so fast?

Opening her door, I ran up the steps. "Maggie?" My voice was high and frantic.

"In here," she replied weakly.

I found her in her bedroom, wrapped in several layers of blankets. Her cough was deep in her chest. It wracked her body, which had somehow become so frail in the last couple of weeks. She was okay when I left. This made no sense.

"How are you?" I croaked.

Maggie smiled. "Dying."

"That's not funny," I cried, wiping the moisture from my face.

"Oh, sweetheart," she said, patting the mattress at her side. "Sit."

I eased down beside her as another round of coughing took hold. Even the old mattress felt the reverberations. I looked at her hair, messy and uncombed. Her face was wrinkled, even more than it was before I left.

"It's just about time for me to go home."

"You *are* home," I argued.

She shook her head. "That's not true." Maggie placed a hand on my heart. "You know it in here. Nothing in this world was made to last forever. Not even night-walkers," she teased, the familiar spark in her eyes easing my pain.

"Ford told me about what you went through."

"And who told my baby brother?" I growled. Roman. Asshole. No doubt he was the one who flapped his big mouth.

"Your brother's no baby, and he's very proud of you, young lady." She pointed her knotted fingers at me. I wished those fingers would heal, that her body would mend itself and allow her to stay with me a little longer. And I wish I deserved to even hope for such a thing.

"He shouldn't be. I did horrible things."

"Some people are hell bent on destroying everything around them, and sometimes they get caught up in the destruction. Don't you worry about helping them along. You did the right thing."

"It doesn't feel right – not all the time. Sometimes it doesn't feel wrong either." It was funny how a scent could define a moment. In Maggie's room, the smell of old, musky blankets and the pine that made her bedframe were the most predominant odors.

Another coughing fit shook her. She coughed so violently that she sat straight up, sinking back into the pillows when it was over. When she relaxed, a high-pitched wheezing could be heard from her throat, rattling congestion in her chest. She was right. She wouldn't survive this.

"What can I do, Maggie?"

She smiled, taking in as much oxygen as she could with each breath. "Would you stay with me for a while?"

"Of course," I answered, grabbing her hand and rubbing away the cold. She was frigid. "There isn't anywhere I'd rather be."

"I've missed you."

I smiled slightly. I'd missed her so much while I was gone, but that would pale in comparison to what I'd feel when she left me for good. My voice cracked, but I needed her to know. "I love you, Maggie."

"And I love you."

MERCEDES WAS DOWNSTAIRS AN HOUR LATER WHEN MAGGIE FELL ASLEEP, her chest rattling with congestion. A pot of water boiled over the flames in the fireplace, alongside a large pot of soup. "Can you carry the water to her room? It seems to help her breathe easier," she asked.

I grabbed two towels and lifted the bubbling water. Steam moistened my face as I climbed the stairs to her. There was a towel on the table beside her, a round indention in the center. I eased the pot down and watched as the vapor rose and spread throughout the room. Within minutes, Maggie's breathing sounded a little bit better.

If it eased her pain or helped her at all, for even a second, it was worth it. Her chest relaxed and she was able to rest peacefully for a time. Mercedes whispered to me from downstairs, "Come and eat. She'll be okay."

I was going to remind her that I didn't eat soup, but she added, "I have meat for you." The fact that Maggie was sleeping and that Mercedes was helping was enough to pry me from the bedside.

In the kitchen, I watched her. Mother never let us help her cook unless she locked herself away, refusing to do anything but sleep. But Mercedes watched her from a distance. She taught herself what to do and how to do it, and she taught me a few things, too.

"You've been helping her?" I asked, watching Mercedes. She nodded, handing me a dish with raw beef on it. "They slaughtered a cow?"

"To welcome the refugees. The council wants to make a good impression, I guess."

"This'll do it." She ladled soup into her bowl and sat it in front of her, sitting to my right at the table. The wooden surface was worn smooth, scarred from years of use, from Maggie's hands and knives. "Thank you for helping her."

"She means a lot to you," she said, dipping her spoon into the hot broth and raising it to her lips, blowing ripples across its brown surface.

"She does." I used the knife and fork she'd set out to cut into the meat. It was fresh and smelled so delicious my mouth watered for a taste. I couldn't talk. Every time I talked I couldn't hear Maggie's breath. If we were quiet and still, I could hear her and know that she was alive.

Mercedes seemed to sense it. Having been a night-walker, she knew the sensitivities. She knew what it felt to be starved, crazed, and half out of your mind with primal needs, but feel like the same you inside.

Her spoon stilled above her soup. "She's been waiting for you, I think. She didn't want to let go until she saw you. Maggie loved you in a way Mother couldn't allow herself to."

I nodded, chewing rapidly to stave off the tears that threatened to bleed out from me. If they carried grief as well as liquid, I would be drained dry in no time.

She patted my hand for a second. "You loved her too. She knows that."

"Doesn't make it any easier," I blubbered, letting the dam of sadness break beneath my eyelids.

"I know. And I'm here for you. So is Tage. He's on the porch and refuses to come inside."

"Why?"

"He wants to be close to you, but still give you time with her. It's really sweet."

"Have you seen Noah?" Before everything had changed, she'd had her very own love.

Mercedes stiffened, grabbing her glass of water. "I don't want to talk about him."

"Why? What did he do?"

She sat her glass down and dabbed at her lips with a cloth. "His affections changed when I did, apparently. He is no longer interested in marrying an Infected or a night-walker."

"You're neither."

"Tell *him* that. He's terrified of me now, backed away like I was Satan himself."

I shook my head. "Then he doesn't deserve you."

"Doesn't ease the pain, but thank you." She stilled and looked at me for a long moment. "It's getting dark. I'll light the candles."

I quickly finished my meal as she set to work lighting a long wooden stick and then transferring the flame to the wicks of the candles around the room. Her soup was still steaming, but her appetite had left.

When she stilled and my bowl was empty, I stood and moved to the wash pan. She came to me. "I'll take care of this."

My hands shook. I was about to burst and needed to tell someone. Whispering to her, I admitted it for the first time. "I… I killed Pierce. It was me. Not those women."

Her breath caught and she tugged the bowl from my hands and turned to look at me with steely eyes that reminded me of Mother. "Good."

TWENTY-EIGHT

TAGE

PORSCHIA STEPPED OUT ON THE PORCH JUST BEFORE DAWN. HER FACE WAS damp from water and not blood. For a moment, I thought everything was okay, that Maggie had just had a rough night. When her lip began to quiver, I knew I was wrong and wrapped her tightly in a hug. She squeezed me back and I felt every ounce of her pain as sobs wracked her body. I'd have done anything to take the pain away. If the bond allowed it, I would have absorbed it all so she didn't have to feel a single second of it.

But there was nothing to heal a broken heart. Hurt like this always left a scar, some more sensitive than others. I'd been sensing danger drawing near and had focused on keeping everyone inside the house safe instead of honing in on what was happening within the walls.

"She's gone," Porschia hiccupped, pulling me closer.

I rubbed her back and hair and tried to make sure she knew I loved her. Because I did. I loved her so damn much it hurt. My heart hurt because hers was torn in two.

Mercedes stepped out behind her and pulled the door closed. "I'll tell Father."

Porschia broke down again. She was broken and I wasn't sure I could put her back together. Maggie gave her love when her own mother wouldn't. She took her in, gave her chance after chance and taught her more in just a few weeks than she'd learned about life in all of her years.

Mercedes' footsteps trailed away. "Do you want to go home?" I asked softly.

"No. I want to stay with her. I just needed you."

A millstone dropped from around my neck. I'd been drowning in my sorrows, thinking Porschia didn't want or need me anymore. With just a few words, the rope was cut and the weight fell away.

"I need you, too. I'll help with whatever you need."

"I know you will," she reassured me. "Thank you, Tage."

"You don't have to thank me, kitten. I love you."

She didn't say it back, but pulled me closer, fisting the shirt against my back. It stung a little, but I knew she would say it in her own time. That time wasn't now.

PORSCHIA

Father came right away. He stepped onto the porch and told me he would be back in a few moments and would get a few men to help him dig the grave. Tage volunteered to help and Father stiffened but thanked him. I wasn't sure what that was about.

"I'll be right back," he promised.

Mercedes stayed with us. "Father didn't want me to tell you, but people are still frightened of the night-walkers."

"Of me, you mean."

"All of you, and me because I was one of you," she admitted.

"For a day or two," I growled. These people were exasperating. "It's not something you can catch."

"They're afraid of the rotation starting back up again. You'll need blood."

"We're fine." We were being fed. I thought of Saul in the forest and hoped he was finding food. My theory was that the animals fled from where they were being eradicated, so the women from The Manor may have unknowingly done us a favor by flushing them to us.

"I know. There's just a lot of change and they're frightened. It's crazy.

The people of Mountainside and The Glen think we're liberators, while our own neighbors see us as captors."

"It's not as if drinking from someone hurts or like we kill them when we do it."

She pursed her lips together. "How scared were you before the rotation?"

"Very," I admitted. "More nervous than anything, but I understand. I see it from both sides now."

Mercedes sat on the steps, her dark skirts fluttering in the breeze. "Why do you still wear your dress?" I asked her, leaving Tage's side to sit next to her for a moment.

"Why do you?"

"They make me feel like me, from before."

"Me too." She stared blankly at the dew gathered on the grass. A light fog sat low on the ground.

When Father returned, Tim Brown was with him. He hadn't changed. He looked at me apprehensively as he stepped onto the walk. Shorter than Father by a head, he bowed it toward us. "I'm very sorry for your loss."

"Thank you," Mercedes and I said in unison.

"We will see that Margaret receives a proper burial. The Colony will gather after she's laid to rest. You're welcome to join us then."

I stood up and Tage's hand found the small of my back. "We can help you with her."

"That isn't necessary, Porschia. We know how close you were with Margaret. We can prepare her."

"Is this about my feelings or your own? Are you frightened of me now? Tim, I've never hurt you or anyone else in Blackwater."

He shifted on his feet and looked to the ground. "I understand, but some people are just apprehensive about..."

"Me," I finished for him.

"Night-walkers in general. You know how you viewed them before joining the rotation for the first time," he explained. "I don't hold their opinion, just so you know – but as a member of the council, I have to do what's best for everyone. And right now, it's best if you let us tend to Margaret."

Every muscle in my body drew in tight, but I knew I couldn't do anything. The council was in charge now. Even if they were wrong, I had to abide by their rules if I wanted to stay in Blackwater. In that moment, I questioned leaving my home now more than ever.

Without a word, I walked past him and my father toward home. "Porschia," Father said.

I turned to him, tears threatening again. "I'm sorry," I answered. "I can't. You take care of her, okay? You do that for me."

He inclined his head. "I will."

I nodded fast and started walking before I lost my composure; Mercedes walking to my left and Tage to my right. He threaded his fingers through mine and I squeezed them in thanks.

We all knew this wasn't right, but nothing was going to change their minds. Nothing was going to show them that we weren't going to hurt them. The divide would never be bridged as long as this much hatred and distrust existed.

IT WAS EVENING BEFORE I STEPPED OUTSIDE. THE SUN HAD FALLEN BEHIND the trees in the hills beyond the Colony. The first lightning bugs began to flicker green through the trees and grass. The scent of honeysuckle floated on the gentle breeze. Bushes were flowered and dripped petals of every color on the ground. Rose bushes bloomed. Gardens were being set in every yard, the plants from Mountainside already bolstering their rows.

No one had come to get us yet. Tage stepped out behind me. "You okay?"

"Not really," I answered honestly. "I don't know what's taking them so long."

He rubbed my shoulders, the tension flowing out of them. The night was filled with the sound of cicadas calling out for their pharaoh. Father always said they searched the land for him, longing to serve him again. Every seventeen years they emerged, and they were only starting to sing. Soon, we would battle them for our own crops.

"Pha-raoh, Pha-raoh, Pha-roah," they sang as one.

Maybe it was that sound that masked the words of the council men and women. Maybe Maggie sent them to shield me from their hatred. Maybe they were just loud, obnoxious bugs who should stay buried in the ground or trees or wherever they came from. Whatever it was, my ears were stronger. They'd begun the funeral without us. Purposefully.

"Get Mercedes. I'm going to get Roman." Tage questioned me with his eyes. "Listen, beyond the noise of the night."

His eyes hardened as he heard what I did. "You've *got* to be kidding me."

I shook my head.

He let out a frustrated growl and stalked toward the house. "Mercedes?" he called out. She answered right away. "They started the funeral without us."

I could hear her angry yelling, much more high pitched than his timbre. Roman must have heard, too. He met me on the street in front of his house. "I'm sorry. Maybe if I'd done better to give the night-walkers a good image, you wouldn't be in this position."

"What were you supposed to do? Be their friends and then feed from them? That wouldn't have worked, either." I waited for Tage and Mercedes to catch up. He walked with her, given she was human. He was thoughtful like that. Most men, let alone vampires, would have run ahead, leaving her behind.

"Maybe we should wait and go see her after they leave," I wondered aloud.

"No, kitten," Tage said, grabbing my hand. "You loved her. You have every right in the world to be at Maggie's funeral."

He was right. So with Tage's hand in mine, the four of us walked toward the cemetery.

TWENTY-NINE

MERCEDES

As Victor Freeman spoke of Maggie, whom he never bothered to give the time of day to even though she made the clothes on his back, we approached the crowd. Gasps and whispers became louder the closer we got until no one was listening to Victor and he stopped to see what the commotion was all about. A cold sweat broke out on my forehead and my legs began to feel weak. I had to hold it together. For Maggie. For Porschia.

Ford stepped up beside me and smiled. "'Bout time you showed up."

"No one told us."

Mouth agape, he said, "Mary Brown went to get you."

"She didn't."

"I should have gone after you myself," he spat, looking at Mary with more anger than a teenager should hold. She straightened her back and stared back at us indignantly, lips pursed.

It was slow. If you didn't pay attention, you wouldn't have seen it until the end, but the humans moved away from our group like prey threatened by a predator. Maybe they sensed the danger, the fury flowing from us all.

When it was clear that we weren't leaving, Victor finished what he was saying: a vague eulogy for Maggie that praised her dedication to the

Colony and lifted her skill as a seamstress. But that was all they knew about her. They didn't know how much she cared, or how she talked to you like you were a human being, capable of errors and dripping with emotion. They didn't say how she took my sister in and how she opened her home to me when I had none, simply because she was kind. They didn't know Maggie, so all they could say was how grateful they were to have her clothing. It was about what she'd done for them, not what they knew about her. And it was disgusting.

Porschia was about to snap. I could feel her body tense and become board-like beside me. I nudged her.

She looked to me and I shook my head. "Don't. It's what they expect," I whispered.

She sniffed, blinking her eyes to the sky. "I won't."

I wanted to yell for her, but again, it was what they expected. We would take the high road and leave the low road to the colonists who used to be our neighbors, friends, lovers. Noah stared at me blankly from across the grave. For a moment I stared back, but that was before I realized that he – that none of them – were worth it. Maybe we should all leave, night-walkers included, and see how they fared in the forest by themselves; see how they could protect themselves. In truth, they might be fine now that the Infected around here were cured. They might be able to fend for themselves now, and maybe a little self-reliance would do them some good.

Slowly the colonists, new and old, made their way back to their homes. My sister was breaking. She began picking flowers, sniffing them and letting her tears drop to the earth. I helped her, trying to keep my balance. Maggie deserved flowers on her grave. She was a saint, the only person in our world who didn't see Porschia as anything but her. She saw the good in her, the human in her. She saw the same in everyone, regardless of what they were: Infected, Human, Night-walker. Maggie saw the person, the soul, beneath it all.

Fear blinded people to the truth. It was as much a curse as anything else.

FORD

. . .

I STAYED WITH PORSCHIA AS THE CROWD THINNED AND THEN ONLY THE people who actually knew and cared for Maggie were left. Mercedes didn't look well. Dark circles hung under her eyes and her skin was almost as pale as Porschia's now. But where Porschia looked healthy, Mercedes' skin was splotchy and bruised-looking. I kept an eye on them both. Porschia so she wouldn't snap, and Mercedes so she didn't fall over dead.

Then she passed out, and the only thing that stopped her from hitting the ground hard was Porschia's lightning reflexes.

"What's wrong?" Porschia asked, looking up at the others for help. Tage crouched beside her as Roman and Father helped ease her down.

"Has she eaten?" I asked.

Porschia looked up at me. "She had soup for dinner last night. I don't know if she ate this morning."

"Could it be the same flu that I had after changing back?" Roman threw out.

Father yelled for me to run and get water, so I ran to the nearest well at the back side of the barn and pulled some up with the bucket, unchaining it and taking the whole thing with me. Water sloshed over the edges onto my pants and shoes, but I ran anyway.

When I came back, Mercedes was sitting up, blinking and holding her mouth. "Is she sick?"

Porschia shook her head robotically, a hollow look in her eyes. "She...the cure didn't work this time."

"What?" I knelt beside her and held the bucket up for Mercedes to take a drink, but she pushed it away, rocking and crying.

"Why wouldn't it work? I fed from an Infected! I did exactly what I was supposed to do."

Tage swallowed. "This makes no sense. Are you sure?"

Mercedes opened her mouth wide. The fangs, which had been gone for days, were growing back, albeit slowly this time. Two sharp peaks erupted from her gums, swollen and angry red.

Porschia stood abruptly. "I'll find another. I'll bring an Infected to the woods tonight. You will feed from them and it'll be okay. Just take more blood."

"My fangs aren't in yet. I can't feed from them."

"There are other ways to get blood from a person. And you *will* feed tonight. We have to stop this."

"My body is hot. Not the inferno of when I first changed, but there's a smoldering heat inside me. I've felt it since I left The Manor."

Roman cursed and stood up. "I'm coming with you, Porschia."

"I'll go, too," Tage said, adamantly.

"Someone has to stay with Mercedes, in case..." Porschia didn't finish her sentence, but everyone knew what she meant.

Father spoke up. "Take her to Saul. She can stay with him while you find someone to cure her."

It was a good idea, if we could find him; if he was still in the forest and hadn't left yet. "Is he still there?" I asked.

Porschia nodded. "He is." I saw Tage tense beside her. Roman told Father and me about the bond she had to him. Tage could get mad all he wanted, but that bond might be the best tool we had right now.

"Can you walk?" Porschia asked, helping Mercedes stand.

"Not fast, but yes."

Porschia nodded. "Let's get you to Saul." To Father, she said, "I'll take care of her."

To Tage and Roman, she nodded. "We hunt."

They echoed with as much resolve. "We hunt."

THIRTY

SAUL

I'D HUNTED LAST NIGHT AND BROUGHT DOWN A RACCOON AND A POSSUM, draining them both. They weren't much, but the Colony could use the meat so I decided to start that way. When I saw Porschia holding up Mercedes, flanked by Tage and Roman, I knew something was wrong. "What's going on?"

Roman ran to me, stopping short of smacking into my face. I stepped back. Personal space and all. "We need you to watch Mercedes," he said hurriedly.

"Why does Mercedes need watching?"

"Because I didn't drink enough Infected blood to completely change me back. My fangs hurt like hell and they think I'm gonna kill the whole damn town if I go into Frenzy in the Colony without another nightwalker to stop me," Mercedes answered, out of breath by the end of her explanation.

Was there a set amount of blood to consume in order for the cure to work? Why would she be turning back? "We don't know any more than you do," Roman said, as if reading my mind.

I held the two animals up. "Thought the Colony could use the meat."

Roman nodded. "The Colony doesn't deserve the meat, but okay. After Porschia has a portion."

"I'm okay," she said, but her eyes locked onto the raccoon and wouldn't let go.

"Eat some, Porschia. You need to be strong," Tage coaxed.

She swallowed and asked Tage to help Mercedes. "I'll take them to Blackwater and feed on the way. Meet back at your home?" she asked me.

"Yeah." She would probably beat us there. And I was surprised she knew where I lived. I'd seen her in the forest, but never saw her near my house—if you could call it that.

She was gone before I could offer to help Mercedes, her scent on the breeze she left in her wake. I breathed her in, aware of Tage's growl and the fact that Porschia probably knew how I was feeling. I didn't give a damn anymore. Trying to hide it was useless.

Roman's voice snapped me out of my daze. "Don't push it today, Saul. Maggie died this morning, and they didn't bother to let us know that her funeral had begun."

My heart stopped for a second, beating slow and hard in sadness and anger. Porschia loved Maggie.

"If we're gonna meet Porschia, we'd best get a move on. She's fast and even faster when she's fed," Tage announced with a clap of his hands.

His hands? I wanted to tear them off simply because they'd touched her. I even hated his voice. How could she love him when he was so different from me? Could he compel her to? Did she choose him because he was my opposite? I'd give anything to undo what I'd done. I'd give anything to have Porschia back again. I loved her, and seeing her with him was killing me. Being anywhere near Tage made me want to kill him.

Roman picked Mercedes up in a fireman's hold and the three of us ran toward my home. Porschia was already waiting on the step when we arrived. The white stucco was mostly green and grey now. Poison ivy climbed up the outer walls and crept into the gutters. "The inside is nicer," I said, trying to erase the look of disgust from Mercedes' face.

"It's fine. We appreciate you letting her stay," Porschia reassured. She smiled slightly, her eyes locking onto mine for a moment. As Roman took Mercedes inside and Tage followed them in, I wrapped my fingers around Porschia's wrist. "I'm sorry about Maggie."

She nodded. "I could tell the moment they told you."

"I wanted you to hear it, though."

"Thank you," she whispered, pulling away and walking into the dimness indoors. Little sunlight made its way through the canopy and into the broken windows. There was an old couch, stained and half moth-eaten. "The cot in the back has clean bed clothes. I stole them from my parents."

"Have they visited you yet?" Porschia asked.

"In a manner of speaking. They met me at the crossing and threw some food across, then they told me not to contact them again. They said they were disappointed in my decision to set the fire in the city, and of my choice to become a night-walker after having been cured from the Infection. Then they said I wasn't welcome in my own home." My father was on the council now. Apparently being seen with your formerly-Infected, currently-vampire son was frowned upon.

"I'm sorry," Porschia said, her brows drawn together. "I truly don't understand. They were always so understanding. They love you."

"Things change. And don't worry, it's not you, it's them," I said, standing up straight and shoving my hands in my pockets. "So no one knows you're starting to change back?" I asked Mercedes as Roman settled her on the bed.

"Not yet," she answered.

"That's good." I turned to the others. "I'll take care of her. You go hunt down an Infected."

I wasn't sure where they'd have to go to find one or how far. We might be here for a few days. Mercedes scrunched her nose up as she looked around my house. It was going to be too long a visit, regardless how short. For her and for me.

ROMAN

SAUL FOUGHT HARD TO HIDE HIS IRRITATION AT MERCEDES' DISDAIN. HE was offering to help, yet she was more concerned with examining her surroundings. Not posh enough for her, I guessed. It wasn't like anyone in Blackwater lived in luxury, though this house wasn't exactly the best in the woods. I'd have to tell Saul about the other houses.

"Where would you suggest?" Porschia asked.

"I've been thinking about that, and the best bet might be south. There's a small town probably fifty miles away. It's not ideal, but we can't go back toward Mountainside. That would be pointless. We could go north, but the village there is probably sixty or seventy miles away." Plus the woods are thick in that area. It would make this evening much more fun…

"We could split up," Porschia suggested.

"No," Tage said. "We stay together." He pinned his eyes on me, and I knew what he was thinking. Bad things happened when people split up. I was actually a fan of splitting up.

"Makes sense, Tage. It would be so much faster."

"No." He was a stubborn one. "We stay together."

It made no sense that Mercedes hadn't been cured. She seemed fine – sick and miserable for about a week, sure – but for days she'd seemed human. Now, her fangs were growing back and she was slowly becoming a vampire again.

Did she just take a sip? Could she have accidentally consumed vampire blood? Or was this something else entirely? It wasn't that I cared about Mercedes at all, but for my own neck, I hoped it was the former. I hoped she'd made a mistake, consumed too little from the "gross" Infected or accidentally took in a drop of vampire blood. If the cure wasn't permanent…

"South it is," I said, cracking my knuckles out of habit. With another round of goodbyes and one forlorn Saul bracing himself against the door jamb, we ran; skirting the city and then turning south.

Fifty miles isn't that long when you can travel as fast as a vampire, but we would need to feed when we arrived. I just hoped the people of Vansburg were still alive and well, and that the Infected that surrounded it were, too.

We could feed from them, or I could feed from Tage before I tore Porschia apart. She thought I didn't know that she killed my brother? She sank her fangs into him and he was gone. Just like that. I heard her and Mercedes talking about it. I felt the sharp blade of the knife turn in my back, tearing flesh and sinew, chipping bone.

Being out in the woods with her alone would be more ideal, but I could take Tage in a fight. I'd wait until Porschia weakened and then pounce. She would regret having lied, having murdered, and ever having laid eyes on me.

THIRTY-ONE

SAUL

Mercedes was miserable. She laid on the bed, crying. "Is there something I can get you? Do you need to feed?"

She raised her head off my makeshift pillow to scream, "I can't feed, you idiot! My fangs aren't in," and then promptly let it fall again.

Her tears were still clear. She hadn't fed. She wasn't going any crazier than normal. Maybe the fangs were just a fluke. Maybe she wasn't turning back into a night-walker, after all.

We would be stuck there for a couple of days at the minimum, and from the looks of things, it was going to feel like two months.

I hunted that night, for the Colony and for me. I drained the deer I took down and then dragged the carcass over to the crossing where Ford waited. I was surprised to see him.

"I figured someone would hunt," he said with a shrug. "But Father forbid me from entering the woods until we figure out what's happening to Mercedes. How's she doing?"

Should I lie? "She's not great."

"Upset or in pain?"

"Both, I think."

Footsteps cut through the silence between us and Delilah smiled, holding a basket out for Ford. "I thought you might get hungry, waiting out here all night."

He grinned and accepted her offering. "Thanks. I'm starving."

She settled onto a rock on the bank beside him. "Do you mind if I keep you company for a little while? I can't sleep."

"No, I don't mind at all. That'd be nice," he said. I could feel his heart beat faster. Ford was already a goner.

Lifting the bridge into place, I carried the venison across the water and sat it on the ground, careful not to take one step onto the Colony's boundary. Ford jumped up to help and met me at the edge of the bridge. "Thanks for the meat, Saul. Do you think they'll be back tomorrow?"

"It's hard to say. It could be a few hours, or it could take a few days to find an Infected. Some roam, but they'll be more likely to find them closer to human settlements than randomly in the forest. Everyone here's been cured or..."

Or I burned them to death.

"Yeah," he said, stiffening. "Will someone let me know about Mercedes? If she's okay? Father will probably ask that I stay here until someone comes."

"Don't stay out here. Go about your business. I'll send Porschia or Roman for you."

Ford smiled. "Not Tage?"

"Definitely not Tage." I stifled the urge to ruffle his hair and turned on my heel, crossing the bridge and lifting it back over to the forest side.

Delilah frowned. "Why don't they leave the bridge up all the time?"

Ford turned to her. "It's safer this way."

"Safer for whom?" she muttered, lowering her head.

As I walked away, I heard him sit back beside her and begin to tell her everything. About the rotation, the screams of the Infected from the forest and city, about how Mercedes fell, and what happened when Porschia turned.

Her heart sped up, pounding fast against her chest, and her breathing became shallow. It was a frightening history, and if anyone knew how to shield their safe haven, it was the citizens of Blackwater. The people of Mountainside and The Glen learned that the hard way. She should know that.

Instead of running back to Mercedes, who'd fallen fast asleep before I left to hunt and didn't want me within fifty feet of her, I climbed a tree close enough to the Colony so that I could keep an eye on Ford and

Delilah, yet high enough to be hidden from their sight. Oak leaves, fat and healthy from recent rains, blew gently around me.

Delilah listened intently as Ford poured his heart out to her; telling her about his fears, the weaknesses he saw within Blackwater, about the new council, and how his Father was different, somehow smaller since everything had happened with his children and the banishment and subsequent death of his wife, their mother. He had lost most of the only friends he had because of it all, and was more of an outcast than should have been tolerated for a neighbor who'd been through hell and back.

When he became quiet, she turned to him and began whispering something that I couldn't hear, but what I did catch bits and pieces of, didn't make sense. It was as if she spoke a different language. Delilah moved closer to Ford, her ramblings getting more intense, and he stood up as she guided his elbows. His eyes were fastened on hers while she spoke, pulling him toward the river bank where the grass was still bent from the weight of the bridge only moments ago.

She waved her arm toward the wooden planks, anchored together with wooden beams and long, steel nails, and the wooden bridge obeyed her; rising from the ground upon which it laid and positioning itself across the angry river water that swirled and churned beneath it. She walked him into the bridge's center and I stood up, ready to jump down and tackle the witch into the water, but she didn't hurt him. She smiled at Ford, brushed his cheek with the back of her fingers, and then with the same hand, gathered her breath in her hand. She uncurled her fingers and blew into Ford's face. Golden flecks of glittering light filled the air between them until he inhaled them, breathing them in until the skin of his cheeks glowed as if lit from within.

As fast as the light came, it extinguished, but the damage to Ford was done. She grabbed hold of his hand and led him across the river into the forest. Careful not to make noise, I quickly climbed down the tree and followed them down the well-trodden path through the woods; the one we'd taken night after night during the rotation. It was the most direct path away from Blackwater.

Torn between helping Mercedes and keeping Ford alive, I chose to help Ford, knowing that if either sibling was harmed, Porschia would never forgive me. She'd come to some sort of understanding about my role in her mother's death, but if anything happened to her siblings, it would solidify her hatred for me and I'd lose her for good. Mercedes *was* growing fangs, but if she was turning back into a night-walker, it was a slow transition this time. However, Ford was in immediate danger. My mind had trouble wrapping around what I just saw. Delilah was a danger I couldn't understand and didn't know how to combat.

Panic filled my veins and I hoped Porschia felt it and came running. Could I drain a witch? Would she spell me, too?

And what did she need Ford for?

One thing was for certain; we would soon find out. And I wasn't letting either of them out of my sight as long as I could help it.

THIRTY-TWO

PORSCHIA

I STOPPED AND GRIPPED MY CHEST; MY HEART FLUTTERING AND THEN stopping, pounding and then icy fear. Panic. Rage.

Saul was terrified.

Bewildered.

Worried.

"What is it?" Tage asked, at my side in a split-second. Roman stopped, too.

"It's Saul. Something's really wrong," I gasped. "We need to go back. Now."

"I smell the Infected. It's not far away," Tage said, pacing in front of me.

"I'll get an Infected. You go with Porschia," Roman told Tage.

I nodded and took off before either of them could try to talk me out of it. Talking took too much time. I could feel that this was a mortal emergency. There was an urgency in Saul that I'd never felt before.

Pumping my arms, I pushed harder, faster, leaping over fallen trees, boulders, streams. Tearing through the underbrush like an angry wind, I ran. I had to find him. Now.

ROMAN

When the two lovebirds left, I ran after them, waiting for Porschia to weaken and slow. We ran back twice as fast as we'd left and she never tired. Fueled by panic and fear, she ran faster than I would ever be able to. Tage fell behind, too, but wouldn't leave her. His bond would guide the way, just as hers to Saul was leading her steps.

I, however, decided on another path. Concerned for my friend, I waited behind Maggie's house in the darkness, listening to her labored breath, to Mercedes and Porschia striving to heal their broken bond…and that's when I heard the ugly truth. That Porschia had killed my brother, severing ours forever. That's when I knew that she was dangerous to everyone, that I would get revenge and that Mercedes, who so quickly agreed to her snuffing out my brother's life, would die. I just had to find her.

FRAUD

ONE

ROMAN

I WATCHED THE CRUMBLING HOUSE FOR SIGNS OF LIFE. THERE WERE NONE. Creeping closer, I eased the front door open. No candle light flickered. Not even a mouse stirred in the leaf piles that littered the corners of the floor. The hinges let out a long, shrill whine. Porschia was still panicked and Saul wasn't here. No one was. Glancing slowly across the sparse furnishings, it looked just as we'd left it. Apparently, Mercedes was on the loose and Saul couldn't contain her.

Pulling the door closed, my boot almost sank through the rotten, slippery porch plank. Something cold bit into my side. Making my breath shallow, I turned my head to see what or whom I was dealing with.

"Were you hoping to find me, or perhaps my sister?" Mercedes asked, her teeth gritted against my ear.

"Honestly? I was looking for you."

"You know about Pierce, then."

"I do." She shoved the knife in further, piercing my flesh ever so slowly.

"You've been a night-walker for how many years and you still don't get it, do you?" she hissed.

"Get what?" I said carefully.

"Not to take on a bigger opponent than you can handle. And you can't handle me, Roman."

"I came to—" I started, but she shoved the blade in another half inch. It felt like a mile, making me cry out. My eyes watered. We might be nearly indestructible, but we could still feel pain.

"You came," she began to finish my words, "to avenge your brother." Mercedes laughed. "And how do you intend to do that?"

She eased the knife from between my ribs and stepped away, dropping it off the side of the porch. "I don't need this to stop you from attacking Porschia."

I did have one thing she didn't. Information.

When she launched herself at me a moment later, I used it to my advantage. She knocked me onto the porch, both of us crashing through it, my back taking the brunt of both of our weight. "Porschia is in trouble, not that you care at this point." Dirt and dust flew up in plumes around us, mixing with the scents of mold and decay.

She straddled me, sitting up straight, her fangs bared. They were so much longer than her sister's, and Mercedes' silken blonde hair hung over her shoulders in a golden waterfall—a waterfall I needed to see turn crimson. "What's wrong with my sister?" she hissed out.

"Something's wrong with Saul. She felt a spike of anxiety from him and then ran away from me and Tage to find him."

Narrowing her eyes, Mercedes watched me, trying to see if I was bluffing. Thank God I wasn't, because the she-devil was going to eat me and enjoy every second of it, otherwise. "She left Tage?"

"She did, but he ran after her. I don't know if he'll be able to catch her before something else does."

She shook her head. "That makes no sense. She wouldn't leave Tage to run to Saul. That wouldn't happen. Ever. So the question is…why are you lying, Roman? Have you already hurt her?"

"It does make sense if you're bonded," I argued. "And Porschia is bonded with Saul."

"She was bonded to Tage before Saul, and you're bonded to her too, so why aren't you chasing after her? Keeping her safe?"

I paused a moment to consider my words before throwing caution to the wind. If Mercedes was planning to eat me, she'd already made her mind up. "Because I'd give anything to break the bond I have with her. I'd give anything if..."

"She were dead," she finished.

"She killed my brother, Mercedes. Think of how you would feel if someone killed Porschia or Ford. Would you ever stop trying to seek vengeance?"

Mercedes swallowed, looking out at the forest that swallowed us whole. "No, I don't guess I would. But I also can't let you kill me or my siblings. I'm sure you understand the predicament I'm in."

I let my head thump back onto the broken, jagged planks beneath it as she jumped up and away from me. Mercedes pinched her bottom lip and began to pace. It was strange. She was pretty and light-haired, but calculating and shrewd, a natural born hunter. Porschia had hair dark as the night around us, and until she killed Pierce, I thought she had a heart of gold.

Pierce and I were both born to be monsters, inside and out. I just didn't expect that Porschia would turn out to be a bigger one.

From the ground one step below, Mercedes stopped abruptly, looking at me and the pile of rubble I laid in. "I think you should come with me."

"Come with you where?"

"To help Porschia."

I groaned, covering my eyes with one forearm. "I thought we covered this. I have no desire to help your sister. To be perfectly clear, I don't want to help any of you Grants." I wanted their blood.

"Well," she said, "since I'm pretty sure you won't stop this nonsense anytime soon, I'll just have to drain you. I can't have you getting in the way or hurting my brother. Porschia could handle you, but Ford couldn't. And you know that." Her eyes darkened. "Is that your plan now that you couldn't best me? To hurt my brother?"

I sat up, draped my arms on my knees, and shook my head at her. "I honestly hadn't thought of Ford at all." That would kill Porschia. Her and Mercedes rubbed each other wrong, but Ford was golden. Ford was also a good kid. *Could* I do it?

"Don't hurt him," she said in a low growl. "No matter what happens. Not Ford, okay?"

"I thought you were just going to drain me and end this."

She shook her head. I could see the glistening red trails on her cheeks. If she was going to be as emotional as Porschia, I'd beg her to end me.

When I stepped out of the hole and onto the ground, she moved fast, embedding her fangs in my neck. I struggled against her in a futile effort as she drank. "Not going down like this," I gritted.

She pulled away fast. "I wasn't killing you; I was bonding to you. Now I'll know your feelings, where to find you...everything."

I stumbled over to a tree, bracing myself against the coarse bark and leathery lichens. "Great." Now I had a half-insane, over-emotional chick following my every move. Well, I'd dealt with Dara, I could deal with Mercedes.

"Let's go," she said, clapping her hands. "We need to find my siblings, get them out of whatever trouble they're in, and then find an Infected to reverse this mess altogether," she said, motioning to her mouth. "I hate being a vampire. I don't know how you can stand it. We need to fix all of this. Quick."

"There is no 'we', Mercedes."

She grinned. "Oh, but there is. Whether you remember it or not, *we* became friends. I helped you when you were at your weakest once, and I'll do it again."

"I'm not at my weakest."

"Matter of opinion, Roman. Matter. Of. Opinion. Let's go," she said haughtily.

MERCEDES

SILLY NIGHT-WALKER. HE THOUGHT HE WAS GOING TO SNEAK UP ON ME AND drain me dry; though, I'd prefer that end to becoming a rotting husk again. Roman was delusional. But when he spoke of Porschia being in trouble, there was conviction in his voice. Roman's bond to her was as strong as Tage's, though his loyalty was questionable at the moment. That meant she truly was in trouble, and if he wasn't going to help, I wouldn't let him stop me from getting to her.

I tapped my foot and crossed my arms.

"What's that supposed to mean?" he asked.

"It means, hurry up. Work your magic. Lead me to my sister and this trouble you speak of."

He huffed petulantly. "You Grant women are more trouble than you're worth, you know that?"

"Tell me about it, bud. Now, chop chop."

He walked down the path that led away from Saul's wretched house. I wasn't snobbish. I'd lived in a shit house my whole life, but there were animals living in that one. Live ones who didn't want a human squatter, much less a night-walking one. And I didn't want to eat them. Rats and opossums were disgusting, and my guess was that worse than those lived somewhere inside the rest of that mess.

I bounced on my feet as I walked behind him.

"Why are you jumping?" he grouched.

"I have all of this pent-up energy and I need to move. Can't we run?"

"I don't know if you can keep up," he teased, quirking a brow. Suddenly the playfulness faded and all that was left was pure dare. He was going to try to get away. No way in hell.

"Try me, Roman."

He didn't waste any time doing exactly that. Blurring through the trees, I followed his scent, the leather jacket on his back, the spice that was intoxicatingly Roman. He tried to lose me, to throw me off his track, but I was fast. I was fast just like my sister, and like her, I'd be just as deadly to those who crossed my family.

Part of me hoped Roman wouldn't learn that lesson first, despite his being hell bent on the same. Part of me hoped he tested me.

TWO

PORSCHIA

I couldn't find him. Searching through the forest, increasingly frustrated, I knew he was near. I could feel him, but I couldn't hear, smell, or see him. "Saul?" I called out, hoping desperately that he and Mercedes were okay, hoping I wasn't too late.

No answer came.

I was in the middle of the forest in a clearing, and through the circular hole in the foliage, I could see the stars had shifted in the sky. I heard the sounds of small night animals and insects. Crickets. Frogs from the creek just beyond us. Water trickling over stones and mud in that same sliver of water.

My heart thundered. Where was he? A bright flash came from the center of the clearing. I shielded my eyes with my arm and stepped back to the trees for cover.

"It's about time, Porschia. I thought you were faster."

I'd recognize that voice anywhere, and my gut feeling about the person it belonged to? It was right. "Delilah," I answered scornfully.

She laughed and stepped toward me, backlit from behind by some sort of bright white light. "You want to see Saul? Your brother?"

"You have Ford?" I saw red.

"I do, and if you want him to live, you'll follow me without incident. Try to kill me, and I'll have to do the same to your baby brother, which would be a pity. He really is a nice boy." She turned on her heel and sauntered toward the light. I had no choice but to follow.

"How do I know they're okay?"

She glanced back at me over her shoulder. "You don't." She paused for a moment, considering, and added, "But I give you my word."

As if her word was worth anything.

I followed her, stepping toward the white light, squinting until my eyes dripped blood from the strain. When I stepped into the sliver of white slashing through the forest, my world disappeared and I entered another. Blue skies. Sunshine from directly overhead. I stumbled over something thick, and then my hands found themselves embedded in warm sand. Golden and grainy, stretching as far as the eye could see. Delilah was changed, too. Gone was her pale skin smattered with freckles. Gone was the red of her hair. In this place, her skin was bronzed, her body taut and toned. She was strong. Her hair was long and dark and straight as an arrow, hanging to her lower back and threaded with gold. Her dingy clothes had been transformed into gauzy white fabric that clung to her hips and breasts. Golden bracelets and cuffs wrapped around her upper arms, around her neck, on her ears. She wore a golden crown fashioned to look like a lion or panther; some sort of great cat. And the tattoo on her neck? It writhed as if the serpent were alive. Her eyes matched every piece of jewelry she wore: gold and glittering.

"It is an ankh," she said simply. "An important symbol in our culture."

Our? Whose culture? Who cared? Where were Saul and Ford? "Where are they?" I asked impatiently.

She motioned for me to follow her. "This way," she answered simply.

But for miles, there was only sand. What was this place?

"This is The Sand," she offered, as if reading my mind.

Yards in front of us a tent appeared, tall as one of the homes in Blackwater and completely made up of black fabric and wooden poles. It was enormous. "Your loved ones are safe." She stopped and waited for me. "No harm will befall you inside."

I had no choice but to take her at her word. If Ford and Saul were trapped in this place, I needed to find them and get out. The dry air burned my nose and the sand pelted my arms as the wind kicked up.

Moving aside some of the fabric, I made my way into the tent. The scents of faraway spices mixed with those of Saul and my brother. When the dark shroud fell behind me, I could hear their voices. I could breathe again.

"Porschia?" Ford chirped and ran to me, tackling me in a hug.

I held tightly to him. "I'm so glad you're okay," I said, relieved but wary.

"We're fine, but you shouldn't have come." He pulled back and shoved his hands in his pockets. "You were right about Delilah, by the way." He leaned in close. "Even about her eyes. She can change her face. It's... messed up."

I'd told him something was weird, right after she first became a camp follower. But it was only after I couldn't find her scent in Mountainside that I began paying closer attention. One day she was talking with Ford and her eyes, the ones that had always been lichen-green, suddenly became dark brown, as brown as the horse's mane that she stroked. I told Ford to watch closely in case they changed again but he waved me off, probably thinking I was imagining things. But oh, ho. Here she was in this awful place, with a brand new face, and she didn't look like the innocent doe I found in the woods. She looked like a woman, a huntress, a warrior.

"It's okay, Ford. I'm just glad you're safe."

Saul stared at us from a few feet away. I let Ford go and threw my arms around Saul. "Thank you."

He pulled away, surprised. "For what?" he asked.

"For taking care of him."

"How do you know I did?"

Ford made a groaning sound. "Because she knows *you*."

Delilah cleared her throat from behind us and we all snapped to attention, facing her. *Always keep your target in your sight.* That was true of crossbows and crazy witches.

"Now that you're here, Porschia, I can send Ford and Saul back to the forest if you'd like."

"Yes," I answered at the same time Saul and Ford echoed their dissent.

"No!" Ford yelled. "No way, Porschia."

"I'm not leaving you here," Saul said adamantly. "We don't even know what this place is, or how to get back here."

Delilah smiled condescendingly. "You couldn't find it if you wanted to. The only reason you are here now is because I allow you to be. There is only one other who can cross the barrier, and I imagine he will be here very soon."

I moved nearer to Ford. "You need to leave, Ford. Go to Father."

"What's he gonna do?" he protested.

"Just trust me. You need to go while you still can." I whispered to him, "Please."

To my right, Saul crossed his arms over his chest, defiant to the last. I pleaded with him, as well. "Please take him home, Saul."

"I agree *he* should go, but I'm staying."

"He won't be safe in the woods by himself."

Saul shook his head. "He'd be safer there than here."

Delilah watched us with alert eyes, taking it all in. "You truly care for both of them," she stated matter-of-factly.

"I do," I affirmed.

She smiled at Ford. "I think you should do as your sister asks."

"I don't give a shit *what* you think, Delilah! You're nothing but a liar. You probably have something waiting out there to eat me as soon as I step foot back in those woods."

Delilah smiled. "There is nothing that will harm you. I'll see to it."

"Do you give me your word?" I asked her.

"I do," she said with an inclination of her head.

"Then send him home."

"Porschia, no!" Ford yelled as he was drawn out of the tent by an invisible force, shouting and yelling for me to tell her to stop. But I couldn't. Ford needed to live. He needed to go back home, stay in Blackwater, and grow up to be a good man with a long life.

"Go straight home!" I yelled, tears choking my throat.

"Do you want to go with him?" I asked Saul.

"Not happening," he said, his fangs bared at Delilah. "I refuse to leave you here with *her*."

TAGE

I'D BECOME AN EXPERT LIAR. I LIED TO PORSCHIA, MY FRIENDS, AND EVEN myself. Because I wanted to believe that for a few seconds, I could feel normal and not be the monster that I was. When I told her I was in frenzy? That it was the reason I bit her neck without numbing her at her first rotation? Lie. When I told her where I was from and how old I was?

Lies. When I told her I loved her? That was the truth. The only truth that mattered now.

Every untruth I'd woven was unraveling at my feet. Porschia was not going to understand any of this and I didn't know if she would forgive me. She hadn't forgiven Saul easily. I'd been confident for so long, but now? My stomach churned with disgust. I thought I had more time. I was wrong.

I could sense Porschia's distress, but that wasn't what immediately worried me. I felt the heat and an arid wind blowing across the clearing, and then from the center appeared a bright light and Ford fell from the shining sliver onto the forest floor. Reaching him quickly I asked, "Hey, are you okay?"

"I'm fine," he said, angrily ripping his shoulder back from my hand. He backed away and stared at me, stunned, mouth agape as he tried to figure out what had happened and what was happening now, his mind tripping over common sense. But then again, nothing about magic was sensical.

Suddenly his eyes glazed over, an opaque film covering his irises, and he stood and began to walk back in the direction of Blackwater. He was spelled and would find his way home safely, under *her* protection. She must have received a vision as well, and now she'd found Porschia. I'd felt her draw near for days; I just had no idea how close she actually was.

I had to reach Porschia before it was too late. I just hoped she would understand. Either way, she was going to be pissed. Omissions were just as hurtful as blatant lies. But sometimes lies were necessary. Sometimes they were shields.

I always planned to tell her everything about my past, the vision… everything. Soon. But things kept happening, going wrong, and then the time was never right. Either way, the time was now. It was forced, but necessary all the same.

Watching Ford until he became part of the darkness, I stepped toward the center of the clearing and called the light. It collected into a ball in the center of my palm and I launched it forward and opened the barrier, toeing off my boots. It had been too long since my toes last felt the warm sand.

THREE

PORSCHIA

THE WIND GREW WILD, MAKING THE TENT FABRIC FLAIL, TUGGING AND pulling against the ties that bound it. Delilah clapped loudly once and it died down again. She looked to me and smiled before exiting the tent the way we'd come in.

"What is going on?" I said, my voice a shrill whisper. My head ached, my heartbeat pounding relentlessly against my skull.

Inside, the tent was sparse, but there were a few items placed here and there; one of which was a black lounger. Sensing my distress, Saul helped me over to it. "Maybe it's the dry heat, Porschia. You should sit down."

I sat on the lounger, letting the back of it hold me up, while Saul stood at the foot of the piece of furniture. He kept his distance; his body taut, like the string of a bow, tense with the arrow pulled across it.

"Hungry?"

"Very," he admitted.

There was nothing to say. I couldn't feed him because I wasn't well. I didn't know how to get food here, or even if there *was* food here—besides Delilah—and whatever this place was, whatever she was, I had a feeling we wouldn't be able to feed from her easily.

His leg bounced nervously, mimicking my feelings. I was weak and undeniably scared.

"How do we escape?" I whispered.

Delilah reappeared soundlessly and answered, "You don't, but this might help ease the pain."

From behind her, Tage appeared. "Tage?" I sat up straight and he rushed to me, making Saul shift and move across the tent a few feet away. His familiar hands held me tightly; his fingers combing my hair, his soft lips comforting me.

Delilah stood back, shrewdly taking us in. She stared over his shoulder, waiting for something, but I wasn't sure what. And then she spoke.

"Tageset, I cannot believe this."

He stiffened and pulled away.

"Do you not think it is time to tell her?" she questioned. He turned to face her, but she continued her lashing. "Have you not toyed with the poor girl enough?"

"Quiet, Sekhmet," he growled.

She bared her teeth and fangs began to grow long and thin from her incisors. She was a night-walker? How did Tage know this creature? What the hell was going on, and why were we in this place? A dam of questions broke inside me.

"Tage, what is going on?" My voice shook, afraid of his answer and fear that it might break me. He hadn't seemed to know Delilah before now, yet he called her 'Sekhmet' moments ago. What did it mean?

"Tell her, Tageset," she said, enunciating his name.

I glanced worriedly at Saul, whose face reflected my concern. We were in trouble.

Tage turned to me and grabbed my elbows. "I haven't been honest with you, Porschia," he began. "I wasn't turned just before reaching Blackwater, and I wasn't in Frenzy when I first fed from you. I'm much older than that."

My lips quivered. "How much older?"

He blew out a short breath. "You know how the Infection began, and then how vampirism rose at the same time? There were two curses: one placed upon the people of Egypt, and one to affect Pharaoh himself. Ramesses was a stubborn man. He refused to let the Israelites leave Egypt, even after so much suffering. The rivers were turned to poison. The crops were eaten away. His people, his family, would starve, but Ramesses was an inflexible man. He stood firm in his decision because the slaves gave him something his own people couldn't, or wouldn't. He always wanted to build bigger, grander, and taller, but nothing was ever enough. However, when his firstborn children were cursed—all the children born to his wife, Nefertari—he changed his mind. It wasn't just one child, his firstborn son…it was seven. You see, Ramesses fathered many illegitimate children with his concubines, but they were spared. It wouldn't have bothered Ramesses if they were turned into monsters. He had nothing to do with the bastards he fathered. However, the children of his true love were made into monsters. They became the first vampires. And that hurt him so deeply that he finally caved. I didn't think he would. My father was unbreakable up until that point."

Tage's eyes faded from the blue I'd grown to love into a honey gold. He waved a hand down his body and his clothes – the fitted t-shirt and jeans – faded away. He wore a skirt of black fabric fastened with a golden belt.

"You're one of them," I said breathlessly. "One of the cursed children… one of the first vampires?"

He nodded. "I am."

Sekhmet laughed. "He is the first, Porschia. He is THE first vampire. I was the second born, the second vampire created."

They were brother and sister. That meant they were older than… I backed away from Tage and moved toward Saul. A line had seemingly been drawn in the sand beneath our feet. "So this was all a game to you?" I asked. "Were you just using me as some sort of sick prize in a contest with your sister?"

"No," he answered immediately. "I wasn't."

"Why are we even here? Why were you in Blackwater?" When I bumped into Saul's chest he steadied me, which earned him a growl from Tage.

"There is a way to stop all of this," he explained. His eyes, roiling honey, begged me to understand, but how could you understand something that made no sense? How could I understand that Tage wasn't really the Tage I'd grown to love?

My heart was failing, its pattern skittish and as flustered and confused as I felt. But my mind was still reeling. "How?" I asked. "How do we end it?"

He pursed his lips together and then admitted, "You."

TAGE

I COULD SEE IT IN HER EYES – THE BETRAYAL REFLECTED BACK AT ME – AND it cut me like a thousand knives. "For years our father made his sorcerers teach us everything they knew. They taught us magic and made sure we fed only from them, hoping their enchanted blood would bolster our budding talent. Over time, our skills with the art grew. We met with seers frequently as part of our ongoing studies, and before our father died, one seer had a vision; a revelation. In the West, one would arise, one who held both curses."

Porschia covered her mouth. I could see her fingers trembling.

"He could see your face," I told her, remembering the man's withered fingers on my temples and how he transferred the image into my mind. Thousands of years had passed, yet I never forgot it. Behind her stood a grove of deciduous trees and a dark curtain of falling water, but what I saw were her eyes and the strong set of her jaw; mere hints of her iron will and determination. I searched for many centuries until I found Blackwater, and the moment when Roman led me to the square and she was there? I felt the weight of the curse begin to lighten. However, she was human. Either the seer was wrong, or she wasn't yet cursed.

"How am I supposed to help with anything? What else did the seer see?" she asked, frustrated.

Sekhmet smiled, walked toward me, and stopped at my side. "We are the only of The First still living, and we have honed our ability to heal over the years. Tageset can heal the curse of vampirism—if he so chooses." She looked at me pointedly. "And I can heal the Infection, as you call it."

Porschia's mouth gaped open. She looked at me and asked, "Is that true?" Tears filled her eyes. "Together you could heal everything?"

"We *could,*" Sekhmet answered cryptically, and then turned to me.

"But brother, I have another idea for you to consider."

FOUR

SEKHMET

I WATCHED AS MY BROTHER'S ANGER REACHED A TIPPING POINT. HE inclined his head to Porschia, a girl not worthy to lick the sand from the bottoms of his feet, before striding toward me and ushering me out of the tent. "What are you talking about?" he spat.

"Let's talk somewhere more comfortable." I flicked my hand toward the dark tent, sealing it. It was, in effect, a cage for the little birds inside—one bird in particular, who'd become very valuable to me. If my brother wasn't on board with my new plan, he would meet the fate of our other siblings. I'd established the pecking order very early on, and wasn't afraid to end it now. Tageset had always been kindred to me; a like mind with similar ambitions. I wondered idly if the hybrid had changed him too much. Had she weakened him? Only time would tell.

Tageset waved his hand imperiously and a gilded tent arose from the sand with walls of solid gold that gleamed, reflecting the sun and his power. The walls of gold began to shimmer and turned into gauzy fabric that let the warm breeze flow through the structure. "You haven't lost your style, I see," I responded dryly, and led the way inside.

There were chaises, lush fabric, pillows, and statues. It felt like home. I walked up to a golden statue of Bastet that stood taller than I. "Thank you for this." Out of all the gods, Father valued the feline deities the most. They were ferocious, fierce in battle, and showed little mercy. They would end anyone who stood in their way. That was why I wanted to be exactly like them, and over the eons had honed my magic to mimic their ability to take human and feline form. It was why I chose to become Sekhmet, the warrior goddess, instead of pretending to be like her, as I did when I was a child.

Tageset smiled. "I thought you'd appreciate it." He walked to a table where a decanter of clear water stood beside two slender glasses. Filling them both, he brought one to me and sipped from his own as we settled into opposite seats. The water turned to blood, thickly slicking the sides of the cup and sliding down the glass. "You've had another vision?" he asked softly.

"Only of you and the doubly-cursed," I replied. "It was how I found you, and her as well." The seer may have told me about the vision, but he didn't provide an image of Porschia. Tageset never divulged it, either; he just begun to search secretively, alone. I killed everyone he loved in my quest for answers.

"What's changed, then? What other possible alternative is there to ending these curses?"

I squinted my eyes to see if anything in his face would tell me of his loyalty. I was so sure it was with the girl, even after all we'd been through. After all I did for him, he was going to choose her and I would have to kill them both.

"Do you remember our father's dreams of a great city?"

"Of course I do," he said, taking another sip of blood. "He spoke of them often enough."

"You also went with him, to meet the architects and builders. You were by his side."

Tageset nodded. "I was."

"Tageset, I was not with you and him, but I can still see his vision. I could see it then, but I see it clearly now. We could bring it to life." Scooting to the edge of my chair, I sat my glass on the carpet at my feet. "We hold everything right in the palm of our hands. We could build an empire and rule it all. The cursed could be cured, and in gratefulness they would worship us. We would become great like Father."

I tried to make him see, creating a shimmer in front of him and showing him exactly how I saw it in my mind. "They would build great cities and temples in our names. Our faces would be everywhere, in their homes, on the great monuments. The statues would be of us; not of the gods, but of us. The people would be indebted to us and would do anything we asked. We would literally rule the world. There is nothing stopping us, my dear Tageset. Of course, we could start here. It's a fairly large continent."

Through the shimmer were blue lakes and rivers with temples on their banks. There were newly-built homes with paved streets in gridded patterns. "The ruined buildings would have to be burned, but in their place pyramids and great buildings would be erected to honor our past and display the strength and power that only you and I possess now."

I showed him how people could rebuild homes and families and be happy again instead of living in these abysmal conditions.

"What about us?" he asked pointedly. "Where would *we* be in all of this?"

"At the center of it all, Tageset. We could rule, side by side, a force to be reckoned with. We could level the gutted cities with a wave of our hands. We could start a new civilization. Together."

"But you would allow the curses to still exist? How would that help anything?"

I huffed in frustration, miffed that his vision and foresight was not as grandiose as mine.

"I'm only trying to see your full design, Sekhmet. Don't get upset with me."

"You speak like a westerner. How many years have you dwelled here?"

He smiled. "Too many, apparently."

Wait. "How long ago did you receive a vision about her?"

He shifted in his seat. "The seers gave me a vision over a thousand years ago, but it wasn't clear. It was foggy," he squinted. "A new one flashed through my mind just six months ago, but I had to search far and wide for her. It wasn't like I was given a map, and when I found her, she was still human."

Was my brother lying? What did he mean, *she was still human?* "When did she receive both curses? Did you inflict one to cause this shift?" If so, he was brilliant.

"I did not. She was bitten by her sister, who bore the plague of rot, and in the middle of the change, she drank the blood of a vampire."

"How was that so readily available?"

He groaned and leaned back in his seat. "It was the way of their people. Hunters and huntresses wore rings with vampire blood in them in case they should meet an Infected in the forest. They considered it better to become a monster than suffer from rot, and Porschia was a huntress."

I hissed at him. "She is no huntress. I should show her what a true huntress is!"

"If you kill her, your plan will never come to fruition. The seer said that in order to release the curses, we each must heal her."

I hated when Tageset was right, but there were other ways. "Why didn't you heal her of the vampirism and then have her bite a person with the plague of rot? Did you try?" He didn't answer, so I prodded him once more. "Do you wish to die, brother?"

He stiffened. "Not at the moment, no."

"Is that why you didn't heal her and release her from the curse? You wish to die now? After all this time?" My brother wasn't a conqueror. He wasn't trying to search for power or to lead a nation. Until now, he roamed the world alone, single-mindedly seeking the bearer of both curses. He wanted to cure her with me, because once we did so, we would both return to the earth. Dust to dust. Well, I didn't care for dust and had no intention of dying.

He was quiet a moment, looking thoughtfully into his glass. "I thought I did."

"And now?"

"Living seems like the only important thing now. And if we think your plan through, it just might work."

Was he feeding me a lie? Telling me what I wanted to hear? Maybe we should up the ante...

"If you die, you'll never be with her. You'll never see her smile, hear her laughter, or smell her scent. If you heal her, she'll never be yours."

His brows touched one another. "I know that, and that's precisely why I want to live. For her."

"And to rule with me?"

"Of course. You're my sister."

I hoped he knew this already, but it was worth repeating: "Family is the most important thing. We are stronger together, Tageset."

"I know that," he said simply.

"Then you will agree to stay away from the girl. We have to keep her alive, but you don't owe her anything. I'll admit, your plan was brilliant. You roped her in with your charm and spells, but then you went even farther, making her love you. Simply ruthless, brother."

"Thanks," he said, standing up and walking outside.

Tageset walked through the sand, the wind blowing his footprint trail away almost immediately. His imprints were blended into the sand, erased from existence. My brother was always thinking, and it often got him into trouble. Overthinking was almost as bad as an instantaneous wrong decision, and much more torturous.

I spirited into the dark cage. Time to poke the bird.

FIVE

MERCEDES

The forest was loud with insects. Buzzing, annoying things. I stopped running when I caught a waft of a familiar smell. "What is that?" I said, trying to place it.

"It's your brother," Roman answered with a smile.

"Touch him and die," I warned in a saccharine voice laced with shards of glass.

Sure enough, Ford was walking alone through the forest. At night. Alone. And sure enough, Roman sprinted toward him. I tackled Roman to the ground as his arms reached out toward Ford's neck, but he only laughed as we rolled through the underbrush and slammed into a tree trunk. I left him lying on the forest floor, still not sure if he was actually planning to hurt him or if he was simply testing my ability to keep him from doing just that.

"Ford?"

No stumble, no flicker of recognition. He didn't even look up at me.

"Ford!" I yelled.

Nothing.

Roman was on his feet in a second, walking toward the two of us like nothing had happened. He smiled conceitedly. "I'm just going to try to wake him up. You're right there, so you can stand guard," he teased. Roman grabbed Ford's jaw and forced him to look up. Ford's eyes were opaque, a white film floating on top of each eyeball.

"What happened to him?" I gasped, but didn't have time to dwell. Ford was angry. He swung out at both of us, blindly searching for what was stopping him.

Growling, he swung again and again, so we stepped back and let him wear himself out. He soon tired, foam collecting at the corners of his mouth. He stopped and braced his hands on his knees, panting and struggling to catch his breath.

"What the hell happened to my brother, Roman? Did you do this? Is he Infected? Did you Infect him so I'd have to feed from him?" My fingers clenched together into tight balls. I couldn't decide between wanting to tear his head off or knocking him into next week.

"As much as I'd like to take credit for that stroke of brilliance, how would I possibly do that? Ford was in the Colony. He isn't supposed to be out here, and he certainly doesn't act like the Infected. Look at him." Roman stared at Ford as he sat on the forest floor, arms propped on his knees, completely spent. His head bowed down and soon he sank into the leaves. Curled into the fetal position, he fell asleep suddenly and soundly.

Roman shook his head in disbelief. I felt the same way. "So, do we let him sleep?" he asked.

"I have no idea what to do."

"That would be a first for you Grant women. I thought you always knew what to do."

I snorted. Mother thought she knew best about everything, but me and Porschia? Nope. "That's the thing, Roman. You think you're so smart and you're angry because of what Porschia did to your brother, but you forget that you made our lives a living hell by torturing our mother. We haven't known what to do with anything for years."

He was quiet after that, thoughtful. I focused on the rhythmic sound of Ford's breathing.

Slowly.

Steadily.

In and out.

In and out.

It was a long time before Roman spoke, and when he did, his words surprised me. "Pierce was a monster, and he was trying to turn me into one. It's why I stopped helping him."

I listened.

"I thought if he were cured, maybe he would be his old self again, just be my brother."

I gave him a tight smile. Mother never changed. Of course, she wasn't cured, either. I didn't think she was Infected or Vampiric, but I think that their experiments on her while she was pregnant sent her one step over a precipice she couldn't help but topple over. Mental illness was just as much a disease and a curse as anything else in this crazy world.

Pierce was much the same. Maybe over time, he crossed a line that he couldn't go back over again. The Infection eventually attacked the brain. Maybe his was too far gone to be repaired.

Roman scrubbed his face with his hands. "This makes no sense. It's bizarre."

"I know." It was. Everything was. I sat up. "Do you feel her nearby? Is she scared?"

"She's very near, but I don't hear or smell her. It's strange..." he said, his words fading away into thought. "She isn't scared or panicked, but she's sad and hurt. Maybe confused, too. She's a swirl of emotions, and none of them are happy."

"Why would she be sad, in the middle of the forest at night?" Did something happen to Tage?

"Is there a better place to feel sad?"

Ford still hadn't budged. As I listened to my baby brother sleep, I told Roman, "I don't suppose there is."

ROMAN

MERCEDES WATCHED ME LIKE A HAWK UNTIL THE SKY BEGAN TO LIGHTEN, and even then, she was ready to pounce if I tried to make another attempt at her brother. She'd made it clear that I couldn't best her. She was too strong…at least, she would be until I fed and she didn't, which was my next plan. Could I kill Ford? It turned out I didn't know, but I had no qualms about feeding from him. Could I drain the life away from him? I'd have to ask my conscience after a few gulps.

It was dawn before Ford began to stir, and when he finally woke, he was dazed. His eyes were clear as he sat up, scratching the leaves and twigs from his hair. "What's going on?"

Mercedes helped him to his feet. "We were wondering the same thing. You were out roaming the forest alone last night. Your eyes were all...white and gross, and you were mostly unresponsive."

"Mostly?" he asked, dusting himself off.

"Well," she grinned. "You tried to beat the hell out of Roman."

He smiled proudly. "I did?"

"You did," she affirmed.

"And he didn't eat me?"

That made me smile. "Oh, I wanted to."

Ford rolled his eyes and then the smile and happiness faded. "Oh, shit."

"What?" Mercedes asked.

"I know who has Porschia and Saul."

I stepped forward. "Who has them?"

"Delilah. But she isn't who she says she is. She's a witch."

Mercedes' shoulders sank. "Ford, witches aren't real."

He scoffed. "Vampires and Infected rotters are; so why can't witches be real? Anyway, I saw her. She worked her magic on me and used me as bait." Thinking more on it for a second, his fists balled up. "That bitch."

I smiled and clapped his shoulder. "Women."

Mercedes punched my shoulder, further proving my point.

"So how do we find Delilah? Do you remember?" Mercedes asked him.

He shook his head. "I'm not sure. That part's a little fuzzy."

I butted in. "She must be close. I can feel Porschia."

"It's not that she isn't close, Roman. She is, but Delilah took me somewhere else, like we went into another world or something. It was sandy and sunny, and not a tree in sight."

"Desert," I said, thinking to myself. "How would she get you to the desert?"

"Because she's a witch!" he said indignantly. "She's a *crazy* witch, too."

"What do we do?" Mercedes asked. Her hair was falling out of its braid and she still looked sleepy. She, like her sister, wore a light dress, muting the effect of her fangs somehow. It made her look sweet and trustworthy. Women had the best camouflage and used their wiles to their advantage. I hated women in that moment, especially ones bearing the last name of Grant.

"We feed, and then we wait for her to come back."

“And when she does, we’ll be ready.” Mercedes smiled. She was ready for a fight.

I smiled.

SIX

PORSCHIA

My mind couldn't wrap around what Tage had divulged. It made sense in a weird way, but then again, it didn't. Back at the rotation where we met, he bit me without numbing me. He had to have known about the numbing factor then, so why didn't he use it? Because he somehow knew that even though I was human then, I wouldn't be in the future? Tage wanted to hurt me. When he came after me in the city, scaring me half to death, he played it off by saying he knew Roman was close and he was only goading him. Was he thinking about killing me then?

And another thing – why didn't he cure me? If he could cure Vampirism, why didn't he cure me of it already? Then I would have been left as an Infected, and a night-walker could have fed from me and healed me.

I didn't understand.

And what about being the first-born son of the Pharaoh? I wasn't a history expert, but didn't another son succeed him? Egypt didn't end with the plagues, and the fact that he had magic completely blew my mind. I never imagined it was real.

Saul paced back and forth. "I don't know how to get us out of here, but this is insane."

"I know."

"Even if we left, they could just spirit us back here. They have... Powers." He ran his fingers through his hair and laced them around the back of his head.

"I know."

He groaned in frustration, placing his hands on his hips. "You know, as crazy as it is, it all makes sense."

"It does?" It sort of did.

"You know, the part about the children of the cursed Pharaoh being the ones tasked to rid the world of the curse their father was responsible for. It's like a punishment, five thousand years in the making." He tested the tent fabric with his finger, but none gave. "I'm so thirsty."

I was too, but Saul was about to snap. He was fidgety. I knew that feeling, where your skin and everything beneath it crawled and writhed with need. Not want; want was something you could contain. Need was primal and aggressive. It sought out. It wouldn't be suppressed.

Sekhmet appeared through the doorway, smiling brightly.

"My brother is quite taken with you," she said. She focused on me as if I were the only one in the room. I kept silent. Saul stopped and watched as she approached me.

"I guess I can see the appeal. You are very pretty. Innocent. And from what I've heard, fierce as well. It is a potent combination. Is that right, Saul? Is she desirable?" She turned toward him just before reaching me. Saul gritted his teeth. I could hear them scrape, top against bottom.

Sekhmet swayed her hips as she circled him, letting her fingers trail over his chest, shoulder, and back. A low rumble came from my throat. She might have magic, but I bet she still bled. The warning went unheeded. "Do you find me desirable, Saul?"

"Not in the least," he deadpanned. I wanted to hug him for that.

Her lips formed a dramatic pout. "I don't believe you."

Saul moved so fast, I barely saw him. Digging his fangs into her neck, he drank. She didn't even blink, didn't stop him, nothing. And as soon as he'd had enough, she simply pushed him away. Stepping back from him, Sekhmet sealed the wound on her neck with a wave of her hand and rubbed the blood between her fingers and thumb. "You are brave, Saul. I didn't expect that from you."

"I was thirsty," he panted, wiping her blood from his lips and chin.

"You are still in Frenzy?" she asked.

"Yes."

Smiling, Sekhmet looked to him. "Then I suppose I will forgive you, this time. Do it again and I'll mummify you. Alive."

"How are we supposed to feed here?" he challenged. I wanted to scream at him to keep his mouth shut, but that wouldn't help the situation.

"You aren't," she said simply, walking toward me.

"Are you hungry, Porschia?" she asked condescendingly.

I refused to let her get to me.

"Answer me," she commanded.

"No. I'm not hungry."

She smiled. "Liar." Walking back to the entrance, she paused before lifting the fabric. "You will not eat until my brother agrees with my plan."

"And if he doesn't?"

"Then you will be in a lot of pain very soon, I imagine. The heat. Much like time, it withers. The warmth dries everything it touches, slowly at first, and then you'll wake up and not understand what's happened to you."

TAGE

When Sekhmet left the tent, I entered it, appearing before Porschia. She gasped and stepped backward toward Saul, who bared his fangs and snapped them at me. There was a scent coming from him, feline and danger mixed together. "You fed from my sister?" I asked incredulously.

"I couldn't stop myself," he said, finally relaxing.

I shook my head. "You're a danger to her now."

"To your sister?" he asked.

"No, to Porschia."

He stiffened and Porschia looked him over. "You drank Sekhmet's blood. She has powers you can't even begin to understand. And with her blood in you, she can control you—everything you do, say, think. You're a danger to *Porschia* now."

"What can I do? I can make myself vomit."

"She won't allow that. You have two options: Either I put you in a cage to keep her safe, or I send you home to keep her safe."

Saul raked a hand through his hair. "But she isn't safe! Nothing is safe. As long as you and your sister are alive, she'll never *be* safe. I'm not leaving and you're not putting me in a cage. If I'm in a cage, I can't protect her from you!"

"I'm not the one you need to worry about," I told him, looking earnestly at Porschia.

"And she should just blindly trust you on that one, huh?" Saul jeered. "Because you've been such a stand-up guy up until now? Because you love her so much you'd never put her in danger?"

"That's right."

Porschia looked away. "Get out, Tage."

I couldn't believe what I was hearing. Why would she want me to leave? I was keeping her safe. I loved her and she loved me. We could get through this together. "Why?"

"Because I don't want to look at your face right now!" she screamed.

I had to make her see. "This is what she wants. Sekhmet wants to divide. Her very name means 'the one who tears apart'! This is what she does!"

Porschia sighed. "What does Tage-*set* mean? Because you're the one who tore everything apart. You weaseled your way into my life with the sole intention of destroying me! Well, mission accomplished. Now you can leave."

Bloody tears fell onto her cheeks. I wanted to wipe them away, but she didn't want me to look at her, let alone touch her. "My only intention was to find you, and with the help of my sister, erase the curses on you and on the rest of humanity—once and for all." I didn't tell her that the only reason I wanted to cure her originally was because I wanted to die; that I'd lived too long and seen too much to keep living like that. But once I found her, she awakened something in me, something I hadn't felt in years. She was both the reason I wanted to heal the curses, and the reason I didn't. Because if we healed her I would die, after her love gave me the best reason I'd ever had to live.

"And now? What plan have you and your insane sister hatched now? Still going to rid the world of the curses?"

I pursed my lips together. "No."

"No, because...?" she baited.

"Because as soon as I do I'll turn to dust and disappear, and I want to be with you, Porschia. I don't want to die when I can still live a full life spent loving you." I needed every second with her. She was the blood pumping through my veins, feeding me life through her love.

Saul growled. "That's not love, asshole! She shouldn't have to live with this shit when you have a way to heal her!"

He didn't understand. For over a thousand years, I searched for her with the hopes that she would bring death to me. Now, I couldn't bear the thought of leaving her. I loved her.

"And starving her is bullshit too, Tage, or Tageset, or whatever your name is!"

"Starving her?"

"Yeah, your sister said she can't eat or feed until you agree to her demands."

"We'll see about that." Waving my arm, I left Saul and Porschia in the tent and walked into the sand again. The sand was as inconstant as the moon, always changing, shifting. Its contours were always redefining themselves. Didn't I have the same right after enduring centuries of turmoil? I'd finally found a reason to live, and even if it was only for the length of her lifetime, I would spend it with her. I would not leave. Not now that I'd found her. Not now that I loved her.

SEVEN

MERCEDES

Roman and I were questioning Ford when we heard footsteps. "It might be Delilah," I whispered, placing a finger over my lips. Ford nodded. We remained still until the noise drew close and we saw a dim figure through the trees, too large to be Delilah.

"Tage?" Ford said, ignoring my warning to keep quiet.

"Yeah, hey. What are you doing out here?" He jogged to meet us, but something was off. He looked frazzled, which was odd because Tage was known for his airy confidence. He was almost as cocky as Roman most of the time.

"Well, we have a problem," Roman said lazily.

Actually, Ford and I had two problems. The first was Delilah, and if what he said was true, I had no idea how to combat that threat. The second was Roman's bloodthirst. I could end it, but I just hoped it didn't come down to that. In this particular moment, I wasn't hungry or angry. Just tired as hell.

"What's the problem?" Tage asked, stopping in front of us. His eyes darted around as if looking for something…or someone.

Roman perked up, looking behind us. "What is it?"

"Nothing," Tage said quickly. Too quickly.

"Our problem," Roman started, "is that Delilah isn't what everyone thinks she is."

Tage stiffened. "What do you mean?"

"She's a witch," Ford threw out hastily.

"A witch?" Tage asked, shifting on his feet. "I don't know about all that."

"It sounds crazy, but she took me to this sandy, hot place. One minute we were in the forest at night, and the next we were standing in the sun and sand. She's definitely some sort of witch." Ford shoved his hands in his pockets. "I understand if you don't believe me. It sounds stupid to even say it, but I promise it's true."

"You've always been honest with me, Ford," Tage said.

I couldn't help but wonder what was wrong with Tage. His eyes jumped to the area behind us, to his right, left. He glanced behind him. "Are you looking for Porschia?" I finally asked.

"Yeah, I am. I can't seem to find her in the forest."

Ford scoffed. "Bet the witch still has her in that desert."

"Why would Delilah need Porschia, though?" I asked.

"I told her to be careful who she told about what she was," Roman said. "Some will want to use her as a weapon. Maybe Delilah is one of them."

"But if she has magic, why would she need an Infected night-walker?" I asked. Nothing made sense.

"Mercedes is right," Tage said gruffly. "Why would a witch need Porschia?"

From behind Tage came a female voice, Delilah's voice; but the woman who spoke it did not look like Delilah at all. "Tageset, you know *exactly* why I need her and that I'm no witch."

The woman looked dangerous. Long dark hair, feline eyes, olive skin...and when she stepped beside him, I noticed his eyes had changed, too. They were molten gold and looked exactly like Delilah's.

"Tage?" I said, cocking my head.

"Bring them," the woman ordered, and with a wave of his hand, we disappeared. The forest was no more. Heat surrounded us, the sun overhead scorching our skin and the sand beneath our feet.

"Welcome to The Sand," she cooed at us. Then, turning to Tage, she added, "Please place them in the tent with Porschia, Tageset."

"Tageset? What the hell, Tage?" I yelled. Roman grabbed my elbow.

I turned to him and he shook his head slowly. "Don't."

"What?" I whispered to him angrily.

Roman's dark eyes drilled into mine. "Keep your mouth shut and your eyes open. If that's who Delilah really is, we don't know what – or who – we're dealing with yet."

Ford nodded. "He's right, Cede."

I swallowed. "Fine." Despite the fact that I wanted to tear the bitch to shreds and Tage right along with her, I held my tongue and my fangs in check. How did Tage know Delilah? Did he already know her when Porschia first found her wandering outside of Mountainside? She looked so different, more like Ford's age, more like a traumatized teen than a confident woman. She was a hell of a lot less intimidating than she was now.

I turned toward Roman. "Why do you care what I do?"

He pursed his lips. "Because your actions, if you don't think them through—which you have a tendency to do—might adversely affect me, too. I'm not willing to let that happen."

"What are you gonna do about it, Roman?" I snapped.

"Try me," he said, his eyes daring me to test him.

"Hey!" Tage barked. "Do you want to stop arguing and go see Porschia?" Slowly, I backed away from Roman and walked toward Ford, who was already obeying Tage's commands. I didn't like it, but what choice did we have but to follow him? Tage led us toward a huge black tent. The hot wind blew the tails of the fabric, let it go and then grabbed it again. Whatever this was, we were all in deep and I worried not all of us would make it back to Blackwater and reality.

PORSCHIA

SAUL AND I WERE QUIETLY TRYING TO FIND A WAY OUT OF THE TENT, BUT the entrance was sealed. Everything was sealed. "There must be something, some weakness," I grunted, pushing hard against the fabric wall. It was like stone, even though I could see it moving in the wind.

"Porschia?" He stopped shoving the tent wall and rested his hands on his hips.

"Yeah?"

"No matter what, I won't hurt you. I don't care if I fed from her. I don't care what the two of them say, I won't."

"I know that, Saul," I answered, but was unable to hide the waver in my voice. I was doubtful, but Saul didn't seem to be. I hoped he wouldn't hurt me, and I hoped he wouldn't allow Delilah to use him to hurt me, either.

"No, I don't think you do," Saul started. "Everything's been so..."

"It's okay. I know. I promise," I told him, continuing to push against the wall. "Maybe if we push together?"

He walked over to me and we pushed against the tent hard, straining to shove through the fabric, but it was no use. It wasn't budging and that meant we were stuck. We were at Sekhmet's mercy, and that wasn't a position I wanted to be in for long.

"You should go home, Saul. If they offer again, you should go."

He scoffed. "Go home to what? My parents? The Colony? What would I go home to, Porsch?"

I was so tired, every muscle overworked, and I didn't have it in me to argue. "I'm sorry. I just want you to have a chance at normal."

"Normal is relative. It's not something I'll ever have in Blackwater, maybe never again, period, and I'm not leaving you here. I wouldn't do that," he said adamantly.

Hands clapping from behind us made both of us jump. "Working together to escape?" Sekhmet teased. "You've found it is a useless waste of time, I assume."

I refused to say anything to this sorceress. She smiled, reveling in my defiance, mostly because it was never enough to do anything to hurt her. "I brought you a present..." she said coyly, just before my brother, sister, and Roman walked into the room. Tage followed them, sealing the tent once more.

"Why?" I screamed at Tage. Screw his crazy sister. *He* was endangering everyone I loved.

The muscle in his jaw ticked. Was he doing this on his own, or was he so scared of his sister that he'd lost all function of his own brain? I'd had it. "Well, surely you've introduced yourself to everyone, right, Tage? Why don't you show them who you are? How about you tell them what a lying son of a bitch you really are," I dared him.

With a flick of his hand, he was back in his white skirt and golden belt, the muscles of his stomach exposed and flexing angrily. "Does this make you happy?"

"At least it's real. Stop pretending to be something you aren't, and you *aren't* Tage. You're Tageset, firstborn son of Ramesses II, the first vampire ever cursed and sister to this freak," I yelled, pointing at his sister. "Sekhmet, 'the one who tears apart', or whatever it is she calls herself. Why don't you tell everyone how the two of you have the ability to end both curses, yet you refuse?"

"I can't—"

"Tell them!"

"I won't let you go! I love you. Whether you understand it or not, I refuse to lose you now that you're mine," he yelled, striding around the trio of friends, now wide-eyed with their mouths hanging open, gaping at me.

I held my hands up. "Don't touch me," I warned.

"Or what? What can you possibly do to me?"

"I'll eat you."

"You can't," he said simply. "Unless I allow it. Out there," he pointed to the flapping fabric of the tent. "you were strong. But you aren't strong here. You are *nothing* against me or Sekhmet. As long as you keep that in mind, you'll be safe. This is a different world, Porschia, and you have no power in it."

"I don't feel very safe right now, Tage, so forgive me if I decide to just trust what I know."

His face softened. "Put your trust in me. I love you. You know I do. You know *me*, kitten."

"Don't call me that."

Sekhmet began to laugh, drawing all eyes to her. "You call her kitten? That's perfect."

"What is that supposed to mean?" I asked her, my eyes flicking to Tage.

"My father loved the feline deities. It's why I chose the name Sekhmet after I was cursed. I was born Minateri, but I saw how he worshipped Bastet and Sekhmet. He said they were with him in battle, that the ferocious felines helped him win wars and slay his enemies. However, Tageset rejected everything our father valued. After Father refused to allow the slaves to leave, after all of the plagues had been sent down upon us and Tageset was the first to turn, he hated our father. Didn't you, brother?"

"I did."

"But you never forgot the power of the feline goddesses. You named your fake lover after them. *Kitten*," she mused. "She might be strong compared to humans, but she is nothing compared to you and I. She is merely a bug, so easily squashed now. If we didn't need her, I'd do just that," she growled. Her fangs were sharp and long, as deadly as the monster she'd become. And the fact that she was a vampire was only icing on her cake.

Tage backed away from me, turned, and left the tent. "Sekhmet!" he yelled from outside.

"Oh, I've upset him," she pouted before turning to follow him outside. She paused turning to Saul, a seductive smirk easing across her face. "Are you still hungry, Saul?"

"Yes," he panted, trying to calm himself down.

"Feed from Porschia," she whispered.

His head turned slowly toward me, chest heaving. Sekhmet wiggled her fingers and disappeared and while I was distracted with that small movement, I forgot how fast Saul was. He pounced on me in an instant, fangs bared, ready to feed. I pushed his face away, grabbed his throat with both hands. He wouldn't stop. I could see the struggle in his eyes, the war he fought as he gnashed at my face and neck. It took Roman and Mercedes to pull him off me.

He shook with exertion, pain and sweat burst over his brow. For hours, they held him back, across the tent from me but not nearly far enough for comfort. For hours, we all strained against Sekhmet's power.

And as quickly as it begun, it ended. His body relaxed and he fell into the sand. Roman and Mercedes still stood between us—just in case. But the spell on him had been broken. Her attempt to show her power over us had worked.

Saul wouldn't look me in the eye for a long while after that. I knew he was ashamed, but it wasn't his fault. Saul wouldn't harm me on purpose. And if he fed from me, as she-witch commanded, he would have drained me dry and blamed himself for killing me.

That was what she wanted. To ruin everything standing in the way of her plan.

Mercedes, finally at ease but still standing in the center of the tent, looked at me. "You need to fill us in. Now."

EIGHT

PORSCHIA

When things calmed down inside, the wind outside began to thrash the tent so hard I thought it might collapse on us. Sekhmet had sealed the tent after she left. Saul tried the entrance just in case, but it was no use. We were entombed.

"I don't know much about the ancient Egyptians, but that right there? That was fucked up," Roman said. "So... you want to fill us in on all the weird?"

Mercedes growled at Roman. "I just asked her that."

My mouth opened, but I didn't even know where to start, so Saul spoke for me after silently asking if it was okay.

"Please," I said, knowing he'd say it better than I would anyway. And he did. He was much more eloquent than I. He didn't ramble or cry or yell or pace; he only stated the facts.

Roman looked at Mercedes and Ford, and then held up a hand. "We understand about Tage now, sort of. But what does Porschia have to do with any of this?"

"We aren't exactly sure," Saul said. "Tage can heal vampirism, and Sekhmet can heal the Infection, or the 'plague of rot' as she calls it. Some kind of prophet or seer made a prophecy about Porschia a long time ago, and knew that she would suffer from both plagues. If they heal her, they can end both diseases for all of humanity, but the pair of them would die in the process. At least, that's what I gathered."

My stomach clenched and I dropped to the ground.

Saul was with me in an instant. "What's wrong?"

"I'm going to be sick," I choked. Heaving and heaving, nothing came up. But it didn't stop my stomach from trying in earnest to expel something. My throat was dry. I couldn't take the dry air anymore.

Mercedes screamed into the tent. "You're killing her, Tage! You are killing Porschia. She needs to feed!"

"Do you think he heard you?" Ford asked.

She threw her hands up in frustration. "Hard to tell. This place is... it makes no sense. How do you turn a fabric tent into stone?!"

My stomach kept revolting. Saul rubbed my back, holding my hair just in case. Eventually, the painful spell stopped and I fell onto my hip, spent and unable to move.

"Can I carry you to one of the couches?" Saul asked.

"Yeah," I answered breathlessly. He lifted me easily and slowly walked to a nearby couch and laid me down on it.

Looking down at me, he whispered, "I wish there was more I could do. I just fed from her, do you want to feed from me?"

"No way. I don't want to risk her being able to control me—if that part is even true. I don't know what's true anymore."

Roman whistled. "I can't see a way out of this situation. Not a single one. They have magic and fangs, and we only have one of those things." He paused and nodded to Ford. "Well, most of us do, but either way, we're screwed. Royally. We automatically lose in this case."

"Well we can't just give up," Mercedes snapped at him.

"We don't have to give up to know we're beaten," he growled back at her.

Ford rolled his eyes. "Let's just shut up and think. There has to be a way."

Roman stared at my brother in a way that made me want to attack him. "What's going on, Roman?"

Mercedes waved me off. "I'm taking care of it, Porschia. Butt out."

What exactly was she taking care of?

"There *might* be a way. At least, there's only one I can think of," Saul said pensively, grabbing his bottom lip between his thumb and forefinger.

"What's that?" Roman asked.

"We get them both to heal Porschia."

"How in the hell do you suggest we do that?" Roman smarted.

Saul shook his head. "I have no idea, but both of them would die and we'd be rid of them."

"Even if that worked, we would still be stuck here forever," I argued.

"There's no way to know, but the cure is more important than we are. We're expendable in this situation." Saul was right, but expendable or not, I didn't want Tage to die any more than I was ready to meet death myself.

TAGE

I WANTED TO TEAR HER IN TWO: MY OWN SISTER! TRUTHFULLY, I HAVE BEEN waiting for her to strike. She wanted nothing more than to build an empire, and I highly doubted she desired anyone by her side while she did it. Our siblings had all died at her hand, and the only reason I was still alive was because I left Egypt and managed to stay clear of her all of these centuries. Now there was no way to get rid of her unless I killed her. If she died, Porschia could be cured, but not the rest of humanity. The ultimate cure comes from the children of Ramesses making amends for his mistakes. At one point, there were seven of us who could heal either one plague or the other, but Sekhmet killed them off, leaving only the two of us to clean up Father's mess.

By healing Porschia, we could heal the whole world. However, Sekhmet thinks we should cure everyone individually, on our own. One thing I'd learned about defying my destiny thus far was that there would be consequences for trying to wiggle out of your responsibility. With every choice, good or bad, there were consequences. Some were just easier to live with than others.

"You wanted to speak, brother?"

"We need to feed her, Sekhmet. We need her to be healthy if we're going to keep her alive."

Sekhmet scrutinized me, sizing up my motives. "She is stronger when fed, which means we should keep her in a weakened state. Eventually we could even suspend her life, keep her in a stasis until we need her again."

"You don't know what you're saying. Even the most experienced of sorcerers knows not to toy with a person's breath."

She waved me off. "I know what I'm doing. I've been studying for years. Besides, there is a spell in one of the Books of the Dead I've found. It was in Father's special collection of papyri. It will work."

"So one spell in one book is supposed to comfort me? Why wasn't it in all the other copies? Why aren't all the papyri filled with this miracle spell?"

"The Book of the Dead isn't the only book you should have been reading, Tageset."

It suddenly dawned on me. I knew exactly where she'd gotten the spell. "Not those of the cult, surely? No, Sekhmet. Those men challenged even Osiris. That's dark magic. We were warned never to fool around with it."

"I'm not *fooling* with anything. I know the dark magic as well as I know the light. Trust me, brother."

She was dark, evil, and not to be trusted. I'd known that since before the plagues, although it was funny how most people don't change. A tiger couldn't change her stripes, I supposed. "Why did you bring them all here?"

"I had to raise the stakes."

"For whom?" I said, exasperated.

She sighed. "For you. I question your motives. Do you really want to rule with me, or will you try to go behind my back and free her the first chance you get?"

"If I heal her, I die, and I don't want that. Regardless of my motives, know that I don't ever want to give her up."

My sister narrowed her eyes. "Very well. I suppose that's all I can expect for now."

She was quiet for a moment and then turned to look out at a vast expanse of dunes. They stretched, burnt and golden as far as the eye could see. "I always felt sorry for you, Tageset. You were groomed for the throne, but cursed never to see your destiny; usurped by an illegitimate child who came from nothing. At least Mother had the foresight to have us trained by the sorcerers. It saved your life in the end. You wouldn't have survived this long without their teachings."

"I know," I admitted. Sekhmet was right. I would have died in Egypt alongside my siblings if I hadn't taken an interest in sorcery.

"Good. Don't forget that we are the last. We can survive together. Forever." With those words, she walked to the golden tent and disappeared inside.

I needed to talk to Porschia, but first I needed to feed her. She weakened a little more with each passing second, and eventually the arid climate would kill her. The Infection within her would weaken her body and would soon become more dominant than her vampire half. In this place, she would slowly shrivel. I could see it beginning in the way she licked her cracked lips, the way her voice would crack as if she just needed a single drink of water to quench her thirst. But one drink would never be enough here.

INSIDE THE DARK TENT, THE OTHERS SPOKE AND TRIED TO DREAM UP WAYS to get out of this place; but there was no way out, except through me or Sekhmet. I'd made myself invisible and strode straight to Porschia, who was alone on the chaise, looking paler than ever, if not a little green. I appeared before her in an instant and then made an invisible, rounded wall around us, impervious to sound or harm. The others figured out what had happened a moment too late, not that they could've stopped me. They beat upon the outside of the barrier completely in vain, their fists falling upon the impenetrable barrier but making no sound. We were alone.

"What do you want, Tage*set*?" she said wearily, enunciating my name. "Here to finish me off?"

"I'm here with a peace offering," I answered, and revealed a hare in my hands. I stroked his soft fur, calming him. "Drink and eat," I said, handing the animal to her. She wasted no time sinking her teeth into the hide. I knew her petite teeth could pierce it. That was why I chose him. Plus, my kitten loved rabbit.

She drank until there was no more blood left and then tore a leg off before stripping it of the pelt and biting into the meat. I watched as she groaned in delight, reveling in the taste and feel of food, fullness, and of a thirst finally quenched.

"You've forgotten your manners, kitten." I smiled. "Where's my thank you?"

"I'll thank you when you and your sister heal me and let my family leave this awful place."

"That's not an option right now."

She curled her lip. "Because Sekhmet says so? What happened to your balls, Tage? Does she have them, too?"

"You have so much fight in you."

"No I don't," she said, stopping her assault on the hare. "You don't see it, but I'll die here, Tage. I won't last a month."

"The heat won't harm you. I can even make it more temperate, if you'd like. I'll provide you with all the food you need."

She huffed, "You just don't get it, do you? I don't want to be a bird in a cage, some kind of pet for you to keep as long as you're entertained. I need more than just a better temperature and food. I need to *live*. I need my family, but not here. I need them to lead lives of their own and to be a part of those lives."

"You need *me*. You need us. I can give you all the love you'll ever need. Just let me try to make this work."

"I don't need you like this! And I can't live like this either, Tage."

She was frustrating. I sat on the end of her chaise and watched her recoil from my touch. "I'm still Tage, and I still love you. Just because I didn't tell you everything about my past, doesn't mean that what I felt wasn't genuine."

"Sekhmet says it was all a game to you, and based on how you're acting now, I have to believe her. You never loved me, Tage. You only loved yourself. And the evidence is that you'd rather damn the whole world for the sake of your selfishness. I swear to you Tage – if you do that, I'll hate you as long as I live."

My heart stalled for a minute. I swallowed. Could I live with her hatred? I saw what it did to Saul.

"Just heal me," she pleaded. "Heal me and let everyone go."

I stood up. Enough.

"Wait," she said. "Isn't that what your father was told? To let the slaves go? It's history repeating itself, Tage, and you have a chance right now to do what should have been done back then! You can change all of this and make the world better...if you have the backbone to do it!" She stood up, dropping my offering to her.

"You don't know what you're asking of me," I pleaded.

"I'm asking you to do what your father's pride wouldn't allow him to. I'm asking you to have balls and do what's right, despite your sister or history or anything else. It's your turn, Tage. You have to make a decision, but remember whatever you choose, we all have to live with the consequences." She sat back down. "I hope you're as brave as I think you are."

I wasn't. I wasn't that brave at all. I'd already run from my kingdom, my duties, my family, my life. But in running, I found her, and she became everything to me. Now she was asking me to let her go, and I wasn't strong enough to do it. I was weak.

She looked at me and moved closer. "I still see you. I see your heart, and as black as I thought it was when we met, I know it's not black at all. You are *good*, Tage. You just have to believe it. Don't let her ruin you. Don't let her darkness smother your light. This isn't you. It might have been you thousands of years ago, but it's not the Tage I know."

Her hand brushed my face and I closed my eyes.

And disappeared.

Dropping the barrier around her.

NINE

PORSCHIA

"WHAT THE HELL WAS THAT?" MERCEDES ASKED, THROWING HER ARMS around my neck. "Did he feed you? What did he say? It didn't seem like he hurt you. Did he hurt you?"

"I'm not hurt." *Physically.*

"What's that?" Saul pointed at my feet. Just beside my toes was a piece of paper.

Picking up the paper, I unfolded it. In bleeding black ink were the words: *My brother will never let you go.*

"She was listening." I held up the scrap of paper for everyone to see.

Ford cursed. "They can make themselves invisible. She was probably in there with you two the whole time."

Saul ripped the paper out of my hands and tore it in two with his teeth. He was fuming. "She's probably here now. Listen, you ancient bitch! We're done with you!"

Sekhmet's laughter filled the air, a ghostly quality that made it echo through the room. "Big words for a simple vampire boy," she taunted.

An enormous cat appeared, its fur black as night. It stalked forward as we inched back until our backs hit the tent wall behind us. The feline jumped at Saul, knocked him to the ground, and licked his face once.

Suddenly, the creature morphed into Sekhmet herself. She straddled Saul, barely clad. "I am not a bitch, young Saul. You should watch your tongue. I might just decide to tear it out."

He panted as she moved her hands over his torso and then he cried out, sweat bursting into beads on his forehead.

"Get off him!" I screamed, knocking her onto the sand beside him.

She sniffed the air, blotting at her busted lip. I knew she would bleed. Someone just had to make her. She laughed once and stood up. "That… was a big mistake. You see, my brother believes you should live. He and I could rule the masses with our powers of healing, except for you. If we healed you, the people wouldn't need us. That damned prophecy," she huffed. "*You* are the factor we need to remove from the equation. And right now, I think you should die."

She spelled the others, freezing them into place so they were unable to combat her, and then pounced at me and clawed at my face. Though frozen, they could still speak. Saul yelled for Tage, who appeared between me and Sekhmet in an instant.

"She isn't expendable, Sekhmet. Learn to control your impulses!"

He caught her wrist as she began to shoot some sort of gold, glittery magic into the air. It swirled around me, tightening around my body like a coiling serpent. "We don't need her!" she fumed.

"*I* need her!" he shouted.

She stopped spouting the golden magic and stared at him. "You need me, not her," she said softly, seductively. Sekhmet pushed the hair from his face tenderly, but he moved away from her. "You need me, Tageset," she repeated, more firmly this time. "We are the last of our kind."

"We are siblings, Sekhmet," Tage answered stiffly.

I was going to be sick.

"The old ways—"

"Never mind the past. Is that all you can think about? You've lived thousands of years since then. The old ways don't matter anymore!"

In a flash, they were gone, and we were no closer to figuring out how to leave this place – this tent, the sand, the magic – as we were when we first got here. The sun through the fabric shifted suddenly toward what I assumed was the west, and then sank beneath the horizon. The air was still except for the sound of locusts. I wondered if they were from The Sand or if their echo from the forest in our world could resonate here. Maybe this place was thin and delicate. Maybe escape was possible, if only we could make our way outside.

"What if we dig under the walls?" Ford asked quietly.

Roman perked up. "It's worth a try." He grinned at Mercedes. "I'll help him. You and Saul dig over there," he pointed across the space to the opposite tent wall.

"No way in hell," she spat, running over to help the pair of them, positioning herself between them.

"What is going on?" I asked Saul.

"No clue, but I think your sister might eat Roman if he keeps it up. We're all pretty hungry."

"I'm sorry. He should have fed you, too."

Saul waved it off, but I could tell that he was already faltering again. He didn't get much sustenance from Sekhmet.

For hours they fought to dig a hole that the sand kept falling back into, but they could never find the bottom of the walls that enclosed us. "This is pointless," Saul said, holding his arm out. I clasped hands with him and hoisted him out, then Ford. Mercedes helped Roman. When we turned around, all the furniture in the tent was gone, replaced with a circle of enormous beds.

Silently, I thanked Tage. Sekhmet wouldn't have cared if we slept on the sand. In the center of the circle of black sheeted mattresses was a table with water, a few pitchers of what smelled like blood, a cooked hen surrounded by vegetables for Ford, and a raw one on a long, white platter next to it for me. Everyone rushed to the bounty and began to feed from what they needed most. We didn't know when we'd eat or drink again. Sekhmet was unstable, yet powerful enough to deny us anything she wanted.

The dry heat was affecting everyone, and so was the feeling of finally-full stomachs. That night, when everyone's breathing became steady, when even the night-walkers needed rest, I stared at the flowing dark fabric above me and wished to speak with Tage. As if he heard me, he appeared beside me, his finger over his lips. His familiar hand filled mine. "Come with me?"

I nodded and removed the sheet that covered me. In an instant, we were standing outside. The air was fresh and the sand was blissfully cool beneath my feet. The night sky looked as thick as tar and the stars twinkled, happily trapped inside it. "I had to see you," he whispered, squeezing my hand.

"I wanted to see you, too." It was difficult for me to admit it, but I wanted to talk to him. My feelings were all over the board, ranging from blissful love to blinding hatred, and he could feel them all through the bond. In the darkness, he looked like the night-walker I'd come to fear, then befriend, and finally love. Some colonists called them night-dwellers, believing for the longest time that the sunshine affected them in some awful way. It didn't unless they were newly changed, but in this setting, on the sand at night, the name fit him. He was as intense as the night, broody and exotic. The night fit him. It became him.

"What about Sekhmet?" I asked, wondering if she was around.

"She won't bother us tonight."

"How can you be so sure?"

"I just am. You have to trust me," he pleaded. His eyes, the ones I'd known as a crystal blue were gone, replaced by ones even more beautiful. I didn't know it was possible. They were like honey trapped in glass, threaded with gold and strength.

I squeezed his hand once. "Okay." I trusted him more than his sister. I knew he never wanted to hurt me or see me harmed in any way. He lied about who he was and it hurt my feelings, because although he said he loved me, I wondered if maybe that was just part of the act to lure me in. He had lied about his identity for so long, maybe he forgot who he was.

Leading me away from the tent, long-trunked trees suddenly sprouted in front of us, a whole forest of them. They only had a few leaves each, but they were beautiful. "Palm trees," he offered.

I couldn't stop staring up at them. The warm wind tickled their leaves, creating a dry, rustling sound.

"Where are we going?"

"This is my own private place inside The Sand. I wanted to talk to you without being overheard or interrupted," he said.

I appreciated that more than he knew. Between Saul and my brother and sister, there was no way to keep a conversation private. Mercedes was able to whisper to me while trying to dig a hole beneath the tent that Roman knew about Pierce. He hadn't tried to kill me yet, but if I knew Roman, revenge weighed heavily on his mind. He was being quiet, which wasn't like him. I couldn't blame him.

In the middle of the forest of palm trees was another clearing, and inside the clearing was a small house made out of palm trees thatched together into a roof and smooth, earthen walls. "This is amazing, Tage." Candles flickered from within, spreading their warm glow into the night.

He tugged me forward when my feet stopped of their own accord, a brilliant smile spreading across his face. This was him. This was Tage. Genuine and happy for a moment.

Inside the cozy house there were lush furnishings; couches, pillows, blankets, tables, and a large canopied bed draped with sheer white fabric.

"Is this where you've been staying?"

"Yes. This is where I hide away when I get too frustrated to stay around my sister. You want to sit down?" he asked, motioning toward a couch.

I gave him a small smile. "Sure." Were things ever awkward with Tage? Even when he creeped me out the first time I met him, they weren't awkward. My feelings were vibrant, even when they were negative.

He sat beside me and let out a long breath. "Can I hold you for a sec?"

Nodding, I sank into his open arms and breathed him in. He smelled different, like sweet spices and something rich and dry, but his arms felt the same. His heart beat in the same distinct rhythm, and I had a hard time wrapping my mind around the fact that it had beat this way for centuries.

"Tage?"

"Hmm?"

"Are you okay?"

"I'm perfect, kitten."

I shook my head and pulled away from his embrace. "I mean with Sekhmet. I'm worried about you."

He furrowed his brows. "Don't worry about me. I can handle myself."

"Your other siblings... What happened to them?"

He swallowed, then answered simply, "She killed them."

"She'll try to kill you," I said. That was one thing I understood about crazy; it was determined as hell.

"I know. I'm ready for her."

But how could he be ready? How could he know when she would strike? How could he prepare for an attack when he didn't know what strategy she'd use this time?

"Calm down, kitten. I can hear your heart racing."

"You seemed so…human before. When I met you at the rotation, the first time you fed from me, you seemed like a night-walker."

"I am a vampire."

"Yes, but you seemed like a new one."

"I wasn't really in Frenzy. I know I let everyone believe that, but I needed to see if you were truly human. Taste is one of the most sensitive senses we have, but I couldn't smell rot on you. I didn't see fangs when I saw you across the pavilion, but I knew your face."

"So you knew it was going to happen if it hadn't already?"

I could feel him exhale deeply. "Yes. I didn't know what you'd be like, and I certainly didn't expect you to be afraid me, but you trembled when I approached. I could feel the pavement beneath your feet quiver ever so slightly. I thought you might somehow know about the prophecy, or be lying about being a hybrid just to stay in Blackwater. But when I tasted you, I knew the change hadn't happened yet."

"Why did you wait so long to tell me who, or what, you were?"

"I had to wait for the change to happen, and then for you to calm down. You had people around you all the time, but even then it wouldn't have mattered. If we were going to heal you, my sister had to be present. She had to find you, too. So I bided my time. I knew she'd come eventually, and thought we might have years before she showed up. Then I got to know you. My fascination quickly turned to infatuation, and you showed me something I'd never been able to allow myself to do."

"What's that?" I looked up, watching his thick, dark lashes fan the skin beneath his eyes.

"You were never loved. Maybe by your siblings, but even without romantic love, you didn't fear it. Most people who are denied that basic emotion are closed off, or they seal their hearts against it. They think they aren't deserving of love. But you saw past my bullshit and gave me exactly that, Porschia. You may not have said the words, but you made me feel loved; at a time when I'd never been loved before in my life. Father only wanted me to succeed him in the throne, but other than that I was a waste of his time. Mother was far too busy with her lovers to pay attention to children. We had many caregivers over the years, but they rotated so often that bonds were never formed. However, you, a simple girl in a simple dress, looked at me. You saw me and on some level, you scared the hell out of me because of it."

"Love is easy, Tage. It's life that's hard."

"But it *isn't* easy. You befriended an old woman who most people in your Colony had overlooked."

"Maggie gave me a chance; a home, comfort, and a bed to sleep in when I needed it. She didn't give up on me."

I could feel him smile, the stubble on his chin catching on the hair at my temple. "But you didn't give up on her, either. You went into the forest when your sister had just turned into a rotter. You faced your Mother on a daily basis. You protected Ford."

I swallowed.

"I don't call you 'kitten' because of my Father's obsession with the feline goddesses. I call you 'kitten' because kittens are small and afraid, but they don't hesitate to claw the shit out of a person if they need to."

"Did you want to kill me?" I was afraid of his answer. "Ever? Did you ever want to kill me?"

"If I wanted to kill you, you'd be dead. And no, I didn't want to kill you. I wanted to heal you so that I could finally die."

"I don't want you to die."

He sighed and hugged me tighter. As much as I needed a moment with him, I had to know. "I need something from you, Tage."

"Name it," he said simply.

"I need you to convince your sister, and then yourself, to heal me like your seer said you should. I need you to end these curses."

"Kitten, it's not that simple—"

"It is, though. I won't live long like this."

"The Sand isn't bad. You'll see. I'll make sure you have everything you've ever needed or could ever want."

I shook my head. "I feel myself dying. The vampire side is in control at present, but it won't stay afloat for long. I'm going to fall prey to the Infection, Tage. Sooner rather than later. And when I do, I'll die, and you won't have me to heal. You won't have me to erase your curse with. I know it's selfish..." my voice broke, "but I just want to live and be normal. I want a normal life, in the Colony, with my family."

I cried then, my voice trembling with emotion and need. "I want to get married one day and have children; to have a chance to be the mother mine wasn't. I want a life, not just an existence, Tage, and only you and your sister can give that to me. I'm begging you," I said, grabbing his hand. Bloody tears splashed onto his skin and his mouth opened as if to say something in reply.

No words fell from his lips, but his lips fell on mine all the same. Warm and harsh, needy and sweet-tasting. Our hands were a flurry of want and they couldn't get enough of what they searched for and found. His hands turned my body to face his. His fingers disappeared beneath my skirt, the fabric bunching in my lap.

My breath fanned his ear as I peppered kisses down the strong column of his throat, reveling in the gravelly noises that came from within his chest.

"Don't stop me," he pleaded.

"I won't," I promised, standing and pulling my dress over my head. His gasp filled the room.

He pulled me into his lap, pulling me as close as our bodies would allow, molding my flesh with his. We spent hours reveling in the feel of one another, my hands gripping his hair, his shoulders, his back. He worshipped every part of me, his fingertips rough but his touch soft.

At the end of the night, as the sun rose and we lay together staring at the ceiling of his small cottage, Tage was quiet. Finally, his thumb brushed my shoulder and he said, "I think I know how to stay alive and heal you at the same time."

I swallowed thickly. "Really?"

"Really. I would do anything for you, kitten. Anything in my power."

I nodded against his chest. "You love me," I cried.

"I do, and you love me, too," he said softly.

"I do."

His sharp inhalation said it all.

My fingers tightened on his side. "Are you sure?"

"We'll soon find out," he said.

TEN

TAGE

I TOOK HER BACK TO THE TENT, THINKING THAT WE'D BEEN STEALTHY enough to avoid detection. She straightened her dress before I landed her back inside the tent, but everyone but Ford was already wide awake and wondering where the hell Porschia had gone. I left her to fend for herself in the middle of a storm of shouts and gestures, because I needed to speak with Sekhmet immediately.

She was waiting for me in her tent. "You've been busy, brother," she greeted dryly.

"I've been thinking," I lied.

"Would you like to discuss?"

I sat on the couch across from hers. "How strong is your magic?" I asked.

"Stronger than anything you can imagine. Stronger than yours," she bragged.

Ignoring the jab, I asked, "What if we can have it both ways? If we cure Porschia, I mean." I paused at this, because Sekhmet began to growl and pace the floor.

"Haven't we already been through this?"

"Yes, but if we heal her and through her, heal the nations, they will love us far more than if we just heal individuals of our choosing. If we go that route, they'll think we're tyrants. However, if we heal them all at once, they'll know our power."

She shook her head, throwing her hands up. "If we heal her, we die, Tageset. End of story for you and me. No empire, no kingdom, no adoration."

"You think you're too weak," I said, narrowing my eyes at her.

"I am not weak at all," she challenged.

"If we heal the world, we can rule it. Think about it, sister. We're stronger than any spell the sorcerers could conjure back then. We can preserve our lives." I left her standing there, pondering the words I'd just sent her. Sekhmet was a woman, and a stubborn one at that. If she was like any of the others I'd met over the years, telling her she couldn't do something was the surest way to get her to do exactly that.

PORSCHIA

"Where did he take you?" Saul yelled.

"Are you hurt?" Mercedes chimed in.

Ford was awakened by the noise and immediately jumped in; yelling something unintelligible, laden with curses and talks about killing anyone who hurt his sister.

Roman was quietly watching, perched on the footboard of his bed.

Suddenly, the room changed again. The beds disappeared and couches took their place. Roman fell onto a lavish carpet now spread beneath him.

All of our clothing changed, too. Mercedes and I wore garments much like Sekhmet's; gauzy dresses baring our stomachs, split up to our thighs, the fabric wrapping around to barely cover our breasts. My fabric was gold and hers was a deep green, like needles on a dark pine.

The guys looked dumbstruck. "We're wearing skirts," Ford finally said, looking down at his new garment. They all wore black fabric, held together and up with a threaded gold belt.

Mercedes snorted. "They actually look pretty hot. Not Ford, of course, but Roman and Saul? Damn."

They did. The garments showed off their toned calves and abdomens. Roman was super pale, but his dark hair made it work somehow. And

Saul hadn't lost all of his tan since he'd changed. He was still handsome as ever.

Ford was still preoccupied with checking out what he looked like, but the other guys were staring at us. Roman was undressing my sister with his eyes and Saul wouldn't stop looking at me. It made me squirm a little, especially after the events of just a few hours ago.

I whispered to Cedes, "Why is Roman looking at you like that?"

The only answer I received was a growl.

Sekhmet interrupted everything, as usual. "You look perfect now," she greeted with a clap of her hands. "And now, I have wonderful news for *some* of you."

"Do tell," Mercedes said sweetly. She almost fooled me.

"My brother and I have decided to heal you, but also to use our magic to prevent death from taking us, as the seer foretold."

The five of us looked at one another. "I don't like this," Saul whispered quietly.

"Can they really stop death?" Ford asked. His eyes darted around to each of us, finally landing on Sekhmet when she spoke again.

"Yes, Ford. I believe we are much more powerful than the seer from our time would have been able to understand."

"What's in it for you?" Roman finally spoke. "If you heal Porschia and make both curses go away..."

"Porschia bears both curses. Through her, we will fulfill the prophecy by curing her and subsequently ridding the world of both plagues. Then, from out of the ashes, the phoenix can rise. My brother and I will take full credit and rule the world. It's brilliant, really. We will have the love and gratefulness of the people and be powerful enough to strike down any who oppose us. That's also a perk." Sekhmet smiled and held out a hand for me. "Please come."

Mercedes grabbed my arm, preventing me from moving. "Can we go with her?"

"Oh, you will want front row seats for this, I can assure you."

Saul stepped in front of me. "What if she refuses to be a part of this craziness?"

Sekhmet smiled. "She has no choice."

"There's always a choice," Roman said, nudging Saul. In unison they leapt forward, attacking her, gnashing their fangs at her, but some force held them away and then slammed them both into the wall to our left.

They hit with an "Ooof!" and dropped to the floor groaning. Roman was the first to speak. "Well *that* didn't go how I planned."

Sekhmet stalked forward and grabbed my free hand. My sister tried to pull me away from her, but it was no use. Then Ford jumped in, trying to help give Mercedes some leverage, and I became a rope in a battle of tug-of-war. However, the loud pop of my shoulder indicated that Sekhmet won. My siblings dropped my free arm as soon as they heard the popping noise, but Sekhmet only laughed as I sucked in a sharp, shrill breath.

"AAAH!" I cried out, falling to the floor, and Mercedes and Ford went to their knees with me. "It's out of place," I gritted out. I'd seen it once before with Meg when she fell off her porch and landed wrong, dislocating her shoulder. It took two adults to hold her down, and another to jerk the appendage back into place. I remembered her screams. Mine were the same.

Looking curiously at me, Sekhmet bent down and hovered her hand over my shoulder. It slowly and painfully retracted, mending itself. The bone was soon back in its socket and I panted from relief of the pain.

"Are you not going to thank me? What has happened to manners in this world?"

"Thank you," I choked out.

Sekhmet extended her hand again. "I would hate to start hurting your friends. Please come with me so we can avoid any other calamities."

I placed my hand in hers and let her help me up. Mercedes and Ford rose from the floor and Roman and Saul tried to pull themselves up; following behind us guardedly. As we walked, our tent was transformed. No longer supported with fabric walls, but stone columns as tall as three houses and a roof of stone. Large statues of people wearing headdresses, crossing their hearts with staffs and whips, graced the corridors.

"That is a likeness of my father. Most pharaohs did not know magic. They had sorcerers and seers, but most could not perform magic themselves. They simply surrounded themselves with it for protection. My father valued it very much. He had no power of his own, but he married well. Nefertari, our mother, was descended from the most powerful sorcerers in our land. She could perform the incantations and read the scripts from the Book of the Dead that most people would never see. A powerful priestess, she was also one that many priests were terrified of. She once brought a boy back to life. He drowned in the river Nile and his mother brought his lifeless body straight to the palace because her power was known throughout the land. It was feared."

"Why didn't they carve statues of her?" I asked. Looking over my shoulder, I saw my friends and family walking behind us. Saul nodded. I gave him a slight shake of the head, hoping he knew not to try anything again.

"They did, but most have long since returned to the earth," she said.

Maybe Tage was able to get through to her. Maybe I really would be cured.

Sekhmet was quiet for a moment. The sounds of our bare feet on the stone tiles were all that could be heard, a shuffling murmur echoing through the place. Torches began to flicker to life around us as we walked deeper into the structure, into the darkness and away from the natural light.

"Where's Tage?"

"Tageset will meet us in a moment," she said. "My brother wants to be with you forever. You may have magic in your blood for the ways in which you have bewitched him. That has never been an easy task for any woman he's had."

That was a low blow. I knew he'd had other women. Obviously. I mean, I knew he was old, but did I really need to hear it, right after we...were intimate?

She knew, and she didn't like it. And I bet Tage wasn't going to meet us anywhere. She was going to kill us all.

Turning to the others, I mouthed the word, "Run."

With the heel of my palm, I jammed her jaw upward, a loud crack echoing through the room. I jumped on her and began hitting her face, and then I sank my fangs into her neck. Instantly I was lifted into the air. With a flick of her wrist, she turned me around and around in a circle. "I thought we were finally getting along, Porschia, and then you go and upset me." She spat blood onto the stones on the floor.

Dizziness set in. Around and around and around she spun me.

"You were planning to kill us!" I screamed.

"I was *going* to heal you, but now I might have changed my mind!" she roared, shifting back into the enormous black cat. "I will devour you, and then you cannot hurt me or my brother ever again!"

"Tage!" Mercedes yelled, and then they all started yelling for him. When he appeared beside them, Mercedes pointed to me. Sekhmet sped up the spinning until I saw black, and then I felt nothing at all.

ELEVEN

TAGE

"SEKHMET!" I YELLED, MY VOICE BOOMING AGAINST THE VAST SPACE. SHE changed back into her true form immediately.

"What?"

"Control yourself! If we are going to succeed at this, you have to focus and control your emotions."

From behind, I heard Roman whispering. Hazarding a glance, I saw that he was talking to Mercedes.

"If female vamps are more powerful, they're crazier, out of control," he whispered. Mercedes' face never changed, but she elbowed him hard in the ribs. It didn't deter him. He just smiled and continued. "What if Sekhmet is more powerful than our boy, Tage?"

"She isn't," Mercedes answered confidently, crossing her arms in defiance.

I hoped she was right, but I had my doubts at this point. I've been able to rein her in so far, but what if she really snapped? Could I stop her if she wanted them dead?

Porschia rubbed her temples as we walked through the remains of the temple. Her head was throbbing. I could hear the blood whooshing through the veins and arteries on her head. My sister was reckless. She could have hurt her. However, as I looked at Porschia, she seemed to be okay other than the pounding headache as she marveled at the sight of the temple. And truly it was grander than anything she'd seen in her lifetime, but it wasn't as grand as it was during mine. What was once smooth and colorful was now rough and chipped away, the colors faded by time.

"Would you like to see what this place looked like when we were children?" I asked the others, nudging my sister. We could bring it back to life.

The two of us joined hands and chanted the incantation to reverse the effects of age. A breeze blew, swirling between us, then around us and spiraling outward. When we opened our eyes, the place was transformed.

"Whoa," Ford drawled. "This is..."

"Beautiful," Porschia said, staring at the hieroglyphs, now in stunning color all around her.

"Come," Sekhmet said, leading the way into the heart of the temple. Soon we were inside, the torches already lit. The room of offerings was even more intricately painted, a midnight sky overhead with thousands of stars. Around us were weighty incantations, ones that Sekhmet believed would also help us remain alive. But I knew they wouldn't. Once we cured Porschia, my sister and I would die. It was part of the bargain struck. No gift, no cure, was without sacrifice.

It was why Mercedes, Roman, and Saul couldn't be cured again. They turned once and the choice was not theirs, and so the cure worked. It healed them. However, when they turned a second time, voluntarily choosing to become vampires, the choice was made and the results were as good as set in stone. No longer could they be healed. I hadn't told Porschia that, because if we succeeded in curing her, their curses would still end along with everyone else's. It wasn't necessary to worry her if we could end it all anyway.

"Porschia?" I said.

"Yeah."

"I need you to lay on this stone."

Her eyes searched mine, scared.

"It's an offering table. We have to do this the ancient way, or else it won't work." I moved in close, brushing a kiss over her lips. "I would never hurt you."

"Just like you'd never lie to her?" Saul asked, crossing his arms over his chest.

Porschia glanced at him, but swallowed thickly and placed her hand in mine. I threw a smirk at Saul for good measure. He didn't know that he was about to get a major leg up on me. He'd been chasing Porschia since the first rotation. We both had. At one point he was ahead, and then I was. Soon, I wouldn't even be in the running. Roman just shook his head, and I thought Ford was going to pounce on me. The kid was not happy.

I helped her lay on the stone while Sekhmet waved her hand over it, black candles appearing all around her, fire sparking from their wicks.

"Are you ready?" Sekhmet asked me.

"I am. You touch her feet. I want to be near her head."

Sekhmet didn't fight me, surprisingly, and moved to Porschia's bare feet; grabbing her ankles and holding on. I grabbed the base of her head, my thumbs brushing her cheeks.

Saul stepped forward, but Roman stopped him from coming near. "Don't."

This was going to hurt. I was leaving her. She would go on without me. Marry someone. Have his children. Have a life. She would laugh. Maybe for the first time in her life, she might be happy. And that was why I closed my eyes. A single tear fell onto her forehead, my blood leaving a stain that ran into her dark hair.

"Tage?" she whispered.

"Shhh, kitten."

"Tage, will this work? Are you sure this will work?"

Sekhmet began to chant and rocked her body back and forth, slowly and then more rapidly. I joined her. In the old tongue, we asked for Porschia to be cleansed, for the diseases to flee from her and from the world. Sekhmet focused on the plague of rot while I focused on the vampirism, imagining her tiny fangs receding, replaced by perfect incisors as pearly white as the others they lined up with. I imagined her skin dark from being out in the sun during a hard summer of work, of her stomach never thirsting for blood. And for a moment, we were transported into the sky, floating among the clouds, staring at the stars that weren't present when we entered the place. Our pleas were heard.

Sekhmet's chants changed. She plead for Osiris to allow us to remain whole, for our tongues not to be removed, for our hearts not to be weighed against us, for our organs to thrive. She asked for longevity, eternal life, saying that we'd earned as much in the thousand lifetimes we'd had to suffer.

I asked Osiris to fulfill the prophecy. I asked him to be merciful to Porschia and to allow us to right our father's wrong in the way destiny intended. In the end, I asked him to ignore Sekhmet and do what was right.

A burst of air filled the space with the scent of spice. Osiris had heard our pleas, but which ones? And then we felt it. The Infection and the vampirism flowed from Porschia's body like water being let out of a drain. I felt it fall away, until even her scent changed. She smelled sweet again, like her blood before she turned. It smelled like it did when I first saw her at the rotation.

Sekhmet began to chant again when the hot wind started to blow and our skin began to dry. We crashed back to earth, the stone landing hard on the temple floor, rocking the foundations. Particles of the stone roof began to shower us. The wind grew angry, scouring everything around us.

"What is happening?" Sekhmet screamed, holding tightly to Porschia's ankles as our garments and hair thrashed in the storm. Lightning struck around the room. I couldn't see anyone but the three of us. Where were the others?

Then it became calm and I knew he was near. Death had come for me and my sister.

The wind completely left the room, making way for a cold, gray fog to filter in. "I love you, Porschia," I whispered. I could feel the hands of death reach out for me and pull me down and away from her. Sekhmet and I had been denied, and our magic was worthless against something so much bigger than ourselves.

But Porschia was free.

She would live.

She was healed.

Free.

PORSCHIA

"What's happening?" Mercedes screamed, but her voice sounded so far away. Sekhmet pulled my ankles so hard I thought they'd snap, and then Tage brushed my cheek with his thumb. "I love you, Porschia," he whispered, and then it was quiet. There was nothing.

I laid there for a moment, too afraid to move. A strange fog rolled through the room, smelling of rot, like a thousand Infected crawling over the floor. But it never rose, never touched me.

When the fog receded, there was quiet. "Cede?"

"We're here!" she yelled. She still sounded so far away.

"Tage?"

No answer. I sat up on the stone and looked around.

"Tage?" He wasn't there.

"Tage?" I began to panic. I knew he was going to heal me. I knew it meant he might die, but I still wasn't prepared for this.

Empty.

Nothing.

A void.

A hole.

I screamed for him. The others ran to me from wherever they'd been.

"Shhh, Porsch. You're okay," Cede said in my ear as she gathered the pieces of me in her arms. I was broken, shattered, torn apart.

"He's gone," I said. Even my voice was hollow.

"I know. It's okay," Mercedes answered gently.

"It's not okay. It is *not* okay!" I screamed. "He said he would live!"

"Porschia," she said, shaking me once. "You're healed. We all are."

What? With shaking fingers, I reached up to my mouth. There were no tiny fangs. Nothing. My teeth were normal. I looked at my skin and while it was pale, it wasn't luminous. "What?"

She smiled, crystal tears flowing down her face. "We're all healed. He did this for you. Tage healed the world just because you asked him to."

But he told me he could do it without dying… Where was he?

I hugged her tight, crying into her shoulder as I sat on the stone. Looking around at the others, I saw that they were watching the pair of us. Roman smiled. No sharp fangs. Saul nodded. They were okay. We were all going to be okay.

Physically we would be healthy, normal young adults who might even be accepted back into society in Blackwater. Maybe now, the shunning of different classes of people based on the curses would end. Maybe now, everyone would be considered equal.

We eased off the stone and my legs were wobbly. I didn't know if they would hold me up. Ford came and gave me a bear hug, and then Saul wrapped his arms around me and I cried all over him, too. They were happy and so they thought I was crying tears of joy too, but mine were heavily laden with longing and guilt. I asked Tage for a normal life, and he died giving it to me. My tears left only watery spots on Saul's skin. They weren't blood-filled anymore.

Mercedes made a funny noise, so I looked up. "How are we ever going to explain these outfits?" she asked breathlessly.

Ford responded, "How are we going to explain what happened?"

How *would* we explain? Would anyone believe us?

What happened was as real as anything I'd experienced, yet it felt like a dream at the same time. Piece by piece, the temple turned to dust and was blown away by the wind. Even the stone I'd laid on moments earlier disintegrated. We covered our faces to keep from getting sand and grit in our eyes, but it still stung our skin as every trace of The Sand disappeared, peppering us as it was sucked away. Opening my eyes, I saw that we stood in the forest once again.

It was over.

My fingers felt strange, cold, and...my ring. It was gone. I dropped to the ground, frantically turning over leaves, shoving my hands through the dark soil below it. "What's wrong?" Ford asked, dropping down to help me look for what he didn't even know I'd lost.

"My ring. It's gone!" I cried out. Turning in a circle, I searched for it, but no glint of silver shone in the sun. No foreign bump lay hidden beneath the fallen foliage. It was as if the ring had disappeared along with The Sand, Sekhmet, and Tage. Looking over at Saul's hand, I noticed that he still had his.

It wasn't *all* erased, so where was it?

I had to find it.

It was all I had left of Tage. Although he wasn't the one to give it to me – Roman was – it held Tage's blood, too. His blood bonded him to me.

It was all I had left of him.

I scrambled around, making long arcs around the small area I'd been standing in, but there was nothing. Ford stopped looking when he saw me pause.

"Maybe we can come back and look later. I think we should go home," he said gently.

"No! I have to find it," I insisted.

Mercedes crouched down beside me. "It won't bring him back, Porsch."

I wanted to cry and slap her damn mouth at the same time. "I know, but I need it. Just go on without me."

"We aren't leaving without you. We go home together," Saul said, leaving no room for argument. I would find it; I just needed to come back alone. I could try to find a magnet in the city, but I *would* find my ring. They waited as I checked again and again until even I realized there was no use.

"We can come back," Mercedes promised, urging me to leave the clearing. Leaving was the last thing I wanted to do, but also the only thing I wanted to do. I was torn completely in two. Half of me would return to Blackwater, but the other half would always try to find Tage. What if he wasn't dead? What if he was somehow able to cheat death and come back?

Collecting myself, I started walking toward Blackwater, stepping gingerly through the forest floor. Bare feet were fine on sand, but The Sand was gone. It vanished when he did.

It would be a long walk home, even though the distance was short.

When we came near the Colony, Saul began to hang back from the crowd. "What's wrong?" I asked.

"I'm banished."

"You know what, Saul?"

"What?" he asked, looking at me.

"Fuck that. You've earned a home wherever you want it."

My mind was numb as we crossed into Blackwater that evening. My feet knew the way, and it was that fact, along with my siblings and friends, that were the only reasons I made it home. The sun was sinking below the hilltops, barely visible between the leaves that fluttered happily in the wind. Children throwing rocks in the river were the first to run into the Colony, spreading the word that we were all home, that we weren't night-walkers anymore. They yelled about our funny clothing and shouted that our fangs were gone. They must have seen the smiles of Mercedes, Roman, and Saul, but I couldn't bring myself to smile. My heart hurt. It hurt worse than it did when I first turned into a monster, because while that pain was sharp and sudden, this was deep; carving a message into my heart that Tage was dead.

We walked to our row of homes and waved at the new neighbors, transplants from Mountainside. Roman cleared his throat. "We should all go to my house until they come for us."

I agreed silently. I didn't know if I could bear to look at the house I shared with Tage.

Ford paused at the sidewalk, hitching his finger toward Father's. "I should go tell him first."

"You should," I agreed. "He'll want to see you."
"He'll want to see you and Cedes, too."
I hoped he was right.

TWELVE

SAUL

ROMAN WAS RIGHT. THE COUNCIL HAD ALREADY GATHERED AND CAME TO Roman's house to speak with us before we could even figure out how to find some food to eat. We were weak and starved half to death. Roman, Mercedes, and I took turns talking so Porschia wouldn't have to; Ford occasionally peppering the conversation with comments.

Her father tried to engage her several times, but she just clammed up, withdrawing further into herself. No one asked why I was in Blackwater. I think she would have stood up and told them all what they could do with their mandates if they did.

In the end, the men and women trickled out of Roman's home; former neighbors, family friends, my own father. He didn't ask me to come home, maybe because I was still unwelcome. Maybe because he knew I didn't want to step foot inside his house again.

Mercedes declined their father's request that she go home, too. "I'm staying with Porschia," she told him gently. "She needs someone."

Porschia did need someone. If she were left alone, she'd wither like a rose in winter.

I knew that someone wasn't me, but I was grateful that Mercedes cared enough to worry about her siblings at all. She and Roman exchanged several meaningful glances and one didn't have to be a genius to figure that one out. Somewhere in the fray, they'd become close. Friends. Maybe more.

Roman groaned out loud, closing the door after Carson Grant and Ford. "Where are we ever going to get something to eat?"

"We could go hunting," I teased.

"I don't think I'd make it over the crossing again. That trunk is slicker than I remember, and the bridge is on the other side. There's no one strong enough to lift it across."

Everyone voiced their sadness over that. The bridge was great, but now we were hard-pressed to move from the comfort of Roman's living room couches.

"We will. In time, we'll be able to make some contraption to get it across and put it in place. There's nothing for us to keep out of Blackwater now." They were the first words she'd spoken in hours, and everyone's attention snapped to Porschia with that surprisingly hopeful statement. "You could figure it out, Saul. If you get to the point where you can work with Brian and the carpenters again, you could," she added.

"That's a big if, Porsch," I said softly.

"Nothing's as big as the obstacle we just crossed," she whispered.

A knock sounded on the front door. Mercedes offered to get it and sluggishly walked to the door, wrenching it open. "Uh, I think you guys should see this," she called out over her shoulder.

My first thought was, *What now? What are they going to do to us now?* but that was before I saw the food. That was before I was thankful that they 'got' it; they understood we'd been through hell. And maybe, just maybe, they could offer our scorched tongues and souls a drink of water.

We feasted on the food our neighbors gave us and then decided we should all crash at Roman's. He had plenty of room. I slept like I hadn't slept in a hundred years—until Mercedes shook me awake. I sat up straight. "What's wrong?"

"Saul! I can't find Porschia," she whisper-yelled.

Groggy, I slipped out from beneath the blanket and followed her out of the room. "Where have you looked?"

"Everywhere. I've been all over this house, the back yard, and even next door in their – er, *her* – house. I've looked everywhere I could think of."

"Would she go to your Father's house?"

Mercedes shook her head no. I scrutinized her a moment, noting the dark bags hanging beneath her eyes and the snarled mess of her hair. Then it hit me. "Did you look in the basement?"

Her eyes widened. "She wouldn't go down there. Why would she want to go back there?" she wondered aloud.

"Give me a few?" I asked.

"Yeah," she agreed.

I padded down the steps and into the cool, damp room of the basement where I saw Porschia huddled on the cot inside the cage, curled up beneath a blanket she'd taken from upstairs. "Hey," I said quietly in case she was asleep.

"Hey," her voice broke.

"You need a pillow."

She shook her head. "I'm fine, Saul. Go back to sleep."

"Nah. Not when I'm on pillow duty. Sit up." When she raised herself, I slid into the space, bracing my back against the bars behind us. I patted my leg. "Pillow."

"I can't lay on you," she argued.

"You can. I'm warm and I'm your friend, so it's completely not weird."

Surprisingly, she laid down, resting her head on my thigh. In a few minutes, her breathing steadied and I could feel the muscles of her body twitch as she fell into a deep sleep. Mercedes crept down, holding a lit candle. She clutched her chest when she saw her curled up on the cot.

"I can stay with her if you want," she whispered.

I shook my head. "I'm good. Get some sleep, Cedes."

She pursed her lips together before she slowly turned, making her way back upstairs.

THIRTEEN

PORSCHIA

One second at a time.

One minute at a time.

One hour at a time.

One day at a time.

One week... it had been a week. Mercedes brought me clothes yesterday. They actually fit. While I loved Maggie's dresses, so had he, and they reminded me too much of him. His hands on my waist. His breath at my ear.

The last thing I wanted was to forget him, but I also couldn't let his ghost keep me from living. He sacrificed himself so that I could have a life, because I'd asked him for just that. He gave up his life to give me normal, and I'd be damned if I was going to waste his gift.

In my jeans and navy blue t-shirt, I walked across town to the carpentry shop. Former neighbors still stared as I passed them by. It may have been curiosity, and it may have been fear, but my decision had been made. I didn't want to stay in Blackwater, but I did want to be near my family. The city was a mess, and I certainly didn't want that. What I needed was help, and I intended to ask for it.

Inside the building, Brian Yankee hammered nails into two long pieces of wood. I walked up close so he couldn't ignore me in case he still held a grudge over his Father's banishment. His eyes caught mine. "Porschia?" He laid his hammer down and stood up straight. "What brings you here?" A mixture of surprise and trepidation swirled across his features.

"I need your help."

He ticked his head back. "Sure. What kind of help?"

"The house-building sort."

"We've never built a house in Blackwater. Sheds and the big barn, yes, but not houses. There might be a few empty. A lot of the people from Mountainside and The Glen are staying in the city. Some of the buildings are run down, but not ruined. Not like those that are crumbling."

I shook my head. "I want to build in the forest."

"Why would you want to do that?"

Standing silently, I let him figure it out. I could tell when he did, because he squinted his eyes and crossed his arms. "You are welcome here. This is your home."

"It doesn't feel the same. I want to be close, but I need space."

He nodded. "We can make the wall joists here, and if your brother can figure out how to get the bridge in place somehow, he could drive the horse and buggy across. That would make it much easier. I expect you'll not go too deep into the woods."

I couldn't help but smile. "You'll help me?"

"Of course," he said sincerely. "Look at all you did to help us. If this is what you need, I'll make it happen."

I thanked Brian and ran for home. Ford and I had to figure the bridge out.

My brother threw his arms around me on the porch, almost knocking me backward down the steps. "It's good to see you out and about, Porsch!"

"I need your genius, Ford."

"Really? I can go get it," he said, hitching his thumb back toward the house playfully.

I punched him lightly and he feigned injury. "So, what are you scheming about?" he asked.

"Who says I'm scheming?" I teased.

"It's in the twinkle of your eyes. You're up to something."

"Nothing," I told him, "except trying to think of how to get the bridge in place." I hopped down off the porch and started toward the crossing.

"You're kidding, right?" he yelled from behind me.

"Nope."

"Aww, Porsch, that's impossible now. You know," he said, catching up with me, "we should've left it up, guarded it or something. Now it's going to rot on the other side of the river."

"Not if you're half as smart as I'm betting you are, little brother."

Once we got to the edge of the river, Ford stared at the bridge across the swirling water. After an hour, we sat on the bank. He picked grass and threw it into the river. "It's steep here," he finally said.

That was obvious, so I waited and listened for him to talk the solution out of his mind. "We can't use horses." He sighed. "Can't lift it without a lot of man-power."

"Could we place it downstream?" I offered.

"Maybe if we find a place it'll fit, but it was built to be used here, at this spot. It would be best if it stayed here."

"Can we make something? I asked.

"To lift it?" he asked with a groan.

"Yeah, to hoist it over somehow."

He picked another long piece of grass. "We'd need a lot of rope, a good pulley, and some strong timber, but I think we could make something to lever it over, Porsch. Then we could have people on this side with ropes to steer it so it didn't swing around wildly and hurt someone. They could guide it into place." He jumped up. "I need to talk to Brian. Be right back."

His rushed footsteps carried him back toward the houses, and I knew it would be a while before he came back. I made my way upstream along the bank to a place where I could descend, to the calm pool beneath the waterfall where we said farewell to Mercedes after she fell. It was where we played, bathed, and managed to find a sliver of happiness in spite of the dismal situation we were in.

Kicking off the new tennis shoes Mercedes found for me in the city, I rolled up the legs of my pants until they were too tight to go any farther and the rolled fabric sat right above my knee, gently squeezing my legs. It had been scorching hot over the past week, no rain, and the bank was sandy and dry. I dug my toes into it and closed my eyes, remembering the feel of his skin melded to mine.

I miss you. I hope you're at peace now.

A tear fell from my eyes, joining the water in the pool as I stepped in.

This is hard. Being without you... I was so angry that you lied, but I understand it at the same time. It's all such a confusing mess. And it's surreal, Tage. Part of me wonders if I've lost my mind like Mother and only imagined you; created the night-walkers and Infected in some world that only existed to me. But if that's true, then I'm glad, because you were part of that world. And if it's not, then I'm so glad your seer saw me and that you were led to me. Because I love you.

A warm breeze swirled around me and I imagined it was his arms, wrapping around my waist from behind.

"Hey," a voice from behind said, pulling me out of my trance. I turned to find Saul walking down the bank along the roots that made little earthen steps.

"Hey."

"I didn't mean to bother you. I didn't realize anyone was here." He slowed his steps. "I can go," he said, hitching his thumb behind him.

"It's fine. I'm just wading."

"I just need to cool off for a few minutes." I noticed his shirt was wringing wet with sweat as he reached down to unlace his boots. "I swear steam just came out," he said, setting one boot aside and then the other.

"It wouldn't surprise me. What have you been doing?" It was just after midday and the sun was already scorching hot. The humidity only made it seem hotter.

"A crew of us are fixing the roof of Town Hall."

That surprised me enough to stop walking through the cool water. "It's about time. How long have they been using it with a broken roof?"

"Too long."

That was about right. We were both quiet for a few long moments until he finally broke the silence. "How are you holding up?"

"I'm fine."

He shook his head, having finished rolling his pant legs up. "You're not now, but you will be."

I hoped he was right.

"We aren't sick or eating our neighbors, so that's something, right?" I teased, releasing a hollow laugh.

He grabbed the back of his shirt and pulled it over his head. I looked to the waterfall, knowing he was splashing his head and body. "I'm going in," he warned, and then took off running to the deeper section just beneath the falling water.

I couldn't help but laugh. He looked carefree and different, too young to have gone through what we all did. Too happy for it to have been real.

He stilled just in front of the water, cocking his head to the side. "Do you hear that?"

The only thing I heard was water and the locusts.

"The bugs?"

"Yeah. They aren't saying *Pharaoh* anymore."

I bent in to listen, realizing they weren't. They were screeching, but in no particular rhythm. It's as if the word had been erased from their biology. I swallowed thickly. Just like him, the word was gone.

"Aw, shit. I'm sorry, Porschia." He trudged through the water toward me, but I was already out and putting on my shoes.

"It's okay. I have to go."

He sighed. "I'm sorry anyway."

Everyone who was there knew that Tage had done the right thing. He lied to his sister, knowing his abilities weren't strong enough to allow them to cheat a death they'd been so long denied. He couldn't magic away fate. And yet he healed me, and through me, the world was made whole.

Climbing the bank quickly, I reveled in the feeling of burning muscles. Being part vampire made everything so simple. We were faster and our senses were more acute; the ultimate predators. But being a predator wasn't fun when it wasn't really a challenge. Normal was much more difficult. Everyday life was hard. Physically. Mentally. But it was a challenge I'd greatly face and be thankful for each day.

One day, as soon as the stone in my chest melted, I'd face it a whole lot happier.

ROMAN

MERCEDES LAID HER HEAD ON MY SHOULDERS AND STARED THROUGH THE open window as the curtains fluttered in the breeze.

"Every star is shining, just like everything's right in the world," she said softly.

"Isn't it?" I asked.

"No. My sister is broken and I still have this sneaking suspicion that you're glad about it."

The fingers that brushed her arm stilled. "I'm not."

"You are. I can tell you still haven't let it go, but I understand. I probably wouldn't have if I were you either. I really like you, Roman, but I can't do this if you're planning to hurt her."

She let out a shuddering breath.

Did I still resent Porschia for killing Pierce? Yes. I'd be lying if I said I didn't. Did I want her dead? Not anymore. I'd seen enough blood shed for a thousand lifetimes. Somehow, when the change happened and the curses were finished, I didn't age like I thought I would, especially after seeing how the women at The Manor shrank and crumbled. I'd been spared. I was young and fit and had Mercedes to spend time with. She and I were friends and lovers now, but maybe one day we would be more.

The thing of it was that there was possibility. A future. Hope.

And I didn't want to lose her. I liked her, too.

I liked the feel of her skin and how her nose crinkled when she laughed. And her body, my God, it was made for me. I was sure of it.

"I want to put it behind me. It's still a fresh wound, Cede. I can't just snap my fingers and forget I had a brother. I can't forget what she did."

Mercedes shifted to face me. "You don't have to forget. You don't even have to forgive her. But I don't want you to hurt her. If you hurt her, it'll kill me."

"I'd never hurt you."

"At one point, you'd have torn my throat out, Roman."

I smiled. "You'd have done the same to me. But I promise you now that we're changed, I won't hurt your sister… or your brother."

Mercedes didn't cry often. She was tough. As the eldest in that dysfunctional household, she held in a whole lot. So when her tear fell onto my skin, hot and then cooling as it slid down my chest, it almost broke my heart.

I wasn't sure I had one left until that moment.

"I promise."

She swallowed and nodded, nuzzling closer against me. And I reveled in the feel of her. The feel of us.

FOURTEEN

PORSCHIA

Roman was waiting near the bridge, as sweaty as Saul. I gave him a slight wave, intending to move away without speaking, but he jogged to catch up with me. Mercedes had spilled the beans about him trying to kill her and Ford to get back at me for killing Pierce. Oops.

I warily watched Roman approach. He pursed his lips before he began talking. "Can we just start over, Porschia? I did awful things to your family. You did awful things to mine. But we're human now, and we have a chance at a new start. Plus, it's harder to kill another person when you aren't a monster with fangs, thirsty for blood. So I guess I'm asking if we can just start fresh?"

I could see the tension in his shoulders as he waited for my reply. I gave it to him in the form of a hug. "As long as you promise never to hurt my family, Roman. If you want to hurt someone, come after me."

He snorted. "I promise. Though, if we're truly starting over, I hope we'll never let it come to that. Besides," he paused. "I think you've been punished enough for a thousand men."

I knew he meant losing Tage, and he was right. My heart felt like a thousand arrows had pierced it, shredding it into nothing.

I WALKED QUICKLY BACK TO MY HOUSE, ALTHOUGH IT WASN'T JUST MINE AT the moment. Once we left Roman's house that first night after the excitement receded, Mercedes and Saul migrated with me. Mercedes slept in the room next to mine and Saul took the couch. I'd only asked him once to be a pillow again since that first night at Roman's. I counted that as a battle won in this drawn-out war.

Somehow I fell asleep on the couch and woke with a crick in my neck. Rolling it from side to side, I tried to remind myself that this was one of the things that made me normal, made me human, and I should be thankful for it. And then I heard shouting from upstairs and got worried. One of those voices was Roman. The other was Mercedes. Could he have been bluffing?

I rushed up the steps and threw her door open. That was a mistake.

"Porschia?! Don't you knock?" she shrieked, quickly grabbing a pillow to cover herself with, although Roman just laughed as I jerked the door closed. I felt like melting into a puddle and disappearing altogether. Roman and my sister? When did those feelings turn from death and destruction to love making?

"I'm leaving. I'll leave," I stuttered. Something banged against the door.

"Knock next time!" Mercedes yelled.

"I didn't know you'd be *banging* our next door *neighbor* in the middle of the *day* in my *house*! And he tried to *kill* you!"

"It's my house, too! And we've already kissed and made up!" She was insufferable.

"Go to Roman's next time!"

She growled as I opened the front door and began to walk, and then I realized I had nowhere to go. The river was occupied, my house was... being used, and Father wasn't home. He was busy helping Brian and the carpenters with something – I didn't know what and he didn't elaborate. Ford was working things out and needed to do it on his own.

My feet carried me down familiar pathways, straight to Maggie's.

I sat on her porch, the familiar worn wooden planks beneath me. The sun filtered through the leaves on the tree in her front yard. "You gonna start sewing for her?" someone asked from next door. It was Meg's mom, and the very fact that she had the ability to wear a smile on her face and carry on a simple conversation after losing her daughter – to my mother, no less – even though it was months ago, astounded me. I hadn't come that far yet.

"Does anyone really need it?"

"They do. Not everyone can fit in the clothes they find in the city. A lot of them are moth-eaten anyway. I'm not saying you should make one style or another, but a lot of people could use some fresh items in their closet."

"Why would anyone want *me* to make them?" She knew why I was asking. People were terrified of me. Would they even want my hands touching the fabric they'd wear?

She sighed. "I think they would. Besides, it's time to leave the past where it lies."

One thing was certain: if a woman who'd lost her daughter to the cold-blooded hands of my mother could find it within her heart to say anything at all to me, let alone something encouraging, it meant there might be hope for us all. Because if the situation were reversed, I'm not sure I could look into the eyes of someone related to the person who slaughtered everything I loved. "I'll consider it once the dust settles."

She inclined her head and then stepped inside the home next to Maggie's. I still felt that things needed time. In general, people weren't willing to change their way of thinking overnight, especially something ingrained from a fear so thick it could be felt.

I stood and pushed Maggie's door open. Stepping inside, it smelled like home. Familiar and inviting, like the dried vanilla hanging on nails in each room, and like sunshine on dust. I couldn't let her home get coated in it, so I grabbed some rags and began to erase it off of everything I could see. I cleaned for hours until I was spent, and then I went upstairs to the bed she'd offered me, curling up into a ball and falling asleep.

It was almost dark when someone pushed the door open with a loud squeak. I jumped up, startled and still groggy.

Saul's silhouette filled the doorway. "There you are."

"Yeah. I was tired and must have lost track of the time." And I felt tired all the time. I wanted nothing more than to sleep this nightmare away.

He smiled. "Your sister is worried."

"She sure wasn't worried earlier," I grumbled beneath my breath.

"She told me everything," he said with a grin.

I laughed ruefully. "At least you didn't have to witness it."

"True. Ready to go home?"

Was I? This was as much home to me as anywhere else. I wondered why someone from Mountainside or The Glen didn't get placed here. I was glad they weren't, but wondered why all the same. The house was big. It could easily house a large family, or maybe even two small ones.

"Yeah, I'm ready. I'm confused as hell about my sister and Roman, but I'm ready to go back if they're…finished."

I laced my tennis shoes and followed him down the hall and stairs. The evening was warm and the sky was only beginning to show the brightest stars. I stared at the familiar patterns.

"You like the stars?" he asked.

"I always have. I like the sky in general because it varies so much, but it's always beautiful."

He smiled at me. "That's an interesting way to think about it."

I shrugged. "It's true. Clouds, the coloring of the sky, the patterns; they're always unique."

"The stars are constant, though," he teased.

"There's beauty in their predictability. The stars are reliable." They're always there. They don't leave.

At the pavilion, I paused near the fountain. Someone had cleaned it out and filled it with fresh, clean water. "Blackwater seems happier now."

"People are finally taking care of it," he replied simply.

"Why didn't they before?"

He sighed. "There wasn't much hope of a future before, but now people can see the possibility of a long, happy life. They want to be surrounded by things that remind them to live. This place was awfully run down, and it's good to see people actually caring about it again."

"I don't remember a time when they did," I said, trying to search my memory.

"At some point someone did. They wouldn't have placed this fountain, the benches, or laid these stones in the ground if they didn't care. Someone created a place of beauty, but because of its use in the rotation, its beauty became tainted. It became a place to fear instead of a place to enjoy."

We walked down the sidewalks toward what used to be the night-walker portion of town. Now, children ran around catching the lightning bugs that flared beneath the dark trees in their lawns, careful not to step into the gardens that were flourishing.

Saul cleared his throat. "Ford told me about the bridge."

"Yeah. I think it would be nice to be able to use it."

"To get supplies across for your new house?"

Ford had a big mouth. "Yeah. I just think I would feel more comfortable out there." He was quiet for a beat. "You know what's weird?"

"What?" he asked.

"I've lived here most of my life, and I only spent time in the forest recently. But I was more comfortable there than I ever was in Blackwater. It's like the forest became a part of me, or me a part of her. Beyond the crossing, I feel like I can breathe. Here, I feel smothered."

"I feel it too," he admitted.

"Have you spoken with your parents yet?"

"My mom came to see me today at Town Hall. She brought lunch. It was awkward and she didn't stay long, but it was a start. I just thanked her and watched her walk away."

"They were wrong to shut you out," I told him.

"They only did what they thought was right. At one point, even you agreed with them. At one point, *I* agreed with them."

I swallowed. "For the record, I'm glad you're here."

He smiled slightly, a smile that didn't flourish or reach his eyes. "Me too, most days."

We paused in front of our houses. Saul chuckled as Roman threw open his door and greeted us. "Hello, neighbors!"

Growling in response, I couldn't help but smack Saul as he laughed at me. "You sound so human now," Saul added.

I did. I sounded like before.

"Is Mercedes with you?" I asked Roman.

"Nah, she's wearing a hole in your living room floor," he replied.

Before I could turn to walk in that direction, she threw open the front door and ran to me, squeezing my neck hard. "You scared me so bad."

"Why?"

"I thought you were going to leave."

"And go where, Mercedes?" I asked. There was nowhere for me to go.

She let me go and stepped back. "I don't know, but when you disappear, I worry."

"I can handle myself," I argued.

"You could. But you aren't... it's not like..."

It wasn't and I wasn't. She was right. "I know, but I'm fine. I was at Maggie's."

She told Roman to go to bed, to which he replied with a snort, insisting that he needed sleep because she'd worn him out. Mercedes gave him an evil look and grabbed my hand. "He is insufferable."

"You fed that fire, Cedes," I teased.

"Well, it's an amazing fire," she giggled, pulling me up the walk to our house.

Saul groaned. "Do you have to discuss this in front of me?"

"You can walk ahead of us if you prefer, Saul," Mercedes smarted.

He groaned again.

THAT NIGHT, MERCEDES SAT ON THE EDGE OF MY MATTRESS PICKING AT HER cuticles. "So, are you mad?"

"No, but I'm wondering what the hell happened. There seemed to be some major tension brewing between the two of you while we were in The Sand, and now you're sleeping with him? What changed?"

She bit a hangnail off her pinky. "I don't know what happened, but after we were healed, Roman and I started talking all the time. Talking led to forgiving, and forgiving led to –"

"I know where it led. Did you know he asked me earlier for a second chance?" I asked, holding a pillow over my chest. I didn't tell her that he also slipped past me downstairs while I was asleep and that they were incredibly loud in the bedroom.

"He's sincere; he just wants to live like a normal person now that he has the chance. We aren't serious, but we *are* attracted to each other. We both have needs, so we're satisfying those together."

"What about love?" I asked.

My sister lowered her head, staring at her nails intently. "Not sure love is in the cards for me."

"I know you loved Noah, but Roman isn't Noah and I'm not sure how I feel about you and Roman. I don't feel upset, but it's just weird. But, that being said, I'm glad he's not Noah. He turned out to be someone who didn't deserve your love. Maybe Roman will surprise us all and become that man. Maybe he'll just be a fling for now, but either way, I'm fine with it and you don't have to ask for my blessing or approval."

"I know he was infatuated with you at one time," she said, watching my reaction. "I just wanted to make sure you didn't ever feel that way about him."

"I can honestly say that Roman has only ever been a friend or an enemy in my eyes. I've never thought of him that way."

"That's a relief," she said on an exhale.

"And I don't think he ever really *wanted me* wanted me. I think he was curious and a night-walker barely under control. As you know, even when you're out of Frenzy, it's still hard to suppress the hunger."

"I hated every second of it. I don't know how you did it. I turned into both, but not at the same time, Porsch. That must have been excruciating." Awkward silence filled the air and she fidgeted, smoothing her jeans.

It was excruciating. Worst thing I'd felt in my life until now, when it felt like there was a gaping hole in my chest, one that would never close and would ooze heartache forever.

She awkwardly reached out for me and we hugged, squishing the pillow between us. "I'm sorry you're hurting," she said comfortingly.

"I'm glad you're healed," was all I could choke out.

FIFTEEN

SAUL

WHEN SOMETHING ENORMOUS HAPPENS IN YOUR LIFE, YOU START TO separate time based on that event. I originally thought it would be pre-Infection and post-Infection, but then when I was cured, pre- and post-cure became the moment. Then pre- and post- vampire. But the moment that took the cake ended up being pre-and post- sacrifice. Tage sacrificed himself and his sister to heal everyone. He didn't mean to be a hero, and he didn't plan to sacrifice himself from the start. He was a bastard. I never liked the guy and I knew if the decision were left to him, he'd have kept Porschia in a pretty, gilded cage just so he could keep her to himself for an eternity.

If she didn't ask him to heal her, he wouldn't have. It was that simple. And everyone would have a different moment to separate our lives, a different one for each person instead of this unifying event.

It had been five weeks since we returned to Blackwater from The Sand. The bridge was now in place over the river, thanks to Ford, Brian, and a host of men who helped pull the bridge into place. My palms still burned from gripping the rope so hard.

The Council was hosting a celebration tonight to celebrate our new beginning. There would be meat, vegetables, fruits, and even music. I hoped Porschia would go. She needed to see that she wasn't an outcast anymore. Surprisingly, none of us were.

My Father tried to speak with me yesterday, but I kept walking. I wasn't ready to make nice. Maybe I would never be ready. Maybe it would just take time.

I guided the horse across the bridge. She got skittish going over the water, but was okay once we got to the other side. I was hauling more wood for Porschia's house. It wasn't far into the woods at all, which made me feel more at ease, but a young woman living alone, away from the town put her at risk. Even if she didn't see it, she was in danger here. There were animals – predators – who still lurked in the woods. There were humans who were inherently bad. Being alone wasn't the smartest idea, which was why I'd been staying with her at her house. I knew Mercedes was there, but daily she was getting more wrapped up in Roman. Literally.

Maybe she would let me stay with her or maybe I could build myself a shack nearby, camouflage it, even.

When I pulled up, she was holding onto a tree. "You okay?" I slowed the horses and tied their reins to a tree branch.

I could tell she was sick. "Porschia?" I asked again.

She gagged and then caught her breath. "I'm fine," she choked.

That wasn't what fine looked like.

A shiver ran up my spine. It felt like the Infection all over again. What if Tage didn't cure her, after all? What if she was sick and would die? She stood up and I could see how pale she was.

"Don't say it," she started. "Don't even think it. I'm not that kind of sick. I think I just ate something that disagreed with me."

From down the pathway, I heard Mercedes' voice. "You could have given me a ride, Saul," she scolded.

"I didn't know you needed one."

"And you," she said, pointing at Porschia. "Are you pregnant?"

Porschia got even paler, if that was possible. Her mouth hung open. "What?"

"I said, are you pregnant? Have you been taking advantage of her, Saul? Because that is lower than low." Mercedes stomped up beside me.

I hadn't touched her, other than her head laying on me once in a while. She couldn't be pregna – oh, God.

"Porsch?" I asked.

"I'm not pregnant," she finally said, sitting down on a nearby boulder. "That's not possible."

"Well, it depends on if you slept with anyone, sweetie." Mercedes sat next to her sister, handing her the basket of food she'd brought.

"I-" Porschia started, but couldn't finish. "It's not possible."

"It's not *likely*, or not *possible*? Like, you've never slept with anyone because you're my baby sister and still a virgin?"

Porschia stared blankly in front of her.

"Oh, shit." Mercedes said. "You need to see someone. When was your last cycle?"

"Before I turned into a fucking monster, Mercedes! When was yours?"

Mercedes winced. "After I started turning human again, but it stopped mid-cycle when I started growing fangs again."

I'd heard enough to know who the father of her child was, and I saw red. Throwing the planks off the cart, I unknotted the reins and guided the horse backward.

"Saul, you don't have to leave," Porschia said softly.

I couldn't look at her. "Yeah, well, I have to help Brian with a few things. Ford is at the barn."

"Okay... thanks."

Nodding was the only answer I could give her. My chest was tight. I couldn't half breathe.

DAMN HIM STRAIGHT TO HELL. HE *KNEW*. I BET HE KNEW EXACTLY WHAT sleeping with her in The Sand would do. His magic probably helped him. He was a damn devil, and while I was sorry Porschia was hurting, I was still glad he was dead and gone.

It was like she was a prize to win, and when he won her, he wanted to cage her up and keep her like a pretty doll. But Porschia was a human being, not a toy. She didn't deserve how he treated her. She didn't deserve how he 'forgot' to numb her, how he almost attacked her in the city, or how he looked at her and then possessed her. Then he turned out to be some thousand-year-old Egyptian prince with a freak sister. What the hell?

I stomped toward town, small rocks skittering down the hill to get out of my way, thinking through the implications of it all. His crazy backstory should have blown her mind. She should have run for the hills, not into his arms. Why did she sleep with him?

Him?

Of all people, why did he have to come into her life?

If he had never come to Blackwater, none of this crap would've happened. Porschia might never have even turned. You never know. He might have been the one to manipulate her mother. He might have driven her crazy.

MERCEDES

We sat in silence, watching Saul run away as fast as he could. Damn him for that. Porschia needed support right now; not to have someone she cared about tuck tail and run. Once the cart was out of sight, the sounds of its wheels slowly fading into the distance and the small clouds of dust that the horse and cart stirred up beginning to settle back to the ground, Porschia cried. Not silently or stoically; she bawled in loud hiccups when he was out of earshot.

"Could this be possible? I was still a monster then."

"You were never a monster, Porsch."

"I was! I was awful and I know it, but how could I possibly be pregnant?"

"You were healed shortly after that. Maybe that had something to do with it," I said, wrapping my arm around her shoulder and pulling her into a hug. "I can't believe you slept with Tage."

"Why not?" she said, pulling away from me.

"I don't know. I mean, I know you loved the guy, but before that night, you didn't seem particularly intimate with him."

"We weren't until then. There was just too much going on," she said. I could tell in her tone that she didn't believe those words either.

"You were scared," I told her.

"I was?" she asked.

"You were. You placed all your faith in Saul and gave him your heart, only to have him disappoint you. His fall from grace dragged you down with him. It was a terrible spiral."

Porschia sniffed and wiped her cheeks. "How will they tell if I am?"

I had no idea. "I guess you'll start showing eventually if you are."

"Saul is never going to look at me again."

I stopped what I was about to say, asking, "Do you want him to?"

She stilled, looking like she knew she'd said too much. Maybe she did. "No," she said adamantly. "Not like you think. He's just so upset."

Uh-huh. Right. She still had feelings, however small, for Saul Daniels. *I'll be damned.*

But this little bun in the oven, if it's there, might cause an issue with that. If she was pregnant and Saul could deal with it not being his child, specifically with it being Tage's, maybe Porschia could be happy again.

I used to think that without Noah, I would never find someone who made me happy. Roman, it turned out, was a fine substitute, and I knew exactly what to expect from him. Noah ended up being a monumental disappointment, and I would happily use Roman as a distraction. I knew that was exactly what he was doing with me.

"What do I do?" she asked, starting to cry all over again.

"You build your house, move in, and then live like you want to live. That's the beauty of Tage's gift. You get to go on."

She opened her mouth, a wide strand of saliva stretching between her lips. "But how do I go on without him?"

I didn't know what to say. It would be hard, so hard she'd want to throw her hands in the air and give up about a hundred times a day, but she couldn't. She had to keep moving forward. That was the only way to keep the past behind her. "One step at a time," I finally answered.

She rested her head on my shoulder. "Thanks for staying with me."

"I plan to be the sister you should've had all along. I'll make everything up to you, Porsch."

"I'll make everything up to you, too," she promised.

And we would. We would keep our promises to one another, because that's what sisters did—especially when life was ordinary.

"Will you help me go look for my ring?" Porschia asked.

I nodded. "Yeah. I can do that."

We walked into the forest together, her arm brushing mine from time to time, to the place we'd entered and exited The Sand – the place where everything fell apart at the same time it was mended.

Ford wasn't able to find a magnet and I hadn't looked yet, but I was optimistic that we would find it. Perhaps under the twisted, gnarled root of a tree, or beneath layers of fallen, trampled leaves. But we didn't find it. We didn't find *him*.

SIXTEEN

PORSCHIA

Mercedes insisted I wear a dress, one of the ones Maggie made, because it was light green and she said it made my eyes look amazing. I didn't feel amazing puking outside of Town Hall. I felt hideous. Luckily, Mercedes had braided and pinned my hair back. "Water?" a deep voice asked.

Saul stood behind me, holding out a glass. I swallowed my nervousness and accepted the drink. "Thanks."

"You're welcome."

I hadn't really puked; it was more dry-heaving. I hadn't eaten in hours, so there was nothing to come up. My plan was to fill up on the feast tonight. Whether I vomited it back up or not, I had to try to eat, or so Mercedes said. Just in case...

"Hey," he said. "About earlier. I'm sorry I took off like that."

I looked at him and sipped again, the water cleansing my mouth. "You had every right."

He shook his head. "No, I didn't. We're friends, and friends should be there for each other no matter the situation. Right?"

"Right. Well, now you're here with water, so as your friend, I forgive you."

He laughed and stuck his elbow out for me. "Ready to get back to the celebration?"

"Honestly?" I smiled.

"Your Dad's asking about you," he said with a smirk.

My eyes widened. "He is?"

"Yep."

Oh, Lord above. Let that be the last time I vomit tonight. I took hold of his elbow and we walked around to the front doors that were literally teeming with people, new faces and old.

Sure enough, Father was searching that sea of faces for mine. When his eyes found their target, he began excusing himself, pushing through the crowd. "I haven't seen you in a few days. How are you?" he asked, hugging me awkwardly.

"I've been fine. Busy, but I'm doing great."

"How's the house?"

"The roof is on and the walls are up. They just have to plank the outside, I think."

Father thought for a second. "What about insulation?"

"Ford's handling it. He found something in one of the warehouses in the city that he says will work."

Father crossed his arms over his chest. "I don't like you living out there alone."

"Would you prefer I move someone in with me?" I asked innocently.

Saul nudged me and I couldn't help but let a giggle bubble out.

"Not unless it's Mercedes or you're married, young lady."

Oh, wow. If I truly was pregnant, he wasn't going to take the news well. Father was traditional. Everyone in Blackwater was, and being seventeen, pregnant, and unmarried was anything but that. Blackwater might shun me again; the citizens happy I'd left their perfection on my own accord before marring it.

Ford yelled for Father, saving me from any further scrutiny. The conversation alone had my stomach turning somersaults, but the smell of the food was too mouth-watering to ignore. I breathed in the aromas, closing my eyes and savoring the smells that were familiar but not common enough.

"Hungry?" Saul asked.

"I'm starving."

"Let's go eat, then." Again, I took his elbow and he led me toward the buffet table. I loaded a plate with more food than an adult should be able to eat, and then we found a quiet spot outside. When Saul went back for our drinks I thought about how he was trying to make up for running away, but he didn't have to. He didn't owe me anything.

Mercedes found me outside. "How are things?" she intoned.

"I've only been sick once this evening, but since I'm about to eat a ton of food, it probably won't be the last time," I laughed.

"Well, at least you're in good spirits about it," she said.

"Where's Roman?"

"Inside getting something to eat. I was heading there, too, when I found you."

I took a glance inside, but I couldn't see anything but a thick wall of bodies. "You should stay with him tonight."

She narrowed her eyes. "Why is that? Your cabin isn't ready."

"You don't have to babysit me. I'm a big girl now."

"You sure are," she teased with a grin. "And maybe I will. We'll see how the evening plays out."

"Oh, I bet I know *exactly* how it'll play out. I can't unsee what I've seen, Cedes."

She grinned. "It was hot, though!"

"Ewww. No, it wasn't."

Saul squeezed out the door and walked toward us. "Mercedes," he greeted.

"Saul. Are you behaving now?"

"I am," he smiled.

"Good," she said simply, bouncing on her feet. "Then I trust you'll see Porschia home? I think I'm sleeping elsewhere tonight."

Saul groaned. "Do *try* to keep it down. We can still hear you from the house when you get really loud."

Mercedes just laughed. "I'll try to remember that when he's-"

"And that's enough of that," I interrupted. My face was on fire. I was probably glowing hot even in the dark.

Mercedes throaty chuckle filled the air as she went to find Roman.

"It's weird, right? It's not just me?" Saul asked. "Those two seem like they fit, but then again, they don't."

"They're different, but in a lot of ways they're alike. I guess all that matters is that they seem to enjoy one another for the time being. I can't tell if it's just a fling or something that might turn into more."

"Time will tell." He began eating and paused when he saw I wasn't. "You scared to get sick?"

"Yes and no."

"You've had the worst luck. You were sick when you turned, and now you're sick again. I think you've had more than your share of sickness for your lifetime."

I giggled, holding my fork to my mouth. "Well *I* agree, but someone up there doesn't." I pointed the prongs into the air, heavenward.

We ate in silence, quietly exchanging the occasional glance. It was awkward on a comfortable level, if that was possible. We'd grown familiar with this feeling. Friends, but so much closer than friends. Saul's jealousy over Tage and his anger at finding out I might be pregnant with Tage's baby didn't surprise me at all. The fact that I wasn't angry with his reaction did. Once upon a time, I would have been mad as hell. Now, I was just tired.

When our forks slowed and our bellies were full, he took my plate and glass back into the crowd. I brushed my arms. It didn't matter that it was warmer than it had been in months. Summer was shoving Spring out of its way, but I was still cold-natured.

"Hey, are you ready to head back?" Saul asked, helping me up and absently rubbing my upper arms to warm me.

"Yeah," I said, stepping to the side.

"Sorry," he apologized.

I gave him a smile. "Nothing to apologize for."

We walked back to my house in the Colony. It would soon be his, or maybe Mercedes' when I left. I guessed they would fight over it unless Cedes moved in with Roman. Either way, it didn't matter. I was close to not having to worry about it. I could almost smell the fresh planks of wood that would make the exterior of my house. Pine. It was strong and the wood was so yellow, it nearly glowed.

"What are you thinking about?" Saul asked as he opened the front door for me.

"My new house."

"Are you excited about its progress?"

"Very," I admitted. "I can almost breathe."

He paused, holding a hand against the door as I walked in, but he didn't follow me inside. When I turned with a questioning look, he peered up at me. "If Mercedes doesn't move in with you, I want you to consider letting me," he finally said.

My brows must have touched my hair. "Um..."

"Just hear me out, Porschia. You'll need help. I mean, if you're—" he motioned to my stomach, "well, then you'll need a lot of help. I can haul water and do anything you need me to. I'm strong and I—"

"I know, Saul. I'll think about it."

He exhaled loudly. "Okay."

"I'm exhausted," I told him, a yawn following closely behind my words. "Do you mind if I turn in?"

"No, I plan to do the same," he said. I looked at his pillow and blankets folded on the end of the couch in neat rectangles of red fabric, the color reminding me of blood. Appropriate, I supposed, but any reminder was difficult to suffer through at this point. Pretending it was all a dream was simpler.

It was simpler until I remembered the smell of the palms, the feel of the hot sand on the soles of my feet and in between my toes. Until I remembered him...and remembered that it was impossible to forget him.

SEVENTEEN

SAUL

Roman, Ford, Carson, and I were loading things into the wagon—Porschia's things. It was moving day. We'd worked to finish her house, which was really just a make-shift cabin. We weren't home builders like the ones in the time before the Infection, but it was nice and Porschia was happy. Over the past several weeks her sickness gradually went away, and I've been holding my breath and praying that her stomach doesn't bulge in the slightest. So far it hasn't.

If she is carrying Tage's child, it won't change things for me. She won't be changed. She's still Porschia. But being that she was still a night-walker and Infected when they... Well, I don't think she could be carrying a child. She wasn't well enough to. No night-walker had ever conceived, and no Infected either, according to Roman. His authority and knowledge was all we had to go on since he had lived the longest and experienced more from both of those worlds than the rest of us.

Recently, Porschia had asked him the strangest thing. At The Manor, she said the women immediately started aging upon being turned back into humans. Then she asked why *he* wasn't aging now.

He shook his head and said he didn't know, but wondered if it had to do with his body being changed from the healing of both curses and not just from an individual. No one knew. No one might ever know.

"That's the last of it," Ford said, hefting a box of kitchen things: plates, bowls, silverware, cups. "Don't break it."

I shoved it farther into the cart and locked the short gate on the back. Hopefully, it wouldn't fall out going up the hill. Ford and Roman climbed into the cart. "We can steady it," Roman said, eyeballing the load. Ford didn't seem as confident, but of course, on his best day he wasn't nearly as cocky as Roman.

I climbed onto the wooden seat as Carson took the reins from the tree branch, handing them to me. "Is she okay?" he asked, holding the small of his back. His hair was much whiter than it had been even last month. His wrinkles were deeper, but he'd also smiled more in the past weeks than I'd ever seen him.

"She's doing great. Excited to be out in the woods by herself."

Carson groaned. "I asked her not to do it."

That made me smile. Porschia was twice as stubborn as any woman I'd ever met. There was no asking her *not* to do something. Maybe when she was a kid, but not now and not again. "I'm looking out for her," I said.

"Not too much," he warned sternly, as only her father could.

"Yes, sir." I chuckled, steering the horse toward the river. Two more trips across the bridge and she could rest for the night.

EIGHTEEN

PORSCHIA

AFTER THE GUYS UNLOADED, MERCEDES AND I ASKED THEM TO GO FIND some dinner for everyone. I had very little—okay, nothing—at my new house. I'd planted a fall garden, but didn't know how well it would produce its first year. Until then, I was dependent upon the kindness of others. Father was very kind, and everyone was willing to pitch in. Saul had begun leading hunts in the forest again, but this time it was only humans and crossbows, muscles and determination. Ford was eager to join him, and I'm not sure he left Saul's side during the overnight hours. When the hunts were over, Saul would come to my house, quietly remove his boots, and crash on the couch. Tonight, I wasn't sure if he would do the same or not. The couch was now at my new house; 'The Cabin', as we affectionately called it.

Ford came back on foot with a basket full of vegetables and fruits. "Roman's getting bread from one of the new ladies from Mountainside. She's amazing!" he said, out of breath from the uphill climb.

"Where is Saul?"

"Saul's with him," he answered.

I don't know why, but I was worried he would walk away and never come back. Especially with what was happening with me. I could feel a hardening of my lower abdomen, just a small lump, but it was there. My period was missing and I knew that one plus one equaled two. I would be having a baby this winter. Swallowing down that truth, I took the basket from Ford. "Thank you for this. There's enough to eat on for a few days." It truly was. All of us could eat for a few days on what he'd managed to round up in an hour.

Ford shrugged. "When a lot of people pitch in a little, it helps us and doesn't hurt them. I think people are starting to understand that now, where they used to hoard every scrap."

Hoarding every scrap was necessary back then, and it might become necessary again. Everyone ate well in the summer. It was early in the season and while some of the items would need to sit in the windowsill and ripen more, time would change them into something amazing.

"Father's pissed," he said nonchalantly.

"About what?" I asked.

Mercedes snorted. "Probably going to have a heart attack when he sees-"

"Shut up, Mercedes!" I yelled.

"What?" she said sweetly. "I was going to say Saul sleeping on your couch when he comes to visit."

"Saul's staying here?" Ford asked with a grin.

"Thanks a lot, Mercedes. And he hasn't said he is or he isn't, so you could be totally wrong." So there. I told them.

"What are you wrong about?" Saul asked from the front door, which my brother left wide open. Roman smiled from behind his shoulder.

"That you're gonna shack up with my sister," Ford offered. I wanted to melt into a puddle and sink between the floor boards. Seriously? My siblings were the worst.

Saul just laughed. "If she'll let me stay, I'd love to."

His eyes searched mine. "We'll talk about it later," I grumbled. "But right now I'm starving. Come help me, Mercedes."

Roman entered the kitchen with us. "I'm great with knives," he said with a wink. "Among other things," he said into Mercedes' ear, all gravely. I was seriously going to kick them out. After dinner.

Because, hunger.

PORSCHIA

. . .

Mercedes and I battled Roman for space in the small kitchen. We built a small fireplace and it worked well, cooking the vegetables into a delicious stew. Roman was even able to sweet-talk an old lady from The Glen into giving us some canned chicken. My mouth had watered since smelling it boil.

When it was finished, Ford and I raced to see who could finish our bowls first. He won. Barely. "Are we going hunting tonight?" Ford asked Saul.

"I'm going to check the snares, but I think I need a night off," Saul answered tiredly.

Ford nodded. "Can I tag along?"

Smiling, Saul answered, "Sure."

Roman and Mercedes finished their soup and then Mercedes cleaned the dishes in a basin of water on the porch. "I can get those," I told her. She ignored me, except for the dramatic rolling of her eyes. I felt useless. I hadn't hunted since I got back, not able to will myself into the woods at night, and now I was too nauseated to do much of anything. Loud, heaving vomiting wouldn't attract animals, it would scare them a mile away in the opposite direction.

Mercedes and Roman took off when the dishes were cleaned and stacked neatly on the wooden countertop Brian made. "See you tomorrow," she said with a hug around my neck.

"I'll be here."

"You can still come into Blackwater, you know."

I *did* know that. It wasn't that I had anything against the Colony or the people in it, I just needed distance right now. Maybe I always would.

Ford hugged me after Mercedes. "I'm going to run home for a bit. I'll meet you at the crossing, Saul. Midnight?"

"Sounds good," he answered. He must be planning to leave, too. Saul stood and stretched his arms to the ceiling. He and my brother were wearing their standard slacks and white button-ups. It wasn't that they needed a dress code anymore, but that they wore what was available.

"Ford, could you help me get some things from Maggie's tomorrow?"

He scuffed the toe of his shoe. "Are you sure we're allowed to do that?"

"I just want some fabric, needles, and thread. We'll be fine. I think you need some new pants," I said, nodding toward the hem along the bottom of his. It was rising more each day because he was growing tall fast.

"I could sure use some," he answered. "And you know I'll help you with anything, Porsch. Well, I'm heading home. Be safe tonight," he said, stepping off the porch and walking fast down the hill. That left only me and Saul.

I turned to see him right behind me and nearly jumped out of my skin. "You scared me!"

"Sorry," he smiled, meaning he wasn't sorry at all.

I turned back to see my brother disappear into the dusk. "He's learning a lot," Saul offered.

"In the forest?"

"In general. He helped us finish your cabin, too. Brian took him into the city to look for cabinets and he helped install them. He's doing great in the woods, learning snares, and he's damn good with a crossbow."

"Maybe Father should have given in and let him hunt after all," I said, but then I remembered the smell of rot, the shrieks from the Infected, the speed of being a night-walker, and the hunger of being both. It was too dangerous for him.

"He did the right thing. The Colony needed Mercedes and you, but Ford was young. He had time to wait."

"Or time for the pair of us to fall before they needed fresh meat to offer up."

"It wasn't a sacrifice, Porschia."

"Wasn't it?" I turned to face him.

His jaw ticked. "It wasn't meant to be, I don't think, but you're right. We were offered up; put in danger. And it could have ended a lot differently than it did, so we ought to be thankful we came out on this side of the daisies."

Daisies made me think of Meg's grave, of Maggie's, of the neighbors my mother slaughtered, of my Mother's grave – the one Father insisted on having erected for her. Love made no sense. Father still loved her on some level, and I missed her as well. Not the hateful woman who hurled daily reminders that I was the bane of her existence, but the pensive one who every so often sat on the porch and just watched the sky. I missed the moments that resembled normal. There weren't many that I could recall, but the ones I could, I clung to.

And Saul was right. It could have ended a number of other tragic ways, with any of us or all of us dying, but it didn't. And when the others went home that night and he and I stood on the porch alone, I was glad he didn't go back to town.

"Sometimes, I think it never happened; like it was just a nightmare." I'd never said those words aloud before now.

"It was a living nightmare, but it did happen." He folded me in a hug and asked, "Can I stay here tonight? On the couch?"

I nodded against his shoulder.

"Thanks," he said softly.

I wasn't sure if it was because he didn't want to be alone or because he didn't want me to be alone in the woods, but either way, I was glad for his company and friendship. Now that we'd gotten that back, I didn't want him to go anywhere. Too many people I loved disappeared.

NINETEEN

SAUL

Porschia was fine when I left her later that night to meet Ford. She was asleep in her bed with three blankets over her, despite the lingering heat of the day. I slipped out and didn't think I'd woken her. Ford was already at the crossing. We made our way quickly through the snares and came back with a raccoon, a hare, and a mink. It wasn't a deer, but it would do. My muscles were sore from working hard to finish Porschia's cabin, so a night off from spending hours in the woods was worth not bringing down something bigger, not that we did every night anyway.

I walked Ford back to the crossing, saying goodbye with a huge yawn. He laughed, then told me I was getting old and should go get some sleep. He was wrong about me being old, but I did need sleep.

I just didn't know I wouldn't be getting much when I got back to Porschia's. I pushed the door open, the hinges letting out a small squeak. But the door didn't wake her. Porschia was already up, sitting on the couch I used for a bed, curled up with her knees propped up and her arms wrapped tightly around them.

"What's wrong?" I said, rushing to her. A single candle provided what scant light we had. "Are you hurt?"

"No," she blubbered, and then burst into tears, angrily wiping her face and nose.

"What's wrong?" I sat down beside her and began to rub her back.

"You left and didn't say goodbye."

"You were sleeping, Porsch."

"I don't care. Everyone leaves. Everyone leaves and sometimes they don't come back, and you left and I didn't get to say goodbye!" she cried.

I pulled her over against my chest, brushing strands of her hair back from her face. "I promise to always tell you goodbye if I have to go. I promise."

She sobbed into my shirt, soaking it, and I held her and told her she was okay and that I'd never leave her. It was a promise I felt confident with making, now that the dust had settled. The curses were gone. Forever. That just left a normal life and a lifetime for Porschia and me, filled with normal promises, if we stayed in each other's lives that long.

I hoped we would.

She raised her head and wiped her eyes. "You might want to leave."

"Why would I want to do that?"

"Because I'm definitely pregnant, Saul, and you left the first time you heard it was even a possibility."

My hands stilled on her back. "Are you sure?"

She let out a harsh laugh. "Positive. I'm starting to show. Just a little, and it's probably not visible from the dresses I wear, but I see it. I feel it."

Swallowing, I reached my free hand out and asked, "Can I feel it?"

"My stomach?"

"Yeah," I answered. I wanted to be there for her, and accepting it was a simple way of showing her I wasn't going anywhere.

"Okay," she said guardedly, wiping the moisture from beneath her eyes. "But we need to stand up."

I was on my feet in a second, helping her off the couch. What if she got dizzy? Mom said she was always dizzy when she was carrying me.

Porschia tried to smile and accepted my hand. She looked down at the space between us that would soon be filled with her child and then grabbed my hands, placing them on her belly. Her lower stomach was hard and slightly rounded. She was right.

I gasped. "It's so hard."

"I know," she giggled. "It's weird."

"I'm not sure how this is possible, but I'll be here for you through...everything. I'm not going anywhere, unless your father makes me quit sleeping on your couch. And I'm sorry I left like that. I wasn't leaving you, I just needed time to process everything."

"You sleeping on my couch is about to be the least of his worries. I just hope everyone in town doesn't shun him because of my decisions."

I hugged her, feeling the tight knot of her stomach meet mine. Whatever ropes were around my heart loosened in that moment. She trusted me again. She cared, on whatever level this was. She didn't want me to leave without telling her. She let me feel her baby, and I was living at her house for the time being.

If she'd let me, I'd be there every step of the way. She might not feel the same way, but she was my best friend. The rotation brought us together, the curses tore us apart. But now that they were gone, we were back to being friends.

Was there anything better in the world?

"You should get some rest," I told her.

"So should you," she said, sniffling. She walked away toward her bedroom. "See you in the morning."

"Are we sleeping in?"

"Absolutely," she said.

Her mattress springs squealed when she sat down and settled, and then the occasional sniffle was the only sound from her room. I removed my boots and socks, stretched out on the couch, and turned my pillow over. Staring at the ceiling until I heard her breathing steady, I finally crashed. We didn't wake till long after the sun came up.

TWENTY

PORSCHIA

It was late July when I first let Saul feel the baby bump. Through August I was able to wear dresses and aprons to cover it, but September was less forgiving. The baby was growing and getting too big to conceal under anything.

I tried to squeeze into another dress. They fit, but were tight around the stomach. There was no hiding it now. I'd been working on dresses with high waists--basically right under my breasts – which were another thing that was blossoming. One of those dresses was almost ready, so I made it my priority for the day. Tomorrow, Father wanted all of us to come to his house for dinner. I had managed to avoid him for the last two weeks, but he wasn't having it anymore.

Ford grinned when he came to invite us. "I'll see if someone has smelling salts for him. He's gonna hit the floor," he teased, glancing at my protruding stomach.

"Thanks for the love, brother," I deadpanned.

He lightly slapped my shoulder. "You're welcome, sis."

All afternoon I worked to finish a dress that would fit me without making what I was trying to hide so obvious. I pricked my fingers seven times. Saul came home as I was trying it on.

"Porschia?" he yelled.

"One sec!" Ford had not only brought my sewing supplies and enough fabric to fill an entire corner of my bedroom, but he brought my old bedroom mirror, too. Part of the shine around the corners had worn away, but the center still reflected. I sighed. I guessed I looked as good as I could, given the circumstances. My complexion looked amazing. *He might think I'm a night-walker again,* I thought idly.

A sinking feeling filled my stomach, making it feel heavier than usual. Was this baby cursed? Was this some sick trick? To heal everyone else, only to bring the curse back again with a newborn?

"You okay?" Saul asked, concerned. "It's almost time to go to dinner."

"I know. Just..." I stepped out of the room, wearing the newly-finished navy blue dress. It had an 'empire waist', according to the Regency pattern, whatever that meant. It was all Ford could find that he thought might work. The fabric was light and gauzy, perfect for summer, and I'd altered the sleeves to make them short. One looked slightly longer than the other, but whatever. I wasn't perfect at this by any means.

Saul's brows raised. "You made that?"

"I did." He was impressed with my improper measurements? That was a good thing, considering the fact that I was in the process of making a pair of pants for him; tan, in a cooler fabric than the wool he sweated in every day. I hoped he liked them, and I hoped they didn't have one leg longer than the other or gathered funny at his backside.

"Wow. You look amazing," he said with a smile. "I don't think he'll be able to tell."

"I think he will, but even if not, I have to tell him. After dinner, I plan to see if I can speak with him alone."

"That's probably for the best," he said softly.

I laughed. "I can't hide it well now anyway, and it's only going to get worse from here."

He tucked a strand of hair behind my ear. "You look beautiful, Porschia."

My face heated. Smiling, I grabbed his arm and tugged him out of the house. "I'm starving," I said with a giggle.

"You're always starving."

Each step through the Colony made me more nervous. I imagined former neighbors looking out windows, staring at my stomach and whispering behind their cupped palms. Saul was by my side every step of the way. Would they think he was the father? Would it ruin his reputation in the community now that he was finally rebuilding his life?

"You might not want to be seen with me," I blurted out. "I didn't think of that, and I'm sorry."

He stopped in his tracks. "What are you talking about?" he asked incredulously.

"When people find out about me, they might make assumptions about you since we're together a lot."

He ran his hand over his freshly-cut hair. "The thing is, Porschia, I don't care what *any* of these people think. Not one of them. I care about you. I care about my friends. I want to live my life the way I want to live it, and if they can't understand that, well, that's their problem. Not mine."

He started walking with hurried, agitated steps, so I did, too. Then he wheeled around. "And guess what, Porschia? I wouldn't mind if they thought that baby *was* mine. Most of the time, I wish it was. And one day —not today—" he said, pointing his finger at me, "maybe you'll let me be more than just a friend. Maybe you'll let me be a father to your baby, and the baby will be ours, because that is all I can think about."

My mouth gaped open.

"Don't say anything. God, don't say a word. I can't deal with it right now, but one day... Just, let's go to dinner," he said finally.

I was shocked. I'd never thought about my baby needing a father.

The fact that he was even thinking along those lines meant he still had feelings for me. I wasn't blind. I could see it in the gentle way he brushed my hair back; in his eyes, stormy gray and blue, roiling as if he wanted to tear apart the forest to stop from leaving me alone in the woods. But it wasn't fair of me to ask anything of him, and the thing that still stood between me and Saul was Tage.

I still ached for him, still loved him. I wasn't sure my heart would ever stop hurting. Would it ever heal? Would I? Should I allow myself to? Because the last thing I wanted to do was forget anything about him. If I let the smallest detail of him slip away, I'd lose a piece of myself. Which piece, I wasn't sure.

"Stop over-thinking it," Saul warned.

It was hard not to over-think this.

"If you want me to tell your Dad I knocked you up, I will, if that's easier than explaining Tage."

"He knows about Tage and what happened," I defended.

"He doesn't know you slept with him."

I felt like slapping him. One minute he made me crazy, and the next he made sense. This was one of the former moments.

"Well, I'll tell him!"

"Don't yell at me. I'm just trying to help."

"Stop trying so hard!" I whispered fiercely. "I can handle this."

"Fine." His broody ass walked straight to Father's house, over broken asphalt and yellow lines so faded, they were nearly white.

When we stepped onto Father's porch, Mercedes and Roman shouted greetings to us. Seeing my face, Cedes' smile fell. "What's wrong?" She turned to Saul. "Did you upset her?"

"Why do you always assume *I* did something wrong?" he snapped.

"Because you're a member of the male species, that's why!" she yelled back.

Roman shook his head and clapped Saul on the shoulder. "There's no winning this fight, man. Let it go."

Saul shrugged his hand off. "Fine. Can we just go eat and get this over with?"

"Absolutely," I replied. He was infuriating.

I decided something in that moment. I was finished walking on eggshells. I'd made a decision and it was the right one for me. Everyone else would just have to deal with it, including my father.

Opening the door, Ford eyeballed my belly and smiled, ticking his eyes to Father. Father wiped his hands on a towel, saying, "Right on time! I'm not the best cook in the world, but I hope it's edible."

He pulled me in for a hug and I purposely pushed my stomach into his. "Uh," he said. When he stepped back, his eyes were wide. "Porschia?"

"I'm pregnant. It's Tage's. I don't regret it," I spouted.

"I can see that," he said, looking at my stomach. The room was so quiet you could hear a pin drop, until he started laughing. "Well, then I guess I'm going to be a grandfather, and I'm willing to bet that you're hungry," he said, smiling nervously.

"I am," I agreed, my shoulders relaxing. I took a deep breath and let Father lead me to the table.

"Sit here and I'll get some water and a plate for you," he said. "Everyone else, find a seat," he laughed.

"I can help—"

"No! You rest. You need to rest." He was going overboard about this. I wasn't helpless. I just had a small watermelon under my breasts.

Mercedes settled beside me on the left and Ford cut Saul off to sit on my right. Saul wound up diagonal from me. Roman sat beside him, and Father's chair was between him and Ford. "He took that well," my sister whispered.

"Better than I expected," I said, so thankful he had reacted positively. If he'd have reacted in any other way, I would have crumbled.

Father put chicken on the table. I didn't ask where he got it from, but Ford grinned. I gave his shin a slight kick. He shouldn't steal and he knew it. Ford just shrugged in response.

Next came squash and tomatoes. From the oven, Father cursed, waving a towel back and forth to fan something that was smoking. "The uh, the bread is a little well done," he said with a smile as he set it in the middle of us. Each of us ignored the smoke and grabbed a lump of the charred bread, placing it on our plates. Mercedes filled everyone's glass with water and told Father to sit down. Roman got up to help her, which was sweet. Saul glared at me from across the table, enough so that Father noticed.

"Everything okay?" he asked, looking between us.

"Yeah," Saul replied.

"Funny, with you two living together, I thought the baby might be yours, Saul."

And thanks a lot for that, Father. Thanks a lot.

Things went from awkward to bad after that, and most of what was to be a fun family dinner was spent in silence. The longer I sat in the atmosphere that Saul ruined, the angrier I got.

When everyone finally finished, Ford said he would handle the dishes. I offered to help but Father wouldn't hear of it. "Get home and rest," he said, eyeballing Saul. "Do you want to sleep here tonight?" he whispered.

"No. I'm going to go home."

He smiled. "There's just something about being in your own bed. You're not sharing a bed with Saul, right?"

I laughed. "No, Father. He sleeps on the couch."

"Tonight or all nights?" he asked, seriously.

"All nights. We're just friends."

He let out a pent-up breath. "That makes me feel better. Truthfully, I'm glad he's staying with you. I worry about you out there by yourself."

Well I wasn't. I was with Saul. Sort of. In a platonic way.

I hugged my Father like I hadn't in years, because in reality, I hadn't allowed myself to get too close to him while Mother was living. He would intervene between the two of us but only to a point, and it disappointed me too often to let him in. But now that we had a new beginning, I wouldn't waste it.

"Thank you for dinner," I told him.

"Don't be such a stranger. Maybe I'll come and visit more often. Or both," he said, letting me go.

"That would be great." Everyone but Ford was already waiting on the porch. Mercedes and Roman, hand-in-hand. I snorted.

"What?" Mercedes asked.

"Never saw Roman as the hand-holding type."

Roman narrowed his eyes. "I'll have you know that I am a gentleman."

"Since when?" I asked playfully.

"Since I became human for good, so it's pretty recent. Maybe you have a point," he laughed.

"Where's Saul?" I asked, seeing that he was noticeably missing from the group.

Mercedes winced. "He stomped off after we came outside, so he's probably slamming your front door shut by now."

"He's infuriating," I said, gathering my skirt so I could walk faster. Mercedes and Roman jogged to catch up with me. They walked with me until I turned to go toward the crossing and Mercedes promised to come help me with some sewing tomorrow. She was still learning, but was better at following patterns and cutting than I was. Maggie would have loved her.

TWENTY-ONE

PORSCHIA

At the bridge, I noticed someone with a fishing pole, watching the water from above. Meg's boyfriend, Jonah turned to face me. "Oh, hey, Porschia."

"Hi, Jonah. How've you been?"

"Okay," he said. "Some days are better than others. I heard what happened with Tage. I'm sure you feel the same way."

"I do." I leaned onto the railing and watched his line bob in the current below. The dark water rushed around it, but the line was strong; thin but made with enough strength to survive. Much like Jonah. Much like me.

"I miss her," I admitted, thinking of Meg.

"I do too. Sometimes it doesn't even seem real. When I'm at home, sometimes I feel like she's going to walk in the back door, asking how my day was."

Nodding in understanding, I stood there with him for a few minutes. "She loved you, Noah. You made her happier than she'd ever been. You made her life whole, even though it was cut short, and that counts for a lot in my book."

His throat was clogged with emotion when he answered. "Thank you."

"You're welcome. Well, I need to get home."

"Take care, Porschia."

"You too." I left him behind, his line fighting the current, his hook baited and ready to catch dinner. Shadows of large fish could be seen just upriver. If they moved a few feet down the river, he and his family would have a nice meal.

I marched to the cabin where I found Saul waiting in the living room, pacing the floor. "You'll wear a path through the boards if you don't slow down," I tried to tease.

"You have to joke. Right now?"

"What else would you have me do, Saul? Cry? Yell at you? I don't want to do any of those things. I just want everything to go back to normal."

"*Nothing* is normal! *Everything* has changed! You have to accept that. At some point, preferably before your child is born, you're going to have to accept a lot of things—things you refuse to even acknowledge."

I didn't have time for a fight, nor did I have the energy to deal with drama this evening. I pushed the front door closed behind me and walked toward my bedroom.

"Stop." His voice was stern.

"Why?" I threw my hands up.

"Because you need to hear this." He was obviously determined to tell me something.

"What? What do I possibly need to hear?"

Saul strode to me and pressed his lips to mine. I shoved him hard, wishing for the first time that I had the strength I'd had as a hybrid. That gesture would have made him hit the wall across the room. Instead, he backed away one foot.

"Don't you ever do that again without asking," I said, my voice low and quivering. I wiped my lips with the back of my hand. "In fact, don't do that again. Period."

"Tage is dead," he said, holding my eyes with his. My lips stung with the fire of his kiss. I pressed them together before answering.

"I know."

"He's dead, and he's not coming back."

Tears filled my eyes. I tried to blink them away.

"Tage is dead," he continued, "but I'm right here. I'm willing to be whatever you need for as long as you need it, whatever you want. I'm here. I'm right here in front of you. Tage is not coming back. This isn't a dream. It's not a drill. It's reality, Porschia. Tage is gone. Forever."

"Stop talking to me like I'm a child. I know he's dead, you asshole!"

I stomped to my room and slammed the door, locking it with the bar latch.

He hit the wooden wall once. “Damn it! Talk to me, Porschia. Don’t shut me out.”

But shutting him out was the only way I knew how to deal with this. If I thought night-walker emotions were all over the board, I had no idea what a pregnant woman was capable of. The last thing I wanted to do was see his face, contorted in anger and without an ounce of compassion—or maybe it was too much. In his way, he was trying to help, but his way wasn’t mine.

I laid in my bed, curled into a ball, and cried myself to sleep as he slammed a few cabinets and then settled on the other side of the wall. I hoped his couch was extra lumpy tonight.

SAUL

She just didn’t get it. She wanted Tage to come back and help her raise this baby, and it wasn’t going to happen. She still looked at me like we were new friends with no history whatsoever, like she’d never uttered the words, *I love you*. She’d told me that again and again, and those three words became my favorite ones to hear. I knew she needed time, and I was trying to give her as much as she needed. Hell, we might just end up being friends in the end, but no matter what, she had to accept that he wasn’t coming back.

He was dead.

I didn’t mean to be cruel, but she needed to hear it.

I knew she didn’t need me to add stress on top of what she was already dealing with, but she had to accept the facts at some point. Living in a skewed reality wasn’t helping her. In the long run, when she woke up, had an infant and Tage never showed up, she would fall apart.

I’d rather pick her pieces up now than wait until she had the baby and let her fall apart then.

Her sniffling and hiccupping from across the wall made me want to tear it down, gather her up, and hold her all night. Instead, I laid on the couch and tried to rest. Ford would be here in a few hours. We needed to hunt tonight.

Three hours and zero minutes of sleep later, there was lantern light from the front porch and a slight knock on the door. Ford pushed the front door open and closed it behind him, and then he opened the glass door of his lantern and blew the candle out.

"You ready?" he asked.

"Yeah, just let me tell her I'm leaving," I whispered.

"You'll wake her up," he argued.

"I promised I would. It's okay." I knocked twice on her door, then heard rustling.

She unlocked it and peeked out, eyes bleary with sleep. "Is everything okay?"

"We're leaving to hunt. I just... wanted to let you know." Ford threw a wave in her direction, which she returned.

"Be careful," she told us, watching stoically as we gathered our things. Ford stepped outside onto the porch, and I had almost pulled the door to when she yelled out, "Saul!"

I opened it back up and looked at her. "Yeah?"

"Thank you for saying goodbye."

"It's not goodbye. I'll be back at daybreak." She nodded. "I promise," I added. "And I'll take care of Ford."

Her eyes filled with tears and she nodded again to keep them at bay, waving as I closed the door behind her.

"Everything okay?" Ford asked as we set out up the trail behind the house.

"It will be."

"Seemed tense at dinner," he said.

"It was, and then I came home and was a complete asshole." It was true. I had been an asshole, but damn if she didn't need to hear the words.

"What did you do?"

I adjusted my crossbow on my back. "I told her Tage was dead."

"She knows that already," he said. I was quiet while he thought about it. "Sort of. She's in denial, isn't she?" he asked. Quietly, he turned to me and added, "Mother used to do that. She'd just pretend that things weren't happening or hadn't happened. I'm glad you told her. I don't want her to end up like Mother."

No one wanted that. I wondered if whatever Miranda had was hereditary. Was it from being a subject in a crazy biological test courtesy of Pierce and Roman, or was it just the way she was? Porschia was not her mother, and I wouldn't let her fall down that cliff.

"Are you still in love with her?" he asked.

"Yes."

He nodded. "She isn't ready yet."

"I know."

"So don't push, Saul."

"I'm not. I just needed her to see that he's really and truly gone. She questions whether any of it happened sometimes." I probably shouldn't have told him that, but I needed him to know why I'd been cruel to her.

He pinched his lips together. "Maybe she can start fresh. With enough time, maybe she'll forget about Tage."

"That will never happen, and I don't expect it to, truthfully. He was someone she loved for a time. You don't forget those things."

"Do you feel like she forgot you?" he asked.

This was getting too heavy. "I'm just glad she didn't shoot me. I know she hated me for a time. She and I are friends now, and that's what I want to be for her. That's what she needs."

"In time, though..." he insinuated.

"In time, who knows?" I finished the conversation. "We'll check snares on the way in. Let's go southeast."

"Sounds good. I'll shut up now." I ruffled his hair, making him groan, and then shushed him for it.

TWENTY-TWO

MERCEDES

"I HEAR THE HORSE AND CART," I SAID. PORSCHIA SNAPPED TO ATTENTION.

"The rest of it's here!"

It wasn't like we'd brought a lot already, just some furniture so far: her bed, a table and chairs, Saul's couch. I hadn't broached that subject with her, but it was time.

"So, where is Saul going to live now?" I tapped my fingernail on the doorframe and then leaned against it to watch her squirm.

"Well, that's between you and him, I guess. Do you want the house?" Porschia dragged the question out like it was painful. Did I want the house? I pretty much lived at Roman's now. Ever since the night Porschia practically shoved me over there, I'd slept there, ate there, done everything else there...

"I don't know. I mean, Saul can stay on the couch for as long as he needs to. Oh, wait." I smiled mockingly. "You brought the couch here. I guess that means he has to stay with you, Porsch."

Her face reddened. "He doesn't have to. He just needs a bed. He could take my old room in the house."

"Yeah, I'm not really looking for a roommate right now, and how would it look? Two unmarried young people living together. Father would be shamed. It would be so scandalous."

"How would it be different if he stayed here?" I tried to whisper, but it came out as more of a shriek, high-pitched and urgent. The horse was so close now. He was going to hear her loud mouth!

I walked to her and saw that not only was Saul outside, but Roman and my brother were, too. I grinned.

"Don't speak another word of this. Saul can decide on his own," Porschia said with finality.

I watched as his face lit up when he saw her in the doorway. Oh, he'd already made his mind up. It was just going to take a little convincing on her part. Not much, just a little. Somehow, I had hope for these two yet.

Saul tied the horse so he wouldn't run away and the guys began carrying all of the boxes inside. Porschia peeked in each box and told them where to put it, not that there were many options. Most of the space was open. Only the bedroom had walls.

"Can I help?" a familiar voice said from the doorway. His arms were full, carrying a heavy box. Good. I hoped they fell off.

"Noah?" Porschia said. "What are you doing here?"

"Hoping to lend a helping hand. Hi, Mercedes," he said with a grin.

I stepped back into the kitchen, putting space between us. However, it wasn't for me. It was for him. I wanted to take a spoon and gouge his eyeballs out. "We have plenty of help, so you can sit that down and run on back to Blackwater," I said sweetly.

His smile dried up fast. "I was actually hoping to talk with you."

Roman emerged from Porschia's bedroom and walked over to stand beside me. His arm snaked around my waist deliciously and Noah's eyes fixated on the motion. "She doesn't want to talk," Roman said to him.

"You talk for her?" he asked defiantly.

"I do."

Noah ignored Roman and looked at me. "Please, just for a second? I don't like how we left things."

I squared my shoulders, ready to fight. "Where we *left* things is just fine with me. You were terrified to be near me, treated me like a piece of trash, and made it clear that we were through. So I'd say I got your message loud and clear, and now I thoroughly agree with you. We *are* through."

Porschia quietly cleared her throat. "Thank you for helping, Noah, but I think it's best if you leave."

"Seriously? Porschia, just let me..."

"Leave!" she yelled. "I'm tired of repeating myself to everyone. Get out. It's my damn house and my sister is always welcome here. She says you are not, and I will honor her decision to drop you like a bad habit!"

Flabbergasted, he set the box on the floor, stuffed his hands in his pockets, and walked away. The crunching of boot steps trailed away from the cabin.

"Holy... Wow, Porsch. I think you made sure he got the message," I said incredulously.

"Well?" She threw up her hands, agitated. "It's true."

I laughed and everyone else joined me. "You have more bark than bite now, but it's still scary as hell!"

"Besides," Porschia said, "you have Roman now, and even he's better than that." She gestured toward Noah's retreating form.

"Gee, thanks," Roman deadpanned.

"You know what I mean," she snapped, walking back into her bedroom, a ball of writhing female hormones. The guys were all starting to doubt that she was pregnant, but they hadn't seen her mostly naked. There was most certainly a tiny bump. That bump would get bigger soon, and she wouldn't be able to cover it with the gathered fabric of Maggie's dresses anymore.

PORSCHIA

THINGS WITH SAUL WERE WEIRD FOR A FEW DAYS AFTER THE NIGHT OF THE big blow up, but they settled down and so did I. The sad part? He was right. I was trying to pretend that Tage never happened, and yet tried to hold onto him tightly anyway.

He was dead.

He lied to me.

He saved me.

He saved everyone.

I was having his child, so a piece of him would never die.

I was scared to have this baby.

I was scared it was cursed.

I was scared.

Those were the truths I repeated to myself every day as the days slipped into weeks. I made pants for Saul and Ford, although Roman still preferred to rummage through the city for his clothing. He liked denim and Mercedes liked it on him. Their relationship seemed to be progressing. If sex was the first step in their relationship and hand-holding was the second, the third was sweet gifts. Roman knew how to make my sister melt. He brought her fresh flowers, cooked for her, brought back interesting things for her in the city. He was always doing something for her. It was sweet.

Sometimes, it made me jealous that I didn't have anyone to love me the way Roman loved her. They hadn't said the big L-word, but it was obvious, as strange as that was. Roman set out to kill her. He and she told me the story at different times, but he wanted revenge for me killing Pierce and he was going to kill Mercedes to get it. Fortunately, she was still a night-walker and fought him off easily. Otherwise, we would both be missing a sibling and I might still be thinking about carving Roman up —human or not.

Summer nights turned cooler and the humidity faded away into crispness. The leaves began to turn from green to bright shades of gold, burnt orange, and red. The canopy was on fire, raining leaves of ash all around the cabin, and I couldn't get enough. I spent more time outside than in. Saul worked during the day, sometimes with the carpenters, sometimes in the city, and sometimes helping Father and Ford with various things. We planted a fall garden and I guarded it from the voracious deer who tried to eat everything in it, simply having to stomp on the porch planks to make them scatter and leap into the woods at breakneck speed.

Mercedes was helping me sew now. Father was the first to place an official request, followed by Mary Brown. She needed a new dress. I sat on the porch, happy to feel the warm sunshine tickling my skin through the leaves that fluttered in the wind. Light filtering onto the porch resembled the colors of a kaleidoscope.

"Mary seemed peppy," Mercedes mused as she considered the measurements we'd just taken from her.

"Too peppy. Did you see her stare at my stomach? I bet she runs to town and tells everyone."

"People have seen you. It's not like you can hide it now. And anyway, who cares?" she said, tucking her hair back into her braid. "What *they* think," she ticked her head toward Blackwater, "doesn't matter. It's what *you* think."

"I think several months ago, I couldn't have imagined you sitting on a porch sewing with me," I teased.

"My fingers might have fallen off, especially since I keep pricking them," she said with a smile. "I'm glad you're doing better, but I can see that you're still angry at him."

"At who?" I asked, stopping my needle.

"Tage. You have every right to be pissed. I would be."

I sat the fabric on my lap, weaving the needle into a safe position. "That he left or that he lied in the first place?"

"All of it. It was a lot to swallow, and everything was such a whirlwind. It happened so fast. I hope the sex didn't happen that fast," she said, obviously picturing it.

"Stop thinking about that!"

She giggled and wagged her eyebrows at me. "That part of everything was great," I answered. "It was just the whole thing. I asked him for this, so I have no right to be angry about it, but I am. I'm pissed that he lied in the first place, but could I have expected him to waltz up and say, 'Hey, I'm the five-thousand-year-old pharaoh's son and I saw a vision of you. You're gonna break the curse and I'm gonna help you. We just have to find my crazy sister'?"

"That would have been weird. You'd have thought he was just as insane as Mother."

Mercedes never had trouble talking about her, but I still did sometimes. This was one of those times, so I changed the subject.

"The baby is moving. Want to feel?" I asked.

She threw her work down and placed her hands on my stomach as the baby rolled its hands or feet across my abdomen. "That little one is a kicker!"

"Cedes?" I said as she smiled, reveling in the happiness a baby could bring.

"Yeah?"

"What if...what if the baby is cursed?"

Her hands stilled. "That's not going to happen. Is that what's been bothering you?"

I nodded. "More than Tage or Saul or anything. I'm scared."

"Porschia," she cried, hugging my neck. "Be scared because this is new and you're inexperienced. Be scared to be like Mother. Be scared because it's normal at this stage, but don't be afraid of this baby being cursed. I believe Tage. When he said he was going to cure you, he meant it. This baby is part of you, and he wouldn't have let anything happen to you or his child. You have to believe that."

"I'm trying," I cried onto her shoulder.

"Shhh. It's okay. Everything is going to be okay. Besides, if she's a she, she'll be strong like us, and all the boys in Blackwater will be chasing her. It's a good thing we're badasses and can scare them all away." She moved her mouth to my belly and cooed, "Especially Uncle Roman. He's terrifying. Yes, he is."

My sister was losing her mind, but I hoped she was right. I hoped the baby was healthy and normal, that the curses were truly dead and behind us. I wanted to breathe and live and move forward, but until this child was born, I didn't know if I could do that.

TWENTY-THREE

SAUL

Roman was always doing something for Mercedes. I knew Porschia and I were just friends, but I wanted to do something nice for her. I couldn't have Roman showing me up, now could I? When Mercedes left for the evening, I asked for some female advice and help pulling off what she suggested.

For the first time ever, a woman made sense. The plan was that Mercedes and Roman would set the scene for us and I would bring the food, which I would get at the bridge where she left it for me, because we were still very dependent on them for it.

I jumped onto the porch. From inside, Porschia let out a squeal, and I saw her clutching her chest when I opened the door.

"You scared me to death!" she cried.

"Sorry." I smiled. "What are you up to?"

She had an arm full of fabric and sewing stuff. "Just putting this away for the evening. My hand is starting to cramp."

"Want to take a walk?" I asked hopefully.

She narrowed her eyes. "A walk."

"A walk. Where we walk around together and talk. A walk. It's a nice evening. The sun is still out and I feel like walking."

"Where are we walking to?" she asked, throwing the stuff on her bed.

I laughed and offered her an elbow. "You'll have to wait and see."

"Oh!" she exclaimed, her eyebrows raised. "So not just any walk, a *surprise* walk."

"Yep."

Porschia smiled, big and genuine. "Then let's walk."

It was a step in the direction of happy. She smiled all the way down the hill, down the widened path and over the bridge, where a burlap sack was waiting for us. I bent to scoop it up and she gave me a look that made my heart stop for a second: half playful, half curious, all Porschia.

"What is that?" she asked.

"Dinner."

Her eyes lit up when I said the word. She was starving.

"I'm starving."

"I know," I laughed. We'd been starving since the day we were born. Sometimes it was just worse than others.

Inside the bag was a long strip of burlap—Mercedes' suggestion.

"Do you trust me?" I asked, stopping to look at her for a moment.

She thought about it for a second or two. "Mostly," she answered.

"Fair enough. Close your eyes." I took the strip out of the bag and sat the bag on the ground. "Blindfolds are required from this point forward."

"Is this really necessary?" she groaned.

"Completely."

Her slight huff didn't erase her smile. She turned around and let me place the fabric over her eyes and tie it into a knot at the back of her head. "Hold onto me."

I placed her arm around my elbow so her feet would be close to mine and picked the bag up again. Then I walked in different directions to throw her off. If I'd have followed the creek, she would have known where we were headed. She knew its bends like the back of her hand.

When we'd been walking for a while, her steps grew slower and more sluggish. "Is this an attempt to walk the baby out? Because I still have a few months to go, I think. It won't work at this stage."

I burst out laughing. I could see the logs, the blanket and a few pillows Mercedes and Roman had set up. It was just like the evening before the rotation where we sat and ate and talked. She didn't want to accept my marriage proposal until she had to, or until she was sure it was what she wanted, desperate or not. I just wanted to remind her that I hadn't forgotten us–

the us that came before all of the chaos. I still remembered her.

A few feet away, I stopped and removed her blindfold. She looked at the logs, at the spread quilt and pillows piled to one side. I didn't want her to get the wrong impression. "It's in case you're tired and want to lay on your side for a while. Mercedes said that helped you feel better. She actually brought those. Roman dragged the log over."

Porschia was quiet, which scared the hell out of me.

"It's just dinner. I just wanted you to have a nice dinner. Or, as nice as it can be for now. I have food." I said, holding the bag up with one finger.

"This is the nicest thing, Saul. The nicest thing in a very long time." When her voice broke, I knew I'd done something wrong. I thought she'd smile and love it, but I made her cry. I hated it when she cried, because she'd done so too many times after the shit storm we were thrown into the middle of.

"Don't cry," I said, dropping the bag onto the blanket and wiping her tears away with my thumbs. "I don't want you to cry."

"They're happy tears." She sniffed and laughed. "Finally."

The tension bled from my shoulders. "Can I ask a favor?" she said.

"Of course."

"Help me down?"

I held her hands as she eased onto the blanket. "Sure the tree wouldn't be better?"

"Nope. This is heaven. Now feed me, please."

I shook my head. "Human. Night-walker. Infected. Hybrid. Human. Pregnant human. You're always hungry."

She giggled and then her face hardened. "Seriously, what's for dinner?"

PORSCHIA

Eating rolls, cheese, and corn and green beans out of glass jars with Saul right by the riverside made me an emotional mess. It was nice. The evening air was cooling perfectly. The fact that Saul even thought to do this was a testament to what a great person he was. He even made my sister and Roman an accomplice. But this? The plan? The dinner and evening? It was all Saul. I couldn't be more thankful that things between the two of us were okay.

"Where do you see yourself in five years?" he asked out of the blue.

I listened to the noises of dusk, almost able to hear the precise second when the sun disappeared behind the hills and the land was bathed in breath-giving shadow. Crickets began to chirp and sounds from the Colony echoed from the houses beyond us. The houses we grew up in were only a stone's throw from us.

Where did I see myself in five years?

"I honestly don't know how to answer that. I'm not sure. I know I'll have a child, but despite the size of my stomach, that fact still seems surreal. I have no plans to leave my home or the Colony, but it's hard to say where life will take a person. We know that well," I said with a wistful smile. "Where do you see yourself?"

He reclined so that his back was leaning against the blanched log. "I'm not sure. If you'd asked me before everything happened, I would have said married to you, one child, maybe two. Living in a house in the Colony. Hunting when needed, with the guardianship of a night-walker, of course. Providing for my family and community. I would have said that my relationship with my parents would be strong."

"That was before," I said softly.

"It was. Now, things have changed. I'm not sure where this road will lead me either, Porschia. But no matter what, I hope you're always a part of my life. That much hasn't changed at all."

I stared into the now-empty jar of corn. The fork I had been using swirled around the rim as I sat it on the ground beside the blanket, steadying it until it stood upright in the grass. "I hope for the same thing. I hope everyone I care about just stays close. They say change is the one constant of life, but I don't like it. Not now. I just want things to stay the way they are."

"Change is overrated," Saul agreed with a grin.

"It is. Everyone gets in such a big hurry to change things, when maybe they're best left alone. Maybe they're right the way they are, and you can't see it until it's messed up."

I truly believed that. Sometimes you couldn't see you'd made the wrong decision until the consequences slapped you in the face.

"Are you nervous?" he asked.

Confused, I crinkled my brows.

"About the baby," Saul added.

My mother was an awful person. I never wanted to be that way, and the thought of being a mother scared me. "I'm terrified," I said softly, unable to change the shift in my demeanor. My shoulders stiffened, I sat up straighter.

SAUL

"About motherhood?" I asked. This seemed like more than just butterflies about a new adventure. If her arms were closer, I bet I would see them covered in goosebumps. Porschia Grant was scared.

"Mostly," she half answered.

"Tell me what's going on." She was silent, so I begged. "Please."

She struggled to get comfortable, ultimately deciding to use the pillows Mercedes had brought, laying on her left side. "Mercedes thinks it's silly."

"I'm not Mercedes. Try me."

She took a deep breath. "You'll think I'm nuts."

"I've never in my life thought you were crazy, and I won't start now. Just trust me, Porsch. Let me in."

Swallowing and laying on her side, Porschia took a leap forward in faith. "I'm scared the baby will be cursed."

What she said took the breath from me. "Why?"

"Because when the baby was conceived... I was still cursed."

It was true. And I understood her concern.

Porschia spoke before I did and when she did, it was like water flooding over a dam, weakening the structure before destroying it all together. "Mercedes said that when I was healed, I was healed completely, so the baby would be healed, too. But what if it doesn't work that way? What if we aren't supposed to be cured? What if it's the calm before another storm and I'm bringing the rain, Saul?"

I looked at her for a long moment. "Then we'll deal with it. We'll protect the baby. I won't leave your side; you can count on that."

"You'd be outcast again," she argued.

"I would be outcast if I were anywhere but in your presence." Her slight gasp meant she finally heard me. Not only did Tage give her a life, he gave her a chance at happiness. I planned to make that happy happen, no matter what.

TWENTY-FOUR

PORSCHIA

EVERYONE WAS GATHERING AT FATHER'S FOR CHRISTMAS. IT HAD SNOWED A few inches and Saul refused to let me walk down the side of the hill. "You'll fall and have the baby early. Ford's bringing the wagon. End of story."

And that was the end of that story. He was so stubborn and insistent that I finally caved. I'd sewn everyone a little something and had tucked the gifts into a large sack, which Saul warned me not to lift. "I'll get it," he said.

He was getting way too over-protective. It was sweet, but it was also overkill. I was pregnant, not helpless.

Wearing the red dress I made to accommodate my rapidly growing stomach, I yelled for him to come get the bag. If he wanted to carry it, fine. I could hear hooves on the frozen earth, which meant Ford was driving the horse and cart up the hill.

Outside, Saul insisted that he help me to the cart and that he sit beside me. Right beside me. In case anything should happen. Ford just grinned over his shoulder. "Ready?" he yelled to me.

"You'll have to ask Saul."

Saul gave me a smart-ass smirk and told Ford, "We're ready."

Ford gave the reins a snap and the wagon lurched, making us rock forward. Saul's hand reflexively fell to my stomach. "Are you okay?" His eyes were wide and concerned.

"I'm fine," I said, swatting his hand away. "Would you stop?"

He helped me inside Father's house and in his defense, the walkway was slick. Father met us with open arms at the front door, and it smelled like cinnamon inside. Mercedes hugged me next as we moved into the room. "Merry Christmas!" she greeted.

"Merry Christmas!" I responded.

This was the first Christmas my family had ever celebrated.

The thought alone made me ache for what could have been, yet be thankful for what was. It made me hopeful for what was to come.

Sure enough, Mercedes had made cinnamon tea with honey. It was now my favorite drink in the world. The baby began to kick up a storm, so I settled on Father's couch. He had a small tree with dried orange and apple slices hanging from branches all around it.

Saul was eyeballing the seat next to me, so as Mercedes passed me, I grabbed her and told her to sit.

"What's going on with you two?" she giggled.

"He's driving me insane. He worries about every little thing."

She shook her head. "He worries about *you*. You realize he still has feelings for you, right? You aren't blind or delusional?"

"I know, but I can't right now, Cedes."

She hugged my neck and whispered, "I know, but he'll wait until you're ready."

Men always needed more than what I could offer, and I knew Saul wouldn't wait around for long. He was young, but ready for a family. He told me as much a month or so ago at the riverside.

"What if I'm never ready?" I said, voicing yet another fear of mine. The fears of childhood, the Infected, night-walkers, starvation, Mother – they were nothing compared to the fear of the future.

What if I just wasn't meant to have a normal, happy life with a man? Some women weren't. Mercedes rolled her eyes. "That boy has loved you since the first time you glanced in his direction." She glanced at Saul, who was talking earnestly with Ford across the room. "He's yours whether you want him or not."

Did I? Could I ever do that to Tage? I didn't know the answers and wasn't sure I ever would.

We ate dinner together: rolls, eggs, and our combined shares of meat from a slaughtered hog and heifer. The mood was light, jovial, and fun. We laughed, clinked glasses in toasts, and everyone more or less said how much they were looking forward to a new year. The winter would be rough, but all winters were. I wasn't looking forward to that part of it, not to mention having a baby in the middle of the snow season, but it wasn't up to me. We didn't get to choose when things in life happened, only how we handled them.

Gathering in the living room near the tree, we exchanged gifts. I was sandwiched between Mercedes and Father, Saul sat in the chair diagonal to us, and Roman perched on the arm of his seat. Ford sat on the floor near the tree itself.

Roman and Mercedes had baked everyone loaves of cinnamon sugar bread. She said that Roman had procured the ingredients, but I wasn't sure how. She also made me and Saul each our own loaf, "so my niece or nephew doesn't have to share," she teased. Ford and Father had gotten everyone a jar of peaches. When it was my turn, Saul got up and handed the burlap sack to me. I gave everyone their new garment: a new pair of pants for Ford, a shirt for Father, an apron for Mercedes – she was learning to cook more and more and actually enjoyed it – and for Saul and Roman, I'd learned to knit. I made Roman a winter cap with dark gray yarn, and I gave Saul a bright red scarf. He smiled as he wrapped it around his neck. "Thank you."

"You're welcome."

He rubbed his hands together fast and said, "My turn!"

I hadn't noticed him bring a bag at all, but there it was, tucked far under the tree. Ford scooted it out and over to him. The first thing he retrieved was a hunting knife, which he gave to Ford, making his smile light up like the wick of a candle.

To Roman and Mercedes, he gave candles, handing them over with a smirk. Mercedes thanked him and giggled something behind her hand to Roman. I knew what those would be illuminating. Probably tonight.

Saul moved on to Father. "I found these in the city," he said, handing him three new pairs of suspenders. Father's age was beginning to show in his middle, and those would come in handy.

He pulled a small, velvety bag from the sack. "This is for you, Porschia."

I accepted the bag and released the draw string. Inside was something hard; a ring. When I pulled it out, I saw that it was my poison ring.

Tears filled my eyes until they spilled over. "Where did you find it?"

"I went back to the forest the next day. It took hours, but I finally found it. And when I did, it was broken. The hinge was torn apart. It took some time, but Garreth and I went into the city and found one that would work. He repaired it for you." I hadn't seen Garreth but a handful of times since we came back, and those were at a distance. He'd waved once, stopped by the river with a fishing pole. I'd waved quickly and walked away, leaving him with a confused look on his face. Garreth didn't do anything wrong. No one did. He was just a reminder. Everything reminded me of Tage, and I both loved and hated that.

Emotions clogged my throat. "Thank you."

"I know how much it meant to you," he said, kneeling in front of me. "I'm sorry that's all I could find."

I knew what he meant. Despite his own feelings, he would bring Tage back if he could, just so I would be happy.

My heart might have melted a little just then.

TWENTY-FIVE

SAUL

Winter hit hard and fast. She wasn't playing around, and unfortunately, I didn't cut enough firewood before she showed her face. With the scarf Porschia made me for Christmas, and its new matching hat, I trudged outside with the axe. Porschia offered to help, but she knew how I felt about her walking around on the slick snow and ice. It was frigid outside, and way too dangerous for her to even be out in it.

Besides, late January was really close to February. She'd already seen Marjorie, an older woman who was the midwife for Blackwater's women for the past fifty years. Marjorie told her she was ripe and the baby would come any day now. That made me more nervous than a cat on a hot tin roof. If she so much as winced, I jumped to make sure she was okay.

She held her stomach a lot now. Pre-labor pains, according to Marjorie. But those, she said, mimicked the real thing, so how would we know when pre-labor turned into actual labor? She told us what signs to look for and said she would come no matter the weather, as long as Ford came after her with the cart.

That afternoon, I all but begged her to let me take her into town. We could stay with Mercedes until after the baby was here, safe and settled.

She promised to think about it, but I wondered if she was too stubborn for her own good.

Wood was abundant but the work had me sweating, and in cold weather, that wasn't a good thing. I took off the cap so my head would cool down, and that was when I heard a crashing noise from inside the cabin. I slipped and slid through the foot of snow that had fallen since I'd been out.

"Porschia?"

No answer came.

"Porschia!" I yelled, sliding across the porch into the door.

When I shoved the heavy door open, I could hear her laughing hysterically. "What the hell?" I murmured.

She was sitting in the middle of the kitchen floor with pans all around her, giggling so hard she couldn't catch her breath. "I'm not..." giggle, "graceful."

I rushed over to her. "Did you fall?"

She just nodded, laughing. "It was a slow fall, though. I'm fine. I just tipped over and sort of plopped down onto my butt. I'm fine." Porschia looked at me; really took a second to look, and then her smile dropped.

"I scared you." It wasn't a question.

"A little."

"I didn't mean to. It was just silly of me and I couldn't help but laugh. I didn't mean to scare you, Saul."

My heart pounded toward her. It and I was just glad she was okay. "You aren't hurt? The baby's okay?"

"Yeah." She tucked some hair back into the braid gathered at the base of her neck. "I'm fine." She waved me off. "I wouldn't turn down help getting up, though. It might take me all afternoon."

She was still so tiny. Even with her swollen belly, Porschia weighed nothing. I wished I could get more for her to eat, but the hunts had turned up empty for more than a week now. Winter was always rough, but this was bad for everyone. However, everyone wasn't my concern; she was. The baby was.

After picking up all the fallen pans, I headed back outside, determined to finish the chore as fast as possible. Night-walker strength would have come in real handy right about then.

PORSCHIA

Saul worried himself sick over me and the baby. I just lost my balance. It wasn't a big deal. When he rushed outside, I heard the axe fall much more frequently. Then I became the worrier. I didn't want him to make a mistake and hurt himself, just because he was trying to hurry up and come back inside with me.

He was saved an hour later when my brother pulled the cart up the slippery hill and stopped in front of the house. I stepped onto the porch to see what he needed.

"Mercedes sent me to get Porschia. Weather's turning bad again. If we get much more, I won't be able to get Marjorie up here, or her back down to Blackwater," he told Saul.

"I'm right here," I said, exasperated that they were talking about me as if I were an inanimate object.

"Mercedes is right, Porsch. You need to come into town where it's safe," Ford said patiently. "Just until you have the baby. I promise to bring you back home when you're okay."

There weren't many people who could break my will, but my baby brother was one of the few who could. The walls around my heart did not seem to apply to Ford. Maybe because he was kinder than most people; he was good. Ford only cared about the welfare of others. He always gave, never took. So when he came to get me and take me to a safer place, I listened.

Saul approached with his hands out. "I think you should listen to him—"

"I'll go pack," I said, cutting off his speech.

His eyebrows shot up. "Really?"

"Yeah. Give me a hand?"

"Of course. Yeah," he sputtered, shooting Ford a thankful smile. "We'll be ready in a few."

Ford laughed and told us to hurry. "It's freezing out here!"

It was a whirlwind of throwing things into baskets and sacks. We took what food we had, changes of clothes, blankets I'd knitted and clothes I'd sewn for the baby.

A strong wave of pain washed around my stomach and across my back. I cried out, clutching the edge of the dresser in my room.

Saul was beside me in an instant. "What's wrong?"

"Just a contraction, I think."

"You've done too much today," he said, softly. "Do you want to sit down?"

"No. Ford's right. We need to get into town, I think. The clouds are already dark." The spell passed and I was able to take a deep breath. "Let's keep packing."

Saul did most of the packing while I waddled around the rooms, telling him what to take with us. He didn't complain about helping or being bossed around, just loaded everything into the cart outside. When he helped me onto the porch, I wondered where we were going to sit. I might have gone a little overboard.

He locked the door behind us with the iron latch and helped me across the planks, already slick with snow and ice. Then he lifted me up into the cart and jumped into the back himself. "Just sit in the middle, that's where the clothes and blankets are. It'll be more comfortable." I was comfortable where I was, I just couldn't get down. That was the problem.

I looked at him and he was already beside me, holding out a hand so I could ease down slowly. "Thanks."

He nodded, made sure I was okay, and then settled beside me. "Go easy, Ford."

My brother just laughed. "Gee, thanks for telling me! I was planning on racing down the hill, but I'll try to restrain myself."

Saul just smiled and put a blanket around our shoulders. "Smartass."

TWENTY-SIX

MERCEDES

I BIT MY NAILS UNTIL I COULDN'T ANYMORE—NOT WITHOUT BLEEDING. Ford told us where he was going before he left to be sure she could stay with us if she didn't want to stay with him and Father. Of course she could, I told him.

I'd never been more relieved that he was going to get her off that hill. The snow was deep and the dark clouds looming overhead meant it would soon be even deeper. I worried about the horse and cart slipping and all of them getting hurt, but she couldn't walk down. This was the safest option, even though it wasn't a great one.

She wanted separation from Blackwater, or from people in general. I hadn't figured out which or if it was both, but I understood. Porschia never felt like she belonged here, and most of that was self-imposed. Instead of defying Mother and making the most of her life here, Porschia hid herself away, too afraid to be embarrassed by the harsh words Mother would fire in her direction. She had felt isolated since birth. But being so far along in her pregnancy, in the winter, in the woods, was dangerous.

Roman came to stand beside me. "You okay?"

"I'm fine."

"Liar."

I smiled. "I'm worried about them."

"Ford's good with the horse. He'll make sure everyone's safe."

He was. Ford was incredible with every animal he came in contact with, but the horses were especially his. They obeyed. "It's just that it's slick and getting dark."

"He's got this, babe," Roman reassured me, turning me around and wrapping me in a hug.

I couldn't help but laugh. "How'd we get here from you wanting to kill me?"

"All psychopathic thoughts were erased when I was healed?" he teased.

"Wish I could thank Tage for that, too."

He nodded outside. "Lantern."

As usual, Roman was right. I could see Ford's lantern hanging from his cart, snow beginning to fall in thick, poufy clumps as they pulled up. It was like the sky was raining tiny clouds. I opened the door to welcome my sister and heard her yell out.

"What's wrong?" I screamed into the frigid air as I slipped on the concrete path. Roman caught me before I fell on my butt.

"She's having another big contraction," Saul yelled.

"How many has she had?"

"A lot. Get a bed ready, Ford's going after Marjorie now. We might need Roman's help for a few."

"I need to help Porschia get inside!" I yelled, slipping again.

"I've got her," Saul said. I kept trying to get to her, but the tone of his voice stopped me. "I promise, Cedes. I've got Porschia."

Swallowing, I caved. He wouldn't let anything bad happen to her. I knew that much. He was like a worried mother hen anyway, the way he hovered.

Porschia cried out again, then roared through gritted teeth. He sat her feet on the ground before picking her up, one hand around her back and the other beneath her knees. When he got to us, Roman held the door while I ran inside to make the bed with extra blankets and pillows. Porschia's lips were already blue, and her teeth were chattering violently.

Roman kissed my cheek. "I'm going with Ford. Be back soon."

"Thank you," I said, squeezing his hand. He was gone in a flash and I wondered if he would always be fast, night-walker or not.

Saul climbed the steps, carrying my sister. I heard his boots fall on the board of each step until he came to the landing and into her room. He laid her down on the bed as gently as possible, every muscle in her body tight as shivers wracked her body. I covered her immediately.

"I'll be right back," Saul said, staring at Porschia. "If you need me, yell."

She nodded. "O-okk-ay."

I shooed him away and then sat beside Porschia as softly as I could. "Are you in labor?"

"I don't know. The contractions aren't super close together, but they sure do hurt."

"Is the baby kicking?"

"I can't feel anything but pain right now," she panted, not even able to shiver through the contraction. I let her squeeze my hand when she needed, flexing when she didn't to keep the blood flowing. My sister was still stronger than I was somehow.

She relaxed after a wave of pain. "Why didn't you want to stay a night-walker?" she asked. "As soon as we freed those people from The Manor, you wasted no time in changing back."

"I hated feeling so out of control emotionally, and I knew that given the chance, eventually I wouldn't be able to control myself. I'd hurt some-one, maybe someone I loved, and maybe for no reason at all except that I was hungry. In the end, I wasn't strong enough to handle it."

"No one was."

"You did," I argued.

Porschia laughed. "I didn't handle anything at all. I was a mess."

"It's good you can talk about it now. You haven't in months; almost a year."

She winced. "I know."

SAUL

Ford and Roman were back in no time, but not with Marjorie. The woman was too ill to deliver a baby. Instead, Garreth stood inside the door, removing his snow-covered shoes. "What's wrong with Marjorie?" I asked.

"She's old," was his reply. She was one of the oldest people in the Colony now that the Elders were gone. I'd asked Brian about his father just the other day. They were still in the woods, only a couple of miles from Porschia, but that didn't comfort me. She'd effectively had them banished, and they weren't doing well. Time was catching up with them quickly, so I didn't think they could reach her cabin—if they even knew about it.

Garreth shrugged his thick coat off and handed it to me. I tipped my head. "She's upstairs. Second bedroom on the right."

His loud steps echoed up the hallway. Turning to Ford, he waved him forward. "Bring my bag, son."

Ford answered fast. "Got it." He hefted a large leather satchel onto his shoulder, bending beneath its weight.

"Good." Garreth opened Porschia's bedroom door, from which heavy panting could be heard. She was in pain and that caused me pain of a different kind. "Breathe through it," Mercedes said to her.

"Gonna be a long night. You bring my bag," he said, pointing to me, "and then all of you wait downstairs."

"No," I said sternly. "I'm staying."

Garreth paused. "You the father?"

"Yes."

He narrowed her eyes. "Fine. You can stay if Porschia wants you to – and *only* then. Understood?"

I swallowed, hoping Porschia would let me stay. She probably wouldn't. "Understood."

"Good."

TWENTY-SEVEN

SAUL

PORSCHIA LET ME STAY UNTIL GARRETH GOT CONCERNED. "THE BABY IS upside down. I need to turn it."

"You should go outside for a little while," said Porschia. Her hair and skin was wet with sweat.

"I'll be right outside the door."

Garreth huffed. "You need to boil some water and find me some rags. Or make them. Tear up a sheet if you need to."

"Porsch, I'll have Roman boil the water and get rags, but I will be right outside your door. You need me, you yell."

She nodded fast and watched as I closed it. I wanted to tell her I loved her, that I loved this baby because it was a part of her, but now wasn't the time. The baby was breech and this was going to be a difficult delivery, especially for a first-time mother.

I sat on the landing, my feet on the steps below me, and prayed to whomever would listen.

Don't take her from me.

Watch over her.

Please, don't take her.

I repeated those words through Porschia's screaming, when I would close my eyes as tightly as I could and say them out loud. I repeated them through the panting and through Garreth's stern instructions.

Then things went silent before a tiny cry erupted from within the room. A small cry became louder. "Oh my goodness," Mercedes giggled. "It's a boy! Welcome to the world, little man."

I stood and paced the floor outside her bedroom door.

Garreth's voice filtered to me. "Praise be. He's a healthy one. Listen to those lungs."

The baby wailed.

I couldn't stand it anymore. "Is everything okay?"

"Everything's fine," Cedes yelled. "But it's going to be a little while. Garreth needs space to work."

"Porschia?" I yelled.

"Yeah?" she answered weakly.

"Are you okay?"

No answer came back to me. "Porschia?"

Mercedes came through the door holding a tiny bundle, but she wasn't smiling. Every line on her face told me she was scared out of her mind. "What's wrong?" I rushed to her, gently grabbing each of her biceps. "Talk to me, Cedes."

She shook her head, tears falling onto the cheek of Porschia's son. "She's lost a lot of blood. Garreth's doing what he can."

"What?" The breath in me was sucked away in an instant.

"He told me to take the baby and go, but he needs us to tear some sheets and boil more water." Mercedes' hands were shaking, her lip was quivering.

"Roman!" I yelled.

He jogged up the steps with a smile. "Is this the little guy— What's wrong?"

"She needs you. Porschia's in bad shape," I said, my voice cracking. "Can you have Ford boil more water? I need to find another sheet to tear for her."

The fact that Porschia needed cloth was the only thing that kept me from breaking the damn door open and rushing to her side. That, and the fact that Garreth needed to help her, not be distracted.

Roman guided Mercedes down the steps, and she closed her eyes tightly once they reached the bottom. "This isn't fair."

"She'll be okay," Roman whispered, wrapping an arm around her shoulder.

"You don't know that, and there's nothing we can do to help her now. There's no magical night-walker blood to heal her body and keep her young. There's nothing."

I never imagined longing for one of the curses to save the one I loved.

I TOOK THE STRIPS OF CLOTH IN AND SAT THEM ON THE BOTTOM OF THE BED as Garreth instructed. "The water?" he barked.

"I'll get it now. It wasn't boiling a few minutes ago, but it should be hot enough now."

"It's close enough. I need it."

Taking the steps two at a time, I listened to the baby cry. "Is he okay?" I asked, using a towel to remove the pot from the fire.

"He's hungry, I think," Mercedes answered, bouncing the little guy and shushing him sweetly.

The little guy was uncomfortable, but he would be okay.

Porschia opened her eyes when I sat the pot on the side table. "Saul?" Her lips were so dry they stuck together, pulling apart when she said my name.

"Yeah. I'm here."

"I'm not doing so well."

Tears pricked my eyes. "I know, but you're going to be okay."

She tried to smile, her eyes glassy and fixed on my face. "Maybe. But just in case, I wanted to tell you goodbye."

I shook my head. "No. Don't you tell me goodbye. This isn't goodbye. You'll be okay and I'll come back as soon as Garreth lets me."

"You always say it's not goodbye, but sometimes it is," she said, her head falling to the side on her pillow. Her pale skin was a testament to how much blood she'd lost. The scent of iron permeated the room.

Garreth kneaded her stomach over and over, working her abdomen like he was making bread. "You hang on for me, girl. I haven't lost one yet."

"There's a first time," she inhaled slowly, "for everything."

TWENTY-EIGHT

MERCEDES

I'd never seen Saul cry. Not when he turned into an Infected. Not when he became a vampire, despite the intense pain of turning. Not when he learned that Porschia hated him. Because Porschia was alive at each of those milestones, and even if she hated him or he was a monster, she was still there. Where my sister was, there was hope.

But when he came out of her room, he was broken. Not in half, two parts separated, but shattered and splintered into a million shards of man. "She's not doing well, Mercedes. If you want to go see her, I'll hold him."

He sobbed, trying to hold himself together. When Roman reached out and took the baby, I ran up the steps.

My sister was fading fast. "Porschia?"

Garreth waved me in.

When my sister lazily opened her eyes, she tried to smile. "Where's Father?" she asked.

"Ford ran to get him. We were so worried, we forgot to tell him you were in labor. It's stupid and I'm so sorry."

She shook her head weakly once. "S'okay."

"Did you think of a name for the baby?" I asked, grabbing hold of her hand. It was freezing. Her fingers didn't have enough strength to grip mine.

"Seth."

"After TageSET?"

She nodded once. "He looks like Tage."

Garreth's concerned eyes looked to mine and I knew we were in trouble. We needed a miracle.

"You'll take care of him?"

"Seth? Of course."

"And Saul. Don't let him hide away. Burn the cabin down if you have to."

I promised I would, but I knew it was a lie. That cabin was all she wanted in the world after things finally calmed. Burning it would be the last thing I would do.

Father burst through the door. "Porschia?" he exclaimed, frantic.

"Hi, Father," Porschia answered. I moved aside, setting her hand on top of the blankets so that Father could visit her. By that point, Garreth had stopped his ministrations and was simply using a damp towel to dab my sister's forehead.

"You listen to me," he said. "I was never stern enough with your Mother, but I am *not* making that mistake again. I need you to live. I need you to *want* to live. If not for me and your siblings, if not for Saul, then live for Tage and that little boy downstairs. Do you understand me?"

Porschia never answered. She'd already closed her eyes, her head supported only by the strength of the pillow beneath it.

TWENTY-NINE

ONE MONTH LATER...

SAUL

"SETH, ARE YOU HUNGRY?" I ASKED AS I BOUNCED HIM AROUND. HE WAS always starving, just like his mother, and he had dark hair and golden eyes like Tage. His nose came from the Grant's. It looked like Ford's and Carson's, strong and square.

From the bed, Porschia groaned. "He's hungry again?"

It was sometime in the middle of the night, the second time he'd woken in the past few hours for another feeding. Porschia was worn out. We both were. But Seth? Seth was happy and alert. Even at four a.m. To him, it was party time.

Porschia somehow recovered from the traumatic birth. I teased her about it now that she was well. "It's you, Porschia. Nothing with you will ever be easy or run-of-the-mill."

She always laughed and told me I was right.

I always sent thanks to whomever listened that I could hear that laughter again.

We were still staying with Mercedes, and would until spring. Both of us stayed in her bedroom; she on the bed and me on the couch that Roman and I had somehow contorted into making it through the narrow doorway. She needed rest and the convenience of having Seth close for feedings. After she fed him, I would take him for the rest of the night.

The winter came in like a lion but was acting more like a lamb lately. It had Porschia itching to go back into her cabin in the woods, but I had a feeling we weren't out of the woods yet. The snow would come again. It always did this time of year, and we didn't want to be stuck up there with an infant and no way to get back down the mountain.

I would argue that fact and Porschia would calm down for a few days, but without fresh snow, she would start asking when we were leaving again. Mercedes would give her a good guilt trip about not wanting to stay with her and that would buy another few days. Luckily, we only had four or five more weeks of winter. Hopefully, we could hold her off that long.

I stayed with her until Seth was finished feeding and then took him to the couch, where he slept soundly on my chest. I think he liked the sound of my heartbeat, or maybe it was that my body heat kept him warm. Either way, he and I got along just fine.

The following morning, Porschia dragged herself out of bed and tamed her hair. I could hear her brush moving through the long strands, but didn't want to open my eyes just yet. Too tired. "I think I'm going to cut my hair off," she said suddenly.

That got my attention and my eyes snapped open. "Don't. I like it long."

Over her shoulder, she threw an ornery grin. "Who said I wanted you to like it?"

"You know you value my opinion above all others." I wished.

Garreth had been checking in regularly with Porschia to ensure that she was recovering physically and doing well mentally. He warned about post-partum depression and gave me a list of signs to watch for, "especially given her mother's condition," he'd said. Everyone in Blackwater knew of her Mom's particular brand of crazy, years before she started her killing spree.

"Leave it long. If you cut if off, you won't be able to braid it and get it off your neck. You'll smother this summer."

"It's a risk I'm willing to take," she said in a sing-song voice. She seemed genuinely happy.

"You're in an awfully good mood," I commented.

"I am. I feel incredible today, for the first time in so long." She certainly looked beautiful. Her skin wasn't ghostly white, her lips were plump and moist, and her cheeks rosy. I was still keeping my distance, living solidly in the realm of friendship.

"He loves to lay on you," she mused, staring contentedly at Seth on my chest.

"Who wouldn't?" I teased, rewarded by her laughter.

"I'm going to see if Mercedes wants to go for a walk."

That surprised me. It was the first time she'd felt like leaving the house since she gave birth.

"That's great. Have fun. We'll be sleeping here when you get back," I told her, my mind already fuzzy and half asleep.

I think she said, "Sweet dreams," and though I didn't hear it, I knew she said goodbye but didn't mean it.

PORSCHIA

MERCEDES WAS EXCITED TO GO FOR A WALK. SHE LACED HER BOOTS AND threw a coat at me, then she shrugged hers on and we were out of there. She didn't even tell Roman goodbye.

"You look amazing!" she beamed.

"Thank you. I feel great today. I figured we'd take full advantage."

We walked down the street, reveling in the warmth the bright sunshine gave us against the cold air. "It's so bright," Mercedes said, squinting.

"I love it."

Mercedes smiled. "I'm glad you're still alive."

I laughed. "I'm glad, too."

"I thought you were going to die. You scared me so bad. Please don't ever do that again," she scolded.

"I'll try not to."

"Not good enough, but I'll take it for now," she snickered.

"Saul was a real mess."

This is the first time we'd talked about it; I was still healing and she hadn't broached the subject. Now I was wondering if I felt well enough to hear it, or if I ever would feel like hearing it. Best to rip the bandage off quickly.

"How do you mean?"

"He cried, and I don't mean that his eyes misted over. He cried hard. And he thought you were going to leave him. He kept saying you'd said goodbye." She paused.

I kept quiet. I didn't know I'd scared him so badly.

"He's amazing with Seth, too," she continued.

"He is."

We waved to James Freeman, who was adding firewood to the dwindling stack on their front porch. I was surprised when he waved back.

"He's a good man," she said.

"James?"

"No," Mercedes said in exasperation. "Saul."

"I know he's a good man. I wouldn't trust him with Seth if he wasn't."

We passed the pavilion and our feet carried us to Father's. The door was shut but he'd left a fire smoldering, only a tiny plume of smoke slithering into the sky. "He must be with Ford."

Father and Ford had become close. Father went to help him in his chores at the barn most days now. We walked out back, staring at the rusted shells of the automobiles after which the three of us were named. Brown, withered vines twisted around each one in a threadbare blanket of decay.

"Saul loves you. Maybe you should give him a chance. It's been a long time since..."

"Tage?" I asked. I knew it had been a long time. And people could say his name around me. I wouldn't break. "I know."

"So... maybe you'll let him in a little?" she prodded.

I smiled, staring at the wall that led into the city. "Maybe someday."

THIRTY

SIX MONTHS LATER...

PORSCHIA

THE AUGUST SUN WAS HOT AND SO WAS THE CABIN. I WIPED THE SWEAT from my brow and watched Seth as he lay on a blanket on the floor. Saul would be home soon and I couldn't wait for him to see what Seth learned today. He'd been rolling from his back to his tummy for a while now, but now he could roll back over. It surprised him every time and he would cry, sticking out his bottom lip, until I picked him up and soothed him.

I was so thankful he was normal. There were no signs of disease. Most parents checked for ten fingers and toes, Garreth told me. But the number of digits he had didn't concern me. When I woke from being unconscious after losing too much blood from having him, the first thing I did was check his teeth. No fangs.

My little man was perfect. He wasn't cursed. And he looked like the spitting image of Tage, with dark hair, olive skin, and golden eyes. I'd hoped they'd be blue, the color I fell in love with before I knew they weren't real, but this was better in a way. This was Tage's way of living on through his son.

Random things worried me. Would he call Saul daddy? Would Saul want him to? Would he correct him? Would I tell him about Tage? Should I shield him from the ugly history of the curses?

We had months to wait for the next step, but for today...tummy rolls.

Saul opened the door with a big grin. "How is everybody?" He found Seth on the floor, on his tummy, his arms and legs in the air like he was swimming. He bobbed around on his stomach until he finally wiggled the right way, gathering momentum and flipping over onto his back. Saul's mouth gaped open.

"Did you see that?" he asked incredulously.

"See what?"

It was a running joke with us. If either of us hadn't seen it, it didn't happen. That way we each saw his firsts together, even if we weren't together.

"You've already seen it," he said, eyes narrowed playfully.

"I don't know what you're talking about," I told him as I worked in the wash tub to launder Seth's diapers. It was a dirty job, but someone had to do it.

"How's the new building coming along?" I asked. The carpenters were busy building a new storage building. It was going to be as big or bigger than the barn, and used to store things from the city we found and wanted to keep readily available in the settlement.

"Great. Walls are finished."

"That's amazing. I can't wait to see the roof on it."

"You won't have to wait long. Brian wants to push forward. We're even working tomorrow."

Most of the time Sunday was a day off, but Brian wanted to get this giant building done before fall so we could stuff it full of things in preparation for winter. Good for Blackwater, bad for Saul. He was bone tired.

He tickled Seth's belly and looked up at me. "I'm going to go clean up," he said, heading out back where there was another full wash basin. Ford used the horse and cart to haul water for us. His idea, but it was so helpful. He'd found giant plastic barrels in the city and used them to hold what we needed for a few days. It was a godsend. On top of the list of things you didn't consider when building a cabin in the woods, was how to get water.

"I'm about to finish up. Dinner is almost ready." It was stew. Again. But stew lasted a few days and was filling, so we ate it often.

After cleaning up, Saul would eat, take a nap, and then lead the hunt that night. I didn't know how he did it, but night after night without fail or enough sleep, he did. I worried that one day soon it would all catch up to him.

I went outside to hang Seth's diapers on the line, completely forgetting that Saul was outside bathing. He faced the other way, whistling a tune that drew my attention to him and the water sluicing down his backside. My God. The man was marble. I needed to go. I rushed inside and slammed the door. A minute later, he came in. "What's wrong?"

"Nothing," I said quickly.

"I heard the door slam."

"Did it? Hmm." I couldn't look at him.

"Did you go outside?" I could hear him grin. Asshole.

"I hung Seth's diapers."

"Did you see something you liked?" he snorted.

"Would I have run back inside if I liked it?"

He nodded. "You would have, yes, so I'll take that slamming door as a compliment."

"Whatever. That's ridiculous."

"So is the shade of red on your face, sweetheart."

THIRTY-ONE

THREE MONTHS LATER...

PORSCHIA

SETH LOVED TO SIT ON THE GROUND AND PLAY WITH THE LEAVES, ALTHOUGH I had to watch that he didn't put them in his mouth because apparently he loved to taste everything. Saul was inside getting ready for the celebration to observe the end of the harvesting season. Winter was coming soon and the council wanted to celebrate another year of health and prosperity in honor of Thanksgiving. It was the second year we'd had something to be thankful for. Seth and I were sitting outside on a blanket, enjoying the fall sunshine, when I heard a small mewling sound from beneath the porch.

Kneeling to look beneath the porch, I saw a dark, furry shape tuck itself behind one of the posts. "Here, sweetie," I cooed, but she wouldn't come.

Her new claws were embedded into the wood of a post and she wasn't letting go, even as I pulled her body away and out from beneath the porch. She was black with green eyes the color of lichens on tree bark. A shiver climbed up my spine, one vertebrae at a time. They were the color of Delilah's eyes, of Sekhmet before she revealed her true self. I dropped the cat, who landed on all fours with its hair standing on end.

Seth blew bubbles at the kitten.

A warm breeze filtered through the air, dry as a bone. Was it Tage? Did he send her? I stared at the cat and she stared back at me.

"Is this a gift?" I asked no one.

"Is what a gift?" Saul answered, but it wasn't him I was asking. Sometimes I felt Tage. I knew he looked out for me and Seth, and I think he had a hand in saving me after Seth was born. Couldn't swear to it, but it felt that way. Or maybe I was just losing my mind.

"Did you bring home a kitten for us?" I asked with a smile, picking up the black ball of fur for him to see. Her claws found my forearm. Rip.

"Ouch!" I held her against me and she calmed down, retracting her claws from the fabric of my dress. I was back to wearing one of Maggie's since they fit again and they reminded me of her kindness and smile.

"I don't know where that one came from, but we should probably take it into town when we go. It won't last long out here." The muscle in his jaw ticked, and I saw his face turn to stone as he buttoned his shirt and rolled the sleeves up. "Ready?"

"Yeah. I just need Seth's bag."

"Fine."

The walk into town was tense. He carried the kitten against his chest, but Saul never said a word until we were near the bridge. "Do you talk to him?" he finally asked tersely.

"Seth?" I asked, pretending I didn't know what he meant.

"Tage. Do you talk to him?"

"No, why?" Lying to Saul was easier than fighting with Saul. I took the low road that day. "Do *you* normally talk to dead people?"

He huffed, started walking and then stopped again. "Maybe this isn't working out."

My chest tightened. "What isn't?"

"Me staying with you. Maybe I should find somewhere else to stay for a while." He wouldn't look at me, just stared at the dark water.

"If you want to leave, that's your decision, Saul." I took Seth's bag from his arm and put it on my shoulder, walking across the bridge alone as Seth babbled at Saul over my shoulder. I walked quickly toward Town Hall so he wouldn't see the tears building, and so I could make them go away before someone noticed they were there. Mercedes was like a bloodhound about these things.

"Just giving you what you want. I can't compete with a ghost forever, Porschia," he yelled from behind.

Giving me what I wanted? Whatever. He was tired of waiting. Just like

I told Mercedes, it would eventually happen. He was pissed about a black kitten showing up at our house. A freaking cat. A cat that he brought into town to give away, and I didn't even care because the animal's eyes freaked me out and I didn't need a cat. Even if it was from Tage, I didn't want it. The animal reminded me of too many things.

The tears never fell. I fought them until they dried up on their own and then I entered Town Hall. If people talked about me while I was pregnant, I never heard. Living out of town probably had something to do with that, but one thing was certain: Everyone loved babies. Everyone loved Seth.

The women cooed at him as soon as I entered the door, and what surprised me the most was that Saul's mom was the first to ask to hold him. Somewhat reluctantly, I handed him to her. Saul might be furious if he saw.... but just before Saul walked in, Seth was passed to another woman and I was saved from more of his anger.

He glanced in my direction before heading to the back of the room, making a plate of food and then exiting out the back. He'd taken my move. That was what I planned on doing, but then my baby was commandeered by Blackwater's female population and I had to watch him like a hawk. Inside, unfortunately.

"He's so precious," Mary Brown said pleasantly as she let him hold her finger. Mary had never apologized for the way she treated me in the past, but she was trying to be kind now, to make amends. Maggie would have told me to leave the past where it lays, so maybe I could do that. Maybe I could forgive. Forgiveness was more for the one doing the forgiving than for those receiving it anyway.

"He's been trying to take a few steps lately. He'll be walking soon," I said.

"Oh, that's wonderful. Don't take a single day for granted," another said.

"I won't." That was one promise I could keep. As long as I drew breath, I would love Seth with all my heart and soul. Whether anyone else loved me or not.

MERCEDES FOUND ME AND SETH IN THE CROWD. "HAVE YOU EATEN?" SHE asked, a strange, pleading but tense look on her face.

"Not yet. Seth has admirers."

"Well, you should eat. You should go outside right now and eat." She tried to tug me along, but I had to get Seth first.

"Sorry ladies," I said, taking my son in my arms. "He's probably getting hungry."

They told me to feed him and then bring him right back. "It's been a long time since we got to hold a tiny one," Mary said.

"We'll be back in a little while, probably wearing more food than we consume. Right, Seth?"

He cooed and pulled a loose strand of my hair so hard it made me yelp. Mercedes was right with me. "Let's get his food and yours and go."

"What's the emergency?" I asked, slowing my feet, realizing she was dragging me.

"Hannah Brandt is the emergency."

"Hannah Brandt? Who is Hannah Bran—"

"The girl who's outside flirting with Saul." I tightened my grip on Seth just slightly.

I didn't want to tell her tonight, but I had to now. "He's moving out, so he can flirt with Hannah or Heather or whatever her name is all he wants."

"He's leaving?" she whisper-yelled. I ignored her and made my way to the food. Seth was already chewing his fingers, and full-on wailing would begin in minutes if he didn't have food to eat and play with. The scents of various dishes floated through the air. Again, our garden hadn't fared well, so I had nothing to spare or bring today.

Mercedes held Seth while I made a plate of food for him and me. She started out the door with him before I could stop her or even protest it, so I had to follow behind with the plates of food. Sure enough, the sight of Saul and Hannah – or was it Heather? – stopped me in my tracks.

He was smiling ear to ear, laying it on thick. I'd forgotten how charming he could be when he wanted something...or someone.

Maybe that was a testament unto itself. Maybe he hadn't wanted me in some time.

I gritted my teeth and watched as Mercedes waltzed right up and handed Seth over to him. "Mercedes, I can handle my own son," I told her, setting the plates down on a nearby bench and walking over to Saul. I reached for Seth, but he clung to Saul, swatting at his nose and blowing bubbles.

"I'm Hannah." Hannah. Not Heather. I liked the name Heather better. Too bad.

"Hi," I greeted her coolly. "Come on, little man," I said, reaching for Seth. He began to cry as I pulled him from Saul. "It's okay, baby. We're going to eat now." With those words, his eyes got round. He knew what *that* word meant. My boy liked his food.

Mercedes laid a blanket on the ground and I sat with my back to Saul. Seth dove in to his food: potatoes that I'd smashed up, cooked broccoli, and chicken that I'd torn apart and then cut again. Chicken was his favorite and he squealed and babbled as he ate, like he was having a big conversation with me and Auntie Cedes.

Mercedes scooted next to him. "I've got Seth. You eat."

"I'm okay."

"You need to eat," she repeated.

"I said I'm okay." I gave her a drop-it look, but she didn't do it. Instead, she set her jaw and said the four words a third time.

"I am not hungry, Mercedes," I said through gritted teeth.

"Since when?" Saul asked. He was standing right behind us.

"Since now."

"Eat," he ordered.

"I will eat when I'm good and ready, and not you or my meddling sister is going to tell me when that time will be! So just go find someone else to bully."

"Bully?" I could hear his lips turn up in a smile.

"Isn't Hannah waiting for more entertainment?" I asked sweetly. "Shouldn't keep her waiting."

"She just left with her parents."

"Well, there's always tomorrow," I cooed. Seth smeared potatoes across my dress. Oh, well. "Isn't there, buddy? Tomorrow's a brand new day."

Saul chuckled, and as he stepped toward Town Hall, toward the din of forks on plates and chatter from hundreds of our neighbors, he turned and looked at me over his shoulder. "You don't have be jealous. She's just a girl."

Yeah, she was just a girl. A girl who saw a handsome, hard-working man who liked babies and was kind to women. That kind of girl would hook her claws right into him and never let go, and…

I was out of my mind jealous about it.

Mercedes held Seth as we walked away from the noise. The candlelight in the room flickered as happily as the laughter flowing out the doors and windows of the building. "Well, that was fun!" Mercedes said with a wicked grin. "Interesting, but fun."

"What was so fun about it?" Personally, I thought it was terrible.

"Watching you realize you still have the hots for Saul."

"I do not."

"You so do, and you know what?" she asked.

"What?" Seth tugged her hair as his head got too heavy for him to lift. It bobbed up and down until finding a soft place on her shoulder. His golden eyes closed and within seconds, my son was asleep. I wished I had that super power.

"I'm glad. You have to let him go at some point, Porschia. You wanted a life and you were right to ask for one, but now you need to live it. It's what he would want."

"How do you know what he would want? If he even thought I had feelings for Saul, he'd have killed him."

She stopped along the street. "That's not true. He knew there was something residual. You can't just turn love off, Porschia. Even when you shot me, I still loved you, you know."

"Yeah, well, you deserved that," I giggled, thankful we'd gotten to a point where we could laugh about it all, because living it sure as hell wasn't funny.

Mercedes began to walk again. "If you let Saul go, you'll regret it."

I knew I would. I just didn't know if I could ask him to stay.

Being a coward was easy. Living with the fact that you were a coward was hard.

"Could you keep him for a while?" I asked suddenly.

My sister's brows shot up. "Like, now?"

"Yeah, at your house?"

"Sure." She grinned. "Go get him."

I shook my head. "I need to do something first."

She gritted her teeth. "You'll be careful?"

"Of course," I said, rolling my eyes.

She told me to go and started walking toward her house with Seth. I walked toward the waterfall, toward the farewell pool, gathering flowers as I went.

THIRTY-TWO

SAUL

Why was Porschia walking away from Mercedes? Seth was conked out. That boy could sleep through a thunderstorm. I didn't know what was going on, but I followed Porschia, keeping my distance. Being stealthy was much easier as a night-walker. I cringed with every snapped branch, every scuff of my boot on the asphalt, every time I tripped over a root that was hidden in the tall hay.

She bent once in a while, pulling up flowers that were probably closed. It was late. She was supposed to be staying with Cedes because it was late.

The river's noise became louder as we got closer to the falls. She eased down the steep bank and I stayed above to make sure she was okay. It was too late for her to be out alone. We didn't know all the refugees yet, and even if we did, her mother was a prime example of why you couldn't fully trust your neighbors.

I stood behind a tree, split in the center from three feet off the ground. She took a flower and tossed it into the stirring water beneath the falls. She was saying farewell, but to whom? Me?

Easing away, I gave her some space. I wasn't going to let her get rid of me so easily. I was angry earlier, and she was jealous. But this wasn't over. I wasn't going down without a fight.

PORSCHIA

I THREW A WILDFLOWER INTO THE WATER, ITS PURPLE LEAVES CURLING IN ON its center. It was getting darker, but I could see it swirl around before sinking.

I have to let you go. I hope you understand.

Another flower: Queen Anne's Lace.

I loved you. I still love you, but I love him, too. You're probably pissed because it's him, but I think we were supposed to go through all of this. Before I met you, it was him. Before I loved you, I loved him. And it's hard to admit, but I never completely stopped loving him. It wasn't fair, but it wasn't fair to me either.

A third flower: one I couldn't name.

I hope you're with Maggie and Meg. Somehow, I hope Mother is with you, too. Seth will grow up knowing you, and Saul, if he stays. He'll have a Dad. I'll have the life you gave me. I'll have normal. And I can't thank you enough, Tage. I'll always love you.

I'll always think of you when I feel a warm, dry breeze. I'll think of you when I look at our son and when the first snow falls, when I pass the pavilion or go into the city. I'm letting you go, but I'm still keeping your memory with me.

You did this for me. You let me live, and now it's time for me to start living, not just existing. For Seth, and for me...but mostly for you. I hope you can forgive and understand.

I turned and began to climb back up the bank. The roots were slippery and I lost my footing for a second, and then I heard a rustling in the bushes from the closest house. That was when I knew Saul was watching out for me. Still.

I saw him duck into Roman's front door as I approached Mercedes'. I let myself in and found her curled up with Seth. "Shhh," she warned.

"He's out."

Candlelight from the nightstand flickered across his angelic, chubby cheeks.

"You need sleep, too. Stay in your room," she admonished.

The thought made me cringe. Although she burned the old mattress and with it, all the evidence of the birth that nearly killed me, replacing it with one from the city, there was no amount of fire that could take the memory of that night away. However, walking back through the woods to the cabin, at night, wasn't something I looked forward to. I needed a crossbow, and Father told me that when I was ready, I should come to him and he would give me the one he taught me with; the one I took on the hunt during the rotation. I wasn't great with it, but wanted to be. And I was getting there.

One night, soon, I'd ask Mercedes to watch Seth and I would take to the woods with or without Saul. I'd find the game, take them down, and help provide for everyone. Not because I had to, but because I wanted to.

I didn't want this existence. I wanted to live. I wanted to fight. I wanted to love.

Easing my bedroom door closed, I sank back against the wood and stared at the moonlight casting shadows around the room. Eerily beautiful, I relaxed, walked across the wooden planks, and sank into the bed. It was actually comfortable.

The following morning, I woke to something warm against my stomach. I thought maybe Mercedes had brought Seth in to sleep with me, but my hand didn't find him. It found fur. I opened my eyes to find the kitten curled up against me.

As I suddenly sat up straight, the feline jumped away from me, but kept her eyes trained warily on mine. The cat's eyes weren't green, they were deep brown, like Delilah's after she met Ford. They'd changed. I remembered telling him the color of her eyes were different, but he thought I was tired and had imagined the whole thing.

"Where'd you come from? I thought Saul took care of you."

She hissed at me, the fur on her back standing straight up.

I jumped out of the bed, grabbed her up, and took her downstairs to the front door, tossing her onto the front step. "Don't come back," I warned her.

She stared at me defiantly.

"What's wrong?" Mercedes asked from behind me. "Aww, a kitty!" She went to push around me, but I stopped her.

"It's evil. Don't touch it."

Mercedes smiled, thinking I was joking. I most certainly wasn't, and told her as much. She looked at me strange and then backed away from the seemingly innocent kitten.

———

Seth loved Ford. Even at such a young age, he loved animals, and since Ford worked with them, I decided to take Seth to see him at the barn. He patted the horses' manes, blew raspberries at the chickens, and patted the ground wildly as he watched them stalk around, pecking at worms and bugs in the soil.

"He's growing up so fast," my baby brother said about my son. I could say the same thing about him.

"It's crazy. He was just born."

"Months ago," he added.

It didn't seem that way. Ford picked Seth up and took him inside to pet a few of the cows who were poking their heads out of the stall they had access to from outside. He laughed as Seth bopped them on the head, the cows blinking patiently at the assault from the smiling baby.

"What's this we have here?" he said, crouching down. "It's a kitten."

I stomped toward my son, knowing what I would find, and saw the cat there, rubbing herself against my brother's leg. If that wasn't exactly what Delilah, Sekhmet, or whatever the evil bitch's name was, had done, I'd be damned.

The black kitten purred loudly as she raked her fur against Ford's shin. Seth reached out to pet her.

"Don't let him touch her!" I yelled.

Ford stilled and stood up. "What's wrong? It's just a cat."

Was it? I grabbed the cat and took her into the sun. Her eyes weren't green or deep brown, they were golden, just like Seth's. Just like Tage's and Sekhmet's. That cat was the Satan spawn of Tage's sister, I was certain of it.

"Whoa," Ford said, stopping over my shoulder. "The eyes."

"I know. I think it's her. I know it sounds crazy, Ford, but the cat is following me, showing up everywhere… or maybe she's following Seth."

My grip on the kitten tightened slightly, not enough to hurt her, but enough to tell her I meant business. "Are you going to hurt my son?"

The animal hissed, clawing my fingers, leaving deep gashes across my knuckles. The blood pooled within the ragged lines.

I dropped the cat and grabbed my son from Ford.

"Do you really think it's her?"

I nodded. "I know it's insane, but her eyes change. Green, brown, and now gold. It's her."

He shook his head. "I wouldn't put it past her."

"I hate to ask you this, Ford, but can you—"

"Consider it done. I'll get rid of her."

I nodded and walked away as he cooed for the kitty to come to him. I didn't know how he'd get rid of her, but I knew he would. Ford was as good as his word, and his word was even more golden than the evil cat's eyes.

The whole way back to Mercedes' house, I worried. Would Seth be normal? Would he be amazing like his father or crazy like his grandmother? Would he be a good man?

Saul was a good man. He had him as an example...and Ford.

I needed a moment. I jogged to Mercedes' house, Seth clutched tightly in my arms. "What's wrong?" she asked as I burst through the door.

"Could you watch him for a little while?"

"Sure. Are you okay?" Her eyes were wide with worry. I'd seen her give Mother the same look many times.

"I'm fine. I swear."

"Is this about the cat?"

"It's not. It's about... so much more. I just need a little while."

"Okay," she said reluctantly, taking Seth out of my arms. "You're probably hungry, aren't you, little guy?"

I didn't see Saul at the barn today, but I hoped he would notice me leaving alone and follow me. It was a gamble, but one I had to take. Town hall was empty. I pulled the doors of the tiny building apart and took my space in one of the back pews, and then I waited. Dust motes danced through shafts of buttery sunlight pouring in from transoms above the kaleidoscope windows below.

Saul never disappointed. Twenty minutes later, he opened the door behind me and walked down the carpet-padded aisle. I could almost feel his heartbeat thundering, or maybe it was just mine. I looked to the ceiling, no longer bearing the hole of abandonment, but fresh-smelling planks of wood, nails, and sweat.

His warm hand found my shoulder. "May I sit with you?"

I scooted over to make room for him and he settled beside me with a sigh. His warmth flowed into my side. "I'm sorry for following you."

"No one's sorrier than me that you have to."

"Why are you here?" he asked in a gentle voice.

"Turns out, I need a husband."

He was quiet for a long beat and my heart drummed inside my chest. I thought he might get up and walk away, leave me there without saying a word. Maybe I was too late and had assumed too much.

Saul nudged me. “How soon do you need a husband?”

“As soon as possible,” I responded, my throat clogging with tears.

“Let’s do it. Marry me,” he whispered. His strong hand tangled in my hair and pulled my mouth to his, and I answered him in kind.

Saul was still mine and I was still his.

In the end, I wanted a future with him.

I loved him and he loved me.

So I freely gave my heart to him—all of it.

And when we finally came up for air, we left the past right there in Town hall, walking out into the bright sunshine, hand-in-hand, to begin anew.

In the distance…

Children laughed.

Birds sang.

Puffy clouds floated over the clear blue sky.

An axe fell upon wood.

Water cascaded over the falls.

Animals bleated.

I smiled, and so did Saul. We walked to get our son.

THIRTY-THREE

PORSCHIA

Saul stared at me from just in front of the river, dressed in his new black slacks, white shirt, and sporting a fresh haircut. He smiled, and when he did my heart skipped a beat. Seth's chubby, sticky fingers held my right hand, while Father held my left.

They walked me toward Saul, toward a new, fresh beginning and a happy one at that. Father's chin trembled when he kissed my cheek and stepped away. Saul took Seth, holding him in one of his arms while our marriage was made official, blessed, and made public in front of all of our family, friends, and neighbors—new and old. Victor Freeman officiated. Fall leaves were thrown at the three of us as Saul and I kissed and then ran through the crowd. Laughter, whoops and hollers, clapping and whistling filled the air.

A hot breeze cut through it all, making me smile, reminding me of who gave me this chance at the ordinary.

We feasted on food the council provided, and then Mercedes took Seth for the night. Then we feasted on one another.

Saul was tender and strong, gentle but possessive, and I loved every second of making love with that man. It was something I was sure I'd never grow tired of. We woke in the morning, my simple, white dress on the floor next to his slacks and shirt. A tangle of skin and blankets and love.

And then we made love again. And again.

SAUL

Damn but she was beautiful. She wore white better than anyone I'd ever seen. It might be the only color I wanted her to wear from now on. That or nothing at all, because as beautiful as she was in her wedding dress, she was exquisite without anything at all.

I've never been happier in my life as I was that day.

Until the day after, and the day after that….

THIRTY-FOUR

THREE YEARS LATER...

SAUL

I'D JUST FINISHED HELPING ROMAN BUILD A CRADLE. HE AND MERCEDES were about to have their first baby and she and Porschia were busy cleaning the house from top to bottom, because Cedes was afraid of germs and her baby touching said germs. Seth was using his tiny hammer to set the last nail in the side of the wood. "You did good, buddy," I said, ruffling his hair.

"I need a wrench," Seth said seriously, looking around the room. He didn't really need one, but he liked to play with tools, so I got up to get the one from my tool bag for him. However, when I bent down, the wrench flew out of the bag and floated to Seth, gently landing in his hand.

I looked at the wrench in my son's hand, then to Roman, and back again. He nodded, mouth gaping open. "It happened," he said quietly, watching Seth like a hawk.

"What was that, Seth?" I asked, crouching down next to him.

"My other Daddy taught me to do that."

"Your other Daddy?"

"Yeah, the one I see when I'm sleepin'," he said.

I swallowed. "What else does your other Daddy say?"

Seth shrugged innocently. "He gave me Boots." Boots was the damn kitten that showed up on Porschia's front porch a few years ago, and the bane of my existence. It hated me with a passion.

"And sometimes he doesn't like you," Seth added.

"Well, buddy, I love you and that's all that matters. You tell him that for me, okay?"

"Okay," he said, tightening an invisible bolt. "I think it's fixed now, Dad."

"Good. Why don't you go tickle Ford before he leaves?"

"Good idea!" he shrieked, dropping the wrench onto the wooden planks of the floor and running down the steps.

Roman shook his head. "What the hell does that even mean?" He motioned toward where Seth had been sitting on his knees.

"I have no idea."

www.ingramcontent.com/pod-product-compliance
Lightning Source LLC
Chambersburg PA
CBHW020304030826
48979CB00027B/2113/J
* 9 7 8 1 0 8 7 9 4 4 7 4 6 *